# DEPARTURE LOUNGE

A Novel

# DEPARTURE LOUNGE

A Novel

## ROBERT LAURENCE

SANTA FE

Sunstone books may be purchased for educational, business, or sales promotional use.
For information please write: Special Markets Department, Sunstone Press,
P.O. Box 2321, Santa Fe, New Mexico 87504-2321.

Book and Cover design › Vicki Ahl
Body typeface › Minion Pro
Printed on acid-free paper
∞

_____

Library of Congress Cataloging-in-Publication Data

Laurence, Robert, 1945 Sept. 19-
  Departure lounge : a novel / by Robert Laurence.
     p. cm.
  ISBN 978-0-86534-863-9 (softcover : alk. paper)
  I. Title.
  PS3612.A9442278D47 2012
  813'.6--dc23
                        2012003566

_____

WWW.SUNSTONEPRESS.COM
SUNSTONE PRESS / POST OFFICE BOX 2321 / SANTA FE, NM 87504-2321 /USA
(505) 988-4418 / ORDERS ONLY (800) 243-5644 / FAX (505) 988-1025

To the artist,
for the spicy asymmetry that she has provided to my life.
And to Abidjan, née Feisty, by Acaroid, out of Some One Finer,
for continually reminding me of the essential balance of the universe.

# PROLOGUE

You should know at the outset that this is a story of the Eighties: No cell phones, no e-mail, no iPods, no caller ID, no Euros. Whether you have a fondness for those days, or think instead that the changes from then to now have been for the good, is not a matter that is particularly important to this story, nor to its characters. But you need to remember that in those days, one didn't know who was calling until one answered the phone. People read newspapers, information travelled more slowly, and it was easier to be out of touch. There was no TSA, and airport security was more relaxed than it is now. Substantially more relaxed. A first class stamp cost 22¢, and people used them all the time.

The world fit together somewhat differently then. The Berlin Wall still stood, as did the World Trade Center. Athens had two airports and the drachma, but no subway. There was a country called Yugoslavia, but there was no Slovenia. Albuquerque, New Mexico sat, then as now, in the desert sun, but its Triple A ball club was called the Dukes then, and was a farm team for the Dodgers; Ron y Marcia's was still dishing up blue corn enchiladas on Yale Boulevard; the city had no casinos and a rather small airport. Tallahassee, Florida, then as now, was more South Georgia than Florida, and, palm trees were, then as now, not native to the place. The palm trees that do grow there are not the tall, stately coconut palms, but are the stocky, Mexican-looking palms, struggling to live in a place that is a touch too cold in the winter. They look more like the palm trees of Athens than of Phoenix. Palm trees do not grow at all in Albuquerque, and never did.

Just as palm trees grow in but are not native to Tallahassee, this story is not a story about palm trees, even though it begins with the palm trees of Tallahassee losing their fans in a tropical storm. This story, you see, is about places, and it is more about travelling to places than it is about what is found there. Late in the story, a character named Marie Cochran will say "Life imitates travel," and that, indeed, is part of what this story is about. It is also about love, youthful equitation, minor league baseball, and bankruptcy law. It is about, in other words, much of what is important in life. It is also about post-modern literary criticism, which isn't all that important, but there you are. But it is mostly about getting to places, and the details, like the presence or not of palm trees, and the friendliness or not of the weather, are secondary to the places themselves and the getting there.

Marie Cochran will make her observation in reaction to something that her friend and sometime lover, Michael Reid, once wrote to her in a letter from who-knows-where. That will happen a lot in this story, as the people to whom Michael writes his letters go about their various lives and get to know one another. Sort of.

Those who know Michael Reid well might say that the entire story will happen almost as if Michael himself had scripted it out. Britt Larsen, even, will think this, although she never knew Michael at all, not really. Maybe she will have an inkling of it the day in the Albuquerque departure lounge under the flight board. Maybe not. Or maybe she will foretell it, in a way, during the fight in Zia School park. Or maybe she should have known it, or something like it, was to happen from the time, before the first dance at the Café Fargo, when she watched the small, dark-eyed woman drink her beer over ice. Maybe not.

It will turn out like this: . . .

*THE SUMMER AND FALL OF 1983*

# ~ 1

## TALLAHASSEE, FLORIDA

The storm was nameless, too weak to merit an identity of its own. It was a mere tropical depression, a meteorological funk, a bad mood with rain. Nevertheless, this anonymous storm shook Pascagoula by the neck and it flooded Mobile, where two boys drowned while their mother watched. Pensacola saw tornados, but they did not touch down. In Tallahassee, the rain fell horizontally, if that makes sense, blown into the sides of buildings, where it flowed in sheets into the sandy ground. Fans were blown off of the stocky palm trees and Spanish moss from the limbs of live oaks. A few wires came down, but the storm was unnamed and Tallahassee was used to such. Tomorrow's *Democrat* would carry news of it back on page 4, gruesomely featuring the drownings in Mobile.

Inside Love Hall at Florida State University, in the classroom on the second floor where the mathematics department faculty was meeting, there was an academic depression that could more than match the tropical depression outside. As the rain flew against the window glass of the room, and leaked where some caulking was missing into puddles on the floor, the faculty—nineteen men and two women—sat around the classroom and variously tilted their heads back and looked at the ceiling, stared belligerently at each other, doodled or read. No one spoke. The meeting was more than two hours old and if there were barometers to measure departmental collegiality and academic good sportsmanship, those instruments would be bottoming out and forecasters as far away as Coral Gables would be studying their dials, nodding their heads and deciding that this storm was about to bear a name.

"Then do we stand adjourned?" The chairman of the math department looked around the table, smiling broadly and without warmth. It was mid-morning, ten-fifty by the clock next to the portrait of Gauss. The meeting had been sufficiently contentious that even Gauss seemed dismayed.

"Not without a motion to that effect." The speaker was the leader of the opposition. His tape recorder was running, and he was making copious notes, which would be sent around tomorrow as *Alternative Minutes of the Faculty Meeting of May 17, 1983*. The tapes he kept under lock and key in his office. Really.

"Christ." An unidentified speaker.

"Move we adjourn." The man sitting to the right of the chairman spoke. He was the informal vice-chairman of the department. That there should even be an informal vice-chairman of the mathematics department was one of the many grievances of the opposition; moreover, the informal vice-chairman was a rather obvious and unrepentant seducer of undergraduate coeds, and that, too, was one of the many grievances of the opposition. This department was one in which academic politics, for now, reigned. The faculty was sharply divided; wounds were open, and for two hours and forty-five minutes now, the salt had flowed freely, notwithstanding the rain.

"Second."

The leader of the opposition wrote the name of the seconder into his notes, then spoke again, staring the chairman in the face. "Move for a secret ballot."

A fence-sitter scraped his chair, rose and walked out of the meeting. The leader of the opposition noted the departure in his notes.

"Is there a second?" the chairman asked, trying to sound sardonic, but managing only exasperation.

Without looking up from the journal she was reading, Anna Browning raised her hand. "Second."

"Assistant Professor Browning seconds the motion," observed the chairman.

"Let the record indicate the emphasis the chair has placed on Professor Browning's untenured status . . ."

"What emphasis? What nonsense. And in any event, Dorothy, the record indicates what I say it indicates . . .," the reference being to the departmental secretary who was taking the official minutes, and who would later complain at length about the meeting to her boy friend, who was a carpenter, bored with

Dorothy's whining about her job, and thinking about calling his previous girl friend.

"Noted," said the leader of the opposition.

". . . furthermore, it is clear that a motion for a secret ballot on a vote to adjourn is offered only to delay the meeting and embarrass me and I take personal umbrage . . .."

"In a department where all semblance of academic freedom has been destroyed by the deliberate campaign of harassment undertaken by the present, and, we can only hope, short-term chairman, there is no motion too trivial that votes should not be shielded from the chairman's retribution. Nor do I particularly give a shit about whether I embarrass the chairman or not."

"How elegant, Professor," said the chairman, who was made uncomfortable by profanity. "You have such a charming way with words. And may I note that, if we are speaking of the harassment of Professor Browning, you, the chairman of her publication review committee, are in a much better position to harass her than am I?"

The chairman and his opponent were now into it again beyond immediate extraction. They grew red in the face as they shouted at each other, interrupted each other and banged the table. No one else spoke. Most of the professors around the table sat back and waited, again, for the argument to subside. No one said "*Gentlemen, please* . . .." Those inclined to make peace had paid the price of peace-making in the past. Most were not inclined to.

Anna Browning turned the argument's volume down by concentrating on the article she was reading in the *American Journal of Probability and Statistics*. The article, she was beginning to realize, might have some impact on her present work. She picked up a pencil and began to underline, circle, question-mark, and sketch out equations in the margin. She skipped back to the first page of the article and glanced again at the author's name. Jablonski. *Never heard of him. Iowa State. Iowa State?* The argument raged on around her. And about her.

*Fellas, I'm not crazy about being discussed as if I were not present.* She didn't say it, but she thought about saying it. *You might find a slightly better time and place to discuss my tenure and my career path.* She imagined her voice dripping with sarcasm; she imagined her colleagues shamefacedly apologizing. She imagined herself walking out of the meeting, aloof. Department politics did not interest her, and it annoyed her that she had been asked in advance to second the motion for a secret ballot. *What horse crap.* But her refusal would have been noticed, and that would have annoyed her, too. Her husband Ben would have known exactly what to say, and how to say it for maximum impact and embellishment of his reputation, but then he had tenure. She kept quiet.

*You jerks.*

*This transformation here does not look correct.* She cocked her head to the right, scratched the part in her hair with the eraser on her pencil, and studied the equation.

"Is it your intention, Anna, to second this motion?" the chairman asked.

Enough of her attention was still on the faculty meeting that she heard the question and did not need to have it repeated nor even to pause. "Yes." She didn't look up, and continued to write in the margin.

*Shit.*

*This second transformation should look like this . . .. He can't mean what he says here. It's too simplistic.*

*Or elegant,* she heard a worried voice in her head observe. *Or it's too elegant.*

"The motion is for a secret ballot. Is there a motion to make *this* vote secret?" The leader of the opposition did not respond, spoiling the irony. The vote was eight to five, in favor of secrecy, six abstentions, one absent and the chair not voting. The chairman now seemed resigned to go through with the thing without a fight. The ballots were passed out. Anna marked hers *Yes* without removing her attention from the *AJP&S.*

"The vote is fifteen yeses, no noes, five blank ballots. We are adjourned. I want to thank you personally, Harry, for that little exercise, and apologize to all of the rest of you for the extra time it took . . ."

"You are no longer in the chair, this meeting has adjourned, so shut the fuck up," said the leader of the opposition. The tape recorder was still running. The chairman stood up and left, and slowly the professors drifted out of the classroom where they had been meeting and back to their offices. Anna let her colleagues leave before she glanced up from Jablonski's article. She spoke to no one, afraid that her annoyance at the whole proceeding would show, and no one spoke to her, though she heard her name mentioned in whispers among three of them. She looked around the room, at the portrait of Gauss, at the puddle on the floor, at the unerased chalkboards, holding proofs from an earlier class in Algebraic Structures, and out the windows, into the raging, nameless storm.

Finally, after several minutes in the empty classroom, she stood up and walked out the door and back to her office, where she tried to regain her composure in the quiet world of stochastic processes.

## TALLAHASSEE

A red wasp crawled slowly up the inside of the window in Anna Browning's office. Every few inches it would pause, let go and suspend itself in the air, making a particularly bothersome, almost sub-sonic buzz. Anna watched it. The wasp was trying to fly through the window. *Thwack, thwack,* was how it sounded when the wasp hit the glass. Its partner, which had been buzzing around the ceiling for the last hour, alighted and clung to the binding of a dusty copy of *Johnson & Kiokemeister,* Anna's original calculus book from undergraduate days.

The Tallahassee summer afternoon was tremendously hot. It was the kind of Tallahassee summer afternoon that caused descriptive adjectives to be stillborn in one's forebrain so that all one could say about the weather was, "God, is it hot." Such afternoons are not rare in Tallahassee, Florida, not in July, and all over town that day people were no doubt shaking their heads to each other in supermarket parking lots, saying, "God, is it hot," and wiping the sweat from their faces.

It was tremendously hot in Anna's office and Love Hall's air conditioning was running at about twenty per cent of capacity. Cause: unknown. Occurrence: frequent. The door from her office into the corridor was open and so was the window to the outside, but no air stirred. Anna watched the wasp on the window, thinking that if it would just walk down, instead of up, it would come to the opening and be gone. She thought she might encourage it to do so with a blue book, but was afraid of getting stung. It was very hot.

The blue books were at hand, all right, twenty-three sets of Advanced Calculus exams stacked up on her desk, a barrier to any sort of creative activity. It was July, first summer session had finished a week ago and there they still sat, in careless violation of department and college deadlines, waiting for the first one to be touched. There was, actually, a kind of reverse snobbism around the mathematics department about being late with grades; only those who had no important research going had time to meet exam-grading deadlines. The Dean of the College of Arts and Sciences was from the political science department, and didn't that say all that needed to be said regarding his reproachful memos about exam-grading deadlines? Important political science research was a concept impossible to imagine. Perhaps if she looked around she could find a fan somewhere in the building to get the air moving.

Anna knew she could not use her research, or any other academically elegant excuse for not grading her exams. True, she had spent a few hours last week re-reading the article by Jablonski and then had spoken for a while to a friend at the University of Iowa, trying to find out who the hell this Jablonski was. But really, she knew, her office was too tidy and her correspondence was too up to date for her to say she hadn't been grading because she had been researching. The last thing, in fact, that she had done just now before sitting down in front of the blue books to watch the wasp thwack its head against the window was to dust the frames that held her various diplomas on the wall. She had done the dusting ritualistically, for she knew that once the dust was removed there would be nothing left to do but grade exams.

By now she was sure that Jablonski's work threatened to preempt about six months of thinking and working she had done on the stochastic applications of Tupelov's Theorem. She looked at the *AJP&S*, which was now lying face-down and open to the article, on her desk next to the blue books. She tossed her blond hair over her right shoulder, away from the part, crossed her legs, and squinted in thought at the *Journal*. She still wasn't sure she understood his second transformation. Her first thought on reading the article during May's faculty meeting was that the second transformation was clearly wrong; the blackboard behind her still held six equations, her first quick attempt to disprove it, written that afternoon, stared-at, but untouched since then. But his error had been harder to show than she had thought it would be and she had had to put it aside until after spring-term exams. Then, summer teaching. Now, summer-term exams. The thinking she had done on the problem since, mostly in the car on the way to and from work or to pick up the children, had changed from a certainty that he was wrong, to a mere suspicion of that and, now, on this hot afternoon, with twenty-three blue books to grade and the air conditioning at twenty percent, the most Anna could work up was a hope that he was wrong, or that, if he was right, there was still something left for her to do. Maybe she should read it again. She fiddled with her watch, which had a tendency to slip around her thin wrist so the face was pointing down, and looked at it; it would soon be lunch time.

The wasp reached the top of the window and buzzed horizontally along the casement.

Anna was pregnant, though you wouldn't know it yet by looking. But she was; by now there could be no doubt. She felt very pregnant on this hot afternoon; she felt chubby and her clothes too tight. Things felt different when she was pregnant; the whole world felt chubby and full of water. She had been pregnant three times before and had two children to show for it. Sam was eight and Janet was five and there had been an abortion, before she had married Ben and about which he knew nothing. Now she was pregnant again and she expected about a year and a half of being tired and sleepy, a depressed, grouchy wreck without so much as a glass of wine or an aspirin to help, until the new child was born, weaned and placed in day care. She looked forward to having a new toddler around eventually, she really did, but she did not look forward to the next eighteen months. The wasp hung upside down from the ceiling and walked toward the fluorescent light.

Instead of picking up Jablonski's article, or a blue book for that matter, she reached for Mike Reid's letter. Maybe there was one last thing to do before she started grading the exams. The letter had come earlier in the week, addressed to her here at the office, but she had tossed it aside without opening it. She had thought maybe she would save it for the next faculty meeting, when she liked to have something to read, in a largely fruitless attempt to cut through the tension. But now twenty-three Advanced Calculus exams threatened and she knew she couldn't let herself start in on Jablonski's article again. *The frames have been dusted, Anna*, she scolded herself, *Deadlines have passed*. She could, though, read Mike's letter.

She really only vaguely disliked Mike Reid. Only vaguely. Enough so that she hadn't been all that anxious to read the letter, but really, she only vaguely disliked him. She had met him a few years ago when they both had taught at Wabash. *Wabash* was what Anna called her previous institution, whose proper name was Washburn University, in Topeka, Kansas, with what she hoped was just exactly the right degree of withering deprecation. Ben had called it that for the first time just after she had been hired there out of her post-doc, for a foot in the academic world's door. It had been a decent start for her, not exactly a lucky break, not exactly as good as she deserved, but good enough, and not so non-prestigious as to hold her career back. Close, though. So she had accepted. She had also suggested that Ben take a leave from Florida State and accept a visiting professorship there—surely they would have offered, or at Kansas or Kansas State, which were close by—but he had called it *Wabash* and had laughed off the suggestion. Ben was eight years older than she and held an endowed chair in the English department, the best department here, and what, he had asked, could he gain from a sojourn like that to the mid-west? Or the far west. Or wherever the hell Kansas was, about which he was both agnostic and indifferent. So Ben had held down the fort here while she had packed up Sam and, like some migrant worker, set out for the Great Plains. She really did see the sense in his position. Ben had deigned so much as to set foot in Kansas, so their conjugal visits had been at home, in Florida, one of which had produced Janet, who had been born the following summer in Tallahassee, before being placed in day care back in Topeka.

Mike Reid had been a couple of years senior in rank to her, an associate professor with tenure in Math Ed, not the Math Department, a teacher whose career seemed to be going nowhere, even then. They had been colleagues while she had produced three well-received papers in five semesters, one of which had been mentioned for the Putnam Award, and then she had been invited back to Tallahassee to join the Florida State faculty, reuniting her family. Ben, she thought, had been proud of her, though it was not his way to show it very much. And he may have exerted his influence to get FSU to offer her a position, which would, very much, have been his way.

Mike was just the kind of academic that Ben and Anna loved to hate: a college teacher, not a scholar. He was so unlike Anna and the boys—that was how Ben referred to her and the other three assistant professors in the math department. "Anna and the boys," he would say, "are at a colloquium tonight." Or "one of the boys is giving a paper at Princeton." The boys were all a decade younger than Anna and the four of them were very much scholars, determined to advance in the academic world, while Mike Reid couldn't have been less concerned about such things. Anna and the boys had a friendly competition amongst themselves over who published where and how often, and who would get tenure first, and who got invited where to present. The boys didn't know yet of Jablonski's article, but they would see the difficulty immediately.

Mike wasn't serious about his career, she thought, still holding the unopened letter by opposite corners, spinning it between her index fingers. He couldn't ever be one of the boys. He wasn't much of a mathematician, to tell the truth, confirming all of her expectations about math educators. Granted, he had an easy enough way about him and had written a time or two in support to her peer review committee, back at Wabash. But his comfort, living and working in Topeka, far from the center of the academic world, clashed with her anxiousness to get out and up. They thought so differently about things that they had never really been what you'd call close. She had left Topeka without saying good-bye, but he had kept in touch over the years, letting her know that he had moved from Wabash to the University of Arkansas shortly after she had returned to FSU. As if she had cared.

Yet, she remembered, there had been one very odd encounter. He had been over at her rental house on a weekend afternoon, looking at some books she wished to sell. Sam had been put down for his nap. Something, Anna was never able to say exactly what, had made her suddenly, after two years of wheat-field celibacy, willing. She had not been eager, maybe, but she had been willing, she admitted it. It had been an unusual moment, a moment of uncharacteristic and reckless spontaneity. (Not unlike, she supposed, sarcastically lecturing one's senior colleagues about faculty-meeting decorum.) It was unpleasant even to remember it now, years later. She had laughed at something unimportant and touched his shoulder with her temple and there had been a moment of silence, and she had been willing. But they hadn't gone to bed, not that afternoon, not ever. Mike hadn't been equally as willing, or was committed to someone else, or, more likely, hadn't even realized he was being invited, or something. They had never even acknowledged the encounter. She certainly hadn't considered the possibility again after that strange afternoon with the sun barely piercing the fog and the irises in bloom, but she still carried a little embarrassment around with her for having thought about it at all. And, she guessed, she carried a little anger that he'd been too slow, too insensitive to subtlety and hadn't caught the invitation. Maybe he had a boy friend, she thought now, for the first time ever. But no, he was married, she remembered. Maybe that was it. How delightfully old-fashioned. But really, she rarely thought of that afternoon anymore, or of Mike at all; they hardly stayed in touch. She'd get a postcard every now and then, usually from some country she had no interest in ever visiting, postcards memorable mostly because Sam saved the stamps. And he'd call now and then, usually to have her explain a recent math development that he wanted to superficialize for some math ed journal. She never instigated the communication.

But now he offered one last respite from the blue books. She opened the letter:

> *Madison County, Arkansas. [It said.] June, nearly July, 1983. Rain, cool rain falls. An owl, hunting, hoots. The almanac says that Jupiter is rising just now in the east, above the clouds. It is 11:20 p.m., Central Daylight Time.*

An owl, hunting, hoots? He always was a poetic little bastard. Anna could only imagine what Ben would have to say about *an owl, hunting, hoots.* She went back to reading.

> *Dear Anna,*
>
> *Emily is asleep upstairs. I was sitting a while ago, listening to the rain and the sounds of the night, and I got to thinking a thought or two that put you in my mind. So it occurred to me that I'd enjoy a bit of time tonight at this small desk here writing to you. If you'd like to imagine me sitting with a glass of straight rye whiskey by my hand, the surface just faintly vibrating as I write, with cigarette smoke rising up to be lost in the shadows between the cabin's ceiling beams and with the cat curled on the cool summer hearth, you may, though little of that is, in fact, true.*
>
> *The axiom is said to be this: never forgo a piece of ass.*

Anna started. Was he going to write about that which she had just been recalling? Did he remember her as a forgone piece of ass? Damn him. She read on.

> *I first heard it stated that plainly from a friend of mine, but I didn't put too much stock in it at the time. We were riding a bus through central Norway, through that enormously beautiful countryside of the strangest purple-green hue, of the most magnificent waterfalls you've ever seen, and of small villages so quaintly Norwegian they made your legs ache. But I didn't put too much stock in the axiom, even later that night, back at the hotel, when my friend picked a tune on his guitar, quietly and without singing, and I played chess, but poorly, with a calm Icelander whose girl friend, with sad eyes and a small scar on her lip,*

*sat even more silently, regarded our moves and smoked. We all stayed up until the morning, talking English and watching it not get dark, I, you may be sure, giving much more thought to the scar than the advice.*

*All of that happened some time ago. (My friend is now divorced, I presume for having taken the axiom a bit too literally to heart.) Two years ago it was, I guess, before this summer, when I bought a ticket to Paris via Amsterdam and jumped in my pickup with the dog in the back, and drove I-40 west—OKC, Amarillo, Albuquerque—then back through Carlsbad, Lubbock, Fort Worth, admittedly the long way around for Paris, but I had a friend from my days teaching in Moriarty whom I wanted to see, I wanted to catch a Dukes game and to duck my head into the Caverns, and I had the time. Emily, contrariwise, had work to do: she had a weekend gig at a small club in Fort Worth, so the plan was that we'd rendezvous there, I'd attend her three shows, then catch the KLM flight to Schipol, and she'd drive back home with the dog.*

*Albuquerque was tasty and dry. The visit with my friend was felicitous (as always), the Dukes played well (as they do now and then), and the Caverns (for the first time) put me to mind of the adage that sometimes real life looks like bad special effects. The last leg through Texas to Fort Worth was dull and hot, but the little bar was all that one could want in a north Texas jazz club. And then some.*

*At this point, however, the gods intervened. The club liked Em's stuff. Their headliner called in sick. More likely wrecked. The club offered her a two-week run. Of course, she took the offer, as the gods of chromatic jazz are not to be trifled with. And who's to take the dog home, and mow the yard, and look after the neighbors' horses, one of whom is old, blind in one eye, and lame, and whose left hind Em promised she'd soak daily while they, the neighbors that is, who look after our animals when we're gone, are in Europe? Me. The gods of travel are puny compared to the gods of chromatic jazz.*

*And so it was that the dog and I found ourselves continuing our journey, as I drove north and east, feeling the ache of 747-deprivation. Jet-exhaust, window-seat, passport-control, blue-money deprivation. And somewhere along the way, somewhere in the east Oklahoma hills, my friend's axiom came back to me. Maybe he had it right, though too specific. You should never pass up a piece of ass, or a flight to Amsterdam.*

*There is no use comparing an orgasm to the feel of walking from the arrival gate to customs at Schipol. There is no accounting for taste. But we all have some experience, I suppose, for which the advice is correct, and we forgo that experience at our own psychic perils.*

*None of which is really to say that I made the wrong choice regarding Europe after Albuquerque and Fort Worth this summer. It seemed so, as I stopped in Sallisaw, a small town in eastern Oklahoma, with a lower-level Thoroughbred track, at the Stuckey's across from which I split a cheeseburger with the dog at just the time when KLM 664 for Adam was due to leave the Atlanta gate. Good Lord, it seemed so!*

"Annie!"

She jumped. Standing at the open door of her office was Jim Finch, the informal vice-chairman of the department, who, by the look on his face and the tone of his voice, had been standing there for some time.

She disliked being called *Annie*, but decided to let it slide. "Hey, Jim," she said, tossing the letter onto her desk, where it didn't stick, and the several pages of lined and punched notebook paper fluttered themselves out of order through the humid air and onto the institutional carpet. Ben said that she had begun to say *hey*, instead of *hi*, during her years in Kansas, and he continually pestered her about it.

"You were gone. Engrossed. Had to speak twice."

It annoyed her the way the informal vice-chairman clipped the beginnings off of his sentences, as if subjects and pronouns were in short supply.

"Yeah, it was nothing. I was reading a letter from a friend. More of an acquaintance, really. A colleague, sort of, from before. Math ed. It was pretty tedious going, if you want to know the truth." With her foot, she nudged the pages of the letter under her desk.

"Too bad you weren't engrossed in reading exams. Something the Dean could take comfort in."

"Yeah. Really. There they are, that's for sure." She gestured at them with her left hand, and then cocked her head to the left, considering their continued and stubborn existence. "I'm hoping they're about to grade themselves."

Jim Finch gave a short unamused laugh, and Anna swiveled her chair around, putting her back to him and facing the blackboard. "Take a look at this; it's what I *should* be engrossed with. Or *in*. Or whatever." She stood up, walked to the board, picked up a piece of chalk, and, still with her back to him, tapped at the third equation. "I know it's not your field, but I can bring you up to speed in a couple of minutes."

"No time for that."

"No time for math, Jim? Tut, tut. Let's keep our priorities straight." She turned to face him, smiling, but her smile dissolved when she saw his humorlessness.

"Way past the deadline, Annie. Not a good thing to do. Not professional."

"You're talking about being professional? Come off it, Jim. What's more professional than doing math?"

She wiped the sweat from her upper lip, and turned and faced the board again.

"Chalk down, Annie. Look here. Not professional to miss the college's deadline, Annie. Last Friday at four o'clock. Extra paperwork for the staff. Looks bad on your record. You let the students down."

"I what? I what?" The heat, the letter, her pregnancy: something made Jim's last sentence completely non-sensible to her. "I *what*?" For a long moment, Anna said nothing more. She could feel the red rising in her face, and perspiration rushed from under her arms. She wished she were wearing something with sleeves, but maybe not, as the sharp stink steadied her. "You've been prowling the hallways, looking for bluebooks, have you, Jim? Or is it just me? Am I the only one who's late?" Finch said nothing, but looked over her shoulder, out the window. "Or is this visit about something else?"

Finch looked at her, then turned on his heel and walked out of her office. "You know what this is about," he said, walking away. In the hallway, he turned back and said, "Get them graded. Don't want to send a memo to the Dean."

"God damn it," Anna yelled, cocked her arm and threw the chalk at the blackboard. It struck, broke in a dozen pieces and fell to the carpet, leaving what appeared to be a star in the middle of the second equation. "God *damn* it." She had to move to the door to yell at his back going down the corridor. "God damn it." A door up the way closed and latched. "They'll get graded. Leave me alone, and don't you lecture me about letting the students down. Or about being professional. What's less professional than screwing the coeds, huh, Jim?" Finch was now all the way to the stairwell, and turned to the right. "And no one calls me *Annie*, God damn it." She slammed the door to her office, opened it, and slammed it again, then walked to the blackboard and broke every piece of chalk there in half. She picked up the stack of bluebooks from her desk, dropped them onto the floor, and walked out of her office, leaving the door open. The wasps were no longer apparent.

It was a short walk across the Quad to the campustown on Tennessee Street, but the day was so sultry and she was so pissed off and tired that she barely made it without giving up. Taking her life in her hands, she jay-walked across Tennessee Street, and looked in the window at Hutton's. Sometimes Ben came here for lunch and maybe she could catch him.

Yes. He was, in fact, sitting in the restaurant with his back to her, heading a table of grad students apparently. Ben was talking and smoking and the students were laughing and eating, and Anna walked on down Tennessee Street. She didn't have the energy, after the hot walk, to play faculty spouse. She would see him at dinner and they could talk then and she could tell him about Jim Finch's visit.

Around the corner from Hutton's, she stepped into a small bookstore. The air was breathtakingly cool inside, and smelled like the Mid-Eastern food that was sold in the shop next door. She browsed the shelves while waiting for some hunger to arise. Did she really feel like shawarma? She bought a mystery by Mickey Friedman, a local yokel who wrote a good yarn, and exchanged pleasantries with the clerk, or maybe she was the owner, who always pretended to know Anna, a pretense she never returned. Today she said little more than "God, it's hot out there." She then sat next door for an hour, picking at a falafel sandwich, drinking iced tea, and read a third of the mystery.

After lunch and a sweaty walk back to the math building, her office presented her with four choices: Friedman, Jablonski, Reid, blue books. Anna did not disparage the list; what she was feeling today was not that she needed more choices in her life. Given perfect freedom, she would immediately have chosen to work on her equations. Mathematics brought her joy. The mystery was a lunchtime diversion; Mike's letter had not caught her interest; Ben she would see tonight. The children, too. She loved her children, and enjoyed their company, but eight hours a day was not too long to be free of their demands.

The blue books, though, changed everything. Jablonski would have to wait, as would Mickey Friedman. With some resignation and no enthusiasm, she picked up Mike's letter from where she had pushed it under the desk, rearranged the pages—he was a letter-page numberer—and tried to find where she had left off.

*Good Lord, it seemed so!*

She disliked exclamation points.

*But it seems less so tonight, some weeks later, sitting, writing, listening to the Ozark rain. Europe seems far away tonight. The Café Metro on the Place des Abbesses, the spot that, for no particular reason, is my favorite spot in Paris, seems no more attractive just now than our upper field, twenty acres of Ozark hillside, once a pasture, but now let go to head-high weeds, oak and dogwood saplings, ticks and quail, two hundred yards from where I sit. Here, right now, seems—well—okay. "Here." I guess there can't be a "there" without a "here." I had never before been aware of a compulsion to travel, but as I sit here tonight I feel for the first time ever I guess, at ease from that previously unknown compulsion. Here is really quite pleasant. One can answer, without any real embarrassment, "Oh, no place very interesting. I stayed home this summer." Hmmm. "Home."*

*Most important, I guess, staying home is not a rejection of the road. There are reasons, it appears, for staying home other than that one can think of nowhere to go. Just as there are reasons for walking in the mountains other than fear of the water. So, no, none of this necessarily means that I made the wrong choice, choosing here over there, home over Paris. Only that it is now woven into the fabric of nature that one trip, pondered, packed for and ticketed, was untaken. That is not sad, particularly, nor tragic nor an occasion for remorse. It just is: I shall die short one flight to Amsterdam, never to be made up.*

*So what does this have to do with you and why do I write like this on a rainy summer night? Because it seems, my friend, it seems to me that you might appreciate the mechanics of this strange mind-balance. On one side lies concern for not coming up short in the end and, on the other, an avoidance of compulsiveness. What a difficult job it is to get through life with such a balance level. Then again, and here's the irony, what an easy job it seems to get through life. When the choice is Paris or the Ozarks, love or friendship, truth or wonder, how can one choose wrong? I remember telling you once the postulate of Eskimo society: life is hard, and the margin for error is small. How different from that is my existence. How pleasant the rain sounds.*

*The question becomes this: what really matters? Do trips to Paris matter? Do orgasms? One's mind and soul, I am inclined to believe, can only really care about eight things, maximum. Before one goes crazy deciding about choices to be made, opportunities forgone, worries to worry, it must be known: is this one of the eight? What really matters, I wonder? Where one goes. What one does. Who one loves and how well. One's ability to turn a double play when the kid pitcher really needs it.*

*Listen. Something has roused the dog, who barks with a long howl, as bird dogs do. I'd better go see, as it might be a skunk. That, to her anyway, would matter. And, I'll admit, to me.*

*Look after yourself and say hello to Sam for me. And to the others too, of course.*

*Michael.*

Anna put the letter down into her lap. Tedious. Her initial appraisal to Jim Finch had been correct. What typical Mike Reid pop philosophy. She could imagine Ben's devastating attack on both the thoughts and the pseudo-literary style. Ben was the smartest person she knew; there was talk, he had told her, that in a year or two the chairmanship at Duke would open and it would be his for the taking. Of course, that would put her in a spot; her career would have to proceed smartly if she were going to be able to find a job in Durham that soon. And, she realized again, Jablonski may have put a substantial delay in those plans, damn it.

The frustration she felt over Jablonski's article and her wasted and too-pedestrian efforts, plus the gross indignity of having been lectured to about her exam grading, plus the overwhelming nonsense of departmental politics, all of this almost led her to take the letter home and to offer it up for Ben's destruction; Mike Reid represented the professional obscurity that Jablonski's piece threatened, and that Jim Finch made her long for. But no, she wouldn't do that. She didn't really dislike Mike, and his letter showed that he had retained a flattering fondness for her. Maybe he had even, finally, acknowledged the encounter years earlier, as subtle an acknowledgement as the original invitation had been. She put the envelope, with its large-denomination stamp, in her purse to take home to Sam, used the letter itself to mark Jablonski's article and tossed the *AJP&S* onto the floor, into the corner, near the blackboard with its six equations, one starred with bits of broken chalk. She took a breath of the humid air to invigorate herself and the little one, and picked up the top blue book from the floor. The wasps had reappeared, buzzing around the fluorescent lights.

TALLAHASSEE

"Another drink, Mrs. Browning?" The wife of the English department chairman was the perfect hostess; she offered to take Anna's glass and refill it from the wet bar on the patio. Anna and the fetus were still teetotalers, but Anna was damned if she were going to do anything that would make her pregnancy a topic of this damn party's conversation.

"Doctor," she replied.

"Beg pardon?" The chairman's wife smiled broadly and stared over Anna's right shoulder, not meeting her eyes. Ben's dislike of the chairman did not extend to missing his parties or forsaking his bar or table. Anna usually declined to join him, but she had relented this time, she didn't know exactly why. But she was equally damned if she were going to put up with being treated like *Professor Browning's Little Pregnant Wife.*

"*Doctor* Browning." She paused meaningfully. "But you can call me Anna, Mildred." The chairman's wife had never invited Anna to call her Mildred, but she seemed not to notice.

"Of course. Anna, could I get you another drink? Is this your first?" she asked, apparently referring to the baby, not the drink. By now, Anna's condition could not be disguised, though she did not get enormous when she was pregnant.

"No." She let the word answer both questions. "Thank you."

"Let's see, now, have you met Ms. Winston? She's the wife of the new assistant professor, Dr. Blanchard." Anna nodded across the circle of women that were standing near the hors d'oeuvres. The chairman's wife put a chummy arm around Anna's shoulders and said, "I just have such a hard time remembering that these young married women don't like to use their husband's names. I guess we're just old fashioned, aren't we, Anna? Please, here, have another stuffed mushroom. You're eating for two, remember." Ms. Winston almost choked on her Trisket and cheese. *Fuck off*, Anna thought, to both of them, as she accepted the mushroom. She was actually eating more like enough for three, than two.

"What do you do, Anna?" Ms. Winston asked.

"I'm a professor in the math department," she replied, after chewing. In certain contexts such as this one, it was considered proper to leave the modifier "assistant" off the title. "I'm a probabilist." She looked around, trying to see where Ben was; her feet hurt and she was ready to go home.

"*How* so very interesting!" gushed the chairman's wife. "Tell us all something about your work. Perhaps we can use it at the race track!" She nodded her head and the women politely laughed at the joke.

*Good God in heaven, get me out of here*, Anna thought. *Make them go away. Please, Lord.* There was no way she could translate her work into terms anyone here could understand, nor did she have any inclination to try. Ben couldn't even understand when she talked about her work. It was abstract mathematics in a very narrow esoteric field and was not *like* anything. Moreover, she didn't have the energy even to explain to this insufferable crowd why she couldn't explain.

"It's a little hard to explain."

"Oh, give it a try," said Ms. Winston, clearly not interested in the least.

"Well, actually, it's secret."

"Secret?" Ms. Winston wondered, her eyebrows rising. "Really? Why?" She sounded oh, so skeptical.

"I'm funded by the National Security Agency," Anna said, reaching with a Dorito across in front of the chairman's wife for the guacamole. "I really can't say anymore."

"But my goodness," said Mildred, "I had no idea that secret military research was going on at Florida State."

"I really can't say anymore."

"Of course, but . . ."

"I really can't say anymore." She made her voice quite serious, and reached for another stuffed mushroom. They were really rather tasty. "You'll have to excuse me; I could get into great trouble saying what I have already said." Wait until Ben heard of her little prank. "Would you please excuse me? And, where's the bathroom, Mildred?"

It was in through the patio doors, Mildred explained, down the hall to the left and through the master bedroom. Anna had to pee about a hundred times a day when she was pregnant and she got very tired of it. She got very tired of most everything, now that she thought of it, and most especially she got tired of English department faculty parties. Faculty parties. Parties. After using the bathroom, she would find Ben and force him to head home.

The door to what might be the master bedroom was closed. She looked left and right; it must be this one. She knocked tentatively, but there was no answer. She was desperate to pee and could hardly retrace her steps to ask again. She turned the knob and pushed through. Inside, a television was playing and a young woman in jeans was stretched out on the bed with her shoes off and socks on, propped up on the pillows that she must have extracted from beneath the covers. Anna nodded to her, assuming that she lived here, and walked past her to the bathroom. The young woman, dark-haired and probably tall when she stood up, was watching the television and talking quietly on the telephone. She seemed to be reciting the National Anthem. *Life is very bizarre*, Anna thought, as she went into the bathroom and relieved herself, no doubt for all of about seven minutes, and checked her hair in the mirror. Her hormones were obviously working overtime, for her hair was thicker than usual, but she hadn't been able to find the energy to wash it before this party, and it looked it. She wet one of Mildred's combs and straightened her part, then washed the comb out and shook her head to scramble the part up again.

Back in the bedroom, the young woman was still talking quietly into the telephone, while staring at the television intently. It *was* the Star Spangled Banner she was reciting, and now Anna saw why: on the TV screen another woman, who bore something of a resemblance to the woman on the bed, was wearing a blue Los Angeles Dodgers jacket and was singing the anthem with some considerable enthusiasm, though the volume on the TV was turned down rather low. The woman on the bed was apparently giving what amounted to a play-by-play, word-by-word, note-by-note description for the person on the other end of the line. Anna stood and watched for a while and listened. The singer could sing, all right. The woman on the bed ignored Anna and tonelessly recited the words to the anthem. "And the rockets' red glare . . .."

When the singing was finished, the camera pulled back to reveal a baseball stadium and a cheering crowd, and the context of the patriotic display became clear. The woman with the jacket walked, waving to the crowd, to the sidelines; the woman in the room moved the telephone away from her mouth and smiled up at Anna. "Hi."

"Hi. Was that your sister or something? She has a nice voice."

"That was Linda Ronstadt, who is not my sister, but who does indeed have a nice voice, thank you." Into the telephone: "There's a lady here, hon, who thought Linda was my sister. She says she has a nice voice." To Anna: "Linda Ronstadt. Francis Scott Key. Tommy Lasorta. Three of the great names in the history of baseball." She then laughed into the phone, apparently in response to something happening on the other end, and then broke into a shaky soprano: "Itsoeasyitsoeasyitsoeasyitsoeasy," then dropping her voice in what to Anna's ear was a decent approximation of a perfect fifth: "Itsoeasyitsoeasyitsoeasyitsoeasy." She seemed to be singing a duet with the person on the other end, at the end of which she dissolved in laughter, as, apparently did the other person. This one, the one on the bed in the master bedroom, wiped tears from her eyes and said into the phone, "Oh, darlin', I miss you so much." A pause, then, "Yeah, I know." Then: "What?" She listened for a bit. To Anna: "My friend wants to know if you know that L.A.'s Triple A farm team is called the Albuquerque Dukes." Into the phone, "I don't think so, Robin; she looks confused."

"Do you live here? Who are you, George and Mildred's daughter?"

"She wants to know if I live here. No, I don't. I come to their parties and drink their whiskey, watch their television, and use their long-distance carrier. I have been doing so for two and one-third years, which approximates my entire lifetime, as I remember it. It comes with the tuition. I told her that I don't live here. I told her I like to drink George's whiskey. I am lying just now in George and Mildred's bed. She wonders, I can tell, whether this is the first time I have ever lain in this particular bed. You wonder, don't you?" This last was to Anna. "The correct answer would be *no, it is not*, a comment which I will leave in that richly ambiguous state. The bed is overly soft. One would complain to the manager about it at the Omni, though not at a Motel 6. I think I shall make poetry about the softness of George and Mildred's bed for next week's poetry seminar."

While the three-sided conversation did not seem to bother the student lying on the bed, Anna found herself becoming increasingly confused. Luckily she had discovered that the mystery woman was a student before she had introduced herself. It was almost always the case at parties such as this, with half-drunk students such as this one, that the name *Browning* brought forth one of two equally disagreeable expressions of opinion: "Your husband is the best fucking teacher I have ever had." Or, "Your husband is the worst fucking teacher I have ever had." Anna had no interest at all into which category this woman would place Ben, so she said, "Tell your friend I said hi," and she walked to the door. On the way out she heard, "The lady says hi. I think she is Ben Browning's spouseperson. She appears to be rather pregnant." And, so softly that Anna, now back in the hallway, could barely make out the rest: "He's an incomprehensible, post-modern, full-of-himself crit. But you didn't hear it from me."

Anna went in search of Ben, knowing that he would be pleased with the mystery woman's appraisal, if she told him about it, and would want to know who the student was. She wasn't sure she'd tell him. Maybe he was in the library playing *Name The Author*, one of his favorite parlor games. A student would choose a book off the shelves of the library, open it and read the last paragraph. Ben would then identify the author. He was amazingly good at this game; she had once seen him get seven right out of ten at a party for a group of grad students in the library at their home. Ben was very well read and had a breathtaking memory and a careful eye for writing style and syntax.

She heard his voice before she saw him, coming, indeed, from the library, but he, not a student, was reading, or reciting, maybe. The words sounded vaguely familiar. She stopped short of the doorway and listened.

"I, you may be thure, giving *much* more thought to the thcar than the advithe." He was giving the words an overly theatrical sound; that, and the lisp, suggested sexual deviance. She didn't place the words until the laughter died down in the library and Ben went on: "All of that happened thum time ago. Two yearth, I geth, before this thummer, when I bought a ticket to Parith via Amthterdam—I jutht *love* Parith—and jumped in my pickup with the dog in the back and drove to Albuquerque . . ."

It was Mike Reid's letter. Earlier, several months ago now, some days after the letter had arrived, dragged down by the new frustration of working in reaction to another's work rather than truly on her own and still using the letter to mark Jablonski's place in the *AJP&S*, Anna had changed her mind and, on a whim, had shown the letter to Ben. His reaction had been unusual at the time. He had read it once, then again and handed it back with barely a comment. She had been crest-fallen, as he had given her none of the satisfaction she had expected. He hadn't amused her with his wit; he hadn't seen that something important was happening in her work that worried her a bit. Nor did he seem to notice her disappointment. So she had placed the letter back in the *Journal*, still marking Jablonski's article, and had forgotten about it. Now she heard the words, issuing forth from the door of the chairman's library, amidst the laughter and interjections by the grad students. She entered the room.

Ben was sitting in an arm chair, with his legs crossed, holding the letter in one hand and his reading glasses in the other. About a dozen other people stood or sat around him; she recognized none of them and guessed they were mostly new graduate students getting their first taste of the *Ben Browning treatment*. They were enjoying the show and Ben went back to reading, without noticing Anna's arrival into the room.

She wondered if she should be angry that Ben had taken the letter without her permission and was now using it to make fun of someone whom he didn't know, and who was at least ostensibly her friend. Just now she was too tired to be angry. Ben had changed his presentation, and sat back in the chair, put on an English accent and was Alistair Cook, introducing a segment of Masterpiece Theater. Anna was the Victorian heroine, he explained, of tonight's segment, and she had received, in a part of the story that he had to summarize, a love letter from a half-wit named Michael, whom Anna disliked but whose advances she had to tolerate for the good of the Empire. He began reading again. "What a difficult job it is to get through life with such a balance level. Then again, and here's the irony, what an easy job it seems to get through life. When the choice is Paris or London, love or friendship, truth or wonder, how can one choose wrong?" He stopped reading, took off his glasses, raised his eyebrows at the camera and asked, "How indeed? And how will our troubled Anna be able to choose, when the future of the British colony in Rhodesia hangs in the balance? Episode Four of *Anna of Kensington; Anna of Salisbury.*"

The audience applauded and it was not until then that Ben noticed Anna in the doorway. She hoped that he would not drawn attention to her, but her hope died immediately, as she knew it would. "Why, here is the dear thing now; gentlemen and ladies, I give you the recipient of this painfully stupid epistle, Dr. Anna Browning, please make a path—a *wide* path—for her, boys." She walked over and sat on the arm of the chair. She couldn't yank him away from the party when he was the center of attention, nor could she ruin his performance, so she did her best to smile, and crossed her arms over the top of her stomach, and said nothing.

Ben folded the letter with a glance at her and put it into his jacket pocket, and it appeared that the show was over, but then a woman Anna didn't know, the wife of one of the graduate students apparently, with long nails and blue eye shadow, said, "I've always wanted to go to Norway . . .." and that set them off laughing again, the grad student spouse hiding his head in shame while laughing as hard as the rest. Ben produced the letter with a flourish and was off again. He cupped his hand to his ear and leaned forward toward the audience: "How *pleasant* the rain sounds!"

A half an hour later, the fun was over and Anna grabbed the chance to tell Ben she was tired and wished to go home and a half an hour after that all the goodbyes had been said and they walked out to the car. The nameless woman watching television had been nowhere to be seen the rest of the evening.

Anna drove, for she hadn't been drinking.

"Here," he said, handing her the letter, once the car was underway. It was a short drive home.

"You could have asked. I would have let you use it, I suppose."

"Spur of the moment. I saw it tonight in your study, and grabbed it on the way out."

If so, Anna thought, it would surprise her. She guessed that he had thought of the idea when she had first shown him the letter. But she didn't feel like having a fight tonight, not over the letter. In fact, now that she thought about it, she felt considerably more like a finger-tip massage, with chilled coconut oil, soothing the tight skin over her belly. Ben could do the job, if he wasn't too tipsy to be interested, and if his coconutty fingers found their way between her legs and brought her to orgasm, she would not, she thought, say *no* to that, either. She looked over at him sitting looking out of the window, and guessed that he was not too tipsy.

"I told Mildred that I was working on a secret research project for the N.S.A."

He chuckled. "Did she take it?"

"She took it."

He chuckled again. "She will henceforth hold you in great respect, my dear, damn her tight little right-wing rectum."

"I thought that was her husband," Anna observed.

"What?"

"A tight, right-wing asshole."

Now he laughed out loud and reached over and put his hand on hers and she knew that she was right and he wasn't too tipsy and she hurried a little to get home.

~

Every night for the past six months, Anna had awakened in the late night not knowing where she was. Literally. Every night. Sometimes the disorientation would be complete and she would be afraid. She would lie motionless in bed and search the dark room desperately for something she recognized, some hint of where she was. Nothing would look familiar. Sometimes she would move about and Ben would wake up; he thought this was good sport and would add to her confusion: he would call her other names like Frieda or Pam. "What's the matter, Pam?" Or "What is it Frieda? Where *are* we? I'm frightened." And when she finally came fully awake and figured the shadows out, he would laugh and go back to sleep, and, a little later, so would she.

Many times, though, it was like this night: a quiet, short-lived minor disorientation. She opened her eyes and saw the dark place on the wall in front of her. It looked like a cave. Why was she sleeping in front of a cave? Where was she? She was naked. Who might be around? She pulled the sheet up to her shoulders. Why was this place lighted? Shortly, in less than a minute, she reached the stage she enjoyed, actually, the tiny instant when she crossed over from confusion to understanding; the moment when her brain began to figure things out; when something whispered in her ear *It's the familiar confusion, Anna. You know, like every night. In a minute you'll be awake and will know where you are.* That instant was fun, and, as the months had gone by and the disorientation had returned in one form or another every night, she had come almost to look forward to it. She could feel herself coming back into control and she enjoyed the feel.

Quickly, tonight, she did. The dark shape was the bookshelf against the bedroom wall; the light was the moon. She lay on her side; Ben slept quietly behind her. Down the hall she heard a comforting silence from the children's rooms. The faucet was dripping into the bathroom tub. Outside, the street was quiet, though a dog barked somewhere nearby. Not theirs.

Often, she went right back to sleep after the confusion, but tonight she seemed to be fully awake. She rolled over onto her back, the small mound of her belly bulging under the sheet. Her mouth tasted of Colgate and Scope, which between them were still not enough to mask completely the aftertaste of Mildred's too-garlicky bean dip, all overlaid with the bleachy taste of semen from their lovemaking. It was a combination that in the abstract sounded unattractive, but which in reality was not all that unpleasant. She felt good and would have suggested sex again, even to the extent of intercourse, if they could have found a way to fit together comfortably, and if Ben had been awake. But he wasn't and waking him up was rarely a good idea.

She thought instead she might do some work. Not get-up-and-get-dressed-and-push-a-pencil-around-at-her-desk work, not detail work, but work here, in bed. Many times a flash of insight came more easily when she just held the problem she was working on in her head for a while, eyes closed, breathing deeply. She thought she might use the technique on Jablonski's second transformation, now that she knew who and where she was.

One's brain, though, had to be made ready for such thinking; synapses had to be warmed up; the sleep must be driven away. Anna's usual exercise was to multiply two three-digit numbers together in her head, which she did, as she quietly eased herself out of bed and down the hall to the bathroom. She chose two, as she sat to pee: 617 times 387 is . . . 238,779. Again. 126 times 752 is . . . 94,752.

She did not pass her own test. The numbers did not flow smoothly enough. She had to strain a fraction too hard. The thinking she did would be compromised if she tried tonight. The flashes, she knew from experience, would be flashes of dead ends and not insights. It was probably the party's fault. Mildred's fault. The garlic's fault. Ms. Winston's fault. The fault of the woman with long fingernails who wanted to go to Norway some day. The fault of the strange woman lying on the bed singing *It's So Easy* along with her friend on the telephone. She tightened the hot water faucet in the tub to stop the drip, turned out the bathroom light, and walked back down the hall.

She had felt, she admitted to herself now back in the dark bedroom, having checked the children in their sleep, she had felt a quirk of something in the first flash of recognition of Mike's letter. It was a strange feeling which she now tried to identify. Well, she thought to herself, it was not betrayal of Mike Reid. He, after all, would never know that his letter had been the brunt of Ben's ridicule, nor did Anna feel the kind of loyalty that is a necessary ingredient of betrayal. She was honest enough to remember that her own first reaction on reading the letter was that it was worthy of Ben's biting sarcasm. No, betrayal of Mike was not what she felt.

But there had been a quirk of something. Maybe, that it hadn't been the deal. She had shown Ben the letter for her own purposes, not so Ben could display his witty talents to adoring students. But no, she had never been jealous of her husband. She herself was amused by his wit, and she remembered when they had first met years ago at a party and he had said, shaking her hand somewhat longer than was necessary, "My, my, my. And here we have the winner of the gold in the Nordic Combined." And when someone, probably her date, asked him what he meant, he had said, "The Nordic Combined: hair, eyes and ass; blond, blue and, well, I can only imagine." If anyone else had said that, she might have been insulted, but there was something in Ben that made such statements, or made things like taking her letter without asking, acceptable. She admired his intellect so much that she was willing to accept that the rules were different for him. Furthermore she admired his success and knew that performances like tonight's were very much a part of the *Ben Browning treatment*, which brought that success. No, she had been as amused as the rest at the reading.

She slipped back into bed and under the sheet next to her husband, lying on her side, face to the outside of the bed.

So the quirk must have been that he had never seen the letter as representing something that she needed to talk about. But it was very much like Ben that he had not seen this need; that he had not seen the Jablonski connection. Ben was not one to understand the uncertainty that Jablonski had brought to her work, nor one to see that there was something attractive as well as distasteful in Mike Reid's life. She could not ask Ben to be that which he was not and the quirk was fading fast as sleep began to come back to her.

617 times 387 hadn't come quite effortlessly enough tonight, and the urge to work was drifting away. The evening, though, had uncovered a bit of renewal and she felt ready to work tomorrow and eagerly awaited the hours back with the problem. Did she have any remorse? Did she, in the end, regret having shown the letter to Ben? Was her mood of weeks earlier when she had initially decided to keep the letter to herself, was that mood with its small touch of fondness—or at least ambivalence—toward Mike Reid reinstated? She thought her feelings over. No, it was not, not really. She turned over onto her other side, her body naked and quietly pregnant, and she went back to sleep.

# THE SUMMER OF 1984

~ 2

# AT JFK INTERNATIONAL AIRPORT, NEW YORK CITY

For about the third time in his life, Michael Reid forgot that TWA's domestic flights into JFK arrive at a different terminal from where the international flights depart, so he was somewhat disoriented when he disembarked his flight from Washington National and walked into JFK's TWA arrival hall, the sweeping ceiling and tall windows were not there and the television monitors did not list his flight to Amsterdam. But he remembered in time, before having to ask like some college kid on junior year abroad, and found the sidewalk that connected the two terminals. He had plenty of time, and he walked across at an unhurried pace, with a beat-up backpack across one shoulder and no other baggage. He travelled light, which was trendy these days: one bag, littered with old baggage tags. The tags, of course, were not thought trendy by those who read *The Sophisticated Traveler*, but to hell with them. He also had a map of the world at home with little lines drawn all over it. To hell with them all, he would take his small pleasures where he found them. A man in a dark blue business suit dodged passed him and ran ahead, carrying an attaché case and with his tie flapping over his shoulder.

He anticipated with some eagerness boarding the 747, and he slowed his pace a bit more in order to savor the feeling. He hoped the plane would not be full; there is no more comfortable way to travel, he thought, than on a half-empty 747. He would also soon have jet lag and he anticipated that, too, with some eagerness. It made him feel like he was moving and it upset the rhythm of life in a way he found stimulating. He thought the schemes one saw in magazines like *Business Week* for avoiding jet lag were a form of heresy. Avoiding jet lag was like avoiding piquant sauce. Jet lag, think of it, was a malady, if that's what it was, unknown thirty years ago.

Michael walked into the TWA international terminal and now the disorientation was gone. It was just as he'd left it. He checked in at the ticket counter, showed his passport and set his backpack on the scale. The agent told him that he could keep it, as the plane wasn't full and there was plenty of room. Michael smiled through his moustache and thought that his luck was running pretty good today. An auspicious beginning. He hoped that the agent would notice that his ticket was for around the world; he would have liked to have smiled at her and said something like, "Yes, I know." But she didn't, and the effect would not have been the same if he had drawn her attention to the fact, so he picked up the pack and walked down the concourse toward security. There he exchanged pleasantries with the guard, sent his pack through the X-ray machine, and himself through the metal detector, and continued, with minimal delay, his quiet and leisurely way to the gate. The plane would not board for more than an hour, so he took a seat at the gate and pulled out a postcard to write to Marie:

> *This is it. Leave tonite for Adam. See you in Phoenix, July 30, TWA 652 from LAX, 12:30 pm, local time. Expect jet lag. What a wonderful perspective, to see Phoenix as east of New York. Here:*
> *Oh, it's Saturday night/ everyone's having fun/ I'm at the laundromat/ tryin' to get my washing done.*
> *Michael.*

His friend Marie Cochran, to whom he was in the habit of sending postcards while waiting for airplanes, was spending the summer in Phoenix, an idea breathtaking in its foolishness, from his perspective. He much preferred Albuquerque, where she usually lived, where he had lived, where they had taught school, hiked the mountains, argued religion and brands of beer together for years. And where they had begun their now years-long, on-again, off-again love affair. Anyway, she was in Phoenix for the summer and they had made plans to meet up at the other end of this trip, but this he decided not to anticipate, it being contrary to his theory of travel to contemplate the end at the beginning and also because he had only left home two weeks earlier and Emily's tender goodbye was nearby.

Just now, though, he couldn't find Marie's temporary Phoenix address in his book. It must be somewhere inside his pack but he wasn't going to look for it now, so he addressed the card to the address he knew well at her Albuquerque duplex on Manzano NE and walked down the concourse to mail it. He had once had his pack stolen, years ago, in the New York Port Authority bus terminal, not far from here, really, when he had left it unattended just about this long. But he didn't think that anything would happen this time; his luck seemed to be running to the good. Back in his seat in the departure lounge with his feet propped on the pack, he sat with his arms crossed, thought about how he liked the smell of jet exhaust and waited for the flight to Amsterdam to be called.

## ALBUQUERQUE, NEW MEXICO

*Neither leisured foreigner seized the weird height.*

Richard Randolph sat alone, between home plate and the coach's box, on the third base side of the Albuquerque Dukes' stadium and watched the clouds over Sandia Crest to the east begin to turn pink as the sunset neared. He and Michael Reid had once sat just about here on just such a summer evening, contemplating the Crest and letting the boys battle their ways to the big leagues, or no, with little in the way of the attention they deserved. Even now Franklin Stubbs was at bat and Richard knew that he should be paying more attention to the hitch in his swing, for soon, it was commonly thought, Franklin would be on TV, playing for the Dodgers, and the color man would be talking about that hitch and Richard would be pleased to have analyzed it some months or years previously. Such was the life of the serious Triple A baseball fan, as Richard Randolph fancied himself.

But just now he was not being a serious Triple A fan, as they had not been—Michael, an occasional summertime visitor, was never a serious Triple A fan—as they had not been on that earlier day, when Michael had stared at the Crest for a while, munched a little contraband Chinese, smuggled into the ballpark, and had said:

"Neither leisured foreigner seized the weird height."

"Just what, exactly, the fuck are you talking about?"

"Neither leisured . . . ."

"I heard you."

"*E before i* words. They all break the rules."

"Christ. Watch the game."

"I am watching the game. Ball, strike, foul, ball, ball, counting backwards; the last ball was a slider away."

"You wouldn't know a slider if you shook hands with one."

"Maybe not, but that," he had said, gesturing at the Crest with a pair of chopsticks, "that sure the holy hell is a weird height."

Indeed it is, Richard thought as he did almost every time he sat along the third base line at Dukes Stadium. And he sat here often for he liked to watch both the Crest and the third base coach. He admired the utter disregard for the law embodied in the coach's abuse of the coach's box. As a law professor he must condemn, or at least eye suspiciously such blatant mocking of the rules. Just now, for example, the coach was easily a foot-and-a-half outside the box, signaling to Franklin Stubbs. Hit and run? Maybe. Down by one in the middle innings at home against Tucson, a lower division team. But would you hit and run Franklin Stubbs? Richard guessed not.

So, maybe as a law professor he should condemn the outside-the-box-straying coach, but as a private citizen he could admire him and think of dozens of outside-the-stadium rules that he, if he had the nerve of that coach, would flout just as boldly. Stubbs took the pitch and the runner held at first. You do not hit and run with Franklin Stubbs, a big, hitch-swinging slugger, at the plate.

Indeed it is a weird height, he thought, as the batter stepped out, the stadium's lights came on, and Richard looked again at the Crest, which was still catching the sun, even as the field itself became dark. Anyone who, one day, wondered what a *weird height* was, should be led to this very seat and made to contemplate the Crest as it rose like a stone forehead over the malls, the watered lawns and the backyard barbecues of Albuquerque's northeast heights. That is, on the unlikely assumption that anyone would ever give a shit what a *weird height* was. But the Crest surely was one and Richard enjoyed the view. There were, he thought, few better places in the world to watch a ball game. Just about then, the Tucson pitcher hung a curve and Franklin Stubbs hitched his swing and mashed a line drive onto the right field wall in the gap, and, though there seemed to be no connection, Richard found himself recalling the glance he had taken at the breasts of Britt Larsen, a second year law student and his research assistant, and he wondered just exactly what the fuck *that* was all about. Franklin Stubbs was thrown out trying for third, and a small, chunky woman several rows up, with platinum hair and black eyebrows and a hickey on her neck, yelled "The ump sucks the big weenie" for all to hear.

Any number of reasons could be given why Richard's midmorning wayward eye in the Forum at the law school had surprised, if not dismayed him. In the first place, (although no real order came to his mind as the top of the fifth came and went with not much to distract him from this train of thought), in the first place, those breasts, rather remarkable though they were, riding apparently freely behind a red silk shirt with large yellow orchids on the front and back, were far from the most remarkable things about Ms. Larsen. The most remarkable things, which he had noticed the first time she had shown up at his office door, inquiring about his search for a researcher, were her eyes. They were a very pale blue and had a look behind them that Richard had previously seen only in pilots and quarterbacks, a look, an expectation, of being listened to, of being in charge, of being one to be reckoned with. *The* one to be reckoned with. She had looked these blue eyes straight at him, as if she knew there was no way she would not be his researcher. This was not a woman used to hearing the word *no*. To this look, he noticed in future meetings, was added a certain extra vision, as if she were able to see what was happening on the far side of the moon. Her eyes, this look, were so arresting that for weeks he had had little other image of her. And so, first, Richard found it somewhat surprising that he had involuntarily today found her attractive below, say, the nose.

Other reasons drifted through his mind as the game went on and the sky became dark, meandered like grounders through the legs of a kid on the way down. For one thing he was rather happily married and he and his wife had sex often and creatively. He had had one divorce, which he considered a lifetime supply, and besides, another divorce was not really in the picture because if Rita, his wife, would ever discover him sleeping with a student she would not divorce him, she'd blow his fucking brains out is what she'd do.

In the bottom of the sixth, the Dukes mounted a bit of a rally, scored twice and took the lead. There was a play at home and the Tucson catcher made the big league play to end the inning. Their pitcher was a shade out of position backing up the plate, and while that had no effect on this game, Richard noted it, as, he supposed, did the Tucson brass.

Where was he? In the fifth place—or is this the fourth?—for two years, from somewhat before his divorce until somewhat before his remarriage, he had slept around and had found it unfulfilling and rather threatening, and he had no desire to begin that again, none. Period. He also considered sex with students to be, if not *per se* unethical, at least very compromising and not to be considered, let alone pursued. Besides, Ms. Larsen was a member of the Law Women's Action League, the macho-fem left wing of the more moderate Women's Law Student Caucus, though the latter group would, in fact, object to any characterization of *moderation,* the center of UNM law school politics being well left of center. He had seen her name last spring on a petition from the Action League supporting the staff's desire—or was it a demand?—the staff's *request* that a break room be found for them somewhere in the building. The request and its supporting petition had ended up in possession of the chair of the Facilities Committee, *to wit* Richard Randolph, and had been a complete pain in the ass, as it had necessitated dealing with the law librarian, who was difficult. In the end, though, the staff got their break room, the library moved its rare book room, and the American Indian Law Center lost one of its conference rooms, leading to many observations, meant to be insightful, about how when European-Americans needed more space the Indians inevitably had to cough it up.

None of this Richard found particularly objectionable, including the positions of the staff, the Caucus, the Action League, the Indians, nor Britt Larsen personally, beyond the inconvenience of his having to deal with it. So Ms. Larsen was in solidarity with her under-paid sisters who manned, if that was the word, the word processors, the telephones and the copy machines around the law school. Big deal. But he couldn't think just now, the top of the seventh having seen the Toros go down one-two-three, what, if anything, the deliberations of the Facilities Committee had to do with Britt Larsen's rather eye-catching breasts. Well, yes, he supposed that membership in the Action League might bring Ms. Larsen's romantic, as well as her political, life into consideration. He knew nothing of her private affairs, but this line of thought made him wonder. Perhaps she was a fuzz. *Fuzz* was Rita's word for a woman who either slept with other women but said she didn't, or who didn't but said she did. But no, there was nothing fuzzy about Ms. Larsen's blue eyes, and he suspected, from the little he knew about her, that, if her preferences tended toward the off-beat, then, forsaking camouflage, she'd say so.

"Ah ha," he said aloud, to himself, wondering for the first time it *that,* in fact, was the attraction, competing with her eyes and other body parts. "Well well well well well. A-hem." Now there was a question the analysis of which promised to keep him busy through the eighth inning at least. He called for the beer man, tugged his Dodgers cap low, down over his eyes, put his feet on the railing in front of him, laced his fingers across his stomach and watched, with the eyes of a serious Triple A fan, as the Albuquerque shortstop went deep in the hole and threw late to first.

## ALBUQUERQUE

Britt Larsen, the object of Richard Randolph's late inning thoughts, was in his sight actually, at least if one takes a broad definition of *in sight*, on top of Sandia Crest, some ten or fifteen miles in a straight line from the third base boxes. Her arms were folded and she leaned over the guard rail and looked at the city below. Albuquerque presents a spectacularly lovely sight from ten and a half thousand feet at sunset, with its lights coming on. In particular, the lighted green and brownery of Dukes Stadium is admired even by non-fans for its lovely setting. (Of course she could not see the Albuquerque shortstop who was just now going deep in the hole and throwing late to first.) The city's street lights shimmered as the desert's late afternoon heat left to warm the stars and give rain to Kansas. Far in the west, beyond Mt. Taylor, a dusty breeze caught the last rays of the sun and made an orangeness that promised a cool evening ahead.

Britt had bought carry-out barbecue in town and had driven the back way up the Crest to dine alone and watch the sun go down. It was pleasant and peaceful up on the Crest, and quiet now, in May, before the tourists arrived. She gnawed the end of a rib, licked her fingers and wiped them on a paper napkin, silently, her eyes fixed on a point over the horizon, a bit south of west. There, well over the horizon actually, in Phoenix, the sun would still be high enough to be hot. But then, it was always hot in Phoenix.

When it was fully dark and getting a little chilly, she walked back to her car and drove slowly down the hair-pinned road, through the piñon, juniper and scrub oak forest and north on highway 14. After about ten miles, she pulled into the parking lot of the Golden Inn, a ramshackle little bar a few miles short of the actual town of Golden, if *town* is the right word for an old, now touristy, trading post, a gas pump and a church. She got out of her car and leaned for a few minutes against its door, breathing the cooling desert air, and looking back down the road to the south. Then she walked through the barroom doors and inside, where the air was smoky and warm, and the country music was turned up loud. A few patrons were dancing to the juke box, but most were sitting at tables drinking and talking: bikers and hippies, immigrants and rancher boys, gays and straights, college kids and old timers. The Golden Inn was very much a live-and-let-live kind of place, and a whiff of marijuana smoke in the air would not be unknown, though the air was so heavy with cigarette smoke that no one would notice, even if anyone cared, which no one did. The small, raised platform was set up for a band, which was nowhere to be seen.

Passing the tables, she walked straight toward the bar.

"Hey, doll!" The bartender and part owner, whose name was Doris, waved at her from behind the bar. "Pull up a stool. Long time; no see." Doris was sixty-ish, wore her hair in a long, grey braid, and had a face wrinkled and weathered by too long in the New Mexico sun. She wore faded jeans and a Grateful Dead tee shirt and somewhere, surely, she had a cigarette, perhaps two, burning in an ashtray. She sipped on a glass of ice water. "Where you been, doll?" She had that bartenders' way of using generic nicknames to disguise the fact that she couldn't remember the names of even the customers she knew as regulars.

"Hi, Doris. Bring me a Tecate."

"Comin' up." She reached into a cooler, grabbed a brown bottle, opened it and put it in front of Britt, who had claimed a bar stool. All the others were empty, though two guys were leaning against the end of the bar, drinking draft beer. "No glass, right?"

"Good memory. No glass, but a chunk of lime, if you've got it."

Doris balanced a small corner of lime on the top of the bottle. Britt squeezed three drops of juice into the beer, then pulled the bite of pulp off the lime peel with her teeth and took the first pull from the bottle around the lime pulp. "Need a light?," Doris offered.

"Naw, I'm trying to quit."

"So, doll, where ya been? I haven't seen you in here much. You still digging for bones down near Tijeras?"

"Get with the program, Doris. We don't dig for bones, we dig for pot shards." She had to raise her voice to be heard over the music.

"Whatever. What happened? Did they close down the dig?"

"No, the dig's still going, but I hung up my trowel. I left the Forest Service, and I'm in law school, now, and I don't get over to this side of the mountains very often. But I was up on the Crest, and . . ." Britt shrugged her shoulders, ". . . I thought I'd stop in here for a beer. How ya been? How's business? Here's lookin' atcha." With a long swig, she took down a third of the bottle.

"About the same. Too many fights; not enough cash flow. Me? Too many cigarettes; not enough sex." Doris laughed, a throaty, smoker's laugh, ending in a phlegmy cough, before she went down the bar to pull two more for the guys drinking drafts. She drifted back. "Law school? I guess I can see that. You like it?"

"Yeah. I get to work in the shade and have a drink of water whenever I want." A pause for Doris's laugh.

"You do have that pale, indoors look."

"No, really, it's fun. And every day that I walk into the school, I stop and remember that it's better than working."

"Sounds good. For you, maybe," said Doris, sounding unconvinced. "Too much reading. Too much reading indoors for me. Say, whatever happened to that little red head you used to come in here with? What was her name?"

"Lorinda." Britt took another long drink from the Tecate bottle. "She went by Rindy."

"Rindy, right," said Doris, faking it. "She was a pistol, that one. I haven't seen her for a while either. Whatever happened to her?"

"Beats me. I haven't seen her since she delivered her one-liner on that stool right over there, and then walked through those doors and out of my life." Britt pointed with her right hand to a stool three down from where she sat, then gestured with her head to the left toward the doors.

"What one-liner?"

"Doesn't matter. Ancient history." She finished the beer. "I'll have another."

A waitress walked up to the bar with her tray. "Hey, Britt," then to Doris, "Three C-lites with," which was bar shorthand for *three Coors Lights, with glasses.*

"Comin' up." Doris pulled the bottles from the cooler, twisted off the caps and put the bottles and glasses on the waitress's tray. "I'll swear. I make half my money serving Coors Light and I don't know how anyone can stand to drink the shit." She then put a Tecate down in front of Britt, who took a long swallow.

"Makin' love on the beach . . .," Britt said, starting the old anti-Coors joke, and tipping the brown bottle in Doris's direction.

"Yeah, . . .," Doris responded on cue, "Fuckin' near water." They clicked beer bottle to water glass, then Doris walked down the bar, dragged on her cigarette, but left it in the ash tray, and wandered back to Britt. "Well, listen honey, if you want my opinion, gettin' blue over ancient history is a bad idea. Let it go, is what I think."

"Who says I'm blue?"

"Honey doll, I'm a barkeep. I do three things: I pull drafts, I sell Slim Jims, and I diagnose the blues. And the blues-o-meter pinned over in here the moment you walked through those doors. Let it go."

"It shows, does it? I didn't know it was that obvious." Britt thought for a minute, and took several smaller sips from her beer, then said, "No, it wasn't Rindy, that's for sure. I let go of that long ago, and she was not on my mind when I walked in or sat down. Not until you asked after her." Doris looked skeptical. "No, really. But I'll admit that I'd been up on the Crest thinking about something that had been said to me on the phone, earlier in the summer."

"Who said what?"

"Oh, nobody you'd know. A new girl friend. Maybe. She said she was going to spend the summer in Phoenix."

"Foolhardy proposition there. I never cared for Arizona myself."

"I hear you."

"But so . . .?"

Britt shrugged. "The summer's getting along."

"What happens then?"

She shrugged again. "We'll see. But the question is whether I want to do this again. Now, I mean."

"Does she?"

"Who knows? She's spending the summer in Phoenix, isn't she?"

"Hold that thought." Doris walked down to the end of the bar to take away the glasses and empty the ashtray of the two guys that had just left, apparently in an attempt to pick up two hippie girls who sat at a table near the bandstand, looking on the whole rather open to the possibility. She wiped the bar clean with her rag, put out the two cigarettes that she had going, lit up a new one, then filled two orders for the waitress with the tray. Those orders then required her to restock the bar cooler with Coors Light, which entailed a trip to the cooler in the back. All the while, Britt sat, sipping her beer, staring into the mirror behind the bar. As Doris returned from the back, carrying a case of beer in both hands, Britt swiveled on her stool and looked around the bar, but at nothing in particular.

"Okay, I'm back." Doris was putting the beers into the bar cooler, four at a time.

"Isn't there a band tonight?" Britt asked.

"Yeah, they're out in the back finishing a joint. Give them time; they're only thirty minutes late. This crowd doesn't begin to notice until a band is an hour late."

Britt stretched and yawned, then turned back to the bar, her nearly empty Tecate, and Doris.

"Here's what I think, doll: You never know what you're getting into when someone new walks your way. What I always say is *look before you leap*."

"You know what, Doris?" said Britt, "I was just thinking exactly the opposite."

"Leap before you look?"

"Actually, look beyond the jump."

"What's that mean?"

"Long story. Old, old equestrian advice. Give me one more."

Doris took a drag from her cigarette, then stubbed it out. "You're alone tonight, right honey? The cops're out."

"You think I'm drunk?"

"I think the Sandoval County deputies are out, tryin' to make their quota, this is a lonely stretch of highway, and you drank two beers, too fast. Blame the blues if you want, but you don't need a third."

"Thanks for the tip. Then bring me a cup of coffee instead, with cream."

"Comin' up."

The coffee came in a heavy white mug, with a spoon in it, and a couple of packets of creamer on the side. "It's been sittin' over there for a coupla hours, probably strong enough to float a nail. Lemme know; I'll make some fresh. We get less call for it than we should around here. Most who I tell to ease up tell me to piss off."

"Would I ever tell you to piss off?" Britt studied one of the little sacks of creamer. "Got any real milk somewhere back there, Doris? I don't care for soybeans in my coffee."

"Hold on, doll, somewhere around here's some half-and-half."

It came in a stainless steel pitcher, cold from the cooler. Britt thumbed the lid open, filled her spoon with the cream, and let it drip, drop-by-drop, into the black coffee. Each drop splotched the surface, until finally, after a second spoonful, the coffee was a mottled, swirled dark brown. Then, without stirring, Britt brought the cup to her mouth, blew on it quickly, and tested the temperature with her lips. Doris drifted down the bar to chat up three new customers that had taken stools, including the one Lorinda had used when she had said it was over, while Britt slowly drank her bad coffee, lightened just enough to be drinkable, then another cup, before she waved goodbye to Doris, laid a five and two ones on the bar, and walked to her car for the long drive back to town.

## ~ 3

# NEAR SKIBOTEN, NORWAY

Michael Reid, a long way from Duke's Stadium and with no baseball on his mind, pulled aside the curtain across the tipi's door and stepped from the warm smoky interior into the midnight brightness of the June snow. His moustache smelled of boiled reindeer grease and he held two beers in his hands by their necks. Sometimes, he thought to himself as he arched his stiff backbone and looked up into the broken clouds racing inland on the cold wind, sometimes life's just too fucking strange to be believed. He turned back and smiled his thanks to the Sami matriarch who had been his hostess. "Thank you. *Toosand tak.*" A thousand thanks. His Norwegian was far from being up to saying *Sometimes life's just too fucking strange to be believed.* He just let it go without saying, dropped the curtain and turned to look around at the midnight-lit scene.

There were three other reindeer-hide tipis set up in the cleared area around him. The gathering of traditional Sami people (whom he had called *Laplanders* until having been schooled in Sami language and sensibilities) had been going on for a day or two and would go on for a week more. Sami etiquette required that before this long, bright night was over he would have to visit the other tents, sample the stew, drink a beer or two and listen to the babble of Sami language and Norwegian, neither of which he understood. The other matriarchs would be insulted, he had been told, if the American stranger favored one tipi over the others. Small enough price to pay, really—no price at all, really—for the chance to stand here and be totally baffled at how unlikely things can turn out to be.

A river ran nearby. He could hear the roar of the rapids, and he walked toward the sound, through the tall, skinny pines, the reindeer lichen crunching under his feet in the places where the snow had melted off. A little cold fresh air would clear his head, he thought, and word was that the salmon were running up that river, so he would have a look. At the bank, he cleared a bit of snow off the ground with his shoe and sat, back up to a boulder. The river was broad and shallow and running fast with the melt. Occasionally a bit of ice would rush by, but no salmon, assuming he would know the look of a running salmon when he saw one, which he reckoned unlikely. The clouds sped by overhead, showing small bits of blue, but mostly a white-grey, issuing, he now noticed, a flake or two of new June snow. He pushed his beer bottles into a snow bank within reach and leaned his head back against the boulder.

*Sometimes life is so ridiculous it's hardly worth living.* A Dustin Hoffman line from the movie *Little Big Man.* He tried to get the entire passage right. *I was just saved . . .* Start again. *My worst enemy just saved me from a violent murder at the hands of my best friend. Sometimes life's so ridiculous it's hardly worth living.* That was close. He preferred to overlook the suicidal implications; times were different in the Eighties: sometimes life was ridiculous enough to *be* worth living. He determined to sit here until he caught a glimpse of genuine midnight sun.

He had not yet seen the actual midnight sun—that is to say, the sun when it was actually midnight—even though he had been about two weeks now above the Circle at near midsummer and so for two weeks the sun had never set. It had been easy enough to miss the actual midnight sun; in Oslo one gets used to going to sleep when it is still late-evening dusk and sleeping through the little bit of washed-out starlight. Farther north one can just as easily sleep through the midnight sun. That, plus the generally cloudy and dreary weather, winter refusing to let go, had kept the sun out of his sight. It always looked like it was about ten o'clock in the morning, simple as that. The Sami events swirled around him now with little concern for the clock, nor for the sun, and he had become comfortable enough with that.

Nevertheless, there was no reason to go out of one's way not to see the actual midnight sun, and tonight, sitting on his cold, wet jeans, leaning against the boulder, with the salmon running and the snow falling, he could come close. It was a little past midnight, really, but he sat facing the north and caught, every now and again, a flash of the yellow disk. All in all, it was fairly unimpressive. Before long, he was asleep.

Mai Kaaren woke him, not many minutes later. She nudged his foot with her boot and smiled when he opened his eyes. Her hair, he thought as he looked up at her, was the color of Saturn, and he thought, too, that he was a little bit in love with her. Of course he had only known her for about two weeks and she was the wife of his friend Svein who had invited him to Finmark, that is to say the northernmost province of Norway, and who had been very hospitable to him, and she was the mother of two delightful little Norski/Sami children, and there was Emily, and Marie, too, but how, he wondered, was one to resist a woman whose hair was the color of Saturn?

"Do we have to go?" Svein and Mai Kaaren had brought him to this gathering and he was dependent upon them for a ride back to the hotel. He didn't get up.

"No. De pardy vill goe on all night long. If you vant to return to de hotel, you vill haf to find a ride. Are you tired?" He adored her accent and the rhythm of the words and he knew that he would unconsciously begin to mimic her speech pattern after about three sentences. He wasn't sure whether her ear for English was good enough to pick up the mimicry. He supposed it was and supposed, too, that she would find it condescending, so he tried to shake off the sleep and concentrate on speaking standard American English.

"No, I do not want to go back," he said. "I came ou'dere to vatch the midnight sun." Not a great start, he thought. Use contractions, go on, she can understand them, even though she does not—doesn't—use them. "I have two beers. Will you join me?"

"Yes." She sat down on her jacket and leaned up against the same boulder, close enough so that their shoulders touched. "Yes, let's have a beer."

"I'll show you a new trick; I learned it from one of the boys back there. How to open one beer bottle with another one." He picked up one beer and held it by the neck in his left hand, just below the cap. The heft was heavier than beer bottles back home and the bottle was bigger. He held the other beer in his right hand, upside down, with a point of the cap under the cap of the first bottle. Using his left index knuckle as a fulcrum, he levered the top bottle away from him. The cap of the bottom bottle popped off onto the ground.

Mai Kaaren laughed. "Hooray. How did you knoe dat the vrong cap vuld not come off?"

"At first I thought it was the cleverness of Norwegians. But now I see that I can do it, too."

"So maybe you haf become a little Norwegian."

"No, I haf decided that it is a principle of natural science that it is always the bottom cap dat comes off. No more strange than that the sun doesn't set and the salmon swim upstream." He handed her the open bottle. "Skol."

"Tak." She took a drink. "So vat do you tink of our midnight sun?" The sun was, in fact, just then gleaming through the clouds.

Still holding the unopened beer, he considered the sun. He held his hand up to shade his eyes. "Unimpressive."

"Ja?"

"Ja. The problem is that the midnight sun is meaningless without a timepiece nearby. There is no midnight sun unless it's midnight and how the hell is one to know that it is midnight when the sun is still shining? I have to look at my watch to know that I am looking at the midnight sun. Otherwise, it looks just like the ten-o'clock-in-the-morning sun." He held up the unopened beer bottle in his hand as if to toast the sun. "No offense. I'm thirsty."

"But how vill you open yours?"

"Ah, yes. That seems to be a problem I haven't thought about."

"Ve could put the cap back on this one and use it to open d'oder one, but then . . ."

They both laughed at the predicament.

"We will have to share," Mai Kaaren said. She took a long drink and handed him the bottle. "Skol."

"Here's to you," he said, looking straight into her eyes. He did not wipe the mouth of the bottle off. "Here's to you, to Norwegian beer, sweet with your spit, and to the midnight sun." He drank. "It's as if the Grand Canyon were not spectacular unless snapshot." He felt dramatic, poetic. "It's as if the enormity of the ocean could not be felt without a Pepsi machine to compare it with; as if a goldfinch were unremarkable when seen without binoculars. Whatever astronomical significance the midnight sun might have, it is the only natural phenomenon that comes to my mind that takes its meaning from humankind's measured tickings."

Mai Kaaren said nothing, but sat quietly next to him, with her arms crossed on her chest. He guessed that she missed most of that last speech. Nevertheless, he felt like talking. He went on, in the same vein: "But, while the midnight sun itself is unremarkable, I find constant daylight, on the other hand, to be an impressive phenomenon. It doesn't get dark in Finmark, it doesn't even get dusk. The rhythm of the day is gone. That's why the parties last so late, right? That's why the kids want never to sleep, right?" He leaned his head back against the boulder.

"Yes, sometimes it is difficult vit dem." Keeping up with his too-long speech in too-complicated English seemed to have tired Mai Kaaren out, and they sat quietly for a while, sharing the beer and watching the light snow fall. She had a heavy sweater on against the June chill, but he wondered if he should offer his arm across her shoulders to warm her. The bright night was full of the kind of sexual tension that Michael found most stimulating. He knew he was attracted to Mai Kaaren, but he could not read her. Certainly he had learned years ago that the fabled sexual freedom of Scandinavia was well overstated, at least in Norway, the most conservative of the countries, and probably especially here in the far reaches of the rural north. He was now as far from Oslo, he remembered, as Oslo is from Rome.

For himself, he was not sure either. There were the other two, Emily and Marie, who would be pissed if they knew. Well, Emily would be disappointed and Marie would be pissed. That, of course, added to the tension, the uncertainty, the not knowing what was ahead, and to the stimulation. It was all more stimulating, he thought, than sex itself. Really, now that he thought about it, the sex itself would be reasonably ridiculous. He could imagine what his white butt would look like, pumping away in the ten a.m. daylight of the northern night, lying here in the snow with who-knows-whom analyzing his technique. Or he could imagine the two of them crammed into the back seat of one of the Saabs parked past the tipis, trying to fit this there. *Wait. No. There. That's right. Wait. My neck. Ouch.* He smiled to himself.

"Vat are you smiling about?" she asked.

"Oh, I was thinking that in a couple of weeks I have to be in Amsterdam to catch a flight to Dubai in the Persian Gulf and how different that will be from all this. It will probably be very hot."

But kissing her, that would be something. Right here in the snow, with the salmon running and the midnight sun shining, a first kiss, lingering, open-mouthed perhaps, full of the potential that sometimes seems so much more than it turns out to be.

Mai Kaaren reached over and grasped the beer bottle so that their hands touched. She did not move to take the bottle away, though, and she, too, leaned her head back on the boulder. "I vould like to go somewhere varm. I get so tired of the snow."

"Greece. It always seems like the Greek islands are full of Northerners whenever I am there."

He knew himself well enough to know that he had no discretion in these matters. If any resistance or discouragement was needed to keep the kiss from happening, she would have to provide it, for he had none, not tonight with the salmon running and the June snow falling.

"Sure. I haf been to de islands. Svein and I haf even been once or twice. I love de sun when it is so varm."

He said nothing. Their hands were still touching on the neck of the beer bottle. He also knew himself well enough to know that he would not be aggressive nor insistent with respect to the kiss. If it were to come it would come almost on its own. And in the meantime, this delightful tension, this not knowing, this knowing that there were many reasons not to go ahead, was so exciting that he had to keep himself from shaking. He half suppressed a shiver.

They did kiss a while later, a kiss that arrived so smoothly that it was difficult to tell who had started it. And it seemed to Michael that her breast came into his hand just as much as his hand reached for her breast. They finished the beer and sat again, backs against the boulder.

"If we leave now, I'm told that the Sami grandmothers will be insulted."

"It is troo. You are the guest from America."

"There is no part of me that could manage a quickie with you here in the snow."

"Kvickie?"

"Uh . . . Hurried lovemaking."

"No."

"It's a little like never being able to open the last bottle of beer." They laughed and sat against the boulder. He reached over and put his hand on her blue jeans, reaching with his fingers to the seam that lay along the inside of her thigh. "Where is Svein?"

"He has already left with a friend. Svein and I are . . . not very happy. You understand?"

"Yes. And the children?"

"They are among their cousins. They will sleep here tonight in their grandmother's tipi."

"What shall we do? Will you come back to my hotel room with me?"

"Yes."

Neither one made a move to get up.

"Can we borrow a car?"

"No. That would be impossible. We haf been drinking. Here the police are very serious about driving after drinking."

"So let's see. I should pay my respects to the matriarchs, including your mother-in-law, and eat some more reindeer stew, we should walk two kilometers to the road and hitchhike through the early morning to my hotel where we will make love for the rest of the non-existent night."

"Ja. I tink so."

"And it will be several hours before we are in bed."

"Ja. I tink so."

"And it will never get dark."

"No."

So he kissed her again, and held her breast, afraid that he would probably die sometime in the next several hours out of the pure anticipation. "There are times, Mai Kaaren, when I am very glad that I am not twenty years old. There are some things that it takes being forty to appreciate and I shall savor this strange Norwegian foreplay as the gourmet dish that it is."

In the end, it did not happen as they had planned, and the whole darkless evening turned out to be less a form of Norwegian foreplay, than Samian-style *coitus interruptus*. One of the children took sick, perhaps from the stew, more likely from sleep deprivation, and had to be taken back to town. Svein showed up from somewhere, looking every bit as if a quickie were very much part of his repertoire. Off they went in their car, braving the threat of the police, leaving the older child in the care of her grandmother. Mai Kaaren said goodnight to Michael with what might have been a touch of wistfulness, but then again, maybe it was his imagination, and she was only concerned about her child and pissed off at her spouse. It was hard to tell. But at the last second, before she climbed into the car, and out of earshot of the others, she turned to Michael and spoke a phrase: "*Jeg kommer til dere*," a phrase he did not recognize, but which she would explain, days later when she lay in his arms in his hotel room, meant *I will come to you*.

But right then, he did not know what Wednesday afternoon held in store for him, so he did the rest of that evening right, first from tipi to tipi, and later a long walk on the rough-cut logging road to the main highway, where, after some measureless time, he flagged down a trucker bound for the coast, and back at his hotel, with the drapes open to the bright sky, he thought perhaps overly long about Mai Kaaren and Emily and Marie, until sleep caught up with him, after which he dreamt of all three.

## PHOENIX, ARIZONA

The Arizona sun was so hot it made the water tepid, as Marie Cochran swam laps in the Escalante public swimming pool. The children waited impatiently through their rest period while Marie and a few other adults, with serious faces and without laughing, paddled up and back, each in his or her own lane and thoughts. There was little to connect what these few grownups did with the water to what the youngsters did; not one adult seemed to be having fun.

Marie certainly was not. No one with any sense, she thought to herself, not for the first time, comes to Phoenix in the summer. It was only late-June, Michael had said he'd be here in late-July and Marie was already tired of waiting for him, tired of the heat, tired of the stupid palm trees and she wanted to be home in Albuquerque. Summer session was half over, she reminded herself, as she tumble-turned into her final lap, and Michael was who-knows-where, somewhere in Asia she guessed, though she hadn't heard from him since he left Europe. It was getting to be time to do what needed to be done, but what that was, she did not know.

She pulled herself out of the pool, just before the life guard whistled the squealing children back into the water, and walked over to where her towel was spread on the cement. She re-oiled herself against the sun and lay back, face up. The Phoenix sun was much hotter out of the water and seemed to press like a weight along her torso. Marie's body is short and lean. Her suit that afternoon was a bright blue, one-piece Speedo. She was proud that now, in her late thirties, she could still kick into a tumble turn and could still swim sixty meters—two lengths plus a turn in this pool—underwater. She was a short, small diet away from her college graduation weight, and the suit she wore that day she could have worn when she swam competitively twenty years ago. Her hair was black and cropped short and threatening to turn grey.

Britt's image seemed to want to form itself on the inside of her eyelids; it was not the first time that had happened in Arizona, and she did not discourage it. She had told Michael, Marie had, she had told him years ago as they had lain in bed staring up at the ceiling, sharing a joint and a warm can of tonic water, he talking about some place she couldn't recall, and she, with the kind of disconnectedness that their post-coital conversations sometimes had, she had told him, apropos of nothing, that, if she ever were to have an affair with another woman, the other one would have to lead her very firmly, and she had been right.

She and three school teaching buddies had, the previous March, been at the Café Fargo, a little jazz club near Candelaria and Wyoming on the east side of Albuquerque. The evening had started early, right after school on Friday, in Blackie's out in Moriarty where they all taught. After one round of drinks they had made phone calls and broken dates, telling their friends and spouses to fend for themselves, and the teachers had driven to Albuquerque, had dined on cheeseburgers and malts at the Owl Café, had seen *The Hustler*, re-running at Don Pancho's, and finally had found themselves drinking beers and discussing the movie at a small table near the back of the Café Fargo. All but Marie had to make the long drive back through the canyon to their homes in Moriarty, so the evening would not be an overly late one. Lanny McDonald was attacking a keyboard and the piano was resisting just enough so that the music was vaguely stirring. Jill was in the bathroom and Al and Susan were dancing and Marie, who drinks her beer over ice, was watching the bubbles collect around the cubes and thinking that she was tired of chaperoning Al and Susan. They were both married to other parties and had, for about the last two years, flirted rather openly with the idea of a tryst. For such an improbable event to happen just the right combination of inclination and opportunity would have to converge, and, Marie observed as she watched them dance, inclination seemed to be running rather high tonight. So, they would count on her and Jill to deny them the opportunity, they would each go home after much elbow rubbing and many double entendres, have sex with their legitimate spouses and the game would go on. Marie took a sip of cold beer. It would serve them right if she and Jill were to sneak away and leave them here to decide what to do on their own.

"Dance with me." It had not been a question; she was sure of that and if Michael would show his ass up from wherever the hell he was, she'd stress that. No question mark.

Marie looked up from the iced bubbles to see a lanky blond woman with her hands in her jeans' pockets, her cowgirl shirt pearl-buttoned two short of the top and her ragged blond bangs hiding her eyebrows. Her ears stood out just enough from the side of her head so that they peaked through her hair, which was loosely pulled back, and her mouth was wide, both guaranteeing that the word *pretty* would never be used to describe her. *Lovely*, though, was a real possibility. When Marie stood up, she found herself, even wearing mid-high heels, a half-head shorter than the stranger. And, still in her school clothes, she suddenly felt herself vastly overdressed for The Fargo.

They danced without touching. When the music stopped, the blond woman spoke: "I'm Britt Larsen." She had a scratchy, lower-register voice.

"Marie Cochran."

They smiled.

"Again?" This time, she asked.

"My friends and I . . .," Marie pointed to the table, ". . . we're kind of having a party."

"Let's have dinner sometime." That firmness again. And her eyes. Her eyes made pale blue seem the most determined color in the universe.

"I don't know . . . ." Lanny resumed the attack; it became difficult to talk.

"I'll call you," this Britt said.

"You don't know me."

A shrug. "I'd like to."

"You don't know my number."

"Tell me. I'll remember."

"Ah, five-two-one, four-double-five-four. Listen, ah, Britt, I don't . . . "

"I know. Neither do I."

⌒

"Who was that?" Jill asked.

"You don't know her . . ." Marie began, not knowing how she was going to finish.

"Who was that?" Al interrupted, helping Susan with her chair.

"Someone I don't know," Jill answered for her, "and now that that sort of ice has been broken, come on, Susie dear, let's have a dance. And Al, Marie needs a beer; the next round is yours to buy."

⌒

Britt called on Wednesday night.

"Hi. It's Britt Larsen. From the Fargo."

"Hello." Marie cleared her throat and then cut short any small talk. "Listen, I'm having a few friends over for dinner on Saturday night. Would you like to come over?" Using the word *over* twice sounded funny and her tongue threatened to tie. She was also about to giggle from the whole idea; she wanted very much not to giggle.

"Sure. What time? Where?"

"Seven. Three-eighteen-B Manzano, Northeast. It's a little up and down duplex."

"Manzano?"

"Yes. It's between Washington and San Mateo. Between Central and Lomas."

"Three-eighteen B."

"That's right."

"Got it. Seven?"

"Yes. And, . . ." Marie could feel herself blushing, even in her own living room, ". . . I'm sorry, what was your last name again?"

There was a short chuckle on the other end. "Larsen. With an *e*. L-A-R-S-E-N. Can I bring anything?"

"No. It's just going to be a small dinner. Just a few friends. Nothing very . . . fancy." *Honest to God*, Marie thought, *I almost said* intimate.

"Okay. See ya then."

Marie hung up. It would have been so much easier to have put her off.

~

Britt arrived last on Saturday, driving an old Corolla with a Forest Service bumper sticker that said *Prevent Grassland Fires*. She wore a blue shirtwaist dress with short sleeves, and sandals, through which her red toe nails grinned upwards, and she carried herself up the sidewalk to the door with a lightness uncommon in tall people. *She's tall, like I remembered*, thought Marie, *but somehow both slender and shapely, which I didn't*. They shook hands at the door, and Marie's dog Ginger gave her a sniff of approval.

"Hi, Marie. You look nice."

Marie had worried her way through the tail end of the week, wondering about this evening. She didn't know, after all, whether this Britt was even a, you know . . .. The word did not come easily to her; she was playing with a fantasy, juggling various feelings. She did not know whether she wanted her to be. If she was, it wasn't necessarily true that she would make a pass and, when Saturday came, Marie still didn't know what she would do if she did. *Dance with me.* Behind everything lay that, and she was driven though the week by that force. Yet she wasn't ready for her friends to suspect that she was entertaining the notion, even if she was, nor was she really ready to be with the stranger alone. So she fretted and carefully invited Jill and her husband, Bob Westwood (that is to say, the Moriarty connection), her old friends the Malones (to show she had friends from outside of work), and an extra single woman, Liz Gonzales from down the street (so that everyone wouldn't be all coupled up). She didn't know how the evening would begin or end, or whether Britt would do something forward at the door and what Marie would do then. But no, just *Hi, Marie. You look nice,* and a handshake.

The dinner party was a great success. She had ordered out hot chicken mole and carne adovada from El Modelo, Greek appetizers from Angelo's, Jamaican beer and Israeli wine. That way, she explained, her guests could have better than Marie could cook, but something that couldn't be had out. Everyone approved and madly sprinkled feta on the mole, washed guacamole down with Red Stripe, and unashamedly sipped a nice Be'ershevan Chateau Margaux with the decidedly non-kosher adovada.

Britt, too, was a great success as she charmed Marie's friends. Marie learned, along with the others, that Britt was a law student, finishing her second year, and that she and Marie had met some time ago at the wedding of a mutual friend. (This last, of course, was a fib, and Marie's pulse increased as she heard it related.) Britt had graduated from UNM in anthropology and had spent seven years with the Forest Service's archaeology survey, travelling throughout the southwest desert, digging, as she said, large holes with small shovels, before entering law school. She was an Albuquerque native and, it turned out, only two years behind Liz through Del Norte High. (That would make her, say, late twenties, Marie calculated, maybe thirty.) And so, as Marie settled these facts in her mind so that she could feign, if necessary, that she had known them for some time, the conversation fell to old what's his name on the football team and what is he up to these days?

The evening wore itself pleasantly on.

"*Brit*," asked Jill, "Is that short for *Britany*?"

"Short for nothing," said Britt, "Two t's. It's my mother's maiden name." And to Marie: "I don't think you knew that." *She's teasing me,* thought Marie, as she shook her head *no,* with a little smile on her lips.

"So, is it Swedish?" asked Liz.

"Dutch, actually," said Britt. "Two generations back. Well, three to me."

The guests talked and passed a joint around, but Britt declined, saying that she was trying to quit smoking, and smoking anything made her want a cigarette. And as the evening wore itself pleasantly on, it became clear to Marie that she wanted Britt to be the last to leave. She was liking her, and wished for the chance to get to know her better. *As a friend*, she thought to herself, *just as a friend*. Britt listened more than she talked, shied away from discussions of law or politics, and later, when they played the movie game, it was she who knew the name of the first song Sam sings in *Casablanca*.

"*It Had To Be You*," she announced to the disbelieving crowd, "Yes, really. A very up-beat version, just as the camera comes in through the doors at Rick's," and she sang a few lines. Then Jill remembered that Diane Keaton sings the same song in *Annie Hall* and that led to a discussion of whether Woody Allen made the connection with his movie *Play It Again, Sam* or whether it was just happenstance, which discussion broke down along typical pro- and anti-Woody lines, with Britt and Marie on different sides. And through this all, Marie fretted on, as she wanted Britt to be the last to leave, but wasn't sure why. And, as she had told Michael—the conversation came into her mind as she stood in the kitchen, the necks of cold beers between her fingers, listening to the buzz of conversation in the other room—as she had told Michael and knew was still true, she was not ready to be the first to commit to this, nor even to be the first to show her hand, if there was anything to commit to, or if there were any hand to be shown, and she didn't know Britt well enough even to know that.

One of the bottles slipped out of her hand, didn't break but bounced on the floor, splashing beer on the tile and her legs. She cleaned it up, decided she was worrying too much and joined the others, carefully sitting across the room from Britt. They were all on the floor, Britt with her legs straight out and ankles crossed, her dress riding just above her knees. Her back was to the couch and one arm was across the seat; two silver bracelets lay on that wrist against the white material. Tim Malone was admiring the bracelets, and, perhaps, the wrist; he touched them and turned them around to see the bottom side. Marie couldn't hear their conversation. Scattered around the floor where they all sat were ash trays, Bob's baggie of weed, a few album covers and books off the shelves. Talk swirled around Marie and she found herself thinking again of, well, you know, later. She wanted Britt to be the last to leave, but—she was worrying about logistics again—she didn't want it to be obvious that she wanted this; she didn't want there to be something for her friends to make anything of on the drive home:

*So who is this Britt?*

*I don't know; she seemed nice.*

*She was still there when we left. Looked to me like she was going to be the last to leave.*

*Oh. Hmmmmm. You don't suppose . . . .*

*Maybe. You know she's not married and she never would go out with Jim from the junior high.*

*Etc.*

Marie dreaded the thought of such a conversation going on while she and Britt sat on that couch and, what . . .? *What they do, exactly?*, she wondered. She wasn't at all sure that she would know how. She and Michael had once or twice fucked on that couch, she remembered. A close look at the underside of the cushion on which Britt's wrist now rested would reveal the evidence.

Her stomach felt like it was trying to digest a chain saw. Partly, she suspected, it was the marijuana, which had increasingly over the years given her indigestion. She attributed this phenomenon to advancing age and figured sometime soon she'd quit. But she hadn't had more than a hit or two tonight, and besides her ears were warm and the backs of her knees cold and she felt like she always had to use the bathroom; these, she knew, were the signs of tension, not grass, and as she leaned back against the wall under the front window and ran her fingers through her hair, she just did not know what the hell to do, with the evening, with her stomach or with her god damned brain which would not let things be as they would become on their own.

Once, later, they passed in the kitchen for a few seconds, alone; the very first time, Marie would remember later, they were ever alone together.

"Relax," Britt said to Marie, who wondered if the others could so easily see where her thoughts lay.

Luck saved her. Three guests left together and the Malones were just settling in for the comfortable late evening's talk which would have left Marie's nerves nowhere to hide, when their baby sitter called and said their kids were okay but she wasn't feeling well and could they come home quickly? Britt jumped up, saying, "I've gotta go, too. I'll let you out." Goodbyes were said and the guests drove away, never noticing that Britt parked her car in the street and walked back up to the house.

"Want to walk Ginger while I clean up the kitchen? Are you okay with dogs? She'll be fine. The leash is there by the door. Once around the block will be all she needs."

Britt smiled, attached the leash to Ginger's collar and closed the door behind her.

*Why all those words?*, Marie wondered, picking up and stacking the dishes in the sink. *Was I really trying to get her out of the house?* She shook her head at the mystery of it all, shook her head to clear it, but still didn't know what she was going to do when Britt and the dog came back through the door.

What they did was to sit on the white couch until after midnight and become the friends they had pretended to be all evening long.

"You're left-handed."

"I am," said Britt, "How did you figure that out?"

"I suspected it when we shook hands at the door. Left-handers have a different feel when they're shaking hands, something that tells me it's not their dominant hand. Then I noticed that you ate with your left." Britt said nothing. "I find left-handedness to be very mysterious. I don't know, somehow it makes me feel all turned inside out, thinking about what it would be like to be left-handed."

"Tell me something surprising about yourself," Britt asked. She sat with her elbow on the back of the couch and her head on her hand. Marie was at the other end, cross-legged, leaning against the arm of the couch. Ginger, a yellow LabX dog, with a doubtful pedigree, exhausted after the party, relieved after her walk, and sated from the treats of the indulgent guests, lay curled between them on the floor, her nose under her tail, her eyes seeming to follow their conversation. "Tell me something that will make me wonder if I should have come to dinner."

Marie thought for a moment before speaking. "I had my picture in *Sports Illustrated* once."

"Really? You're an athlete? Let me guess. Gymnastics?"

"I swim. Not any more, of course, not competitively, but I swam in college and the magazine wrote a story about the team."

"What college?"

"Allegheny. A small school in western P-A. We were pretty good for

Division III, but SI's hook was that there were three sets of identical twins on the team."

"You?"

"No, I'm an only child."

"So, what was it like?"

"The story? Not very special. It was nice at the time, though. Our coach made the photographer take a team picture, a pick-out-the-twins kind of thing. There were only ten of us on the team, so it wasn't that hard to do. Eight of us had four-point-oh GPAs, which would have been a better story, but they ignored that part."

"You?"

"Me. February something. Sixty-six. Jean-Claude Killy was on the cover."

"Jean-Claude Who?"

"Killy."

Britt shook her head.

"A big-deal French skier at the time. There's a copy around here somewhere." Marie knew exactly where it was, but she had no intention of bringing it out to show her guest.

"What did you study in college?"

"French. And European history was my minor."

"So, you speak French?"

"*Oui.* Like a hick."

"What do you mean?"

"My folks started buying me French lessons when I was eight, and my tutor was a Canadian. Then, on his urging, we started to spend a month every summer in Gaspé, so by the time I began taking classes in high school, my Canadian accent was cemented in my brain, and I couldn't get rid of it, despite my teacher's urging. By the time of college, I stopped wanting to. French speakers from France are totally snooty about Canadian accents, so naturally I became proud, if defensive, of mine."

"And what was it like being a nationally famous athlete?"

Marie chuckled. It was really very comfortable here, now that the others were gone and her stomach was at ease. "My recollections of being on the college team are not all that great, actually. It was awfully boola-boola, do you know what I mean? *Alligator Pride blah blah blah, sink Denison.*" She clenched and shook her fist, laughing again. "But I do have some fond memories of one summer in particular. I got a job for the summer in a library in Worcester, Mass., and spent the weekends driving around New England, entering myself in small AAU swim meets. *Marie Cochran, unattached.* That's how the program would list me to show I wasn't representing any team. It was a fine summer—that would have been in sixty-seven—driving around by myself, sleeping in cheap motels or in the back of my car, swimming pretty well, seeing some new places." Marie put her left arm along the back of the couch and rested her head on her shoulder, about to lose herself in the memory. With one index finger, Britt reached over and touched the back of Marie's hand, between the two middle knuckles, a very short and light and non-lingering touch. Marie looked at her down the length of the couch. She did not move her hand, neither did she acknowledge the touch. "What were you doing in the summer of sixty-seven?"

"I was ten. Braces and pig tails. Biking around the northeast heights of Albuquerque."

"Ten." Marie shook her head. "I was twenty. . . ." They allowed the thought to rest for a while. "Do you need another beer?"

"No, I'm fine."

Later on, when Britt kissed her, Marie thought, *I've kissed women before,* and let her arms reach around Britt's neck, *I've hugged women before. What's the big deal?* But Britt licked her front teeth and Marie opened her mouth, and Britt brushed her left thumb across Marie's right nipple, which perked up at the touch, and Marie could no longer deny that things were changing, and changing very quickly.

"Put some music on, why don't you, that we can hear in your bedroom." What extraordinary directness this woman had. Marie didn't exactly feel frightened or invaded, still, she wasn't sure.

"You put some music on. I have to go to the bathroom." Hoping that sounded ambiguous and equivocal, she stood up, rearranged her shirt and ran up the stairs. Halfway up, she stopped and said, "I'll be right back down," turned and walked the rest of the way up the stairs, thinking that hadn't sounded equivocal enough.

In the bathroom, she peed, ran the water into the sink, and spoke to herself in the mirror. "Well, my thirty-eight-year-old-virgin-in-such-matters, the time to decide is here." She would be violating no commitments, dishonoring no trusts; there was no one close enough to whom fidelity in such matters was owed. Nor would she be choosing sides, casting her lot with radical feminism, not tonight, not in this. Whatever was in the air downstairs, where she could now hear Bob Marley singing, and where *something* was surely in the air, politics were not. The only question was this—she was still looking into her own somewhat dilated eyes—this: did she want to get undressed with that beautiful and entertaining young woman downstairs and to have done and, yes—this was harder—to do that which she expected would be done? She lifted her left eyebrow and spoke aloud to herself: "What the hell."

She splashed water on her face, brushed her teeth, washed between her legs and walked downstairs. In the living room, Britt was dancing to Bob Marley, a very small little dance, her feet hardly moving, her hands in her dress pockets, swaying slightly in time to the reggae. Her head was cocked over to the right as she looked through the bookshelf, her back to the stairs when Marie came to stand by her. Britt put the arm with the bracelets across Marie's shoulders and said, without looking, "Say whatever you want, but don't say *I'm not sure if we should do this.*"

"Why not?"

"Too ordinary for the occasion."

"It's been said to you before?"

"Once or twice."

"I had Chinese food on Wednesday night and the fortune cookie said *The last wish you made will come true.*"

"What had it been?" Britt smiled, still looking at the books; the irony of that fortune seemed to strike her fancy.

"I don't remember, but you were on my mind."

"What would it be now?"

Marie shrugged under Britt's arm. The bracelets tinkled into the reggae. She put her own arm around Britt's waist. "Total destruction's the only solution," Bob Marley sang.

Marie looked up and their eyes met: pale blue and brown, almost black. "*Total destruction's the only solution,*" she said.

Britt took her hand and they walked upstairs to Marie's bedroom, left the lights off and shut the door. $\sim$

Knowing without being told that Marie needed the morning alone to deal with The First Time, Britt left about three a.m. In the quiet of the early morning, Marie heard the Corolla head down Manzano and right on Copper and, after a bit, she fell asleep. ⁓

In the morning, Marie sorted pretty carefully through her feelings and found herself whole, intact, no different, not queer. Well, okay, a little queer. The sex, though, had been exquisite. Exquisitely unconventional. If not exactly, well . . . penetrating. But with all that had been new, and plenty had been, she had been surprised most by what was missing. Maybe there was a certain dark unknowing, a little unsureness that was there, somewhere, each time, the first few times a man came into her, but she had never known for sure of its constant existence until it was not there. With fine blond hair lying lightly across Marie's face so that her eye lashes caught in the strands, her body bearing a weight not so different in mass but quite unfamiliar in contour, she awaited its arrival. She lay there, the nails of her right hand gently running the length of Britt's back and her left arm lying straight out on the bed, with a window-square of moonlight on the wall over their heads, and she looked for that darkness in her mind and it was not there. In its absence, she was suddenly afraid for the times it had been there and she had passed over it. Britt, who seemed to know Marie's thoughts, leaned up on her elbows, looked into her eyes and talked softly of nothing.

Yes, the sex had been splendid. And the baggage, what of the baggage? What of the fact that she had had sex with another woman? What of that? How did that feel? She thought the question over as she sat alone with the *Boston Globe*, a plain bagel and a pot of Earl Grey at Hippo's on Harvard Street near campus the next morning. In the abstract it felt fine, and she looked forward to seeing Britt again. She looked forward to going to bed with Britt again, let's be honest. True, Marie had been the recipient of the evening's most-intimate caresses, and she knew that there would eventually have to be reciprocation, but that idea, she was a little surprised to find, was no longer entirely off-putting. On the other hand, she knew at the back of her mind why she was here at Hippo's and not three blocks away at the Rising Moon, a campus feminist-Lesbian hangout. Before last night, she knew, her choice of a place to sit and read the *Globe* would have been made solely on the freshness of the bagels; she was comfortable at the Moon and would have chosen one over the other without a thought. And, she also knew, this morning she had given some thought to the choice. *Will the counter-girl somehow know? What if she's there? What if this? What if that?* And that, she reckoned, was a reaction that needed some pondering. If sex with Britt feminized bagel selection, what else would change in her day-to-day thirty-eight-year-old school teacher's life? What *wouldn't* change? What would Jill, her closest friend, think? She couldn't imagine telling her. What would Michael think?

Reciprocation came the following Saturday afternoon. At first Marie felt bashful, self-conscious about taking the initiative, and then fumbly, on unfamiliar territory, but finally she thought, what the heck, she knew what she herself liked, and Britt responded. Afterward, she pulled Marie up into her arms, and Marie worried that her technique was about to be criticized, or, which would have been just as embarrassing, complimented. But no, Britt just brushed her lips across Marie's forehead, and then began to talk softly about a bay Thoroughbred gelding named *T-man*, official registered name *Transnational*, whom she and her older sister Beth had ridden as young girls.

"Where's Beth now?"

"Kansas City. Divorced mother of two. The family likes her new boy friend."

Marie snuggled herself more closely next to Britt's smooth side, and laid her hand softly between Britt's breasts, a gesture, she thought, more intimate in its own way than anything that had gone on in the previous forty-two minutes.

"Go on."

She listened while Britt told her the story of the time when she had been thirteen and T-man had taken her over a one-meter oxer on her way to the blue ribbon in Open Equitation, front hooves tucked under and ears pricked forward, in front of two thousand people at the Albuquerque Convention Center. And Marie drifted off to sleep, imagining a young teenage girl in a helmet and jodhpurs with blond braids down her back, a little clumsy and hesitant in her movements on the ground, but on horseback, through a mysterious process known, it seems, only to young teenage girls, melding with the animal into one being, so that it's difficult to tell where the girl ends and the horse begins.

She awoke around two o'clock in the afternoon, alone in the bed, covered by a light quilt. She stayed naked, but wrapped herself in the quilt, and went down the stairs. Britt was gone, but there was a note on the kitchen table, in a bold, untidy hand, something better than a scrawl, straight up-and-down letters, a mixture of printing and cursive. *She's left-handed*, thought Marie, *but she doesn't write back-handed.*

*Hi.*

    *I didn't want to wake you, but I've got a memo due on Monday and I have to spend some time at the library. While I was waiting to see if you'd wake up, I took the dog for a walk, and I made a sandwich for you, since we skipped lunch. [Here Britt had drawn a small smiley face, with its left eyebrow raised.] I'll call you tonite.*

    *Xs,*

    *B.*

And yes, there was Ginger's leash across the back of a kitchen chair, instead of on its hook by the back door where she kept it, and yes, inside the fridge was a corned beef sandwich with mustard, cut on the diagonal, an open Heineken, short a couple of swigs, and a cold glass full of ice cubes. Wrapped in the quilt, naked and sexually content, Marie slowly ate the sandwich, sharing some of the beef with Ginger, and slowly drank the beer, watching the shadows begin to get long in the afternoon. And after a bit, she turned on the television to whatever channel it was already on, and walked upstairs to shower and dress.

Their next time together—Marie still had a hard time calling them *dates*, even now, later, in Phoenix—had been for a mid-week dinner, a week and a half later. Marie had gotten her period in the meantime, *and what the hell do I say to her about that?*, she wondered, but it had turned out not to be an issue. They had met in two cars in the parking lot of El Norteño, out east on Zuni, a place Marie had never been, but had found easily enough on her drive home after work. Britt was dressed in a jean jacket over a plain hooded sweatshirt, blue jeans and sneakers, with her hair pulled back into a ponytail that was coming loose. She had on a pair of aviator sun glasses, which she took off, folded and put into her jacket pocket as she walked over to Marie's car. She wore no make-up, and that made Marie self-conscious about her own lipstick, which, in fact, she had just touched up in the car's rear-view mirror as Britt was pulling into the parking lot, having come from the opposite direction.

Inside, they took a booth near the back, ordered, clinked plastic ice-water glasses and smiled at each other across the table. Britt pulled off her jacket, laid it next to her on the bench, and now pulled the sleeves of her sweatshirt up to her elbows.

"I hadn't noticed that before," Marie said. In the garish fluorescent bulbs of the restaurant, she could see a thin white scar running along the inside of Britt's right arm, about three inches long, between her wrist and her elbow. Two-thirds of the way toward her wrist, the scar forked, with a smaller branch pointing toward her thumb. "How did you get that?"

Britt let her arm fall onto the table, her hand palm up and extended toward Marie, and she ran her left hand along the length of the scar before speaking.

"Transnational declined a jump in practice one day when I was fourteen and tossed me over his head, into a wing. Bad horse! . . ."

"Wing?"

"The thing on the side that holds the cross-poles up. The poles are actually called the gate. The whole thing is called the jump."

Marie nodded.

"So, I broke my arm when I hit the wing. That's where the bone came through the skin."

"Yeeeow. That hurt."

"Plenty. But it hurt more when my trainer, who had some experience with such things, tucked the bone back in, under the skin."

"Man." Marie reached out and, with her right index finger, traced the length of the scar. "I can see it, but I can't feel it." Britt smiled and accepted the caress, which lingered.

"Sarah, my trainer, bound it in Vet-rap, which we used on the horses' legs. I remember it was bright yellow; I suppose I was sort of in shock. Anyway, she took me to the emergency room at Pres, where they set the bone, put two screws in, and stitched me up. It didn't hurt too much after the first day or so. I was quite proud of the cast."

Across the restaurant, the waitress headed their way with the orders, and Marie removed her finger and folded her hands together in front of her. Britt left her arm lying where it was.

"And the scar?"

"Yeah, I kind of like that, too. It's a nice reminder."

"Reminder?"

"Of those days around the stable. Riding. Jumping. My friends. And of learning not to be afraid to get back on T-man."

"It's lovely."

Britt smiled broadly. "I think T-man tossed me years ago, just so I could hear you say that tonight."

Marie felt herself blush. "Whatever happened to T-man?"

"Oh, that's a sad, sad story, and I don't feel like being sad right now. How was your day?"

And over their meals Marie told about her day at school, and the faculty meeting, and the Pintos' softball game, which was why she was just now getting into Albuquerque, and why she hadn't been home to change. Britt listened, saying little, her eyes bright and sparkling, sipping iced tea, her right arm back on her side of the table.

Britt said goodnight by Marie's car in the parking lot, without so much as a suggestion that the evening should continue somewhere else horizontally, nor even an embrace, but with an affectionate, if discreet, squeeze on Marie's right shoulder

She had seen Britt three times more in the next three weeks. Once they had met at the multiplex at Coronado Mall, where Britt had suggested that they see *Entre Nous*, but Marie, worried about whom they might run into, had countered with *Repo Man*. Britt had smiled and agreed, making Marie feel completely transparent. And once they had gone hiking out on the west mesa, amongst the volcanoes and the petroglyphs, and then, sunburned and sandy, to an art exhibit of a friend of Britt's downtown, under-dressed for the opening, but Albuquerque is not a place where such things matter much. Neither time had they ended up in bed again. In fact, Marie was just beginning to think that Britt had cooled off on her, and that they were becoming Just Friends, until after a tennis match on the following weekend, they had showered together back at Marie's, and then had made love all afternoon. Later, they had ordered out for pizza, and had eaten it, naked and sitting cross-legged in bed, and then, for the first time, Britt had spent the night. But in the morning they had divided the check for breakfast at the Garcia's on 4th Street, and then split up to spend the rest of their Sundays doing whatever. Alone, in Marie's case.

This ratio between sex and no-sex meetings seemed an unlikely one to Marie, and left her in a generally unsettled state. And as she drew closer to the other woman, the threat to her comfortable and set life became by degrees more real. It seemed as though everything she did was done with a view toward camouflaging the relationship that was developing. She watched her words carefully with her friends, clammed up in *what are ya doing this weekend?* conversations, invited a male friend to dinner and made sure they were seen together by her neighbors. She remembered how she had felt as a college sophomore when she had moved in with her boy friend, but had posed as a virgin living in the dorm when her parents were near.

They talked of none of this. Britt had once invited her to a party which, it had been clear, would have been a women's party but she had begged off and she figured Britt had known exactly what was going on, but they talked of none of it.

Exams for both of them intervened and made it more difficult to get together. And, it would be honest to say, it was with some unspecified relief that Marie heard her principal say that he thought it would be a good idea if Marie, who was single and all, would sign up for a course at ASU in teaching about the Soviet bloc to junior high schoolers. The superintendent would help with expenses and she had agreed to go. She sprung the news to Britt on the phone, that she would be leaving in ten days to spend the summer in Phoenix, embarrassed that Britt would sense her relief and see her as politically weak.

When she hung up the phone, she was out of breath with the enormity of what she had heard. The words themselves had been quite ordinary: "Oh. I didn't know you were thinking of that. . . . Yeah, it sounds like a really good opportunity. It'll be hotter than hell of course in Phoenix in the summer. . . . Well, should, can we get together before you go?"

It was not the words, it was the voice behind the words; it was the feeling of disappointment. *My God and holy shit*, Marie thought after she had hung up, one hand still on the receiver, the other clutching her opposite shoulder, *this isn't about feminist politics or unconventional sex at all. This is about love. I've surprised and hurt her and I had no idea. I really had no idea.*

And so she had fled to Phoenix, to study, swim, buy bagels without a thought, more than occasionally to think of Britt, sometimes of this or that they had done in bed, sometimes of something funny she had said, or of the girl on T-man's back, sometimes of the voice on the phone. And to see Michael as he passed through on the way from who knows where back to the Ozarks.

There was much to talk over with Michael, and many times before they had done so. He somehow gave her perspective that she lacked on her own. Their history was a long one: they had met very casually soon after she had come to Albuquerque to do her Master's degree at UNM, in a course in test design. Nothing had come of that meeting, as one would expect from a course in test design, but when she was hired the following year to teach at Moriarty Middle School, she was pleased to find an acquaintance among her new colleagues. And they had become close friends. After he quit teaching junior high to return to graduate school full time, the friendship had taken an odd turn; they saw each other less, but had become lovers. She hadn't slept with all that many men in her life, not really. In the high single-digits, say. Well, the mid-to-high single digits. Seven, actually. Eight, if you counted that thing on the bus ride back to campus after the swim meet at Baldwin-Wallace, which she didn't. At any rate, Michael was different from the others. She didn't love him, and never had, not really, not as she had loved two of the others. Nor was he a lark, or an imprudent fling. There had been a couple of those, too. *Sex with a friend*, Marie called her relationship with Michael, when she called it anything at all, which she usually didn't.

Then he had left Albuquerque to teach college, first in Kansas, then in the Ozarks. They stayed in touch by letter and postcard and the rare phone call. Michael would drop back into town occasionally, and when he was travelling by himself, which was sometimes, but not always, he would spend some time at Marie's. They had never lived together, and hadn't very often, in fact, slept together, literally speaking. But over the years their relationship had become one that they were comfortable with: long-range close friends and occasional, sporadic, reasonably intense lovers. And they had talked things out. He would listen and later she would know what to do. A week or so talking to Michael, and getting regularly and well laid, would put Britt and this flutter in her heart and this worry in her brain all, she trusted, back into perspective.

But now—she turned over under the hot sun by the Escalante pool— right now, she was tired of waiting. Michael was not due for a several weeks yet, her course was only half over, Phoenix was already intolerable and the flutter was still there. She stood up and ran her fingers through her hair; it was dry in the hot desert air and she mussed it up so it could lie as it wanted to, with a crooked part on the left and slightly cowlicked on the right. She put on her glasses, picked up her things and decided to look for a good Mexican meal. It was harder than hell to find a good Mexican meal in Phoenix.

CORRESPONDENCE

Oslo. June 12th. Rainy and cold out; warm and smoky in. Smokey?

Smoky. I sit in a small bar, wet from the rain getting here, with a warm, expensive beer.

Dear Marie,

Damn. I have apparently left your Phoenix address at home. Damn. Well, actually, writing to you in Albuquerque, to your familiar little home, will be very much like writing to you in Phoenix, in who-knows-what sort of dreary apartment you're renting. It's the receiving that will be different and I guess, my friend, that's your problem. Ah well, time in fact goes slowly here and it seems right that you will receive this, forwarded from Albuquerque, some leisurely time after I've written it.

I'm winding up my visit here in Norway, taking it easy, until-next-time good-byeing, having a last look at Vigeland Park, a last beer with a good friend. I like this place—I call it the Columbus, Ohio of Scandinavia: quiet, small, provincial, conservative, all in a sort of rich, socialist way. I once nearly fell in love here, and probably should have, with a girl sunning her legs in the park. She was a girl named Birgitte, and I still think of her occasionally, even now, almost twenty years later. That was in '65.

A couple of weeks ago, I took the night train from Oslo to Stockholm, the ferry to Finland and met up with a couple of Sami people—Laplanders you would call them, but they prefer Sami, their name for themselves in their own language—late one night, at a small jazz club, very clean, very white, very expensive and very well-lighted, in a town whose Finnish name is Turku. It is called Åbu in Swedish. The musicians played jazz from sheet music and it was not bad. These new Sami friends invited me to visit their town in the far north of Norway and I thought I'd do just that, as I had some time on my hands and I had never been to the far north before.

A couple of days later I caught the train north to a place near the Circle, called Roveneimi, still in Finland. It was snowing and I had to buy a cap to keep warm, liking the fact that I had to buy a winter's hat only a few weeks before I am due in the Persian Gulf. I also liked the looks of this Roveneimi; I could imagine it in the winter, lying under cold, squeaky snow with the northern lights well-displayed.

My new friend, Svein, met me at the train station and we drove for many hours north, out of Finland and into Norway, to his town, called Kautokeino. It is called Guov'dagaeid'no in Sami-language. Svein, like I said, is Sami.

Kautokeino is a small town in the inland north. There is one old church, but most of the town is new and non-quaint, the old one having been burnt by the Nazis in their WW II retreat. This is true of much of the North. I understand it is very cold in the winter and it was still cold and snowing when I arrived in late May. When summer comes, the snow melts and the bugs are bad. Like Alaska, I'm told, though I've never been to Alaska.

The folks up there were very friendly to a stranger who required them to speak English most of the time. (You should know, though, that the bus drivers in Norway speak better English than most of my students.) Anyway, they threw a party for me a few days after I arrived, a party at which we all got very, very drunk. I mean very, very drunk. I remember sitting at one point watching someone wander out into the yard and take a piss in front of the window. It was about three in the morning, but it looked like it was ten a.m., for, check your map, the sun never sets up here in the summer. The conversation at this party had turned a little ugly and political, as conversations with drunken radicals will. These drunken radicals were radical Samis, sort of Scandinavian AIM members. Mai Kaaren—that's Svein's wife—and I were the only non-Samis there. She was sitting in my lap, and I could guess by the tenseness in her body that she, at least, was taking something of a beating, maybe for Norwegian attitudes in general, maybe for her own blond Norwegianess, maybe for how she was raising her half-Sami children, I couldn't tell. She could be shut out of the conversation at any time, when the others would switch to Sami language, which she doesn't speak, and then she would turn to me and catch me up with the conversation, which had become, with the alcohol, to be rarely in English. I felt a little sad for her situation, and for the fact that from where we sat I, and presumably she, could see Svein with his hand down the pants of a young woman in the kitchen, as he was wont to do, I knew, whether in a northern homestead or in a clean little jazz club far to the south of where I now sat.

At about six o'clock in the morning, we left. "I must sleep," I said to a young Sami woman who wanted us not to go yet.

"You will sleep with me?"

Her smooth face glowed in the early morning light—it actually still looked like ten a.m.—and her dark hair was eye-catching in the North, though really Scandinavia has never been as blond as myth would have it. She had brown eyes, I remember, and while communication is always chancy in such situations, I think she meant what she asked, that is to say I think she meant that for which *sleep* is a common enough English-language euphemism. On such an overcast Scandinavian morning, strung out on vodka and strong coffee, it not having been dark for going on a week at that point, and some spot in one's mind never having really relaxed in that time, it is hard to do anything but react to a suggestion like that. As much as I hate admitting it to you, dear one, I am never sure from which bodily unit such a reaction will come.

"No." I kissed her on the cheek and thought about trying to explain to her that she was too young and I too drunk for anything very good to come of such an early morning undark coupling. I made no such explanation though, and Svein, Mai Kaaren and I walked home together, they quarrelling in Norwegian and I storing for later the image of the sad-eyed invitation.

A week later, at a traditional Sami gathering at a place called Skibotn, with tipi tents, matriarchs, boiled reindeer meat and beer, the sky cleared and for a moment, I got my first real glimpse of the actual midnight sun. It looked, of course, like the sun would look through a clearing ten a.m. sky, alone in the North with the salmon running.

Finally, after Svein took me to a Sami political rally at a place called Nesseby in far northeastern Norway, near the Russian border, I caught the south-bound coastal ferry boat and once aboard, claimed an empty cabin. It was an inside cabin, and it struck me that if I closed the door and turned out the light, it would be dark. It was, for the first time in three weeks or more, and I felt some strange place, behind and above my eyes, relaxing. You know how it feels to let your face relax after smiling too long? It was the same, but inside and not muscular. I looked at the dark for a long time, letting this place relax, before going out to watch the ten a.m. coast slip by. I have no idea what time it really was.

The boat took me to Hammerfest, then to Bodø and the train back to Oslo, where it rains and is cold. It is now, in fact, two days after I began this letter, but the weather refuses to become nice. Tomorrow I catch the train to Copenhagen and then Amsterdam and by next week I should be in the desert and the hot, hot sun.

I hope all's well with you and I look forward to seeing you in Phoenix, although why anyone would want to leave Albuquerque and the Dukes for Phoenix in the summer I can't imagine. But then, as I recall, you are not a baseball fan, are you? A pity. Anyway, I'll see you on July 30th, if my schedule holds and will write if it doesn't. One never knows when travelling. Oops. I don't have your Phoenix address. If plans change in July, I may have a hard time getting word to you. We'll have to play it by ear. It will be good to see you.

Adios, amiga.

Michael.

# ~ 4

# TALLAHASSEE

I t was never possible, really, for Anna Browning to describe to others what work she did. Not her teaching, which to her was the least part of her work, but her mathematical research. It was too esoteric to be understood by anyone save the thousand or so men and women in the world who worked in the same field. She worked with entirely theoretical mathematics, and she worked on the cutting edge of pure thought. The concepts were so abstract that they would not stand translation into the language of laypersons; she could not say to non-mathematicians that her theorems were about this or like that; for her, there was no metaphor to her work.

Not even Ben could understand her work, but he could understand and express his non-understanding. "It is like," he would explain to his colleagues, "a man who speaks only English attempting to describe to a child who speaks only Japanese what Faulkner was trying to accomplish in the first chapter of *The Sound and the Fury.*"

Anna worked in the field of probability, but that explained too little to mathematicians and too much to laypersons. Probability is a broad field and that on which Anna worked had nothing to do with gaming odds, weather predictions, or other ordinary uses of the word. Her field of stochastic processes dealt with optimal filtering, continuous-time Markov chains and queuing theory, but while these terms were already beyond the understanding of most lay persons, they were only the most elementary of the foundational terms for her work. She worked, let it be said, with thoughts, thoughts expressed in formulae, abstract thoughts that had application only to other equally abstract thoughts. Some day the formulae with which she worked might have application to some physical phenomena, but for the formulae themselves or for the eventual physical applications, Anna cared nothing. She cared for the pure thoughts, for the act of thinking, for the ability to think about things that, quite literally, no one had ever thought about before in the entire history of the human race.

And too, it must be said, she cared for the secondary matters: the competition with the boys, her name in lights as her thoughts were published, the awe her less-gifted colleagues showed when she made advances in her field, the points that her publications counted in the minor, and the not-so-minor, academic wars that were fought out in the halls of the college, the wars between those who could, and did, think and those who couldn't, or didn't. And, as much as any of these, she cared for the respect that her advancement earned her in the eyes of her husband.

Jablonski's work interfered with all of this. It threatened most directly those secondary pleasures, but it also had sent a shudder through those first concerns of pure thought. It is impossible to describe, of course, the actual stochastic matters where their works came into conflict, but, just as Ben was able to explain his non-understanding without being able to describe that which he didn't understand, it is possible to construct an analogy to capture the threat that Anna saw in Jablonski's work. (Anna herself, of course, had no need for such an analogy, nor would this one have occurred to her. Nor would she have spent one speck of energy trying to construct such an analogy for the aid of non-mathematicians trying to understand the conflict. She understood the conflict directly, abstractly, and she had understood it since her first glance at Jablonski's article.)

Anna's work, one might say, off and on for three years, and more or less continuously for eighteen months, had involved her in the careful description of a certain scene, a certain place, say a small Greek island, at a certain time, say late August, 1965. She had described with care, analogously speaking, the look and feel of the village: the climate, the colors, what crops were growing and in what stage of development they were, the wine that was to be made. She had then focused in on one resident of that village, say a retired British expatriate nurse, living alone and simply, on a small pension, in a tidy, white-washed house, walking to and from the market and bakery, taking her first cognac a little too early in the day. She—Anna, that is—had described the nurse's library of cherished books in English, brought from home, begged from passing tourists, collected from an English-language bookshop in Athens. She had described the woman reading about Picasso in one of those books. The Blue Period. The painting of the twisted man with the mandolin.

Jablonski, by comparison, was a composer and in his article he had written music for the mandolin.

Now, of the thousand or so people in the world who could understand Anna's work, only a tenth of those, maybe, had the sharpness of mind and the subtlety of thought even to see the connection between the two works. But to Anna there was no doubt. If Anna's mandolin was indeed tuned for Jablonski's music, and as the weeks went by she was becoming more and more convinced that it was, then the impact of his article on her work would be enormous. The subtlety of the conflict meant that hers would still be valid and worthwhile; as the analogy suggests, her work had a richness and density that his lacked. But the directness and the efficiency of Jablonski's work made her seem, in her own eyes and the eyes of the ones that mattered, a plodder by comparison. A careful plodder, true, but that was of little comfort to Anna.

So, as the weeks went by, as her belly swelled and she could not find a comfortable position in which to work and ended up doing most of her thinking while standing at her office window, as she took the spring semester off and worked at home, and as she gave birth, smoothly, easily, to a girl baby they named Rachel, who seemed happy from the first instant, as the weeks and months went by, Anna worked on her problem. She had first to complete her own work, for the Greek island scene was not yet fully described, and she had to confirm Jablonski's work, for one never knew, and, all at the same time, she searched for the next step beyond Jablonski in her own work. Perhaps to push the analogy one step too far, she explored the nurse's small home in the hope that somewhere amongst the books on the shelves or the stacked correspondence would be, say, the score for a full symphonic opera, into which Jablonski's music would fit, as Act Two, Scene Two: *Salvatore serenades Gwendolyn (song with mandolin)*.

The job of simultaneously finishing her own work, checking the accuracy of Jablonski's and discovering the broader principle was largely impossible. Anna's talents were formidable, but few indeed have minds that formidable. A more experienced mathematician would have gone about it more slowly, but then great advances in mathematics are seldom made by patient, experienced mathematicians. It is also likely that most of her more experienced colleagues had attacked in exactly the same way when they had, early in their careers, encountered their own Jablonskies.

Anna sat at her desk at home, none of this on her mind, on a Wednesday, late afternoon, while the rain outside fell straight down and steamed off the surface of the street, leaving a smell of hot, moist macadam, which is an odor lying somewhere between pleasant and unpleasant and is decidedly a feature of the Tallahassee summer. The older children played quietly in their rooms, for they knew the rules when Mother was working, and they wished for the rain to stop. Rachel did not know the rules, but was nevertheless allowing Anna a respite, entertaining herself, quietly, on a blanket on the floor of Anna's study, trying to fathom the connection that seemed to exist between her left foot and the rest of her body, a task no less abstract than Anna's own struggle with Tupelov's Theorem and Jablonski's transformations.

Anna sat with her left hand loosely clenched and held against her pursed lips, her elbow resting on a stack of several dozen yellow pages of her notes on the problem. Her right hand held a green pencil whose point stood an inch or two off a piece of yellow paper that was not yet ready to be added to the stack, half-filled with equations. Her stare was out the window, unfocused, in thought, through the rain. She sat forward in the chair with her bare feet pulled back and her toes curled under, beneath the chair. She sat like this, without moving, for ten minutes, occasionally sniffing at what was threatening to become a summer cold. Her concentration was complete. Finally, after five minutes more, she lowered the pencil point and wrote a new equation below the last one. She blinked her eyes and pushed the pencil through her hair and behind her ear and wiped her nose on a Kleenex. She picked up several loose papers, of which the one she had just written on was the only one marked, and shuffled them together, tapping them against the desk top. Then she placed the papers neatly in front of her, rested her cheek in her right hand and read over the half-page of equations. In terms of the analogy, the afternoon's work had described a potted carnation on the nurse's window sill in the Greek sunshine; the last equation had made its color a dark, mottled pink.

She swiveled her chair around and looked down at Rachel, on the floor. She seemed content enough for now. To pick her up would remind her instantly that she was hungry and Anna had learned that, for reasons too intimate to stand analysis, she could not think about mathematics while Rachel was nursing. She had used the months of feedings to reread the Hornblower novels, usually sitting in the rocker in the bedroom with her feet on the bed, the baby crooked in one arm, her shirt pulled up or wide open, holding a book and turning the pages both with one hand. The older children were getting used to seeing her in various stages of undress and they seemed to be managing, though Janet was embarrassed for her. Ben, on the other hand, didn't mind how she looked, but he was embarrassed that she read Hornblower.

After a minute, she pulled the pencil from behind her ear and turned back to her work. She erased a symbol from the last equation and wrote it back in, more neatly, then brushed the eraser crumbs away. It was a measure of the quickness of her mind that she had taught herself to write first, before brushing the crumbs, so that no thought would flee. She pulled her chair up closer to her desk and unfocused her eyes through the rain. Rachel gurgled pleasantly at the beginnings of her language.

CORRESPONDENCE

6/13
The Dubai Airport
Dear Anna,
    They don't use Arabic numbers in Arabia. What's that do to your sense of propriety? All the best, and I hope Sam still saves stamps.
Michael

TALLAHASSEE

The library in the Browning house on Hillcrest Court was in the sun room off the back, the east, side. It had small-paned windows from floor to ceiling on the north and east and book shelves covered the west and south walls. In the summer, the room was shaded by several large, dense mulberry trees and in the winter, it was pleasantly sunny and warm. Unlike Ben's library at the university, which was book-lined and window-less, like a dark and dusty desert cave, the library at home was open and bright.

Anna stood in the doorway with the baby on her shoulder and looked around the room. The drapes were still open and the windows reflected the room's lights back inside; out beyond the reflections the night was black and nothing of the yard could be seen. Ben was sitting on the couch, with a lap desk on his knees. His work was lighted by a table lamp, a cigarette burned in an ash tray near his left hand and a book lay open on the couch to his right. He held a fountain pen and his letters made tidy, straight tracks across the white, unlined paper. "I write," Ben liked to say, "I do not process words. Writing takes both ink and intelligence; processing words takes neither." Anna walked to the couch, put his cigarette out, for the sake of the baby, picked up the book and sat down. She nestled Rachel into the crook of her right arm while holding the book with her left. She was dressed in jeans, with no shoes and a light blue short sleeve shirt, with only one button fastened, and stained on the left front with dribbled milk.

"What are you working on?" she asked.

Ben was a very productive scholar, a literary critic, nearly always working on something for publication. He was the kind of northern, atheist, intellectual that southern universities with visions of national reputations feel compelled to hire, and who then confirm the southerners' impression of themselves by detesting all thing southern. To this model, Ben added a typical Browning twist, making southern literature his specialty, "thereby bringing northern sensibility and intelligence to southern writing," he liked to say. Thus he had the expertise to criticize with authority that which, at heart, he disliked.

Now, he propped his glasses above his eyebrows, capped his pen and put his arm across the back of the couch behind his wife. "A review of a biography of Faulkner by a certain young Dr. Robinson, of SUNY Buffalo. For the *Georgia Review.*"

"How is it?"

"Brilliant."

"Which?"

"My review. Professor Robinson, I'm afraid, doesn't get it."

"Doesn't get what?"

"Doesn't get *it*. Doesn't get what Faulkner is about. Doesn't get what biography is about. Doesn't get what the English language is about. Doesn't get what either subtlety or ambiguity is about. *It*, he does not get. I have said so, with some elegance, I believe."

"Will they publish the review?"

"I should suppose so. They solicited it from me. If they don't, Cornell will. I don't really care; actually, I'd rather place it in Cornell. What are you doing? Taking a break? How's the babe?"

"Okay. She just now went to sleep, so I wasn't able to do any work. She felt like walking, so I wandered around the house, tucking the children in, pinching brown leaves off the plants. She's just restless, I guess."

"Why don't you put her to bed now?"

Anna shrugged. "I don't know. She might wake up if I put her down right now. I'm restless too, I guess."

The conversation lapsed for a bit. Then Anna put the book on the floor, reached up and took his hand in hers. "I got a postcard from Mike Reid today."

"How *pleasant* the rain sounds?"

Anna smiled. "Yes, him. He's somewhere. He's always on a trip somewhere. "

"So?"

"I don't know. Nothing. I went over to school today to pick up my mail. There wasn't anything of interest, except the postcard."

"So?"

"So he's playing while I'm working."

"Of course he is. By the way, is this conversation going somewhere? Somewhere in particular, I mean?"

"Oh, it's Jablonski's work again. Still. I can't seem to lick it. I wanted to give up today and then the damn card came. From Dubai, for Christ's sake. Where's Dubai?"

"Persian Gulf."

"It all made me wonder why I'm doing this."

"What is this? Post-partum or post-feminism?"

She gave a short, tired laugh that contained no genuine amusement. "Both, maybe. I'm not sure. Is it okay if I wonder if it's all worth it? It's hard to try to think like Jablonski thinks, especially when I don't get to sleep more than a few hours at a time."

"Why, honey chile," Ben mocked, "you go on ahead and quit that theaha hard work." He was doing a character out of what he called *early Tennessee Williams*. Ben thought Tennessee Williams was overrated and that early Tennessee Williams was, as he put it, "interesting, but not very." When he wanted to put someone on and simultaneously to put down one of his least favorite writers—a double mocking that Ben delighted in—he often did *early Tennessee Williams*. "You'all oughta just stay home and drink lemonade and mind the chil'n and let ol' Big Daddy heah take care of yo."

"Come on, be serious."

"Why, Ah *am* serious, honey. Ah've nevah understood why you should worry yo' pretty little hayad over this heah Fluboski. Ah'll provide for yo' deah."

"Ben, come on. It just seems like my work is, for the first time . . . I don't know. It's that I'm out of touch with my work. So much seems to depend on what's going on inside this Jablonski's mind and I don't even know him and I can't figure him out. I don't like not being in control. It's like being in a race where you can't see the other runner. It hasn't been like this before. I don't know how fast I have to run. I'm not even sure of the direction. I don't know if maybe he isn't right and I'm wrong. No, that's not it. I don't know if I can think hard enough. I don't know if I'm as smart as he is. That's what it comes down to; I've never felt that before. Do you ever feel like that?"

"Anna, you are whining."

"Do you?"

"No."

"Did you when you were an assistant professor?"

"No."

"Why not?"

"Now how in the world am I supposed to answer a question like that?"

"What do I do?"

"You beat this Zilkowski. You out-think him and out-publish him, or you out-flank him. Get it done. Leave him in the dust."

"Simple as that?"

"Simple as that."

"And if I can't?"

"*Anna Browning showed early speed, but faded at the three-sixteenth pole.*"

"Will you still love me if I fade at the three-sixteenth pole?"

"Just don't."

"Will you?"

"Honey chile, . . .."

"Come on."

"*O! Tempore. O! More.*" Ben put a dramatic hand to his head, palm out, and rolled his eyes. "Married to a woman who can't out-think Fibek Krumski from Cornland U. And who dresses, I must say, like white trash. Still, you do perform fellatio adequately, or at least it is my fading recollection that you do. Sure, honey, I'll still love you."

"Fading recollection?" She tossed his hand back to him, swung her feet up on the couch and rearranged Rachel so she lay, still asleep, on Anna's chest.

She used Ben's right thigh for a pillow; her legs were not long enough to reach the end of the couch. "*Fading recollection?* It was, I believe, only last Saturday." She laughed. "But then, who's keeping track? And I don't recall that *adequate* was the adjective that you used to describe the process."

Ben stroked the baby's head and then left his hand rest on Anna's right breast. "Now, let me think. Ahh, yes, I remember now. No, indeed. *Adequate* would understate it some, though I don't recall exactly what term I used at the time."

"*Jesus.*"

"That sounds right. Say, why don't you offer to suck off this pollack at the next math convention? He might agree to slow down the scholarly pace in exchange."

"Ben, don't be vulgar in front of the baby. She is not yet aware of what an asshole you are. Besides, I'll bet he's a faggot."

"Oh?"

"Yes. I can tell by his writing. His transformations are rather effete, I think."

"Atta girl. That's my Anna. Go for the knockout. You can't be beaten when you get mean." He squeezed her breast. "I believe you're leaking a little, my dear."

"You're not exactly helping." She removed his hand and held his thumb resting against her shoulder. After a minute, she spoke again. "Still, wouldn't you like to go somewhere? Overseas, I mean, maybe?"

"What is this? Has that lightweight Mike Whatshisname gotten to you?"

"No. . . . No. He doesn't matter. But a trip would be nice."

"Your recent delicate condition, my dear, and our new offspring, has made travelling a bit difficult of late." He picked up his pen and uncapped it. "Next summer, though, why don't I take Oxford up on their offer to lecture? Unless you'd rather go to, say, Dubai?"

"Ugh."

"Oxford?"

"God, Ben, I'd love to go to Oxford. Shall we?"

"Of course we shall."

"Hoopla!"

"Hoopla, indeed, Stephen Dedalus."

"I thought Brecht."

"Joyce, first. In English. Now, why don't you go tend your hemorrhoids and let me decide what further insightful things I am going share with the readers of the *Georgia Review*?"

"I think I'll lie right here, if you don't mind, and close my eyes for a minute. Bend that lamp shade a bit to the left, won't you? Wake me when you go up to bed, okay? Rachel will be hungry by then." And Anna folded her hands over the baby's feet and soon they were both asleep to the sound of the scratching of Ben's fountain pen.

## ON A BUS TO TRINCOMALEE, SRI LANKA

Sri Lanka is a country small enough so that the buses that run the streets of Colombo in fact go everywhere, or nearly, on the island. They are enormous red vehicles, with wooden floors and hard seats and their destinations are written on the front in two languages, both of which are absolutely incomprehensible to the average tourist. These buses charge approximately nothing to take you between any two points on the island. The minuscule fare is paid in Sri Lankan rupees, usually in tiny, red folding bills that have been in circulation so long that they have more the feel and smell of dirty oilcloth than of paper. Through the dirt and between the creases and rips are barely visible images of exotic birds and fish and Tamil women picking tea.

Michael Reid sat on the driver's side, that is to say the right side, of the red bus bound for Trincomalee on the east coast and felt like the rankest of tourists. He had hopped on this bus with his backpack in a town called Kandy, set for the hours-long journey to the east coast, only to discover that he had no small bills in his pocket, nor any coins either. He had paid the fare with a bill twenty times larger than was needed and, of course, the conductor had pocketed the bill, unable to make change, promising in a hard-to-catch, sing-song English that when a few more passengers boarded he would return with the money Michael was owed. Right. Michael sat, the bus jolting through pot holes, up the side of the mountain, and stewed over his mistake.

It was true enough that twenty times nearly nothing is still nearly nothing and that Michael was worrying just now, and had been worrying for the past half an hour, about a truly, breathtakingly, insignificant sum of money. Nevertheless, it was the principle of the thing. He counted his bill as surely gone. He had been reading in the *Mirror* about claims that bus conductors were cheating even their fellow citizens, let alone tourists. *Forget it; the money is gone.* And it was gone through a mistake that would be made only by a rookie tourist on his first trip away from North Platte. It would have been so easy to buy a Coke or something before he got on the bus and made sure he had some change. *God damn it.*

The bus honked once and pulled around an elephant that was slowly working its way uphill, under the prodding of its handler, pulling an enormous sawn log with a heavy chain that chimed and sparked against the macadam. Cars coming the other way on the curving road swerved to their side to avoid the bus, and walkers along the road scattered to avoid the swerving cars. Small homes and small businesses stood along the roadside; people on the porches hardly looked up, for such driving was the norm in this country. Behind the buildings, the forest grew up the hillside, more blue than green through the smoke and the humid, dusty air.

Damn it. He shook his head and tried to be reasonable. The money was not great. It wasn't even lost for sure yet. Who cares? Who cares? *Who cares?* Forget it. Enjoy the sights. Damn it. He hated this feeling. He felt like an idiot. A hot, uncomfortable, soiled, rookie idiot. He knew that little bastard was going to keep his money and tell his family about the tourist he cheated today. He tried to narrow his eyes into slits to send the message to the conductor that he was not from North Platte and he could not be ripped off with impunity.

The day was hot and dusty and Michael was bound for the ocean to wash himself clean of the grime and the dust and the heat. Later on, before the swim, a Sri Lankan student would sit down next to him on the bus and they would discuss here and home and the fighting in the north, and the conductor would walk by and hand him his change with a smile as if there had never been the least possibility that he wouldn't and then the hotel keeper would be friendly and accommodating and the sea water would be cool and clean and dinner would be papaya, shark meat and Lankan beer. And all of it—bus ride, hotel, dinner, beer—would cost approximately nothing, and in the morning the sun would rise here while it was setting at home, and he would walk the beach, watching the fishermen, and everything would be just fine. But before then, for several minutes more yet, Michael would grind his teeth and sour his stomach and spoil this bus ride through the highlands of South Asia, all over an amount of money that at home he would piss away without a thought. And he would share with no one his thoughts about this bus ride and how sometimes, through some combination of rhythms either internal or external, he seemed out of control of his own mind.

## TALLAHASSEE

As part of the compensation package that Ben Browning was awarded with his endowed professorship, in addition to a lavish salary of which his colleagues were jealous—a jealousy that pleased Ben to be a party to—and the more meager salary of his own secretary, he was also entitled to a suite of offices on the fourth floor of Williams Hall, overlooking Westcott Plaza. His secretary, with whom his relations were cool, worked in a small anteroom, off of which opened his office proper, as well as an annex that he used as a library. It was into this suite that he strode, mid-week, at precisely ten o'clock, as was his habit. He and his secretary did not greet each other, as was also habitual. He would have her fired if University personnel regulations permitted it, which they did not, and she knew it, both that he would and that he could not. He noted, but did not acknowledge, the presence of the student who was sitting, apparently waiting his arrival. Tall, a wavy brunette, with red fingernails, a skirt above her knees and flip-flops. Nice tan.

He said, "Five minutes," to no one in particular and walked into his office and closed the door behind him.

The inner office was large and high-ceilinged, with windows on the north and east sides. It held a large desk, which he kept tidy, a credenza, a work table, two chairs for visitors and a wing-backed easy chair with a floor lamp and side table, where he liked to sit, read and smoke. His various diplomas, honors and awards covered the walls, while on the credenza behind the desk stood a photograph of Anna and the children, taken at the beach soon after Rachel was born. Ben sat himself in the chair behind the desk and began to organize his day.

Out in the anteroom, Nikki Wallace looked at the clock over the secretary's desk, re-crossed her legs, and waited, flipping her right flip-flop and wishing she could have a cigarette, but there was no ashtray to be seen. She did not know Professor Browning well, though his reputation, she knew, was of irascibility. She had missed his dramatic reading of Michael Reid's letter at the English department party, a year ago now, while she had reclined on George and Mildred's double bed, sipped their Scotch, used their long-distance carrier, and watched the Dodgers' game on their TV. She had, indeed, written about the softness of the bed and the smoothness of the Scotch, about the distinctiveness of Linda's voice and the pleasure of an unhurried, paid-for, long-distance conversation with one's best friend, for the next week's poetry seminar. Her principal classmate critic in the class had pronounce the poem *diverting*, while the professor, whose only real qualification to be a poetry professor was that he usually managed to be drunk by the two-thirty p.m. starting time of the seminar, seemed satisfied with it, though it was hard to tell, as always. That professor was her MFA advisor, which meant that she was certain to get her degree, as it would be less trouble for him to approve of her portfolio than it would be to read it and decide whether he liked it. Which was the real reason, it turns out, that she had made the appointment to see Ben Browning at ten this morning, well before her next class, at noon.

Precisely, as best she could tell, five minutes after he had walked into his office, the secretary, without looking at either Nikki or the clock, said, "You may go in now," and went back to her typing. Nikki stood up, picked her papers off of the chair next to her and approached the door.

"Should I knock?" The secretary said nothing, so Nikki tapped quietly on the office door and let herself in.

Ben looked up from the book he was reading. "You are?"

"Nikki Wallace. I was in your Faulkner class last spring."

"Yes, you were. I thought I recognized you. Come in. Do you smoke?"

"Yes." She walked over to the front of Ben's desk, as he held out the pack to her, with two smokes protruding. Regular-sized, unfiltered Lucky Strikes. She took one, then leaned across his desk to accept the light he offered. With her left hand she held the top of her scoop-neck pull-over to her chest so as not to display her breasts to him. He noted the gesture, but said nothing. "Thanks," she said.

"L.S.M.F.T.," Ben said. "Sit down."

She took the chair across the desk from him, and pulled it closer to the desk so as to reach the ashtray that he put on the corner for her use. She took a drag from the cigarette; the smoke was harsh on her throat, and heavy in her lungs, but she was determined to mention neither the strength of the cigarette nor the pretentiousness of smoking unfiltered Luckies. She exhaled toward the floor, then used her thumb and ring-finger nails to remove a bit of tobacco from her tongue, an act she had seen performed dozens of times in the movies, but had never before done herself.

"What can I do for you, Nikki Wallace?"

"I'm doing the MFA, but I'm thinking of switching into the PhD program in literature. It was suggested that I get your advice about the switch."

"Why me?"

"Like I said, several people suggested it, including the chairman of the department. And I enjoyed the Faulkner class."

"What did you like about it?"

"Starting with the fact that we didn't read any Faulkner at all for the first four weeks of the course."

"And why did you like that?"

"I don't know. I guess the contrariness of it. Lots of the students were complaining, as I suppose you know, but the more they complained, the more I found myself getting what you were doing."

"And what was I doing, do you think?"

"Giving us a context into which to fit his writing."

"Of course. But I also made you, if you'll recall, . . ."

At that moment, the door to the office burst open, and Anna Browning came raging into the room. She did not look at Nikki, and it was not clear that she even knew she was there, as she stomped over to Ben's desk and threw a piece of paper onto it. "How the hell am I ever going to get any work done with that kind of teaching schedule?" Her voice was loud, high-pitched and shaking. "How? The son of a bitch is trying to get me denied tenure."

"You'll excuse us?" Ben said to Nikki, who rose quickly and walked out of the office and into the anteroom, closing the door behind her and leaving her papers on the chair and the cigarette in the ashtray on the corner of Ben's desk. She raised her eyebrows to the secretary, whose expression did not change even to a tenth of a degree in response. Nikki sat down in the chair she had occupied earlier.

It had taken her about the time that it took to walk back to her chair in the anteroom to identify the small blond woman in a blue blazer and skirt who had barged in on them. She had seen Anna only twice during her time in Tallahassee, and at one of those times Anna had been quite pregnant. Now a good deal thinner and a good deal more distressed, she looked much different, but, then, who else could it be? Through the door, she could hear only one side of the conversation, as Anna stormed and shouted, but Ben's quiet responses were inaudible in the anteroom. "God damn it, Ben, he's out to destroy my career. . . . How can I do *that*? . . . And what will *he* do? . . . Right. . . . Not bloody likely. . . . Oh, thank you very much. . . . Well, how the hell do you expect me to react? . . . What? . . . What I came by here for is a little sympathy from my husband, not to hear that he'd call his good friend the Dean. . . . Great. It was the same God damn thing last semester. . . . Well, that's very fucking easy for you to say. . . . Oh, really? You seem to have forgotten that I have a baby in diapers to take care of. . . . Sure. . . . Right. Except that you're going to be in fucking New York for ten days starting tomorrow. Who's going to take care of her then? . . . You're damn right, I am. And Sam. And Janet. And the fucking house. And my work. . . . I've got to put up with that kind of horseshit from my chairman, but I don't see why I have to put up with it from my own husband." A long pause here, while she apparently was listening to Ben. Then, "Oh, fuck you." And the door to the office opened quickly and Anna rushed out, her face red and covered with tears. She slammed the door shut, wiped her eyes on the sleeve of her blazer, then composed herself and walked into the corridor, never looking at either Nikki or the secretary.

Once again, Nikki's look of amazed embarrassment in the direction of the secretary was not returned and, moments later, the door to the office opened and Ben said, "Where were we?" Nikki got up and returned to her chair; the cigarette was still smoldering in the ashtray.

Ben walked around his desk and sat down. "Do you have an actual adult name, Nikki Wallace, or is it just Nikki?"

*Well*, thought Nikki, *he's not above being a little flirty, moments after he's had a spat with the Mrs.* But what she said out loud was, "Just Nikki."

"Of all the stupid things that our parents can do to us," Ben said, "the names they give us do the least harm." Nikki said nothing. "Ever been married, Nikki Wallace? Have any children?"

"No."

"To which? No husband or no children?"

"Both. I mean neither."

"*Both* would be proper. So, where did you go to undergraduate school, Nikki Wallace?"

"St. John's."

"New York or Maryland?"

"Santa Fe, actually. It's an adjunct of the one in Maryland."

"Yes. The Great Books curriculum. Spare me the usual gushing, please."

"Actually, I was going to say I found it rather mundane."

"No, you weren't, but I appreciate the thought. Name one book in the program you found non-mundane."

"*De Revolutionibus Orbium Coelestium*."

"Trying to impress me by being erudite, not to mention literate in Latin?"

"Yes, a little, I guess."

"Keep it up. Who, by all means, wrote that impressive sounding work?"

"Copernicus. *The Revolution of Celestial Spheres*."

"You lost points there. The more erudite thing would have been to assume that, with the hint of the author's name, I could have translated the schoolboy Latin."

"Sorry."

"Welcome to the big leagues. Presumably that is your c.v. that you're holding in your well-manicured fingers. May I see it?" She handed it across the desk to him, then put out the stub of the cigarette in the ash tray. "Want another?" he asked, as he began to read. "You didn't get much of that one."

She had her own, but didn't want to admit that the Luckies were too strong. "Thanks."

This time he handed her the entire pack, and his lighter, a gold-plated one, with his initials on it, and which burned odorous lighter fluid, not butane. She lit up while he studied her c.v., and set the lighter beside the ashtray on the corner of his desk.

Without looking up, Ben said, "You were about to explain to me why I had the Faulkner class read things written after he wrote."

"I was?"

"You were. What does that have to do with the context of his writing?"

"Well, I guess you were giving us a context for our own criticism of his writing."

"Please don't say *I guess* again during the course of this interview. What did you get in the Faulkner class?"

"An A."

"Well, that's a start. Have you gotten any B's in the MFA program?"

"No."

"Where are you from, Nikki Wallace?"

"Albuquerque."

"Um hmm," he said, not looking up, and without apparent interest. "And what do you write?"

"Poetry, mostly."

"Um hmm." Now he put down her c.v., took off his reading glasses and looked across the desk at her. "So, why switch?"

"I think I'd like to teach."

"You want my job, do you?"

"Yes. Well, one just like it. Tallahassee itself doesn't do much for me."

"Nor for me."

"I think the opportunities to teach would be better on the literature side. Maybe I can still write some poetry."

"Your career, or not, as a poet does not interest me. But perhaps we can make a critic out of you. Perhaps. Now, here's what we'll do: when we get finished here, walk back into the anteroom, turn left, and to the right of my secretary's desk you'll see a door that leads to a room that is just on the other side of that wall there." He pointed with his left hand to the wall that contained his framed diplomas. "That room is a library. Pick yourself any work of fiction, just as long as it was written in the last fifty years, and write an essay for me analyzing one of the secondary characters. Pick something you've never read before, and for God's sake don't pick something that you read at St. John's. Don't try to cheat, because I'll be able to tell. Pick something difficult; this process begins with the degree of difficulty of the task that you've chosen for yourself.

"Now, prepare that essay and turn it into my secretary by nine in the morning, a week from Monday. As you no doubt heard from my distraught wife while you were eavesdropping through the door, I will be in New York City on that Monday, but never mind, as my secretary will carefully note the day and time that you turn the essay in.

"Are you with me?" Nikki nodded. She thought, correctly, it turns out, that he would think it silly of her to be taking notes while he was giving her these tasks. "Good. Now, when you turn in that essay, return the book to the library, and pick yourself a work of criticism, this time one written in the past twenty-five years, and write an essay for me discussing the author's theory of literature. Submit that essay one week after you turned in the first."

"How long?"

"That question counts against you. As long as it takes." She kept her face blank. "Okay. Ten pages will certainly be too few. Fifty, too many. Does that help?"

She nodded. "Is this part of the admission process to the PhD program?"

"Of course not. The admissions committee is not allowed to inquire into your marital status, more's the pity. This is, instead, a little test to see if I'm going to support your application to the admissions committee. If the first essay is of the quality that I would expect from a St. John's undergraduate, then I will oppose your application, which means that you will surely be turned down. But if I like it, then I will support your application, which means that you will surely be accepted, and will begin the PhD program immediately. And if I like the second essay, then I shall be your dissertation advisor, and that will ensure that your rise through the ranks of academia will be swift as well as certain. Any questions?"

"What about the MFA?"

Ben shrugged. "Complete it if you want, but it will add two years to your course of study."

"Why?"

"Because if you switch now, the credits you've earned working on the MFA will transfer over and satisfy much of the coursework requirement for the PhD. Complete the MFA and you'll have to start over for the PhD. If you're allowed to make the switch, about which at the present time I am still uncertain, we'll load you up on courses second summer session and in the fall, you'll take your prelims at Christmas time, and you'll be working on your dissertation in the spring. They'll probably give you an MA for good attendance in the process. If you're serious about this, make the switch now, and you can be as poetic as you want on the side. If you're not serious, then you've wasted my time. Now, do you have any other questions?" She shook her head. "Good. One other thing: I've already read my decade's quota of feminist claptrap, so spare me. Got it?"

"Got it. No feminist claptrap."

"Then we're done. Goodbye. Whether we talk again depends on how well you write."

Nikki stood up, stubbed out her cigarette, brushed some ashes off of her skirt and onto the floor, and turned to leave, her flip-flops smacking against her heels.

"Oh, and Nikki Wallace?" She turned to look at him, as he lit a new cigarette for himself. "I hope you pass the test. I like your . . ." Here he paused to take a drag, which he held for somewhat longer than was absolutely necessary; then he exhaled, and with it the word, ". . . style."

"Thank you."

"You're welcome. Close the door behind you."

Nikki walked out of the office, and back into the library on the other side of the wall where, after about ten minutes, she chose Thomas Pynchon's *V.* Then, exiting the Browning Suite, as she had decided to call it and where, she was determined, she was going to spend a good part of the next several years, she said *good day* to the secretary, who said nothing in return.

# ~ 5

# CORRESPONDENCE

June 12. Hill Top Lodge, Kandy, Sri Lanka. 80° F, I'd guess; the monsoon bends yonder palm trees across the valley; spicy aromas wander up the stairway from the kitchen and across the balcony. 3:00 p.m., local time, which makes it 3:00 a.m. in the Ozarks, I think, but whether that's 3:00 a.m. yesterday, today or tomorrow, I do not know.

Dear Richard,

It's odd, isn't it, that there should be a city in Sri Lanka called Kandy, pronounced just like the confectionary? Odder still that in that town stands a temple said to house one of the Buddha's teeth, hence the Temple of the Tooth. Oddest of all that I am here, have seen the temple, though not the tooth (I remain skeptical), and now sit writing, fighting a half-hearted and losing battle against an afternoon nap, even while anticipating the meal that I smell being prepared below. And finally, so odd as to leave one awash in oddity, I find myself sitting here not contemplating this or that listed above—all surely worthy of contemplation—but rather wracking my brain trying to think of the name of the game that is played by several ball players before the real game begins: several tossers, one hitter, you know, little slaps to improve the reflexes. The one that appears so effortless, but is in fact so difficult. The one about which are stenciled messages in front of the boxes at Dukes stadium and elsewhere:

"NO _ _ _ _ _ _."

Perhaps I'll remember it before I finish writing. Likely you'll know what I mean right off and will have said already several lines ago yet several days from now in the future, "of course, he means _ _ _ _ _ _." But little good that does me now and less good it will do me later when you say it. Since I can't figure out if *now* here is yesterday, today or tomorrow at home I see little hope of receiving useful psychic help from you.

Pepper. Of course. Son of a bitch. I'll be damned.

Anyway, a few days ago, on the bus from Colombo to this place, I saw some cricketers playing pepper. I hadn't known they did that.

How I came to be here in Sri Lanka is a story worth telling. I am possessed, see, of a plane ticket around the world. *Around the world.* That has a nice ring to it, doesn't it? Yes. *Around the world.* TWA and Singapore Airlines, US $2000, good for longer than I've got to spend and subject to any number of restrictions that I needn't go into. So I left the Ozarks on a small prop commuter plane; Emily stayed behind, more interested in the fledging of the two small owls in the oak tree out in front of the cabin, than in the charms of my compulsive traveling. I nearly missed connections in St. Louis, which I thought inauspicious. I saw my folks and one of their old pals in Nashville, which was pleasant, spent a weekend in Our Nation's Capital, visiting the standard white marble and, don't ask me why, the National Building Museum, then made connections to A'dam at JFK, and hopped the Pond, comfortable on a half-empty 747. I spent five weeks in Europe, seeing some friends in Oslo and some sights in the far north, and then, back in Amsterdam, made a visit to the drawing gallery in the Van Gogh Museum. That afternoon, the day before I was to leave for the Middle East, I stopped by the Singapore Airlines ticket office to check on my flight and was told that my visa for the United Arab Emirates was incorrect, they—meaning the UAE—wouldn't let me out of the transit lounge, so they—meaning Singapore Airlines—wouldn't allow me on the plane with an Amsterdam - Dubai coupon and, well, what would I like to do?

My original itinerary was A'dam → Dubai →Karachi →surface to Bombay → Singapore. That was now out, or rather I had two hours before the UAE embassy closed to get things straightened out. In any case, the Hindus, Sikhs and Muslims are fighting in Northwest India, what else is new?, and the plane to Dubai goes on to Colombo, Sri Lanka where Americans are welcome without visas. So the change was made. I thought about scouring A'dam for an English-language travel guide to Sri Lanka, but gave up the notion as ridiculous, and decided instead to take a stroll by Anne Frank's house (wherein, if you don't know, lies a letter from the US State Department denying her family's application for a visa) ate lunch at an inexpensive Dutch restaurant, which is rare, across the street from a porno theater, which is not, and wondered for a bit what Anne Frank would think of porno theaters in her neighborhood. I wondered a bit more about the wisdom of arriving in Sri Lanka, a place I had only vaguely even heard of, without a travel guide. Then I finished my beer, claimed my pack from the hotel and rode the trolley and train to Schiphol, the departure lounge of which, as far as I'm concerned, is holy ground, not unlike the Temple of the Tooth.

(Do Buddhists dislike blasphemy? I'm not sure, but who doesn't? I cover the paragraph above and glance around. I'm alone. In any case, the guests here are mostly foreigners, non-Buddhists: An Australian painter and his young—too young—boy friend. A Belgian couple with a motorcycle.)

I meant no blasphemy. I strolled around the Schiphol departure lounge feeling the breathtaking enormity of the earth. Unheard-of destinations. Larnaka. Feel the sound of that place on your tongue. Taste it on your palate. Larnaka. It's in Cyprus, I think. At Schiphol, if one had the time, money and inclination, one could walk up to a counter and say, "I'll have a ticket to Larnaka, please." Hallowed ground. Transit passengers asleep or wired, in all stages of jet lag. Tour groups standing together, uttering strange or familiar sounds. Airplanes, jet exhaust, tax-free liquor. I walked twice up and down the concourse to my gate, savoring every step. The sight of the sign over my departure gate: SQ 003 Dubai, Colombo, Singapore. The sense of going, of being free. This, I think, is what birds must feel like. The flight took off in the afternoon, but it was dark before we flew out of Europe, so there was no particular feeling of entering the East. After a brief, middle-of-the-night stop in Dubai, which looked mysterious, rich and attractive, I arrived in Colombo.

The tale, you see, is not so much of Sri Lanka itself, where they drive on the left, read their strange letters from left to right, have a difficult time getting along with one another and call me *Sir*, an honorific I'm uncomfortable with. Oh, there are many such stories that will eventually have to be told to you and to the others: of cricketers playing pepper, of Tamil women making gravel by hand along the side of the road, starting with very large rocks and ending with very small ones and bleeding fingers, of elephants on the road and of the Temple of the Tooth. Such stories need desert air and beer, not ink and long-distance. For now my friend, as I sit here, the nap forgone, writing a letter that does not reflect the pauses that I have paused to wonder about what you, Rita, and my other New Mexican friends are up to this summer, for now the story is one of travel, of last-minute changes, of hassles that work out well, of standing in the Colombo airport knowing that no one in the entire world has any idea of where I am right now and of the freedom that brings, of approaching the frosted glass doors into the arrival hall having no knowledge, nor any expectations, of what lies beyond, of walking through those doors (the exchange is on your left) to be struck by the heat, the noise, the smell, the strangeness and excitement of it all, of the unequalled rush of a bus ride into an unknown city to a nice little tucked-away hotel called Lake Lodge, where I collapse in the room's heat, under a spinning fan, in the glorious agony of jet lag and over-stimulation. (*Glorious agony*? Forgive me. It's the swaying palms. It's the spicy food. It's being half-way around the world, for God's sake, and not knowing if this is the farthest east or the farthest west I've been. It's not knowing if it's yesterday, today or tomorrow at home. "But *glorious agony*?" you say. I know. I know. Forgive me, my friend.)

The first day in Colombo was hard. I wrote a card to Em: "Remember the bus ride into Bandung? Remember the first night in Bamako? . . ." It was hot and I was tireder than I realized and, of course, I'd forgotten what the third world is like. I always forget. I walked from the hotel along one of the main streets and felt over-dressed, white and uncomfortable. Everyone wanted to sell me something or to beg something. The dust and the dirt, the heat and the sun, the cars and the crowds and the noise. Colombo is not Oslo. Nor Albuquerque.

At the hotel, a young French woman awaited her boy friend. He was several days late in arriving from India and she was very frightened, both for him apparently traveling in the war zone to the north, and for herself alone in this place. She speaks no English, but the innkeeper, who speaks a little French, made her know that she shouldn't walk in Colombo alone, so she sat and read and smoked and waited. One night we ate dinner together, very quietly as we had only about seven words in common. *Sortie* was one and she was happy to take a walk, after several days inside the hotel. So we left the hotel and walked through residential neighborhoods to the main road by the sea. From there we found the cornishe, called the Galle Face, once a race track and now a tree-less park on the seaside, with an old colonial hotel, kites in the constant breeze, and vendors of nuts and ice creams. We shared a soda, silently, and watched the kite fliers at their sport and the waves crash on the beach. She would hold my arm when we approached men on the street and I felt sad that she was so afraid. The next morning we said *bon jour*, smiled, and silently ate breakfast.

What now? I don't know. I have a visa for India and there is a train north from here every day, but there is fighting in the north and all the Lankans say to stay in the central or south. The monsoon doesn't blow on the east coast and a swim in the Indian Ocean might be nice. There are enormous Buddhas and beautiful vistas everywhere I turn. There is a national exposition in a place called Andrahanapura. And near here, just out of view down the hill and to the left, on the other side of the lake, is the temple with the Buddha's tooth and farther on, women who make gravel on the side of the road by hand and who don't believe Buddha was anyone real special. And that, I'm told, is what the fighting in the north is about. In any case, my flight to Singapore is in three weeks. Here the palms sway and all is well and I hope the same for you.

My best to Rita and the kids,
Michael.

Richard Randolph sat in tee shirt, shorts and deck shoes, in his office at the law school, with his feet on the desk, a Vernor's in his hand, his eyes closed, and Beethoven on the stereo. Ragged, sandy hair; clean-shaven, though not today, nor yesterday. At the moment he was quite enjoying the summer life of a law professor. No classes, no deadlines, no committees, few students, fewer colleagues. Beethoven on the stereo. The Dukes at home. Of course, strictly speaking he was not being paid at the moment; his next pay check would not arrive until September. But Rita, a personnel officer for the city, was being paid and the kids weren't starving and, while at any given moment you couldn't be sure what the jokers at the campus radio station were going to play, at this moment they were playing Beethoven.

He sipped his ginger ale and closed his eyes.

He and Christina were going to the ball game tonight. Alone. Just the two of them. Christina was Rita's child, a serious and precise little twelve-year-old whom he had heard answer the phone like this the other day: "Hello, Christina speaking. . . . My father doesn't live here. You must want my stepfather. Just a moment, please." So he had asked her to go to the game, just the two of them, and for ice cream after. He'd fix the little twit; he planned to be so charming it would curl her hair.

A knock came on his open door. He kept his eyes closed and managed a gesture with his free hand that said come in, but quietly.

"Professor Randolph?" He opened one eye; it was Britt Larsen. He raised a finger to his lips.

"I can come back . . . ."

"Shhhh. Come in and listen. Beethoven's Fifth . . . ."

". . . I don't want to bother you."

"Shoosh." A very gentle shooshing. She walked into the office, sat on his couch with her books in her lap and listened. He flipped the volume up; a nearby office door closed, not gently. He shut his eyes again and, with his right hand, directed the woodwinds.

When the music subsided, if that's the word, Richard quickly reached over and snapped the stereo off. "You never know. KUNM is likely to follow that up with a Romanian folk tune. I'd die right now if I heard a Romanian folk tune."

Britt laughed. "That had me fooled. I thought I knew the Fifth." She hummed a little: "Bump-bump-bum-baaa . . ."

"You're thinking of the Fifth Symphony. That was the Fifth Piano Concerto."

"Oh. I don't really know that much about classical music. I do like the Ninth Symphony, though."

"The Ninth is the single greatest piece of music ever written. Period. And we're not going to argue about that, now or ever. Got that? But the Fifth Piano Concerto is pretty good for a summer afternoon in one's office, I'll say that much. The problem with the Ninth is that it's too commonly used in the movies, and the characters are always directing it, standing in front of a mirror or something. It's considered sensitive film-making."

"*Sophie's Choice*?"

"For example. One should never direct music to which one is listening; it takes away from the experience; it focuses one's mind too much on the rhythm, to the detriment of the rest."

"Actually, I don't really care for the singing part of the Ninth too much . . . ."

"You don't care for the *singing* part. I see. Baseball is nice, but you don't care for no-hitters." Britt shrugged. "Okay. You like the theater, but don't care for Shakespeare. Eating is fun but French food isn't special. God damn it, Ms. Larsen, excuse my language. Next time you listen to the last movement of the Ninth, concentrate on the soprano part. It is truly wonderful. If there is anything to this karma notion, and how can a half a billion Buddhists be wrong—did you know there's a temple somewhere with his teeth in it?—if there is anything to karma, I shall be rewarded in the next life with a body that can sing the soprano part of the *Ode to Joy*."

Richard closed his eyes and began to recite, in an unmusical monotone, but with the rhythm of the Ninth Symphony: "*Wer ein hol-des Wieb er-rung-en, mis-che sein-en Ju-be-lein! Ja, ver auch nur eine See-le sein nennt auf dem Er-den-rund! Und wers nie ge-konnt, der steh-le wein-end sich aus diesem Bund. . . .*"

"What's that?"

"I told you. It's the soprano part to the Ode to Joy. Want to hear the rest? *Kusse gab sie uns und Reben, einen Freund, geprüft in Tod; . . .*"

"You know it all?"

"Just the words; I can't manage the notes. I like to be prepared. Someday

I might be rewarded and granted the voice, but only for an hour and I don't want to have to be searching for the words then. Finding the orchestra will be hard enough. The reward will be for having tolerated with perfect good humor law students and others, *like you Garcia . . .*"—this last was shouted at the closed door nearby—". . . who don't appreciate the soprano part of the Ninth Symphony. That's kind of circular, isn't it?"

"Yes, but I'm impressed that you know the whole thing."

"It wasn't really that hard. It repeats a lot. It was one of my two great acts of memorization."

"The other?"

"Uh . . . I can recite the complete works of Emily Dickinson?"

"Really?" She sounded impressed.

"No, not really, but I have thought of memorizing them. I admire Emily Dickinson."

"You're a credit to your gender."

"Why? Because I admire her, or because I told the truth?"

"Either way. And you were directing during the music."

"No, I wasn't." He put his feet on the floor and swiveled to face her. "Now, what did I send you to look for?" He had several researchers who were always running about on some errand.

"Cases on warehouse receipts. U.C.C. section seven-dash-five-oh-three. I didn't find very much."

"Right. What've you got?" He sipped his Vernor's. "Sorry, I can't offer you one. Besides, you're working."

"As best I can tell, only three cases have ever interpreted that section."

"Hmhmm. Lemme see." She handed him the Xerox copies. "By the way, that was a *non sequitur*."

"What was a what?"

"A *non sequitur*: one thing that doesn't logically follow from another. *Non sequitur*. N-O-N second word S-E-Q-U-I-T-U-R. I can't offer you a ginger ale, and besides you're working. See?" She didn't answer, but wrote the Latin phrase down on her notepad. Richard leaned back again to skim the cases. Britt sat quietly on the edge of the couch, balancing her notes on her knees.

"Do you understand what these are about?" He gestured with the stack of Xeroxes.

"Not really. No. I just found the cases for you."

"You read them of course."

"Of course, but they were confusing."

"Have you studied Article Seven?"

"I had the Uniform Commercial Code course, but we must have skipped Article Seven. "

Richard sighed, got up, shoved some files on the floor and sat next to her on the couch. He sketched a diagram on a yellow pad. "George sends his lawn mower out to Bev to have it sharpened. Bev stores it with Acme and gets a receipt. Bev sells the receipt to Tom. Who owns the lawn mower now, Tom or George?"

"George, I guess. It was his."

"Yeah, but Tom paid good money for the receipt."

"Tom ought to sue Bev; she shouldn't have sold the receipt to him."

"Sure. Bev's a crook and should go to jail. That's the junior high answer." Britt looked crestfallen. "But suppose she takes Tom's money, spends it on silk underwear and leaves town. Between Tom and George, who gets the mower?"

"George, I guess." She shrugged. "Tom only bought a scrap of paper."

"*A scrap of paper* she says; that receipt is what Article Seven is all about. Substantial rights are tied up in that receipt. Generally speaking, paper trades more freely than goods."

"I don't know what that means."

"Which would you rather pay good money for: a lawn mower or a receipt for the same lawn mower?"

"A lawn mower."

"Right. Anyone would. So, if we want people to deal in paper—and we do, because it's a very efficient way to do business—then we've got to set up a legal system that gives them at least some protection against a person who buys the actual goods subject to the paper. Of course, lawn mower receipts aren't very important, but suppose it's five tons of soybeans sitting in some elevator in Iowa, being bought and sold via paper in Chicago. What then?"

"I don't know who should win."

"Of course you don't. Neither do I. It all depends on just exactly what the hell seven-five-oh-three means and you tell me . . . ," he held up the Xeroxes, ". . . that I've got to get advice from judges in Mississippi, Kansas and South Dakota, for crying out loud. *You* know more than they do and you only know what I just told you."

"So, what do you want me to do now?"

"Check the law reviews. Check the treatises. Check *White & Summers*."

"Who?"

"The leading treatise."

"Oh." She wrote the names in her notes.

"Check the bankruptcy reports. Have you had bankruptcy yet?"

She shook her head. "But why bankruptcy?"

"It's the legal equivalent of Bev's purchase of silk underwear and her exit from the premises. But forget the bankruptcy reports for now. You'll get confused. You will take bankruptcy from me in the fall."

"Well, uh, I haven't looked at the schedule too closely for the fall yet."

"You *will* take bankruptcy. How can I have a researcher who doesn't know any bankruptcy?"

"Ummmm," she squirmed in her seat, "I wasn't sure I'd be your researcher in the fall."

"And why not?"

"Well, I'm going to be one of the editors of the *Law Review*."

"Congratulations. I saw the memo. Good, that will make you into a proofreader and office manager. But if you want to do some actual law, take bankruptcy and be my researcher."

"Can I think about it?"

"Sure. Think about it. Ask around. Ask anybody. Well, don't ask the Dean; what the hell does he know? Listen. Editing the *Law Review* will give you a prestigious resume and hone your editing skills. Prestige is over-rated and editing is boring. Working for me on the other hand will improve your research and writing skills and you'll learn a bunch of commercial law. So decide what you want," he smiled at her and handed back the cases, plus his yellow sheet with the diagram on it, "then take bankruptcy and be my researcher. Do both, if you must, but you *will* be my RA."

"Okay. Maybe. Thanks for asking. I'll let you know. But when do you want this stuff?"

"I won't be back in the office until . . . ," he checked the calendar, ". . . next Tuesday. " He stood up and so did she. "At which time you will know section seven-five-oh-three better than the guy who wrote it. Start with *White & Summers*, but I'll tell you in advance: they don't know what it means either. Now, goodbye. I'm taking my stepdaughter to watch the Dukes game." He shooed her toward the door.

Britt packed up her books and Richard watched her leave. A short while later he walked home, whistling tunelessly, thinking of George's lawnmower and Britt's eyes and the Buddha's teeth and thinking that tonight, if it was all right with Tina, they'd sit in the third base boxes.

CORRESPONDENCE

Kota Bharu, Malaysia. The Travelers' Inn, an ant-infested little US$2 hotel. July 10. 11:00 p.m. Hot.

Dear Richard,

Singapore was disappointing. The botanical gardens are nice, but Kandy's are nicer. (Watch out, my friend. There are cocktail parties from which one can be asked to leave for such extreme place-dropping as *Kandy's botanical gardens are nicer than Singapore's*. Be careful with this information, and use it judiciously.)

So I took the night train north to Kuala Lipis, a spot in the Malaysian highlands, across a wide river from a wall of jungle. Rather off the beaten track, this place was; no postcards were for sale that I could find, though John McEnroe was playing tennis on the TV in a little bar, where I ordered soda and got cream soda, and playing well, too. I was enjoying myself in this little town. The local mosque is a quiet, cool, and rather male place for reading and talk, while the places of Chinese religion are dark, smoky, exotic, magical, and less male. I was enjoying myself, as I was saying, but I was pestered by my itinerary. Should I stay here, then take the train back to Singapore? Must I make a trip to Kuala Lumpur, though generally speaking I have found small places, on this trip and others, preferable to large ones? Or should I try the east coast by bus? How far north could I go and still return on time to Singapore for the flight eastward?

I do not travel for the chance to think such questions as these.

I chose wrong. I left my highland town by bus for the east coast. It was a pleasant enough ride, though long, but the coast itself was not the isolated Malaysia it appeared to be on the map. Singaporeans are rich and they vacation on the beaches of southeastern Malaysia. Likewise rich Aussies. My hotel was dear, hard on a Hyatt, for God's sake. The food was uninteresting. Tourists abounded. I hated it; I might as well have been in Syracuse.

I swam a bit, in the South China Sea, check the map. Floating, I wished to be back in K. Lipis in the highlands. But to return there would mean a long bus ride, only to catch the train almost immediately back to Singapore. Stay here the extra days? But I don't want to be here. Etc., etc., so forth and so on.

Some years ago, I spent a summer in the Caribbean. I was coming from New Mexico, where I had seen you and Rita, and a school-teaching pal you don't know. I rented a motorcycle on St. Lucia, burned my little North American body on Antigua. I hopped the islands south—Guadeloupe, St. Vincent, Bequia—pursuing the sun and little else. I finally rendezvoused with Em in pre-Reagan, socialist Grenada, she flying down from KC. We rented a little beach-front bungalow on the back of the island, with a glass front door and tiny tree frogs clinging to the kitchen windows. My memories are of hot peppers and sweet mangoes, of music on the night breeze, the tune coming up short as a band practiced somewhere across the way, of diving pelicans and greasy turtle soup and of a yacht full of fat, pink Belgians and one very lovely, very naked Swedish girl who helped me up the side of the yacht, and offered me a beer.

And of questions: Should we stay here? Should we go on? Where? Questions like those that dragged my feet as I bobbed in the South China Sea off the southeast Malaysian coast.

We left, and moved on to Trinidad. Emily was not taken with Port of Spain, so after a week, during which we spent most of our time at the track, she returned to the jazz clubs of Kansas City, and I woke up at the Pelican Hotel, a comfortable place near the park and city center, with two more weeks on my own, before I had to be back home.

It is rare, I suppose, that one gets to try out one's dreams. A date with Debra Winger. Turning the pivot on a double play in the ninth to win on Opening Day. Snorkeling with Jacques Cousteau. All impossible. Yet, soon after Emily headed north, I got to the POS airport without a taxi (no mean trick) and said, more-or-less, "I'll take the next ticket anywhere." *More-or-less* because the reality was more complicated than the dream. For example, the next flight was to

Miami, and who would choose Miami over Port of Spain? Or London, which struck even me as truly, impossibly, extravagant. And so on. But only more complicated, not less soul-satisfying, as if the date with Ms. Winger required considerable running around on a hot and muggy Cleveland afternoon to get the tickets she wanted. In any event, it pleases me just now to concentrate not on the details and complications but on the dream, or what I perceive to be the dream of every traveler: to go where chance alone dictates. I went to Guyana, had a wonderful time, drank strong liquor with some fishermen, ate curried crab in a restaurant with neither lights nor napkins, ran aground on a river ferry, hunted iguanas (iguanae?) with some local boys, and returned to the north with a small spark in my left eye for having done what I had done, a spark that lives there still.

None of this was particularly on my mind as I bobbed off Malaysia in the South China Sea, ignoring unsuccessfully the Hyatt and the Aussies and pondering the alternatives. Something swam by, a spirit, I guess, the spirit who looks after travelers, who had looked after me so well in Trinidad and since, who may once have been called St. Christopher but whom I now think of as a more friendly red-headed spirit named Chip, who lives under the spring near the cabin in the Ozarks, who bites his nails and grants the wishes of people on the road. This Chip swam by and wondered why, exactly, I had to return to Singapore at all? There lies the road north, up the way Thailand and Laos. Why not take it? What are roads north for, anyway?

So here I sit in Kota Bharu, having departed from my itinerary and ended up as far north as one can go in Malaysia, and into the common room of a hotel, with a several months old copy of the *New Yorker*, which I have read cover-to-cover, including the article on dance, and keeping company with a few heebie-jeebies in my lower gut and a sense of adventure that walks into my Ozarkian life damned rarely. It is now well after midnight, still hotter than sparrow shit, and I sit alone and write, surrounded by the rhythmic sounds of passion behind one wall and, I'm afraid, the scurrying sounds of a rat in the bathroom behind another. One of these days soon I'll take the bus to the Thai border and see what happens there.

I had no real intention to tie the three places I've spoken of in this summer's two letters into any kind of tidy package. But here goes: just now, I am struck by my three traveler's tales I've told to you—the happenstancical arrival in Sri Lanka in the last letter, the choosing of chance in Trinidad and the abandonment of well-laid plans in Malaysia, in this one. Travel, it seems to me, is made up of portions of chance and control. Like most everything, I suppose. Chance put me in Sri Lanka, and to Colombo itself was added surprise, a tangy combination. Contrariwise, the choice to head north for Bangkok was an exercise of control. I had originally set the itinerary, sure, but it had been Made in America with no notion that Singapore could possibly look like the inside of Coronado Mall. The itinerary had become bigger than itself, had taken over, had made me forget that *I'm* in charge here. Chip, or whoever, reminded me that I, not any itinerary, decide where I go. Trinidad was a hybrid: a deliberate, and perhaps artificial, choice to put chance in control.

And so it goes. Chance and control. If my luck holds, I'll continue to have some of each.

The hotel has become quiet, for how long depends on the nocturnal urges of several entities beyond my control. My beer sits with one last large swallow, the warmth and bitterness of which will dispel the notion that any universal truth lies in the paragraphs above.

Goodnight, my friend.

Michael.

## SUPERIOR, ARIZONA

The Arboretum—officially the Boyce Thompson Desert Arboretum State Park—had become Marie Cochran's favorite place in Phoenix. Well, technically speaking, it wasn't in Phoenix proper, but about fifty miles east of campus on US 60, but that didn't bother Marie, as she enjoyed the drive and it saved her from having to admit that there was anything about the city itself that she liked. She had found it mentioned, not in the *What's Happening* section of the weekend *Republic*, but rather in the business section, in an article about the fiscal troubles of the U of A down in Tucson, and there had been a mention of various remote-from-Tucson research facilities, including the Arboretum, that were especially feeling the pinch. She had seen the article one weekday, and it had painted the place as kind of an anti-tourist-attraction, and feeling a little anti-touristy herself, bored and restive, she had made the long drive out to Superior, and had liked what she had found there, including most notably, few visitors other than herself. It was a quiet, contemplative place, and on her second visit, she had met the Assistant Park Manager, a heavy-set, bearded young man named Chuck, who had given her a tour, pointing out that there were more than thirty-two hundred species of desert plants in the Arboretum, an impressive number, she had to concede. When she had mentioned that there might be more guests if the place were featured in *What's Happening*, Chuck had laughed and said, "What's happening at the Arboretum? Cacti, growing slowly," and they had become friends. And after that, her Arizona life had begun to circulate from her apartment, a dreary little efficiency, in a half-empty complex of dreary units that supposedly filled up with snowbirds in the winter, furnished but just barely with a cigarette-burned kitchen table, a threadbare couch and a bed that someone else had slept in, to the ASU campus, which she found both sterile and pretentious compared to UNM, to a couple of restaurants and movie theaters she frequented, to the pool for exercise, and to the Arboretum. And of these, the only one she could say she truly enjoyed was the Arboretum.

And so it was on a late, mid-week, class-less morning as mid-July approached, that Marie sat on a wooden bench in the breezeway of the Arboretum's Visitor Center, with a book in her lap, scanning a plaque honoring the generous contributors to the Arboretum, and listening to the quiet sounds of the desert birds—more than two hundred and thirty species, Chuck had told her, though not all at one time. Another impressive number, no doubt. Ginger, who was not allowed on the grounds, was tied with a long rope to the car door handle, with shade and water within reach, and was ministered to by a woman Marie knew only as Kitty, a retiree from up North somewhere, who volunteered at the Arboretum and looked after the gift shop, giving her plenty of time to be over-indulgent toward Ginger, who didn't mind the attention at all. Marie had seen and waved to Chuck on her way through the turnstiles, as he went about on some Assistant Park Manager business, and if the usual pattern held, he would look her up before long and they'd have a chat, which she wouldn't mind, though right now she was enjoying the quiet.

The book in her lap was *One Day in the Life of Ivan Denisovitch*, which was to be the subject of the final exam in the course she was taking. She had first read it years ago, then again this summer, and she had brought it along today to skim through, early prepping for the exam. There was actually not much to worry about concerning the exam, as the professor, a young man with a freshly minted PhD, just out of a post-doc spent in Leningrad, had practically winked at the class when he had announced well in advance that the final exam would involve *Ivan Denisovitch*. He clearly did not see it to be his job to pass out anything except A's to this class of middle-aged, experienced school teachers, all older than he, and all having been classroom teachers when he was still playing intramural basketball at Northwestern. The class as a whole was both relieved and annoyed by this attitude, Marie included, in her case more annoyed than relieved. As both a teacher and a student she was used to taking examinations seriously, and found this youngster's slap-ass manner to be off-putting. *Ivan Denisovitch* was surely too old for her students, and she wouldn't be using it in her classes, but still, she would have preferred that the professor not fool around.

Tucked away in the still unopened *Ivan Denisovitch* in Marie's lap were two documents that she had brought along with her to the Arboretum. The first was Michael Reid's latest letter, and which she now pulled out and unfolded. He was staying at a beach house called French Chateau, a collection, he wrote, and notwithstanding its glamorous name, a collection of grass huts on the beach, serviced by an open-sided, tin-roofed restaurant, on the east coast of Sri Lanka. And, the letter, written while sitting at a small table in his grass hut, had described in precise detail a Buddhist temple he had visited, and which he called *The Temple of the Tooth*, though whether that was the official name of the place, or merely Michael's own construction, she couldn't tell. He was skeptical, it was clear, of the claim that the temple contained one of the actual Buddha's actual teeth, nevertheless, it appeared that he had spent hours exploring the temple, had been intrigued by its mysticism, and he had included in his letter a floor plan of the place, which he had hand-drawn, with arrows and marginal notes on the map explaining the various sites: *Here fruit and rice were sold to make offerings. This was where five monks sat, chanting. This room was filled with incense and chimes. Visitors, including me, sat here, waiting to be taken to the altar.* In the end, he had written, armed with an offering of rice, he had entered the innermost sanctuary, in which, behind a rail, stood a number of monks accepting the gifts, and behind them an altar with candles and incense, and behind the altar a small door, now closed, behind which was said to lie the tooth. On the back of the floor plan he had made a clumsy sketch, from memory, of the altar room, and the door into the inner sanctum, to give her, he wrote, a sense of the place, and below that, another sketch, apparently of where he sat days later to write, showing nothing more than a porch rail, with his two feet propped up on it, and the straight line of the horizon, and written below: *The Indian Ocean—Lat. $8^oN$, Long. $81^oE$.* And below that, a piece of cellophane tape holding a sprinkle of Indian Ocean sand, and he had signed off, anticipating, he wrote, their rendezvous later next month. *Roughly three weeks now*, she thought, the letter, forwarded from Albuquerque, having taken its sweet time getting to her. She was anticipating the event more than a little herself. *He seems a long way away to be arriving in Phoenix in three weeks.*

She refolded Michael's letter, put it back into *Ivan Denisovitch*, took out the other document, and began to study.

"May I join you?"

Marie looked up. "Oh, hi, Chuck. Sure. Sit down. How's your day going?"

"Normally. No unexpected events. There's a group of Japanese botanists coming tomorrow, but I think I'm ready. Say, how's your Japanese? I'll give you a job serving lunch. Assistant to the Assistant Park Manager for East Asian Hospitality."

"Sorry. I'm not your gal." Her eyes glanced back to the paper in her hand.

"What are you doing?" He nodded at the paper.

"Studying. Here," she handed him the paper. "Quiz me."

He looked at the diagram on the page, and then back at Marie. "I thought the course was in Russian history or something."

Marie giggled. "This is something else. I'm trying to learn it to surprise a friend. Go ahead, quiz me."

"Okay," he said, "Let's see. Fetlock."

"That's the joint just above the hoof. Kind of like a wrist."

"Correct. Croup."

"The part of the back just forward of the tail."

"Hock?"

"Like the knee, except on the hind legs. The back of the hind legs."

"Poll."

"Top of the head, behind the ears."

"Pastern."

She paused, stumped. "Let's see. The pastern. Damn it. Pastern. Okay, tell me."

"Between the fetlock and the hoof."

"Right. Pastern. Hey, do you know all of these terms?"

"Without the diagram. Impressed? I grew up on a ranch up near Flagstaff."

"Lucky you. Okay, go on."

"Let's see if you can do it in the other direction. What's the bump between his shoulders, just behind the mane called?"

"Easy one: the withers."

～

Four hours later, she had passed her own horse-parts quiz, had shown to Chuck, over two bottles of Pepsi in the staff workroom, Michael's floor plan of The Temple of the Tooth, had taken Ginger for a walk around the parking lot, had walked the High Trail by herself, had reread the final chapter of *Ivan Denisovitch*, and then, revived, was ready for the drive back into the city.

# ~ 6

# HAT YAI, THAILAND

Michael Reid sat, leaning against the footboard at the end of the weak-springed bed, watched a cockroach walk boldly across the headboard at the other end, and tried to figure out what day it was. He had been having some difficulty lately figuring out what day it was at home. Is today here, tomorrow at home or is it still today? Or yesterday, maybe. He had sat, several weeks ago now, on the Galle Face, by a west-facing beach in Colombo and watched the sun set beyond the crashing waves of the Indian Ocean monsoon. Sri Lanka, he knew, was roughly halfway around from Topeka, where Emily was, visiting friends and playing music, and so the sun would have been rising there and Emily, an early riser, might well have been looking, weather permitting, at the same sun, at the very same time. She had felt close.

He got to thinking though, sitting there on the Galle Face, about whether Emily was watching this morning's sunrise, or yesterday's. Or the next morning's. He couldn't figure it out, then, and he had tried to think through the problem off and on through the weeks since. Here is how he was beginning to have it figured out: *now* here is *now* at home. Simple enough. He called *now* night, sitting in this roachy little hotel room in Thailand. In Kansas right now, Emily would call *now* late morning; that's because we live on a globe. Still simple. So, okay. Does Emily call *now* Tuesday morning, like he calls it Tuesday night, or does she call it Monday morning? Or Wednesday morning? He wasn't sure. Moreover—here comes the insight, he thought, such as it is—it's arbitrary anyway, and depends on where you put the line called the international date line. It could go anywhere. So, the difference between Monday and Tuesday, the difference between yesterday and today, a difference Michael had always reckoned to be rather fundamental, turns out, he had decided, to be arbitrary. It would take some getting used to a world in which the difference between yesterday, today and tomorrow is arbitrary.

While Michael had a reasonably high tolerance for arbitrariness, he had a low tolerance for cockroaches, and he had decided to sleep with the lights on in the room that night to discourage them from getting too bold. He had done so before, on this trip and others. Bedbugs were worse. He remembered his first bedbug: in a small hotel deep in Venezuela, he had awakened with the knowledge that something was biting him and it wasn't flying. He had gotten up and left the room, and had drunk warm gins and bitter tonics, which are good for malaria and, indirectly at least, for bedbugs, in the lobby until dawn, contemplating, among other mysteries, why it mattered if the insect that was biting one was flying or crawling.

No sign of bedbugs here though. But he disliked roaches, too, and would sleep tonight with the lights on and that meant, he knew, that it was best to read or write letters late into the night so when he fell asleep, he would fall hard. He turned his attention back to his pad, to the letter to Marie, writing that he probably wouldn't be meeting her in Phoenix.

At about 11:30 there was a knock on the door. He looked back over his right shoulder. Who could that be? "Come in." The door swung open and a young woman stood there. She was short and wore what looked like an ordinary house dress. She seemed young, though he found it hard to judge such things in the East. She was barefoot and padded over to stand by the bed.

"Like a massage?" she asked, with a strong Thai accent, and reached out and lightly touched his right wrist, perhaps because he was wearing a saffron thread around it to show he had visited the local Buddha. It was quite a delicate gesture, two fingers on top and her thumb under, on his pulse.

"Suck cock?" She made a circle with her other hand and held it to her mouth, a tremendously obscene gesture and the contraposition of the two hand motions was startling.

Actually, a massage would feel good. He had ridden a long hot train most of that day, north from the Malaysian border, sitting on a hard wooden bench, nodding off through hot fields with water buffalo, and through only slightly cooler highlands with rubber trees. He was stiff and sore and his head ached from squinting into the sun. Now that he thought of it, a blow job would not be entirely unwelcome either. But the lights were ablaze, the roaches were aggressive and the night promised neither relaxation nor romance. He declined; she did not insist, and quietly closed the door as she left. He watched her go, doubting that she wore anything at all under her dress. He wadded up his first attempt at a letter of explanation to Marie, tossed it across the room in the direction of the waste basket, and started anew on a fresh sheet of paper. He wrote on for a while.

Later, he put his pen down, shook a cramp out of his hand and stared out the window at the movie marquee across the street. *Raiders of the Lost Ark* was playing and Harrison Ford was looking directly into the hotel window from a two-story-tall billboard. It was odd that he was sitting here writing this letter to Marie, his friend and sometime lover, but not to Emily, his long-time companion and mate. "That *is* odd, isn't it, Harrison?" He addressed the marquee. "May I call you Harrison?" The cockroach appeared to eye him suspiciously. Emily, though, would not care when he showed up back in the States; she was with her friends and her music in Kansas and was not due back in the Ozarks until September. When she went to Kansas, she stayed in the otherwise unoccupied farmhouse of some friends, with the phone disconnected and she composed jazz, the only interruptions being excursions to some not-entirely reputable clubs on the Kansas side of Kansas City, or some student haunts in Manhattan and Lawrence. He suspected that she didn't even open his letters until she was ready to come home, though she denied it. Their long-standing relationship allowed each of them much time alone and she did not need to be told that he was running late.

Marie Cochran, on the other hand, ran a tidy, well-ordered life into which he was allowed—*tolerated* was probably a better word—as a random irritant. It would probably be best for all three of them if he and Marie stopped having sex and went back to the way it had been at the beginning. She was probably his best friend, and sex was not necessary to that, neither did it seem to get in the way. He found her strong, hard little body irresistible and he would never, on his own, stop fucking her, he supposed. Thinking of her even now did nothing to bring on the sleep he needed. He went back to writing.

A half-hour later, sleep had still not come and the letter, after two more false starts, was done. Various little Marie-isms peppered his imagination and tightened the crotch of his jeans. He walked to the window and looked out on the street below. The cinema was letting out and the street bustled with patrons and vendors, noise and strange smells. He eyed a roach—the same one? He had a colleague who had once advanced the notion, sitting around the faculty lounge, that one never saw the same cockroach twice. "(A) wrong," had said another colleague, "and (B) irrelevant." Anyway on the headboard stood a roach who appeared to be the same one. The roach stared straight back, its feelers testing the hot breeze from the window.

"Okay, you little fucker, the place is yours for . . ." he checked his watch, ". . . two hours. Be gone when I get back." He put on his shoes, left the lights and ceiling fan on and walked down the stairs and into the lobby. His visitor was watching television and filing her nails. She waved to him with the nail file as he walked out the door and joined the crowd on the street.

## PHOENIX

It was hot in Phoenix on the next-to-the last day in July; 107 degrees, the radio said. The lunchtime traffic on the I-10 had been worse than she had expected, and Marie was late to meet Michael's plane. Then she drove by mistake into the remote economy parking lot, and had to jog from her car to the terminal, which left her shirt wet and sticky under her arms. In the shockingly air conditioned arrival hall, she about froze and began to shiver.

Wrong terminal. *Shit.* When she had at last found the right arrival gate, no one was around. She was about twenty minutes late. *Shit.* She ran to the baggage claim, vaguely remembering that Michael hardly ever checked his bag. No one she recognized was there. Hardly anyone was there at all. She asked around about a short guy with a moustache and a backpack, but nobody knew anything.

*Fuck.*

Now she sat on a bench near the baggage carousel and tried to figure it out, eating too quickly some stale and greasy popcorn, which, it appeared, was to be her only lunch. If he had arrived and she hadn't been here, he might have called, but she would have missed the call anyway, in traffic. Or he might have taken a cab, but he didn't know her address, unless he had remembered it or found it. Unlikely. Besides, Michael didn't take taxis. He wouldn't have given up so quickly and called some other Phoenix friend, if he had one, would he? She assumed her charms would have been worth a half hour's wait. So, he ought to be here in the terminal. Where? She walked in search. Nothing.

*Shit.*

Well, maybe he had missed his connection. He was coming from overseas, after all, and connections were probably not as smooth as the Central Avenue bus, which weren't all that smooth anyway, another thing not to like about Phoenix. And the Olympics were on in L.A., and so even with the boycott, there was no telling what a zoo LAX was. So maybe he would be arriving later. In that case, the place for her was by the phone, at home. She wasn't in the book, but 411 had the number. She couldn't meet every fucking plane from Los Angeles, could she? No, she could not. She walked out of the artificial cold, into the breathtaking heat, back to her car, burned her bare legs on the hot car seat, and drove to her apartment in Tempe.

The apartment was practically empty. She was packed, except for a few dishes, a few clothes, the sheets and towels. She poured a beer, opened a book and sat on the couch by the phone. She was trying to read *The Secret Sharer* and was having a hard time with it. She was hardly in the right mood, packed and waiting for the phone to ring, her stomach grinding away on the popcorn. She wanted to be out of Phoenix and wanted Michael to arrive. She half hoped to talk him into driving to Albuquerque with her and then flying on from there. In any case, she was ready to be done waiting for him; she was ready for the phone to ring; she was ready, God damn it, for something to happen.

That night she went to sleep hungry; the fridge was empty and she had been afraid to miss his call, and she hadn't wanted to tie up the phone even to order out for a pizza.

"This is crazy, this is crazy, this is crazy. I'm going nuts sitting here. Two fucking days. I'm leaving tonight at eight and fuck him."

Ginger, with the incredible patience inscribed within her yellow lab genes, diluted though they were, trotted across the room toward Marie, head down, ears back, wagging her tail.

"Yeah? Well, fuck you too."

Marie had imagined over the summer any number of ways she might leave Phoenix for Albuquerque and home. She had imagined a slow drive east, through the White Mountains, sexually exhausted, with the warmth and closeness that Michael always left behind with her when he departed. Or she had imagined a long week's drive home, with a stop at a spot she knew in the Gila, where a windmill pumped water for her and the range cattle, and where she could stay for days and never see another person, camping, hiking, and getting Phoenix out of her system. Or she had imagined Britt flying over to drive back with her.

She had not imagined packing her car in ten minutes on a hot Phoenix night, her stomach in a knot, her nerves chopped in small pieces, the two nails she had permitted herself to chew, gone, sexual frustration off the scale and her so pissed off at Michael she could not, hardly, speak, if there had been anyone around to speak to, which there wasn't. She slammed the apartment door behind her, discovered she had locked the car keys inside and had to hunt up the manager.

Twenty minutes later, with the dog in the back seat, she pulled out of the parking lot, put the Pretenders on the cassette deck, turned up so the high-end guitar hurt her ears, and headed east out of town, toward Globe. The haze of the city smudged the brightest stars and exhausted the others, the palm trees had their usual stupid, confused look, as if they were not sure even whether they were trees or not, and the rock and roll did not soothe her soul: *I went back to Ohio /But my city was gone /There was no train station /There was no downtown. /Hey, ho, way to go/Ohio.*

CORRESPONDENCE

Hat Yai, extreme southern Thailand. July 17. 11:00 p.m. or so, I sit, dressed, in bed; hot, hot noodles and mystery meat lie easily enough, for now, on my stomach. The weather is hot, too.

Dear Marie,
I am in Thailand.
Here is a major discovery: I find that this trip has affected my time-sense more than my space-sense. There is really no around-the-world feel to it. In that, I guess, the trip is a disappointment. I get on planes; I get off them; cultures do not merge one into another; the lines are sharp, drawn at departure lounges. I can see on a map that I continually head east, but there is no feeling of that. I have repetitive jet lag.

Time, though, is different. For instance: I am about to write that I have deviated from my itinerary and fallen off course and behind.

So, I am about to tell you, it is unlikely I'll make our rendezvous in Phoenix, and I'm about to advise you that if I were you, I wouldn't wait around, enjoying the Phoenix summer, just on the chance that I'll show. So, all of that I'm about to say. But I realize that because I'm in Hat Yai, Thailand, a long way from the main post office, and because I left your Phoenix address at home, by the time you get this and read what I'm about to say, I will likely already have missed our rendezvous and you will be in Albuquerque, knowing it.

So why say it? What the hell. I've come to Thailand on the spur of the moment, via a slow, hot train yesterday to here and won't be seeing you and you probably won't know why until it's too late. Makes one feel a tad fatalistic.

Here, all is pleasant and I hope the same for you. After a slow ride all day on that hot train, I am about to sleep with the lights on in my hotel room in what I hope will be at least a partially successful tactic to keep the roaches in the walls. Tomorrow I'll relax and walk the city. I had something of a hectic time in Singapore and Malaysia; getting my act together required the expenditure of megawatts of psychic energy. Now I'd like to slow down a bit and savor the feel of being unexpectedly here. A saffron thread rides lightly on my wrist, showing that I have visited the local Buddha (reclining), the hot noodles continue to rest comfortably, I have just been solicited by the house prostitute, and I am waiting for sleep to arrive, thinking of you. There is every indication that the wait will be a long one.

So, my friend, I'll be in touch when I get back to the States. I have written this letter to you as I imagine you sitting right now, that is to say in my *now*, July 17, sitting in Phoenix with a beer, icy-cold and watered down as is your strange custom, thinking ahead, with some eager anticipation, maybe, of our getting together for the first time in, what is it? A year, plus or minus. It is not so pleasant for me to imagine you, not as you are in my *now*, but as you are in yours, that is, the *now* in the future as you are reading this, your specs slipping down your nose, back in Albuquerque, our rendezvous fumbled. Are you pissed? Are you calling me *shithead*? Have you even read this far? All I can say is this: a week or so ago when I spotted the road in Malaysia and it led north to Bangkok, it had to be taken, for it is along this road and in this unheard-of town and even in this roach-filled hotel room that a good part of my life lies. Emily will understand, but then she knows me better than you do. Emily would also know, you little shit, and without asking, that I said *no* to the hooker.

        Adios and best regards,
        Your complete, if tardy, pal,
        Michael.

## EASTERN ARIZONA

After midnight, in the White Mountains of eastern Arizona, on the land of the Apaches, exhaustion overtook Marie. She pulled off on the side of the road, set the brake, locked the doors and put her head down on the seat. She was instantly asleep, surrounded by dreams she would never remember.

And Venus passed behind the sun and entered the evening sky.

# THE WINTER AND SPRING OF 1985

# ST. GEORGE ISLAND, FLORIDA

T he new year's fog off Apalachicola Bay enclosed Anna Browning in a world thirty feet in radius. The only inhabitants of that world were Anna and Rachel, the little one, and a half dozen or so small, long-legged birds, who pecked at the sand, dodged the bay's quiet laps and eyed her warily. One bird was one-legged. A blue crab about the size of Rachel's foot had formerly inhabited this world, but now it lay lifeless, upside down on the sand.

Above, the ceiling of the world was also thirty feet high. The sun did not shine through the fog bank and no noise came to Anna from beyond the fog. The only sounds in this world were the peeps of the small birds, the lapping of the water and the breeze in her ears. A gull drifted slowly through, over her head, barely flapping its wings against the breeze and looking weightless. It spotted the crab and landed near it. The gull had orange feet and a yellow bill with a bump on the top. It stood over the crab and looked with one eye at Anna, about twenty feet away. Then it gobbled the crab in one bite, squirted a white turd onto the white sand and looked around again, first at Rachel, then at Anna. It spread its wings and was lifted by the breeze and was gone.

The wind came, off the water, from beyond this small world. It carried a dampness that wet Anna's hair, so that it stuck to the sides of her face. She could feel small beads of moisture collect on her eyelashes; she pushed her hair behind her ears and wiped her face with the back of her glove, then dug a rubber band out of her pocket and pulled her hair into a pony tail.

Rachel played about halfway to the fog, off to the right, toward the water. She squatted in her baby-squat and poked a short finger at the shell of a horseshoe crab. Anna had always thought that horseshoe crabs looked prehistoric and someday she would explain about history and prehistory and crabs to Rachel. Rachel rolled the shell over and proceeded to fill it with sand; she used only her right hand and held her left straight out behind her for balance. Anna could see the fingers of the left flex sympathetically as those of the right squeezed handfuls of sand.

Ben, Sam and Janet were somewhere on the beach, outside of this world. They had walked faster and explored more quickly, and Rachel had been unable to keep up, so Anna had stopped to sit and watch her. Soon someone would scream and run, or smoke and walk into this world, or she would get cold and they'd meet back at the car.

Somehow it struck her that the grey of the fog was just the right grey for the day. It was a neutral grey that could not be seen itself, wasn't a thing itself, but obscured that which was not here, nearby. She had once heard a photographer lecture that there was a certain grey that was exactly the same color in both the positive and negative print and she was sure it had to be this grey. This was a very quiet grey.

Through some of this fog, now near the edge of the world, Rachel's bright yellow coat looked dull and far-away. Another yard or two and she would disappear. The crab shell, now filled and patted carefully, was behind her and forgotten, and she walked away from Anna, toward the wall of fog that was the edge of this world.

"Rachel . . ."

The little girl turned and looked at her mother. A few strands of blond hair strayed from under her hood and into her mouth.

"Stay where I can see you."

Rachel turned her head and looked into the fog, turned back to Anna and pointed out, off the world, toward the water. She didn't speak, but in a way that was somehow both clear and ambiguous—and it was like magic that it could be both simultaneously—her eyes and hand said, "?" Anna couldn't make out what she asked, but it could not have been clearer that she was wordlessly asking something. Apparently she could see something from over there that Anna couldn't see from where she sat.

"No, honey. Stay where I can see you."

She looked again, then trotted back and sat down at Anna's side.

"What was it?"

Rachel still spoke very little and now she just looked up at Anna.

"A bird? Bird?" Anna pointed at the small birds on the shore. Rachel watched her silently, then leaned her head on Anna's lap, put her thumb in her mouth and, with both eyes opened, one above another, watched the birds run in and out of the small waves. Anna tucked the stray hairs back under her hood and let her hand rest on the child's shoulder.

Right now she found the idea of a small grey world where both positive and negative were the same color to be an attractive one. She closed her eyes and imagined such a world. She smelled the sea and heard the small sounds of the waves and the birds and imagined the fog thickening so that everything was that special neutral grey and the world only contained Anna and the silent child with her head in her lap. She imagined a world only six feet in radius, then six inches. Slowly, her mind began to clear of mathematical formulae and academic politics and domestic quarrels. In this small grey world, she relaxed.

Far off, she heard a car horn. She opened her eyes and turned her left ear in that direction. There it was again. It was probably Ben signaling her to head on back, but it was faint enough so that she could ignore it and then later deny having heard it and be believed. She closed her eyes again and let her mind approach the neutral grey. The tide, not great here in the northern reaches of the Gulf, turned and headed in.

Later, she walked back to the car, with Rachel in her arms and asleep on her shoulder. Ben was angry for having to wait and worry, he said, about where they had been. She told Ben she wanted to hold Rachel on the drive back to Tallahassee, instead of strapping her in the plastic child's seat in the back and he said that was stupid and besides it was against the law and she said she didn't care, God damn it, she was just going to do it, and she did. Janet and Sam sat quietly in the back and said nothing. For dinner that night she made short beef ribs with a sauce made of coffee, wine and peppers, and then worked until midnight on her equations.

CORRESPONDENCE

February 4, Πάρος, Κυκλάδες, Greece. 10:00 p.m.; in the upper 40s F; wind from the south, easy and damp; the moon, a couple of days past full, is rising; the night ferry, the ΝΆΞΟΣ, from Athens, eases into the harbor.

Dear Anna,

I'm sipping a brandy as I write. *Full 40 years old* the bottle claims, which, I note, describes me as well, or nearly. I think I shall try always to drink brandy older than I. The weather today was quite pleasant and even now it is comfortable outside, in a sweater, but the house, with its marble floors, always seems cold. I can see my breath as I write by candlelight and my fingers are cold.

I've taken a leave of absence and Emily and I have come to this small island in the Aegean. We have rented a house overlooking the principal village, a quiet, comfortable place but not quite as charming as it sounds, for Paros is definitely on the tourist path and the place has less the feel of unspoiled Greek life than of a Greek Cape Cod in the winter. It is a good time away from normalcy for us—for me more than Emily, as she makes and talks music with both the Greeks and the foreigners, as we are called and call ourselves, while I limit myself to one mathematical thought per week and didn't use last week's quota. You don't understand the joys of that, do you? Anyway, we are here until Easter, or perhaps June. That is a lengthy time, but it is not indefinitely, as is true of many of the foreigners and, I find, makes all the difference in the world.

Time moves slowly here. I read novels; I just finished *Jude the Obscure*, about which more later. I study Greek: Μαθάινω τα Ελλήνικα. I study Greek. Μαθάινω, μαθάινεις, μαθάινει, μαθάινουμε, μαθάινετε, μαθάινουν. I study. You study. Etc., etc. And I write long rambling letters with deteriorating handwriting but, I trust, impeccable spelling, long, rambling letters, as you can see, in some cases to old friends with whom I've shared only a postcard or a letter or two, in three, or is it four years? A long time. Too long.

Last week I was in Athens, a busy, noisy, ugly city which I still love for my first view of the Parthenon, appearing unexpectedly in the window of the bus from Piraeus early one August morning in '65. I had a few errands to run, needed some space, as we say, and, after six weeks on Paros, wanted to be moving around. The city in some ways was particularly unpleasant this time—it was cold and I seemed always to be hurrying. I don't remember even one glance at the Parthenon. And ignore what you've heard of Athens in the summer or in the daytime;

Athens on a winter night is cold and grey. The air is heavy with smoke and exhaust, and cold from the north. The people look grey—they have dark hair and dark skin, they dress in dark clothes. I put my hands in my pockets and walked from my hotel, near the Plaka, and around Syntagma Square, where you can now buy *USA Today* (one of the great modern desecrations, which hints that the Elgin marbles should stay in London). I turned my collar to the grimy wind; pulled my cap down low. Only a few customers sat over coffee at the outside tables at Syntagma; the bar of the Grand Bretagne looked warm. I walked past the University—that night someone had built a fire on the steps and students were huddling close, singing, protesting—to Omonia Square.

Ομόνια, in the daytime, is remarkable in its ordinariness, if that makes sense. Kind of a Trafalgar without Nelson. This Monday night, though, it had the sort of comfortable seediness that I sought, so I walked around it and through the streets behind, surveyed the movie houses and night clubs and had dinner in a down-below-street-level restaurant with a drunk talking to us all from the corner table and a dishwasher who looked like Einstein. *Jude*, as I said, was in my pocket and there was a strangeness in the air.

At about 9:00 I was having a brandy in a cafe that dominates one corner of Ομόνια. I still think of this place as the Café Neon, from the first time, years ago, that I sounded out the letters over the door: ΚΑΦΕΝΕΟΝ. (I now know that that is simply the Greek word for *café* and the actual name of the place is a difficult to pronounce Greek family name.) It is a huge place, this Καφένεον, two stories tall inside with enormous and drafty windows, and mirrors held in place by some sort of beast in *bas-relief*. These figures are as large as I, and they rise from the walls—creatures with the legs and back of a lion, the breasts and head of a woman and the wings of an eagle. They, the marble table tops and tiled floors all speak of an earlier elegance but, if so, that elegance has faded, replaced by dinginess. Bare light bulbs hang down on story-long cords. Grime from the grease and the smoke and the Athens smog coats the top surfaces of the beasts, adding to their three-dimensionality. The marble floor is thick with grease and dirt. The windows and mirrors have been washed, but not very well and they remain streaked and coated with film. There is an old, old price list on the wall, amended to add beer and Coca-cola to the offerings.

Nearly fifty patrons, I'd guess, sat around the small tables. They were nearly all men. Over here a gentleman with a well-trimmed goatee sat in a fur coat that cost more than my plane ticket. Over there, an old drunk with a weeks-old beard and a well-worn hat did an odd little dance, scratching this and that, and moved from table to table, ordering nothing. My grey coat and brown cap fit in with the dress of the patrons and the feel of the winter night, but under the coat, against the cold wind, I wore a red sweater, easily the brightest garment in the place.

At about 9:30, a brandy and a half gone, you walked in. Well, no, she was not quite you. She was about your height, but she was heavier, without being heavy. Above the waist of her skirt, a hint of a soft belly, unlike you, as I remember you. Her hair was the right length, the right style and, discounting that it was dirtier than I ever saw yours, the right color—oh, maybe a half-shade darker. She had the same way of tossing it back from her face, always to the right side, away from the part, back over her shoulder.

The mouth was right, with the same downward curve of the lips when she wasn't smiling—not a frown, exactly, but a contemplative look, as if life were a bit more complicated than the rest of us saw. The eyebrows were right.

I don't recall that you smoked. She did and, yes, she smoked like I'd guess you would, if you smoked—all five fingers of her right hand extended straight out, with the cigarette held between the last segments of the index and middle fingers. Short, nervous puffs, little inhaling, the cigarette always near her mouth.

She never laughed. I would have known for sure it wasn't you if she had laughed; I remember your laugh. But she never did. She just sat at a table with five or six Greek men, talking, gesturing like a Greek—once, she pointed up the street with her chin. She drank Greek coffee right to the bottom, including the dregs and then for several minutes slowly picked the grains from her teeth and chewed them.

I listened closely for her voice, above the hubbub of the place, but I was more than half-way across the large room and at best I caught a phrase or two—no, less than a phrase, a sound, a bit of voice. I couldn't even tell the language, the voice was so small, though I suppose it was Greek. What I could catch was as one would expect from a small blond woman in a καφένεον in Athens and, yes, could have been yours.

Quickly she rose, grabbed her packages and hurried outside. It seemed as though in seconds she was gone. And, I think, just as she reached the door, she glanced quickly over her left shoulder at me. No pause, no hesitation. If she glanced, it was probably because of my bright red sweater, which does catch the eye in Athens on a winter night. Or, worse, maybe my staring had been obvious, for the resemblance was so remarkable, I could hardly look away.

Or maybe, just maybe, it was you and you had recognized me. *Jude*, as I've said, was in my pocket and there was a strangeness in the air, so there leapt to my mind the possibility that some Hardyesque twist of fate might have placed you, a little heavier, a little dirtier, down on your luck to my view, in a Greek καφένεον that winter night. As ripped as I was by the fate of Sue Bridehead, and by two glasses of too-young brandy, I wondered, I admit, was it you?

Or maybe . . . Quantum physicists tell us, some of them do anyway, of other places, of alternate universes. One, perhaps, is very much like this one, but in it Anna Browning frequents a καφένεον on Ομόνια square and gestures like a Greek, and Albert Einstein washes dishes in a nearby restaurant. Maybe, on that cold night in Athens, I was there.

I don't suppose I'll ever know. I didn't follow her when she left. I could have—she was wearing blue and white without a coat—it was too cold that night to be without a coat—and she would have been easy to follow in the dark Ομόνια crowd. But I didn't. The decision to do so had to be made right then and I wasn't quick enough. The thoughts had not yet clearly formed; to the extent they had, I felt silly; my brandy wasn't finished; it was warm inside, cold out. So she got up, glanced, maybe, and left. The doors swung in, out and back in again and she was gone. If she had laughed, I would have known for sure that it wasn't you, but, as I said, she didn't laugh.

Several days have come and gone since I started this letter. The wind has backed around to the east, bringing an uneasy feeling to our little island, as the east wind often does. I've drunk the original brandy and several others. I've done a number of quite ordinary things. I've also watched

Venus set, right down, all the way into the Aegean Sea; she turned quite orange in the process.

I hope this reaches you and Sam happy and healthy.

Your friend,

Michael.

## TALLAHASSEE

The exact moment when Anna decided to leave is rather easy to describe with precision, but it is much harder to describe the making of the decision itself. The thought of leaving had drifted through her mind once or twice, but never as something that could actually be done. When the work went roughly, when the children got on her nerves, as Ben became insensitive at impossibly high levels, as her colleagues became increasingly insufferable, she would play with the notion of leaving but never in a way that moved her one inch closer to a decision to leave. The letter from Mike Reid in Athens had done something to her; it had disturbed her and pissed her off; it had felt like an invasion of her privacy that he should remember so well her smallest mannerisms, for she remembered none of his. So she had played with the incredible notion of somehow telling him that she had not appreciated it and would he please leave her alone, but that had seemed impossible to do. Even when once, on a whim, she had withdrawn some cash from the children's trust account, and had watched in fascination as the teller had counted out the fifties, the most that could be said as to her state of mind was that she had a vague notion that there were many ways that such money could be used, but she hadn't really thought about leaving and figured that she would eventually put the money back and no one would notice. In the meantime, she put it in an envelope and stuck it in a drawer at home and would take it out every now and then and hold it, when she was alone.

But, while Anna's thoughts about leaving during the weeks after the arrival of Michael's letter were very sporadic and unformed, the exact moment of her decision to leave is rather easy to describe. She sat in the mathematics department faculty lounge with some of her colleagues, over coffee and donuts. They were entertaining the University's Provost, who was spending the day at the department, visiting classes and interviewing professors and students. The day of the Provost's visit was Thursday, February 20th and the coffee was put out at ten-thirty in the morning and so Anna's decision to leave was formed almost exactly at ten-forty-five a.m. on that day. She sat with a cup of coffee and her mind on nothing in particular and the talk that pulsed around her was of politics, legislative funding, Seminole basketball and the like. There was also the usual by-play of department politics and back-biting. The chairman's memo inviting the faculty to meet this morning for coffee with the Provost had been distributed in two waves; some got it one day, some the next, for reasons that were either benign or suspicious, depending on whether one was in the chairman's camp or not. In the midst of the discussion of trivialities over coffee, one of Anna's colleagues among the anti-chairman forces said to the chairman, "It was good of you finally to invite all of us to this gathering." And the chairman responded with a huge, if frozen, smile, "I'm happy you were able to join us, Harry." Now, this sort of exchange was a regular part of mathematics department communications, where few things were left to lie and no scab was left unpicked. And honestly, Anna herself had at times been an active participant in such jousting, she drifting increasingly into the anti-chairman camp, ever since having been singled out, she thought, for the exam-grading-deadline sermon. But on that day in February, the forces that move Anna were poised to be abruptly shifted by such a small and petty exchange and she decided to leave. She picked up her purse, carefully folded her blazer and placed it on the back of her chair and left the room. A few of her colleagues might have noticed that she stood up, folded her blazer and walked out with particular deliberation, but most probably assumed she would soon return, for she left her books and coffee sitting on the conference table and she had a class to teach in a half an hour. But instead of returning to her office, she walked directly out of the building and up College Avenue, toward downtown. Back at school, when the coffee was finished and the Provost was back to his rounds, one of her friends picked up Anna's things and brought them to her office, but she was nowhere to be found.

At the post office, on the corner of Park and Duval Streets, Anna retrieved a thick envelope from her mailbox, the box she had rented a month earlier, the envelope she had mailed to herself two weeks ago. It contained sixty-five hundred dollars in cash and her passport. She took her wallet out of her purse, placed it in the mailbox and closed and locked the little door. She walked around to the counter, where she bought a stamped envelope, and mailed the box's key to the same box number. On the way out of the post office, she dropped her purse in the trash can and walked the rest of the way downtown, holding the fat envelope in her right hand. It was an early Tallahassee spring day, for late February is indeed the beginning of the Tallahassee springtime, and it was warm and sunny enough to make the walking comfortable. She bought an ice cream cone for lunch and caught a cab to the airport.

~

Later that same day, Anna sat with her eyes closed and imagined herself in an old Florida mansion, like the ones along Park Street in Tallahassee. White, it was, with clean, sharp architectural lines and pillars in the front. The house was empty. No people, no furniture. It had fifty rooms. In each room were seven closets. Three hundred fifty closets, all told. Each time a thought came to her, she put it in a closet and closed the door. She carefully visualized the door closing; she heard the solid click as the door knob mechanism caught. She then relaxed, with her eyes closed, sitting back in the reclining aisle seat, until another thought would pop unbidden into her head, then she put that in a closet in the white house and closed the door. She wandered from room to room in this Florida mansion. There were many closets. There were no people. The drone of the 747 in overdrive filled the background, and slowly she closeted her thoughts and worries, so that, later, when she stood in the line for passport control at the Athens airport, she was, in a real sense, a person standing in line for passport control and nothing else.

ATHENS

In 1985, Athens had two airports. They were called the east and west airports, but the directions indicated their orientation to each other, not to the city. The two actually shared the same runway, and lay to the south and west of the city, south of Piraeus, where the boats dock. The west airport, closer to the sea, was the one for Olympic Airlines and was served from the city by Olympic's private buses. They are blue and white and say Ολύμπια on the side. The east airport was for all other airlines and was called the *International Airport*, a reference to the airlines, not the destinations. Of course, Olympic flies international flights and they landed at the west airport. Nearer to the sea. To get from Athens to the east airport, one took the city's express buses from Syntagma. These buses were yellow and the ride cost sixty drachma.

Very early one morning, two weeks, more or less, after Anna Browning arrived and stood in line for passport control at the west airport, Michael Reid walked from his hotel on the Plaka, through the empty streets to Syntagma, to catch the yellow bus to the east airport. It had been a long, late night, the previous night, and he had slept only about two hours, and slept poorly, too. He had met Chris, an acquaintance from Paros, at her hotel at about eight the previous night and they had talked until midnight, waiting in her room for a phone call from her college roommate. Chris was 19 or 20, an American in Europe for the first time, who had lived for two months on Paros with her sister and brother-in-law and was now going to *do Europe* on her own: from Athens by boat to Italy, then by train to Rome, Milan, Zurich, Paris, London, and back to Athens to catch a plane, two weeks hence, for the US in time for the summer term at her college. Two weeks. It made Michael tired just to think about it. They sat on her bed and he listened to her talk and sniffle at her cold; she talked about the trip, Paros, home, her friends and what she wanted to see, and Michael found himself envying, if nothing else, the magic of the first time, with more to see than time to see it.

As luck would have it, she was out of the room in the bathroom down the hall when the call from her friend came through, now near midnight.

"Εμπρος!" Michael answered the phone, showing off.

"Hello?" A young, female, American voice.

"Yes, hello?"

"Do you speak English? Chris? Christine? Is there a Christine Bailey there?" Michael had not known her last name until then. He wondered if the friend would wonder who he was and why he was answering her phone.

"She's out of the room right now. I'm a friend. Can you hold on for a minute while I get her? She's been waiting for your call."

"Shit. No. I don't have enough money to talk long."

"Can she call you?"

"I'm at a public phone."

Kids. Broke, ignorant kids. It made him remember '65. He was going to have to take charge here. "Okay. Where are you?"

"Amsterdam." Amsterdam. In '65, he and his compatriots were not calling from Amsterdam to Athens to arrange meetings in Rome. The Americanization of Europe. Michael did not approve.

"Okay. Chris is leaving Athens tomorrow and should be in Rome by, let's see, Wednesday."

"Yes. Rome. That's where we're meeting."

"Do you have a hotel picked out?"

"No."

"Of course not. All right. She'll be at let's see, . . ., she'll be on the steps of St. Peter's at noon on Thursday. Have you got that?"

"St. Peter's."

"Right. Noon on Thursday. And if you miss connections, she'll be there at noon on each following day until you do meet. Okay?"

*Click.* The telephone went dead. Chris's friend probably didn't know how to keep putting coins into the pay phone. Well, he had done his best. That last bit had come to him from some novel, science fiction, time travel, he thought, but he couldn't quite place the story right then.

When Chris came back from the toilet, she was mad and worried and uncomfortable with the rendezvous and all of the other things that would be expected of a nineteen year old American, on her own in Europe, who had only one friend outside of Greece, and who wasn't at all sure she could even *find* St. Peter's on her own. She had wanted to meet at the train station. Michael let her wonder for a while about what she might do now, other than be at St. Peter's at noon on Thursday. Later, he suggested that they wonder while they walk to find something to eat.

So they finally had dinner, well after midnight, in a grill near Omonia with little to recommend it other than its accessibility, and he tried to calm her over fried chicken, fried potatoes and beer, and as he walked with her through the deserted streets back to her hotel, the greasy food lay heavy on his stomach. In the lobby, she invited him up to the room again, to what end exactly, it was hard to tell. Nor would he ever know, as it was by then nearly two and he had a plane to catch at 6:30, and he declined. She, for that matter, had an early train to Patras and a date in Rome two days hence, so she was probably just being polite.

The fried food and, maybe, the ambiguous invitation caused him to toss and turn through the short night until his watch beeped him awake at four in the morning. He took a cold shower, dressed in jeans, a Greek sweater and knee-high rubber Wellington boots and set out to get himself to the international airport, feeling, if the truth be told, every bit twice Chris's age. Nevertheless, he was not of a mind to complain, walking the dark streets of the Plaka before the day's traffic got going, only a few shopkeepers up and around, preparing to open. At one shop he tapped on the window, spoke some halting Greek with a smile—there is damned little that cannot be had in Athens with a little halting Greek and a smile—and a middle-aged man wearing a white apron opened the door and sold him a rice pudding, to go, with cinnamon. He paid, and the man said "Brrrrummmppppp. Rice pudding," as if he were imitating a brass band's flourish, and on Michael walked to the bus stop, eating the pudding with a small plastic spoon. Eating rice pudding for breakfast while walking with a pack over one's shoulder courts—no, guarantees, actually—a gooey moustache, but that was a price that Michael thought worth paying on what was becoming, as he woke up, a fine morning.

It felt good to be going. He was flying to Sophia, or, as the brochure he had picked up at the Bulgarian Embassy called it, София, which didn't look all that much like *Sophia*, he thought. That was okay by him. The less София was like *Sophia* the better. He wondered what the city would look like. He had no idea, which was, really, why he was going. What would the arrival lounge look like? What would socialism look like? Would there be a behind-the-iron-curtain feel? What would book stores look like? It felt good to be moving.

At the bus stop, the ticket kiosk was closed. The sign said the first bus would leave at 5:30 a.m. If there was any traffic by that time, and there might be, the trip could take a half an hour and that would cut it close for his 6:30 flight. So he flagged down a taxi, hopped into the back, and, after a moment's thought, realized that he didn't know how to say either *international* or *east* in Greek. He tried "Στό άεροδρομίο, πάρακαλώ , δεν Ολύμπια," which means roughly "to the airport, please, but not Olympic's", but the driver spoke English, of course, and sped off through the empty streets. Michael sat back and smiled at the irony of knowing just enough Greek only to be able to ask for the wrong airport and of grabbing a cab that was speeding to get him to the airport with hours to spare. A trip that began with such double, pre-dawn irony was destined to turn out well. Of all the world's ironies, pre-dawn ones were his favorite. He went about finishing his rice pudding breakfast, watching the city streak by, and wiping, for now, his moustache on the back of his hand.

~ 8

# ALBUQUERQUE

"Four down," Britt looked across the breakfast table. "*Kiwi's treaty*. Eight letters. The third one is an *i*." A pause. "I think."

Marie looked up from an article she was reading in the Sunday *Boston Globe* about the up-coming Canadian elections. She enjoyed reading the *Globe* on Sunday over breakfast and old jazz, and, now that there was someone to go out and collect the paper, in her pajamas. Everybody reads the *New York Times*, she thought, but she liked the *Globe*'s greater provincialism and diminished pretention. She had pleasant, contra-desert, memories of her summers in New England while in college, which the *Globe* often managed to bring back, via a story from Worcester or Manchester. Britt, who was not fond of lounging, was already dressed in jeans and an Oxford-cloth dress shirt, with the sleeves rolled up. Her feet were bare. She spread some brie on a piece of French bread and gave it to the dog. She was doing the puzzle in the *Albuquerque Journal*.

"Waitangi," Marie said, without hesitation.

"Y-what?"

"Waitangi: w-a-i-t-a-n-g-i."

"W-a-i-t-a-n-g-i. It fits."

Marie put the *Globe* down on the table. "Of course if fits. It must, being correct. *Kiwi's* means *New Zealander's*. And there's only one treaty between New Zealand and the Maoris who lived there before the Europeans. It was signed in Waitangi." She looked across the kitchen table and smiled.

It hadn't taken Marie long to decide, on the drive back from Phoenix, what had to be decided. She had spent several hours distilling her pissed-offedness at Michael for not showing, but by the time exhaustion overtook her and she had pulled off on the side of the road, after midnight, deep in the Apache reservation, she had been too tired any longer to support serious anger. And the next morning she had awakened with Britt, not Michael, on her mind. After a breakfast of huevos rancheros red and weak coffee in Show Low, Arizona, she had headed east on US 60, and had driven to her favorite campsite, really just a spot along a little-used Forest Service logging road near Old Horse Springs, New Mexico, there to begin sorting things through. But after a day walking in the forest with the dog, and sitting staring out across the San Augustín plain, she had decided not to spend another night in her car and so, as darkness began to fall, she had gotten back on the road to Magdalena and Socorro, then north on the Interstate to Albuquerque. From her duplex she had called Britt after midnight.

"Hi, it's me. I'm home. I know it's late, but I wanted to talk."

"I'll be over in ten minutes."

"There's nothing here at my place. The bed's not even made and there's nothing in the fridge. Would it be all right if I came over to yours?"

"Of course."

"Did I wake you up?"

"Yes, but it's okay."

"Are you sure?"

"Yes. Come over right now. Bring Ginger, too."

"You can't have pets in your apartment."

"Bring her anyway."

"Okay, but I look a mess."

"Please."

"Okay." She started to hang up. "Oh, and Britt?"

"Yes?"

"I missed you."

"Me, too."

She stayed at Britt's apartment for three days, as much as anything sleeping off her exhaustion, and allowing herself to be pampered. Two weeks after she got back to her own place, Michael's letter from Thailand caught up with her, having first been to New York, coming, oddly enough, across the Atlantic, the long way around, then to Albuquerque, then forwarded to Phoenix and then forwarded back to Albuquerque. The letter was full of half-hearted excuses for why he hadn't—or wasn't going to—show up in Phoenix. *Half-hearted* was generous really and the strange way in which she did not become less pissed off at him seemed to draw her closer to Britt, to whom she did not explain the circumstances of her departure from Phoenix. They saw each other regularly throughout the fall.

Michael had finally called in September, a little sheepish but with the nerve to be surprised that she had been and was still angry. "Why didn't you just call?," she had asked, to which he had responded "I was in Thailand," as if that explained everything, or as if there were no telephones in Thailand or something. He had then gone on and on about his aversion to telephoning home from abroad, and she had hung up in the middle of a sentence.

Britt gave up her apartment and moved in after Christmas, following Marie's holiday visit with her parents in Canton, and on Marie's third invitation.

*Are you sure?*

*Let's see.*

It was now February. School was going well, spring break lay ahead and Michael had blown the country again, without Marie's having seen him.

Britt looked up from the puzzle. "Couldn't it be some other New Zealand treaty?"

"Nope. They all refer to that one simply as *The Treaty*. Trust me."

"How do you know? You've never been to New Zealand." She sipped her coffee. "Have you?"

"I lived there. Didn't I mention that? For seven years. The South Island. With my second husband."

"Second."

"Vladimir."

"Vladimir."

"Yes. When we were doing that illegal gun-trade thingy."

"Where is old Vlad these days?"

"Still in jail, I presume. I had the marriage annulled when he was convicted. For failure to consummate."

"Well, that's something, at least." This time, Britt ate the bread and cheese herself, followed by handful of green grapes.

"No, actually . . ."

"No. Actually."

". . . World Geography. Seventh grade. We do New Zealand and Australia in about two days. The textbook mentions the Treaty of Waitangi, noting that there were no treaties at all with the Australian Aborigines." Marie thought for a minute. "I think it was Michael, though, who told me that they just call it *The Treaty* down there."

"I liked the other story better."

"Maybe it was in the Teacher's Manual."

"I think Heloise is an alien."

"There's a clue in your puzzle about Heloise?"

"Nooo. *Ask Heloise*. Same page. I got distracted in the middle of the seventh grade lesson." Britt turned the piece of the *Journal* that she was reading so that Marie could see the picture at the head of the household advice column. "Look at this picture. Have you ever seen anyone trying harder to look human? And here," Britt took the paper quickly back, before Marie had a chance to study the picture, "she's saying that you can get ballpoint pen stains out of clothes by spraying them with hairspray, which is clearly bogus. Besides, who uses hairspray anymore? That's definitely some kind of coded message to her home planet, that's what I think."

Britt put a spoonful of Nescafé in her empty cup, then stood up and walked over to the stove, where she poured herself a cupful of hot water, then returned to the table. Then she poured half-and-half gently down the side of the cup. She studied the cup, but didn't stir the cream in.

Marie put the paper down, looked over the entire breakfast scene, and said, "I still can't believe I'm having breakfast with you. More than that, I can't believe I'm living with someone who feeds my dog four-dollar-a-pound imported French cheese and who thinks that Heloise is a space alien. Why do you never stir your coffee?"

"Well, *look* at it!" Britt leaned on her elbows and inspected her coffee through the clear glass cup. "It's beautiful. It looks like a damn Georgia O'Keeffe painting. Look here." She was on her feet now, bent over, hands on knees, her eyes at table level, getting the best possible vantage on the cup.

The unstirred coffee with cream did, in fact, look a bit like a brown-on-brown O'Keeffe print. The layers of color were separated by smooth, clean curves. The hills of Abiquiu could be seen, if one looked for a while. Marie put the paper down, pushed her glasses up on her nose and lowered her eyes to table level.

"Okay, so it does. But it's *Nescafé*, for crying out loud, when there's a pot of perfectly good organic Guatemalan roast right here on the table." She shook her head.

"*Hecho en México.*"

"Yes. I've learned to be careful about that when I shop. *Nescafé.* Georgia O'Keeffe would not approve. Michael for some reason had the same ridiculous preference." After a pause, "The only thing, I might add, that you and Michael Reid have in common."

"You mean other than finding you irresistible?"

"Yeah, right. He found me plenty resistible last summer."

"Hard to imagine." Britt bent over the breakfast table, used both hands to hold her hair out of the way and, without lifting the cup, sipped the top stratum of the darkest brown, her eyes bright and on Marie.

SOPHIA, BULGARIA

"Do you speak English?"

The attractive young Bulgarian woman behind the information counter in the departure lounge of the Sophia airport looked up and shook her head. "He." She pronounced it *nay.* Ναί, also pronounced *nay,* means *yes* in Greek, and for a moment he was confused.

"Ναί?" he asked.

"He," she answered.

Michael shook his head. "Μιλάτε τα ελληνικά;" *You speak Greek?* While Greece and Bulgaria do border each other, he had no real expectation that anyone north of the border would speak Greek. Nobody speaks Greek. Including, really, Michael Reid.

"Nyet." Maybe she thought his Greek sounded like Russian.

"Kanst du Deutsch?" He felt reasonably trilingual.

"Ja," she said.

"Ich suche das autobus nach centrum." *I'm looking for the bus to the center.* That should do. He had not spoken German for some time and never particularly well and he hadn't thought far enough ahead to realize that he might be speaking it on this trip. Here was another indication that this trip seemed to be starting out well, after last night's early morning, greasy dinner with Chris in Athens, and a sloppy rice pudding breakfast this morning. Here he was, after all, in the departure lounge of the Sophia airport, surrounded by early-rising skiers, bound home for Russia, if his ear heard right, he having arrived in Sophia only a half an hour ago. But the arrival hall had been totally empty, abandoned, closed, who knew what?, when he had emerged from customs and passport control, so he had walked around to the departure lounge to change money and ask directions to town. He had walked by two old taxis to get here, but the thought did not occur to him to take the easy way into town. He did not take taxis, well, hardly ever.

The buzz of the woman's German response was too quick for his ear to pick up.

"Bitte?" *Beg pardon?* "Noch einmal?" *Once again?*

"Autobus nummer sechs und actsig, außerhalb an der Bordsteinkante . . ." the woman began again.

"Sie müssen langsam und einfach sprechen, bitte," he interrupted. *You must speak slowly and simply, please.*

"Sechs und actsig." She wrote *86* in the corner of a small tourist map of Sophia. "Außerhalb." She pointed through the window to the curb, and began slowly to tell him about catching the No. 86 bus and the number 10 tram to Lenin Square. She changed some money for him, smiled and wished him a pleasant stay in Bulgaria.

Outside the terminal, No. 86 sat idling at the curbside, blue diesel smoke drifting up from the undercarriage. He bought a ticket at the kiosk for practically nothing, but even so, he thought about not cancelling it in the little machine on the bus's inside wall, thereby doing his part to send the commie regime to economic ruin. But the other passengers seemed to be honest, so he inserted the ticket into the machine, which stamped a hole in it, and shortly afterward the bus pulled away, on its way into a strange and unknown city.

The bus filled quickly in the first mile, past seemingly endless, indistinguishable blocks of concrete apartment buildings. Public transport seemed popular and cheap, and autos on the road were few. At the major intersections stood ugly, formidable observation posts, undoubtedly for traffic control, though there was little traffic. But a thought had been planted in Michael's head by a friend on Paros who couldn't believe that one would go on holiday to Bulgaria. "A holiday? In Bulgaria?" he had asked, first across the small table where they sat drinking ouzo, and eating feta, tomatoes and olives, then, louder, to the Portside Cafe at large. "Οι διακοπές; Στήν Βουλγάρια;" The friend, who had apparently once spent a particularly unpleasant night and day in Sophia, involuntarily held up by bad weather or airplane repairs or something during a cheap flight from Athens to Copenhagen, had laughed at

Michael's plans and announced to the bar that the movie *1984* was, or should have been, filmed in Sophia, a place that he never intended to revisit, as he had never intended to visit it in the first place. Michael, now on the bus into the center of Sophia, shook his head to dispel the nagging predisposition. Still, he had to admit, the place did have an Oceania feel to it, especially that day, passing by tall, cement traffic observation towers rising against a low-slung sky and with dirty, gritty, slushy snow around, in some places burying cars that appeared not to have been used since the fall.

The people who boarded were dressed as many Americans dress, Michael noted—such passes for major discovery when one confronts Socialism for the first time—and they stared at him as he sat with his pack on his knees. He could imagine himself in Cleveland; a tourist would get just these sorts of looks from K-Mart-dressed people aboard a bus from the airport to Public Square, sitting, saying nothing, with a backpack on his knees, and, on a day in March, with the sky low and the wind from the west, the view outside would not be totally unlike this one. Wondering whether seeing a similarity between Sophia and Cleveland was a positive development, Michael smiled and said hello in German to the man sitting next to him, still feeling trilingual and not yet knowing how the Bulgarians hate the Germans.

## ALBUQUERQUE AND MORIARTY

Downstairs, music was playing, though what exactly was playing Marie couldn't have said, as her belly was in the process of trying to turn itself inside out. Again.

"Stop. Oof. Stopstopstop. Please stop."

Britt stopped. They were in the bedroom, which was bright in the afternoon, becoming late afternoon. The Crest was just visible to them on the bed, above the half-closed curtain.

"I have never come four times in succession." She had to breathe before going on. "Never." Breath. "I didn't think it was possible." Breath.

Britt moved her arms under Marie's thighs, folded her hands across her belly and rested her chin on the backs of her hands, looking up along the length of Marie's body to her face. She stretched her legs out behind her on the bed and hung her feet off the end. Marie's eyes were looking up, at the ceiling, as her chest rose and fell, still catching her breath.

"I'm still not sure it *is* possible, and I just did it. Maybe the second and third were really the same one, you know, merging into one another? Maybe? . . ."

When she lay on her back, Marie's small breasts were hardly visible, too small even to be called mounds, just minor, slightly curving fleshy deviations from the flatness that ran from her pubic bone to her collar bone. But with her nipples swollen like now, there was no possibility of thinking of her flat chest as boyish. Britt, without moving her hands or her chin, placed her left thumb on the top of Marie's clitoris.

". . . Sort of? Like thunder," Marie wondered.

"Thunder?"

"Don't do that. Thunder. You know how lightning strikes are discrete, but how thunder can just kind of roll, one rumble into the next? Maybe it's like that."

"What is?"

"Coming. Maybe it's too, I don't know, western even to count."

"Maybe."

"Ginger doesn't like the thunder . . ."

"I know."

". . . but I do. If it thunders in February, you know, it will frost in May."

"It's not February."

"I know."

"I've never heard thunder in February. What was that again?"

"If it thunders in February, it will frost in May. Or maybe April. I forget. It's some expression of Michael's. Maybe it only applies in the Ozarks."

Britt removed her thumb, her hands and her arms, and got up, kneeling now between Marie's legs, her hands on either side of Marie's hips, her breasts hanging down.

She looked up into Marie's face, at the slashes of her black eyebrows, at the curl of her eyelashes. "You know, you have a very special look about you when you take your glasses off. It's a special intimate look, like it's reserved only for me and only for times when we're alone together. Like now. I feel sorry for all those whose lovers don't wear glasses." She was smiling. "Roll over; I'll give you a back rub." Marie did. Britt straddled her thighs and began massaging the small of her back. "You were thinking of Michael while we were making love? How flattering."

"Actually, I was thinking of thunder while we were making love. Which you *might* take as flattering when it comes to that. Michael just sort of popped into my head, relating to thunder, not lovemaking."

"I'll be *he* never noticed how special you look with your glasses off. Never get contacts, okay? I'd be crazy with jealousy thinking that everyone was seeing you that way. "

"I can't believe you'd ever be jealous." Britt made no comment, but continued massaging. "I got a letter today. He writes a nice letter." Marie turned her head to the right and looked out the window to the east and the Crest. The spring afternoon sun made the shadows long and the foothills looked green, as only desert dwellers know green; others would say grey-by-green. "You shouldn't worry, you know. It's you I love." She looked back over her shoulder, arched her back, and felt Britt's finger press a little deeper in response. "You know that, right?" Britt smiled but said nothing. "I never loved him, not really. Only a little bit, now and then, before I knew you. But he writes and when he writes, I think of him."

"What's he write about?"

Marie chuckled. "Actually, this time he sent me a copy of a letter he wrote to someone else, someone I don't know, named Ann. It was a strange letter, full of mysterious references, about seeing someone that he thought was this Ann, but maybe wasn't and probably couldn't be. He sent me a greasy, smudged Xerox copy of the letter, with a note saying that he thought I'd be interested in the experience. He does funny things like that; makes me wonder if he ever sent this Ann a copy of a letter to me." Marie contemplated the possibility, pretty sure that she didn't like the idea.

"It seemed like you were pissed at him for a while."

Marie snapped back from the Athens cafe, remembered last summer in Phoenix and blushed. "Because he stood me up back when I was trying to decide how I felt about you."

"Really? You never told me that. When?"

"Last summer in Phoenix. We were supposed to meet there at the end of his trip. But he fell behind and I came home to you. The rest is history."

Britt moved herself up so that she now straddled Marie's butt, and began running her thumbs along either side of Marie's spine.

"Do you think you would have decided differently if he had shown up?"

"Do you want me to say no?"

"Yes."

"No. Maybe I wanted to compare this . . . ," she moved her head to show she meant the two of them, ". . . with the other."

"Do you still?"

"No. But I wish I knew why I was so hurt. It puzzled me how pissed off I was at him, it seemed to go against the rules we had established." Britt spread her hands and worked her thumbs under Marie's shoulder blades, her fingers extending along Marie's ribs. "I was never able to figure that out. That feels good right there. Maybe it has something to do with us, I mean you and me. I don't know. Finally, . . ." she shrugged, "it just went away and we made up. I'd like to see him, talk to him again. I don't miss him in bed, not really, but you have to know, he's a special person."

"Where is he now?"

"Bulgaria."

Now Britt was straddling the small of Marie's back and working the muscles of her shoulders. Marie could feel Britt's weight, and the pressure of her crotch against her back. That pressure became rhythmic, in time with Britt's breathing and the massaging of her hands.

"Bulgaria?"

"A short excursion, it sounds like, from Greece, where the two of them are spending the spring."

"The two of them?"

"His wife, Emily, is with him."

Britt said nothing in response to this, nor anything for some time after. Marie could feel her arousal from the warm dampness against the small of her back, and from the increasing depth of Britt's breathing. When she shuddered, leaned forward, and pressed her breasts into Marie's back, Marie turned over and held her close. Then she slipped her right leg between Britt's and behind her right knee; she tensed the muscle along the front of her thigh, giving Britt the smooth, hard surface against which Marie knew she liked to press. With her right hand she provided a bit of pressure behind Britt's butt, in time with Britt's rhythm, and with her left hand she turned Britt's face to hers. Britt's mouth is wide and large and must be kissed carefully and in sections for the job to be done right. Marie set to the task, unhurriedly, with her eyes open, looking out the window. And a little while later she whispered *baby baby baby* into her lover's ear, while Britt, neither a moaner nor a shouter, quietly but strongly, came in her arms.

~

Later, the room now dark, and nothing having been said for many, many minutes, the two lovers lay side by side, face to face, holding four hands between them, watching each other, listening to each other's breaths and to the on-coming sounds of the city at night.

~

Marie had gotten up to use the bathroom, and when she returned, Britt had turned on the bedside lamp and was lying on her back with her hands behind her head. Marie came over to the bed and lay down on her belly, resting on her elbows, her hip touching Britt's.

"Does she know?"

"Who? What?"

"Michael's wife. Does she know he fucks you?"

"Sometimes I can't believe how straightforward you are. You also know that I don't fuck him anymore. I haven't seen him for almost two years."

"Okay, Marie," she turned over onto her front, raised her feet from over the edge of the bed, crossed her ankles and bounced her heels on her butt, "Okay, did this Emily know that you were fucking him when you were fucking him? Hmmmmm?"

"I don't think so. I assume not, no."

"Did you ever meet her?"

"Sure. Long ago. At various Moriarty functions. Football games, Christmas concerts, faculty parties, that kind of thing. That was way before I was fucking him, of course, as you so indelicately put it. She's okay. Jewish, I think."

"What does she do? Or did?"

"She was an accountant, and did the books for, like, small businesses. I think she did contract work for the school district, too, but I'm not sure of that. But she's a musician, and when he got the university job after his PhD, she quit bookkeeping to concentrate on the music."

"She performs?"

"Mostly I think she composes. I heard a UNM jazz group play one of her compositions once. Weird, atonal, arrhythmic stuff. I didn't like it. That's about all I remember. Actually, it's more than I want to remember."

"How did she feel about trading New Mexico for . . . where did you say?"

"Kansas. She was a mid-westerner, and never really cared for the desert, I think. I don't know. He never really told me very much about her."

"He doesn't sound all that much committed to her. Is he?"

"That's the way Michael is: he has commitments; he just leaves town and lets them take care of themselves for a while. He used to say it was good for commitments to look after themselves for a while instead of always being looked after. Like teenagers."

Britt shook her head. "Nice. We have to get up."

"Why?"

"The League has a meeting at six that I have to attend; something about some event with the Women's Center down on the main campus. Then three of us are getting together to study for Leibman's Ethics mid-term."

"I thought you didn't have mid-terms at law school."

"Mostly we don't, but Leibman's the exception. Randolph says that when Leibman gives a mid-term, nobody shows up for Bankruptcy. I think it's an issue about which they yell at each other at faculty meetings. Come on; get dressed. Don't you have to get prepared for your classes tomorrow?" Britt jumped quickly out of bed, pulled the curtain shut, flipped on the light, then turned back to the bed, where Marie had now rolled over on her back, with one knee up and her hands behind her head. "What are you doing?"

"Lying here naked in front of you. I like the feel of being naked in front of you. I like the way you look at me. There is something completely different about the way you look at me, but I can't put my finger on it. You go ahead and get dressed; it just occurs to me that I'm going to like even more the feel of being naked in front of you while you are fully dressed."

"Didn't you get the message," Britt asked, "probably in junior high, not to pay too much attention to the other girls getting dressed after gym class?"

"I don't recall it, but maybe it was delivered so subtly that I got it without ever hearing it."

"A savvy point."

"Did you get the message?"

"I sure did, yes."

"And did you follow it?"

"You bet."

"But that was then; this is now. I *teach* junior high; I'm not *in* it. I plan to pay attention. And to enjoy it."

And it was true: there was something erotic, if inverted from the usual, in lying on the bed watching Britt pull her clothes on piece-by-piece: low-cut, lace-trimmed panties, a C-cup bra that fastened in front, a long-sleeved rugby shirt, pulled over her head and left unbuttoned, blue jeans, the material worn, but not yet through, in the knee. Britt, a feminist and blond to boot, did not shave, but from across the room Marie could hardly notice that, and had lost her aversion to it anyway. Her mind felt fuzzy after the afternoon's lovemaking.

Britt walked over to the side of the bed and sat down to put her socks on, then reached over with her right hand and inserted her finger tip in Marie's navel, and gave her belly a little pinch. Marie reached up, pushed the sleeve of Britt's shirt up to expose the scar on her forearm, and then, pulling the arm to her lips, traced small kisses from one end to another.

"I gotta go."

Marie ignored her. "Was it hard getting back on the horse after the accident?"

"Yes. Which was the reason that my trainer insisted that I take the same jump, cast and all, the next weekend."

"Sarah."

"Sarah."

"But why so soon? What did the doctor have to say about that?"

"The doctor was not consulted. My mother almost had a stroke."

"So what was the rush?"

"Okay, slide over. Ten more minutes." Marie moved over on the bed to make room for Britt, who lay down on her back, fully clothed but still without shoes, and arranged a couple of pillows behind her head. "Come here." She pulled Marie against her side, but instead Marie climbed on top, stretching out along the length of Britt's body, the jeans rough and scratchy against her bare legs. She pulled the bedspread over her back and laid her left ear on Britt's chest. "The thing you have to remember is that T-man could read my mind." Marie looked up, skeptical. "Well, okay, I suppose technically he was reading the smallest little body-language messages, or maybe smelling faint little stress-induced odors, but for all practical purposes, he could read my mind. Fr'instance, T-man never liked shots, so I'd practice on him, with a used syringe with a toothpick instead of a needle, and I'd walk toward him holding either a fake one or a real one behind my back, and honest to God he'd know what I had."

Marie lay her head back down. "Maybe."

"So, anyway, T had to be shown that shying from a jump was not okay, and I had to be shown how not to be afraid of the jump. Or him. So, the next weekend, Sarah got all of her students gathered around, and my folks, and Beth, and my best friend, and I was to re-jump the jump he'd missed."

"Why make such a big deal of it? I think it would be better with just you, without the audience."

"I thought the same thing, and I remember standing in the tack room with Sarah, saying *why can't I just do this without everyone watching?* And she took me by my skinny shoulders—I was almost as tall as her by then, but pretty scrawny—. . ."

"How old were you again?"

"Just turned fourteen. So she said, *What is secret number one?* And I said, *Be confident.* And she said *Are you confident?* And I said *No.* So she asked, *What's secret number two?* This was a routine she used on all of us."

"And what was secret number two?," Marie asked.

"Fake it. *So Okay,* Sarah said, *now here's a little trick: don't try to fake Transnational. Fake out all of those* people *out there. Get it? All right? Now put on your helmet and let's go.* And at the entrance to the arena, I saw what she meant: no way was I going to let those people, and especially my mother, see that I was afraid. She gave me a pat on the butt and said, *Don't forget to let him have a look at the cast; he'll be curious. And remember, keep going counter-clockwise.*"

"Why counter-clockwise?"

"It would be easier on my right arm. See? Because I'd pull the horse's head around to the left with my good left arm. So T was standing in the middle of the arena next to the jump, which was set at low cross-ties, and everyone was watching—the other girls standing outside the boards and everyone else sitting on the risers—and I walked over to him and held out my right arm." She did so now, lying on her back bearing Marie's weight. "He took a long, long sniff of it, then faced front, as if to say, *So, what's the program?* And Sarah threw me up into the saddle and we started. I flexed him . . ."

"What's that?"

"Pulled his nose first to my left knee, then to the right to make sure his neck was loose. It hurt a little to pull him to the right, but not too much. He was always pretty light. Then I started him out at a walk. Half-way around, I asked for a trot. He took about four steps, stopped in his tracks, and looked back up at me over his right shoulder. I can still remember his right eye staring at me as if to say, *What's going on?*"

"Why?"

"The cast must have changed the way I held the reins, and he felt the difference in his mouth. But I got him straightened out and after that he was all right. I trotted around the arena once, then, at the far end, turned him toward the jump and asked for a canter. I looked at the jump and knew I was afraid, but luckily I saw my mother sitting in the stands, looking like *Please Lord, look after my baby and forgive me for what I'm letting her do,* and that was enough to remind me to fake her out. So, the fear of the jump went away, just like that. I said the mantra and over we went."

"The mantra? What's that?"

"We called it Sarah's Mantra: *heels-down-toes-out-squeeze-with-your-calves-shorten-the-rein-grab-his-mane-look-beyond-the-jump-be-ready-for-anything.*" She laughed. "I'll never forget that."

"Say it again."

She did, and they laughed together, Marie's head moving up and down with the laughter coming from Britt's chest.

"Look beyond the jump? Why?"

"That's important. Looking at the jump is the most effective way to get the horse to shy from it. Look beyond, at where you're going, and the horse will, too. We took the jump three times and that was that. Sarah started the regular class—which was good psychology again, because the other girls knew not to make a big deal out of it, and if we'd taken a break my folks would have gotten all gushy, and I would have been mortified. Sarah must have been a good child psychologist, because I was never afraid of T again. Or jumping. Or anything, really, I guess."

Britt let the last thought rest without comment for a minute, then said, "Come now, roll off. I gotta go."

"Will you take me riding sometime?" Marie rolled onto the bed, but made no move yet to get up.

"Sure. Have you ever been?"

"Once. The horse didn't want to get going, but when we headed back at the end of the hour, he ran fast and that scared me. That must have been twenty years ago."

"That's what we call being *barn sour*; it's common in rentals. They don't like leaving the barn, and if you let them they'll run back to where they know their hay is and to where their buddies are. It can be dangerous, actually. No, we'll go back to the barn where I rode and get you on a good, manageable horse. You'll like it. You'll probably be good at it."

"But we won't see T-man, right?"

"No. We won't." Britt sat up, put her feet on the floor and put her sneakers on. "Okay, that's that. Now I've really got to go. I'm going to make a sandwich to eat down. I'll be late. Don't wait up. Kiss me." And just like that, she was down the stairs and, after a very quick clattering around in the kitchen, out the back door.

Marie listened to her go, then got up, did her own solitary version of the inverse strip-tease: cotton briefs, no bra, a Moriarty Pintos tee-shirt, then changed her mind, took off the tee-shirt and put a sports bra on, then the tee-shirt and a pair of running shorts and shoes. And she and Ginger hopped in her car and drove over to the golf course behind the law school, where they ran a lap around, then walked one, then ran the third, which should be about six miles, thinking that she might catch a sight of Britt in the large law library windows that look out over the golf course, but she didn't.

⁓

"Can I read it?"

"What?"

It was breakfast later in the week, Thursday morning, and Marie was dressed for work in a green and black paisley dress with a touch of red, a little below the knee, hose, medium high heels and a little light make up; Britt wore a shapeless striped blue-on-brown sweater and khaki shorts. Her knee socks—Marie's knee socks, actually—would have been too short had they been pulled up, but instead they were clumped at her ankles, above her sneakers. A barrette pulled her hair behind one ear, but she hadn't been able to find the other barrette, so on that side her hair hung straight, with her right ear peaking through.

"Michael's letter, can I read it?"

"No."

"Why not?"

"Because you asked. 'Bye."

"Your underwear's showing, Cutie."

Marie adjusted her slip and replied, "And you're going to freeze today in those shorts."

"Naw. It'll be warm in the law school. 'Bye. See you tonight. Oh, we need Tampax. And grapefruit juice. If you get by the store." They brushed lips, touched fingertips, five-to-five, Marie's right and Britt's left, and Marie exited through the backdoor to her car, parked in the alley.

Marie's daily commute, through the Tijeras Canyon and east across the plains to Moriarty, took about an hour. Before, it had been only barely tolerable, the sun in her eyes both ways and the hot wind from the south buffeting the car. She had tolerated it at first for her career, because it had been the only decent job she could find, but she wasn't willing to isolate herself on the New Mexican plains. Later on, as she came to like what went on in her classroom, as she tried to get country boys and girls to think about the world beyond Torrence County and as she tried to get Anglos, Mexicans and hippies to learn to admire, or tolerate, at any rate, the others' differences. She became committed to her little rural school district and thought a time or two about moving to Moriarty; she had been encouraged to do so, as well, by school board, parents and children. But she had always resisted; Moriarty was too small, too public and she was afraid that she would end up being too lazy to commute to the west for the stimulation of the city. She couldn't imagine being a thirty-seven year old single woman living in a trailer in Moriarty, New Mexico, hanging out at Blackie's, watching satellite TV and listening to the wind moan through the barbed wire. So she stayed in Albuquerque and fought the sun both ways for two hours a day for seven years.

Now, of course, she thought, as she headed out of the canyon, the back of the Crest sloping down on her left, and toward Edgewood, the road heading straight, now, all the way to and past Oklahoma City, now, she thought, she had a reason to commute. If she moved out there now, there was no reason to expect that the good, right-thinking citizens of Moriarty would not notice that she brought a blond-haired woman and only one double bed with her. Nor could she expect them to approve. *Crimes against nature!* She winced as she imagined the school board meeting; Moriarty was a pretty conservative community. No, she needed the isolation of the commute and the anonymity of the city. She also needed, she knew, the hour's transition from what had become one life to another. She couldn't yet imagine living in town, where she would kiss Britt good morning and good bye and, fifteen minutes later, walk into a classroom full of kids trying to get through a normal adolescence full of zits, wet dreams and cheerleader tryouts. A *normal* adolescence: she bit and held her tongue gently between her teeth and silently reproached herself for having even thought the word. *Normal.* Anyway, it took a while for her to shift out of the new part of her life and to resettle comfortably into the old one.

And she didn't know whether she could or should go on with the shifting. Britt had been encouraging her lately to re-study her own personal history, to see if maybe the shift was smaller than it seemed to be. Marie had so far resisted the suggestion and, for now, the commute kept her from answering many such questions and she was grateful. For all that Britt had brought her that pleased, she had certainly brought, from that very first dance in Fargo's until just this morning, a shit load of disorientation.

For one thing, she thought, as the road flattened out, it was somehow crazily intimate to be sharing a box of Tampax with one's lover.

On the other hand, take age. She had never planned, never considered, being involved with someone younger than she. Every lover, boy friend, whatever, that she had had before Britt had been her age or older. How in the world was she supposed to know how to deal with a person who had fewer memories, less experience than she? It had always been comfortably the opposite. She was unprepared for all of this, all of this exploration, all of this fumbling around, all of this newness.

And there was the meeting with Britt's parents, which she had been putting off, but which she knew must come. It wouldn't be difficult in the clichéd way; rather it would be a nice evening with two oh-so-understanding PFLAG members, being *Britt's new girlfriend.* She couldn't imagine what she would say, or how she would act, or what she would call them. Still and all, the meeting was sure to come.

And on this note, she exited the interstate, drove along the strip that passed for downtown Moriarty, past Blackies and Mike's Store and the park and the municipal court, to the school. She pulled into her parking spot and waved hello to the elementary school music teacher, with whom one time years ago she had spent the night, and how much easier that had been, she thought, forgetting that it hadn't been at all. She also thought that it served school teachers right to have to deal with hard, disorienting, energy-sapping questions. That, after all is what she dispensed for a living. A car horn made her turn around, and she watched Jill Westwood pull in and unload herself and her books.

Jill was ten years older, and had children starting ten years younger, than Marie and their friendship had developed over time into one that seemed to want to wander effortlessly between older sister and close friend, between mentor and colleague, between advisor and confidant. Jill needed to be told, she knew, but she wasn't sure how, or when.

Marie watched Jill walk across the parking lot, lugging about a half-dozen books and two briefcases. She was a soft woman, not fat, but a large, soft woman whose bones did not show. She wore her hair, which was a grey-brown-black mixture, in a sort of modified pageboy and she favored blazers, skirts and penny loafers, all of which made Marie think of Vassar '58. She was very precise, with undercurrents of both concern and humor that made the nuances of her speech hard to catch sometimes. Marie waited for her, trying to imagine how she might tell her about Britt. "Jill, there is something I've got to talk to you about . . .." Or "Hey. Good morning. Have a nice weekend? Britt Larsen and I—we're lovers, you know—we went camping in the Gila." Or "Listen, Jill, I have to tell you: exactly two hours and twenty minutes ago I awoke in the arms of another woman."

*Aye-yi-yi*, Marie thought as Jill reached her and Marie offered help with one of the briefcases, *this is all ridiculous*. They walked together across the parking lot and into the Middle School.

Their classrooms were in an old and singularly unattractive cinder block building, painted inside and out in a light green that one suspected had been a real bargain. The middle school was surrounded by a hard dirt playground and, farther on, sage brush and tumble weed. The district was poor and the building was unfancy. Inside her room, though, it was at least colorful. She had done the best she could and tried to make the room cheerful. Just now, she smiled to herself, not everyone in town thought her room cheerful, decorated as it was with bright posters from the USSR. Travel scenes, onion-topped buildings and smiling red-cheeked peasants were everywhere. And, right in front, there was Lenin, looking somewhere into the twenty-second century, or, if you were the president of the school board, he was looking into south Texas and maybe even Roswell, making plans for May Day, 1986.

But what the hell, the school board had sent her to ASU to take the course, so how could they complain? Besides, she knew that they knew that most of the parents knew that she was good, she was fair and what she taught needed to be taught. They'd disagree on the details, but she had been there long enough to gain their confidence. Their admiration, even, maybe. Lenin, perhaps, pushed it near the limit, but not over, not this time, she was sure.

Besides, she thought, as she straightened up the room and lined the desks in rows, they'll approve of today. Over the weekend, as Britt had played a Linda Ronstadt CD upstairs, and as Marie had worked on her lesson plans down, she had found herself inspired by Linda's—or actually Chuck Berry's—words: *Oh well oh well I feel so good today/I just touched down on an international runway/ Jet-propelled back home from overseas to the USA . . .*"

It was time, she thought, to salute the flag, so to speak, and the students would have a chance to say what they liked about the good old USA. After two weeks of socialist propaganda, it would be interesting to hear what they had to say. Would they think the county lending library down in Estancia was first-stage socialism? What about Amtrak? Medicare? The EPA? She intended to make them think about it. She went happily about her class prep, singing to herself: *Detroit, Chicago, Chattanooga, Baton Rouge .*

An early bus arrived and her home room students began to drift in.

"Hi, Miss Cochran."

"'Morning, Shirley. Yikes, you got your hair cut!"

"Don't you like it?"

"Well, let me see the back." She leaned down to be eye-level and put her hands on her knees. The little girl turned slowly, her whole visage a definition of *hopeful*.

"Sure, I like it." She patted Shirley's cheek in time to the music in her head, and sang *"Everything you want we got it right here in the USA."* She ended with a flourish on the air guitar.

"You're crazy, Miss Cochran," Shirley said, and she ran out to the playground before classes would begin.

ALBUQUERQUE

At ten minutes after two that same day, as Marie, in Moriarty, was teaching her way through her sixth period, eighth grade Civics class, the Fourth Amendment to the US Constitution, Richard Randolph ran across the Forum at the law school, through the double doors and down the steps, two at a time, heading for his office. He had scheduled two meetings for the same hour and he was ten minutes late for both. Administration was not his strong suit and he knew it. If the dean and his colleagues didn't know it by now, well . . . they should.

Outside his office door, Britt Larsen sat on the corner of his secretary's momentarily empty desk, looking a little disaccomodating.

"Oh, damn it," he said, "Do I have an appointment with you?"

"It's nice to see you, too. Yes, at two." She looked at her watch.

"I've got two meetings right now and I'm late for both of them. Sorry. Can we put it off for until later?"

"Sure. It's your research, not mine."

"Right. What is it you're working on?"

"The Riley case."

"Right. How's it going? Wait. No time now. Can we put it off?"

"*Sure*, she said again."

"Thanks. Hold on. Slow down, Randolph, be polite. How are you? Long time, no see."

"Like every Tuesday and Thursday, including today, ten-thirty, in Bankruptcy class?"

"In the sea of faces . . . I meant you and me, face-to-face, prof-to-RA. Say, how's life as the editor of the *Review*?"

"Associate editor." She grimaced in a way that made him think she didn't like being someone's associate. She'd better get used to it. "Articles Editor."

"Right. How is it going?"

"You were correct; I haven't learned anything yet. I'm glad I can still work for you."

"Me, too. Listen, I've *got* to run."

"When should I come back?"

"Can't tell you now. Come on, walk with me to the Dean's office; we can talk on the way." He looked at his watch. "God, Ned's going to kill me." They walked briskly out of the suite of faculty offices and turned left at the corridor. It was really only a short zig and a longer zag, up the half flight of stairs, across the foyer and into the administrative suite. It gave them little time to carry on the conversation.

"Is there anything else I can do before . . . before whenever it is we're going to meet again?"

"Let's see. I can't think of anything. Yes, there is. In re Sullivan." As they passed the receptionist's counter, he was handed a fistful of pink *WHILE YOU WERE OUT* messages. "Thanks, Gert." He glanced through them and stuffed the lot into his rear pocket.

"Yes? A bankruptcy case?"

"Mmhuh. It's in your casebook. We'll get to it in class next week. Probably Tuesday. Be prepared on it?"

"I'm always prepared for class. Sort of."

"Be *well* prepared. Get my drift?"

"No."

"Think."

"You're going to call on me?"

"Right." He pointed an index finger at her.

"Why tell me in advance?"

"I want someone I *know* is prepared."

"You want me to be a ringer."

"Right."

"What's in it for me?"

"What?" He stopped and held the door into the Dean's suite for her.

"The *quid pro quo* as you taught me to say in Contracts class. How about a free pass in exchange?" *Pass* was student lingo for saying in class that one was not prepared to recite.

"No deal."

"Why not? You're asking me to help you put one over on my own classmates. I ought to get something in return."

"I don't give free passes."

"Never?"

"Never. Hi, Jane, . . ." the frizzy-haired Dean's secretary looked up, ". . . am I in trouble?"

"They've been waiting."

"Good." He turned back to Britt. "You were saying?"

"No free pass?"

"No."

"Afraid of losing control over the class?"

"You bet."

"Then what?"

"If you prepare In re Sullivan then you save yourself the embarrassment of having to say you aren't prepared."

"Some deal."

"Who ever said law school was a deal?"

"Toss in an Eskimo Pie."

"What is this?"

"*Randolph!*" Ned Bradley, the associate dean, stuck his head out of the door into his conference room. "For God's sake, . . ."

"Unlax, Doc, . . ."

"What!"

"*Unlax.* It was Bugs Bunny's line. I like it. See? *Unlax* instead of *relax.*"

"Bugs Bunny, my eye. Come on, the meeting should have started fifteen minutes ago."

"Cool your retro-rockets, Ned, this is a student we have here. You remember them, right? Students? Tuition? Classes? Like that? Surely you've seen them around the halls. *They*, not committee meetings, are what education is all about, Your Excellency, so mind your manners and stop being such a dean. Britt Larsen, this is the Associate Dean. Dean Bradley, Britt Larsen: third year student. Associate Editor of the *New Mexico Law Review.*" He glanced at Britt and realized that one jibe about her not being Editor-in-Chief was all he would ever be allowed in any one day.

"I know Ms. Larsen." Ned put aside his rough manner and slid smoothly into decanal posture. "How are you? How goes the *Law Review?*"

"Fine, thanks. We're on schedule, at least."

Richard interrupted. "You'll excuse me, Ned, but I've got a meeting to attend. Two, in fact. No time for chit-chat. Ms. Larsen. Go look up Professor Johnson. Do you know Professor Johnson? Good. She should be in the faculty library. Apologize for me, tell her that I am aware of the meeting of the Curriculum Committee but that I am in Malaysia. Then see my secretary when she gets back from her break. Set up our meeting on the Riley case for tomorrow or early next week. Tell her to leave me a note reminding me of when that meeting is. Then, and only then, buy yourself an Eskimo Pie and prepare In re Sullivan. Scoot now; Professor Johnson doesn't like to be kept waiting. Now, . . ." he sighed, ". . . Ned, can we get this meeting going? I haven't got all day. Have you got fifty cents? Give it to Ms. Larsen; I'll pay you back." Richard walked into the conference room, leaving Britt, Ned and Jane looking at one another.

"Okay," Ned Bradley broke Richard's spell, as he dug into his pants pocket. "What did he say he owed you?"

"Never mind," said Britt. "He was just joking. It was nice to see you again. 'Bye, Jane."

She left the administrative suite and retraced her steps back to the *cul de sac* that contained Richard's office, the pool secretary for him and the other nearby faculty, and the faculty library. The door to the library was closed, so she said to Harriet, the secretary, "Can I go in? Professor Randolph gave me a message to deliver."

"Sure," Harriet said, not looking away from her computer screen. "It's just some kind of committee meeting."

Britt walked through the door and into the rather gloomy interior of the faculty library. It was actually more of a meeting room than a library, for all it had in the way of reading materials were periodicals: the *New York Times*, the *Wall Street Journal*, the *Washington Post*, the *Los Angeles Times*, the *Denver Post*, plus new issues of several law reviews. At the table in the middle of the room sat four faculty members, one of whom was speaking.

". . . every damn year for the last four years. So, we'll do it again this year, with the . . . Yes?"

Britt had interrupted the meeting merely by her presence, standing in the doorway, without saying anything. Cynthia Johnson looked up from the papers in front of her, looked over her reading glasses, and said again, "Yes?"

"That's Britt Larsen," said one of her colleagues, who had had Britt in Property class her first year.

"Yes?" said Professor Johnson again.

"Professor Johnson?" The professor nodded. "I'm Professor Randolph's RA and he asked me to give you a message. He's sorry about being late for the meeting, but he's got another meeting that was scheduled at the same time in the Dean's office. He apologizes, and will catch up with you later."

"If Richard Randolph apologized for missing a committee meeting, it would be breaking news, but I appreciate your sensibilities, Ms. Larsen. Thank you." She turned back to her notes and began speaking again. "Where was I? Yes, we'll prepare something again for the faculty's review, and . . .." Britt walked out of the room and across to Harriet's desk.

"Professor Randolph told me to set up an appointment with you for tomorrow or early next week. About an hour, I think."

Harriet looked at the calendar in front of her. "Well, he's probably forgotten that he'll be meeting with the AG in Santa Fe all day on Friday, but how about next Monday or Tuesday? He's pretty free then. Say, Tuesday after lunch?"

"That works for me," said Britt. "I've got him for Bankruptcy just before lunch, so that will be easy." She put her backpack down on the floor, pulled out her weekly planner and wrote the engagement down. "He also said to make sure you leave him a note to remind him of it."

Harriet nodded knowingly. "Will do. As if that works. I'll make sure he's here."

"'Bye."

"'Bye."

Britt now exited the *cul de sac* and headed up the half-flight of steps to the main floor of the law school. On her right was the snack bar, and she went in, put two quarters into the machine and bought herself an Eskimo Pie, peeled the wrapper off and walked through the double doors and into the Forum, the large open area in the law school into which the classrooms and law library emptied. Scattered around the moot courtroom in the center of the Forum were clumps of cushy black leather chairs and low wooden tables, and the Forum served its function of being an informal gathering place for students, staff and faculty alike. Just now, several groups of students, and a few solitary individuals, argued, laughed, studied or, in two cases, slept, here and there around the area. Between her and the library entrance sat a group of her classmates that she knew, so she made her way over, nibbling at the chocolate on her ice cream.

"Hey, guys. What's up?"

"Britt. Pull up a chair."

"Can't do it. I've got to study. See ya' later." She headed toward the library doors.

"Wait!" Keisha Wilkinson, one of her friends, jumped up out of her chair and walked over to Britt. "Can I get your notes from Bankruptcy class Tuesday? I had to miss."

"Sure. Come on by my carrel."

"I'll be there in a minute or two; I've got to finish up what we were talking about back there."

"See ya."

"Just a few minutes."

Britt walked through the library doors and to the left, heading toward the *Law Review* office.

"Ms. Larsen! No food in the library, please." It was the attendant behind the desk. But he was one of her classmates, serving work-study time at the circulation desk, and there was no force to his demand. Britt stuck her tongue out at him, took the last bite of ice cream off the stick and dropped the evidence in the waste basket as she headed down the stairs. The *Law Review* office was to her left, and she stopped in to see if there were any messages for her. In her mailbox was a fat manila envelope, with a return address from the University of Oregon, and a note written on the outside of the envelope in the handwriting of Alexander Rivera, the Editor-in-Chief of the *Review*: *Britt—I like the looks of this, and I think that if we act quickly, we might get a commitment before the competition even offers. Can you give me a placement memo on it by Monday?* Instead of signing the note, Alex had, as was his practice, used a rubber stamp: *A.E.R., E-i-C, N.M.L. Rev.* Without opening the envelope, she quickly left again. She had an Associate Editor's office in the suite, but the common room tended to feel like an elite members-only club, filled mostly with students just out of undergrad school—barely out of high school, it seemed sometimes—and she had found it to be an unpleasant place to hang out, and an impossible place to get any work done, except for the endless meetings that her editorship required. Besides, if she ran into Alex, he would take fifteen minutes to explain that which was perfectly clear from his note, that she would be busy this weekend writing him a memorandum on whether she thought the *Review* should make an offer of publication for the article in the envelope.

As a place to study and work, she preferred her carrel, which was at the back, on the lower level of the library, in a bright and quiet spot near the windows looking out on the golf course that bordered the law school to the north. She could see, sitting by himself in a lawn chair outdoors and to the right of her carrel, the director of the American Indian Law Center, wearing a sun hat and smoking a cigar. She didn't really know him, only by reputation, but he saw her looking his way and waved to her, so she waved back.

Her carrel was really just a large desk, surrounded on three sides by blond wooden partitions, about chest high. In the small area enclosed, just barely big enough to turn around in, there was a chair, a desk lamp, a waste basket and shelves for books. Most of the books were the brown and red *Bankruptcy Reporters* that contained the cases that her research on the Riley case had uncovered. Several were unopened on the shelves, the cases marked by yellow index cards, others lay stacked on the desk. The bookshelves also held her course books and notepads from class. She had added the personal touch of a few cut flowers, surreptitiously picked from the garden at the golf course club house and now a little past their prime sitting in a paper coffee cup, and she had pinned up three pictures on the far partition, near the window. One was of Marie and Ginger, taken soon after they had met, when they had gone hiking on the West Mesa to see the petroglyphs. Marie wore a Dukes' ball cap, pushed back on her head to show her face, an *Allegheny Alum* sweatshirt, a sleeveless vest jacket, open because the day had started desert cool but had turned out warm, khaki shorts and hiking boots. She was squatting next to the dog, with one knee raised and the other in the dirt, one arm held out straight, palm outwards, shading her eyes from the sun, and the other on Ginger's collar, who was standing, ears perked up, and panting. You could see Britt's shadow crossing the foreground of the scene. The second picture was of a group of Forest Service diggers, Britt included, from when they had been working the dig down in the Gila four years ago. And the third picture was of a young Britt sitting atop Transnational, with Beth and Sarah on the ground; Sarah was holding her blue ribbon and looking very proud.

Britt sat down in her chair, opened the manila envelope from Oregon, and began to read.

"Hey."

She looked up to see Keisha standing, leaning on the top of the partition, looking at her.

"Hey, back. So, what do you need?"

"Bankruptcy. Last Tuesday."

Britt pulled her Bankruptcy binder off the shelf and opened it to the back, snapped open the rings and took out the last three pages. "Here. Don't lose them."

"I'll make copies and bring them right back." She leafed through the pages. "How do you take such tidy notes the way he rambles on, always shooting from here to there?"

"Those aren't my raw notes, dummy. Those are the re-writes."

"You re-write you notes?"

"Sure."

"Every day?"

"Don't you remember how Randolph preached to us in Contracts first year about after-class study? Like it's the secret to success in law school?"

"Vaguely."

"Well, it turns out he's right. Here're my raw notes . . .," she picked up a manila folder and fanned the pages with her thumb. "Even I can't read them anymore."

"Then why keep them?"

"In case I lose *those*. Or lend them to someone who shreds them, by mistake, instead of copying them."

"You're a maniac. I'll be right back." She ran off toward the copy room, and, knowing she'd return soon, Britt looked outside instead of going back to the article submitted by—she checked the front page—Professor Judith Wilson of the University of Oregon. Whoever she is. Cigar apparently finished, the director was not to be seen, though his lawn chair and coffee-can ashtray still were.

"I'm back. Here. Thanks."

"You're welcome. Guess what? I'm to be Randolph's ringer next Tuesday."

"Ringer? Meaning what."

"He gave me a heads-up that he's going to call on me for the Sullivan case." She pulled her Bankruptcy casebook off the shelf and opened it to show Keisha the spot.

"So, not that you don't already look brilliant compared to the rest of us, now you get advance notice that you're going to be called on? The rich get richer. What's up?"

"I don't know. He just said that I should read the case carefully."

"As if you don't already?"

"*Very* carefully, he said."

"I wonder what he's got in mind."

"We'll see on Tuesday."

"You nervous?"

"Naw. What's the worst that could happen?"

"If it were me? I could faint. I *hate* being called on. I think he's got something up his sleeve on Tuesday. Be careful."

"Why think that?"

"He's a *law* professor?" Eyebrows raised and shaking her head, Keisha allowed her voice to drip cynicism.

"Come on, Keisha, they're not the enemy."

"Not to you, Ms. Editor-of-the-Law-Review/full-ride-scholarship/third-in-her-class. How many books did you write last semester?" *Writing the book* was what the law students called writing the best exam in the course.

"Just one."

"*Just one.* Which one?"

"Estate and Gift Tax."

Keisha shook her head. "Estate and Gift Tax. You *are* a maniac. The rest of us live in a different world. You work for Randolph, don't you."

"Yeah. We get along. He's funny—quirky funny. I like him, actually; he makes me think."

"Think away, my friend. You're good at it." She turned to go, then turned back. "Say, where you been?"

"Me? Here mostly. Seems like my butt is glued to this chair."

"No, I don't mean around school. I mean after hours. We don't see you for beers, at dinners, parties. What's going on?"

Britt shrugged. "Just busy, I guess. Who said third year was going to be easier than first?"

"Nobody. Rumors are rampant, you know."

"What kind of rumors?"

"Mostly inchoate, as your friend Randolph would have it. She wasn't here. She wasn't there. She wasn't at that, either. Where is she? Doesn't she like us anymore? That kind of thing."

"You know how law school rumors go. Like I said, . . ."

"And there was a sighting."

"A sighting?"

"Yup. Britt and an Unknown Female shopping for groceries at the Albertson's on Eubank."

"Roommate."

"Whose picture you keep in your carrel?" Keisha gestured with her eyes to the picture of Marie. Britt said nothing, looked first at the picture, then back at Keisha. "The sighting came with a description: short, dark hair, wears glasses."

"Yeah, well, she's kind of flying under the radar right now."

"Who among us hasn't been there? She looks nice. Who's the dog?"

"Ginger. Marie's dog." Britt said nothing for a minute, while they both looked at the picture. Then, "Listen, what I don't need right now is one of Gretchen's all-politics-are-personal lectures."

"You mean *the closet is the breeding ground of misogyny*?"

"Spare me. It's just the two of us, and she's trying to figure things out." Britt paused, looking out the window toward the golf course. "She needs some time and some slack, and if Gretchen were to out my sweetheart, she'd have a train wreck on her hands."

Keisha reached over and squeezed Britt's near shoulder. "Oh, I don't think you have to worry. She'd out a two-faced politician, that's for sure. Or maybe even a two-faced classmate. But not the friend of a friend; I can't believe she'd do that."

"Anyway, we just want to live quietly for now, okay? No confirmation of the rumor, okay? Might have been a cousin from out of town, mightn't it have been?"

"Cousin from another branch of the family. But hey, mum's the word with me. And don't worry about Gretchen; if I hear her getting mouthy, I'll tell her to clam up. But there are a few of us getting together at our place on Sunday night. Make your own tacos. Coupla beers. Small talk. Bring her around, we'd like to meet her. Very quiet. Tell her no politics, no speculums."

"I'll ask, but I doubt that she's ready. Anyway, I'll be busy."

"You can't read that Bankruptcy case from now until next Tuesday."

"No, with this." She picked up the *Law Review* submission and read the title out loud. "*Re/structuring the Modern Paradigm for Union and Non-Union Employment Relationships in the Public Sector.*"

"What do you have to do with that?"

"Read it and write Alex a memo explaining why I don't think we should offer to publish."

"You already know?"

"I don't care for the word *paradigm*." She showed Keisha the title page and re-read the title, this time pronouncing the slash. "*Re-slash-structuring the Modern Paradigm* and so on, blah blah blah. I'm bored already. But Alex likes that kind of shit. That's the problem. One of them. Anyway, I think the weekend has been trashed by the combination of Judith Wilson, Alex Rivera and In re Sullivan. But thanks for the invitation."

"Okay. Let me know. Or don't; just come by around seven. And listen, babe, if—what's her name? Marie?—doesn't feel up to it, that's okay, too. Come by yourself."

"It really does sound like fun. We'll see. Now git. Re-slash-structuring awaits, with In re Sullivan in line."

"See ya' around. Thanks for the notes. I'm coming to next Tuesday's Bankruptcy class for sure, just to see what happens."

"No heckling."

"Bye."

Keisha walked off, back through the library and up the steps to the Forum. Britt sat for a minute looking at the picture of Marie, then changed her mind, put Professor Wilson's article back in the envelope, and wrote Alex a short note, saying that she'd get him the memo by next Wednesday. Then she opened her casebook, turned over a fresh sheet on her yellow pad, and began to prepare In re Sullivan for class.

## ALBUQUERQUE

"It wasn't a love letter, you know." Marie rattled the ice in her glass and watched the bubbles from the beer be trapped by the ice cubes on their ways to the top. Her turn, Britt was cleaning up the Saturday lunch dishes, filling the dishwasher, and diverting the occasional table scrap from the trash can to Ginger's mouth.

"Which letter is it that isn't a love letter, I know?"

"You know, Michael's latest."

"Michael? The name is vaguely familiar."

"Michael Reid."

"Oh, Michael Reid. The guy you don't love. And haven't seen for however many years. But who still writes dreamy letters to you. That Michael?"

"Yes, that one," she laughed and tried to figure out if Britt was trying not to. She decided she was.

"And whose name sometimes comes up in otherwise intimate conversations."

"You will never let me forget that, will you. I only mentioned moustaches, sort of generically speaking, you know. I didn't ask you to get one." Marie paused for a minute. "That would be way too kinky for me."

"How deliriously pleased am I to hear you say that."

"Do people *do* that?"

Britt shrugged her shoulders. "Someone does everything, I suppose."

"But anyway, that's not what we were talking about."

"What were we talking about?"

"The letter."

"What letter is that?"

"Michael's letter. You're being difficult."

"Where's this one from?"

"Bulgaria. And it wasn't a love letter, but you still can't read it so don't ask."

"Ah, but maybe I already did, sneaking home early from the law library, while you and the Moriarty-ites were hard at it over the troubles in South Africa, or wherever. Or Bulgaria, for all I know."

"I don't believe for a second that you read my private mail."

"There's nothing I want to do less."

"In that case, maybe I'll let you sometime."

"You want my advice?"

"Sure."

"Go back to Bulgaria."

"Me? What? What are you talking about? I've never been to Bulgaria."

"That, my dear, was the best single line in *Casablanca*. Rick to the young Bulgarian girl who is about to sleep with Inspector Renault in exchange for an exit visa and she wants to know from Rick if Renault will keep his word. *Yes*, says Rick, *he'll do what he says.* The girl receives this assurance with decidedly mixed emotions, so Rick says, *You want my advice? Oh, yes, Mister Rick,* she says, dark eyes brimming. *Go back to Bulgaria*, he says. It's so chillingly cold and heartless. But, of course, in the end Rick shows he's not heartless at all by letting her husband win at roulette by playing twenty-two black twice in a row, giving the Bulgarians enough money to bribe Renault for the visa without requiring the young wife to screw the creep. There you've got it: the most interesting by-play in the entire movie."

"I suppose you know who played the Bulgarian woman."

"Actually, I do. It was an actress named Joy Page. She had eyes not unlike yours."

"Want to go to the movies tonight?"

"Can't. I've got a case to prepare for Bankruptcy class, and a memo to write for the *Law Review*. But if you go ahead if there's something you want to see. Bring me back some carryout Mexican and I'd be as pleased as can be."

⌣

Later, Marie having passed on seeing *The Breakfast Club*, which was on her list, and the two of them having eaten burritos from Sadie's, which was a long drive for Marie, but worth it, Marie lay on her stomach on the floor with *L'actualité*, the French-Canadian newsmagazine, which she read to keep her French current. But her attention was on the Steichen portrait of Amelia Earhart. A poster, of course, not a real Steichen print. It had come with Britt and hung on the wall over the couch. An amazingly strong, modern woman looked out of that frame, staring straight into Steichen's camera. It mesmerized her. Under it, Britt reclined on the white couch, a law book propped on her drawn-up knees. Marie watched as, without looking up from the book, Britt reached out her left hand. She clicked her tongue for the dog, her hand offering an ear skritch. Still looking at the book, she spoke:

"Trover; c'mere, baby."

"Would you stop calling my dog that? Her name's Ginger. You're gonna drive her crazy."

"She asked me to call her *Trover*, didn't ya, Trover?" The yellow lab flopped her tail against the floor and looked from one to the other, her expression approximating confusion.

They both spoke:

"See?"

Britt went back to her reading. After a minute, Marie spoke. "I don't even know what *Trover* means."

"I doubt that she does either."

"Come on. What's it mean?"

"*Black's* is upstairs on my desk. Look it up."

"*Me* look it up?"

"I already know what it means, Angel. Besides, I'm reading."

Marie got herself up off the floor and wandered up the stairs to the study. She poked through the odds and ends on Britt's desk, looked for a minute at her own portrait sitting in a small silver frame, then looked on the bookshelf and saw *Black's Law Dictionary*. She pulled it down and found her way to this: "In common-law practice, the action of trover is a species of action on the case and originally lay for the recovery of damages against a person who found another's goods and wrongfully converted them to his own use. Subsequently the allegation of the loss of the goods by the plaintiff and the finding of them by the defendant was merely fictitious, and the action became the remedy for any wrongful interference with or detention of the goods of another." She read it again, then put the dictionary back on the shelf and walked back downstairs.

"That made no sense."

"Nope. It's kind of an old-fashioned term. I'm not sure why Trover likes it. Why do you like it, girl?" This last to the dog, who once again flopped her tail on the floor, then got herself to her feet, shook, walked over to the couch and nuzzled her head under Britt's hand.

"But what's it mean?"

"Well, let's see. It's an old form of action that we learned about in History. See, the British common law was very formalistic, and in order to sue you had to fit your case into one form of action or another, and they were pretty strict. So, in the beginning, trover was for when you lost your property and someone found it and used is as their own."

"Finders keepers."

"Right. Which turns out *not* to be the law. So, the loser could sue the finder in trover to recover whatever damage was done to the property."

"Not get the property back?"

"That's *replevin*. Different deal. And who would name a dog *Replevin*?"

"Okay, but the dictionary mentioned something about fiction."

"Right. After a bit, the judges started letting you sort of pretend that you had lost the property. So suppose someone takes my horse out of my barn and uses it without my permission, and the horse comes back lame. I get to sue in trover by *pretending* that I lost the horse, and *pretending* that the defendant found him. The defendant doesn't get to dispute the fiction. See?"

"Sounds like nonsense."

"Blame the British. You're the one who reads *The Economist*."

"So, why have you renamed my dog after such legalistic British nonsense?"

"I *told* you; because she *asked* me to. Now let me read, will you?"

Marie returned to *L'actualité*. After a few minutes, though, she began chuckling to herself.

"What are you nickering about?"

"Want to hear a joke?"

"Sure." Britt left her casebook open, but lay it on her chest.

"Ready?"

"Ready."

"This horse walks into a bar. And the bartender says, *Hay, why the long face?*" She chuckled.

Britt laughed.

"Did you like it?," Marie asked.

"Yes. That's funny. Want to hear another one?"

"Another joke?"

"Another horse-walks-into-a-bar joke."

"Sure."

"Okay. A horse walks into a bar. *What'll it be?* asks the bartender. *Give me a beer*, says the horse. So the bartender pulls him a draft and sets it down in front of the horse. *That'll be five dollars.* So the horse pays and is sipping his beer and a few minutes later the bartender comes back to chat. *We don't get too many horses in here*, says the bartender. *Well*, says the horse, *at five dollars a beer, I'm surprised you get any at all.*

Marie laughed quietly. "Okay. My turn. This one's kind of vulgar."

"Where did you hear all these jokes?"

"At the girls basketball game. A bunch of us were sitting together in the stands and some of the men teachers from the high school started telling jokes. Okay, so a guy walks into a bar with a monkey on his shoulder. Before the guy can make an order, the monkey jumps off of his shoulder, onto the bar, grabs a handful of popcorn and stuffs it into his mouth. So the bartender throws them out onto the street. Have you heard it?"

"Can't tell yet. Go on."

"So the next day, the guy walks into the bar again with the monkey on his shoulder, and the bartender says, *No fooling around*. But the monkey jumps off the guy's shoulder and onto the bar, and stuffs first a handful of popcorn into his mouth and then a handful of peanuts. So the bartender throws them out onto the street. Okay?"

Britt nodded. "Go on."

"The next day, the guy walks into the bar with the monkey on his shoulder, and the bartender says, *I'm serious now. No fooling around. Keep that monkey under control.* But the monkey jumps off the guy's shoulder, eats a handful of popcorn, then a handful of peanuts, then jumps onto the pool table, grabs the cue ball and eats that too. So the bartender throws them out onto the street.

"With me? Okay, so a week goes by before the guy comes back into the bar, again with the monkey on his shoulder. And the bartender says, *I was hoping you wouldn't be back.* And the guy says, *He'll be good.* And for a while the monkey just sits on the guy's shoulder looking around, but after about fifteen minutes, he jumps onto the bar, eats a handful of popcorn, then a handful of peanuts, then he runs down the bar to the dish of maraschino cherries. He takes one, bends over and sticks it in his butt, then pulls it out and eats it, and then he eats a whole handful of cherries.

"So the bartender says, *You're out of here, buster, and don't come back ever. But first tell me what that thing was with the maraschino cherry in his butt.*

"*Well,* says the guy, *ever since the cue ball he likes to size everything before he eats it.*"

Britt laughed so hard she had to wipe away her tears. "That's very funny. I never thought I'd hear you tell a joke like that."

Marie looked pleased with herself. "I thought it was funny, too. A little gross, though."

"Okay," said Britt, "I've got another walks-into-a-bar one for you. This guy walks into a bar and there are two pretty women sitting at one of the tables. So he goes over to the bartender and asks what they are drinking. *Scotch on the rocks, and a margarita,* says the bartender. *Send them over a round on me,* says the guy, and the bartender does. But when the guy looks over, the women don't even acknowledge the two new drinks sitting on the table. So after a minute, the guy walks over to the table and says, *Which of you two beauties is going home with me tonight?* And one of the women says, *Neither of us.* Then the guy pulls up an empty chair and says, *New in town?* And the other woman says, *Nope.* And the guy says, *I'll bet you gals are football fans, aren't you?* And the first woman says, *Not really.*

"So this goes on for a while, as the guy tries pick-up line after pick-up line, and the women just answer like that. And finally the guy says, *Listen, girls, I give up. But I'm usually much more successful than I've been with you two. At least tell me what I'm doing wrong; I'm afraid I've lost my touch.* And one of the women says, *We're Lesbians.* And so the guy says, *Oh. Well, how're things in Beirut?*"

Marie didn't laugh, and sat up cross-legged on the floor. "Is that funny?"

"Don't you think so? I do."

"Why is it funny?"

"I don't know. Because the guy won't give up and is still trying to pick them up at the end. Don't you think it's funny?"

"I don't know what to think. I don't know what I would have done if one of the guys at the basketball game had told that one. Should I laugh, or tell him it's offensive? I feel like I don't have any instinct about such things."

"What would you have done a year ago if one of the guys at a basketball game had told that joke?"

"I don't know. It's hard to even remember a year ago—who I was; what I thought. I guess I would have thought that the mistaking *Lesbian* for *Lebanese* was funny. You've made me pretty much rethink such things though, you know that don't you?"

"Should I be sorry?"

"Are you?"

"I love you and am very happy to be with you, so, no, I can't say I'm sorry. But I hate to see you struggle with the difficulties I have caused."

Marie crawled slowly on all fours over to the couch where Britt lay, feeling her nipples brush against her shirt. She wasn't wearing a bra and the only time she could ever feel the least bit busty was on her hands and knees like this. She swiveled around to sit with her back to the couch, looking across the room and toward the closed drapes on the front window. "I love you, too, Britt, but it's a little confusing not to know whether to laugh at a joke or not."

"I know it is, but I don't know how to help."

"You're patient with me, don't force me to go anywhere, and you teach me stuff, like when it's okay to laugh at a joke about Lesbians."

"Speaking of not going anywhere, we were invited out for make-your-own-tacos at Keisha and Liz's tomorrow night. I've mentioned Keisha, haven't I? She's in my study group for Remedies."

"I think so. Who's Liz?"

"Liz Taylor. They're a couple."

"Liz *Taylor*? Who would name a child Elizabeth Taylor?"

"A funny story. You should get her to tell it, but here's the short version. She was born Elizabeth Sturgis, nicknamed Lizzie early on. But her father died when she was a toddler and later her mother married a guy name Taylor, and they began making little Taylors. So, when Liz got to the age when kids begin to know each other's last names . . . when would that be?"

"Oh, say the third grade. Second, maybe."

"Right. Liz began to wonder why she was the only Sturgis in the family. Her mother explained it, but Liz had no recollection of her father. So, they changed her name officially to Elizabeth Sturgis Taylor. If it had been anything other than Sturgis, they would have called her by her middle name, but can you imagine being called little *Sturgie*? So, Liz Taylor she became. She's cute."

"How long have they been together?"

"Two years, about. It was kind of a law library romance. But they don't study together, so Liz isn't in the Remedies study group."

"What did you say to Keisha?"

"That I was pretty busy with school and *Law Review* work, but that I'd ask."

"Would you like to go?"

"Yes and no, depending on whether you were comfortable with it. But tomorrow night, the bottom line is this—even if you were, I've just got too much work to do."

"Next time, maybe you should say *yes.*"

"For me, or both of us?"

Marie shrugged her shoulders. "Both of us. It won't be a big deal, will it?"

"Not as long as you remember to put the meat in the taco shell before putting the salsa on top. If you do it in the other way around, the salsa runs out of the shell and down your arm."

"Please. Well, let's just play it by ear. Like you said, this weekend is pretty busy."

"Okay."

"Would people there know about, uh, *us*?"

"Well, nobody *knows*. But yes, they'd suspect, if we arrive and leave together. And why would you be there with me if we weren't?"

"Would everyone there be coupled up, you know, Lesbians?"

"I don't know who got asked. If it was the Remedies study group, then no. Debbie is married to a guy named Ralph, whom I haven't met. Linda and Jenny . . . I don't know."

"You don't talk about it?"

"Mostly, we talk about Remedies."

"Can't you, I don't know, . . . tell?"

"I can't. Some women say they can, but I can't. Of course the world is full of guys who say they can, but I don't believe them. Can you?"

"I guess not. Did you think I was gay when you asked me to dance at the Fargo?"

"Lesbian."

"I thought it was okay to say *gay*."

"Sure, it's okay, but when you're talking about an individual, not a group of people, you'd might as well use the term that fits."

"Well, did you?"

"I don't remember even thinking about it. I liked your looks, sure, but I was most drawn to your bizarre habit of drinking beer over ice. I watched you pour three glassfuls before getting up the nerve to ask you to dance."

"I'm glad you did. I never would have, you know."

"I know. That's okay. I probably didn't even catch your eye, did I?"

"I never thought about that. No, I guess not. But you would now."

"Thanks."

Britt went back to her reading and Marie reached over, picked her *L'actualité* from the floor and tried to find her place in the article she was reading. But after a minute, she closed the magazine and put it on the floor beside her. She reached back and took Britt's free hand, her left, and brought it around in front of her, Britt's thumb on her right collar bone.

"Wait," Britt said, "Let's reverse everything. I've got to be able to write." So she changed the direction she was lying on the couch and lay back, now with her right arm across Marie's chest, her Bankruptcy book open to the Sullivan case, and her left hand making notes in the margin. Marie held Britt's right hand with her right, and pressed it against her collarbone.

"Do you remember what I was wearing that night?"

"That night at the Fargo? Sure. Grey striped skirt, plain blue blouse, maybe silk, non-sensible shoes."

"You probably thought I looked like a school marm."

"What I thought was that you looked adorable."

"Yeah, right."

"Adore-able. Don't argue."

"Well, I hadn't gotten dressed that morning thinking that I was going to be picked up by a lanky blond in a cowgirl shirt."

"I'm not sure *picked up* precisely explains what when on that night. I asked you to dance; I didn't pee on the table in front of you."

"What? That's gross."

"That's what fillies do when they're in heat and trying to get the attention of a gelding."

"You mean a stallion."

"Gelding. Stallions don't need much in the way of encouragement."

"But what can a gelding do?"

"Nothing, but she doesn't know that. For that matter, he doesn't know it either. A gelding doesn't know he's a gelding. They seem to have some sort of weird testosterone memory, like *I think there's some kind of reward behind that smell there, but what was it? What was it? Ahhh, never mind; I wonder if there's anything to eat around here?* So the mare gets kind of frustrated at his lack of focus and usually either bites him on the ass or pees in front of him."

"You as a filly in heat: it's not an image I ever would have thought of applying to you."

"Well, in a cross-species, homoerotic sort of way."

"You're crazy." Marie laughed and kissed Britt's thumb, feeling the book re-open behind her head, and hearing the scratch of Britt's pen as she made a note in the margin.

"Can I ask you another question?"

Britt looked up from her reading. "Umhmm."

"Maybe we could, umm, get to bed a little early tonight?"

"Sleepy?"

"You know what I mean."

"How nice it is to be asked."

"What do you mean?"

"It's nice to be asked, that's all. It makes me feel pretty."

"I think you're pretty."

"More than that. Sexy. Desirable. Desired."

"Those, too."

"More even than that. Desired as in sweaty-palms-and-damp-panties desired."

Marie rubbed her palms together. "No sweat, I'm afraid." Britt looked down at Marie, who turned her head so their eyes could meet. "However . . ."

"Truly?"

"Sopping. Will you take one out of two?"

"Any day."

"Don't we have sex often enough for you?"

"Yes, but it's nice when you suggest it."

Marie put her hands behind her head. For some reason, she felt a little nervous having this conversation, though oddly enough, it seemed to be increasing, rather than diminishing, her arousal. "I suggest it sometimes."

"Sure, with your eyes. Or with what you put on, or take off. But you don't often use the words, which are nice sometimes."

"Sometimes I say it."

"Twice since I moved in."

"Great. She's a goddam memory bank."

"The occasions were memorable; I remember every detail. One was a weekend morning. One was mid-week, after dinner, two weeks ago, maybe three. *The soldiers wore grey; you wore blue.*"

"What?"

"*Casablanca.* Again."

"Okay, so here. *Je veux faire une demande de permis de conduire.*" Marie moved Britt's hand down so that it covered her left breast.

"Does that mean what I think it means?"

"Probably not."

"What's it mean?"

"*I want to apply for a driver's license.*"

"Why did you say that?"

"It was the first thing that came to my mind. I was reading about corruption in the Montreal license bureau."

"How do you say *You may have your way with me?*"

"*Ce permis est valide pour sept ans.*"

"Are you telling me the truth?"

"*Peut-être que.*"

"What's that mean?"

"*Perhaps.*"

Britt let her hand lie where it was for a moment, then moved it to the top of Marie's head, where she ruffled her hair, then smoothed it back into place. She leaned forward and kissed the part, then spoke, mumbling into Marie's hair. "I like hearing you speak French. It makes me quiver."

Marie reached her right hand up over her head, searching, without looking, for the back of Britt's head, which she pulled into the corner of her neck. "*Oui? Quel chemin au bureau d'immatriculation des véhicules ?*" Another pause, then Marie took her hand back and continued, "Your finger, I'll bet, is still in the book."

"Yeah, it is. That's because I know for a fact that Randolph is going to call on me Tuesday for this case and I'm going to nail it and his ass to the wall."

"Is that why you aren't down here on the floor checking the moisture content of my underpants?"

"Yes. Do you mind? Can we wait a bit?"

"I can wait. In fact, it's good to wait."

"Good? Why?"

"That's what I liked least about sex with men."

"What?"

"Too goddam predictable." Britt laughed, as she opened her book and began to read. And Marie put her glasses on and went back to reading the *L'actualité*, trying the fathom the intricacies of *la politique québécoise*.

~

Around eleven, Britt finally closed the book on the Sullivan case, went upstairs, took a shower and slipped on her night shirt. In the bedroom, the overhead light was off, but the small table lamp lit the scene of Marie lying on her back in the middle of the bed, wearing nothing except, done up into the tiniest little G-string, her driver's license.

# 9

## ON THE NIGHT TRAIN FROM SOPHIA TO BUCHAREST

When Michael was planning the trip to Bulgaria, Romania and Yugoslavia, or his trip Behind the Iron Curtain, as he liked to think of it, spending a day in Athens at embassies and airline offices, he spoke by phone to the Romanian embassy. The embassy itself was outside of the city center that Michael knew well and a visit in person would have required a complicated bus ride. Actually the most complicated thing about the bus ride would have been finding the correct bus number and stop. That would be complicated because it would require Michael to explain why he didn't just take a taxi, taxis being very numerous and cheap in Athens. Such an explanation is beyond the English or patience of all Greeks and most tourists. So, Michael, who prefers both buses and trains to taxis, called the embassy of Romania.

"I plan to visit Romania. By airplane; perhaps by train."

"Yes?"

"Do I need a visa?"

"From where do you come?"

"America."

"No, of course not. Holders of United States passports may obtain visas at the border."

This sounded right, to Michael, sounded like acceptable diplomacy in early 1985. The L.A. Olympics with the Romanian defiance of the Rooski boycott was a fresh memory. The embassy woman on the phone sounded like a capitalist at heart; his mind's eye saw a thirteen year old Romanian gymnast twisting through the air, her tidy little body coming to a halt on the money, with a jiggle of neither baby fat nor womanhood, and mobbed by dozens of other little boycott-busters, to chants of "Russia sucks" and scores of perfect ten point zero. Ah, Romania, it was like coming home.

"Thank you very much."

The night train from Sophia to Bucharest was nearly empty, almost a month later, and none of this was particularly on Michael's mind as he watched out the window in the corridor of the sleeping car at the occasional lights of rural Bulgaria flashing by. If anything was on his mind, it was that the occasional lights of rural Bulgaria were essentially indistinguishable from the occasional lights of rural Oklahoma, flashing past the window of his Toyota pickup, heading west on I-40 toward a rendezvous with Marie. A Nigerian, studying medicine in Romania, shared the car—that is to say the sleeping car on the night train to Bucharest, not the Toyota pickup driving him west to see Marie—shared the car with him and a sleepy East German conductor. The ticket cost only US $12, payable in greenbacks in Sophia, and the sleeper was only US $10 more, payable ditto on the train, though the conductor eventually returned his entire twenty, unable to change it. His two travelling companions were at the opposite ends of the spectrum of talkativeness, in the obvious directions, and Michael had spent hours listening to the admittedly fascinating, though tiring, insights of the third-worlder on the socialist world, rendered in a sometimes difficult-to-follow west African accent. The train slowed as it approached the border, and pulled into a small, empty station at a town called Giurgiu, the last stop in Bulgaria, early in the morning.

Michael disembarked to stretch his legs and to let the Bulgarian customs people stamp him out of their country and show him where to change his Bulgarian money back to dollars, which he did not bother to do, as the exchange rate in that direction was so disadvantageous as to make it hardly worthwhile. He would, he thought, send his wad of Bulgarian cash to Marie, who could show it to her students. He stood on the steps of the car, then, while the train rolled across the Danube and into Romania. The spring night air was fresh and cold; the lights above the train, on the bridge, glowed with a dim greeny light, like the faces in a Toulouse-Lautrec painting, and were reflected in the water below. If he had been a smoker, he would have chosen just that moment to snap his cigarette over the bridge's railing, to *tsssst* in the Danube. In the station on the Romanian side, the train stopped and waited and the German conductor told him curtly to return to his compartment and await the customs people.

The Romanian border guard who knocked on the compartment door was no gymnast. He probably had supported the Rooski boycott. He clearly thought that obtaining visas at the border was an idea whose time had not come.

"Passport, please." Michael handed it over. It was now about two in the morning and he had fallen asleep waiting for this man's arrival. He felt disheveled and groggy.

"Where is your visa?" They were both speaking German. Michael was speaking it poorly, as always, and it was not the Romanian's first language either, of course. Besides, he hated Germans, and disliked speaking their language, even to Americans. Especially to Americans, maybe.

"I haven't one. I was told I could get one at the border."

"No, that is impossible." Impossible to do it or impossible that he had been told that? Michael didn't know.

"I was told I could get one at the border." Michael's German required that explanations were often redundant. The guard shook his head in—what? Disbelief? Dismay? At crazy Americans? Incompetent embassy staffers? CIA operatives who thought him a fool? At the general hopelessness of the human condition, socialist and capitalist alike?

The guard pocketed the passport. Michael had become rather used to officials taking his passport and disappearing for periods of time. He decided not to worry.

"Your luggage." He pulled his pack off of the rack over his head and set it on the opposite seat. The guard made a bored, one-handed gesture and said "Open." Michael unbuckled the straps and laid the top back. He started to unpack, but the guard, for the first time, smiled and shook his head *no*. He reached under the top layer of clothes and searched the pack, but perfunctorily. In the top pouch he found four books, the *Alexandria Quartet*, and he inquired about them. Michael could not understand the question in any real detail so he just shrugged. "About love." The guard studied the covers; it was impossible to tell what he thought Michael meant.

"What is your work?"

"Professor." That was a mistake and Michael knew it as soon as he said it.

"Professor?" The guard managed to insert substantial disbelief into that one word in a foreign language he disliked speaking. Perhaps Romanian for professor is *professor*. In Europe, Michael wouldn't be called a professor at all, and he knew it. *Instructor*, maybe, or *lecturer*, or *tutor* or some other obscure title. *Professor* in Europe is reserved for a relatively few senior scholars of distinguished reputation, not for youngish college teachers who can keep from being embarrassed in class and have written an article or two only their mothers have read. "*Professor?*" the customs guard repeated.

"*Ja.*" He was in over his head.

"Why are you not working?" Apparently Romanian professors don't run around in blue jeans and Wellingtons being tourists in March. Michael's German was not good enough to extract him; he couldn't explain leave-of-absence. "Holiday," he said in German.

"In March?"

"Ahhhh, . . . holiday."

"Professor of what?"

"I don't know the word. Well, mathematics. Sort of." This last phrase was in English and there was no reason to expect that the guard understood it.

He shook his head; with one gesture he managed to refer to Michael's entire outfit: jeans, tee shirt, no shoes, no socks, moustache, tattoo.

"Okay, so I looked a little bedraggled, but it's two in the morning, for Christ's sake. Cut me some slack." This was all in English.

"*Was?*" the guard wondered. Sometimes a spray of English will hurry things up at the border, sometimes not. The guard continued in German: "Look at you. Look at this." The backpack. "You don't look like a professor."

"My mother agrees with you in this regard." Michael's German wasn't up to this, either, and the English didn't seem to intimidate the guard, who shrugged.

Eventually he disappeared with Michael's passport and with much Romanian muttering. Michael fretted a bit, but the train was moving again and he figured that neither of them could get off, so he went back to sleep.

The two of them went through the entire process once more at about seven in the morning. It was as if the guard thought he must have been dreaming earlier. They repeated the same conversation. He disbelieved the same things. He muttered the same mutterings. As they pulled to a stop in the Bucharest station, the guard visited the sleeper once more, spoke some rapid German, or maybe even Romanian, and left, but Michael missed his command to follow. So a few minutes later the conductor put him in the custody of the foreign exchange agent and he gathered his things quickly, and hurried after.

The station was cold, crowded and grey. There were lots of soldiers around, not on duty but going somewhere, maybe home for the holidays. Exactly what holiday would be unclear. Spring Equinox. Trains were coming and going with much whistling, but the international car Michael was leaving behind was barricaded off from the rest. He caught up with the border guard, asked in German if he still had the passport and followed him into an office with a desk, two chairs, a bed, a map of Romania and a leaking roof. The guard apologized for the leak, offered a cigarette and the chair and sat behind the desk and turned to some paper work. While Michael doesn't smoke, he thought it would be impolite to refuse and this didn't appear to be the time to be impolite, so he took it and accepted a light. He smoked the cigarette, finding that it was not bad, though it made him cough and dizzy. After about a half an hour of silence and no more cigarettes, the guard stood up, stretched and left the office without a word.

"Good deal I'm not a chain smoker," Michael said to the closed door. He took off his shoes, lay down on the bed and stared at the ceiling, wondering if it was getting close to time to worry. He remembered his grandfather needling his grandmother back when he was just a child: "Now, Lorie," his grandfather would say, "if you want me to, I'll sit in that chair over there and I'll worry for a while. I don't think it will do any good, myself, but I'll do it for you." "Oh, Jack," his grandmother would say. His grandfather died of heart failure at 63; his grandmother at 79.

Eventually, the guard returned to the room and took him to the tourist bureau, there in the station, and the tourist agent, who spoke English, translated, and all the confusion was worked out. Michael explained that he taught at an important American university, which was a major overstatement, and was on leave to study in Greece, which was almost true if one read the word *study* very broadly. He declined a Greek verb for them, going for broke and assuming they would not know what he was saying. Finally the guard seemed satisfied, the integrity of the Romanian border had been protected and Michael got his visa and was on his way. Outside the station a man offered him black-market currency at four times the official rate. *I was not born yesterday* is a difficult concept to convey in rusty German, and he didn't try. He hopped the bus for city center, a bus so crammed with morning commuters that it hurt to breathe, and, with a stimulating awareness of where he was, and why, and reckoning that he had done better than some Romanian schmuck without a visa would do at the middle of the night at the American border, he rode through the unfamiliar streets of Bucharest.

ATHENS

Anna Browning sat and watched the traffic swirl around Omonia Square. A yellow No. 1 trolleybus, bound from Syntagma to the train station, swerved to miss a little Fiat and derailed itself. Sparks flew from the overhead wires and the loose antennae bounded on the springs and crossed over each other. The bus coasted to a halt and traffic piled up behind it.

She wasn't real sure where she was. Her mind had been playing tricks on her lately and sometimes she knew where she was and at other times she didn't. Tonight, she wasn't sure. The café itself had a familiar look to it, but where in the world the café was, or where all those cars were going, she didn't know.

Sometimes it bothered her not to know, but not tonight. It was worse when she couldn't remember where she had left the children. Then it was like she was crazy with worry that she had left them where they might be hurt. But not tonight. She knew she had left them with Ben and she knew they were safe, though she couldn't remember exactly who Ben was, or where.

The man sitting next to her at the small marble table was not Ben, she knew that. She laughed to herself. Somehow it was funny even to imagine that he might be Ben. She hoped she knew him, for his eyes were brown and gentle and when he spoke, his voice was soft. Of course he spoke a language that she didn't always understand. But there, those words right there meant did she want a cigarette. She took it and smoked.

Time passed in the way she had come to learn that time passes in Greek cafés. Her mind was clean, cool, clear; she thought of nothing. Time passed. She sipped her sweet Greek coffee, chewing the grains, and the traffic swirled around Omonia Square. It was really quite peaceful here. At last the man spoke quietly to her in that language she didn't always understand. His eyes were gentle and she hoped that she would soon remember who he was. He ran his fingers through her short blond hair and, later, he took her home.

～

The man with the brown eyes lay on the bed beside Anna. He had not really been all that gentle. Now he slept, and she knew that she had not known him before tonight, before he had bought her the coffee in the cafe on Omonia

Square. She sat up in the bed and lit a cigarette, looking around the room. This apparently was not a hotel room, for there were family pictures on the walls and a crucifix over the bed; out the window the street was tree-lined with cars parked on both sides. She dried between her legs with the corner of the top sheet, got up out of the bed and walked, naked, to the sliding glass balcony door. She pulled open the drapes.

Across the street, a wall—no, a wooden fence—covered with Greek graffiti, ran across the front of a lot between two apartment buildings. She smiled when she remembered how the co-eds back home would carefully paint the walls in front of their houses on College Street with the names of their sororities. It looked something like that fence across the street. Except that these words meant something. She now knew where home was and who Ben was and why the children were safe with him. She stood with her left arm across her chest, under her breasts, her right elbow on her left hand, the cigarette near her mouth, and she stared out the window. The smoke stung her eyes.

The building to the left of the fence across the street had a store of some kind on the ground floor, a bookstore, it looked like. Above the store, on the upper floors, were apartments, with small balconies, like the one on the other side of the glass door in front of her. Most were cluttered with bicycles and chairs and other stuff, but one, a story above her, had a table and two chairs and a man stood, leaning on the rail and smoking a cigarette. The end glowed red in the dark and his outline was indistinct in the street light. Mostly she could see his image against the lighted apartment behind him. Still, if she could see him smoking, he might be able to see her. She picked up the man's shirt from the floor at her feet and held it in front of her.

The man on the bed stirred and rolled over onto his back. He still slept, and sleep had brought him a new erection, still bloody from Anna's period. She eyed him, and his hairy little pot belly and his bloody dick with a detached distaste, then turned back to the window.

Behind the fence with the graffiti, a building was being constructed. Concrete had been poured for about two stories and wooden scaffolding stood that high. Above the incomplete structure, the Acropolis stood. A lucky accident let Anna look at it through the gap between the two buildings, a gap soon to be filled. The Parthenon glowed in the moonlight as if the marble were translucent and on the hillside below she could see the lighted nightclubs and hotels of the Plaka.

It was likely, she supposed, that she was a little bit insane. She had left many things behind when she had decided to come here, and many things undone. She had cut loose, left without a word. She knew that people were worried and angry and upset, but a point had come when it had been time to leave. Time to come here, for she had known that if she had not come here to go a little insane, she would have stayed there and gone mad.

Anna was pretty sure that she had originally decided to come to Athens to find Mike Reid and to tell him to stop writing and to leave her alone, but that feeling had gone away. She had found easily enough the café that Mike had written about and she had taken to going there at about the right time each night, thinking that maybe she would see him. She wasn't sure, of course, that he was even still in Greece, but she sat each night, under the beasts in *bas-relief* on the walls of the café that said *KAΦENEON* over the door, and watched for him. She could, she supposed, go to the island he had mentioned, but that would take a kind of energy she didn't have and besides, the café seemed to be the place to wait. She wasn't sure anymore why, exactly, she wanted to see him.

She never met him, though, not really. One night she thought she had seen him. He had come in and sat across the room and drunk a brandy and stared at her. She had started to get up to go over to him, but the man at the table with her, not this man here in the bed but another one, had put his hand on her shoulder and had spoken Greek and gestured as if to say, *No, play it as it is written*. So she had stayed and a bit later had picked up her packages and left, but at the door, when she looked over her shoulder, he had not looked up and had gone on reading. She suspected, standing now, looking at the Acropolis, that it had not been Mike there at all. Or anyone. Her mind played tricks on her sometimes.

She continued to go back to the café, to drink coffee and to wait. It was really quite peaceful there. Is it possible, she wondered, for something to be both the cause and the cure for one's insanity? A car went along the street below, flashed its lights at the next intersection, and was gone. It reminded her of the sea gull that had glided out of and back into the fog that day when she and Rachel sat on the beach on St. George Island. She wished that she could move as effortlessly as that gull or the car along the street below. She would gobble a blue crab, or flash her lights and be gone from this world or that one and on to another. And those that stayed behind and watched would see her come and go and think it perfectly natural that someone could move so freely and effortlessly.

Is it possible to see someone without being seen? Anna looked at the man across the street on the balcony, a story above her. He was looking, perhaps, at her standing in the window, lighted by the street light; she couldn't tell. She stepped closer to the balcony door and dropped the shirt she was holding. The street light gave her body a washed-out color and lightened her hair even more than was natural. She had lost weight since coming to Athens—she found she disliked Greek food—and her ribs showed. Her breasts, now that the nursing was over, had become small again. And her hair was now short; she had had it cut off, above her ears. She guessed that from across the street, if she could be seen at all, she would look like a fair-haired boy standing naked in a dark apartment. She stepped closer to the door, reached her hands up over her head and put her palms on the glass. It was cool to the touch, holding back the March night. She pressed her body against the door and could feel the glass with her knees and thighs and hair and belly and breasts and elbows. She felt clean and cool standing there, except for two fingers, where the cigarette now burned close to the filter. She leaned her forehead on the glass and stared at the man across the way.

The man was too far away for Anna to see his expression and there was really no way to tell if he could see her or not. It was really quite dark and she knew it was possible that the very same street light that illuminated her body might reflect from the glass door and obscure her from his eyes. He continued to look at her, or maybe not, and to smoke. She stood in the light that both lit her and hid her, and watched him.

Finally he finished his cigarette, flicked it in a red arc to the street below and went back inside and closed the door. Anna put her own cigarette out in the ash tray by the bed. The man slept, now on his stomach, with his face turned toward her. The sheets, she saw, were really a mess and he would probably be unhappy when he awoke on them in the morning. She picked up her underwear off the floor, walked into the bathroom, where she made herself a pad out of toilet paper, and walked back to the bedroom. She had placed her wrist watch and her silver necklace with the small sapphire carefully on the table by the bed, and she put these two things on first. She tossed her head with a little flick, for the gesture had remained even after she had cut her hair, and she finished dressing, slowly and quietly. For a few minutes she wandered around the bedroom and out into the living room of the small, nicely-kept apartment, holding her shoes in her hand and looking at the pictures on the walls and the books in the shelves. It was a small, pleasantly furnished apartment, she thought, with a homey feel to it. She picked up some pillows they had left on the living room floor and arranged them on the sofa; she straightened the magazines and knick-knacks on a coffee table. She wondered whether the man would awaken, but he didn't as she let herself out of the apartment, put on her shoes and walked to her hotel through the deserted streets of Athens.

## SIBIU, ROMANIA

It was one of those situations in which you realize, in a flash, how bad something might have been at the very same instant you realize that it isn't going to be that bad. It was a situation without anticipation and with neither fore- nor after-boding; it was one in which you knew it was all over and would turn out well at the same moment it began and you knew it could have been disastrous.

Michael Reid stood in the concourse of the train station in Sibiu, a small city in central Romania. He had just disembarked the train from Brashov, on which he had ridden the spring evening through the Transylvanian highlands. The concourse was busy with passengers rushing this way and that, and he stood still in the hectic environs and enjoyed the feel of the strangeness of the place. His pack was slung over one shoulder and his hands were in his jeans pockets, his cap on the back of his head, as he reconnoitered and began the search for a hotel. He was about to step with his right foot toward where the tourist bureau might be, reckoning that it was probably closed anyway and rolling the appropriate German phrases around on his tongue. He felt no foreboding, nor any disquiet.

A hand tapped his shoulder from behind. He turned around and a man stood there holding out toward him Michael's wallet. He immediately knew he had left it on the seat next to him on the railroad car. It hadn't slipped out of his pocket; hadn't fallen from his pack. He immediately recalled placing it on the seat when he had pulled his pack down from above and he recalled then walking away without picking it up. He immediately knew how close he had come to what passed for tourist disaster. And he immediately knew that everything was to turn out all right.

It was all over that quickly. Anxiety and relief rushed over him simultaneously and produced the strangest sensation on his skin. The man, who was so non-descript that Michael could not have recognized him in the crowd five minutes later, handed him the wallet and they shook hands. Michael was so nonplused that he was nearly speechless. He did not say, as would have been sensible, *Do you speak English*? Or *Kanst du Deutsch*? He did not offer a reward. He stood with one hand over his heart and with the wallet in the other and said only "Thank you, thank you, thank you" in English. The man offered a small wave and a smile and was gone.

As soon as his wits returned from wherever they go at such times, which was about as long as graciousness required, though he wasn't thinking of being gracious, Michael checked the inside of the wallet. His passport and his money all were obviously still there. He stood in the concourse with the passengers still swirling around him and shook his head at the experience.

For the novice traveler, the loss of a passport may seem the ultimate misfortune. Michael knew otherwise. He had lost his twice—technically only once, for he had faked it the other time, just to see how the replacement system worked—and he knew that, in general, inconvenience, not tragedy, followed. Likewise money, assuming one is savvy enough not to carry too much cash. But this was his first trip into the socialist world and the rules seemed different here. For instance, he was running rather regularly into the police and was being made to exhibit his passport on the street, something that happened approximately never to him elsewhere in the world. And he was carrying most of his funds in cash on this excursion, having been told, quite inaccurately it appeared, that travelers checks were not liquid enough where he was heading.

He checked the clock on the station wall. 20.32. Eight-thirty. Sure enough, the tourist bureau was closed. But Romanian for *hotel* is *hotel* and after a few inquiries he found his way to the trolley stop in front of the station and there got advice to hop the No. T1, which would take him by the Hotel Boulevard, or so his ear told him. That could be the name of a hotel, or a street on which there were several. He would have to see. There were no empty seats when he climbed on, so he stood with his pack between his feet, bent to watch out the window for the hotel, and with an electric jolt the trolleybus started off, threatening to rattle itself apart before it made one more circuit. Not for the first time he found himself amused at the great commie empire as it was perceived at home. If this bus were any indication, the hegemony would fall into rusty dust all by itself before long. If the stranger on the train were any indication that would be too bad. The trolleybus left the station behind, lumbered past a high wall enclosing, he would discover later, a fascinating old town, and headed into the modern, rather grey streets of Sibiu.

Relatively soon after arriving in the Soviet Bloc, that is to say, on the first full day he was in Sophia, that is to say about two weeks ago, Michael had begun attracting the attention of the police. The first time—the first time *ever* in his travels—had been while he was taking a random walk through the city and found himself in a pleasant park on the overcast spring day. The dirty slush on the sidewalk made the going unsteady, and he was concentrating as much on his footing as anything. Two policemen approached; he was about to tip his cap and pass by when one of them spoke.

"Bulgarian, bulgarian, bulgarian, bul . . . "

"I'm sorry. I don't speak Bulgarian."

"Passport, p'leess."

"Am I doing anything wrong? I don't want to do anything wrong."

Silence.

He handed over his passport, then had to help them find his Bulgarian visa. He was vaguely proud that it was difficult to find, sandwiched between stamps from India and Thailand and the Caribbean. Apparently the police were satisfied.

"Go that way, p'leess."

"But I wanted to go over there, to see that." In the distance, across a park was some sort of . . . what? . . . a gathering. A group of about fifty people were standing off to the side of the path. He thought he could hear singing. Children's voices?

"That way," one officer said, firmly.

Middle-aged white men are not used to such treatment in the USA, and it did not go down easily with Michael Reid.

The next time was at the train station. He had decided not to use his Sophia-to-Bucharest airplane coupon, which had been practically free anyway, due to an odd pricing scheme, and was determined to take the train to Romania. The business had to be done at the shiny, nearly new train station, with signs in Bulgarian and French. At the international ticket window therein, tickets to places outside Bulgaria were bought with hard currency and with some formalities. So after he had set his plans on the Sunday night train, Michael returned to the station for the ticket, but first he roamed the concourse, looking for something to eat.

"Bulgarian, bulgarian, bul . . . ."

"I'm sorry. I don't speak Bulgarian."

"Passport, p'leess."

Maybe it was his clothes. It was much colder in Sophia than in Athens, so on his first morning there he had visited the large state department store and bought a warm coat, not the brightly colored K-mart-like ski wear that many people wore on the streets of Sophia, nor an expensive fur, which were also seen, but a bottom-of-the-line, Rooski-made pea coat, knee length, double-breasted, with a big collar. He tucked his jeans into knee-high black rubber Wellingtons, wrapped a bright scarf around his neck, turned the collar up, pulled his cap down low and put on sun glasses. His untrimmed moustache meant that his mouth was essentially invisible, and you couldn't see his lips move. He looked, in other words, exactly like the kind of fellow the police—whether in Sophia or the Ozarks—would never let near a Girl Scout field trip, if that was what the gathering in the park had been. Now, again, in the train station:

"Passport, p'leess."

This time, he had his wits about him. He pushed his cap back on his head, but purposefully left his sun glasses on. "May I see your badge?" The plainclothesman was about his height, thus short, nicely dressed in a leather jacket and turtleneck sweater. He produced an impressive looking plastic card with his photo. It could have been his YMCA card. He smiled. "Was I doing anything wrong?" Michael asked. The plainclothesman inspected his passport. Without any fuss, they were gradually surrounded by several plainclothesmen. They handed his passport around. "I don't want to do anything wrong."

"Thank you," the policeman said in English, and handed it back. There, that hadn't been so bad; I'm getting good at this. Michael returned his attention to finding a snack to eat. Maybe a pastry.

"Passport!" This fellow was much bigger than the other one. He did not smile. He did not say *P'leess*. Michael's wits fled and he handed it over. This one did not even look at it, but rather put it in his pocket and set out across the station. Michael started to say, "But, I just showed it to that one . . .", but the other one was nowhere to be seen and, in any case, the new one was gone, heading across the main concourse, who-knows-where with his passport. Over his shoulder he said: "Follow me."

This fellow had mastered a stride so that he could appear to walk easily while quickly, but Michael, behind and with shorter legs, had almost to run in order to keep up. The public area of the station disappeared as they were quickly through one set of frosted glass doors, then more. Finally, outside another pair of swinging doors, the policeman, if that is what he was, turned and said, in English, "Wait."

There was nowhere to sit, so Michael leaned against the wall of the corridor and tried to figure out if he should be worried. He decided against it, for now. He looked up and down the hallway; it was mostly empty and could have been downstairs in the Madison County Courthouse at home. The Sophia County Agricultural Extension Agent was probably housed just around that corner. It was amusing to imagine the commie equivalent of Agent Boger at home, who thought that if God had not intended that forests be clear-cut, He wouldn't have created chain saws. What could go wrong here? Occasionally someone would walk in or out of the doors through which the policeman had disappeared and he could catch a glimpse of him at the counter. Reading and writing. Michael waited. For some reason, it popped into his head the time on the Sri Lankan bus the previous summer when he had fretted away a pleasant afternoon's bus ride worrying about getting ripped off for twenty cents. Less than that. Now he was facing the Gulag or something and he was overcome with calm. Richard would appreciate the irony of that.

After ten minutes or so, the policeman emerged and handed Michael his passport, pocketing a scrap of paper on which, in careful block Roman letters, was written "RICHARD RANDOLPH", copied from the *in case of emergency* box on the passport's inside front cover. Michael smiled to himself. He supposed this meant that his friend had become *persona non grata* in Bulgaria. *Sorry, Richard, I shall have to warn you of this before you visit Coфúa.*

"Was I doing anything wrong?" he asked, as they walked, more slowly now, back toward the public part of the station. "I don't want to do anything wrong."

"Ordinary police operation." As he showed Michael the way out, the policeman asked if he was enjoying his visit to Sophia. In fact, Michael was, and said so. The policeman apparently believed it, not supposing that fifteen minutes to establish one's identity would spoil an otherwise enjoyable holiday in Bulgaria.

That same afternoon, Michael sent a postcard to Anna Browning: "Here, isst *no* margink for error!" But of course she did not receive it until much later.

All of that had happened roughly two weeks before he had nearly lost his wallet on the evening train from Brashov to Sibiu, and before he checked into the very nice and more-expensive-than-he-usually-chose hotel, called, in fact, the Hotel Boulevard on the T1 trolley line. Spring had begun in earnest here and the entire day's experience made the police seem far away and the margin for error, once again, if not large, at least manageable.

## TALLAHASSEE

At about the same time that Anna was finding her way through the quiet, dark streets of the Athens night from the stranger's apartment to her hotel, and at about the same time that Michael was having himself a nightcap in the long bar at the Hotel Boulevard in Sibiu, Ben Browning was joking with his graduate students over beers at the Flamingo Cafe on Tennessee Street in Tallahassee. They were comparing quotations from the latest batch of English 1101 papers, which were spread out on the table in front of them. Ben supervised the required freshman English course and was teaching one section, penitence for having offended the chairman in some departmental battle. *Fuck him,* Ben thought, *my chance will come.* In the meantime, teaching the freshmen was only marginally injurious to one's sanity. Pathological. *The pathological characteristics of the freshman English student.* The plan for a satiric essay took shape in his mind, as he listened to one of the TAs read an excerpt.

The rest of the 1101 sections were taught by the grad students, mostly MA candidates, and this year, all male, and they had taken to meeting like this once a week to rehash the papers over a few beers. Unbeknownst to them an author or two of the papers sat nearby and knew exactly what they were doing, but Ben's and his students' spirits were sufficiently high that they wouldn't have cared much if they had known. It was Ben's turn again, and he had to be going.

"I have saved, my friends," he said over the din of the bar, "I have saved the best for last. I offer this for your consideration: *Blooming azaleas in the Tallahassee March look like my head used to feel on acid.*" They all laughed. "Let's drink," he lifted his glass, "to freshmen. To Southern freshmen. To all things Southern. To pinheads. To Southern writers and the nitwits who aspire to be them. To knuckleheads and dimwits. To persons whose heads are too small, whose eyes are too close together. To ignorance. To in-breeding. To cleft palates. To Jesus H. Christ in all his Southern forms. To the curse of affirmative action, with which the South has burdened us all. May the future hold better for each of us than that which the present offers. *Blooming azaleas in the Tallahassee March look like my head used to feel on drugs.*" He shook his head. "God damn it, but it's hard not to feel superior to these people. Why try? Gentlemen: The South!" He drained his glass. "Now, worms, I've got to go. As you know, I am still living the life of bachelor father, and d'chillun muss be tended to."

"What do you hear from your wife?" one of the grad students asked.

"She seems well. Her sister is improving, apparently, so there's some hope that she will soon be home."

"A lot of trouble for you, with the kids and the baby."

"No more than can be handled by the unusually superior parent."

"I'm surprised she didn't take the baby with."

Ben practically slammed his empty glass onto the table. "My God, Hamilton, when are you going to shed that disgusting upper-Midwesternism of taking or going *with*?" He stood up while he let the words sink in. "You're as bad as some fucking freshman. How in the world did you get to be a TA? Oh, yes: you went to Iowa, didn't you?" He turned to go, then spun on his heel and came back to the table. "And don't worry about the baby. I can do anything, post-partum, that the absent Dr. Browning can do, except lactate, and it was time the child ended that particular practice anyway. And finally, not that it is any of your fucking businesses—or, as they say in these parts, *ewe-all's fucking business*—you will have noted the absence lately from the byways of Williams Hall of your colleague Ms. Nikki Wallace, soon-to-be PhD, aspiring literary critic, and, you have always suspected, for I know the graduate student mind, an excellent piece of ass. That dear womanchild is this very minute probably powdering my little one's rashy ass, even while checking on the roast in my oven, all quite voluntarily, I assure you, and out of gratitude for the help I have given her over the years and, I might add, the least that she might do for the chairman of her dissertation committee." He picked up Hamilton's unfinished glass of beer. "Gentlemen, I give you the future Dr. Wallace, no Southerner she."

Ben drained the student's beer and backed away from the table, bowing, as they all lifted their glasses and cheered the speech. And they admired him, they really did, and when he left they shook their heads and wondered whether he really *was* putting it to Nikki Wallace—whom, he was right, they had all lusted after—while his wife was nursing her sick sister. "God damn the old bastard," they said, shaking their heads, "and here's hoping he is."

~

When Ben walked in the front door of his house, it was almost like Anna was home. Nikki sat comfortably in the living room, holding Rachel and reading. He could hear the television playing for the older children in the back room, and he could smell dinner cooking. It was about eight-thirty; he and Anna generally dined late.

"Hi," he said.

Nikki looked up from her book and smiled. "Hi." She put Rachel on the floor and patted her padded behind. "Go say hello to your father, Rachel." The baby waddled, silently smiling, across the room and allowed herself to be picked up by Ben. Of all the things he wondered about Anna's absence, he wondered most about what Rachel thought. Sam and Janet were old enough to be lied to and, while they missed their mother, he had insisted that they act their ages. But Rachel could only know that one who was once here was no longer here and wonder why.

As he picked the little girl up, he took the cigarette from his mouth and held it out to Nikki. "Here, finish this if you like. What are you reading?" he asked, gesturing at the book lying on the couch.

Nikki stood up from the couch, walked over and took the cigarette. "DeLillo's latest." She took a drag.

"*White Noise*. Any good?"

"I'm actually enjoying it. No reason to expect that you'd like it, though. God, you smell half-brewery, half-ashtray. Where have you been? The Grand Finale?"

"Flamingo. With the 1101 TAs. They said to say *hi*. They said little else of interest."

"So why do you spend time with them? I wonder if they suspect we're sleeping together."

"Do you care what they think?"

"Of course, I do. I have to be around them all the time. I still go to school with them, you know, even though I'm spending most of my waking hours over here just now."

"Complaints?"

"No, but still, I wouldn't want them to get the wrong idea about us. I've had to discourage the attentions of a couple of the boys, you know. What I don't need now is to have to deal with a flurry of just-out-of-undergrad jealous ire."

Ben reached out with the free hand and stroked her brunette wave. Rachel imitated the gesture, but couldn't reach Nikki's head. Then with his index finger, he placed her hair behind her ear, while stroking her cheek with his thumb. "We could, of course, make their suspicions real. There is so much inaccuracy in the world these days, I hate to promote more. I'll bet you are just spectacular in bed."

She put her own hand up and pulled his away from her face, and held it in front of them. "I believe we've discussed this. You are the smartest, best-read person I know, and you are the kind of crit I hope to be. I'm in the process of writing the best damn dissertation that you will ever have supervised, and you will have a feeling as close to pride as you ever get when I get my degree. Furthermore, I love your children and am happy to help out and to keep my mouth shut about Anna. But, recall, you're married. And while it is sometimes such a bother, I don't sleep with married men. Ever. There's no future in it." She patted his hand and dropped it, then tickled Rachel's exposed belly button.

"While it may sound heartless to mention it in this context, you may have noticed that my technically marital bed is cold and empty just now, and that my wife is not among those present."

"*Technically* is enough for me. Now . . . Rachel, entertain your father. I'll open the wine and let it breathe before dinner. I bought a very nice seventy-eight Mont-Redon Chateauneuf du Pape with a mid-range two-figure price tag, which, I assume, your budget will be able to afford. I also fed the children. The dinner will be ready in forty-five minutes and we can sit and discuss DeLillo's new book in quite civilized peace. How's that? The *Times* is on the table over there, in which there's a review of Byatt's *Still Life*, which you will not like as it refers to her *acute and supple mind*. Nevertheless, you should read it. Or play with the baby for a while before I put her to bed."

"Perhaps I should read her the op ed page instead? Or do you think the stock quotations would be better? You seem to have some considerable expertise when it comes to my children." *Bitch*, he added to himself by way of silent punctuation.

"Why, I've put you in a bad mood, haven't I?, by reminding you that my sweet and lovable, if not-exactly virginal, nether regions are unavailable to you, not least because of your present marital condition. Poor darling. Bounce her on your knee while reading the paper. She doesn't take much entertaining. You know, one of the things I admire about you most is that I doubt that sleeping with me or not makes one whit of difference in what you think of me. Your standards are incorruptible, I think; I am going to pass my orals with honors whether or not you get into my pants, am I not? Making me think like you is more important to you than screwing me, isn't it?"

He turned to look at the little girl in his arms. "Do you know what she's talking about, Rachel? No? Well, I haven't the slightest idea either. She seems to have the idea that I care whether she ever becomes a doctor of philosophy, or not. That's odd, isn't it?" Rachel began to get bored with the conversation, and squirmed to be let down. She still said nothing. Ben shifted Rachel to the other side and looked back at Nikki, as if to study her. "Still, there *is* something at stake here. Yes. A career in literary criticism. A future book reviewer, perhaps, for . . . oh . . . the *Grand Forks Herald*, has been changing your diaper today, Rachel. Cherish the thought. She may have shared with you judgments that will someday influence the entire literary community of northeastern North Dakota. Honey chile, . . .", he put his free hand on the top of Nikki's head, "your allegedly agile mind and your self-described sweet—more likely pungent— pussy are of roughly equal and passing concern to me. I may recall in the morning which one—or both—I engaged while chewing the roast beef, but I doubt it. Now, *do* let the wine breathe; I have a child to entertain."

Nikki backed away from him. "Avert the baby's eyes," she said, and when Ben turned Rachel's head toward his shoulder, she gave him the finger, two fingers, actually, one with each hand, then turned and walked through the dining room to the kitchen. Ben watched her go and he had to think that she gave her ass just a little extra flick as she turned the corner. She really was an extraordinary young woman, by God, just extraordinary. He lit another cigarette and bounced the baby on his knee until it was her bedtime, not bothering to read the *Times*.

# ~ 10

## ALBUQUERQUE

Three weeks earlier, Britt and Marie had spent a Saturday night making marinara sauce and stuffed manicotti for the freezer, and now, after a long day at school, Marie had taken it out and heated up a plate for each of them, with green salad and Italian bread from the market, warmed and buttered. Britt had not arrived by seven o'clock, so Marie set the table, lit a candle, and helped herself. She ate slowly, and was just finishing when she heard the sound of Britt's car pull in behind the duplex. A minute later, she came bursting through the door, dropped her backpack full of books on the floor and came over to kiss Marie on her part.

"Sorry I'm late. Randolph is not giving me a minute to turn around."

"That's okay; sorry I didn't wait."

"I'll be down in a minute. Let *me* clean up after."

"That's all right. I've got nothing to do tonight."

Britt ran up the stairs two at a time. Marie heard the sound of her peeing, then a flush, then water running in the sink. She was back down in a minute, like she said, by which time Marie had taken her warm plate out of the oven.

"Sit. Want a glass of red?"

"Better not; gotta study. Water with bubbles. Thanks."

Marie poured a glass, then sat down across from Britt, put her elbow on the table, her chin in her hand, and smiled. "You're hungry."

"Had to skip lunch," Britt said around a mouthful of manicotti. "I wasn't prepared for Antitrust. Got the cases read, then didn't get called on. How was your day? You talk, so I don't have to talk with my mouth full."

"Nothing really very interesting. The seventh graders are supposed to be doing papers on the geography of an African country, pick one, and mostly they're copying stuff from the encyclopedia. It always amuses me that seventh graders are surprised that I can tell they didn't write what they copied word-for-word from the encyclopedia. Don't feed the dog at the table."

"*You* feed the dog at the table."

"I feed her only if she doesn't beg; you feed her only when she begs. That's the difference."

Britt leaned down and got nose-to-nose with Ginger. "Oooo, mamamamam," she hummed and smacked her lips, then allowed Ginger to lick the marinara off her fingers. "Go on, Virginia. Go lie down now." The dog walked to her bed and lay down, on the look-out for any crumbs that might fall.

"There was an odd message on the machine from sometime this afternoon."

"What?"

"Quote: *Robin*. Then a number. Then a dial tone. Maybe it was a wrong number. Area code nine-oh-something, I think. I left it on the machine; maybe you can recognize the voice."

"There's only one person in the world who calls me *Robin*: my friend Nikki Wallace."

"Robin? How did that come from *Britt*?"

"My uncle gave it to me after watching me chase robins across the lawn one day at their place back east. It stuck. As I got older, I hated it, and I convinced everyone else to give it up, even my parents. But Nikki ignored my wishes and kept with *Robin*. I adore her, notwithstanding."

"How'd she get this number?"

"I called her the other day, got her machine, and left it."

"May I call you *Robin*?"

"No."

"This Nikki. She's just a friend? Or . . .." Marie left the thought hanging.

"Careful, Angel. Being jealous of my women friends is the first sign that you may have jumped the fence for good."

"Did she say *I'm not sure if we should do this*?"

Britt laughed, covering her mouth to keep the manicotti in. "Decent guess, but no."

"Who was that?"

"Girl named Rindy. End of discussion. But Nikki was the first one I told about what Senator Dominici calls my *sex-shul or-ee-enn-tay-shun*."

"How did you do that?" Britt looked up, a fork of salad greens, dripping vinegar and oil, half-way to her mouth. She said nothing. "Well, you know, I'm going to have to do that, I guess. Someday." Marie's voice was very small, and she looked down at the table when she said it.

Another pause, then Britt spoke, "Well, I guess it's different for everybody." She took a sip of soda water. "Let's see. Nikki and I have been best friends since we were the tallest kids in fourth grade, boys or girls. You know how little girls are: we talked about everything, including a couple of confusing crushes."

Marie interrupted: "Sarah?"

"Of course. Most girls end up being in love with their riding instructor, in my experience. Anyway, by junior high we were inseparable, and by high school, obnoxiously so. We did everything together, except that I rode and she played soccer and softball. She was the All-City shortstop our senior year. So, we went to each other's competitions, and she was there, not when I broke my arm, but the next weekend when I went back over the jump. We started smoking together, and started dating at the same time. In high school, can you believe it?, we even dated a set of twins."

"Really?"

"Yup. Probably just so we could always double date. Anyway, we graduated from high school, both virgins. I went to UNM. She went to St. John's up in Santa Fe. We saw each other a lot, and burned up the phone lines.

"So, during my freshman year, I slept with a couple of guys, then kind of settled back in with my twin. After one typically uninspiring date, during which I spent most of my time thinking about the TA in my Chemistry course, I sat up all night in the commons room at the dorm, thinking and smoking. By morning, I knew it wasn't him, or them. It was me."

"The classic line." Marie reached over and filled Britt's glass with club soda, then topped off her glass of wine out of the same bottle, making the red wine a pale, fizzy pink.

"A cabernet cooler? Yeah, the classic line, except I meant it a bit more profoundly than is usual. So, about four in the morning, I called Nikki and told her."

"What did she say?"

"*You woke me at four in the morning to tell me something I've known for three years?*"

Marie laughed. "Did she? *Know*, I mean."

"Maybe. I don't know. I didn't. Maybe she didn't mean three years literally. But it doesn't surprise me at all that she suspected before I did. She's like that."

"Whatever happened with the TA?"

"Nothing. I knew I liked hanging around after lab talking to her, but that night sitting up all night smoking, I realized that what I'd really like was to go out on a date with her. Dinner and a movie, that kind of thing."

"That's it? Dinner and a movie?"

"I didn't really think much beyond that. I was nineteen. A goodnight kiss, maybe."

"So . . . ?"

Britt shrugged. "I tried to let her know very indirectly that if she asked me out, I'd say *yes*. But she never did."

"So, when did it happen?"

"How much do you feel like talking to me about the first time you got laid?"

"Not much."

"Me neither."

"Fair enough. But it never happened with this Nikki?"

"God, no. Nikki's as straight as the homestretch. So, anyway, we don't see each other as much as we used to, but we still burn up the phone lines. She's probably calling to coordinate our Oscar phone call."

Marie got up from the table rather abruptly and began clearing the dishes. "Oscar phone call?"

"Hold on. Wait. I'm not done here." Britt took her salad plate, still half-full, back from Marie's hand.

"Oh, sorry. What Oscar phone call?" She turned her back to the table and began scraping the plates into the sink.

"In high school and college, we would sit up and watch all the awards together, but when we graduated and moved away we couldn't, so we began to watch them together, so to speak, long distance, sitting in front of different TVs in different cities, talking on the phone while the show was going on. The presenters, the gowns, the songs, whatever. Just like we used to do. A huge phone bill, but don't worry, I'll pay you back."

Still with her back turned, Marie began rinsing the dishes and putting them into the dishwasher. "So what happened to the two of you after graduation?"

"Well, I joined the Forest Service, and she got admitted to some brainy Master's program at Princeton. But she dropped out after a semester, and then kind of beat around. She worked at a bank in New Jersey, then sold ads for *Ms.* magazine in New York City for a while. . . ."

"I thought *Ms.* magazine didn't sell ads."

"This was before. Then she came home and moved back in with her folks. Finally, she decided she wanted to be a writer, and got herself admitted to the writing program at Florida State, and she's been there for quite a while now. Several years. But now she's switched from writing to literary criticism. *Lit crit*, she calls it. I think she'd like to teach. We haven't spoken for a while; I'll catch up on Oscar night and bring you up to date."

"I've been meaning to tell you, there might be a problem with Oscar night." Marie now turned around from the sink, but busied her hands clearing the rest of the dishes from the table, not catching Britt's eyes.

"A problem? What kind of problem?" Britt sopped up the last of the oil and vinegar with the last piece of bread.

"Well, some of the teachers from school sort of invited themselves over here to watch the show, and I thought, well, you'd probably be at the library anyway, and that it would be okay." Marie turned back to loading the dishwasher.

"The library." Britt stared at Marie's back.

"Yeah, you know, it's a school night, and I figured you'd have to study, you know. And we'd be making such a racket. I figured that we'd disturb your studying, and you'd have to head off to the library." Her voice trailed off at the end.

"The library." Britt's voice was flat, emotionless.

There was silence in the kitchen, except for the clattering of the china and silver. The fridge clicked off, increasing the silence. A car went by on the street outside, but even its departure seemed to increase the silence. The dog looked up from her bed at the quiet, glancing from one of them to the other.

Marie finally broke the silence. "Hey, listen. Never mind. It'll be okay. I can beg off or make an excuse or something. There's no reason to have a party on a school night. Us or you. Never mind. It'll be fine."

Neither said anything for a few moments, Britt sitting at the table with her hands folded in front of her. Then she spoke, "No, no. You go ahead, tell them yes. Actually, I think it will be a pretty busy time at school and I probably will have to spend the night at the library. That's what I was going to tell Nikki:

I don't know how she can find the time to watch the Oscars and be working on her PhD at the same time. Go ahead. I'll be okay. Really."

"We'll see."

The silence weighed heavily on the kitchen, until Britt pushed back her chair, carried her glass over to the counter where Marie was standing, put the glass down, patted Marie on the shoulder, and turned and walked upstairs to the room they had set up as a study. There was still a single bed in the room, which, of course, could make the room pose as a second bedroom. She left the overhead light off, sat down at her desk, but rather than opening her books, she stared out onto the street, illuminated by one flickering streetlight.

She waited.

Marie finished loading the dishwasher and cleaning up the table. That, she knew, had not gone well, and she hated herself for the entire thing, starting from the time when Jill had said *Let's do the Oscars at Marie's* and she had not taken either of the two honorable approaches, of telling Jill about Britt, or of begging off immediately. Now, she was terribly embarrassed, and guessed that Britt was waiting upstairs for her to come up and for them to talk. But Marie didn't know what to say, other than that she hated herself for the whole mess, including, especially, that conversation in the kitchen. She wanted very much to walk up the stairs and talk about it, but instead she clicked to Ginger, and took her leash off the hook by the door. Talking quietly up the stairs, she said, "I'm going to take the dog out."

Silence.

"Okay?" Again, a little louder: "Okay?" And from the study, a small flat response: "Okay."

And, when the door to the outside closed, Britt picked up her notepad and began the process of translating her scrawling notes from Richard Randolph's bankruptcy class into something comprehensible.

〜

Marie went to bed at about ten that night, saying *Good night* quietly to the closed study door. There was no response, but maybe she had said it too softly to be heard. She undressed, put on her pajamas, and lay in bed on her left side, watching the red lights on the radio towers blink from the top of the Crest, trying to think about nothing, letting sleep come.

It still had not when, nearly midnight, she heard Britt open the study door, use the toilet, brush her teeth and walk into the dark bedroom. Marie listened while she got undressed, and heard her slip on the night shirt she wore to bed, then felt the mattress move as Britt lay down and got herself settled on her side.

"I'm sorry." Marie said it with a very small voice, not turning over.

"I know. Go to sleep."

"I'm sorry."

"I know. It'll be okay. Go to sleep."

"When I was learning . . ."

"Shhhhh," Britt shushed her, "let's not talk tonight." She moved over so that her head was on Marie's pillow, and their bodies were spooned together, Marie's back to Britt's front. "Go to sleep. It'll be okay. Really. I'm not mad."

But Marie kept talking, softly, toward the wall and out the window and toward the blinking red lights on the Crest, still not turning over to face Britt. "When I was learning how to scuba dive, he started us with snorkels. In fact, on the first day, we weren't allowed masks, either. He wanted us to see that a mask was not really necessary, which is important later. So we stood in the shallow end, and you'd take a breath through your mouth, then swallow, to close off your nasal passage, then you'd start breathing with your mouth, through the snorkel. And you'd bend your legs and lower yourself into the water, so that it rose up your throat to your chin, then over your mouth, to just under your nose. But the last little bit was hard. It was like your lungs rebelled, and refused to go on breathing when you wanted to put your nose under water. I can still remember the feeling of this catch in my chest when the water came up to cover my nostrils. I had been in the water my whole life and wasn't scared of it at all, and I *knew* that I could keep breathing through the snorkel even with my nose under the water, but still there was something about me that was scared that I wouldn't be able to breathe."

She paused for a moment, and pushed her little body back closer into Britt's, and Britt put her right arm over Marie, and held Marie's left shoulder.

"It's like that," Marie said. "It's like I'm not sure I'm going to be able to breathe."

"I know," said Britt. "Go to sleep now. It'll be okay."

And Marie lay there, against the warm softness of her lover, and felt Britt's arm relax and get heavier across her side, and felt Britt's grip on her shoulder relax, and heard Britt's breathing become deep and regular, until she was asleep. But Marie lay there, listening and thinking almost until the sky became grey, before she herself finally drifted off into a fitful sleep.

## CORRESPONDENCE

Somewhere in Romania, aboard the afternoon train to Timisoara. March 21, the Spring Equinox and, as the sun is just setting, 6:00 p.m. or thereabouts. The train awaits a connection, so I sit with a sausage, a bit of bread and two beers and, as the light fades, write as follows:

Dear Marie,

Yesterday I missed the afternoon train from Sibiu to Timisoara. Any number of excuses might be given: I might say that it was warm in the waiting room, and it was, and I was dozing after a rather late night, watching the spring moon rise over the old part of town. Or I might say that a band of gypsies shared the wait with me and entranced me with their wild-eyed brash- and boldness as they went about their business. Gypsies have a way of looking tomorrow in the eye and saying *Oh. Yeah? Sez who?* Gypsies get through life with expectations different from the rest of ours. Or I might admit that really, if the truth be told, in spite of all of my traveler's pseudo-sophistication, the time 15.35 still makes me think of five-thirty, not three-thirty. And so on. But no, I think instead that there is truth to the notion that brain cells are lost with increasing ease as one approaches forty years, as you, my friend, will know soon enough. It was only a few days ago, for Pete's sake, that, on arriving in Sibiu, I gathered up my pack, smiled goodbye and, surrounded by godless commies, disembarked the train, leaving my wallet with US $400 cash, my passport and your last summer's Phoenix address, which I shall never again be without, in the train compartment. That mishap turned out okay, which may show that my *luck* holds, but no, no, my mind is clearly going. So I sat yesterday in the second class waiting room, nodding off and watching the gypsies, while the 15.35 to Timisoara came and went without me.

So it came to pass that I had an unexpected extra day in Sibiu and what ensued will, I think, interest you.

A common tactic of travelers, on the cheap in a strange town, is to hop on a bus and see where it goes, which I did the next morning after missing the train. That would be this morning. Trolleybus T1 in Sibiu starts its run at the station, swings near the old town and the Hotel Boulevard, the classy, class 1 hotel where I stayed. I ordinarily do not stay at class 1 hotels, but I had been told that there is no class 2 hotel in Sibiu, a tale with which I'm not quite comfortable for any number of obvious reasons, as well as one other, my German, which, while perhaps not obvious, will not surprise you, bi-lingual as you are. Anyway, Trolleybus T1 runs past the Boulevard, through some shabby residential areas that reminded me of North Hill in Akron, where my grandmother used to live, and terminates near a very large graveyard somewhere on the outskirts of town.

From there, tracks led on out of town, paralleling the road. A trolley car waited, so I climbed aboard. It was very old, this trolley car, and very small. One car with two antennae; two rows of single wooden seats, all taken by now, so I stood. A driver and a conductor, both old and tired, like the trolley, and smoking short cigarettes. We waited ten minutes or so, then rocked and clanked for about fifteen kilometers through the Romanian countryside, past a park and an army camp, but mostly just through low grey hills, half-covered with snow and spotted with farms and farm animals, to a village whose name I never caught.

This village, scrunched on its heels up against the Transylvanian Alps, had an old and comfortable look to it. Non-descript shops without names, in one of which I took a cup of warmed wine, though it was early; a small bridge over a river rushing with the spring flood; a blue monument in the village center. Coal smoke issued from chimneys; cats stalked the alleyways. Each house's threshold had a date in stone above; some were new and some were from before the war, and all seemed, well, cozy after a string of hotels and the cold marble of the house on Paros. They reminded me, in a way, of home. There were people about and they exchanged greetings and eyed me curiously. The streets were ice-covered and the horses wore metal cleats, but still walked gingerly, as did I.

I found myself walking up and out of town, toward the mountains. I had no purpose in mind except a walk in the country. The day was sunny and the snow was melting as I walked up, tipping my hat, over-smiling through my moustache and trying not to look like a German. The road narrowed and became a path, passed fields and smaller villages and led toward the mountains. Cows chewed their cuds, lying, when they could, in spots where the snow had melted off and the earth looked warm. Overhead, birds flitted about, as birds will do on a sunny spring day.

Ahead, an old woman walked, carrying a sack on a stick over her shoulder. The sack was heavy, I could see, for she was bent pretty low and limped to that side as she walked up the path. We were walking in the same direction and she would stop now and then and, sometimes, look down the path at me. I caught her easily, though to tell the truth, I didn't hurry any to do so. She was old, but no specific age came to mind then, nor does one now. She wore a dark coat, below which showed a green dress, dark stockings and shapeless shoes. She had a scarf, with flowers, I think, over her head. But really all of this, only this morning, is already poorly remembered. I only remember that she was an old woman, with wrinkles, hard hands and a heavy load, which I offered to carry. And so we walked up the Romanian mountain.

It was a pleasant moment, Marie, this walk up the mountain, and one that made me think of you, for it was a moment that you might have enjoyed, too. We walked at the old woman's pace, which was slow, with stops to catch her breath. She jabbered away in Hungarian, for this used to be a part of that country, and languages have a way of lingering on. I had picked up a few words of Hungarian some years ago while travelling for a couple of weeks with a business student from Budapest in back-country Alberta—*igen, nincs, kérem, köszönöm, jó napot, gomba leves*—yes, no, please, thank you, good day, mushroom soup—that kind of thing, which caused the old lady to misjudge my fluency in her language by two orders of magnitude. So, she jabbered away and mostly in response I smiled a lot and nodded where it seemed appropriate, and let my eyes and mind wander. This was Transylvania and maybe she spoke of vampires and wolves, of blood and bats. But maybe she spoke of the spring day and the ailments of old age. It didn't seem to matter much. The sun warmed my back; I took off my cap, and the breeze, which had seemed cold in Sibiu, was now comfortable and blew through my hair. I felt a pleasant scratchy sweatiness across my shoulder where I carried her stick. We passed a shrine beside the path and we both crossed ourselves, she left-handed, and I with the self-consciousness of which you would approve.

We walked for an hour, a mile or maybe two at her pace, slowly uphill through the ice, snow and sun until she turned off through a pasture to her house. It was tiny and sturdy, two rooms, warmed by a wood fire and with a dozen Christian icons on the walls, above head high. Against one wall was her bed, waist-high; in a corner, a man I guessed to be her son fiddled with the innards of a TV set.

On the way down the mountain, I tried to make something of the TV set—a jolt back to the twentieth century, maybe—but the day did not really welcome such thoughts. Rather, my mind lingered on our goodbye, when she had kissed my hand and had spoken her language quietly to me, saying all that needed to be said. And on the view of the village from above. And on the 15.35 to Timisoara, which I was now on my way, again, to meet. I did, and it brought me here, to where I write. It is now quite dark outside and the car is poorly lit. Soon it will be too dark to read or write and I will have nothing to do but to sit and stare out the window at the night, and to wonder where gypsies go. It is very still. Very still.

The train should soon be leaving, to arrive in Timisoara around ten p.m. I have no hotel reservation, no guidebook and the tourist bureau will be closed, so there lies ahead, perhaps, an eventful evening. Romanian for *hotel* is *hotel*, so that helps, though I don't know what Hungarians say, and Hungarian will again be the language of Timisoara. At least I'll be able to order a bowl of mushroom soup, if the need should arise. In a day or two I must be heading for Belgrade and Athens and back to Paros. Emily will be wondering where I am.

Take care, my friend.

As ever,

Michael.


ALBUQUERQUE AND TALLAHASSEE

When the phone rang at the Browning house, Nikki Wallace was reading *The Camomile Lawn*, Mary Wesley's novel, whose most notable claim of achievement was that, while it had not been short-listed for the Booker Prize, there was at least talk that it should have been short-listed for the Booker Prize. Ben had reacted to her having liked DeLillo's *White Noise* by requiring that she read all the short-listed books, and he was now starting her on the ones that had not made the list. Nikki was not liking it, neither *The Camomile Lawn*, nor the entire ridiculous exercise.

Rachel was sleeping soundly in her crib, and the older children were not yet home from school. Ben was not expected for another couple of hours, and she enjoyed the peace and quiet of the empty house. Yes, she could have been working on something more directly related to her dissertation, but Ben had assured her that in the end there would be a connection between the present exercise and her dissertation on mid-twentieth century British critical theory. She doubted it, but would see. In any event, she was a quick reader and would be finished with *The Camomile Lawn* this afternoon.

On the fourth ring, Nikki put the book down on the couch, put her cigarette in the ashtray and walked over to the phone. The answering machine would pick up after the sixth ring, and as much as she wanted to let that happen, Ben had been insistent that the phone always be answered when he wasn't here, in case it was Anna. Of course, he had given her no idea of what to say if it were Anna, and she had not figured that out for herself yet either. She picked up the receiver.

"Brownings."

"Hello? Who's this?"

"Robin! How I love to hear your scratchy voice. I wondered if you were going to get the message. I wasn't sure I had the right number."

"*Brownings*?"

"Long story."

"*Brownings*?"

"Yeah, so who are you to talk? *Hi. This is Marie. I can't come to the phone right now, blah blah blah.* What's up with that?"

"You first."

"No, you first."

"Okay, I'll go. I've moved in with my new girl friend. There."

"Yeowza. That's news. So who is this Marie?"

"School teacher. Social studies. Thirty-eight in June. Short. Dark."

"How long's it been going on?"

"Since the end of the summer. Well, last spring. I actually moved in over Christmas. I'm smitten, kiddo, a real goner."

"So what am I? The last to know?"

"We've talked before from this number. In fact, you've called it. I guess you just didn't get the answering machine."

"Weak. And you just kind of forgot to mention that you had moved in with your new girlfriend? *Moved in*? I'm not buying it."

"Well, . . .."

"Well . . .?"

"We're still getting some things sorted through. Like, I'm probably going to miss Oscar night with you. I'll be on the lam."

"On the lam? Where? Why?"

"Studying at the library. Make that *quote* studying at the library *unquote*. There's a Oscar watch party going on here to be attended by certain Unsuspecting Friends, and . . ."

"Oh my God, Robin, she's a decider."

"She is, yes."

"How long has it been since what's-her-name?"

"Rindy. Three years."

"Which makes it three years minus about two minutes since you swore to me that you would never ever date another decider. Absolutely not. Period. Full stop. Over and out."

"She broke my heart."

"Whatever happened to her, anyway?"

"Rindy? Beats me. She doesn't exactly keep in touch."

"She's probably off somewhere praying."

"That's ungenerous of you."

"She broke my best friend's heart. I'm not feeling generous. Maybe she's breeding."

"Well, you're a breeder, too. At least potentially."

"Did I ever break your heart?"

"No, darlin', you didn't."

"Well, there then. So I say you give this new straight chick the heave-ho."

"I don't think she's actually straight. She's very passionate, and she says she loves me. There's just a part of her life that I'm not part of. Yet. Someday. Maybe."

"Which reminds us of . . . ?"

"Right. Lorinda."

"Who . . .?"

"Broke my heart."

"Right. Heave ho. Don't do it again, Robin, not to you, not to me."

"But you should meet Marie."

"Let me guess. The usual trifecta: she's smart, pretty and funny."

"You're such a cynic. Actually, while she laughs at my jokes, she doesn't really have much of a sense of humor. Though she did tell me a joke the other day. Horse walks into a bar. . .."

"Why the long face?"

"That one. I pretended I hadn't heard it, it was so charming to hear her tell it. But really, she spends most of her time in the neighborhood of *wry*, maybe, more than *funny*. But she is smart. And tough. She's tiny, Nikki, but can keep a class of seventh graders in line. Remember what we were like when we were seventh graders?"

"I do. And you're shacked up with Miss Laska."

"Oh, stop. She's adorable, I tell you, completely adorable. She wears glasses that slip down on her nose. And lipstick. She speaks French with, she tells me, a French-Canadian accent. She drinks beer with ice. And she has this tidy, tight little flat-chested body that is irresistible."

"Well, that's not Miss Laska, I'll give you that."

"How could I toss her out? I can't, that's the answer to that one."

"Marie who?"

"Cochran."

"Irish. Catholic, too, I suppose."

"Lapsed."

"Right, just like her heterosexuality has lapsed, lurking in the closet waiting to jump out when needed. She's met your parents?"

"Not yet."

"Oh oh. Bad sign. And she has Unsuspecting Friends. No not-very-ex ex-boy friend, I hope."

"Well . . ."

"Ho boy."

"There's this guy—this married guy . . ."

"Jesus."

". . . whom she doesn't see much anymore, but who writes her long letters from here and there."

"What kind of letters? What's new in Albuquerque letters? Love letters? Explicit sex letters?"

"I don't know. *I* don't read them."

"Don't."

"She gets a little bluesy for a few days after she gets one. But she hasn't seen him for a long time . . .." Britt's voice kind of trailed off.

"So give this undecided Mick chick the heave ho, you want my advice."

"Can't do it, hon. Even putting aside the fact that this is her house not mine, and she's pretty much supporting me right now, no questions asked."

"So, you're not paying rent? That's a good sign, I guess. I can read a modicum of commitment into that." Sarcasm edged her voice.

"Less than you think, actually. She owns both sides of the duplex, and a couple of college boys rent the other half. I think their rent pretty much covers her mortgage. I pitch in for groceries, and each of us buys her own ticket to the movies. But it's all pretty informal, and I don't really know all that much about her personal finances."

"Why would you?"

"The important thing isn't whether I'm paying rent. Like I told you, I'm a goner."

"Then at least give her an ultimatum: *The exit ramp is approaching, sweetie. You either get off or stay on the highway. You can't just pull over onto the side of the road and wait.*"

"Up ahead. Green sign, white letters: *LESBIANAPOLIS. NEXT 4 EXITS.*"

"You're hopeless. Why not make it six?"

"Okay."

"I was kidding, actually."

"Don't be a poop. Be optimistic; it won't kill you."

"Right. Invite me to the wedding."

"And don't come crying on your shoulder if she breaks my heart, right?"

"No, honey, *do* come crying on my shoulder *when*, not *if*, she breaks your heart."

"I hope not. But anyway, enough of my complicated life. What about yours?"

"Hold on, this may take a while. Let me check the baby."

"*The baby?*"

"Hold on, I'll be right back." Nikki put the receiver next to the phone and walked to the nursery at the back of the house. Rachel was sleeping quietly on her back, sucking her left thumb. Nikki took her thumb out of her mouth and rearranged the blanket over her, tucking her left arm under the blanket. She rewound the mechanical music box that tinkled quiet music and rotated a flock of birds over Rachel's head, and returned to the living room. She put her cigarette out, lit another one and picked up the phone. "I'm back."

*"Brownings? Baby?"*

"Yeah, okay. Ben Browning is my dissertation advisor . . . "

"You're answering your dissertation advisor's home phone and looking after his baby? And I thought my life was confusing."

"Shut up and listen. So, he's my dissertation advisor, and Robin, he's the smartest person I've ever known. He's taught me to understand post-modernism, and it's opened up a whole new field to me."

"You used to say it was incomprehensible."

"That was before I started working with Ben. Well, of course it *is* incomprehensible. It has to be. That's the whole point. It's a theory explained in words, isn't it?, and words are *inherently* incomprehensible. What, after all, do words really mean? What, even, is the meaning of the word *meaning*? It's a goddam freak accident anytime that we ever communicate with each other at all. Once you see that, you look at everything ever said or written differently."

"The guy I work for thinks it's bullshit."

"What's he know about literary criticism?"

"Nothing, I suppose, but we've got post-modernism, too, you know."

*"Post-modern law?* What's that?"

"They call it Critical Legal Studies, and the law school here is loaded. But Randolph—that's my guy—thinks it's bullshit. Actually what he calls it is *post-modern mumbo-jumbo.*"

"Maybe he doesn't get it."

"I don't know, he's pretty smart. But I'll admit he's on the practical side of the law. Says this is a legal engineering school, more than it is a jurisprudence school. I think he thinks the crits don't help with that. I think maybe he's right."

"I think he doesn't get it. Tell him to read Derrida. Tell him to read Empson."

"Maybe. I'll tell him. But none of this has anything to do with why you're answering your dissertation advisor's home phone and looking after his baby. I presume it's his baby."

"It is. Her name is Rachel, and she's a delight. Oh, and I cook dinner for them, too. And see that the two older children have someone to come home to."

"Are there functions you *don't* perform?"

"Well, I'm not boinking him, if that's what you mean. I'm just like his housekeeper."

"How do you stay in school?"

"I'm not doing much these days anyway except working on my dissertation; I've finished all my course work. And for my purposes, Ben's library here is almost as good as the one at the department. The old lady next door looks after Rachel in the morning before I get here, and if I have to run over to school for something in the afternoon. Otherwise, I hang out here from about two until about ten."

"Doing what?"

"Smoking and reading, mostly. Writing. Thinking. Keeping Rachel happy when she's awake. Making sure Sam and Janet do their homework when they get home from school. Making dinner. Talking with Ben about what I'm reading."

"Nice gig, I guess. Does he always get his advisees to look after his household?"

"That's the strangest part of the story. No, this is special. Get this: the Mrs. has vanished."

"Vanished?"

"Gone. Disappeared without a trace. Flew the coop, probably. Abducted, maybe."

"You mean foul play?"

"Conceivable. But Ben doesn't think so. He thinks she just left, but he doesn't seem to know where to. She's some kind of brainy math professor. I met her once or twice and she seemed, I don't know, brainy for sure. But also, I don't know, pressured. Yes, under pressure. Once, she was blowing her stack in his office while I cooled my heels in his waiting room. I don't think I ever spoke to her, certainly not that day."

"What happened?"

"She left in a huff."

"Was she disturbed? I mean, you know, clinically."

"Not that I could see. I don't know. Maybe just the super mom kind of thing: perfect children, perfect wife, brainy career. Married to an asshole. . . ."

"I thought you admired him."

"Okay. Married to a smart, successful asshole, who is admired by certain of his devoted students, and to whom I would not want to be married. From one perspective, she's got it all. Then, apparently, something pops and she walks out of the math building and vanishes. No phone calls, no credit card receipts. Nothing. Ben has this theory that some friend of hers from where she used to teach or somewhere has been pestering her and that she's gone off to see about that."

"A long-distance stalker?"

"Maybe, all I know is that the Mrs. would occasionally get long letters from this guy . . ."

"Small world."

"How so?"

"I told you: my Marie gets long letters from her married ex, too."

"*My Marie*. Heartwarming."

"Fuck off."

"Anyway, Ben thinks that his wife's correspondent is (a) an idiot and (b) messing with Anna's mind. I don't know what your Marie thinks about hers."

"Anna?"

"The vanished Dr. Browning. Ben said he has filed a missing person report with the police, but I doubt it, or you'd read something in the paper: *Math Prof Goes Missing*. Something like that. Instead all there is is a transparently ridiculous story for general consumption about her going off to deal with some family emergency leaving poor Professor Browning with his hands full."

"Just as long as his hands aren't full of you, sweetie."

"That's not an option. Oh, he'd screw me in a minute if I gave the go-ahead. But he won't press it, nor show any remorse, either way. And let's just say that he doesn't seem exactly heartsick over Anna's departure. He's worried, sure, and inconvenienced, but I'm not sure he misses her all that much, at least not the way most people miss their vanished loved ones. He's pretty detached. But he's still the smartest person I've ever met, and I'm going to write a hell of a dissertation, with his help. Bank it. He says my route to the top will be rapid. In exchange for that, looking after his children is a small price to pay. Plus I get an easy two hundred a month."

"Remind him it's illegal to tie your dissertation to sexual favors, if it comes to that."

"Yes, Counselor. But no, he's way too smart for that. Besides, he knows I'd slice 'em off if he tried." A pause, then, "Oops, there's Rachel. Gotta go. Listen, you tell your Marie to decide, and I'll tell my Ben to come clean on the missing person details. Okay? We'll talk later. Oscar night."

"I'm not sure I can pull it off, but I'll try."

"Oscar night. 'Bye, Robin. I love you and always will." And she rang off, before Britt had a chance to say goodbye.

ALBUQUERQUE

Richard Randolph stood in the well of lecture room 2401 on the main floor of the law school while the fifty or so bankruptcy students filed in and got themselves arranged. He was dressed in a jacket and button-down shirt, striped tie and corduroys and his hair was reasonably well combed. With his hands in his pockets, he chatted with the fellows in the front about the weekend's basketball games. When the clock showed ten-thirty, he walked behind the lectern where his notes lay and held up a hand for quiet. It took only a few seconds. He distained the seating charts that were popular among his law school colleagues, and he did not take attendance, thinking both were more fitting of, say, middle school than professional school. The students could sit where they wanted, and the exam would take care of those who forwent the opportunity to come to class.

Although the fix was in, he still made a show of studying the class list before scanning the audience. "Ms. Larsen?"

"Here." She raised her hand so he could find her, to his left and near the back of the stadium seating. It was a large class and she and some of the others moved around day to day. Most, though, sat in their usual places.

"Have you read the Sullivan case?"

"Yes."

"Why don't you start us out on it?" From where he stood, he thought he could sense his minor conspiracy reflected in what went on in front of him as Britt shuffled her papers and found the case in the text. Students are always more savvy in such matters than they were given credit for being. He allowed himself a small smile and noticed that there was missing from his voice a tiny edge, the one that came from his usual anticipation that the called-upon student might not be prepared. It was such a pain in the ass to have to deal with an unprepared student, while the rest of the class, a third of whom were equally unprepared, listened nervously, and hoped not to be called on next.

To his right, Keisha Wilkinson cleared her throat and said something to a classmate.

Britt launched into her brief of the case, starting with the facts that gave rise to the controversy, the procedural history of the case, and then discussing the holding. Richard interrupted her now and then to clarify a point, but mostly he gave her a slack rein. She described in detail what the Court of Appeals had done, how it had refused to follow an earlier Tennessee case; how it had followed an old Supreme Court case decided under a different statute. She ended after about fifteen minutes by describing what the Court of Appeals said was left to be done by the Illinois bankruptcy court, where the case had begun.

She looked up. He nodded. Keisha, across the room, smiled broadly and clapped silently to Richard's back. Britt winked at her.

"Well, what do you think?"

"Sir?"

"What do you think? Do you like the result? Does is make you feel warm inside? Proud to be an American?"

"Well, I don't know." Off her brief, she tightened up a bit and became less sure, less smooth. "What do you mean?"

"I mean how did you react to this case? When you got done reading it, did you say *okay, I get it* or *wait a minute*?"

"Uhh, neither really. I think it's a good decision."

"I'm suspicious." Richard walked to the other side of the room. "Mr. Gordon, does In re Sullivan make you feel proud to be an American?"

"I'm *always* proud to be an American."

"Take American Indian Law and get back to me. Ms. Lamarra?"

"I think it's okay."

"Do you care?"

"Sure I care."

"Do you really know what's going on in this case?" To the class as a whole: "How many liked the result?"

A few hands went up.

"How many not?"

A few more. Thirty students at least had not voted. "How many don't care?"

There was a spattering of laughter, and twenty hands in the air. "Shame on you. Education is the only commodity that people spend good money for . . ."

He paused, allowing the students who had had him for first year Contracts to respond in unison, ". . .and try to get *as little* as possible."

"Right. You may have heard that from me before. Ms. Larsen. Let's start again. You understand this case as a law student, but let's see if you understand it as a lawyer. What's it about?"

As she started in on the facts again, he saw her nervously wipe the palm of her left hand on her jeans.

"No, no, no. No detail. No facts yet. What's it *about*? One word."

"I'm not sure I know what you mean. It's about whether or not Congress could . . . ." She had her eyes buried in her notes, looking for the answer.

"Stop." He cut her off, an index finger in the air. "Put your notes away. Look down here. At me. Come on. Down here." He waited until she looked up from her notes. "One word."

"I don't know." She looked back down into her notes.

With the one finger still in the air and his eyes on Britt, he pointed across the room with his other hand.

"Gordon?"

"Bankruptcy." The class laughed.

"Cute. Anyone?"

From the left somewhere: "Uniformity."

"Right. Uniformity. Who said that?" A hand went up near the back. "Apodaca, right?" Mr. Apodaca nodded. "Good. Larsen, uniformity of what?"

"The bankruptcy laws across the country," Britt said, looking up from her book. Richard was now getting into the class, feeling what he thought a conductor of a good symphony orchestra must feel.

"Correct. Why?"

"The Constitution says so."

"Correct. Article one, section eight, clause four: *Congress may establish uniform* . . .," he paused for emphasis, ". . . uniform *laws on the subject of bankruptcies throughout the United States.* Are they?" His back was now to Britt, as he paced back and forth in front of the room. When she said nothing right away, he stopped walking and looked over his shoulder at her.

"Sir?"

"Are the bankruptcy laws uniform across the states?"

"Well, yes, they have to be. I mean the Constitution says so."

"Right. Does Mr. Sullivan's attorney think that they are uniform?" He boosted himself up and sat on the first row of empty desktops, facing her and most of the class, with his feet dangling down the front.

"No. He thinks they aren't."

"Who's right?"

"He is."

"Who?"

"Sullivan's attorney, but . . ."

"But?"

"The Seventh Circuit Court said he's wrong."

"Confused?"

"A little." She gave a short little laugh; her face was serious with concentration. Keisha Wilkinson across the room had a pained expression on her face.

"What are we doing here, Ms. Larsen?"

"Sir?"

"Right here, now, in this class, ten-fifty-seven on Thursday morning, March, what is this?, the twenty-first. The vernal equinox. What *should* we be doing? How can we get rid of this confusion?"

"I know." She smiled. "We should be explaining the case to an intelligent non-lawyer."

"Why?"

"You told us to."

"I tell you to over and over and over again, don't I? Do you know an intelligent non-lawyer, Ms. Larsen?"

"Yes, I do."

"What's this person's name? Never mind. Did you try to explain In re Sullivan to him or her?"

"No."

"And so you end up knowing the details, not the *guts* of the case. Mend your ways, Ms. Larsen." Another laugh from the class. "Don't laugh! *She* knew the details, at least. How many of you knew them that well?" Pause. Silence. "But that's only the beginning. If you can't explain a case to an intelligent non-lawyer, then you don't understand it yourself. . . . So, where are we, Mr. Gordon?" Richard turned to look at the student sitting two rows back and to his right.

"The Constitution requires uniform laws."

"And is the Illinois exemption law the same as New Mexico's?"

"No."

"Larsen?"

"Sir?"

"Do you agree?"

"Yes, but . . ."

"But?"

"Those are state laws."

"Incorporated into the federal bankruptcy code, right? Gordon?"

"Right."

"And does the Seventh Circuit strike down the bankruptcy law because Congress let Illinois and New Mexico have different exemption schemes, Mr. Gordon?"

"Nope."

"Well, we'd better figure out why, hadn't we? One of you may have to make the same argument to the Tenth Circuit one day. Ms. Larsen, back to you . . . ."

~

In re Sullivan took the full fifty minutes to unwind. At eleven-twenty, Richard was just putting on the finishing touches, telling them that the scholars had debated the same points they had been dealing with in class and were as split as the class was. Pleased with the session, he gave them an assignment for next time and let them go.

Britt sat back in the blue plastic chair, let her arms hang limp and exhaled to the ceiling. The students called what she had been through being *up*; she had been *up*, speaking and answering questions, for most of the session.

"Shit. I thought I knew that case."

"I thought you did a good job, Ms. Larsen," said the fellow sitting behind her and to the right, one of her not-well-known classmates, a year behind her, actually.

"Britt."

"Dick Maxwell. You did."

"Thanks. Gotta cigarette?"

Keisha Wilkinson walked by. "You were great, kiddo. But you were sandbagged, the bastard sandbagged you for sure. Did I tell you, or did I tell you?" She took the unlit cigarette from Britt's hand and broke it in two. "She's quitting."

"You told me. Yeah, maybe I was, but I shoulda known. God, I really wanted to nail it. I've got to go see him this afternoon about some research I'm doing for him. Shit. Just one. Really." Dick Maxwell produced another cigarette.

They walked and smoked out into the Forum. Finding seats on the overstuffed furniture, feet up on the low wooden tables, they flicked their ashes in the direction of the ashtrays and continued the conversation from the class. Other students would drift by; some, hearing that bankruptcy was the subject, would leave, others would stay.

"Look," said Dick Maxwell. "if uniform means anything, it's got to mean the same. New Mexico, Texas, Illinois. Uniform's uniform. Sullivan's got to be wrong."

Richard, walking by their group after answering questions in the well of the classroom, heard the observation. "Good job, Ms. Larsen. And you, Mr. Maxwell, are confusing uniformity with equality. Balance with symmetry."

"Huh? I don't get it," said Dick.

"Many people don't. No offense. Ever been to Notre Dame?"

"No, unless you mean the one in Indiana."

"I was thinking of the one in Paris. Hop a plane, get off at DeGaulle and take a cab to Notre Dame. You should expect it to be an expensive cab ride. Then stand . . . wait, I've got a better idea. Cheaper, too. Let's see, who can I get to do this for me." He paused. "Ah, here's my research assistant now. Ms. Larsen, we need a handout for next class, showing the main façade of Notre Dame cathedral. You'll have to visit Zimmerman to find a picture."

"So," inquired Dick, "this isn't related to Touchdown Jesus?"

"I'm not sure I like the way your mind works. Well, actually, that might serve a similar purpose, but I'll have to have a look. Ms. Larsen, add a picture of Touchdown Jesus to the handout. Two pictures on one page, and we'll make one for every two students, so as to save paper and to admit to the frivolousness of the entire exercise."

"What, or who, is Touchdown Jesus?" Britt asked.

"I'm sure Mr. Maxwell will bring you up to speed on that topic. Wait. Since we're on a Christian theme, add a picture of the Christ of the Andes—the one overlooking Rio—to the handout. Three pictures, one page. You'll have to cut and paste. Now, I've got to go. Don't forget, you're coming by at two-thirty to work on the Riley case, aren't you?"

"Two-thirty. I'll be there." Richard turned to go, but she called him back. "Wait. How many copies do you want?"

"Never mind that. You make the original; my secretary will make the copies. Okay, see you later."

Richard walked away, in the direction of his office, and Britt took a hit on somebody's Diet Pepsi. "God, how do you drink that shit? *Good job*, he says. I'd like to see a screw-up." She then bent her neck back and looked over her head; a friend was leaning on the couch behind her. She reached up and held the friend's elbows. "What're ya doin' for lunch?"

"A bunch of us are going to M & J's. Green chili cheeseburgers? Yummy."

"Damn. I can't go off campus, I've got work to do before I see Randolph. Doesn't anyone want to go to the Bin?" Oddly enough the closest place to the law school to eat was the cafeteria in the county mental hospital. The students called it the Bin, short for Loony Bin, which embarrassed everyone, but nobody could manage to shake it.

"I'll go," said Dick. "But not if we're going to talk bankruptcy."

"I like bankruptcy. But come on, I'll restrain myself. Anyone else?" There were no takers.

∿

Dick Maxwell, of course, asked her out.

"Sorry," she said, "My intelligent non-lawyer . . . you know how it is."

"Married?"

"No. Well . . . goin' steady, you might say."

"What's he do?"

"She's a school teacher," Britt smiled over a banana pudding, just exactly the kind of banana pudding you'd expect to find in the cafeteria at a mental hospital.

"Oh. I see. Sorry."

Britt shook her head, still smiling. "It's always nice to be asked."

∿

Britt spent an hour at Zimmerman, the main campus library, putting together the Bankruptcy class handout, then another hour in the law library researching for Richard before, at precisely two-thirty, she made her way into the lower level faculty suite where his office was. His office door was open but he wasn't in. She sat down on his couch and fiddled with her papers for a few minutes, shuffling copies, index cards, notes and a well-thumbed copy of the bankruptcy statute. Then, she sat back, tucked her hair behind her ears, crossed her legs and waited. She was wearing a pale yellow oxford cloth shirt with the button-down collar not buttoned, jeans and sneakers. She looked around the room.

The office was a mess, as always. No spot of table-top, desk-top or credenza-top could be seen. File folders lay strewn about. Books lay open, stacked five or six high, each book showing a case and marking the place in the one below. She frowned and shook her head. "I couldn't work like this," she said quietly, to the mess. A computer screen glowed in one corner, the cursor flashing in mid-sentence. She stood up from the couch, went over and read the display. Tentatively she touched a button, which did nothing. Propped up on the keyboard was a picture postcard showing the Acropolis, and some writing in Greek letters. She picked it up and turned it over; the reverse was almost blank. Richard's address at the law school was written in ball-point ink, and there was only one other word, printed in all capital letters: *DEITY.* No signature. She replaced the card on the keyboard, sat back down and pulled Professor Wilson's article out of her backpack, along with her yellow pad on which was written the outline she had decided on for her memorandum to Alex Rivera.

A few minutes later, Richard walked through the door and sat down behind his desk. "Whatcha reading?"

"*Re/structuring—actually Re-slash-structuring—the Modern Paradigm for Union and Non-Union Employment Relationships in the Public Sector.*" By Judith Wilson of the University of Oregon. Ever hear of her?"

"Re what?"

"*Re-slash-structuring* . . . here." She stood up and handed the article over the desk to him.

"No. Never heard of her. Professor Wilson's a crit, though, isn't she?"

"How did you know?"

"The slash is the giveaway. Crits love the slash."

"Well, yes, I guess she is. I think. Sometimes I'm not sure."

"Does she cite Derrida?"

"Multiple times."

"With approval?"

"Fawning."

"She's a crit, then. Hence, full of mumbo-jumbo."

"I was telling a friend of mine in Florida that just the other night."

"You were talking to your friends about critical legal studies the other night? You, Ms. Larsen, need to get out more."

"Actually, she brought it up. My best friend is studying literary criticism at Florida State, and she's come under the influence of a post-modernist. I told her that critical legal studies is like post-modern law . . ." She looked up at him, and Richard nodded, ". . . and I used your *mumbo-jumbo* line. She suspected that you didn't get it. She said to tell you to read Derrida and some guy named Emson, or Emerson or something."

"William Empson, probably. *Seven Types of Ambiguity.* There are those who think it's the most important book of the century. It's in the library somewhere. I've read part of it but not the whole thing. It's very intelligent. And Empson was younger than you when he wrote it. Probably."

"It's post-modernism, and you think it's *intelligent?*"

"True. The thing you have to remember about the crits, and more broadly the post-modernists, is that they are right, on a very fundamental level."

"My friend says it has to do with things like the meaning of the word *meaning.*"

"She's right. And how in the world can we or a court hope to figure out what the word *uniformity*, say, from the Sullivan case, means, without first figuring out what the word *means* means."

"So then, you're a crit, too?"

"Hell, no. I just concede that they're right. Fundamentally. But on a fundamental level, so are the quantum physicists, who say that every tiny bit of that couch you're sitting on is nothing but a blur of probabilistic uncertainty, and no single particle in that couch *is* anywhere until it is observed, which observation, in turn, interferes with its location and speed. That is correct. Still, you are able to ignore all of that quantum stuff and sit on the couch without thinking about it. Quantum physics is true on a fundamental level; it just doesn't have much to do with the world we actually live in, you and I. It's like the meaning of the word *meaning*, which turns out to be a very slippery word to define. But still, day-to-day, we get along fine, not really knowing what it *means* to say something *means* something. It's like truth."

"Truth?"

"Ever study epistemology?"

"No. I don't think so."

"Oh, you'd know it if you had. It turns out to be quite difficult to nail down the meaning of what is true. You're a horseback rider, yes?"

"Yes, at least I used to ride. How did you know that?"

"My sister rode. And I thought I recognized that horsey look about you." A pause. "I meant that as a compliment."

"I took it as one."

"Barrels?"

"I rode English."

"Were you ever thrown?"

"More often than I can remember."

"Atta girl. Ever get hurt?"

"I broke my arm once." She gestured with her left hand toward her right arm. "And once the horse clipped me with his right hind on my way down and broke my helmet. I saw stars, but no real damage."

"So," Richard asked, "how do you know that you aren't right now in some nursing home with a feeding tube down your nose, in a coma from that blow to the head, and all of this . . .," he glanced around the room, ". . . isn't just a dream that your addled brain has produced?"

"I don't know. I guess because consciousness has some aspect to it that is not sensory."

"Nice answer. You might be right. Okay, take that guy there." He nodded his head toward the radio, from which had just come the usual announcement: "You're listening to KUNM, 89.9 FM, Albuquerque."

"So?"

"Suppose he'd said, *you're listening to KKOB.*"

"Not true. He'd be wrong."

"But someone right now is listening to KKOB, no?"

"Yes, but that's not whom he was talking to. Whom he meant by the word *you.*"

"So, what does the word *you* mean?"

Britt made air quotes with her fingers and said, "*Most of the ambiguity in the law is related to pronoun use.*"

"Who told you that?"

"Professor Matthews. She kind of harps on it, if you want to know the truth."

"Well, she's right. But it's not just the law. Once you begin to notice it, you'll be interrupting everyone you listen to, saying *he who? They who?* Jane Austen was famous for using feminine pronouns to refer to two or three different people in the same sentence. God, Austen is almost impossible to read."

"Maybe. My friend in Florida doesn't agree with you."

"Don't get me started on her."

"Who?"

"*Touché.* Austen. Anyway, where were we? So, the truth of *you're listening to KUNM* depends on who's hearing it? How comfortable are you in saying that the truth of a statement depends on the audience that hears it?"

"Not very."

"Well, okay then. Truth is slippery. Still and all, we get through the world day after day being pretty much able to know what is true, and what is not. Right?"

"Right."

"Nevertheless . . .," he handed the article back across the desk to her, "*re-slash-structuring* is very likely to be gobbledygook. Which brings us back to where we started."

"Right."

"Or should have started."

"Right. But first . . .?"

"But first?

"Are you going to fill me in on this handout?" She handed him the paste-up she had done with the three photos from Zimmerman.

"Nice work." He handed it back to her. "What do you see?"

"Jesus."

"Well, go on. The topic, recall, is symmetry."

"This one . . .," she pointed to the Christ of the Andes, ". . . is very symmetrical."

"Very."

"And this one, ah, Touchdown Jesus, is not. Well, Jesus himself is, but the entire mural isn't."

"Right? And Notre Dame?"

"Symmetrical."

"Look more closely, while I find the *Michelin Green Guide*."

She studied the handout, while Richard looked through his bookshelf. "Okay, so the thingy over the left door is not the same as the thingy over the right door."

"Right. Listen to this: *the Notre-Dame Façade. . . three stars . . . The façade's overall design is majestic and perfectly balanced. The central portal is taller and wider than the others; that on the left is surmounted by a gable. It was the mediaeval practice to avoid monotony by dissymmetry.*"

"Yes, okay, I can see that."

"Well, the jurisprudential point is the most important thing you'll learn at law school this week."

"Important? You said *frivolous* earlier."

"Did I? The *handout* is frivolous; the principle is profound. Something can be, as the *Guide* says, *perfectly balanced*, even though it's asymmetric. Think, for example of the impact that such a proposition has on, say, issues of gender equality. Balancing the rights of the genders does not mean making everything symmetric. Title nine, for example, can mandate different treatment for men and women's sports teams, in order to *create* balance. So UNM doesn't have to somehow come up with a female equivalent of football. Likewise, uniformity under the Bankruptcy Code does not, the Sullivan case says, mean that every state has to have the same exemption laws. Balance is not the same as symmetry, as the architects of Notre Dame, and the Touchdown Jesus artist knew, but as the designers of the Christ of the Andes forgot. Or ignored, at least."

"Got it. I think. Though His robe is a little crooked. Does that count?"

"Maybe. And now may we get to . . ."

". . . the Riley case."

"Right. So what did you find for me? The perfect case?"

And so they got down to business.

"I think so," Britt said. "In re Greco, a case out of California on almost exactly the same facts as Riley."

"Tell me." He sat down, put his hands behind his head, his feet on the desk and closed his eyes to concentrate while she talked. At one point he made her back up and tell the facts of the case again. "Nope, too tricky. It's a nice argument, but the court won't buy it."

"Why not? This court bought it." She went through the argument in another way. Richard noted a confidence in her voice; she was well-prepared for this meeting, she seemed comfortable with the sophisticated bankruptcy concepts and knew what was going on in the case. "*Collier's* says this: . . ." She read to him from a Xeroxed page out of the leading bankruptcy treatise.

"*Collier's* can't say that."

"It does too. Look." She handed him the copy, which he scanned.

"I'll be damned. That's a very three-six-four piece of work."

"Beg pardon?"

"Three-six-four. It's a baseball reference. Do you know what a three-six-four double play is?" Britt shook her head. "A double play?"

"Two outs on the same play?" She wrote *3/6/4 DP* into the margin of her notes on the Greco case.

"Right. Well, a three-six-four double play is an especially elegant version, but I don't have time to explain it to you just now. Anyway, maybe we can make your elegant argument work. Draft that part of the brief for me, okay? Five pages max. If it reads all right, we'll put it in. What else?"

And so it went for an hour, then two. They debated points; once they had to walk up to the library to read the exact words of a case. Once they had to track down one of his colleagues and snare his thoughts on a procedural matter. By five o'clock they were back in Richard's office and she had a lengthy new assignment, including the drafting of several parts of the brief he was submitting to the Second Circuit Court of Appeals in New York.

"I've never written for an actual federal appellate court before. Thanks for the chance."

"This is a draft, remember. We'll tear it apart several times before it goes off to New York."

"What's this case doing in New York, anyway? How did you get involved?"

"My client is the Bank of Commerce, downtown. The deadbeat is Riley—a limited partnership, really, but Riley's the key guy—and we're into him for fourteen million and change to build a complex of condos down in Belen. Know where Belen is?" Britt nodded. "So, Riley is from New York and when he went down the tubes he filed for bankruptcy there, and now we've got to litigate everything back east."

"Isn't there local counsel back there?"

"Sure, and they're handling all the matters before the bankruptcy judge. We won at trial and the other side appealed these issues, so I said I'd take care of the briefs to the Court of Appeals."

"Will you be doing the oral argument?"

"We probably won't get any; we're supposed to hear next week. This feels to me like one that the court will decide on the written briefs alone. That's why what you're doing has to be done right. Sorry, but you'll probably be spending some late nights in the library until we get this brief hammered out."

"I don't mind. Shoot, you're paying me so well."

He laughed. "What do you get? Three-fifty an hour? The joys of work-study. I remember them well. You like this stuff, don't you? You're very good."

"Maybe. It didn't seem like it in class today. Sorry I messed up. A couple of my friends told me that I should be angry with you for setting me up."

"Are you?"

"No, but you could have told me what you wanted. Then I wouldn't have looked like a fool."

"A fool? Don't be silly. You looked like a goddamned genius. You'll probably be the talk of all the guys down at Jack's tonight. You were great. Just right. If you'd known in advance where I was going, you would have been too glib; you and I would have had a pleasant conversation and the rest of the class would have been left in the dust. In awe of your brilliance, perhaps, but still lost in the dust."

"Still, if I had read the note cases more carefully."

"No. Wrong. You're missing the point from class yet again. You did *not* need to know more detail about the case, or those other cases mentioned in the notes. Learn the lesson: *understand* the case. Don't drown in the details."

"Right."

"So why do you like bankruptcy; somehow that strikes me as odd."

"I don't know, I guess I like the complications of the statute. It seems impossible, with all those words, that you . . . I mean a person . . . could find her way through it to the key points. And when you can, it feels good, like solving a puzzle."

"It's not very sexy, not very glamorous. Not the kind of topic designed to catch the attention of a bright young feminist. You are a bright young feminist, right?"

"Why not?"

"But a lot of lawyers who know the Bankruptcy Code a lot less well than you are making a lot of money on other people's financial misfortunes. Want to practice it?"

"Maybe. I don't know. I haven't thought much about after graduation."

"Got a job?"

"I've had a couple of offers, but nothing has really struck my fancy."

"You'll stay here in Albuquerque?"

She shrugged. "I don't know. Maybe. I grew up here. Maybe I'll stay."

"Not my business." He was a little embarrassed by her reticence.

"No, it's not that. It's just . . . . oh, I don't know. Shit. I've lost my ability to talk. I'm almost thirty years old, is all, . . ."

"Older than William Empson, when he wrote the most important book of the twentieth century."

"Thanks a lot for the reminder. I think maybe I ought to be getting on with it. You know, big cities, east coast, power, influence, adult stuff. Like litigating the Riley case in New York City."

"And leaving the boring part to the hicks back in the boondocks?"

"Yeah, maybe."

"Don't worry. That feeling will go away. In my experience, anyway."

She smiled. "Anyway, I can't leave Albuquerque, not right now. So . . . I don't know. I'll take the bar exam here and then decide. I don't guess I'll starve."

"Have you thought about a judicial clerkship?"

"I started that process last spring, and got a nibble from the Tenth Circuit in Denver. And another one from the Eighth in St. Louis. But, like I said, right now I don't want to leave New Mexico, and there are no federal clerkships open in either Albuquerque or Santa Fe."

"Have you thought about bankruptcy court?"

"Not really. Isn't it too late to apply?"

"They run rather less formally than district or circuit courts do, so no, it's not too late. I know for a fact that Judge Hernandez is looking for a clerk; he called me last week, in fact, and I gave him your name. Give him a call. Better yet, call his present clerk, Andy Stevens, and tell him that I said he should buy you lunch, then introduce you to the judge. You'll like Andy; he graduated two years ago."

"Thanks for the tip. I will. How do I get him?"

"US Bankruptcy Court. Downtown. Andy Stevens."

"Do I go through Career Services?"

"Don't bother. I'm not constrained, as they are, by the need to treat you equally with your classmates."

"Is that fair?"

"Balance, you'll recall, is not the same as symmetry." He stood up, "Now, I've got to go. I'm about to be late for a date with my wife. We're going to an amateur play and . . ." He checked his watch. "Whatever it is that you will be doing four hours from now, you'll be having more fun than I."

Britt packed up her books and headed out of the office. She turned at the door: "One more thing?"

"Sure." He smiled.

"That postcard there on the key board. I read the back before you came in. I shouldn't have, maybe, but . . . what's it mean? I've gotta know."

Richard walked over and picked the card up. He looked at the front and flipped it over in his hand. For a few seconds he said nothing.

"Never mind," she said.

"No, it's okay. What did you think when you read it?"

"I'm not sure. Very dense, I guess. Disturbing, almost."

"No, it's hardly that. I've got a crazy friend who sends me postcards from odd places. On the back he puts words that break the *i before e except after c* rule. He's really pretty crazy. *Deity*. Last year he sent me a card from Thailand that had *caffeine* written on it."

"Why's he do it?"

"Oh, I don't know. Whimsy, I suppose. Or his way of saying that the going is as important as the being there."

"Haven't you ever asked him?"

"Sure. He says it's to improve my spelling. He's really pretty crazy. Do you like the picture? Here, take it." He handed the postcard to her.

Britt admired the Acropolis for a moment. "I'd like to see the Acropolis sometime, but no, I couldn't take it, he sent it to you."

"It's just cluttering up my office. Really, take it if you want."

"There's no hope for your office, if you want my opinion, and you can hardly blame the clutter on one postcard. It belongs here somewhere." She looked around. "Here." She stuck the card on the outside of his office door, behind the corner of his nameplate.

"Right. It looks nice there. Thanks for helping me straighten up my office."

"Anytime. Enjoy the play."

"Fat chance. See you in class."

Britt walked up the stairs into the Forum, called Marie, smuggled a Coke and chips into the library, settled down in her carrel and read bankruptcy cases until 1:30 in the morning.

∿

While Britt slowly turned the pages of the *Bankruptcy Reporter*, and Marie, at home in the duplex, watched television and sketched out her lesson plans for the following week, Richard sat on a folding metal chair in a cramped little studio theater and listened to the actors shout Sam Shepard's words at one another. His shoulder touched Rita's to the right and a stranger's to the left and he couldn't cross his legs without kicking the chair in front of him. In spite of his discomfort, though, he had to admit that this was not an ineffective performance. The two principal actors were really rather good. The leading male actor was tall, good-looking and exuded maleness. The woman was small and wiry with veins that stood out on her neck and a high, squeally voice and she—well, this *is* a Sam Shepard play, he told himself—she too exuded maleness. The tiny studio was advantageous to this play; he sat in the second row of folding chairs, less than ten feet from where the actors walked, and on the same level. When Eddie walked by you could see and smell his sweat; when they kissed, you could hear the slip and slop of their tongues.

All-in-all, his prophecy to Britt in his office several hours ago had been wrong and he was having a good time.

∿

He had been wrong as well about the conversation down at Jack's tonight, where Britt was the topic, but not her genius. Rather, the talk was running just now to dykes, deviance, pushy broads and the good old days. "Why else did God invent closets?" asked Dick Maxwell, and they all laughed and drank to that.

∿

It improved Richard's mood a bit more even, sitting uncomfortably in the small studio theater, when he realized that Sam Shepard probably didn't want him to be having a particularly good time, such being the playwright's general attitude toward humanity. After the play, on the way back to the car, he held Rita's hand and actually whistled a little tune.

"You seem happy tonight."

"Just my own little protest against high-snoot, New Mexico celebrity immigrants. May the south wind blow this evidence of my good spirits and optimism all the way to Santa Fe and into the waiting ears of Sam and Jessica and their ultra chic friends. Zip-adee-do-dah."

"You didn't like it?"

"I *loved* it. The Old Man reminded me of my Uncle Joe, God love him."

"Sarcasm."

"No, really. I expected to be miserable tonight but I had a great time. The actors were good, really good, I thought. I got to watch a perfect stranger get dressed. I've got you to myself and a babysitter until midnight. What more could I ask for? What will it be?" He rubbed his hands together. "Expensive steaks in Old Town? You got it. High speed sex, heading towards Grants, accelerator on the floor, the Grateful Dead on the stereo, your face in my lap? You got it. Pac Man until the joint closes? Unlimited quarters? Name the place."

"Pizza."

"Pizza? Pizza. You got it. Whataya say we get it to go, drive up to the Crest and look at the lights?"

"Hot pizza."

"Okay, hot pizza. Then let's get it at Leo's downtown. Then we'll eat it, off our knees at the bus station, drink Chianti out of a bottle wrapped in a sack and pretend we're waiting for Michael to roll into town on the next Trailways. Okay?"

"Let's go. Pepperoni and mushrooms. No anchovies."

"Anchovies and tomatoes, no green peppers."

"Green chilies and sausage."

"With extra cheese."

"Done. Who's driving?"

~

The bus station's architect had been working, Richard thought, harkening back to his conversation with Britt, in, say, early Post-Modern Greyhound. He guessed it had looked sleazy about forty-five minutes after the ribbon cutting. Now, several years later, the florescent panels were filled with dead moths and some of the lights were dark in the middle and blinking on the ends. The floor had been mopped, but the corners were dirty and littered. A few folks loitered, a few others made deals, while some waited for buses, suitcases at their feet, magazines rolled in their hands. A couple of Border Patrol guys stood in a corner, eyes moving. A pinball machine was being played, sounding electronic and annoying, unlike the mechanical and pleasing sounds that pinball machines used to give off.

The two of them still had their good clothes on from the play, but Richard's tie was undone and the ends hung loose around his neck. He sat with his legs out, ankles crossed and his arms on the backs of two chairs. Rita had shed her panty hose in the car and now wiggled her bare toes in his lap, sitting the long way across three seats, leaning against the far arm rest. The pizza box was on her legs between them and the neck of the Chianti bottle stood up between her calves. Her mouth was full of hot pizza, a cheese tendril fell off her chin and her empty right hand was held, with the fingers spread and shaking, in the universal gesture of people who have their mouths full of too-hot pizza. Richard passed her the wine bottle to cool off.

"Okay?"

"Yeah. God, that's good!"

They sat and ate and talked about the play and work and the kids. Jack, the middle one, had come home from school with both his top front teeth in his fist, very proud and very adorable. The pizza cooled, they got a little drunk and watched the late night buses come and go. Michael was on none of them.

"He told me . . ."

"Who?"

"Michael."

She nodded.

"He told me a story once, a story he had read somewhere. I suppose we were at a Dukes' game and the going was slow. Doesn't matter. Anyway, it was about, let's see, a middle aged guy, our ages, say, professional, successful. He's the narrator, see? And the narrator tells of this uncle he has, a very ordinary guy, an old bachelor, quiet life, unexciting job, an optician maybe. The brother, I guess he was, of the narrator's mother. The narrator never was very interested in him, you know, got socks and underwear from him at Christmas and didn't know anything about sports, that kind of uncle. Got it? A real boring sort of guy. Now that the narrator is grown, the uncle is the last member of his mother's generation, so he feels a little responsibility toward him, but not much. The uncle comes for a yearly visit and bores the narrator and the narrator's wife with his consuming blandness.

"Well, the uncle dies, and the narrator is the only one around to settle his affairs, so he sets off to do it in whatever boring city the uncle lived in. Say, I don't know, Topeka, say, or maybe Buffalo. There's not much to do. A funeral to arrange, which hardly anybody attends. A small bungalow to clean out and sell. It's full of boring furniture and the magazine racks have only *Reader's Digest* and *TV Guide* and, I don't know, *Consumer Reports*. Like there is nothing in this house to show why this uncle did not die of complete boredom decades ago.

"But it all kind of gets to the narrator and he tries to find out something about the old man. What was his life about? He talks to the neighbors, but they hardly know the uncle, he was so quiet and unassuming. In the house there are no letters, no diaries, no photo albums. Nothing. No will. No insurance. Nothing to show that the old guy ever had been alive, ever had been connected to anyone, ever had done anything. The narrator sits on the uncle's bed and looks at all this nothingness around him and, of course, gets this real superior feeling about his life, *vis a vis* his uncle's."

Richard took a drink out of the wine bottle. Rita's eyes were closed, but he knew she was with him. She nodded, "Go on."

"Well, just as his smugness is maxing out, in one desk drawer, he finds an old passport, issued before the narrator was born, with a photo of the uncle, looking younger but every bit as boring as the narrator had always known him. He pages through the passport and it's mostly unused, in fact it looks like it was only used once and then stuck in this drawer. There is only one visa stamp, but that one is a doozy. It covers a full page in the passport, with several multi-colored ink stamps and several stick-on revenue stamps, signed across with official-looking signatures. And this visa is very old, he knows because of the date on the passport, but the colors are still bright and that sparks the narrator's interest and he studies the visa. The language is a strange one; he doesn't even recognize the alphabet. So he gets a magnifying glass and looks at the revenue stamps and then he puts down the passport and glass and sits back in the desk chair and stares out the window at the boring Topeka street scene."

A pause. Rita opened her left eye and reached in the direction of the wine. "Well?"

Richard handed her the bottle. "A double sun setting behind low hills is on one of the stamps. An unknown animal with six legs is on the second; a fantastic city skyline on the third. It is immediately clear to the narrator that the uncle once, somehow, had taken this passport and visited, he doesn't know, somewhere, the Sirius system maybe. And he had come back, fifty years ago and put the passport with its visa in the drawer . . ."

"... and that had been enough," Rita said. Her eyes were open and she was smiling.

"Yeah. Enough. One trip that made him happy to spend the rest of his life the way he had."

"And without ever having to tell anyone about it."

"Just sitting reading the *Reader's Digest*, alone in Topeka, and every now and then to look off and remember having seen Sirius set behind the mountains of an unknown planet."

"Whew. Nice story. What happened to the narrator?"

"I don't remember. That's a good question, isn't it? Does he understand? Does it make his life with Colorado River raft trips and two weeks in Europe now and then intolerable? Or is he too shallow to appreciate what the uncle had done? I'll have to ask Michael next time I see him."

"When will that be?"

"Who's to say? This summer, I hope."

"Is that what he's looking for, with all this travelling around he does? Sometimes I think he's compulsive."

"Is he looking for the one trip that will make his life complete? Want to know what I think? I think he's already taken that one."

"Really? Where to?"

"Nowhere special. I think one time something very trivial happened, like maybe he was bumped from a flight and had to catch another one and he ended up in an airport where he didn't expect to be, and walking down the concourse he felt this sense of movement and that was it. That was his trip to Sirius. Michael's so aware, so much more conscious than the rest of us, conscious of what is happening around him, appreciative of the small things, that I think that's all it took. One small moment full of the sense of movement, and ..."

"And?"

"... the rest of life is topping, double pepperoni, maybe, on the house. I think he decided during a moment like that, that he had gotten what life owed him and whatever came later was extra. That's the only way I can explain the way he eases through life while the rest of us struggle. Like he's walking downhill and the rest of us uphill. Want the last piece?"

"No, I'm stuffed. I liked your story. I like your friend."

"He does."

"Who does what?"

"Him. He wants the last piece." Richard gestured with his head across the room where a down-and-out Hispanic gent sat eyeing their pizza with admiration.

"It's his." Rita closed the box and swung her feet down, slipped on her shoes and walked across the waiting room, the clicks of her heels echoing across the empty space. The man accepted the pizza box eagerly, and Rita chatted with him for a minute; Richard could catch bits of their Spanish drifting across the lobby. He took another sip of wine, wishing, as he always did when he heard Rita speaking Spanish, that he was as bi-lingual as she. He never felt less educated than when he was around bi-lingual people. His pathetic attempts over the years to learn to speak German left him able to memorize the words to *Ode to Joy*, but unable to translate them. Immersion, as Michael was doing on his island in Greece, he thought, was the only way to get it done, though why one would want to learn a language that is hardly spoken by anyone outside the home county, Richard didn't know. One might as well study Navajo.

When Rita walked back, she said, "Got any cash?"

"Why?" he asked, pulling out his money clip.

"Don't ask." She extracted a twenty.

"Jeeze. Why not just give him your MasterCard?"

"Loosen up there, darlin', you'll be rewarded in heaven. Or, at the very least, later this evening."

~

They got home after one to find everyone asleep. They awoke the babysitter, put her in her car and pointed her toward the dorm. Inside, they checked the kids, exchanged teeth for coins under Jack's pillow, doused the lights and took showers, Rita first. She was sitting on the edge of the bed in the tops of her pajamas when Richard walked into the room. She watched him for a minute as he finished drying.

"So, it's true?" she asked.

"What's true?"

"That the erections of men past forty are just slightly above horizontal."

He stopped and looked down. "Is that true? I never studied the matter. How do you know?"

"I read it somewhere—in line at the grocery, I think. I just don't see you walking around like that often enough." She tilted her head to the side and looked at him in the dark. He stood still, pulled his stomach in slightly and let her look. "It looks kind of, I don't know, clumsy. Do you think you maybe could manage another, say, ten degrees? Just for tonight? I promise I won't pester you about it every night."

Richard squinted his eyes and squeezed. His penis bobbed up and down and settled back in, like she said, slightly above horizontal. "Doesn't look like it. It appears that this, along with the usual combination with other appendages, will have to do."

"Walk over here a minute." He did, and at bedside she put her index finger under the head of his penis and pushed it up to about seventy degrees above the horizontal. "Profile, please." He rotated a quarter turn to the left, her finger still propping him in a teenager's enthusiastic erection. "Well, let's see, . . ." she said, now bouncing him on the end of her finger. ". . . we could make love for two hours, sleep for three and still get up at six-thirty."

"Yeah, or we could make love for ten minutes, sleep for five hours and get up at six-forty." He turned back to face her and began to unbutton her tops.

"Now you're talking like some school boy with a seventy-degree hard-on." She removed the prop, flopped on her back crosswise on the bed and finished the unbuttoning herself. "Let's split the difference."

"It's a deal. Did you put the cat out?"

"Fuck the cat. We'll give the sparrows a break in the morning. C'mon. The clock is running. I expect to be orgasmic in twelve minutes."

She was, with time to spare, and woke Todd in the process; he snuffled himself back to sleep and, somewhat more quietly, she was again.

~

Britt drove home, red-eyed and brain-tired. Marie was asleep on the couch in front of a movie she didn't recognize with Cary Grant, who was overplaying it, and Ingrid Bergman, who looked chubby and bored. Britt poured herself a straight rye whiskey, put Marie's feet in her lap and watched until near the end. One minute, it seemed, she was thinking of waking Marie up and the next she too was asleep, sitting up, her head straight back on the couch, snoring quietly. About three, the static of TV snow, which is said to contain evidence of the beginning of the universe, finally woke Marie and the two of them staggered upstairs and slept the rest of the night, in their clothes, Britt's arm crossed over Marie's chest.

## ALBUQUERQUE AND TALLAHASSEE

The Oscar night watch party turned out to be a complete non-event. Marie sat in the lunch room at school and listened without saying a word as the plans disintegrated before her eyes. Really. She didn't have to say a word. Jill announced that her husband wasn't interested in driving all the way to and from town on a Monday night, and if she came without him, then she didn't want to drink because of the drive home late at night, and who wanted to watch the Oscars without a beer? Then Susan, who taught art, announced that she thought the Oscars were dumb and she wasn't going to watch the show at all, and of course Al didn't want to come if Susan wasn't going to be there, so Jill said, "Aw, to hell with the whole thing," and the idea completely fizzled after about seven minutes of discussion. Marie felt an intense sense of relief, but didn't think that it showed.

So, when the actual TV show came on, it was just Marie and Britt sitting on the white couch, with the curtains drawn, Marie's feet in Britt's lap, being gently rubbed with Absorbine. *Not that watered-down human shit*, as Britt put it, but the real horse liniment, which burned up the sides of Marie's legs as Britt massaged her calves. Another *Law Review* memorandum to Alex had been finished before her own mid-week deadline, and she had declared that she could take a night off from Randolph's work and class prep to watch the show. "I think," she had said, her blue eyes sparkling over Friday's dinner when Marie had said that no one from Moriarty was coming over to watch, "I think, I don't need to go to the library anyway," and Marie was put at ease by tone of her voice and especially by the sparkle.

"Lift your feet a minute." Marie pulled her knees up toward her chest, and Britt stood up, took off her jeans, then sat back down in her panties, cross-legged, then took Marie's feet back into her lap and began to rub them again. "Okay, that's better. Who have you got?"

"Malkovitch and Crouse."

"Me, too." They had liked *Places in the Heart*, though Marie planned to differ with Britt and pick Jessica Lange ahead of Sally Field for Best Actress.

So, they were 0-2 after the first two awards, though they agreed that it had been nice to see Linda Hunt present, and how good she had been, cross-dressed as Mel Gibson's male friend, Billy, in *The Year of Living Dangerously*.

They had seen that movie separately, of course, as that was before they had met, and so, as the night wore on through the lesser awards, they found themselves discussing that film, and, in general, the presenters more than the nominees. Britt wondered aloud why it was called *The Year of Living Dangerously*, because it hadn't felt all that dangerous until the very end. Marie, who had read the book, explained it.

At Best Animated Short, they moved to the kitchen, warmed up some left-over barbecued chicken in the microwave, which they ate standing up at the kitchen counter, and got back in time for Best Foreign Film, none of which they had seen, nor would they in Albuquerque for years probably, were they inclined, which they weren't. Settling back onto the couch with a beer split between the two of them, Marie's half over ice in a glass and Britt's half still in the bottle, Marie said, without a second's consideration, "Why don't you call your friend Nikki?"

"Really? It's okay?"

"Of course it is. I'll turn this down."

"Want me to go upstairs?"

"No. How can you talk about the awards from upstairs? Use that one." She gestured toward the wall phone in the kitchen.

Britt got up from the couch, picked the receiver up, and then paused. "I'm not sure what number to use." She dialed from memory Nikki's Tallahassee apartment, but only got the answering machine: "*I'm not here. Deal with it.*"

"Hi. It's me. Monday night. I'll try that other number. Love ya." Then she had to run upstairs to the study to find the other number, left by Nikki on the answering machine, which she had written in her day planner. Back downstairs, she dialed that number, and when it picked up she stretched the cord across the back of the couch and sat down, pulling Marie's feet back into her lap.

"Brownings."

"It's me. It's Oscar night, and we're doing so poorly I've lost track."

"Where are you?"

"At home. Where are you?"

"Uhhh, you're the one who called? I'm at Ben's. Sitting in the family room with the two older children. To my right, this is Sam. Say hello, Sam." Nikki held the receiver out at arm's length and Sam, sitting on the floor at her feet, said "Hi." "And to my left, this is Janet. Say hello, Janet, this is my best friend

Robin." She moved the receiver across to the other side and Janet, on the couch and leaning affectionately into Nikki's side, said "Hi."

"So," Britt said, "the kids you're looking after must be reasonably precocious, if they're sitting quietly and watching the award for. . ." she checked the TV screen, ". . . for Best Sound."

"They certainly are that, but tonight it is more like having a chance to do something that they would never, ever do with their parents. Nix. Ben's opinion of the Oscars is scathing."

"Any news from the Mrs.?"

"I can't really talk about that right now. But the short answer is *no*."

"Gotcha. New topic: what's a three-six-four double play?"

"You're becoming a baseball fan? Part of your new, how shall we call it?, *situation*?"

"No. The professor I work for used the expression the other day in his office, but didn't have time to explain it. So, tell me."

"Okay. Runner on first. The batter grounds into the hole—the space—between first and second. The first baseman—who plays the number three position—moves to his right and fields the grounder, and throws to the shortstop—position number six—for the first out. But the trouble is that the first baseman is now out of position, too far to his right to get back in time to cover first. So the second baseman—position number four—who had been moving to his left after the grounder, continues to his left, covers first base and receives the throw from the shortstop to complete the double play. Very elegant."

"*Elegant*. That's just what Randolph said."

"About?"

"An argument I had constructed for a case he's working on."

"Wooo-eee. High praise, that, from a baseball fan."

"Maybe I should have blushed. I'm glad I have you to fill me in."

"Next time he says it, you say *Tinker to Evers to Chance*. Repeat that."

"Tinker to Ever to who?"

"Tinker to Ever-za to Chance."

"Tinker to Evers to Chance."

"Right. Then pause, and after a moment, say *Of course, that was six-four-three*."

"Six-four-three. Got it. I'll try to remember.

"And you might mention to him that I, myself, once witnessed a five-two-five. Very rare, that one."

"Five-two-five?"

"Third baseman to catcher and back to third."

"Elegant, too, I guess?"

"Less elegant than bizarre. Choose your spot carefully."

"I'll try to remember. Oh, oh. Another win for *Amadeus*. It's their night. I didn't like *Amadeus* as much as Marie did, and I've been pulling against it all night long. We both liked *Places in the Heart*."

"*We*. So everything is all right? You're not on the lam? What happened to the watch party?"

"No show. Everything is cool. Marie is right here on the couch, in fact, with her feet in my lap."

"Lucky girl."

"She smells like a horse."

"Oh?"

"I've been rubbing her calves down with Absorbine. She's on her feet all day, you know, wearing ridiculous shoes. Want to say *hi*?"

"Should I? You're not worried about what I might say?"

"Why should I be? Remember what happened in the sixth grade. Hold on." She handed the phone to Marie. "Meet Nikki."

Marie took the phone and found that she was not uneasy at all. "Hi. This is Marie."

"I'm Nikki."

"It's nice to meet you. Sort of. I mean to sort of meet you. On the phone. Not that it's sort of nice. Britt's told me a lot about you."

"Nice to meet you, too. Ditto. Robin raves. You know, right?, that I call her *Robin*?"

"She told me the story. It's very charming; I can see her chasing the birds right now."

"Did she tell you about the salt shaker?"

"Salt shaker?"

Britt, applying more liniment, groaned.

"Yeah," Nikki continued. "One of the adults had said something to her about how you could catch a robin by shaking salt onto its tail. She hadn't quite gotten the point that if you're close enough to shake salt on its tail, you could just reach down and grab the bird. So, anyway, there she was running around the well-kept yards of suburban Philly . . . I think it was Philly; ask her."

"Philadelphia?"

Britt nodded. "Uncle Steve and Aunt Lynn's."

Into the phone, Marie said, "Philly. Uncle Steve and Aunt Lynn's."

"Right," said Nikki, "Philly, with a sterling silver salt shaker, trying to get some salt to stick to a bird's tale. The neighbors—and, one would suspect, the birds—probably thought that she was nuts, but her family was charmed. As you said. Uncle Steve called her *the robin chaser*, which got shortened to *Robin*."

"She won't let me call her *Robin*."

"She hates it. Or hated it, at least. Which is why I did it, of course." The two of them laughed quietly. Then Marie heard Nikki say, off the telephone, "Time for bed, Janet. Brush your teeth, and wash your face. I'll be in when I hear the toilet flush." A pause. "Sam will be along in half an hour. Remember? That was the deal." Another pause. "Go on along now." Then, back into the telephone, "Listen, Marie, do me a favor and ask me how school is going."

Marie paused; then said, "How is school going?"

"Thanks. I hope you don't mind but I want to tell you something and I don't want Robin to know that I'm telling you. Okay? Don't say anything. Just pretend that you're listening to me talk about the travails of the PhD program. Say, *hmmm*."

"Hmmm."

"The thing that I want you to know about Robin is that she is not afraid of anything. Somewhere along the way, she lost her sense of fear. And that gets her into trouble now and then. I think it's way too late for her to regain that sense, and there's no telling what it would do to her if she tried. So, instead, those of us around her have to watch to see that she doesn't get hurt. Okay, say something non-committal, like *huh*."

"Huh."

"Remember, I'm talking about school. Nod your head like I'm saying something that you could agree with."

Marie nodded her head, feeling manipulated and vaguely uncomfortable.

"And there isn't really much more to say. Except this: be careful with her. Fearless people are oddly vulnerable. She's a very important person in my life. Remember that. Okay, now say *it sounds like they're keeping you busy*."

"It sounds like they're keeping you busy."

"Right. And now we're back on the record."

"Okay. It was nice to meet you. I hope we can do it face-to-face sometime."

"Me, too."

"Here's Britt back." Marie handed the receiver back to Britt, picked up her glass and Britt's bottle and carried them back into the kitchen, while only half listening to Britt's side of the conversation with her friend, now about the awards ceremony, now about so-and-so's dreadful gown, now about this movie or that one, now about their various study regimes, and with little, as far as Marie could tell, about either her or her relationship with Britt.

Walking back into the living room, Marie made hair-washing motions with her hands and pointed upstairs. Britt nodded, while listening to Nikki talk. Marie walked upstairs, decided not just to wash her hair but to take a shower and get ready for bed. In the bedroom, she tossed her clothes into the laundry basket, took a fresh set of pajamas from the dresser drawer and walked naked to the bathroom. In the shower, she shampooed, washed and shaved, all the time thinking about what Nikki had said to her. She wasn't sure what the point of the one-sided conversation was, and knew that they would have to talk again, this time without Britt around, so she could ask Nikki what this was all about.

Dried off, she put on her pajamas and, toweling her hair, heard the phone ring downstairs. "You getting that?" she hollered down the stairs.

"It's Nikki calling back. She had to put the kids to bed." And Marie heard Britt pick up the phone and start talking, almost in mid-sentence. She walked downstairs, where commercials were playing on the TV. Britt swung her feet onto the floor to make room for Marie to sit down, patted the cushion right next to her with her hand, and collected Marie under her arm as she sat down. Marie snuggled comfortably in and put her head on Britt's shoulder, and listened to Britt's side of the conversation, now back to the Oscar ceremony, mostly about the decent job that Jack Lemmon was doing as the host.

After a while, their talk wound down, and Britt said, "Okay, sweetie, I've really got to go now. Marie's back and at some point the interesting awards will be on." She listened for a minute, and then said. "Of course. . . . Love ya, too. . . . Bye."

The conversation over, Britt disengaged herself from Marie, stood up with the phone receiver and walked around back to the kitchen to hang up. "Wow. Listen, let me pay the phone bill this month, okay? That was longer than I thought it would be."

"It's all right. Besides, the two of you split it."

"Yeah, but not fifty-fifty."

"I'm glad you got to talk to her. She's okay?"

"Seems to be. I think I told you she's working as the housekeeper for her dissertation advisor, whose wife has run off or something." Britt sat down again, with her arm around Marie; commercials still ran.

"What happened in the sixth grade?"

"What? Oh. We got into a fight and I gave her a bloody nose."

"Why did you remind her of that?"

"Broken, actually. She claims it's still crooked, but it isn't."

"Why did you have to remind her of that?"

"I didn't want her to say something snotty to you."

"She would have, without the threat of violence?"

"You never know. Nikki has high standards with regard to my lovers. She doesn't always approve, and when she doesn't she says so."

"Doesn't she approve of me?"

"She never approves of *anyone* at the beginning. She'll come around."

"She seemed nice enough on the phone. Pleasant."

"She *must* like you. Nikki is too blunt to ever be called *pleasant*. What did she tell you when you asked about her schoolwork?"

"Oh, you know, she just told me about her classes; what she is taking and how they were going. That kind of thing." Marie lifted her head from Britt's shoulder and fluffed her hair on that side, letting it dry. "I've gotten your shirt wet."

"Good," said Britt. "Now I know what it looks like when you lie to me."

"What do you mean?" Marie looked at her, hating the fact that she'd been caught. It was all this Nikki's fault.

"I know for a fact that she has finished all of her course work and now is just working full-time on her dissertation. She hasn't had an actual class in six months."

Marie pivoted on the couch to face Britt and said, "I'm sorry. She told me something that she didn't want you to know she told me. Do you want me to tell you?"

"You bet."

"That you aren't afraid of anything. But I knew that. You told me the broken-arm story."

"Well then, that's okay. I didn't want to have to give her another bloody nose anyway. Listen: I trust her and I trust you, and I shouldn't have asked you what she said. Next time, it's okay to keep it to yourself. Really. Besides, it was a cheap shot. I, in fact, told you a fib just the other day."

"When?"

"You asked if anyone in the study group knew about us, and I said *no*, though people would suspect it if we went somewhere together. In fact, Keisha knows. She figured it out, when she saw your picture in my carrel in the library. It seems that someone spotted us shopping for groceries at Albertson's."

Marie contemplated the fact that an unknown classmate of Britt's knew that they were lovers.

"It's okay," she said.

"Sure."

"No, really. Okay."

"Your story the other night about not being able to breathe was touching."

"This seems, I don't know, different. The thought of introducing you to my friends at school makes my breath catch, I'll admit. Still. But the thought of meeting your friends at school seems . . . different. Michael once wrote to me about the feeling he gets when getting off an airplane somewhere that he's never been before. Especially if he knows little about the place; sometimes he doesn't even buy a guide book. He likes the feel of walking into the airport's arrival hall not knowing what to expect. Well, I'm not the traveler that he is, but I get the point. And that's what I think it will feel like to meet Keisha and the rest of your study group."

"Kind of like getting off a plane at the Beirut airport?" Britt laughed.

"Exactly." Marie chuckled, too. "*Exactly*. How are things in Beirut?" They laughed together. "See, I think I can do that, though I'm still no Michael Reid . . ."

"About which I am more than pleased."

". . . no, I mean I won't be either as comfortable nor as stimulated as he is arriving at an unfamiliar airport, but I think I can do it. For whatever reason, meeting that husband will be the hardest, and I don't know him from Adam. But you're not nervous about meeting my straight friends?"

"Hey, I've been like this for a long, long time. I'm okay with it whenever you are. Say the word."

"I will. Soon. I promise."

"Don't make promises you can't keep."

"Speaking of which, what do I look like when I'm lying?"

"You fiddle with your hands, then you fluff your hair. I don't know where your eyes were looking, but not at me. And I don't think you were blinking. Here, let's practice. Look at me. Okay, now: what do you miss about making love with men?" Marie said nothing for a long moment, causing Britt to say, "I'm not sure I like this silence."

"I'm doing you the favor of taking the question seriously."

"Fair enough."

Marie thought for a bit more, before speaking. "The thing is, Britt, that I can't separate having sex with a woman from having sex with you."

"I'm glad."

"No, it's more profound than that. For me, it's not sex with men *versus* sex with women. It's sex with you *versus* sex with anyone else. *Anyone* else. I have no interest in anyone else. And that may be the difference between me and your friends."

"Wait . . ."

"No, you wait. What I mean is this: if we were to split up, I have no doubt that you would eventually find your way into the arms of another woman. And I'm completely okay with that, even though, of course, I hope we never split up. But see?, I'm not sure I would. I can't and don't look beyond you, and can't generalize from you to all, or even other, women. And I think that's what your friends will find weak in me, that I'm lacking in commitment. That they'll see it in me, or know it about me just by looking, or will learn it about me or will hear it in my voice. Somehow they'll know, and will think that, I don't know, I'm not true, not true to you, or to them or to . . ."

Britt interrupted. ". . . to Beirut society?"

"To Beirut society. I don't want them not to like me because I'm not committed to their society."

"Listen to me." Britt took Marie by her shoulders and turned her so they faced each other. "*That*, my dear, dear Marie, was one of the loveliest thing that has ever been said to me. This is not some Lesbo-feminista political game. This is you, and me, in love. That's enough for me, and let's not worry about what anyone thinks of our love affair. And if I have my way, we will never, either of us, ever sleep with *anyone* else again. Okay? Male or female? Never again. Okay?"

"It's a deal."

"Okay," Britt said, "now this is trickier: What about this Michael?"

Marie looked across the room at the television screen; she had completely lost track of what was going on at the Oscars. "Michael? That's harder."

"Why?"

"Because we were friends, before we were lovers, and will still be I think—I hope—after we stop being lovers. I *want* to talk to him about you, and tell him that I'm in love with a younger woman, and I wonder what he'd say about that. But I don't know what he'd say, and I don't know what he'll do, now that I'm with you. I don't know. I don't know." Her voice drifted off.

"Well," Britt said, "you're not lying to me, I now know that. And I'm thankful for it. I guess that'll have to do for now. My arm is asleep." She rearranged them on the couch, now sitting side-by-side, their thighs touching and holding hands. "Where are we?"

Marie was grateful to let the topic of Michael fade into the ceremony. "It's *Amadeus*'s night, that's for sure. Too bad for you. Ha! Did you ever spend the night in T-man's stall?"

"Sure."

"When he was sick?"

"How do you know he got sick?"

"I'm guessing."

"Yes. I stayed with him those two nights. But several other times, happier times, when we were at shows. What brought this up?"

"I just want to make sure that you know that our resolutions not to sleep with anyone else doesn't include the horse that I plan to buy you for a graduation present."

Britt stood up, walked over to the TV and turned the volume down. "Wait, wait, wait, wait. This is serious, now. You are *not* to buy me a horse for graduation, or any other event. Okay? Look at me." She walked over to the couch, took Marie's chin in her left hand and made eye contact. "It's a nice thought, but *don't do it.*"

"Wow. You're serious, aren't you?"

"Totally."

"Don't you ever think about getting another horse?"

"Only every day, including this one."

"Then . . . ?"

Britt sat down on the couch. "I continued to ride after we put Transnational down, but my mother refused, absolutely refused, to own another horse. So I road stable horses, and even continued to compete. But it wasn't the same. Then, late in high school, I stopped competing, and eventually stopped going by the stable, where the girls all seemed so young. In college, I don't know, I just never started riding seriously again. I thought about getting a horse after college, but in the Forest Service my lifestyle was so itinerant that it didn't make any sense. I rode some in my job, now western. It was fun when we had to document a site in a wilderness area, where no vehicles are allowed. We spent three months on one down in the Gila; it's actually not all that far from that place that you told me you liked, down near, where was it?"

"Old Horse Springs." Marie paused. "I never knew if it was named for an old horse or an old spring."

"The latter. I asked. We had to pack all of our equipment in on horses and mules, and then ride in and out for food and other supplies. I rode a Quarter Horse mare, about two hands shorter than T-man, but she was a sure-footed thing, that's for sure. And she was game.

"Anyway. I couldn't have my own horse when I was moving all the time from site to site, and then I quit and went back to school, where, as you know, I became broke, until I found my present salaried lover . . ."

". . . who wants to buy you a horse for graduation. What's the objection, now that the surprise is gone?"

"First. One should never, ever give another person a pet for a gift. Period. Second, I know a lot more about horses than you do, and when the time comes, I insist on picking him out."

"Or her."

"Or her. And not having you and some guy who's trying to get rid of his injured or drugged up horse pick for me. For instance, you probably think that color would be an important consideration."

"It isn't?"

"No. Not for me. Where was I? Third. When T-man died, I swore I'd never have another stable horse, who has to spend twenty-two hours a day in a stall. So I won't buy a horse until I own a couple of acres, at least, and can keep the horse in the backyard, at which point, fourth, we'd have to buy two, because they are herd animals and get lonely if they're the only horse around. And fifth, and most important, which Randolph says is a lousy way to structure an argument, buying a horse is like adopting a retarded child . . ."

"What? How shocking a thing to say."

"Okay, so I wouldn't make the point that way to just anyone, but look, they can live well into their twenties, they're totally dependent on you, and they won't grow up and go away to college. They'll be dependent on us until they die. That's a commitment that must be undertaken carefully. And together, in our case. I'm not saying don't buy me a horse; I'm saying let's do it together. And carefully. Okay? Almost as if we were adopting a child."

Marie let the thought sink in for a while, then paused for a minute, took a breath and said, "Okay, since we're asking each other hard questions, here's one: Do you ever think about having a child?"

Without hesitation: "Yes."

"Would you adopt?"

"I guess that's an option, but I had more in mind using the equipment I've got. You know, the phrase *giving birth* has a certain ring to it." When Marie said nothing, Britt continued, "Lately I've thought about having one with you."

"*With me*? That would be a little difficult, wouldn't it?"

"Except for the first ten seconds, it would be entirely *with* you."

"Okay, I concede the point. But what about those first ten seconds? I'm fresh out of Y chromosomes." Marie paused. "Actually, now that I think of it, saying I'm *fresh out* doesn't adequately reflect the shortage of my supply."

"You've got your biology wrong. You don't need a Y chromosome to make a baby; half of all the sperm in the world are Y-less."

"I guess that's right. So what would I need?"

"A gay egg, I guess."

"And a way to introduce her to yours."

"Like maybe a drink and a dance at the Café Fargo? In a petri dish kind of way, I mean. There are probably feminist repro physiologists working on the introduction as we speak."

"The stuff of James Dobson's nightmares. So, short of that, how do you arrange those first ten seconds?"

"Well, you can pick a friend . . ."

"A friend?"

". . . or do it anonymously. Or you go gene shopping."

"Which would you do?"

"That would absolutely be something that we'd figure out together." Britt turned to face Marie and once again put her arm across her lover's shoulders. "Don't you think about having a child?"

"I haven't thought about it for years. If anything, I thought that plane had boarded and pushed back, leaving me at the gate." She laughed to herself. Then, "Boy, of all the disorientating questions that being with you has raised, the zinger has to be this: which of us would get pregnant?" She laughed again, shaking her head.

"First one of us; then the other. You're senior; you can go first" said Britt. "What's disorientating about that?"

"When you put it that way . . . ." Marie left the sentence unfinished. "I'm not sure . . .," and that sentence, too, faded away to nothing.

"I'm not sure, either, Angel. Heck, I've known you for less than a year. I think it's a little early for us to be planning a family together. And I suggest that we stop asking each other squirmy questions and recover the mood of Oscar night, in which our favorites are taking a beating, except that my gal is going to win Best Actress, you watch."

Shortly thereafter, Sally Field did indeed win, but spoiled the night by giving her gushing acceptance speech.

Marie said "That's it. I'm going to bed. Not only did Jessica not win, but Sally disappoints. *You like me!* How smarmy can you get?" She stood up.

"Come on," Britt said. "It showed she's an actual person, who sometimes has to make up her own clunky lines, and not just deliver a well-crafted screenplay. She's still okay, in my book. It made her seem human."

"You're just saying that because you didn't want Jessica to win anyway."

"It's more like I didn't want Sam Shepard's wife to win."

"Well, I'm still going to bed. You coming?"

"You go. I'll watch to the bitter end, and be up in a bit. Kiss me now, in case you're asleep later." She leaned her head back on the white couch and accepted Marie's lingering goodnight kiss. "Mmmm. See you in the morning, Angel." And Marie mounted the stairs to the bedroom, thinking of horses, children and what the heck Nikki had meant on the phone.

# ~ 11

# ALBUQUERQUE

"Nine-fourteen."

Richard sent his serve into the right front corner, then behind him and into the left rear corner. His partner, Ned, played it smoothly, but weakly, off the back wall, to leave Richard a drive to the front and down the left wall for a winner.

"You're out." He and Ned had changed the scoring scheme of their racquetball games to make it more like baseball. Hence, the server was the pitcher, and when he beat Ned on the play, he didn't get the point, but put Ned *out*, so that it was now Ned's turn to serve to him, giving Richard the chance to score.

"Fourteen-nine," Ned announced, and then served to the backhand side; Ned always served to his backhand. Richard probably should have gone to the ceiling, but instead played hard down the left, but failed to pass Ned, who put the shot away easily. "You're out."

"Nine-fourteen."

Richard served softly, high into the right corner, looking to hit the dead spot in the left rear corner behind him. Ned smacked it on the short hop against the back wall, the ball nicked the ceiling on the way to the front wall, just barely made it there and then spun forward to a dead stop, impossible for Richard to get to. Game over.

"Nice game," said Ned.

"Right. You too."

"You played well today." Richard had, in fact, played pretty well. He had won one of three and had stayed close in the others, always an accomplishment against Ned.

"Thanks. You too."

They slid their backs down the wall and sat on the floor outside the racquetball court. Platitudes, maybe, jock talk, but Richard enjoyed the moments after the game. Exhausted, sweaty, breathing hard, there was a definite intimacy to post-racquetball talk, not unlike post-sex talk. Not to be analyzed for literary merit or insight, maybe, but still thoughts were exchanged with a partner when both felt good, tired, vulnerable. The same chemistry was at work, Richard was sure. He always felt a little embarrassed just after playing against a stranger. *What was your name again? I'm sorry.*

Ned was one of his closest friends, his closest racquetball friend, anyway. His closest friend among his colleagues, surely. They played regularly and had times like these.

"At six-four, I had a chance to put you away."

"Yup. I was on my heels."

"But I couldn't get anything on my backhand return."

Their games were not overly competitive. They enjoyed playing hard, but since Richard ordinarily lost, not much was made of that. Individual shots, rallies, points, runs, fades, made the game.

As they caught their breaths and cooled down, their conversation would turn to other things: teaching, the law, families, friends. Today, Richard brought up Michael's latest letter: "Did you ever meet my friend Michael Reid? He passes through town every now and then."

"Law professor?"

"No, he teaches education at Arkansas. Used to live here; used to teach school somewhere around here, I forget where. That was before I knew him. We met at a Dukes game years ago, when he was in grad school, and we became third-base-line friends. Then, outside-the-stadium, beer-drinking friends. That was before I married Rita, and before he got his first tenure-track job, and moved away. Passes through now and then and looks me up."

"Don't think I know him."

"I just got a letter from him; he's in Eastern Europe. Bulgaria. Travelling around. He travels a lot."

"Sabbatical?"

"No, he doesn't work when he travels; just sees the sights."

"Disenchanted middle-aged college prof searching for his identity in far-off places? I've seen the movie. Or maybe not. Read the book, anyway."

"Maybe. I'm not sure that's the way he'd put it."

"*Kicks just keep getting harder to find*?"

"Maybe that's it. So, when did you take to quoting rock and roll lyrics?"

"Actually, I'm an old Rolling Stones fan."

"Actually, you are a complete dork. That was not the Stones."

"Who was it?"

"It would embarrass both of us for me to tell you. Leave it at this: it was a group that no one ever, ever, *ever* mixes up with the Stones."

"Who?"

"I am *not* telling you."

"Whatever."

They walked up the stairs to the locker room.

"Sounds like a nice life. How's he afford it?"

"I don't know. No offspring. Cheap tastes, except in airplane tickets."

"So what's he think of commieland?"

"That was what the letter was about, sort of. He's having a good time, off the beaten path, at least off the beaten capitalist path. He seems to find things to appreciate wherever he goes. He keeps running into the police, though. *Normal police operations*, or so he's told. Talked me out of Christmas in Sophia."

"Sophia?"

"The capital of Bulgaria, of course."

"Of course."

"But he apparently doesn't mind the attention he's getting from the criminal justice system. He's not outraged, anyway."

"He's in trouble?"

"I don't think so. He doesn't seem worried. Never does. You should read the letter; getting picked up by the Sophia police is the kind of thing you criminal law types ought to experience. As he points out, there are people here in the good old USA who get picked up in so-called *normal police operations*."

"Huh. I'd like to read it." Ned was clearly skeptical that he could gain any insight into criminal law through some tourist's observations. "Did you ever see *Midnight Express*? Terrible movie, *Midnight Express. . ..*"

The topic shifted in the shower room.

"What are you working on?" Ned asked.

"Right now, mostly on that bankruptcy case I've got before the Second Circuit."

"Ahhh, the heartbreak of bankruptcy."

"Doesn't apply. I represent the Bank of Commerce downtown."

"I don't want to know about it. I don't deal in areas of the law that use lower case Roman numerals."

"The court just granted oral argument, so I've got a trip to New York City next month."

"Now, I'm interested. Before or after Opening Day?"

"After. I checked. The Mets are playing the Dodgers, twi-night doubleheader on Friday, after the argument on Thursday."

"Gee, tough luck, you bastard."

"Actually, I'm not sure I'll get to the game. I'm thinking of taking my research assistant, Britt Larsen. And I'm not sure she'd be interested in the ball game."

Ned stopped drying his hair. "I urge caution, my friend."

"Why?" Ned just looked at him. "Come on. It's a business trip. A *business* trip. Period. I think I can get the court's permission to let her have a bit of the argument. I can't deny her that chance just because she's a woman. It's the Eighties, Ned, we have women law students, lots of them."

"Is Rita going?"

"I don't know. She has to work. I didn't ask. It's a *business* trip."

"If it were you and I going to argue a case in New York, you'd ask her, right?"

"Maybe."

"Bullshit, *maybe*." Ned went back to drying his hair.

"What are you worried about? The way it looks?"

They were standing, naked, in a small alcove formed by the lockers, with a wooden bench between them. Ned put down the towel and pointed his finger at Richard's face. "I don't give a shit how it looks. You're right, these are the Eighties. Lots of things look normal now that didn't in the Sixties. Both ways. I'm not worried about looks, I'm worried about the actual, below-the-belt reality of the world. I'm worried about the power that teachers have over students. Watch your step."

"The advice of my senior colleague and dean?" Richard asked, a little stiffly.

"The advice of one who has mastered your serve to the back left corner, shithead."

"Okay. Look. There's nothing. Honest."

"Right."

～

Ned's reaction had, in a way, solidified what Richard now recognized was his determination to invite Britt to accompany him to New York to argue the Riley case. Not to do so would acknowledge the legitimacy of Ned's concern, which he refused to do. For him to extend the offer to her, though, would need some arranging. She was not, after all, a lawyer yet, and it would be well out of the ordinary for her to be allowed to present even a part of the oral argument in a case to the federal Court of Appeals, the second highest court in the country. Sure, she could always just tag along, sit at the counsel table, take notes and hand him papers. But the only legitimate reason to invite her along would be if she could actually present part of the argument, and that would take some arranging.

But, actually, it turned out to be easier to arrange than he had imagined. He called the judge he had clerked for just out of law school fifteen years earlier, who was now the Chief Judge of the Fifth Circuit Court of Appeals in New Orleans, and that judge had presented Richard's request to the Chief Judge of the Second Circuit in New York City. A couple of days later Richard heard from the New York court that it had agreed to respect New Mexico's student practice rule and to grant permission for Ms. Britt Larsen to appear in court, *pro hoc vice*—for this case only—under the direct supervision of Richard S. Randolph, Esq., in the case of In re Riley, Docket No. 85-23495Civ. Richard was very pleased.

Ned's concerns, though, had made him defensive and, he decided, the thing would have to be done very openly and with a certain flair. So he showed the letter granting permission to the big Dean, Ned's superior, bragged on Britt a bit and asked that he extend the invitation. The Dean agreed, with apparently none of the concerns that Ned had expressed, and Richard returned to his office, pleased with himself. As a second thought he tacked a message to Ned's door, for the world to see: "2d Cir. granted perm. for B. Larsen to argue."

An hour later, Britt tore into his office, dropped her backpack on the floor and sat on the couch. "What's going on? What's this about?"

He swiveled around from his word processor. Her eyes said *Yes!* He rarely saw such eagerness, such sparks in a law student's eyes and he felt the satisfaction that such sparks bring to all teachers.

"Yes? What is it you want, Ms. Larsen?" he said, trying to sound coy. He hadn't told her of his plans.

"I just talked to the Dean. Do you think I can do it? Argue to the Second Circuit?" She sat back; then up again, "Oh, God, do you think I can do it, Professor Randolph?"

"You can do it. I wouldn't have arranged it if I didn't think so. This is not some silly law school simulation, Britt; remember that. I've got a real client that has fourteen million real dollars at stake here. This is really the United States Court of Appeals. You can do it, but it's not a game. It will take hard work and lots and lots of practice, until you're sick of the case and then more practice. But, if you're willing to work that hard, then I want you to do it, the Dean wants you to do it, the client wants you to do it and the court says it's okay. So think about it."

"What is there to think about? I'll do it. Oh, God, I'm excited already. When's the argument?"

"Mid-next month. We'll spend a couple of days in New York; we'll fly over one day, argue the next, and fly home the third. And, ahem, you'll have to dress like a lawyer, something you've managed rather successfully to avoid doing so far, at least in my presence."

"Like what? Like a suit?"

"Yes, like a suit. I assume we're talking about something in grey or blue, pinstriped, white blouse, some kind of neck do-dad, probably blue with little red specks. Stockings, shoes that are neither fashionable nor comfortable. All the appropriate undergarments."

"Skirt or trousers?"

He paused, considering the question. "Skirt, I think. But talk to Professor Johnson; she was practicing in New York a couple of years ago. Can you manage all of that? Within the next month?"

"I guess I'll have to. What about expenses in New York? I'm sort of broke."

"The client pays. I'll spring for Broadway tickets, assuming you're good enough to take along. That is to say, if you master the case well enough to argue it." *Damn it*, he thought, that was just the kind of stupid double entendre he wanted to avoid. He could imagine Ned, nodding meaningfully.

"Okay." She apparently hadn't noticed anything amiss in his choice of words. "What do we do, besides go shopping for clothes?"

"You give me every Tuesday and Friday afternoon from now until we go.

Starting tomorrow, when we'll divide the case up. First we've got their brief to tear apart and evaluate before we can write our reply brief. Then we practice and undertake to persuade the court orally with our silver advocacy."

"Golden."

"We'll see."

"I'll do it." She reached out her hand and they shook. "Thanks for the chance and I'll do it well."

She walked out with her right fist clenched and, up the stairs to the Forum, she snapped her fingers. "Hoopla!," she said, quoting, without thinking, an expression she had picked up from Marie, who had picked it up from Michael, and Michael, in turn, from Anna.

⁓

"Do you think I should shave for the trip to New York?" They sat, side by side on the white couch, both in shorts, four bare feet on the coffee table, Marie's just reaching the edge and Britt's in the middle, their shoulders just touching. Britt was looking down at her legs.

"I've gotten used to your fuzziness."

"Do you think I should shave for the trip to New York?"

"Is there an echo in here?"

"*Do you*?"

"Yes."

"Thank you. I'm a little out of practice."

"I'll show you how. When's the last time you shaved?"

"Uh, high school? Freshman year of college? Ten years, maybe."

"What about under your arms?"

"I'm not going to be wearing a damn sun dress."

"Still. Once you start, why stop?"

"We'll see. When?"

"Two nights before you go."

"But what if I cut myself?"

"That's why two nights before. You'll heal. Do you have the tools?"

"What do you think?"

"Okay, I'll pick up some stuff at the grocery, so you won't have to be seen publically violating all of your feminist principles. I use soap, but I'd better get you some shaving cream, 'cuz your skin will be tender after all these years. You're very happy about all this, aren't you? Even the shaving part?"

"Un huh."

It was unusual for Britt to take an entire mid-week night off from her studies and Marie would have enjoyed the evening in any case, just being at home, alone, together. But in addition, Britt was almost giddy with the excitement and the flattery of the New York trip and her giddiness was infectious. Add to that that they had cracked a bottle of champagne, which now sat half-empty in a four-quart saucepan full of ice water, and then had split a half a joint about an hour ago, and Marie was experiencing the usual profundity in ordinary things that often came to her with a buzz. It seemed as though Britt's happiness was tangible, tastable, chewable, huggable. She tried to form the words that would describe this ooze and glop of happiness that flowed from her lover, but she could not.

"You are so happy."

"Can you imagine it, Marie? The United States Court of Appeals for the Second Circuit. *May it please the Court. My name is Britt Larsen and along with Richard S. Randolph, I represent the New Mexico Bank of Commerce in this action. . . .* Can you imagine it, Marie? This is what the big time must feel like. The big time. I think we should buy a house. When I get a job after school, I mean. An old adobe one, out in the country. Placitas or Corrales. Maybe an acre or so. Trover would have room to run."

"Ginger. And she doesn't like to run. She likes to sleep." She gestured toward the corner of the room where the dog confirmed Marie's appraisal of her needs. "And do you know how long it would take me to drive from Corrales to Moriarty?"

"All right, then: Cedar Crest. We could commute in opposite directions, get fat on piñon nuts and watch the eagles soar. We could have horses. Two. You can't have just one, you know."

"You mentioned that."

"They get lonely."

"I've been learning about horses from Al the biology teacher. Do you think we should finish that joint?"

Britt lit the stub, took a drag and passed it to Marie. "'Ere."

"Thanks." She took a smaller drag and passed it back. "Al bears some considerable responsibility for our having met, know that?" And Marie told her about the years-long, and as yet unconsummated, as best she could tell, flirtation between Al and Susan, and how she had been on informal chaperone duty the night at the Fargo when they met.

"I'll try to forget that when I meet them, but it will be hard. *Hi, Al. So you and Susan are the would-be couple, oops.*"

"Don't you dare. 'Ere." She exhaled the smoke. "So anyway, Al's been teaching me about horses."

"Like?"

"Like that they can't puke."

"True. That's why they can, and will, eat themselves to death, given half the chance. And why intestinal problems are so serious. Everything's got to keep moving front to back, or they get in trouble. It's called colicking, when things get jammed up and stuck. That's how T-man died . . ."

"Oh."

". . . which we aren't going to talk about now. What else have you learned?"

"No muscles below the knee."

"Right. Tendons and ligaments only. Speaking of which, make that muscle."

"Which muscle?"

"You know good and well which muscle I'm talking about. That one right there." Britt poked a forefinger at the middle of Marie's near thigh. "That one."

Marie tightened her quadriceps. "You should have seen me when I was really in shape."

"Except, of course, that I was a child then, not much interested in the thigh muscles of adults. Thank God."

"You know what I mean. Swimming three thousand meters a day is good for that muscle right there, among others."

"It's funny. I always think of swimmers as being big across the shoulders, not strong of thigh."

"Strong of thigh?"

"Strong of thigh. But your shoulders aren't unnaturally broad, and they weren't in that *SI* picture either."

"That's why I swam Division III, not Division I."

"It's called the *rectus femoris*, you know."

"The which?"

"The *rectus femoris*. I looked it up at the library." Britt moved her hand onto Marie's leg. "Makes me damp just to see it," she said, rubbing the tightened muscle with her palm. "*Rectus femoris*. I like saying it." She lifted her hand and traced the muscle with her fingertips. "And this is the *vastus lateralis. . .,*" she traced along the outside of Marie's thigh, ". . . and this is the *vastus medialis* on the top of the inside. Somewhere under there . . .," she poked with her finger, ". . . is the *vastus intermedius*. Four of them, see? The *quadriceps.*"

"You looked it up?"

"Yeah. I figured if I was going to be so intimate with them, I ought to know their names. I wonder if it ought to be *recta fermora* when it's your leg?"

"In the *law* library?"

"In some med mal loose-leaf service."

"Med mal?"

"Medical malpractice. Presumably there are multi-million dollar cases involving malpractice on these muscles right here. Such a waste; I don't like to even think about it." With her thumb on the *medialis* and her little finger on the *lateralis*, Britt stroked the length of Marie's thigh.

"I like the way you say that. Can I relax now? It's hard to keep it tense."

"Not just yet."

"So have you always been an admirer of *rectus femoris*?"

"You're my first."

"Really? How flattering."

"If you want to know the truth, I never dated a girl before you whose thigh muscles were quite so, let's see, visible. Actually, I'm not sure how I ever got along without one. Or two, rather. Now, tell me what else you have learned about horses."

"Where were we?"

"No vomiting, and no muscles below the knee."

"Right. And they can't breathe through their mouths."

"Right. What else?"

"That's it for now." She lay her hand over Britt's, which was still on top of her thigh. "Can I relax, now? I'm shaking."

"Take a break. Momentarily. But I may need to see it again later. They have thirteen gallons of blood."

"That's a lot."

"Yup. Every year Sarah would throw a Fourth of July party at the stable, and she'd have thirteen milk jugs full of strawberry Kool-aid. And she'd pour two of them out onto the floor of the arena."

"The point being?"

"That a horse can lose a lot of blood and not be in serious danger. To keep us from panicking if one got hurt and started bleeding like mad. Remember that."

"Thirteen gallons. Don't panic. Check. What else?"

"They also have peckers as big as a your arm." Britt reached and held up Marie's arm for emphasis.

Marie studied the improbable comparison. "Well, Al didn't mention that part. He probably thought I'd be shocked."

"It is shocking when you're eleven. Trust me."

The joint had gone out again, now about two-thirds gone, and Britt asked, "Do you want to finish this?"

"Not me. I've had more than enough. Soon I'll be grey, you know. Look here . . ." Marie bent to let Britt see the top of her head. "I'm starting to find more and more grey hairs. Would you want to live back of the Crest with a forty-year-old, grey-haired school teacher?"

"Forty doesn't seem so old. Thirty seems older." Britt laughed, "I thought that was true just the instant before I said it." She picked up Marie's left hand. "God, your thumbs are adorable." Marie's left thumb is what is known as a hammer head thumb, very short between the knuckle and the end, the nail short and wide. "Have I told you that? It was the first thing I ever noticed about you, that your thumb was so damn cute and you drank your beer with ice. I watched for ten minutes at the Fargo before I asked you to dance. If you had been drinking right handed I'd probably never have made my move."

Marie held their hands up and looked for a while at her thumb. "Michael once wrote me a card from some post office where he had just read, you know, one of those wanted posters. It described some convict's thumbs and Michael wanted me to know. He said never to rob a bank without gloves on. What *is* this that we're watching on television?"

"I know for a fact that this one commercial has been playing for twenty minutes."

"What do we have to eat? If I don't eat soon, I'll starve."

"Popcorn. Let's make popcorn."

"Risky, risky, we may burn the fucking house down."

"Let's try. Where's the kitchen?"

Later, buttered and salted and drinking the rest of the champagne straight out of the bottle, they turned the stereo up, took off their shoes and let the Linda's *Greatest Hits* blast. Britt danced a restrained dance, mostly hips and shoulders and blond hair, knees and toes and finger tips and eyes, but Marie, that night anyway, a little stoned and a little drunk, happy and in her own house, danced an exuberant, prancing dance, high stepping, arms straight down, one fist clenched and the other holding the champagne bottle by the neck, her every muscle, it seemed, tightened by the music. She shook her head and messed up her hair and her feet rocked the furniture when they hit on the down beat, and she sang along with the songs. She danced, in other words, like someone who had learned to dance dancing with the girls to rock and roll records, Saturday night at the American Legion hall in the early Sixties, dressed in black leotards and a skirt above her knees, the hot taste of one gulp of whiskey in her throat; a lean, hard, unrestrained dance, an in-your-face dance, a dance that dared the boys, who couldn't dance like this, not yet, an athletic dance that was more muscle than flesh, more rhythm than tune, more fight than love.

*So, you see/I really care, 'are, 'are/without you/I'm nothing/whoa-oh, oh-oh.*

"You're sweating." Britt ran her fingers straight back through Marie's damp hair.

"Mmmmmmm." She closed her eyes and, still moving to the music, she slowed the pace down and let herself be stroked. "It feels good. We should do this more often."

"The next one is slow . . .," Britt said.

"Oh oh. What'd'ya want to do?"

"Dance with me."

"I've heard that before." Marie looked up at Britt and could see that her lover didn't remember the significance of the straightforward command. "The first words you ever spoke to me. I knew I was a goner. It wasn't a slow dance though. I'd never have said yes to that."

"Come on."

"Oh, I'd feel funny."

"Here? In your own living room? The drapes carefully pulled?"

"Well, . . . Who will lead?"

"Don't worry about that. Come here." Britt pulled her toward her, put her elbows on Marie's shoulders and folded her hands on top of Marie's head. "Just dance with me."

"Somebody has to lead."

"That's a rule the boys made up. Here. Put your head here." Britt pulled Marie's head to her so that her ear rested on Britt's collarbone; she kept her hands on top of Marie's head and began to sway with the music, not yet moving her feet. Marie stepped closer, put her hands around Britt's waist and slipped her thumbs into the back pockets of her jeans. One hand still held the champagne bottle, which bounced a little against the back of Britt's leg as she moved gently to the music.

"I'll bet I smell like sweat," Marie murmured into Britt's shirt.

"Umhmm."

There was really nothing to be self-conscience about, Marie thought. Shit, she had lain every which way in this woman's arms. She had put this here, and that there. They had been nipple-to-nipple. Nose-to-toes. Taste-buds-to-nymphae. Why did dancing seem so much more intimate? She immediately stepped on Britt's toe.

"Oops." She apologized.

"Shhhhh," said Britt. "Boys' rules. Girls' rules are that it's all right to touch toes. See?" Marie felt one foot be enveloped by Britt's sock, which then slid down the side of her foot to the floor. Britt was humming along with the music, saying "There. That's right," and she was right, Marie discovered. They were dancing and no one was leading. It felt very satisfying, very coordinated, very . . . well, feminine. When the music stopped, they stood in each other's arms for a moment. Marie's eyes were closed, but she felt Britt kiss her part.

"Tired?" Britt asked.

"No!" The music had started up again and Marie danced away. "Not yet. More dancing. More champagne." She took a drink; there was still enough fizz to make her choke a little, then sneeze. She shook her head, laughed out loud and sang along with the next song.

Finally, after another side of Linda Ronstadt and nearly exhausted, their buzz winding down, they went upstairs where, sitting naked and cross-legged in bed, facing each other, they finished the bottle of champagne. Out the window, lightning crackled over the Crest. "There's magic in this house tonight," Marie said. "You cannot lose."

Richard and Rita had put the kids to bed and were sitting reading, enjoying the quiet.

"You know that bankruptcy argument I've got back east next month?"

"Umhm."

"Want to go?"

"During the week?"

"Yes, but we could stay the weekend. Dodgers *versus* Mets."

"How am I supposed to get off work, not to mention who gives a shit about baseball?"

Richard shrugged. "I was just asking. Just wanted you to know I thought it would be fun."

"Thanks, but I can't. Why don't you take the boys?" Rita grinned over the top of the paper.

"Okay, but I'll probably have to leave them hanging out in Times Square while I'm in court. It'd just be for a few hours, of course. They'd probably be all right."

"Oh, what the hell. I'll keep them. We'll go to the zoo."

"I'm taking my researcher, Britt Larsen."

"To the zoo?"

"To New York. The court's given her permission to argue part of the case. Quite a compliment to her. And to me."

"Have fun."

"Jealous?"

"Nope. Sleep with her and I'll blow your fucking brains out."

"For Christ's sake, Rita, she's my student. Besides, I slept with you when I was married to someone else. So were you for that matter."

"Different."

"Why?"

"Still don't have it figured out, do you? Why do I always end up with such stupid assholes? Because, my dear husband and the father of most of my children, you were very, very lucky to get me and write that down so it doesn't slip your mind again. And yes, now that you ask, I'd like a dish of ice cream and I know we haven't any, but I can wait until you get back from the store." She wrinkled her nose and blew him a kiss over the paper. "Häagen Daz coffee. You'll have to go to Smith's, because Albertson's won't have it. Bye."

## CORRESPONDENCE

March 23. In a second-class sleeper, heading south through central Yugoslavia, bound for Athens. I have just awakened from a numbing nap and still feel groggy. Between *and* and *still* in the sentence above I sat for several minutes, my eyes unfocused out the window. The compartment is empty, except for me; the cars ahead are full of gastarbeiters heading home, but this is a more expensive couchette, and is empty, except for me. Last night, a few minutes before I went to sleep, some Turks played a shell game in the corridor, hoping to rope me in. It is early afternoon and I am sixteen hours north of Athens.

Dear Richard,

When I found myself standing in the Sophia airport early one morning a couple of weeks ago, speaking German to an attractive young Bulgarian woman, I was a little confused. I hadn't actually expected I'd be speaking German on this trip, and had not got myself prepared with the usual phrases. Furthermore, it was very early in the morning after a very late night in Athens, so when I found myself asking directions, I was a bit confused, as much by my ability to speak at all as by the shortcomings of my German. But it worked out okay as such things have a way of doing and the attractive young Bulgarian woman got me started into town and didn't even ask why I didn't take a taxi. My German would not have been up to that.

I rode to the end of the line on bus 86, made the connection to the No. 10 tram, all of this free info in case you ever find yourself in Sophia with only small change in your pocket, for I fear, my friend, that you would be a taxi-taker. I got lost getting off the tram, and ended up, by chance, in an office of Balcantourist, the state tourist agency. Inside it was quiet and empty; many little glass booths with Bulgarian posters for an impossible-to-imagine tourist rush. Soft classical music played from the speakers. Two attendants waited on no one; only one felt comfortable in English. I asked for the hotel I had chosen from a brochure, back in Athens.

"No, that one is only for Bulgarians."

"Why?"

Her English was not so good to explain.

"What do you suggest?"

"One of these. How much do you wish to spend?"

I was placed in a US $15 hotel a short walk away, right downtown on the main street. While the phone call was made and the forms filled in, I admired a bright red and white bauble pinned to the sweater of the other attendant.

"Isst olt Vulgarian traditionink. Red unt vite. Vor de cheeks. In de sprink." She unpinned the bauble and tied it to my sweater.

"But no, you mustn't . . .."

"I haf many," she said, with a smile that shall always dominate my recollection of Bulgaria.

The hotel was not nice. Easily the worst I've ever had in Europe, though no worse than what $15 would bring you in downtown L.A. Better probably. Later on, when I got to Romania, I would say, "The room must be clean."

"Clean? Of course."

"In Bulgaria the rooms were not always clean."

"Yes, but that was Bulgaria."

The toilet, down the hall, was not nice; the shower that worked, one flight up, stood by itself in a very large room, with drafts and a door that didn't lock. A sports team of some sort shared the hotel with me and throughout the night there was much Balkan scampering about. Outside the window, dirty snow fell through the polluted sky, and yellow trams squeaked and clanked by until I fell asleep.

I have no particular insights on the Socialist world, I'm afraid, even now, rushing through the relatively capitalist fields of Yugoslavia, three weeks since I first arrived in Sophia. Insights must be very substantial to bear transportation from here to New Mexico, for it's a long way and the journey can be arduous, as I should know, for I've made it. My tourist's eye spotted no slums or porno book shops in Sophia or Bucharest, neither any interesting newspapers nor political demonstrations. Women walk alone and safely through dark public parks at midnight in those strange, large cities; they also get stopped at random in the daylight by the police and made to exhibit their papers, and for all I know they get beaten by their husbands at home. People on the street smile and frown in about the same proportion as at home. Teenagers flirt, babies are spoiled, life goes on. Make what you can of all of this, but I have no particular insight. Travel, I have found, tells me more about myself and the way things are done at home than about how exactly Sophia works and why. What I have discovered is that I am not crazy about being stopped by the police because I look out of place, a reasonably regular occurrence, as I wrote to you once before, I think.

From Bulgaria, I continued the trip through Romania and Yugoslavia. Sights and sounds along the way I found quite interesting; more later, perhaps over pizza and beer, perhaps watching the Dukes Triple A their way through the Albuquerque summer. I would enjoy that. For now, I think I have finished this letter and will read a bit. Or perhaps I'll try my hand at that Turkish shell game. Just kidding. I have a feeling that my nap will lead to insomnia tonight, listening to the rails click and contemplating a trip through the friendly and familiar streets of Athens by trolleybus from the train station to Syntagma. Such a trip through a spring morning in a known and loved city can hardly be topped, except, of course, by such a trip through an unknown and surprising one. Even comfortable and familiar Athens, though, is always able to offer something unusual. Lately I have been spotting someone I think I know. An old friend, not a close friend, really. Well, it's not all that clear. I have actually seen her only twice, a small blond woman, who looks like a former colleague of mine, sitting with some Greek men in a cafe in Athens. While the similarity is striking, once the woman was a bit heavier than my friend and once a bit thinner. They both looked like Anna, but oddly enough, they didn't look very much like each other. They dressed differently; their hair was different. The one who dressed like Anna wore her hair differently and vice versa. They/she can't be her, I guess. I haven't approached her. For now, it is enough to know that everything is not as it appears to be, and whether it is Anna or not is a question that does not yet need an answer. I have always wanted to be sitting in Athens and to have someone I know walk by. This strange resemblance may be as close as I'll ever get.

Anyway, tomorrow night I shall be in Athens, to eat lukewarm food and drink piney retsina and to walk up Lykabettos where, with luck, I'll see the Aegean Sea reflecting the setting quarter moon. I wish you the Albuquerque equivalent.

All the best,

M.


## MORIARTY AND TALLAHASSEE


Staff members in the Moriarty School District were not permitted to make personal long distance calls on the district's WATS line, which was a pain in the neck to Marie and the other teachers who lived in Albuquerque, as it could be annoyingly expensive just to cancel a dentist appointment. However, if one had been in the system long enough, knew the right person, did not abuse the privilege and knew the appropriate bribe, one could occasionally find a way around the rule. And Marie met all four of these criteria. She had been teaching in Moriarty long enough to know that the right person was not her supervisor, the principal of the Middle School, but Maria Sandoval, the secretary to the District Superintendent. She asked for the privilege only rarely, and knew that, just now in March, Maria's daughters would be selling Girl Scout cookies for their Brownie troop.

So, just after lunch on a day when she did not have playground duty, mid-week the next week after Oscar Monday, Marie walked across the gravel parking lot that separated the Middle School and the High School from the District office, an old Depression-era building that had once been the Moriarty school house, a down-on-its-heels, but still usable, WPA building, rather handsome if one liked the style, which Marie did. Sitting as it does right on old Route 66, it reminded her of Tom Joad, Rose of Sharon and candies 3-for-a-penny. Up the front stairs and through the first door on the right was the Superintendent's office, where Maria Sandoval sat, typing on an IBM Selectric typewriter, the district, a poor one, not having yet converted to computers.

"Hi, Maria. *Como 'sta*?"

"*Bueno*, Marie. What's new?"

"Your girls selling cookies? I need a batch."

"Sign here," Maria said, handing her a list, and Marie put herself down for two boxes of Tagalongs and three boxes of Thin Mints, more than she and Britt would ever eat, but she'd give a couple of boxes to the tenants.

"Listen," Marie said, "I've got to make a long distance phone call. Any chance of pulling that off?"

"Where to?"

"Florida."

"Business?"

"Purely personal."

"Oh, I think I could arrange that. What city, so I can cover for you?"

"Tallahassee."

"Ah, the capital. That makes it easier."

"Why?"

"You don't want to know."

"Just what I was thinking."

"Use the boss's office; he's up in Santa Fe all day, and tomorrow."

"Thanks."

"Use line two. Don't forget to dial nine first."

"Thanks. Line two." Marie walked through the inner door and into the superintendent's office and took his chair behind a remarkably orderly desk, whose orderliness, Marie suspected, was Maria's doing. She picked up the phone, punched the button for line two and dialed the only number that she had for Nikki, the one that had been left on the answering machine at home.

The phone rang just as Ben, home on a day with neither classes nor appointments, was walking by. "Hello?" he said.

"Oh. Hi. I was trying to reach Nikki Wallace."

"Hold on." Ben put the receiver down on the table and called, "It's for you."

Nikki emerged from the library with her finger marking the place in the book of literary criticism she was studying. "Thanks." Then, into the phone, "Hello."

"Nikki, this is Marie Cochran. Britt's, uh, . . ."

"Right. Is Robin all right?"

"Yes. Or at least I presume so. I'm not at home, but at school. I teach outside the city."

"I think Robin told me that. Estancia or somewhere like that?"

"Moriarty. Oh, right. You're from Albuquerque. Right. Do you know where Moriarty is?"

"Somewhere out east."

"Right. About forty miles east of UNM, through the canyon. Twenty miles or so north of Estancia."

"A long commute."

"Yeah, with the sun in my eyes both ways. I've gotten used to it."

"Why Moriarty?"

"Long story, but here's the short version. After I graduated from college, I taught school in Pennsylvania for two years and then thought I needed a Master's degree. The guy I was with at the time, he and I sort of opened the atlas at random and picked UNM out of the blue, packed up and drove out. He didn't like it and split after about three months, but I stayed on to finish the degree. I met a woman named Jill in one of my classes and she taught at the Middle School out here, and brought me out to meet the principal and superintendent. It turned out that Albuquerque itself was pretty over-stocked with social studies teachers, so, when I got the degree and Moriarty offered, I took the job. By that time, I was pretty much hooked on New Mexico, and couldn't envision going back east."

"So you must like it out there?"

"I do. It's small. And poor. There aren't enough textbooks for each kid to have his or her own, so they share. Which makes it hard to give them homework. Some of the children struggle, but that's true everywhere. They're about half white and half Hispanic, and, I don't know, they've kind of grown on me. The town itself, less so. So I still live in Albuquerque."

"Hold on a second. I need to get a smoke." Nikki put the receiver down and carried her book back into the library, where Ben was now sitting at his desk. She returned the book to the shelf, picked up her pack of Kools and an ashtray and walked back to the phone in the living room. Ben said nothing, nor did he look up from his writing. "Sorry. I'm back."

"What I was calling about," Marie began, "was what you said to me on the phone Monday night, about Britt's not being afraid of anything, and how that can get her into trouble. What did you mean? Is there something I should know about law school or something? What are you worried about?"

Nikki paused to light up and inhale, and then said, through the smoke, "You."

"Me?" Marie was shocked by her bluntness. "Why should she be afraid of me?"

"Because you're straight."

"Well," Marie cleared her throat, "present circumstances would indicate otherwise."

"Which is a very strained way of saying that you're gay. What?, is there someone there within earshot?"

"Just a minute." Guiltily, Marie got up from the superintendent's chair, walked around the desk to the door. Maria was no longer at her desk, but Marie shut the door to the office anyway. Back behind the desk, she picked up the phone and said, "So, okay, she's the first for me. Why should she be afraid of that?"

"You are not, I hope you know, the first for whom she's the first. What do you know about Lorinda?"

"Never heard of her."

"Rindy?"

"Oh, okay. I have heard that name. But still I don't know much. Only that Britt doesn't want to talk about her. And that she once said *I'm not sure if we should do this.*"

"Yeah, so she did. The problem was that they had been doing *that* for almost two years before she developed her, uh, misgivings."

"What kind of misgivings?"

"Moral, I believe. She got religion, and the religion she got did not approve of Robin or her ilk. *Your ilk* was the term Lorinda used. *Ilk*. It has a real nasty ring to it, doesn't it? But her exit line was better: I believe it was something along the lines of *You're going to hell, Britt, and I'm not going with you.*"

"Why would she say a thing like that?"

"Beats the shit out of me. A heaven that won't take my friend Robin is not one that I'd be interested in attending." Ben walked through the living room where Nikki was now sitting and smoking, and he cocked his head in inquiry at the comment. Nikki ignored him. "Ask St. Paul."

"He's unavailable."

"He left notes. Phyllis Schlafly will fill you in. Anita Bryant is an adherent to the philosophy. And under the influence of such creeps, the vivacious Lorinda primly re-discovered her heterosexuality and walked out. What it did to Robin was not easy to watch, and I'm not eager to watch it happen again."

"Why do you think I'm going to do that?"

"I generalize. Girls like you, playing on the wrong side of the street, have a way of reverting to their customary ways."

"You don't have a very high opinion of us, do you? Britt says you're straight as the homestretch."

"Does she, now?" Nikki chuckled. "It's true, I am, but when your best friend's a dyke, it changes your perspective." Marie winced at the word, as Nikki continued. "Being straight doesn't mean that I think that the way you and Robin make love is immoral or disgusting, it just means I like sex with men. And I suspect that, deep down inside, you do, too."

"Deep down inside?"

Nikki gave a flat laugh. "Ah, it appears that I made an unintended joke." Marie wondered if the double entendre was going to lighten the tone of the conversation a bit, but it didn't seem so. Nikki went on, "I just don't want Robin hurt by another Lorinda."

"Nor do I. You know, it's possible to over-generalize. They say that once a cat sits on a hot stove burner, he'll never sit on another one, but he'll never sit on a cold burner, either. Britt seems to know enough not to over-generalize. At least not from this Lorinda to me."

"Yes, and Robin says that a horse has one solution to every problem."

"Which is?"

"Run. And that is what I think you should do. Break it off now while you can. Your straight friends will understand. In fact, they'll admire you for coming to your senses. The guys you date in the future will find it attractively kinky that you once fooled around with another woman. And your married ex-boy friend will take you back, wherever or whatever *back* is."

"She shouldn't have told you about him."

"She didn't tell me anything, Marie. Girls who cross the street to play on the other side almost always have a married ex-boy friend. It was just a lucky guess."

"I don't know what to say, Nikki. Only this: I love your friend, I truly do . . ." Marie glanced at the closed door to the office, and realized that she could now hear Maria typing at her desk again. "I'm not playing and I wouldn't hurt her for the world. I know that you aren't going to like this, but you're just going to have to trust me. Maybe someday you will."

"Maybe I will. But for now, my advice is to go back to the life you've been living up until now. My Robin and your Britt will get over it better now than later."

Marie gave a disbelieving little laugh. "I'm not sure she's *my Britt* just yet."

"Holy shit," said Nikki, "this is worse than I thought. I hope to hell that is false modesty, because Robin is in *really* serious trouble if you don't know the extent to which you, sister, have won her heart."

"Okay, so maybe it was false modesty. Or maybe I'm superstitious and think it's bad luck to presume too much. It's just very, very difficult for me to believe that such a remarkable woman is . . ., well, *mine*. But I'll remember what you said. I can't tie up this line any longer, but you've given me a lot to think about. I'm sorry that you feel this way, but maybe we just need more time."

"*We* as in you and Robin, or *we* as in you and me?"

Marie gave another small laugh. "Britt likes to heckle me over my pronouns, too. I guess in this case I meant both, because I intend to stay with her, and I think you come as part of the package."

"Maybe so. Handle her carefully, and don't let her fearlessness fool you."

"I promise to do both of those things. And thanks for sharing them with me."

"Goodbye."

"Goodbye."

Marie hung up the phone and sat back in the chair behind the superintendent's desk. Then she took several deep breaths and walked to the door, ashamed of the nervousness that she felt as she opened it to face Maria. But the secretary seemed oblivious to the entire conversation that had ensued, so that when Marie said, "Thanks, Maria," she just looked up from her typing, smiled and said that the cookies should be here in two weeks. "*Adios*, Marie." Marie then walked back to her classroom in the Middle School and put aside for later consideration all that she had heard from, and said to, Nikki. Five minutes later her students tumbled into the room, and her day resumed.

Back in the Browning house, Nikki stubbed her cigarette out and realized the futility of what she had just tried to do. *Middle-aged love*, she thought, *there's just no arguing against it*. Maybe everything would turn out all right. She walked back to the library to reclaim the book she was studying, and found Ben looking at her as she walked through the door.

"Your best friend's a dyke?"

She wondered how long he'd been eavesdropping.

"The word is *Lesbian* to you."

"You said *dyke*."

"So I did, but the word when used by you takes on an evil, demented connotation."

"Thank you."

"I knew you'd be flattered. But yes, she is. A law student, back in New Mexico."

"And you?"

"I study English." He gave her a look. "Oh. Well, I was just told I am as straight as the homestretch."

"True, I trust."

"Entirely true."

"What a relief. But how does it change your perspective?"

"It makes one suspicious of one's friend's otherwise straight new lover. Thanks for letting me use the phone, but beyond that comment, your interest is not legitimate."

"Who were you talking to? The new lover?"

"New topic: you remember that I'm not going to be here tonight for dinner. I've made sandwiches for the children, which will please them. Your dinner is in the microwave; just push the start button about fifteen minutes after you get hungry."

"When are you leaving?"

"Forthwith." She picked up her cigarettes, her backpack and her jacket.

"Wait. Where are you going?"

"Not that it's exactly your business, but I have a date. A double date actually."

"Who's the lucky fellow? Are you rewarding one of the TAs?"

"No. He's a guy I met some months ago, who does marine water quality at the Department of Environmental Protection."

"How extremely exciting for you."

"Listen, this guy knows more about coliform levels in Apalachicola Bay than I know about anything."

"Does this get any better?"

"Connor, is his name, and a colleague of his from work, and a woman I don't know are going for fried fish at Shingles . . ."

"I don't know how you can stand to eat at that place."

". . . which I suppose explains why it is that you never go there. After that we are going to a poetry reading at that bookstore downtown whose name I can never remember, across the street from that other place that I can't remember."

"Followed by a night of passion, I suppose." Nikki was not, in fact, sleeping with the guy, but saw no reason to give Ben the satisfaction of knowing that, and so, said nothing. "Well, I'm sorry to spoil your evening, but I need you here."

"Nope. Did I mention that I have a date?"

"Break it. There's a reception at the chairman's house for a visiting lecturer, and I really must attend."

"Sorry, but no. I have a date. Furthermore, I told you last week that I was not going to be available on Wednesday night of this week. Check the calendar on the fridge; it's marked there: *Nikki off.*"

"What's so special about tonight? Reschedule. The fried mullet will be just as disgusting tomorrow night."

"Tonight. Open-mic poetry at that bookstore place."

"God Almighty help me; open-fucking-mic night. What's next? Karaoke night? It makes me want to puke. Change your plans."

"No. You will recall the deal, Ben. Weekends off, and other days if I give you plenty of notice. A week is plenty."

"With exceptions for emergencies."

"Appendicitis is an emergency. *Hors d'oeuvres* at George and Mildred's is not. Get Mrs. Lutz next door; she'll look after the children."

"I don't want Mrs. Lutz. I want you."

"Sorry. I have a date. I think I mentioned that. 'Bye. I'll be here tomorrow at two." Nikki left the library and walked out the front door, turned right and walked the eight blocks west from the Browning house to her apartment complex. It was easy enough to put aside the sparring with Ben, who needed her beyond this Wednesday night, had no real alternative, and knew that she had been entirely right that the reception at the chairman's was not worth anyone's changing a single plan for. Even open-mic poetry night. But the conversation with Marie Cochran was harder to put aside. *Was* she over-generalizing? Was this Marie going to commit to Robin? Had she been too hard on her? Would word go from Marie to Robin and back to Nikki, resulting in another busted nose, or the long-distance equivalent of one? She would just have to see. She reached her apartment, checked through the mail, which was uninteresting, then stripped and stepped into the shower.

She was looking forward to her date, even though strictly speaking she wasn't even sure if Connor Williams himself considered it to be a date. She had met him at that bookstore about six weeks earlier on a night that he had read into the open mic, and she had told him afterwards that she had liked his poetry, which was true. She had also liked his looks, but she hadn't mentioned that, not that night, nor since. They had taken to running into each other at the bookstore most weekends, and an odd collection of congenial people had begun to identify itself as a group that met for poetry, then later for fried fish and poetry, mostly on the weekend, but sometimes during the week, like tonight. Connor often did come with a colleague from the DEP, and often there were unknown women at the table, so the tale she had told Ben had been literally true, but she wasn't sure that Connor considered her his date, and she was to drive herself to dinner and then to the reading, then home. Alone. Connor was four inches taller than she, and three years younger, a combination that Nikki was finding nicely asymmetric, and while Nikki wouldn't mind, she thought, being his date for the night, she was slow about taking it farther or faster than it seemed to be proceeding on its own.

So it was that shortly after six o'clock, she hopped in her Saab, adorned with a bumper sticker saying *Xmas Shop in Tucumcari*, and drove back behind the Florida A&M campus, literally across the railroad tracks and into the parking lot at Shingles, a run-down and disreputable looking place, that served, in her estimation, the best fish in town, the best non-pretentious, non-gourmet, fried fish, anyway. She trotted up the front steps and into the dining room, where the air was full of smoke, grease, and music from the juke box. The walls held large posters for Kools and Colt .45 Malt Liquor, most featuring sleek black women, cleavages displayed, often accompanied by equally sleek wild animals. The clientele was mostly black, although there was a short, bald white guy with a beard sitting at the counter, chatting with Mr. Shingle, who was sweating among the fryers in the kitchens, and there was the table full of her friends and acquaintances sitting across the room, away from the juke, all white except for a south Asian woman she didn't know. There was no empty seat next to Connor, so Nikki claimed a chair diagonally across from him and greeted the group.

"Hi, y'all."

"We didn't wait for you, Nikki; we ordered."

And sure enough, Darrell Shingle, son of the proprietor, showed up as if on cue with his pad and pencil, his muscles and gold, to take her order.

"Hey, Darrell."

"'Sup?"

Nikki had learned that Darrell's '*sup?* was no more a question than a more formal *how do you do?* and so she responded, "What's on?"

Darrell knew she was a fish eater, not chicken, and replied, "Bream, cat and mullet."

"Bream and a Bud."

"Gotcha."

The Bud came cold, in a can with no glass. Nikki popped the top, took a drink, and when she noticed Connor looking at her, she winked at him, then inserted herself effortlessly into the conversation at the table, her opinion being that Reagan was a goofball.

~

Ben Browning's view of the evening that lay ahead was not nearly as optimistic as was Nikki's. In fact, the thought that leapt into his mind as she walked out of the house was *worthless cunt*. He had, in fact, little interest in attending George and Mildred's ridiculous get-together. The guest of honor was an idiot whose second-rate work he knew, and who was uninteresting to boot, a dreadful combination. Suffering through the lecture itself tomorrow would be hard enough, without having to listen to his almost certainly inane off-the-cuff remarks over cheap wine. Ben's plan had been to make just enough of an appearance to let George take attendance, as was his way, then to disappear. Otherwise, the air surely would have filled itself with cloying concern over Anna's absence, and the fiction of her family emergency would have been fodder for everyone there. He could hardly stand the thought that the fiction would be discussed even if he were not present, but it would be worse to be there, and have to live within the fiction.

Still, he was pissed at Nikki for leaving him on his own with the children. As she had said, the neighbor lady, Mrs. Lutz, would have been happy to watch the children for a couple of hours, but damn it, he didn't want Mrs. Lutz. He wanted Nikki. She was smart, attractive, entertaining to have around, the children liked her, and there was no denying the considerable sexual tension between the two of them that she brought with her into the house, even if she herself denied it. He felt it, and on the off-chance that Anna would walk up to the door from her space-needing sojourn to wherever, it would very much suit Ben's fancy for a good-looking, long-legged brunette to be sitting, smoking, on the living room couch when she walked in. That would give Anna something to think about.

Still in his sour mood, he strolled into the kitchen and deliberately re-set the microwave to four times the minutes that Nikki had set, sure to spoil whatever she had put in there for him. He would blame the mistake on her, and she would not be able to deny it, for how could she?, and he would have to have sandwiches with the children. She would owe him for that one.

~

If Nikki's mood for the evening was anticipatory, and Ben's was sour, Marie, two hours earlier in the afternoon than they, could best be described as unsettled. She did not know what to think, either when she left the superintendent's office, or when she greeted Maria, or when she walked across the parking lot to her classroom. Unsettled. Uncertain. Confused. Ill at ease. On tenterhooks. However, her fifth period class was soon to commence, and she had learned, over the years, how to put all such distractions—all distractions entirely—aside while her classes ran. Middle schoolers, she had learned, were exquisitely good at sensing a teacher's distraction, and were at all times ready to explode. Utter chaos always stood about an eighth of an inch outside the threshold of every middle school classroom, and it did not take much to invite it in, and thinking about an unsettling phone conversation that one had just had with one's Lesbian lover's best friend while the students were learning about American government would surely do the job. Michael had once told her that she reminded him of Pete Rose in her ability to concentrate her entire being on the task at hand. She had no particular interest in baseball, but had listened to him go on and on about how when Rose was playing baseball he was doing nothing other than playing baseball, and she had gotten the point, long before he had stopped making it. She had taken it to be a compliment.

Thus, it wasn't until seventh period, which was her prep period, when she ordinarily would have been catching up on the day's paperwork, that she found herself instead standing at the windows of her classroom with her hands in the pockets of her slacks, staring out across the parking lot at the high school in the distance. The problem was that she needed someone to talk to about what Nikki had said on the phone. But who? Michael was out of the country, she wasn't sure where. Britt? How would she react to what Nikki had said? Probably by saying it was foolish. Jill? Jill had not been told about Britt yet, and it would not work to announce the relationship at the same time that she raised the question of whether Britt should be afraid of her, as Nikki had said. She needed someone to talk to, and there was no one.

"Cuppa coffee?"

"Huh?" Marie jumped and looked around, finding Jill herself standing at the door to the classroom.

"We could get a cup of coffee and you could tell me what you're stewing about."

"Who's stewing?"

"I walked the other way down the hallway, let's see, . . ." she checked her wristwatch, "about ten minutes ago, and you were standing right there, with your hands in your pockets, looking out the window at nothing. What's up, gal?"

Marie shook her head, and with it her mood, and turned to face Jill. "Nothing, really. I was just thinking that sixth period hadn't gone very well. But sure, let's grab a cup and I'll tell you about it." And together they walked toward the teachers' break room, where they had ten minutes before eighth, and last, period.

Thus it was not until she started the long drive home that Marie could get back to what Jill had rightly perceived to be her stewing over the phone conversation with Nikki. The unsettling thing about the conversation, she now saw, was that it seemed entirely backward. Cockeyed. Britt as the one who should be was afraid? Britt, the experienced one? The self-assured one? The confident one? The one who had the perfectly understanding friends and the perfectly understanding parents?

The freeway ended and Marie exited and began the twisting drive through Tijeras Canyon.

In fact, the perfectly understanding Larsens, Bill and Maggie, had been over for dinner the previous weekend, and, as Marie had anticipated, they were, well, perfectly understanding. It was as if they had consulted Miss Manners, and knew exactly how to handle the situation. Hell, it was as if they had written the damn chapter. *Meeting Your Lesbian Daughter's Heretofore Straight Lover.* A hug or handshake at the door? (Hug.) Do we say *our daughter has told us a lot about you*? (No, because that would draw everyone's attention to the fact that this meeting should have happened months ago.) Do we look around the house? (Yes, if invited.) Which Britt took care of early on. "Here, Mom, let me show you the upstairs." And up they went, while Marie got Bill settled in on the couch with a beer—"Out of the bottle is fine, Marie. No need to get a glass dirty."—and Marie listened intently to the upstairs conversation. "Here's where I study, excuse my messy desk. . . . And here's the bedroom. See? We have a view of the Crest."

And later on, after a perfectly pleasant and relaxed meal, Bill said, "Can you kids come over for dinner next Friday? We'll do some steaks on the grill." *You kids.* And just like that, boom, Marie was part of the Larsen clan, leaving Britt to beg off, saying that she was working with her professor on the Riley case, and ". . . you have a softball game, don't you Marie?" both of which were true, but really she was giving Marie a chance to ease into the situation, and both of them a chance to talk about it.

Through the Canyon now, and back on the I-40, Marie noted that, in the meantime, her own parents, who knew that she now had a roommate, did not know the rest, and she hadn't a clue how she would tell them, nor what their reaction would be, nor—she hadn't thought of this before, and it made her nervous to do so now—whether they had in fact guessed it already. *They*, she was pretty certain, had *not* read Miss Manners on handling the situation and . . .

She heard a squeal of tires and a horn behind her, and realized that she had cut off someone, who, when she looked in the rearview mirror, gave her the finger. She waved at him, trying to say that it was her fault and she was sorry, but he interpreted her wave as dismissive, floored his car and pulled up alongside her, shouting. She couldn't hear his words, but his anger was plain, and she decided to exit the freeway at Juan Tabo. Albuquerque commuters are a serious bunch of drivers, and not to be amidst when one's mind was distracted. So, she took the slower drive down Central Avenue, missing half the lights, and tried to use the extra time to think through the quandaries created by Nikki's phone call. She wished, again, that she had someone to talk to about all of this, and Michael was her first, and her only real choice. But he was still in Greece, and she had no way to contact him, other than by writing a letter to him at his home in Arkansas, and who knew how or when or whether such a letter would get to him. Certainly not in any time to do her any good. She thought maybe he had said that they were staying over there through Easter, but she wasn't sure. And if he were to show up here alone in Albuquerque sometime, say in early summer, he, if she were unable to advise him in advance, would be ready to take her immediately to bed, and how would he react to the new regime and to Britt's presence in the duplex, on the couch and in the double bed?

How would she? She thought she knew the answer to this question, but suddenly, driving west along Central into the setting sun, right in her eyes now that it was near Equinox, suddenly she wasn't sure. Would her resolve weaken and would she end up having sex with Michael? She couldn't imagine that she would, but she had to admit to herself that, once or twice in the past, similar resolve had evaporated. Once she had delivered a carefully rehearsed speech to him about how it had to end and go back to like it was before, until, at least, she saw a copy of the divorce decree. He had said, appropriately enough, "You call the shots, Marie; I have no defense." But, surely as night follows day, it had been she herself, later that weekend, who had asked him to spend the night in the duplex. The recollection of both the speech and the retraction only added to her unsettledness. But surely this was profoundly, fundamentally different. Wasn't it? But how could she know for sure, until he was standing in front of her?

*Straight as the homestretch.* The phrase came back to her as she stopped at the light at Eubank and Central. Is that what she wanted? To be known and called *as straight as the homestretch?* Could she be both straight and in love with Britt? Could she be in love with Britt and still be uncertain of her resolve with respect to Michael? She would just have to wait and see, when he next appeared on the duplex's threshold. And with that, she consciously set her mind to be ready when Britt, with her usual good humored, if lame, excuse for being late for dinner, came bursting through the back door from the alleyway, and into the duplex. And on the spur of the moment, she detoured and turned left on Zuni to El Norteño, the site of their first outside-the-duplex date, and bought chicken mole to go, with cheese enchiladas and sopapillas on the side, all of which she knew would please Britt.

## ALBUQUERQUE

"Okay. Read what we've got so far."

"Where do you want me to start?"

"I don't know." Richard was tired, and he stretched and yawned, sitting on the edge of his desk, with his feet on the chair in front of him. Britt was facing away from him, at the keyboard of the computer in his office. A low table in the corner held the reminder of their dinner, such as it had been: a pint of guacamole and a nearly empty bag of tortilla chips from the little grocery on Girard, and Cokes, none of which was setting particularly easily on his stomach. He didn't know about hers. He put his face into his hands, his elbows resting on his knees, rubbed his eyes and tried to think. By now, the drafting of this brief in the Riley case was getting very old, but this was sure to be the last night of work; it had to be Fed Ex'd to New York tomorrow. He and Britt had worked more than fifty hours together on it, had each gotten to know how the other's mind worked, and he half expected her to know where he wanted to begin. He tried to concentrate. "Let's see . . . Start back at . . . ahhhh . . . how does it go? . . . *The debtor argues that section* . . . ahhh . . . *thirty-seven-dash-twenty-one-dash-oh-six is an increase in Commerce's rights beyond* . . ." He gestured *and so on* with his hand; Britt couldn't see the gesture, but didn't need to.

"Just a second." She manipulated some keys and the cursor repositioned itself. "Here it is." And the text appeared on the screen: *The debtor argues that N.M. Stat. Ann. §37-21-06 is an increase in Commerce's rights beyond that permitted by the New Mexico Constitution and hence not available to Commerce under the Bankruptcy Code. As we have demonstrated in Points I and II, that argument ignores New Mexico case law precisely on point and misinterprets the requirements of the Bankruptcy Code. However, even if the court accepts the debtor's argument under the New Mexico Constitution the court should still find §37-21-06 available to the creditor in this case.* She read it aloud.

"Stop. Something is missing." He walked behind her and read the passage himself. "Hmmmmph," he said. "What do you think?"

"I think it needs a comma right *here*." She placed one after the word *Constitution* in the last sentence.

"I think it needs an exclamation point right there."

"What do you mean?"

"What we're doing at that place is moving to our alternative argument; conceding something that we really don't want to concede. Let's remind the court of that, one last time. Add this for emphasis: *even if the court ignores the seminal case of First National Bank v. Taylor.*"

"*Ovarian.*"

"What?"

"*Ovarian,* not *seminal.*"

"Please."

"Why not?"

"I'm too tired to argue. How about *germinal*?"

"*Germinal* will do. But the whole thing's a fragment."

"Poetic license. Put it in."

"Where?"

He leaned over her shoulder and pointed to the screen.

"There."

She typed the words in. "It looks funny there. The sentence is too complicated now."

"Try setting it off between dashes."

"Won't that be too informal for the court?"

"Fuck 'em. Excuse me." Richard generally tried to watch his language around students, especially his female students. A few years ago he had gotten a little too slap-ass in class one day and had said *What if the debtor had told the creditor to go fuck himself? What then?"* Someone had complained to the Dean, and the complaint had been correct, he had decided; the vulgarity had been gratuitous. Tonight, though, it had slipped out after an hours-long working session with an older-than-average student who was as tough, he thought, as galvanized nails. It was eleven-thirty on a week night, he was tired, the brief had to be Fed Ex'd tomorrow morning and they weren't nearly done yet. A venial offense, at best. Nevertheless, he wished he hadn't said it. Britt made no notice of the vulgarity.

"Wasn't it just two weeks ago that you struck out like every other sentence in my draft as too informal?"

"Yes. Students are overly prone to informality. Lawyers are overly prone to formality. *That* . . .", he gestured at the screen, "is just right."

"Class is still in session?"

"Class is *always* in session, Ms. Larsen. You're here to learn how to be a lawyer, not to be one. Read the whole thing again." He turned away and walked back to sit on the desk, as she read the paragraph aloud.

"Change the first *is* to *represents*."

"*The debtor argues that* . . .", this time she said *blah, blah, blah* instead of reading the numbers, ". . . *r-e-p-r-e-s-e-n-t-s, represents an increase in Commerce's rights beyond* . . ."

"What do you think?" he asked.

"Three-six-four."

"What?"

"Tinker to Evers to someone. I blew it."

"Chance. Tinker to Evers to Chance. Who told you that?"

"My best friend is a baseball fan. She primed me to show off to you, but I'm too tired to get it right."

"Of course, that was six-four-three."

"What was?"

"Tinker to Evers to Chance."

"I'm in over my head, and I can't think straight enough."

"Well, what do you think of that?" He gestured at the computer screen.

"That you are very good at this."

"Thank you. I shall be warmed in my old age with the recollection of that compliment. What do you think of the paragraph?"

"It's good, I think."

"You're right, it is. Okay, read the next one."

Three hours later they were still at it, though the end was in sight. Richard now sat at the key board with his chin in his hand, reading the entire brief through. He made no sound except the regular *click* as he pushed the key that made each new line appear at the bottom of the monitor's screen. Britt was stretched out on the couch with her feet propped up on the far arm and her jacket over her head.

"Are you asleep?"

"Yes."

"Tell me what you think of this: I think we need another paragraph right here . . ." He looked over at her on the couch and saw that her head was still covered. "Here." Pause. "*Here.*" He waited until she swung her feet to the floor and stood up, pulling the jacket around her shoulders and walked over behind him.

She yawned. "Why?"

"All we've done in the previous paragraphs is to brief the cases we've cited. There isn't anything to pull it together. We need another paragraph to say to the judge, *Look here, judge, here's what all these cases mean together.*"

"*The essence of legal reasoning*, as my Contracts teacher used to say."

"I'm surprised to discover that you were awake for that lesson."

"A cheap shot. I was in your class every fucking day and I never went to sleep, even though it was at some ungodly hour, and I'm only sleepy now because it's after two in the morning and we've been working on this for eight hours, not to mention my entire life as I remember it."

"Go on home. I'll finish it."

"Ha. I can only imagine the abuse I would suffer if I did that. Besides, I'm learning a lesson I *was* asleep for, I guess: that briefs are to be completed the night before they are due in court."

"Jeeze. Hit a guy where it hurts. Come on, how about this paragraph?"

"What's this new paragraph have to say?"

"Well, what do all the cases mean together?"

"Let me read the previous paragraphs." She stood behind Richard with her hands in her pockets and watched as he made the lines on the screen move up one at a time.

"Too fast?"

"No."

They were both silent for a minute. She rubbed her eyes. He waited. He already had the paragraph sketched out in his mind, but she would learn best by working through it on her own. The work they had done together on the Riley brief had brought her a short ways across the line from student to colleague, but not very far across, and he had been serious earlier about this being a learning opportunity for her.

Finally, she spoke. "All those cases, let's see, the court ignored the precise wording of the statute and looked instead to the legislative history or the surrounding circumstances."

"Right."

"Shouldn't we say that as a lead-in to the case briefs? Back, say, . . .", she laid her right arm above his shoulder blades, resting on the chair back, reached over his left shoulder, then switched everything and with her right hand pushed his hand away from the control keys. "It's a goddam right-handed world." He did not respond, while she made the cursor retreat several pages. When she found the place, ". . . *here*."

"You're right. What shall we say?"

"*Courts have not always read the language of section eleven-twenty-nine precisely.*"

"No. *Precisely* is the wrong word. See why?"

"I'm not sure."

"No court wants to be encouraged to be imprecise. We need a word that means *precise* in sort of a pejorative sense, so we can urge the court to avoid that kind of obsessive precision. Got one?" He leaned back in the chair, forcing her to step back a step. He leaned all the way back and looked at her upside-down. For God knows what reason, he had an over-powering urge to say *I can see up your nose.* He closed his eyes and concentrated on the problem through his exhaustion, and barely kept from laughing.

Finally, she spoke: "*Overly precise?*"

"Not bad. *Hypertechnical* is better."

"Wow. What's that mean?"

"*Embarrassingly over-precise.*"

"Nice word. *If* it's a word. Which I doubt. Is it?"

He sat up and typed it in. "Of course it is. See? There it is right there in a brief to the Second Circuit. Now, what about this paragraph at the end?"

"Say it again. Something about . . . *as the court can see, the cases do not require a hypertechnical reading of the statute.*"

"Nope. You only get to use *hypertechnical* once a month. Besides, we need in this paragraph to give the court something to hang its hat on. *Hypertechnical* is negative; it tells the court what not to do, but doesn't tell it what *to* do. It's nice as a lead-in, but we need *positive* reinforcement here." He paused and thought for a second. "You know, there's a Holmes aphorism that would fit here. What is it? Something about seeing what Congress is driving at, even though they haven't said it. Let's see, where I could find it at two-thirty in the god damned morning? Lordy, I hope we don't have to walk all the way to the library. It must be in here somewhere."

He stood up and Britt stepped aside to let him out of the corner where the computer stood. When he looked at her, she shrugged her shoulders, as if to say that she sure didn't know where to find it in the mess, even if she had known what he was looking for, which she didn't.

"Keep quiet about my office."

"I didn't say anything."

"I know I've used it before," he went on. "Let's see. God damn it, I'll never remember the name of the case if we have to go look it up. Here, sit down, let me think." She sat back at the key board and started to skim the surrounding paragraphs. He was deep in thought, out loud. "I think Garcia used it in that last article he wrote. There's got to be a copy of that around here somewhere. . . . Ummhmm . . ." He ran his eye along the bookshelf. "Here. . . ." he flipped through the pages of the *New Mexico Law Review*. "That's right, Rehnquist quoted it in some case that Garcia was writing about. Here it is. Type this: . . ."

She interrupted, "Wait until I get to the right place. . . . Okay."

"Quote. *The Legislature has the power . . .*"

"Slow down."

"*The Legislature has the power to decide what the policy of the law shall be, and if it has intimated its will, however indirectly, that will should be recognized and obeyed.* Put in an ellipsis here. *It is not an adequate discharge of duty for courts to say: We see what you are driving at, but you have not said it, and therefore we shall go on as before.* Close quote. The cite is: Johnson against the United States, one-sixty-three-eff-thirty-comma-thirty-two. First Circuit. Nineteen-oh-eight." Britt typed the last bit in correct citation form: *Johnson v. United States*, 163 F. 30, 32 (1st Cir. 1908). Then she said, "It needs a lead-in; you can't start a paragraph like that. Something like . . .", she typed as she spoke, "*. . . As Justice Holmes once said . . .*"

"No, start with your sentence about legislative history and surrounding circumstances."

"I don't remember it."

"Yes, you do."

"Okay. Let's see. *These cases . . .*"

"*The cases just mentioned . . .*"

"*Discussed.*"

"Okay. *Discussed.*"

"*The cases just discussed show that the courts do not . . .*"

"Make it positive, not negative."

She backspaced and started typing again. "*The cases just discussed show that the courts have looked to legislative history and surrounding circumstances, as well as the exact wording of the statute to determine the legislature's intent. As Justice Holmes once wrote, . . .*"

"*Admonished.*"

She backspaced. "*. . . admonished, comma, the Legislature has the power, blah, blah, blah.* That works pretty good. One final sentence, then: *In the present case, it is easy enough to see what Congress was driving at in enacting section eleven-twenty-nine of the Bankruptcy Code, and . . .*" She ran out of steam.

Richard picked it up: "Good. Go on. . . . *and, as Commerce has shown, the courts that have addressed the issue in the past have not required that this legislative intent be ignored.* You will notice, please, the tasteful use of the subjunctive mood. Read the whole thing again."

She did.

"Save it," he said.

"What?"

"The entire brief. Save it, back it up and sign out. We're done."

"Thank God." It only took a few seconds and a couple of key strokes to do that. "There."

"Tomorrow, my secretary will run it off first thing. Two copies. You'll be here at eight and we'll give it one more proof before Fed Ex arrives at nine." She groaned. "Come on. Last time. Then it'll be in and you can sleep all you want. Make it eight-thirty."

"Eight-thirty."

"We have done well, I think. I owe you a lot for your help. I'll buy you a dinner sometime."

She stretched hard and collapsed onto the couch. "Who can think of food? What time is it now?"

"Two-forty-two, a.m. Go home."

"Right."

"You have a car, yes?"

"Well, my bike."

"I'll give you a lift."

"I'll be fine."

"You'll be fine as soon as we get your bike into the back of my pickup. Come on. Leave that stuff . . ." she had started to pick up her books, ". . . you can fetch them in the morning." He turned out the lights, locked his door and they walked through the dark halls, and outside, where she unlocked her bike from the rack near the entrance, and walked it across the empty parking lot to his truck, the only vehicle in sight. The night was clear and cool. The Milky Way was well-displayed and on the top of the Crest the flashing red lights of the television towers were bright and seemed nearby.

They hardly spoke during the drive through the empty streets to the duplex on Manzano Street. Albuquerque is not a town, not here to the east of campus anyway, and off Central, which in any sense seems alive at three in the morning. The wide, straight, flat streets were deserted and looked as if they were meant to be. The businesses were closed; the houses were all dark.

Nothing moved. They passed no other cars. The traffic lights on Lomas changed colors almost randomly, as if they sensed that there was no traffic to control. Their changing, and the passing of the side streets as Richard drove east, were the only indicators that time was flowing by at all.

Quiet jazz played on KUNM and Richard adjusted the volume. He guessed Monk by the easy way the artist had with the keyboard and by the small grunts of humanity between the notes, but he didn't recognize the tune and no announcement was ever made identifying the piece. The student DJ was probably dozing at the switch.

"Don't fall asleep." Britt had put her head back against the seat and he could see by the street lights as they went by that her eyes were closed, her hands were folded in her lap and her legs were straight out, or as nearly as they could be, under the dash. "Hey. Don't fall asleep."

"Right." She didn't change her posture, but she sang, over the jazz, slowly, in a scratchy voice that was closer to tenor than alto: "*Don't it make you want to rock and roll/all night long?/ Mohammed's radio.*"

"Who's that?"

Her eyes were still closed. "Warren Zevon. I was thinking of Linda Ronstadt's version, though." They were quiet for a moment. Then: "*I heard somebody singing sweet and soulful/on the radio/Mohammed's radio.*" She sat up and looked to see where they were. "It's the second right, after the next light, just before the shopping center. Three blocks south. Fourth duplex on the left." She laid her head back against the seat again, now with her eyes open.

In front of the duplex, he waited for her to get out of the truck, but at first she did not move, nor look at him. She spoke with a quiet, tired deliberation. "I have spent a majority of my adult life with my ultimate career goal to sing backup to Linda on *It's So Easy*. I'm beginning to fear that it is not to be." Finally she turned and looked at him with those eyes that seemed to give off their own light. "And you, dammit, you're a slave-driver, a compulsive perfectionist and a disorganized procrastinator all at once, but I love working with you. Good night."

Before he could think of anything to say, she was out of the front seat, lifting her bike out of the bed of the pickup, and running with it across the street and up to the duplex. She ran, he thought, very differently from the way Rita ran, more like a dancer than an athlete. More toe, more ankle; less arm, less thigh. He watched while she opened the door and turned to wave. He sat, after she rolled her bike inside and closed the door, waiting for a light to come on. After a minute it did, and he drove away.

At home he got as far as the side of the bed, dressed in a tee shirt and boxer shorts before Rita woke up. She was sleeping under a blanket, on her stomach with her face turned toward him. His eyes were now adjusted to the dark and he could see that hers were still closed.

"Mumpf taam zit?"

"Three."

"Ooo's'nice." She took a deep breath, then deeper, before she exhaled. With her eyes still closed and her lips barely moving, she mumbled a conversation. "Thought hmmf time gmmmn gedup."

"No. I just got home."

"Nnnnaa'd's'nice. H'lo, dear," she said.

"You know," he said, "I've seen about a thousand movies in which a character wakes up in the middle of the night from a sound sleep, and not once has the actor managed to look like what someone waking up in the middle of the night looks like. You, for instance, look very sexy."

She opened one eye, the top one. "Uuuuump. Y'don't." She closed the eye and put her arms under the pillow, under her head. He watched her body, beneath the sheet, give a compact stretch. He knew her ways well enough to know without seeing that her toes were curling and when she relaxed she would wiggle them and then rub the bottoms of her feet one at a time against the tops.

"Especially," he turned on his front and crawled over toward her, under the covers. "I especially like this little patch of spit on your pillow." He felt with his finger the little wet spot right where her lips lay, open and relaxed. "It smells like the innermost you." He put his nose on the pillow next to her lips and sniffed; he reached his right hand under the covers and put it on her bare butt.

"G'sleemp, dear," Rita said with her eyes still closed. She sniffed. And sleeping seemed just the right thing to do, sharing the pillow with her, smelling her smell in his sleep.

# ~ 12

## TALLAHASSEE AND ATHENS

The phone call that Nikki had been dreading came a few days later, late in the afternoon, the children home from school, playing in their rooms. Nikki's plan was that they should all eat together that night, which would mean earlier than Ben liked, and after the children would already be hungry and grouchy, and that she would have to make something that everyone would eat. She had settled on chicken cacciatore, to be served at around six-thirty, and so at four she began preparations, in order not to be hurried. Making dinner for a family, she had discovered, could be fun, but not if one were hurried.

Thus, when the phone rang, the chicken was just in the oven, but her hands were still greasy with chicken fat and covered with flour from the dredging, and she began counting rings as she cleaned up, knowing that the machine would pick up after the sixth ring. At four, she was still a mess, so she picked up after five, wiping her hands on a towel and tucking the receiver between her ear and her right shoulder.

"Brownings."

At first there was nothing, making her think that it might be one of those telephone marketers that dial automatically and whose computer would connect once she was on the line. She almost hung up, but instead spoke again. "Hello?"

The voice then came through, quiet, in the mezzo-soprano range. "Perhaps I mis-dialed."

"This is the Browning residence." Nikki waited, but the caller did not respond.

The wait got uncomfortably long, but still the caller did not hang up.

"Hello?" Nikki asked again. No answer. Then, beginning to guess who it might be, she said, "Dr. Browning?"

Silence.

"Anna?"

Silence. Or no, Nikki began to realize, the line was not exactly silent, though the caller still had said nothing after her first sentence. There was the sound of wind against the mouthpiece. The caller was using a telephone that was outside. And she could hear traffic in the background. Then the sound of a bus accelerating past, perhaps leaving a stop. Urban traffic. And something else. Music. A bit removed from the telephone, she thought, and live music, she thought. A nearby outdoor café, perhaps, or a concert? She couldn't place the music, but it was electric. And hard, with a quick rhythm. New York, maybe? Or New Orleans? Seattle, maybe. Somewhere with an outdoor music scene.

"Anna?" She asked again.

Silence.

When Ben had initially told her that she must pick up the phone whenever it rang, for it might be Anna calling, Nikki had spent a bit of time trying to figure out what she would say, a problem about which Ben had given her no guidance. She had soon given up, figuring she would have to play it on the fly, and now here she was. (She never would have guessed that the caller would hold the line for this long, this silently, so anticipating the problem would have been fruitless in any case.) Right now, then, the question became this: What to say? Why was she calling? Where was she? Was she in some kind of danger? What would she want to know, if she wasn't going to ask or say anything? How could Nikki possibly guess, this being a woman she knew not at all?

The question then became, as the two of them stood silently, connected so delicately, what *she*, that is Nikki, would want to know? That was easy.

"Anna? The children are well." She thought quickly of what she should add to that. *They miss you?* No. *Where are you?* No. *Are you all right?* No. *Ben is worried about you.* No. There was nothing more to be said. Back when her father had taught her how to play chess, he had drilled her on the principle of *when in doubt, move a pawn*, and it had become the lodestar of her life. If you're not sure what to do, do as little as possible. So, she merely repeated herself.

"They are fine."

And from what she now thought was far away, came a very small voice that said, "Thank you."

Followed by the near silence of before. The music stopped. A motorcycle went by, too loudly. Voices spoken by passersby. Then, after a moment more, "Goodbye."

But the caller—surely by now Nikki knew it was Anna—still she did not hang up. Until Nikki herself said, "Goodbye, Anna," and the line went dead.

Nikki hung up the receiver, and found that she was shaking, and she wiped her hands on the kitchen towel that she had draped over her shoulder, trying to calm them, and herself. She needed a cigarette quite badly, but she couldn't remember where she had put the pack down, nor was she sure she could move from the spot where she was standing. *Thank you*, she had said, and that was all Nikki had to go on, guessing whether she had played the event correctly. *Thank you.*

"Who was that?" It was Sam, standing at the archway between the living room and the hallway.

*Shit*, she thought, *I haven't planned for this, either.* "Your mother. I think, buddy."

"What did she want?" His voice lay somewhere between anger and sobs.

"I think she wanted to be sure you kids were okay."

"Is she all right?"

What could she say, except the truth? "I don't know."

"Where is she?"

"I don't know that either."

"Did she say when she would be home?"

"No, buddy, she didn't." She walked over to the couch and sat down. "Come. Sit here next to me." He walked over and climbed onto the couch, and Nikki put her arm around him. "Where's Janet?"

"Reading, I think." He paused. "I don't think we should tell her. She's too little, and she'll get upset."

"I don't think we should either."

"What are we going to do?"

"I think that you and I should just sit here until we know how we feel, and then maybe you'll help me get dinner ready."

"I don't feel like talking about it."

"Good. Neither do I."

*Thank you.*

"You don't know my mother, do you?"

"No, not really."

"Are you sure it was her?"

*Pretty sure* would be the honest answer, but she suspected that Sam did not need equivocation at a time like this. "Yes."

*Thank you.*

The two of them sat together on the couch, Nikki's arm around Sam's shoulders, neither saying anything else, for nearly twenty minutes, before, still without saying anything, Nikki got up and walked back into the kitchen. Then, "Could you set the table, buddy?" And that is where they were—Nikki checking the chicken in the oven, and Sam laying out the silver—when Ben walked in through the front door, put his briefcase down and hung up his coat in the closet.

"Maybe you'd better wait in your room, Sam."

"Okay." Sam knew exactly what was going on, as he put a handful of spoons down on the table cloth and quietly left, saying nothing to his father.

"What was that about?" Ben asked.

Nikki wiped her hands again on the towel, this time knowing in advance what she was going to say. "Anna called, I think."

"*What?*"

"Your wife called."

"What did she say?"

"Almost nothing. *Hello and goodbye.*" And *thank you*, Nikki thought.

"Did she say where she was?"

"I told you. *Hello and goodbye.* She was mostly silent. But I'm pretty sure it was her."

"Did you ask her where she was?"

"No."

"You should have asked her where she was."

"Next time when she calls, you be here and ask her."

"That's why I'm paying you to be here."

"Ben, you didn't tell me what you wanted me to say to her, so I just did what I thought was best at the time. You'll have to trust me. In any case, there's nothing that we can change now. Oh, and I told Sam that his mother called."

"You *what?*"

"I told Sam his mother called."

"And why the fuck did you do that?"

"He asked me. I decided to tell him the truth."

"Why, you stupid slut. Don't you have an ounce of sense?"

Nikki put down the towel that she had been wringing between her hands. She walked into the living room, got her jacket from the closet and walked to the door. "I quit."

"You can't quit."

But, without another word, she left the house.

She walked the long way home, in no hurry to get there. Before, she had thought if she could have gotten away from the early dinner and cleaned up, she might have called Connor and suggested that they get together, but that was out now, as she had no energy for anyone other than herself. She stopped at the Publix on the corner of her street and bought cigarettes, Diet Pepsi, some chips and three Snickers bars, which was about all that she could think of buying just then. She left the store and walked counter-clockwise, three sides of her block, in no hurry to get home, as she suspected what she would find there.

And she was correct: the phone was ringing when she walked in the front door. She allowed it to ring until the machine picked up. *I'm not here. Deal with it.* The caller left no message, but the phone rang again while she lit a cigarette and opened a soda, and again while she went to the bathroom and changed her clothes.

Finally, she picked up. "Yes?"

It was Ben, of course. "I need you."

"I'll be back tomorrow, at about two."

"You don't want to hear my apology?"

"Fuck your apology. But listen here. There are two words that you are not to use to describe me, or any other woman, known or unknown, in my presence or not. *Slut* is one of them."

"What's the other one?"

"You'll have to figure that out yourself. It shouldn't be too difficult. If you don't know, it is best to err to the conservative side, because if you ever use either one of them, I'm gone. Period."

"Why did you tell Sam?"

"It doesn't matter anymore. I did. You'll have to deal with that reality.

You're his father; you can figure out what to do. If you want to blame me, go ahead, but don't use either of those words to do it."

"If I didn't need you so much, I'd fire you."

"Go to hell." She hung up.

Ben was an asshole, and she found herself caring nothing for him. He surely didn't *need* her, not in the ordinary sense of that word. Was she going back because of Sam and Janet and Rachel? Maybe. But more than anything, she knew, she would be there at two tomorrow and cook his food and clean his house and dress his children, all out of some unimaginable obligation to that so, so small voice saying *thank you* from somewhere far away.

⁓

When Anna hung up the phone, she found herself in a phone booth just outside the American Express office, off Syntagma Square. She remembered that she had placed the call on the spur of the moment. No, that wasn't quite right, because she had needed to get change for her paper money and had walked into American Express to do that, coming out with fifty 20-δραχ coins. And then she had had to go back into the American Express to be told how to place a call to the United States from a pay phone. Nevertheless, it had been almost on the spur of the moment. And now she stood inside the phone booth, which was really just a clear plastic bubble, open to the street, and which covered her from above her head to about her waist.

After a moment, and not thinking about the phone call at all, she walked the half block to Syntagma and turned left, and hopped a bus that would take her to her hotel near Omonia Square, leaving the unused coins behind.

⁓

Nikki picked up the phone and called Albuquerque, but the machine answered. *Hi. This is Marie. I can't come to the phone right now, but leave a message and I'll call you back.* She hung up, without leaving a message. Then she dialed Connor's number.

"Hello."

"Hi, it's me."

"Hey, you. What's up?"

"What are you doing?"

"Right now? Cleaning up after my dinner. Why? Want to get together?"

"No, I'm a mess."

"I'll give you time to clean up, not that it matters to me what you look like."

"No, I don't mean the way I look. I've had a bad day and just need to talk. But not to see anyone, okay? Better yet, I'm going to turn off the lights and let you read to me."

"Read what? Poetry?"

"I don't care. Just something that will take my mind off the last couple of hours of my life."

"I've got something that I brought home to read tonight, how about that?"

"It doesn't matter. Words in a row."

"I'll be right back." She heard the sound of the phone being laid down, and she put her own receiver down, walked into her bedroom and took the extension there off the hook, went back into the living room and hung up that one, then walked back to the bedroom, turned off the lights and lay down, fully clothed, but with her shoes off, then picked up the phone.

"Where did you go?"

"I'm ready."

"Okay." He began to read. "*Factors Affecting Projected Harvests of* Crassostrea virginica *in Apalachicola Bay, by B.A. Townshend, R.M. Fox, S.L. Burgess and C.S. Gupta.*"

"Perfect. You are a wonderful, wonderful human being."

"You, too. Now shhhhh. I'm reading. *Abstract.* No, we can skip the abstract . . .."

"No, read the abstract. I like knowing how a work is going to end before I begin to read it. Like *Romeo and Juliet.*"

"*Romeo and Juliet?*"

"First two sentences. Read."

"*Abstract. Historical data on the economic performance of the oyster industry have been reported by Wilson and others, and up-dated by Simes and others. According to those data, in the year nineteen-seventy the Apalachicola (Franklin County) oyster industry was valued in excess of two million dollars which was approximately three-quarters of the total Florida income from the oyster industry. Projections concerning this industry into the twenty-first century, however, have been rare, due to the complexity of the predictive paradigms. This paper attempts to quantify the parameters that will influence oyster harvests well into next century, and determines that, first, population growth in the Atlanta area, and second, possible but unpredictable adverse events related to off-shore oil drilling in the Gulf will be the key determinates of the future health of the industry.*

"*Historical background. Since mid-century, the state of Florida has been involved in restocking oyster shell into Apalachicola Bay to create new oyster beds...*"

Connor read to her in this vein for more than an hour. His voice she found soothing, in the baritone range, and possessed of a comfortable southern accent. With her eyes closed, she listened to his words, concentrating on his voice until it seemed to inhabit her skull more than her ear, driving out her exchange with Ben, and calming her concern for Anna. And for Sam and Janet and Rachel. The *thank you* was still there, but it was as if it were being buried under the newly falling, powdery New Mexican snow of Connor's words. He concluded. "Want the footnotes, too?"

"No, I'm going to sleep, now."

"Sure you don't want me to come over?"

"Yes, but no. Here, write this down." She gave him Ben's address. "I'll get off work tomorrow night between seven and eight, depending on . . . well, depending on lots of things. Come by a little after seven. Park on the street in front of the house, but don't come up to the door. You can take me out and we'll split a couple dozen, what are they?, *Cassosteria* something."

"*Crassostrea virginica.*"

"Right. A couple of dozen of those, with hot sauce. And a martini or two. Okay? Is it a deal?"

"It's more than a deal. See you tomorrow night."

They hung up, and Nikki found herself able to drift off into sleep, without wondering about where Anna had gone when she hung up the phone, and what she had done there.

ATHENS

The day after she had spoken, however briefly, to Nikki, Anna sat in a dark theater, eating chocolate and smoking. This was the first showing of the day, on a work day, and the theater was empty except for her. The smoke from her cigarette curled up through the light from the projector, but she was alone, and no one seemed to mind that she smoked. She had counted the rows and the seats carefully, and she sat in the exact center of the theater. She had been ready to fight for the seat, but the theater was completely empty and she had taken the one she wanted, right in the center. Well, *almost* the exact center. There was, in fact, an even number of seats in the middle row of the middle section and she had stood for several moments studying the problem before she had told herself that it didn't really matter anyway. So, actually, she sat just to the right of the exact center, facing the movie screen.

She was watching a Swedish movie, with Greek subtitles and was enjoying the feeling of not really knowing what was going on on the screen. It was about these farmers and their children. That was all she could figure out. She enjoyed not being able to figure out the rest; the feel of the theater was just right for a weekday, early afternoon, and it seemed just right to have no more idea about the plot of the movie than that it was about these farmers and their children. She didn't even know the title. Outside the theater it was rainy and cool, but in here it was warm and quiet. The Swedish being spoken added, in an odd way, to the silence, as if the strange words covered up some louder noise that would be heard in a totally quiet room.

Someone had died on the screen. The mother was crying and people were dressed in black and were sad. Anna thought maybe it was the mother of the mother that had died, but she wasn't sure. She watched a while longer, flicking ashes onto the floor of the theater. The youngest child, there on the screen, reminded her a little of Sam. Anna found herself crying, too, which was funny because her own mother had died long ago, when Anna was in college, and she had hardly cried even then.

Anna was no longer going to sit at the café that said ΚΑΦΕΝΕΟΝ over the door. She had decided that. She had given up on the possibility of Mike's ever showing and, besides, her anger at him was slowly fading, so that, as before, she only rarely thought of him. She was no longer even sure, really, if she had stopped going to the cafe because she had given up on his ever showing. One thing that she had never figured out and that she occasionally wondered about was whether she had begun to go to the café only because Mike had suggested it in his letter. She hated the thought that he was in control of her. She had never really liked him all that much; they had never been close friends. "I never really liked him very much," she whispered aloud. "We were never very close."

She was tired of fucking men she didn't know, and she had decided not to do that anymore, either.

She stopped crying, for the scene in the film had left the funeral and the two parents were now talking at the table in the kitchen. She studied the screen, but it was impossible to know what was going on.

One night sitting at the café at a table with a group of men, only a few of whom she actually knew, and one other woman, a strangely quiet person who constantly twisted a strand of her black, dirty hair, Anna had excused herself, picked up her packages on the table and walked out the door, just as she had dozens of times before, but this time without looking back over her shoulder to see if Mike was there. She had run across the street, between the lights, dodging traffic, and had run down the escalator into the train station under Omonia. The escalator itself didn't work, nor did the turnstiles, so she had walked directly to the tracks without paying, and had climbed on the first car that came in either direction. She found herself heading west and she rode to the end of the line in Piraeus where she spent the evening sitting, drinking strong coffee at a café on the street, across from where the ferries docked. She had quite enjoyed herself, watching the ferries load and depart, arrive and unload, and she had not been back in the ΚΑΦΕΝΕΟΝ since then.

Avoiding—no, she did not feel as if she were *avoiding* the café—in fact she still occasionally walked by it and looked in through the windows at the beasts holding the mirrors on the walls, but she never saw anyone she knew, so *avoiding* was not the right word—but not going to drink coffee and watch for Mike at the café put more time on her hands than she was used to in Athens, so she had taken to going to the movies. They were inexpensive and kept her entertained and sometimes she would go to two or even three in one day, or sometimes, like she planned to today, she would sit through the same movie several times. Even when she couldn't understand the words spoken or written on the screen, she enjoyed watching the characters move past and talk to and deal with one another, although the relationships on the screen often seemed as foreign to her as the sounds of these Swedish words.

In all honesty—and Anna had become nothing during her stay in Athens if not honest with herself—in all honesty, she had learned to enjoy being alone. She enjoyed being here, right now, alone in this large hall with only the shadow-people on the screen. But more than solitude itself, she had come to appreciate the freedom that came along with being alone, a freedom that had nothing much, in fact, to do with whether you had people around you. Maybe it wasn't so much *freedom* as it was *control*. She discovered that she was whispering these words aloud, though there was no one but her to hear them. Trying the words out: *alone, freedom, control*. While walking through the streets of Athens, she could turn down the street she chose, or go straight; she could step, or not, into a store that looked inviting; enter, or not, a building and ride an elevator to see what was on the floors above; it was all her choice alone. She was rarely alone in the strictest sense of that word, but she could turn down a certain street with no explanation to anyone of what, exactly, she thought was down there and why she chose this street and not the next one. She could attend a Swedish film with Greek subtitles with no explanation to anyone of why, just now, that seemed a most attractive prospect. She could walk without an itinerary through the streets of the city, with no concern for where she was going, no explanation for why she was taking the step she was taking except that at each instant that was the one she wanted to be taking.

"Itinerarilessness." She tried out the word aloud. "Itinerarilessness." She lit another cigarette, closing her eyes against the flair of the match and finding the end of the cigarette by feel. She was smoking too much, she thought. "I-tin-er-ari-less-ness."

"*I*. I am Anna Browning." She was now no longer whispering, but rather talking in a normal conversational tone.

"*Tin*. Periodic table symbol: Sn. As in tin can and tin pan and . . . Tinnessee Street." She laughed. Tennessee Street was one of the main streets of Tallahassee.

"*Er*. Errrrrr," she noted an usher walking down the aisle. She hid her cigarette and watched him out of the corner of her eye. He walked a few rows past her, made a show of picking up some non-existent paper on the floor and turned and walked back up the aisle. Anna was not fooled and knew she was being watched because the usher or his boss thought she was crazy. She lowered her voice to a conspiratorial whisper again.

"*I*."

"*Tin*."

"*Er*."

"*Ari*."

"*Less*."

"*Ness*." She said the syllables in time with the retreating steps of the usher.

She giggled a small, covered-mouth giggle and turned back to the front. For a while she sat quietly and watched the action on the screen. It was winter and the family seemed to be packing up for a trip somewhere. Maybe they were leaving home.

Anna found herself thinking of the impulsive phone call she had made yesterday to Tallahassee. The impulse had been out of the blue; if she had thought about it, she wouldn't have done it. But she had. She had. She did not think for an instant about the voice of the woman who had answered, nor about the circumstances that had led that woman to be there when Anna had called, but she liked that the woman had told her, without having been asked, that the children were well. She summoned up the images of each child in turn. She could remember every detail of each little body; she could remember exactly what each sounded like when he or she talked, or cried or laughed. She remembered how each one smelled. She remembered how surprised she had been when Janet had smelled different from Sam; she had been certain at the hospital that they must have gotten the babies mixed up and brought her someone else's little girl, and she had made not a small fuss, but then she had figured out that babies were supposed to smell different. And, she remembered, Ben hadn't been able to tell the difference and said she was imagining things, but she was right: Janet had definitely smelled different, and Rachel different again. If she had the right system of notation, she could describe to people the tiniest little variation in the smells of Sam against Janet. She could say, "Now, see here? That little squiggle followed by a doodad? That is the smell of the inside of Sam's elbow. And this, . . ." she would write some more notations, ". . . and this is the smell of the inside of Janet's elbow. See how it is different?" She could imagine holding Janet on her lap and reading to her, smelling her hair. The child's smell seemed to fill the entire auditorium. She could feel the small, almost undetectable increments of relaxation pass through Janet's little body as she reluctantly fell asleep before the story was over. Rachel, on the other hand, still fell asleep more quickly, less reluctantly, as if sleeping were little different from being awake. And, with a start, she felt a small bite of Rachel's teeth on her left nipple.

Anna sat up quickly in her seat and looked around. She realized she had fallen asleep, just like the girls in her dream. The lights were now on in the theater, and people were entering for the next showing. She looked behind her and discovered that her neck was stiff and she wondered how long she had been asleep. She secretly slipped two fingers inside her shirt between two buttons and touched her left nipple. The dream sensation had been so real that she couldn't believe that it was hard and dry, but it was.

The movie was about to start; there would be a long string of advertisements for wine and cigarettes and motorcycles and what-not, all presented in a buzz of Greek with a background of rock and roll or bouzouki music. Then her Swedish friends would begin again their battle with the forces at work in the film, most of which Anna could not understand. There were more people in the theater with her this time, but Anna could still decide for herself alone whether she would stay to the end, with no thought for what the others would be doing. She returned her attention to the screen, her hands folded peacefully in her lap.

～

Anna sat through the entire movie again, not falling asleep this time, and left with the crowd into the late afternoon light. An easy rain was falling, with no wind, the kind of rain in which the drops seem more to float down than fall. She had a bright yellow nylon pullover that she used for a rain jacket and she put it on, over her head and pulled the hood up. She stepped out from under the marquee, into the rain, to decide where to go and what to do. She was near Omonia and she thought she just might get on the Piraeus train again, so as to avoid getting wet in the rain. She ran the three blocks to the square, jay-walked across the slippery street and ran down the still-stationary escalator steps. The train was slow in coming, and packed with commuters and she had to stand the whole way, about thirty minutes.

At the end of the line in Piraeus, she disembarked and walked along the cars in the enormous, high-ceilinged terminal building. There was an agent collecting the tickets of the exiting passengers and a line was forming that was fifty people long. The commuters were in a hurry, and resented the wait. Several people ran ahead and jumped line, near the front, but Anna patiently took a place at the back. There had been no ticket checker the last time she had come this way, without a ticket, but this time she had bought one and now here was the ticket checker. She felt very much in sync with the world around her.

It was raining harder outside, so, once through the line, she walked around the station, looking at the newspaper displays. Athens must have ten different dailies, all very political, she suspected, for she had come to know the Greeks as people who liked to talk politics. *Maybe because they invented it,* she thought. The headlines on the papers were huge and frantic, many of them ending in enormous semi-colons, which Anna had figured out was the Greek question mark. "**WHERE DID THE MONEY GO**;" she imagined one of them saying.

The rain didn't look to be letting up, and Anna decided it didn't really matter if she got a little wet anyway. She walked out of the station, down a few blocks and ducked into a small café. Inside it was very smoky and the windows were steamed so that you couldn't see out. Several groups of people, all dressed in dark clothes with dark caps and the men with unshaven faces, sat with wrapped packages and suit cases around the small tables. Against one wall there was a gas heater running, and the people waiting were clustered around it, leaving the only empty tables on the chilly side of the room. Anna took one, sat down and lit a cigarette.

After a minute, a waiter, dressed in a white shirt and black pants, with a white, dirty apron, came by.

"Ορίστε." Anna hadn't figured out the exact meaning of that word, but it was the one waiters used when they wanted your order.

"Ενα κάφε, πάρακαλώ, μέ γάλα." One coffee, please, with milk. She had only learned these last two words in the past week, having read them off a menu that had an English translation. Actually, sometimes the last words did not seem to work and she got a larger than usual cup of black coffee and she would have to ask again for the milk. And it came in a flash this time to Anna that μέ γάλα must sound, or rather she must sometimes say it to sound, like μεγάλα, which must mean *large* or something like that, like the prefix *mega-*. She smiled to herself for having figured that out. This time, she got the milk; the waiter put the cup on the table and spoke the price. She couldn't understand Greek numbers yet, but 100 δραχ would be plenty. She pulled her roll of money out of her jeans and peeled off two blue fifties. She was carrying, she supposed, a couple of hundred dollars with her, but it never occurred to her to be nervous about that, not in Athens. The waiter took one of the fifties and laid her small change on the table.

As she sipped her coffee, she watched her fellow patrons, who were talking quietly, the men drinking brandy or ouzo, the women mostly just sitting. Anna ran her fingers through her short hair, a little damp in spite of the rain jacket's hood. She supposed her haircut was too young for her, but she was enjoying the effortlessness of it. Besides, here no one cared how she looked. After all, she didn't know anyone.

At some point in the next hour, Anna decided to take the same boat that one of the groups in the café was waiting for. It didn't matter which group or which boat, she decided she would just follow the first group to leave and buy a ticket and ride the boat that they were going to ride. She supposed that she decided that because of the talk she had had with herself in the movie theater. It did not seem to matter much what she did right now; it seemed to matter most that she think to herself, *What do I want to do right now?* She asked herself that question, and decided that a ferry ride to an unknown destination would be nice, and she would do it.

So, a few minutes later, when an older woman, a husband and wife, apparently, and one small child, about Janet's age, got up to leave, Anna followed them. She wondered about none of the things that would bother the usual American tourist in Greece, like whether and where she could buy a ticket and for how much, and when the boat would leave and when it would get there and where, even, that it was going. She only put her hands in her pockets and walked in the rain, about a half a block behind her family, past the street-side kiosks selling everything a traveler might need. Anna quickly stopped and bought a navy blue beret to put on against the chilly rain, then ran a bit to catch up with her family. They walked across a busy street, Anna trailing behind, a busy street where the cars seemed to speed up when they saw you, in hopes of intimidating a blond tourist, and through a gate in the tall fence that surrounded the docks.

They walked past the square sterns of several ferries, where the boats had backed into the docks to unload the cars and trucks, Anna still following a bit behind the family. She had to slow herself down to match their pace; she was not burdened with any luggage, or a grandmother or small child. The pace gave her time to eye carefully the ferries as she walked past. Most were white, sitting quietly waiting to be loaded, their tailgates—Anna didn't know the nautical term and was sure the suburban American term was the wrong one—their tailgates lowered, displaying the empty caverns of their lower decks. She sounded out the names of several, written across their sterns. ΓΕΟΡΓΙΟΣ ΈΞΠΡΕΣΣ. GEORGIOS EXPRESS. She was aided in her struggle with Greek by the fact that she knew the Greek alphabet from her math studies. ΆΤΛΑΣ. ATLAS.

It soon became clear which boat was their boat, for one lay ahead around which activity swirled. Cars were lined up and trucks, issuing blue smoke, sat in line, smaller trucks than the big semis at home, with their cargos wrapped in tarps, as if Christo, the *avant guarde* artist, had been at work. There was nothing, she decided, that looked more non-American right now than those trucks with their wrapped cargos.

Inside the ring of cars, honking, drivers yelling, packed with people and possessions, was a mob of people on foot, all shouting and gesturing at one another. It appeared that the arguments going on were so major that in the US blows would fall and shots would be fired. It appeared that such offense was being taken that civil war might ensue. Anna's family entered the fray, pushed through the crowd to an officer dressed in white, standing behind a small white desk, chest-high. The father of the family thrust a handful of white papers that must be their tickets into the face of the officer, who pushed them away, continuing to write at the desk and to yell at three different groups of people standing in the crowd in front of him.

Anna hung back to watch and to figure out how she was going to get on this boat, which was orange, unlike all the white ones that lay around it, and which said on the back ΝΆΞΟΣ. NAXOS. She had no idea what the word meant, nor any idea of how to get on the boat.

After a minute of shouting, her family's tickets were accepted by the officer and they picked up their luggage and packages and walked up the tailgate and disappeared into the ferry's cavern. Anna watched a while longer and began, she thought, to understand what was going on, and why her family had finally managed to walk through so easily. Most of the arguing, she decided, was about space for the automobiles and trucks, and thus irrelevant to her travel plans. It looked as though more tickets for cars had been sold than there was space, and the man with the uniform was having to allocate the places that were available. She thought that this was the case, because he would stop arguing every now and then and accept tickets, but only from people who then walked onto the boat. So she shouldn't have any trouble, if she could get a ticket.

Outside the fence, across the street where she had walked, there were agencies with signs in the window saying *Tickets* in English, waiting for the tourists that would arrive in the spring. But somehow Anna thought that she could probably buy a ticket from the officer at the desk, so, after a minute more of waiting and watching, she entered the crowd and squirmed her way toward the front. "Pardón. Pardón", she said, accenting the second syllable, as if Spanish were closer to Greek than English, which it is not. And often the men would stand aside for the small, blond European with a haircut like a boy. After a few minutes she was standing right in front of the desk which was so tall that only her head and shoulders showed over the top. People were reaching over her head, shoving papers at the officer and yelling as if she were not there. Nor did the officer bother to notice her. She squirmed around to the side and reached out and grabbed his arm. She had to shout to be heard: "A ticket. Can I buy a ticket?"

Without looking at her, he responded with a stream of Greek she could not understand, nor, really, know whether it was directed to her.

"I need a ticket."

More Greek.

"A ticket." She pulled out her money roll, which was the only way she had of showing that she wanted to buy something.

Finally, he looked down at her and said in English, "Where are you going?" He gave her ten seconds to answer and while she was realizing that she didn't know where the boat was going or why it mattered, he went back to his business and began shouting at the others. The crowd closed around her and she found herself quickly several persons away from the desk. She retreated to reconnoiter.

*Where are you going?* he had said. Now there was a question that would take some thought. *Wherever this boat is going*—even if she could say it in a way that he would understand, which she probably couldn't—is a statement just too bizarre to be believable. Maybe she should give up on this plan, walk across the street and buy a ticket from an English-speaking agent. But that seemed to require a kind of energy that she didn't have yet. It had to be done this way, or not at all.

She looked around and found that she was standing next to a chalk board filled with a list of Greek words and times. Of course. The ferry made several stops; she should have realized that, and it would make the officer's inquiry make sense. This list of single words probably was the itinerary and arrival times. She looked down the list of words, sounding them out. They did sound to her like place names: Σίρος. Νάχος. Πάρος. Ίος. Θήρα. She recognized the second one; it was also the name of the boat. And the third. Paros. That was Mike Reid's island, from which he had written to her about *Jude the Obscure* and the café that said ΚΑΦΕΝΕΟΝ over the doorway. Small world. She was suddenly frightened and not at all sure that she wanted to ride on this boat to that island. But if she bought a ticket all the way to the end—to Θήρα—Thira, she sounded it out—then she could get off wherever she wanted, she supposed. Quickly, she shoved her way back through the crowd to the desk and grabbed the officer's arm again.

"Θήρα."

"Ενδάχει." He pulled out a book of tickets and wrote illegibly on one. He then spoke some Greek that would have to be the price. She shook her head that she didn't understand. He pointed to a place on the book, which showed a price that was easily within what she had in her pocket. She paid, took the ticket and the change, and walked up the tailgate and into the ship. She found her way to the passenger deck and to the second class lounge, which was crowded, smoky and filled with noise. Every seat seemed to be taken already, even though there were still many people outside. She spotted her family, spread out across an entire row of seats as if they were to be camped there for weeks. The grandmother appeared already to be asleep. There was nowhere to sit.

But, she discovered, there were plenty of seats outside on the deck, under an awning where she would stay dry. So she bought herself two cheese pies and a beer, talked a steward out of a blanket, and sat wrapped up, in a deck chair, her sneakers propped on the railing, and watched the final stages of loading and embarkation. Then the dock slipped past, then Piraeus itself, then the coast of Greece. About a half hour after leaving—it was now dark and the rain still fell but she was warm and dry and the food and beer tasted good—she recognized the airport sliding past and she watched the planes land for as long as she could. Then it was night, and there was nothing to see and only the steady roar of the diesels. As they left the mainland, the rain stopped falling and the clouds broke enough so that she could watch the moon rise in the east, over Turkey out there somewhere, she guessed.

After about four hours, which she spent entirely sitting in the same chair watching the moony waves go by and thinking of nothing, they came to what must be Siros, the first stop. There was a short bustle of horn blasting, docking, departing passengers, off-loading vehicles and they were going again. An hour later they approached another island in the dark and an hour later another one. If the list back in Piraeus showed the stops in the correct order this would be Paros, where Mike Reid was living. An announcement came over the loudspeaker which would have confirmed that, had she understood it. She walked to the rail on the dock side and looked out through the dark.

Little could be seen beyond the bustle on the dock immediately below. The dock itself was only a long strip of concrete with places for boats to tie up. About three or four trucks were getting off here, and a few cars. Twenty passengers or so were walking away from the boat, along the dark dock, through the patchy pools of light from a few street lights, toward the town. A few on-lookers hung around; a few casual longshoremen, boys really, looked for jobs carrying suitcases or crates. She could pick out a few cafés and a hotel in the village, and over there a church and a disco. A broken-down windmill stood at the base of the dock. But that was all. Only street lights and house lights were visible against the dark hills rising above the town. A few cars and a motorcycle or two buzzed along the road by the sea, around a traffic circle at the end of the dock and inland, past the church. She heard a rooster crow, even though it was not yet even midnight. A dog barked somewhere.

She could get off here, she supposed, get a room at that hotel there and ask around for Mike tomorrow. But she couldn't think of any reason to do that. What would she say? What would they talk about? What would he think about her being here?

Her reaction to these questions popping into her head was so violent that she was almost ill at the ship's rail. It was as if the night were full of such questions. She walked to the opposite side of the boat, where it seemed to be quieter, and looked out on a hilly peninsula, across the harbor from the town and lit with only a very few house lights. It *was* quieter over on this side, and not just because she was crazy, she knew; the noise of unloading was left behind dockside and here was only the sound of the idling diesel engines. Even so, she knew that she could not get off this boat and spend tomorrow looking for Mike. It might be sort of fun to sit over there, away from the lights on the peninsula and spy on the village and Mike and what's-her-name, his wife, but that seemed to her to be impossible to arrange, so she stood on the quiet side of the boat until it stood off from the dock and headed out through the harbor, sounding its horn, and Paros was left behind.

Emily, reading by candlelight in the cold marble house on the side of the hill, overlooking the harbor, heard the blast from ΝΆΞΟΣ and looked at her watch. If Michael was on the boat, he would be home in about a half an hour, walking up the hillside in the dark, unless he stopped for an ouzo at the

Portside Café, which was likely. She guessed, then, that if he was on ΝΆΞΟΣ, he'd be home in an hour, but he wasn't, of course.

~

Anna rode the rest of the way to Thira and spent the night in the closest hotel to the dock. The next morning she found that she had no desire for touristing around the quaint charm of the white-washed village, with steep, narrow roads, and walls plunging down to the sea, so she took ΝΆΞΟΣ early that day back to Athens. She stayed locked in a stall in the women's restroom during the boat's stop at Paros, she wanted so badly not to see the island in daylight, and when the boat started up again and she left the restroom she was afraid that Mike would have, by some impossible chance, gotten on board. But she searched for him and he was not on the boat that she could find.

She arrived back in Athens early in the afternoon and went directly to her hotel room and stayed inside for two days, not eating and sitting by the window, hoping she wouldn't see him pass by. He never did, for, instead of riding the train straight through to Athens, as he had written to Richard he would, he had stopped for a while in the cold mountains of Macedonia. By the time Michael was back in Athens for a day and a half on his way back to Paros, Anna had become comfortably alone again and was walking the streets wherever she wanted. They did not run into each other, however, for Athens is a very big, very busy city.

ATHENS, TALLAHASSEE AND ALBUQUERQUE

This time, Anna planned the timing carefully, checked her watch and walked into the OTE telephone office on Stadiou Street just as it was turning two o'clock on Saturday afternoon at home in Tallahassee. She had thought quite a bit—she seemed to be thinking more clearly after her ferry boat ride through the islands, down and back to Thira—she had thought quite a bit about what the best time would be and had decided that two o'clock on Saturday afternoon would be just right. She had given little thought to the woman who had answered the phone the last time, the one who had told her that her children were okay. Of course, Ben would have hired someone to keep the house and babysit, and Anna was pleased that Helen Lutz, their usual sitter from next door, had not answered, for she would have been chatty and nosey. So she hadn't minded that a stranger answered, and of course, Ben would have hired a student to do the job. Of course, she would be a female student, a pretty female student. Maybe Ben would be sleeping with her, but given the present situation, Anna would have little room to complain about that. But this time, she had planned the timing carefully, because she wanted to talk to Ben, not the unknown student housekeeper, and at just after two on Saturday afternoon, Ben ought to be at home.

The lady at the counter assigned her to a booth and wrote out for her the string of numbers to dial. The booth was made of heavy glass and had a door like a regular room door, not one of those funny collapsing doors like phone booths used to have at home. She stepped inside, where it smelled of old cigarette smoke, picked up the phone and dialed. There was no overseas sound to the ring, to which she listened so intently that she could almost pick out the individual segments of the sound. Her finger stayed near the disconnect button.

"Hello?"

"Ben. It's Anna."

"Where are you?"

"That's not what you were supposed to ask first."

"What? Where are you? Oh, I'm sorry. How are you?"

"I was only kidding."

"How are you? Anna. It's been two months. I thought you were, I don't know, dead, I guess."

"I'm okay. Now Ben, I can't talk long and I need to have a very matter-of-fact conversation. Okay? How are the children? How is Rachel?"

"My God, Anna, where are you?"

"How is Rachel?" she repeated. There was no answer. "Damn it, Ben. Talk to me about the children. Just like normal. I've called you at home from my office. I'm working at the library, all right? It's that damn second transformation of Jablonski's again, all right? But never mind about that; how's Rachel?"

"How can you do this to us? I've worried. The children don't know what to think. I don't know what to think."

"Ben. I'm going to hang up." She put her finger on the button. "Now, how is Rachel?"

Silence.

"Ben!" She made her voice sharp. She couldn't remember ever having taken such a tone with him.

"She's fine. Still quiet, though she said something last night at dinner. *Milk*, I think; I don't remember."

"Where is she right now?"

"Asleep in the nursery. Her nap."

"How exactly?"

"What do you mean? Anna, this is crazy."

"On her back?"

"Yes. I don't know. Yes, on her back."

"What color is she dressed in?"

"Blue. A double hand-me-down from Sam. You know the blue sleep suit with the feet?"

"I know the one. Go on. Talk to me."

"Anna, my God, what's wrong with you? Where the hell are you?"

She broke the connection with her finger. She sat for a moment in the glass booth and imagined Rachel asleep in Florida, on her back, in blue. Right now that's the way it was. Is. It was hard to believe that simultaneously Rachel was asleep in Tallahassee and Anna sat in an overseas telephone office in Athens. It seemed to mean something profound about the structure of the universe that such things happened simultaneously. That now was now, even though here was not there. Even more, it seemed important that things were happening here under a grossly different set of rules from the ones that applied to the things happening simultaneously there. How could it possibly be that the universe contained such diversity? She shook her head. How was one supposed to know where to be and when and what rules applied?

She noticed that she was still holding the phone. She replaced it in its cradle, left the booth and paid at the counter. Outside the telephone office, the traffic rushed along Stadiou Street between Syntagma and Omonia. The air was heavy with the traffic's exhaust. The shops were open on this Saturday night and the city was alight with excitement and commerce. She knew a taverna called the Lemon Tree, a small place not far from here, a place where, later on, bouzouki music would be played and the men would dance and she and the Greek women would sit in chairs around the room, backs to the wall, arms and ankles crossed, and watch. The Greek women would talk without using words, their hands expressing the finest nuances of feeling above the high, hard, loud music which would rip Anna's eardrums and thoughts of Rachel would be driven away.

Anna stepped into the stream of the pedestrians on the sidewalk, heading right, away from Omonia, her hands in the pockets of her Greek jeans and her eyes on the neon signs flashing high over her head. She took a skip step and ran ahead to catch the light at the intersection and she continued to run until the ache of her short breath made her intimate parts stop longing for home.

∼

At almost exactly the same moment that Anna was dialing her home phone number from the government telephone office, Michael was sitting in the small lobby of the Acropolis House, the hotel near the Plaka where he regularly stayed when he was in town, and which was located a few miles from the hotel that Anna was using. He knew the owner of the Acropolis House well, and so it had been easy enough to arrange to have the overseas phone call placed for him, to be taken here in the lobby, with the TV playing in the background. It was just after nine in the evening, and he sat for a moment deciding whether to tell the owner, yes, now place the call.

Michael's aversion to phoning from overseas was of long standing. When he had first gone to Europe, in the summer of '65, it had been both difficult to call home and prohibitively expensive, especially for a college sophomore hitching around the continent on a budget of twenty-five bucks US a week. There were a lot of American kids in Europe that summer and, well, they just didn't call home. Michael had quickly adapted to being out of touch, and then began to like it, even if his mother didn't, and as he continued to travel over the years, as it became easier and easier to call home, and less and less expensive, relative to his resources, he continued the practice of staying out of touch. Eventually it became more than a practice, rather an obsession, then later a principle, though some, Marie for instance, would call it an affectation. Part of the attraction of travel to Michael was the very state of being out of touch, and he continued to be attracted to that even after his reluctance to call home had become an artifice at best.

And now, on a Saturday night, when it was two in the afternoon in Tallahassee, and noon in Albuquerque, he sat in the lobby of the Acropolis House, deciding whether, for no reason that he could put his finger on, he would abandon his principles for the sake of a chat with his friend Marie. *What the hell?* he said to himself, stood up, poked his head around out the door and toward the front desk.

"Okay, Mr. Choudalakis. Place the call please." The proprietor's English

∼    317

was much better than Michael's Greek. "Πάρακαλώ," he added for effect. *Please.*

The house phone in the lobby rang once, and when Michael picked up he could hear the ringing from far away. Several rings. Then Marie's voice. *Hi. This is Marie. I can't come to the phone right now, but leave a message and I'll call you back.* And a beep.

"Well," he spoke into the phone. "This is unprecedented. I just felt like chatting. I hope you're well. Bye."

He hung up the phone and sat back, smiling to himself. How terribly bloody typical. The abandonment of one's principles to absolutely no earthly effect. It would, he thought, be crazy to keep trying. Not crazy, maybe, but silly. If calling the US from one's hotel lobby in Athens was ostentatious, continually calling an answering machine was brazen. He stood up from the couch, tossed an "Ευχάριστώ" toward the front desk, got a "Πάρακαλώ" in return, and headed out the door of the hotel to the street. The Plaka was not yet beginning to come alive with Saturday night activity, for the Greeks are late partiers, but in any case he felt more like a quiet walk up towards the Acropolis than a noisy night of wine and music. The monuments themselves would be closed, but to sit alone on a bench, above the traffic and the noise seemed just perfect for this night, his last one in Athens before catching the ferry boat the next day back to Emily on Paros.

∽

When Anna's call came through to Ben, the two older Browning children were at the Springtime Tallahassee Grand Parade under the supervision of Nikki and Connor. Janet sat on Connor's shoulders, the better to get a look at the paraders; there were jugglers and fire breathers, unicyclists and stilt-walkers, flipping and tumbling cheerleaders, frat floats with pretty co-eds throwing candy to the crowd, policemen on horseback, and soldiers in fatigues. And here was the main attraction: The Florida A&M Marching 100, high-stepping and blasting away in their gaudy orange and green uniforms, festooned with rattlesnakes, the school's mascot. Sam had squirmed his way through the crowd to be in the front row, while Nikki stood several rows back, keeping an eye on him, and holding the leash of Tim, Connor's brown dog with an intelligent face, a disreputable pedigree, and one perky ear, the other having been nearly torn off and now flopped, the result of a fight he had lost years ago with a bad dog from the next street over. Janet had tied an orange and green bandana around Tim's neck, in honor of the band, and both the dog and the two children were well on their ways to various forms of digestive difficulties due to the overly indulgent nature of their supervisors.

The Springtime Tallahassee excursion had been Nikki's idea, and she had asked Ben if he would mind if she and Connor took the children to the parade. He had said he didn't mind, commenting on the irony that it was only, what?, a few weeks ago when she had abandoned him on a night when he needed her, and now it was she who wanted to take the children on the weekend. Nikki ignored him, and it was arranged. Rachel had threatened to frustrate the plan by being sound asleep when Nikki and Connor came by on Saturday, so, rather than wake her, they had taken Sam and Janet, leaving Ben to watch over the baby while he prepared for his next week's classes.

Now the Marching 100 had stopped in the middle of the street, and was blasting away, while cavorting in place, the crowd was swaying and dancing with them, and Nikki's hand found its way into Connor's and she lay her head against his shoulder, still keeping an eye on Sam through the crowd.

~

Shortly after noon in Albuquerque, Britt was studying while Marie was grocery shopping, soon due home for lunch. She was lying on the bed in the study, reading a *Law Review* submission, in preparation for a staff meeting to begin at one o'clock. Ordinarily, she did not like to be doing school work on Saturday, but the regular staff meeting had been moved from Friday afternoon, to accommodate the work she was doing with Randolph on the Riley case, so she was in no position to complain. She was liking the submission she was reading, a short, quirky, informally written little essay about American Indian law, which meant, if patterns were to hold, that Alex, the Editor-in-Chief, would dislike it for exactly the same reasons. So, when the phone began to ring, she was getting her thoughts in order for what she hoped would be a successful attempt to get the staff to extend an offer to the writer. Screening, she let the machine pick it up. *Hi. This is Marie. I can't come to the phone right now, but leave a message and I'll call you back.* A pause, then a male voice she didn't recognize.

"Well, this is unprecedented. I just felt like chatting. I hope you're well. Bye."

Giving the message little thought, Britt went back to her reading and, a half an hour later when Marie came in the back door and asked for some help carrying the groceries, she had thought no more about it than anyone would of a message on a telephone answering machine not intended for her. After helping with the groceries, and grabbing an orange and a bag of chips out of the bag for her lunch, she said, "Sorry, I gotta go. *Law Review* meeting, about to begin. I should be back by three. Let's go out somewhere tonight. There's a message for you on the machine," and she was out the door with her bike, and that was the end of that. Marie listened twice to the message and then erased it.

~

At noon on that Saturday, Richard and Rita were walking around the Old Town Plaza with their children, except for Christina, who was in Las Cruces with her father, her step-mother, and her half- and step-sibs, except for her oldest step-brother, who was visiting *his* father in Amarillo. Richard had bought Rita a nice strand of turquoise-and-shell heishi beads and now the kids were picking out small charms for themselves, not forgetting to pick something nice for Tina, from off of the white sheets that the Indians had spread on the sidewalk, under the portal of La Placita. Later the plan was to walk over to the Museum of Natural History.

~

When Ben hung up the phone after Anna had disconnected, he lit a cigarette and sat for several minutes trying to figure things out. Where she was? Why she had called? What was he supposed to do? Unable to answer any of these questions, he got up and strolled into the nursery, where he discovered that Rachel was not sleeping in blue, at all, but rather in green.

Back in his study, he picked up his copy of *Middlemarch*, which he was having the students in his Joyce seminar read. He had an esoteric—and, by design, largely inscrutable—theory that Elliot was a precursor to Joyce, and he enjoyed requiring the students to plow through her nearly impenetrable prose. However, Anna's phone call had so irritated him that he himself was unable to concentrate and was finding the going difficult, events so remarkable that they would have baffled anyone who knew Ben Browning, if there had been anyone there to see it, which there wasn't. Eventually, he put the book down and sat smoking cigarette after cigarette, lighting the next one from the previous one, staring across the room for the next hour, until he was brought out of his stupor by Rachel's awakening, and by the return of Nikki, the children and her nearly mute, lab-assistant boy friend.

~

Two days later, Marie had still not said anything to Britt about the message on the answering machine. Britt noticed that the message had been erased, but did not ask about it.

CORRESPONDENCE

Πάρος.
Whenever.

R –
Greek for *yes* is Bulgarian for *no*. It's a richly ambiguous world we live in.
M.

## ~ 13

## ALBUQUERQUE

The lots were small on Manzano Street where the duplex stood, so there was not much of a yard to look after, only a bit of grass to be mowed with the push machine that Marie kept in the storage shed in the back, and two flower beds below the front windows on both sides of the duplex. The tenants took care of the mowing, while Marie kept the flower beds in decent shape, though truthfully, she had never been much of a gardener. There was room for a small vegetable patch in the back, by the alleyway, and Britt had some plans to put tomatoes out later in the spring, which Marie had said was fine, but don't expect her to pull the weeds.

Thus it was that late Sunday morning, after Michael's message had been left on, and then erased from, the answering machine, she and Britt were on their hands and knees in the yard in front of the duplex, digging in the garden and putting out some yellow and red zinnias, and white daisies, which would, no doubt, be totally burned up in the afternoon sun by the time June rolled around. Marie was in jeans and a long-sleeved tee shirt, but Britt wore shorts and a bikini top, trying to get a little sun. They dug in the dirt, pulled weeds and the tendrils of tough Bermuda grass that wanted to take over, and they argued about which plants went where and how far apart they should be. They waved to their neighbors and talked quietly of this and that. Ginger was constantly in the way, wanting her nose in every hole being dug for the plants, until she had been exiled to the corner of the yard, where she now sat, looking rejected.

When they took a break for lunch, Marie changed into shorts, but kept her long sleeves on, and brought out chicken sandwiches, chips and quinine-laced tonic water. They sat on lawn chairs pulled into the sun, as the air was a bit cool. A breezed drifted in from the north strongly enough so that the airport was using the 0-180 runway, and they watched the planes take off, accelerating through the desert air a few miles to the west of where they sat, near Girard Avenue.

"Would you do something for me?" Marie asked.

"Sure. Want another sandwich? I'll make it." Britt started to arise.

"No. Sit still. This may sound silly, but do you think you could explain that Riley case to me?"

Britt turned her head and pushed her sunglasses up onto her forehead. "What a nice thing to ask. Sure. Let's see. What do you know about bankruptcy?"

"I don't know. Not much. When people go broke, the government helps them out, sort of."

"Sort of."

"Except sometimes they aren't *really* broke. Like Continental Airlines."

"Or that Dalkon Shield company."

"A.H. Robbins, right?"

"Right."

"Or that asbestos company, whose name I forget."

"Johns-Manville. Right."

"So that's all I know. The news people think I know what something called *chapter eleven* is, but I don't."

"Okay." Britt paused to get her thoughts in order. "Where to begin? When a company gets into financial trouble, or thinks it's going to be, like, say, Robbins, it can ask for relief. That's called *petitioning*."

"What kind of relief? Like corporate welfare?"

"No. The government doesn't give out any money. I mean that the company seeks its relief from the bankruptcy court. The court makes the debtor—that's what the broke company that wants the relief is called, the *debtor*—makes the debtor's creditors back off for a while. The company gets kind of a breathing spell, because all of its creditors have to stop trying to collect their debts."

"Is it only for companies? I thought that real people could go bankrupt, too."

"Sure. That's consumer bankruptcy, which Randolph thinks is small-time stuff, but in a way I'm liking those issues in class just as much."

"Like maybe that's what you want to do after you graduate?"

"Maybe. The up-side is that when the economy is down, bankruptcies are up, so the business is kind of recession-proof."

"And the down-side?"

"Your client is broke." Britt took a sip of her tonic, now mostly gone. "Now sometimes the company—or the individual—is in such bad shape the court will just sell everything it owns and pass out the money to the creditors and the debtor will go out of business. The creditors don't often get much; usually nothing; ten cents on the dollar if they're lucky. That's a liquidation, and it's called a *chapter seven*, because that's where the rules are found, in chapter seven of the Bankruptcy Code."

"What happens then?"

"Well, if it's a corporation, it just goes out of business, vanishes, leaving behind an empty corporate shell. Individuals get to start over with a fresh start, we call it. But that's not what happened to Riley, or Robbins, or Continental Airlines."

"No?"

"No. Those companies are what are considered going concerns and the idea is that if they can just reorganize their financial affairs, then they can get back on their feet and go on about their businesses."

"Like ripping up the insides of women?"

Britt looked at Marie and raised an eyebrow. "Well, you know there *are* ways of not getting pregnant other than wearing a plastic and metal cockroach in one's womb."

"So I'm learning."

"Did you ever wear one?"

"A Dalkon Shield? Are you nuts?"

"An IUD."

"No. I was on the pill for a while, but then that started to seem silly when I wasn't in a steady relationship. So, I had a cervical cap. Still do, somewhere around here."

"Medicine chest. Third shelf, on the right. I stumbled across it a couple of weeks back. I didn't mean to snoop, but I saw the little container and peaked inside. I'd never seen one before, and wasn't exactly sure what it was."

"A relic from the past, I guess."

"How's it work?"

"You insert it all the way up to the top, then push on it to squeeze the air out, and release. The suction holds it in place. My fingers are almost too short to do it right."

"I happen to think your fingers are just exactly the right length."

"Yeah, well, I almost couldn't get it out the first time I put the damn thing in. It can get a little gooey in there, especially, you know, after sex."

"So I'm told. Okay, so back to chapter eleven, before I get distracted."

"I suppose I could toss it away."

"I suppose you could." A pause, then Britt continued. "The idea here is that the company can make up for bad business decisions that it made in the past, get its feet back under it, and become successful."

"Corporations don't have feet, but I know what you mean. But do the guys who made the bad decisions get to stay on?"

"Depends. Sometimes they are tossed out at the beginning. Sometimes during the process. But, yes, sometimes—often really—they get to say *we'll do better this time around*."

"I'm not sure I like that, but go on."

"Well, theoretically, the creditors—including injured women in the Robbins case—can always complain, and try to get the judge to remove management and appoint a trustee. But I'll admit that some pretty rotten corporate managers have been allowed to stay in control of the company when it reorganizes. Anyway, these reorganizations are called *chapter elevens* because that's where *that* law is found in: United States Code, title eleven, chapter eleven. In a chapter eleven—and that's where Riley is—wait. I guess I should tell you about Riley. He's this New York dude who builds golf course condos in the sun belt. Basically he's got no assets of his own, borrows money whenever he can, uses the money he borrowed for one job to pay off the last one and makes his money turning over the condos to retirees from the north."

"How come I can't believe you're telling me this? You work for this sleazebag?"

"Well, actually, Randolph tells me that it's not that unusual a situation in the construction business. He says that no one has any money, and everyone uses the money from one job to pay off the last one. As long as they can keep building, they do okay. Such is the American construction industry. But Riley got caught short, and the ends didn't meet. In any case, Randolph and I work for the good guys. The National Bank of Commerce." Britt smiled and took a sip of tonic.

"What a relief," Marie said with more than a touch of sarcasm. "Maybe I should transfer my checking account to them?"

"I wouldn't bother."

"Go on."

"So Riley borrows fourteen million from the bank to build condos in Belen, but really to pay off the one in Texas, which incidentally isn't selling, as he had hoped, to pay off the one in Georgia. Maybe the Veep at Commerce knows this and maybe he's on the take, or maybe he's just stupid, anyway Commerce makes the loan, the money disappears, the Belen condos never get built and Riley's business collapses. So he petitions back in New York where he lives. In chapter eleven. And he says he's a going concern and can get himself reorganized if given the chance. So he files his plan."

"What plan?"

"His plan. His chapter eleven plan. His reorganization plan."

"What's his plan?"

Britt took another sip of tonic. "The plan is to pay Commerce sixty-three cents on the dollar over the next three years and forget the rest. That's it, minus the details and without any reference to his other creditors, of which there are bus loads."

"Some plan. Commerce loves it, right?"

"Right. And here it gets technical. Stop me if you're confused. Commerce gets to vote on the plan. To accept or reject."

"They vote to reject, right?"

"Right. But they don't exactly get a veto. The plan can be crammed down their throat, so to speak."

"Is it?"

"That's what the New York argument is about. We say that cramdown . . ."

"Cramdown?"

"That's what it's called."

"*Cramdown?*"

"Yup."

"That's stupid. You go to law school to learn about something called *cramdown?*"

"I do."

"Go on."

"Well, we say that cramdown isn't allowed unless we'd get as much as we would have gotten if Riley had liquidated."

"Sold off everything, right?"

"Right. Chapter seven. Riley basically agrees and so the argument is over what counts in determining whether we would have gotten more in liquidation. Ahhhhh, . . ., that's all. I don't think I can explain the rest. It all has to do with the legal implication of Riley's having lied to the bank when he borrowed the money."

"Lied about what?"

"About having paid off the Texas condos. Here. This should do it: we think Riley should have to pay us back a hundred percent of the money he got by lying, not sixty-three percent as he has proposed. They say there's no connection between the fact that he lied—if he did, which they deny—and what the plan proposes."

"Do you think you'll win?"

"Randolph says he thinks so. There's some rough case law from the courts, but we think we can get around it."

"How so?"

"Well, okay, let's see. Lesson two. The problem is *discharge.*"

"Robbins has a problem with discharge? Wonderful."

Britt sighed. "*Discharge*, Squirt, is the forgiveness of debt. Everything that the debtor owes, but doesn't pay is discharged—forgiven—with a few exceptions."

"So?"

"So, one of the exceptions is for debts obtained under false pretenses."

"I'm not with you."

"We say Riley lied to Commerce and any debt obtained by lying will survive the bankruptcy and won't be forgiven. Won't be discharged."

"So Riley says you should take his sixty-three percent and he'll still owe you the other, ah, forty-seven percent after the bankruptcy."

"Right! You've got it. Except that it's thirty-seven percent. You forgot to borrow."

"Thirty-seven. Right."

"And we want to argue that we have to get the full hundred percent under the plan."

"Why do you care?"

"Well, of course, a hundred percent now is better than sixty-three percent now and thirty-seven percent later. But really, we care because we want to veto the plan, and keep it from being confirmed. So we can get a better deal now than the sixty-three percent and not have to wait until he's done with the bankruptcy."

"But either way you get your money."

"Theoretically."

Marie shook her head. "It seems like a lot of effort to spend on something that has nothing to do with building condos." She noticed a small deflation in Britt's eyes. "It's pretty interesting stuff, though. Thanks for explaining. Where does the work stand now?"

"We've finished our reply brief and we're preparing the oral presentations now. I've never worked on one project so hard, not since I was digging holes in the desert with a brush, anyway. Sometimes I dream about cramdown."

"You need to put a shirt on; you're getting burned."

"It feels good." Britt collapsed the lawn chair flat, and rolled over onto her front side. "But I'd let you put some sunscreen on my back, if you want to."

"Sure." Marie stood up, creamed her hands and rubbed down along Britt's shoulder blades and the small of her back to her bottoms. It would have taken a careful eye to spot Britt's hand as it slipped off the edge of the seat and rested on the grass, cupping the back of Marie's heel. "Thanks," Britt said and squeezed, then put her hands under her chin and closed her eyes. "Thanks. I hope we win, too."

"Did I say I hoped you win?", Marie said, taking off her long sleeves in the sun. Underneath, she, too, wore a bikini top. She rubbed some sun screen on her own arms.

"No, but I know you do."

"How important is winning?"

Britt tilted her head slightly and looked up at Marie. "Entirely."

"Entirely?"

"Entirely."

"Important enough to cheat?"

"Of course not."

"Important enough to take a bribe?"

"Come on, I'm not a judge, I'm a lawyer, sort of. Who'd bribe me?"

"Important enough to lie?"

"The DRs—the disciplinary rules—tell me I can't lie in the representation of a client. So, no, not that important."

"You guys need a rule to tell you that lying is wrong?"

"Feisty today, aren't we? Can you imagine ever lying in the classroom?"

"I deal with thirteen-year-olds. The rules are different. I am not always absolutely forthright."

An airplane blasted through its take-off into the northerly breeze. They paused until the noise died down, and even then the conversation lapsed after it was quiet again. Finally, Britt turned over, propped herself up on her elbows, and looked over at Marie. "Okay. Any number of things are more important than winning the Riley case, including sitting here in the sun with you. But winning is pretty important."

"I know it is, Britt. I do hope you win. I hope you knock the New Yorker on his ass."

And while the sun finished up its Sunday afternoon's work, Britt went to sleep and Marie sat, holding her knees, watching the planes take off, thinking of what a strange and peaceful thing it was to sit in the Albuquerque sun, putter around in the garden, and listen to Britt talk of bankruptcy law.

ALBUQUERQUE

Marie had only been in the law school a couple of times in her life. As she pulled into the parking lot late the next Friday afternoon, only two times came to her memory. Once, years ago, before Britt, she had come to the law library, looking for a book she needed for an ed admin class she was taking. That time, she recalled, she had almost been caught by the place. The mystique of the law had been all about that day, a Saturday, she remembered, and she had felt the enormity, the sophistication and the secrecy of the law. The veneration of words. *Books constitute capital* it said over the library entrance. And the place was full of people who moved comfortably and without intimidation through all of it. People speaking an unknown lingo outside the library in the Forum; people inside who didn't need the librarian's help, as she did, to find what they were looking for. She had been tempted, that afternoon, to try her hand, to apply to law school. That feeling had passed, but she still understood those affected by it.

The second time had been after she and Britt had become lovers and her entry into the law school had been with that uneasiness that many new lovers have when they enter a world that belongs to the other; she had felt it before with other lovers. That unease had been exacerbated by Marie's misgivings about a physical disembarkation into what they called *Beirut society*, the radical feminist-Lesbian community of Albuquerque in general and the law school in particular. Actually, around Britt's women friends, Marie was comfortable enough. But in public, she had a harder time. It was like not knowing what to do with your hands at an eighth grade dance, and just as silly, she supposed. Typically enough, Marie's unease bothered her more than it did Britt.

So, all of these thoughts were bouncing around in Marie's mind as she walked into the law school that Friday afternoon and stood at the end of the long, open Forum and tried to decide how to find Britt. They were to meet here after school and then drive to pick up Britt's car at the shop, and then go on to dinner in town. Marie was a little early and a little eager. She had hurried out of school, stopped at home to shower and change and rushed to the law school. In the glove compartment was a red carnation for her friend, who had been working so hard for the past month. It was getting near the New York trip and Marie hoped to slip a special payday evening into Britt's schedule. So she stood and scanned the Forum, and felt, as if she had taken odd-colored pills, both the unease of this place and the thrill of expectation. A shiver ran over her skin.

One of Britt's friends, a chunky black woman whom Marie knew to be Keisha, was walking toward her, toward the exit door, she supposed, and the unease jumped up, stronger now, probably because Britt wasn't with her. This would be the first time, she realized, that she would meet one of Britt's friends unaccompanied, her first trip to Beirut, if you will, alone, since she had disembarked the plane in Lebanon. The first time she would play the solo role as Britt's partner.

Marie spoke first, "Hi."

"Hi," Keisha said, continuing to walk. Then recognition hit her and she stopped and turned around. "Oh. Hi, Marie. How are you?"

"Fine thanks. You?"

"Late, I'm afraid. I'm supposed to put in a couple of hours at the firm where I clerk before the lawyers leave for the weekend." She glanced at her wristwatch. "I should be downtown right now, and who knows how bad the traffic is going to be on Lomas."

"Hurry, then. I'm supposed to meet Britt. You haven't seen her, have you?"

Still facing Marie, Keisha started to back toward the exit, while talking. "Not since Remedies. Try her carrel. Or the *Law Review* office. I gotta go. You guys want to go dancing with me and Liz Saturday night? Give us a call if you do." She backed her way through the exit door. "Bye."

"Bye," Marie said to the now-closed exit. "Nice to see you."

Instead of following Keisha's advice, Marie decided to wait for Britt here, rather than to hunt for her, so she took a seat in the Forum and opened the *Tribune.*

She sat for a half hour or so, until four-thirty, reading some, while glancing over the top of the paper every now and then, watching for Britt and seeing people going by, mostly in a Friday afternoon hurry. Finally, she decided to look around; she thought she had the rendezvous right, but it was in her nature to wonder about such things when someone was late. She wasn't sure, of course, where to look, but Keisha had suggested Britt's carrel, which she knew to be in the library, and which allowed her to start on familiar grounds, relatively speaking. She went in, under Jefferson's wonderfully compact quotation, and wandered around, upstairs and down. The library was large, open, quiet and almost deserted on this Friday, not yet near exams. There were many twists and turns, stairways and closed doors in the place, and she was soon turned around, her orientation lost, when she walked past one door marked *New Mexico Law Review.*

She knocked.

"Come in!" A male voice, shouting.

Marie opened the door and walked into the midst of what appeared to be a sort of basketball game, with five guys sitting in chairs around the room, simultaneously tossing wadded-up paper balls at three wastebaskets scattered about. There was much shouting, as each player apparently kept his own score. *Mayhem* is the word that first came to Marie's mind to describe the scene.

"Help you?" asked the player closest to her, immediately followed by "Bank shot! Eighteen."

"Never mind," said Marie, and she backed out of the room, closing the door behind her. It was clear that Britt was not in there. Keisha's next idea was the carrel, which she recalled Britt mentioning was on the lower level, and had a view of the golf course out the back, to the north, she guessed that would be, northeast, maybe. She decided to look there.

She found the row of carrels easily enough, with Britt's identified by the piece of masking tape on the outside wall with *B. LARSEN* printed in black. But no Britt. The carrel and all the others along the windows looking out on the golf course and the Crest—yes, the orientation of the building must make that the northeast—were all empty. Marie sat for a moment in Britt's chair, looked at the papers stacked on the desk, and the books on the floor, waiting. She looked at the picture of herself and Ginger, remembering that warm afternoon last spring, out on the West Mesa, before they had driven into town to attend the art opening, early, early in their relationship. It had been a wonderful day, but from there to here seemed, looking back on it, an unimaginable journey.

After a few minutes, she decided that Britt wasn't coming by here; it looked to her as if she had left nothing behind that she would have to get before leaving the building. She wandered back up to the main floor of the library and, at the circulation desk, she asked directions to Richard Randolph's office.

She got lost on the way there and blundered into a meeting room full of Indians. A tall man, with dark skin and two long, thin braids down the front of his nicely tailored grey suit, stood in the front of the room lecturing. He had a piece of chalk in his hand and several large turquoise and silver rings on his fingers. He stopped talking when Marie opened the door and the mostly brown faces of the audience turned around to look at her. The man at the front asked what she wanted. She apologized, asked directions again and left the room, wondering what the meeting was about. One way or another, she guessed, they were plotting to keep what they still had left.

Retracing her steps, she discovered that she had turned right instead of left on her way from the library. Back in the Forum, she got herself straightened out and went down the stairs to the faculty office wing.

Richard Randolph's office was open but empty. She looked into the mess and saw no clue as to where he or Britt might be. The desk outside the door, which looked to be a secretary's, was empty. She noticed the postcard stuck on the door, above his name, the postcard with a picture of the Acropolis on it. Marie had once received one just like it from Michael.

She turned and headed back to the Forum, got lost again—was there no square corner in this entire building?—and had to ask directions in what must have been the faculty lounge. An older man with a grey crew-cut sat reading a journal of some kind.

"You aren't Professor Randolph are you? Richard Randolph?" She didn't think Randolph was that old, but she just realized now that she had no idea what he looked like.

"No. Did you try the moot courtroom?"

"No. Actually, I'm looking for his research assistant, Britt Larsen?"

"Sorry. I don't know her. Go right up those stairs there and through the doors and you'll be back in the Forum."

"Thanks. I keep getting lost."

He looked up from his reading one last time and smiled, but said nothing.

On her way back to her seat, she stopped to use the restroom, sure now that she had missed Britt while she had been looking. Of course, car-less, there was nowhere Britt could go, so Marie headed back to the chair where she had first sat to read the *Trib* and wait. She suddenly caught the sound of Britt's voice, oddly electronized, coming from around the curve of a wooden wall in the center of the Forum. She followed the sound to a small room in the wall. A pony-tailed man of middle age sat in a chair, reading *Time* magazine, his feet in socks propped on a control panel. Britt's image was on a television monitor in front of him. He was not watching the screen, nor did he notice Marie.

She stood quietly for a moment and watched over his shoulder, through the door into the control room. The monitor was black and white; the shot was a severe profile. There were actually, Marie now noticed, five little Britts dotting the control panel, on smaller black-and-white monitors, each with a different view of her. One image was oddly scrambled, like a puzzle that had been put together wrong.

Marie tried to pick up Britt's speech in the middle. She listened carefully and found that it was easier to listen if she did not look at the monitor. While much of the speech was highly technical, legally technical that is, with a bunch of numbers and letters thrown around that sounded like *seven-oh-six-eff-three-bee*, there was enough familiar for Marie to figure out what was going on. She could tell that Britt was speaking to a court, and when she heard the name *Riley* she knew that Britt was practicing for New York. It was rather enjoyable to watch, as it might be enjoyable to watch one's lover deliver a speech in a language the watcher only slightly understands.

Once Britt stopped and listened to a voice coming from off-camera, too indistinct for Marie to catch. That was even more fun, watching Britt listen, watching the intentness in the one eye, the right one, that she could see. Watching a slow nod. I've seen that nod, Marie thought. It means that she doesn't get it yet, but that she's starting to understand.

"Damn it." The technician came awake over his *Time*, reached forward and pressed a button. A man's image replaced Britt's on the large monitor and his voice became understandable. But, Marie noticed, his words indicated that he had not understood the nuance of the nod. He had thought it meant *I see*, instead of *I'm beginning to see*, as Marie knew it did.

"This must be the famous Professor Randolph." Marie felt warmly superior.

"Huh? Can I help you?" The ponytail flopped over the technician's shoulder as he turned to look at her.

*Did I really speak aloud?*, Marie thought. "I'm waiting for my friend." She nodded at the screen.

"No telling how long he'll be."

"No, the other one. Britt Larsen."

"Ditto. Want me to ask?" He leaned toward a microphone.

"No. Don't bother them. Do you mind if I watch?"

"Not at all. Come in. Have a chair. You can look through the window here. My name's Dave Montoya."

"Marie Cochran. Nice to meet you." They nodded to each other; Dave didn't offer to shake hands.

The control room was small, dark, warm and cramped; it had an electric smell that Marie decided was ozone, though she didn't know why, mixed with a little garlic, whose source had to be Dave Montoya. The heat and smell made her dizzy. The room had a small, tinted, double-pane glass window, through which showed a dimly lighted circular room that looked like a courtroom. Richard Randolph sat where the judge would sit and Britt stood on a lower level behind a lectern, empty tables to her left and right and empty chairs behind her, behind a rail, where the audience would sit.

"Is that what they call the something courtroom?"

The technician reached up and flicked a knob counter-clockwise. The sound went off. "What?"

"The courtroom. Is that it?"

"The moot courtroom. Yes, that's it."

"Moot?" Marie had never heard Britt use the term.

"Mostly it's for make-believe cases."

"Oh."

It was especially unsettling, with the sound off, to watch Britt and her professor silently talking, through a tinted window in a room smelling of electricity and garlic. Marie wanted to ask the technician to turn the sound back up, but she didn't; he seemed in control here with all these knobs, switches and screens. Now, on the other side of the window, Britt and Randolph were laughing about something.

"Are you Britt's friend?"

There was a question loaded with meaning. Did he mean friend as in *friends*? Or *Friend*, that is, *lover*? For once, though, it didn't seem to matter.

"Yes."

Maybe it was his looks, this Dave Montoya, his old-style hippie looks. Marie had always felt comfortable around people of the Sixties. Or maybe it was because he seemed an outsider, too, a non-lawyer in the law school. Whichever, it was easy to answer. *Yes.* Simple as that. Expressing no surprise, he went on:

"She's very good. You probably don't think I know, but I do. I watch hundreds of practice rounds like that one every year and I get to know. She's very good."

Marie just smiled pleasantly. What was one to say, after all?

He continued, "I like her, too. She doesn't put anything on, you know? She's got all this power-trip in perspective. She's always very nice to me. You know? Always says thanks for working late. Most of them don't, you know. Law students can be assholes, you know? I should know; I'm around them all day long. But Britt's all right. Randolph's being kind of tough on her tonight, really putting her through the paces. But she's doing fine. She's good. Listen, why don't you just go into the courtroom and wait and listen there? They won't mind. "

"Oh no," Marie said, "I don't want to bother them."

"Oh, go on. A half an hour ago there were two or three people watching. She'd like to have a friend in the lion pit with her. Go ahead, the door's just around there."

Marie didn't think Britt would mind and she would like to see the real thing, so she walked out of the control room, around the curving wall and into the double doors. She was then in a small anteroom, a space between a double set of double doors, presumably to muffle the noise of the Forum and keep the courtroom quiet. It was dark and close and now, through the next set of doors she could hear Britt's natural voice. She pushed the door to the courtroom open.

The moot courtroom was round, and not as dark as it had appeared through the tinted control-room window. A skylight over Britt's head lightened the room. Most of the fixtures were in dark wood but some color was added with turquoise wall hangings and the bunting of various official flags. She could see the window through which she had been watching and saw that it was a one way window—on this side it was a dark mirror. Three or four remote control cameras hung on the walls; one of them buzzed, as Dave must have made some adjustment.

Britt was about thirty feet away, her back to Marie, and she continued to talk, unaware of Marie's quiet entry. Richard faced her and looked up when she came through the door, but then, without any reaction, returned to his notes. Marie took a seat and scraped the chair slightly pulling it out, but Britt seemed not to notice. Marie sat in Richard's line of sight, but not Britt's. She listened.

It was clear to her that Britt and Richard Randolph were going segment-by-segment through a speech. *Through an argument*, Marie corrected herself; Britt had told her that lawyers' presentations to judges are called arguments, not speeches. Britt would say part of it, looking directly at her teacher, only rarely at her notes and he would interrupt, asking questions. These interruptions, Marie had learned, were an important part of the argument, as the judges would insist on answers to their questions right then, not later, not *I'll get to that, your honor*. So Britt would respond immediately to a question from the bench, and then carry on. She stood rather stiffly behind the lectern. Her jeans, button-down shirt, vest and sneakers looked rather out of place in the formal surroundings, and her Forest Service ball cap, with her ponytail sticking out the back probably meant that she hadn't had time to wash her hair that morning. She gestured with her hands, when speaking, but she never moved from behind the lectern. When she listened, she kept her hands clasped behind her back. Marie, who had debated a little in college, knew a very formal presentation when she saw one, though this one was much less structured than a debate, what with all of the interruptions.

After Britt had delivered a bit, Richard Randolph would stop her and they would evaluate what she had done. Before, when he had interrupted her argument, he had been stiff and formal; he called her *Counsel* and *Ms. Larsen* and after a while Marie realized that at those times he was playing judge. She called him *Your Honor* in return. But when he stopped her and they evaluated the argument, he sat back in the black chair, with his hands behind his head, his tie loosened and his dress shirt unbuttoned at the collar, the sweat showing under his arms. During these times, she leaned forward on the lectern on her elbows, and he called her *Britt*.

"That's better, but you've still got to make it smoother. You've got to be ready for that question about dischargability. I don't know when it will come, but it *will* come. And you've got to have section five-twenty-three and Greco right there, right *then*." He leaned forward and slapped his hand against the desk top. "*Then*. No beating around the bush. *Then*. Right?"

"Yes, sir." She wrote something in her notes.

"Okay, try that part again."

Britt took a deep breath, dropped herself back into the lawyer's role, and continued. And so it went, as the two of them proceeded slowly through the argument. Britt's explanation of the Riley case, along with the sheer repetition of the argument, allowed Marie to follow what was going on. *Discharge*, she remembered, was the technical term for the forgiveness of Riley's debt to the Bank of Commerce and she listened closely for the connection between *discharge* and *cramdown*, if there was one. She couldn't quite remember. *Greco* was apparently the name of a case like theirs in which the court had made the connection that Britt wanted to make. And apparently Randolph expected one of the judges in New York to ask about dischargability and Britt was to have Greco in her pocket, at her finger tips, and to present it to a court, like a genius. Once, about the fifth time through this part, she recognized Britt's use of the Greco case at just the right spot and she thought she sensed that all three of them were both proud and relieved. She was, she knew. Britt still did not know she was there.

Once Randolph interrupted her with anger in his voice: "NO! God *damn* it, Britt, that's not right. You've got those two cases mixed up again. How is the court going to keep them straight if you can't?"

Britt breathed deeply, hung her head and gripped the lectern with both hands. Marie was uncomfortable and embarrassed for her.

"How?"

Britt shook her head and put her right hand under her ponytail in the back and massaged her neck. Marie looked down at her hands, folded on the table top in front of her; they were sweaty with the embarrassment she was sharing with Britt.

"*HOW?*"

"It won't."

"No, it won't. Now look. Glenn came first, then Martinson. You can keep that straight, can't you? Glenn, like John Glenn, the first astronaut. First. Right? You'd think you'd know that by now. Let's do it again."

*Fuck you, Randolph*, Marie said to herself and sat back in the chair, crossing her arms. Britt went on with her argument.

Six o'clock came and went. Outside it was getting dark and the skylight lost its glow. An afternoon thunderstorm rumbled somewhere.

Finally, Richard Randolph sat back, stretched and looked right straight at Marie, over Britt's shoulder and said, "I think that was a good one. What do *you* think?"

Marie was surprised and looked behind her. There was no one else in the room. She didn't know what to say. Britt turned around, looked at her, then at the clock.

"Oh, my God. Marie. I forgot. I lost track of the time. I'm sorry."

"It doesn't matter." Marie's voice from her seat in the back echoed in the courtroom. "I was enjoying the argument." She felt reasonably sophisticated, saying *argument*.

"How long have you been here?"

"It doesn't matter. Since about five."

"Oh God, I'm so sorry."

"Never mind, really. Go on with what you're doing."

Britt turned back to Richard, who had been sitting quietly in the front of the room, behind the judges' bench. "Oh, sorry. This is my friend, Marie Cochran. She was going to take me to pick up my car. I guess it's too late for that now."

"I think we're done, Britt. A good afternoon's work. But we should do it again on Tuesday. And you should watch the video tape before then."

"I'll get it from Dave. Thanks, Dave," this last she said with a wave toward the mirrored window. And shortly, a voice boomed from the courtroom's loud speakers, "You're welcome. Have a nice weekend."

Britt and Richard walked to the back where Marie was sitting and they all walked out the way Marie had come in, to stand in the Forum, now empty. The only sound was Dave closing up the video control room around the curve of the wall. Marie wasn't sure if there would be a more-formal introduction to Richard Randolph, and a hand shake. She didn't know if one of them would say *I've heard a lot about you* or not. But no, Britt just said:

"Man, I'm tired and hungry and have bankruptcy grime in my pores. What should we do for dinner?"

Marie said in a voice she hated for being so small, "Anything's all right with me." She had actually planned to suggest, back about five, that they drive up to Santa Fe to the Pink Adobe for dinner, but now it was too late for that, and besides Marie couldn't tell from Britt's question whether *we* meant *you and me* or *the three of us*.

Richard assumed the latter. "My wife's out for fast food with the kids and their grandparents, so I've got nowhere to go but home to an empty house. Mexican? Ron y Marcia's?"

"That sounds good. Okay, Marie?" Britt had often enough at just that point in a similar conversation put her arm across Marie's shoulders, so that it was noticeable to Marie that this time she had not. She wasn't sure what to make of the omission. She wasn't sure if she was glad Britt had not.

"Sure. Shall we go in one car or two?"

They all went together, Richard sitting in the back seat of Marie's Chevy, outfitted on the back bumper, by Britt's hand, with a Smokey Bear sticker saying *Prevent Grassland Fires.*

There was a tangible tension at the restaurant, or at least Marie felt one. Her psyche was engaged in reading as much as possible into the fact that Britt hadn't touched her in the professor's presence. That must mean, she analyzed, that they were to be friends tonight, not a couple, even though it was usually Marie who invoked that posture. So, Britt wanted him not to know that they were lovers. She would have to be very careful what she said. Ordinarily she would have been entirely at ease in front of a male stranger taking such care, but knowing that Britt too was being careful—Britt, who usually was so open and self-assured—made her uncomfortable.

The conversation was also disorienting to Marie, as she was alternately closed out and then made the center of it. When they first sat down, Britt and Richard made an obvious effort to bring her in and she had to talk about her teaching job and what was going on in her eighth grade Civics class. Randolph feigned interest, she thought. The conversation would then slowly swing back to bankruptcy or the law or the law school and the two of them would be talking about things or people Marie was ignorant of. At first she tried to keep up with the discussions of the Riley case, but she noted a measure of condescension in Randolph's voice when she made some comment that was, she supposed, hopelessly superficial. So she quietly dropped out and then they would realize that she was sitting looking off across the adobe-walled room and the conversation would self-consciously snap back to her and her life, and she would be in the center again. If it would just settle down, she thought, settle down and talk about politics or movies or something that we could all talk about, then I could relax. She thought maybe she would try to turn the topic to travel, to talk of Michael's trip to Romania, but the chance never arose.

By the time the food came, Marie had already stuffed herself with chips and salsa and beer. Britt had insisted that she get her beer as usual over ice, but that would have become a topic of conversation, so she just quietly said to the waitress, "No, just a regular glass is fine." Britt had given her an odd look, but was otherwise quiet about it. She had also really bitten her lip during one of the periods of her silence, munching on chips. The pain had been sharp, her mouth filled with saliva and she tasted blood; her eyes had filled with tears and she had covered her mouth with her hand, but Britt and Richard had not noticed. So she wasn't really very hungry when the blue corn enchiladas were put before her, but eating gave her an excuse to turn the conversation back to the others, who were soon again in the depths of the Riley case, well beyond Marie's understanding of it.

Before her dish was done, Marie realized that she was in danger of becoming ill. Her stomach was knotted around the hot, cheesy beef and all she had to calm it was the last of her beer, now warm. She breathed deeply and concentrated on the painting above Britt's shoulder on the wall. It was a desert scene, with browns and grays and a light blue New Mexico sky and mesas in the distance. She focused her attention on the far mesa and tried to settle her stomach and she missed Richard's overly polite question about what she had done last summer. Nope. It wasn't going to work. She excused herself and headed for the restroom.

Around the corner, the cashier's station lay ahead. Marie had to ask directions and, about fifteen feet short of her goal, her head went light, her face pale and she vomited into her cupped hands. Pushing through the door and into the restroom, she ran the water into the sink and continued to throw up.

Back at the table, the waitress interrupted Britt and Richard. "Miss, your friend is sick in the ladies room."

Britt hurried after her.

In the restroom, Marie was still heaving into the sink, which was about to overflow with cold water and slimy, puked-up Mexican food.

"Oh God, honey. . . ." Britt put her right arm around Marie's shoulders and plunged her left hand into the mess to clear the drain. Water and vomit slopped onto the floor and their shoes. Finally, the sink started to empty and Britt was able to wipe her hands and Marie's face with a paper towel. The front of Marie's dress was filthy with vomit, saliva and water from the sink; Britt wiped as much as possible off and sat her on the commode.

"Sit there. I'll tell Randolph and be right back to pick you up. Are you all right now?"

Marie nodded. Britt knelt down on one knee in front of her in the stall.

"Are you sure? You look so pale." She took off Marie's glasses and put them in her jacket pocket; she wiped Marie's nose with a piece of toilet paper and ran her fingers through her hair, wet with cold sweat. "Will you be all right?" Marie nodded again, but almost as soon as Britt walked out of the ladies room, she gagged and spit up onto the floor between her feet. She tore off a wad of toilet paper and covered the mess up, then crossed her arms over her stomach. She had cramps and was miserable and her mouth tasted like vomit and she didn't want to leave the restroom and see that Richard Randolph again. As much as anything, she disliked being without her glasses and not being able to see clearly, especially when he was there. But Britt's removing them had been such an intimate act, the kind of gesture she had missed all night, that she hadn't objected. She leaned forward with her chin almost on her knee and held her stomach and waited for Britt to return.

Of course, transportation was a complication with no easy solution; Albuquerque is not a city in which Richard could grab a cab back to school and no one thought to suggest it. So Marie was lain in the back seat and Britt drove back to the law school to drop Richard off. The trip around to the back of campus, down Lomas and to the school was mostly silent:

"I'm embarrassed," Marie said.

"Nonsense." Richard tried to comfort her with the usual lie. "It's happened to me, too. To all of us."

"How do you feel? Tell me if I should stop," Britt spoke into the rear view mirror.

In the parking lot, Britt said goodbye to Richard, "I'll see you next week."

"I hope she feels better." Then, he turned back and put his hand on the car door, "Oh, I forgot. Your car's in the shop. Will you need a ride home?"

"No. I'll be okay."

"Well, call me at home if you do. G'night."

"Goodnight, Professor."

Back in the car, Britt looked into the back seat and said, "How're'ya doing, Angel?"

"My clothes stink."

"Let's get you home."


ALBUQUERQUE

Marie was somewhat relieved that she was sick twice more through the night and was running a low-grade temperature in the morning. At least she had the flu or had eaten bad meat, she told herself, and had not been felled by the gremlin of fear and tension that she had felt the night before. And they both enjoyed the nursing that Britt did, brewing strange concoctions of teas and soups to settle Marie's stomach and warm her chills. Saturday night, Britt crawled under the covers and read a law book, while Marie slept beside her and, on Sunday morning, she went out to fetch the *Boston Globe*.

Richard was standing in line at Newsland on Central Avenue when Britt walked in the door, carrying a bunch of yellow daffodils in her hand. Rita was browsing the magazine stand and looked up when Britt came over to chat with Richard, but then went back to her browsing. Richard admired the flowers, which Britt held up for a sniff, and then, as if it went without saying whom they were for, inquired about Marie.

He, of course, had seen on Friday that they were lovers, even before Marie had become sick. There had been a quiet intimacy between them—he had seen it going one way when Marie watched Britt practice and the other way when Britt carefully kept Marie in the dinner-table conversation. There had been other things too: the way they discussed the menu items, the order in which they ordered their meals, the way Britt had dealt with the waitress, all these things had a setness about them which came, he knew, from people being together a lot, from having other things decided. He had found himself developing a gentle fondness for the two of them and, noting that only their eyes and smiles touched and that Marie was called a friend, he had respected the convention of the evening and had asked if Britt needed a ride home. But he had never questioned, from early on in the evening, exactly where Britt would be spending the night.

So this morning at Newsland, he had asked after Marie, trying not to reveal that he had found Britt's friend to be distracting somehow, tightly wound, he guessed was how he'd say it. Not nervous, nor fidgety, but somehow expansive inside a small, tight frame. He could imagine her on a stage, fifteen years younger, a hard-muscled, small-breasted young woman dressed in black, playing three-chord rock and roll like her life depended on it, her eyes on her left hand, her face concealed by her beat-out hair, her self turned inward to the music, not out to the audience. It was a distracting image that would not go away. He kept wanting to look into her eyes to see what was happening inside.

As the line moved forward and Richard finally paid for the *Times* of Los Angeles (for him), the *Times* of New York (for Rita) and the *Journal* (for the TV section), Rita came over and he introduced the two women. They exchanged pleasantries and then Rita said she'd be waiting outside, in the sun. After a few minutes more, Richard sent his best to Marie, told Britt he'd see her on Monday and walked outside to find his wife.

She had her hands, one over the other, on top of a parking meter. Her feet were spread wider than her shoulders and she bent forward, and lowered her head, stretching some muscle or ligament in her legs, he supposed, first to this side, then to that. She was tremendously lovely doing it, as a fellow inside the store was saying just exactly then to the guy behind the counter.

As he walked over to her, Richard knew that she sensed his presence without looking at him, as she sometimes did. Her eyes were fixed across the street and she spoke to him without ever looking to see that he was there:

"If there are out-of-state plates on that bike, it is the stuff of which dreams are made."

Across the street, pulled up by Yale Park, was a motorcycle, a Suzuki, it looked like, probably a 750, maybe bigger. It was scratched, mud-splattered, had seen some road, and would see some more. This was no rich lawyer's trendy Harley; this was a bike that had been ridden. A pack was strapped to the back and a woman leaned against it, eating a sandwich. She was dressed in black leather, not fashionable black leather, but used and worn black leather. A cherry red, full-face helmet sat on the left mirror.

"Do you think she's alone?"

Rita shrugged, still looking, still in her stretching pose.

"It's probably not as much fun as you think," he said.

"Few dreams are."

"Want to go check the plates?"

"No need. The dream's been dreamt. That's enough."

"You're crazy. I'm going to look." He jogged across the street. Rita walked to the car and waited.

"Want to know?" he said when he climbed in.

"Nope."

"Liar."

He wondered on the drive home if Rita was going to make some observation about Britt. He was especially curious if she'd identified her as a *fuzz*. But she didn't, or at least she made no comment, but only paged through the *Book Review*, slumped in the seat with her feet on the dash, unconcerned, it seemed, that his research assistant and companion to New York was an attractive woman younger than she, unravaged, apparently, by pregnancy, motherhood or chocolate mousse. But then maybe she had guessed at Britt's preferences and relaxed. He wondered.

He thought as he pulled into the driveway with the papers, and again as his mind wandered a bit over the scouting reports, about mentioning to Rita what he suspected about Britt. But he had decided not to, not now; the fondness and the convention of Friday night, as well as, really, Rita's disinterest all made him respect their privacy. Inside, he turned his attention to the sports pages and tried to construct in advance the Dukes' likely lineup when they returned from their road trip later this month. The serious Triple A fan must carefully balance his loyalty to the parent club with his desire to watch good, winning baseball all summer. And the boys' careers had to remain the prime concern. No sense in keeping a youngster in Albuquerque for the entertainment of Richard Randolph if he was ready for the big leagues. No sense either in sending him up too soon. Spring was a time for careful thought.

A half-hour later, he sat cross-legged on the living room floor, reading the funnies. Rita was in her sweat clothes, out of breath on the couch, back from her run. Her arm was around Todd's shoulder and she was encouraging him as he poured grape juice over his corn flakes. Richard looked away from the disgusting mess and back to the paper. He had already read *Prince Valiant* three times for Jack, the middle one, and guessed it would take a couple more times before he was done. Christina was reading Mary Worth out loud, to herself, with some dramatic effect.

Richard found himself thinking of a night a few summers ago. Michael and Emily had blown into town unexpectedly and had stayed a couple of days before parking their pickup in Richard's driveway and leaving for Guadalajara, if he remembered right, by bus. They had all climbed the La Luz trail up the front of the Crest, and gone to a Dukes' doubleheader and Michael had read the funnies out loud on their last day in town, a Sunday, like this one, describing the background scenes carefully before reading the words. That night, after Rita and Emily and the kids were asleep, he and Michael had talked for hours and had drunk many beers and, well after midnight, Richard had put his hand on his friend's shoulder and said, "*Wohin du gehst, da werde ich auch sein.*" *Wherever you go, there will I also be.*

"How very Ruthian of you," Michael had replied.

"As in the Babe?"

"As in the Bible. You know. *Whither thou goest blah blah blah.*"

"Actually, I was thinking more along Brechtian lines. Mackie Messer, in particular."

"*Die Dreigrossen Oper,*" Michael said dramatically, playing the role of the Street Singer.

"*Ja wohl.*" They and their wives had seen a German-language version of the play some years before, at the Albuquerque Light Opera.

"But Brecht would surely not have been Ruthian. Anti-Ruthian, more probably. Doesn't he have someone, probably Macheath, call it something like *that wohin-du-gehst bullshit*? Something like that."

Richard had tugged at his right earlobe. "My ear for German is far from subtle enough. Maybe the subjunctive is required . . ."

". . . which is well beyond me."

"And me. What I had in mind was not that, Ruth-like, I'd book a ticket to come along on your next trip, but only that, strangely enough, sitting right here in this living room, I sometimes feel like I'm along for the ride."

"Meaning that you read my letters?"

"Indeed I do, bullshit-laden though they are."

His reverie was interrupted by demands for more comic-reading by the boys, and by Rita, who, looking for the Arts section, said, "Where were you?"

"At *The Three Penny Opera*, if you want to know the truth. You, me, Michael and Em. Coupla years ago. At Popejoy."

"Whatever is your attraction to that morose operatic effort?"

"Sukey Tawdry. I never could resist her." Richard broke into song, "*Could it be our boy's done somethin' rash?*"

"Well, okay now," said Rita, beginning to snap her fingers to the rhythm. "I'll admit that your attraction to Bobby Darin is legitimate."

"*Didja hear about Louie Miller? . . .*"

Rita chipped in. "*. . . hep, hep.*"

"*. . . He disappeared, babe,. . .*"

"*. . . after drawing out. . .*"

"*. . . all his hard-earned cash.*"

"Dad." It was Jack. "Are you going to read, or not?"

"*. . . could it be our boy's done somethin' rash?*"

"Dad."

"Come on, Toddeo, get up and dance. You can be Sukey Tawdry. Tina, show your brother how to dance."

"Who can I be?" asked Christina.

"*Oh, Jenny Diver. Sukey Taudry. . . .*" Richard was now on his feet, using a rolled up copy of *Newsweek* as a microphone.

"You can be Jenny Diver. Come on. Everyone up to dance." Christina and Todd joined hands and began hopping around the floor, vaguely in time to Richard's singing.

"*Miss Rita Randolph, and old Lucy Brown . . .*"

"Jack. Come on; you can be Lucy Brown," Rita said.

"I don't want to be some girl."

"Okay, you can be Mackie Messer," Richard said. "*. . . scarlet billows start to . . .*"

"Richard!"

"Never mind that. You can be Tiger Brown. He's the chief of police."

And soon, the whole family was dancing on the living room rug, while Richard sang and Rita clapped the rhythm. "*Now Jenny Diver/ hep, hep/ yeah Sukey Tawdry/Miss Rita Randolph, and old Tiger Brown/Oh, the line forms on the right, babe/now that Macheath's back in town.*"

And after seven renditions, the comics and Michael Reid long forgotten, Richard switched to *Splish Splash*, which Tina thought was a riot.

Back in Marie and Britt's duplex, with the *Globe* and the flowers, Britt reported: "I ran into Richard Randolph and the Mrs. at the newsstand. He sends his regards, although he does not admire your taste in newspapers. But he was buying the *Los Angeles Times*, so what does he know? Probably for the sports."

"You told him you were getting the paper for me?"

"Of course, but I'm guessing he already knew. Now drink this juice and tea. I expect continuous pissing from you today."

Later, in Richard's house, it was absolutely pitch black in the bedroom, past midnight, the house was filled with sleep.

"Rita."

"What?"

"That bike?"

"Yeah?"

"The tag was from Maine."

"I know."

"You knew? *Maine?*"

"Umhmm."

"*Maine?*"

"Umhmm."

"How?"

"Had to be. Go to sleep."

## ALBUQUERQUE AND MORIARTY

Marie's friend Jill found out about Britt by accident, the worst possible way, on a Wednesday night, just as Marie was getting close to telling her, honest to God. When the phone rang, Britt was studying upstairs, and expecting a call from one of her classmates, and Marie, watching television, heard her answer the upstairs extension. After a few seconds, she called down, "It's for you."

It was Jill, confused. "Hello? Who was that? Your sister? You don't have a sister. Never mind. How are you doing? *What* are you doing?"

*Oh oh.*

"I'm doin' okay. Sitting here watching Dynasty. Blake appears to be going blind."

"Ever notice how people tend to go blind in those soap operas a lot more often than they go deaf? Why is that, do you suppose?"

"Blind is heroic. Deaf is old-man-y."

"You're right. It's hard to imagine Blake Carrington going *Eh? What? Come again?* all the time. Jimmy Chavez threw up in third period English today."

"Lot of that going around. I got sick in a restaurant a week or so ago."

"Yeah? What happened?"

"Bad enchiladas, I guess, at Ron y Marcia's. Lost my cookies right by the cash register. Real embarrassing. In front of people I just met, too." She had no idea where the conversation was going to go from here, and maybe the fact that Britt had answered would just be dropped and go nowhere. Jill was a special friend and this was a hell of a conversation to be having with your special friend, sort of winging it, off the cuff, with the television playing in the background and your lover upstairs studying. *I should have told her before now, damn it.*

"Who?"

"Who what?"

"Who were you sick in front of? That's what you just said."

"You don't know them."

"Well, Jimmy Chavez's problem is not bad enchiladas. He did it just to disrupt the class and aggravate me."

"Oh, Jill, Jimmy's not a bad kid."

"Shut up, Marie. Jimmy is a bad kid and you know it. Did you ever see the movie *The Bad Seed*? Jimmy's got it, I swear he does. I can see it in his eyes. He got a little bored in class today, looked me square in the face and puked all over Winnie Higgins. She, of course, about died. It was pretty funny, actually."

They chatted on about school, until Jill brought the subject back to why she had called. "I was going to call Britt Larsen, that friend of yours from the party? Bob's good-looking, divorced, relatively-rich-if-you-want-to-know-the-truth youngest brother is coming to town and I was going to fix him up. Do you have her number? The number in the book doesn't work, and I thought you might know a better one."

The little fellow with the chain saw gave Marie's stomach a rip. Her mind was thinking ahead, and had been, she realized, ever since Britt had answered and it had been Jill on the line. The television was still playing, now back from a commercial, and she found it hard to concentrate. There was, she guessed, nothing to say but the truth, and see where they ended up. Now was not the time to tell her, though. Not like this.

"The number?" Jill broke into her reverie.

"You know it. Actually, you just dialed it."

"What?"

"This is Britt's number, too. She lives here. That was her who answered."

"*She.* Oh. You've got a roommate? Well, let me talk to her. Do you think she might be interested in a blind date? Zack's nice enough. Really. You wouldn't like him but he's nice enough. Is she going with anybody? Let me talk to her."

"Hold on a minute." Marie didn't know what exactly would be gained by putting Britt on the line, but she couldn't think of anything else to do right then. She covered the mouthpiece. "Britt."

From the room upstairs: "Yeah?"

"Phone."

"I'll take it from up here."

"No, come down here for a second." Britt walked down the stairs; Marie sat with her feet under her on the coach holding her hand over the receiver. "It's my friend Jill; . . ." Britt reached for the phone. ". . . she wants to fix you up with her brother-in-law." Britt dropped her hand.

"What do you want me to do?"

"I should tell her."

"Why give me the phone, then?"

"I didn't know what else to do. I needed time to think of what to say."

"You've had six months."

"I know. I need a minute or two more."

"She's going to find out, Marie. No matter what I say, she's going to figure it out. Tonight, probably. What do you want me to say?"

"That you're busy."

Britt took the phone; Marie listened to one side of the conversation.

"Hi, Jill. . . . Sure, I remember. Marie talks about you a lot. . . ." Britt was looking directly into Marie's eyes and Marie could not look away. "Ohhhhhh, I don't know, . . .," she spoke this part very slowly, then, ". . . my lease ran out and I was looking for a place. . . . Yeah, it is." She turned around and faced the bookshelves, put her right hand under her hair and massaged the back of her neck. She listened for a while and when she spoke next, her voice was low and gentle, so Marie had to strain to make it out. "Listen, I don't really think so. I'm sure he's a nice guy; I liked your husband, Bob, right? But, . . . yeah, I know. . . . . it sounds like fun, but, . . ., you know, I don't really *date* much, anymore, you know what I mean?" The good-natured inflection in her voice made the word sound like a teenage ritual. "A few years ago I figured out that I'd been going out on *dates* for, I don't know, fifteen years. . . . Yeah, exactly, . . . . ." Britt laughed. Her back was still to Marie, who felt her own body release a small bit of tension when she heard the laugh. Still, she was not anxious to have Britt turn around nor to resume her conversation with Jill. "So, you had better look for someone else. . . . Oh, no. That's okay. That's fine. It was good to talk to you again. . . . I'd like that. Okay, here's Marie."

She turned back around and handed the phone to Marie, her expression a hard one for Marie to read. She started to take the phone back and to cover the receiver, as if she were going to say something, but then shook her head quickly and handed it over. Marie covered the mouthpiece and said, "Thanks." Then, "Hi. I'm back."

"Yeah," Jill said, "Well, it was a nice idea, but it didn't work out."

"I heard."

"Got any other ideas?"

"I don't know. Alice?"

"Busy. I asked. I don't know, I'll ask around. Hey, how about you? Never mind, last time I fixed you up, you were mad at me for years."

Marie laughed. She felt relieved that everything was going to be all right. "Last time you fixed me up I had to sit for three hours on a hard bench at Okie's watching the guy clean his fingernails with a tooth pick."

"It wasn't that bad, was it?"

"Not for you. You and Bob danced the night away to some hot licks band. I got to tap my foot and drink warm beer."

"Well, I didn't know he didn't like to dance. And I said I was sorry about a decade ago. Never mind. I'll find some other date for Zack."

"If you want to fix me up, why not with Bobby?"

"My son? For God's sake, Marie, he's only seventeen."

"Yeah, but he's cute." Marie had ribbed Jill for a couple of years about her youngest son's sex life, and the conversation pattered along easily as they exchanged jibes.

"And less than half your age."

"So, I'll wear knee socks. We'll go to the drive-in. We'll drink Cokes. It would be fun. Tell him if he goes with me, we can get into all of the R-rated movies."

"What I have in mind for my baby is not a twilight appointment at the East 66 with a knee-socked Ms. Worldly Wisewoman. If your mid-life crisis requires you to put the old ankle-lock on some juvenile, find somebody else's kid and leave my blood pressure alone. God. He'd probably do it, too! Listen, I've got to go. See you tomorrow."

"Bye." Marie hung up.

Britt was sitting in running shorts and a tee shirt on the top stair with her elbows on her knees and her hands clasped together. Marie stood at the bottom and looked up at her. She tried to sound contrite, but it was difficult; she was really quite relieved that it had turned out the way it had. "I'm sorry I made you do that. That just wasn't the way I have it planned that she will learn about us."

"Did she figure it out?"

Marie shrugged and gestured *I don't know* with her eyebrows. "Maybe. I don't think so. Not yet. I'll tell her soon. I made you wimp out, didn't I? You would have told her straight out if I hadn't asked you not to, wouldn't you have?"

"I'm not ashamed to be here, Marie. But shit, I didn't announce it to Randolph. It's the business of the people we want it to be the business of. She's your friend. You get to decide. I hope she understands."

"I think she will. She understands a lot." Marie paused for a minute, feeling the relief wash over her. Then, "Say, you know, you're awfully cute sitting there like that with your underpants showing. Do you have more studying to do?"

Britt glanced over her shoulder, back toward the room where she had been, as if she were thinking about what was piled up on the desk there. She looked back down the stairs at Marie and said, "I have to type up a *Law Review* memo, but it'll wait."

"Is there anything you wouldn't do for me?"

"Nothing that comes to mind right now."

"Go type your memo; I don't want to be responsible for your getting kicked off the *Law Review*. But thanks."

"Sure."

Britt stood up, turned and walked back into the study and Marie went into the living room, turned the television off, poured herself part of a beer into a glass of ice cubes, clicked on the stereo and sat down on the couch. She really did need to figure out how to tell Jill. She'd give it some thought. A dinner, just the two of them, would be the way to do it. The phone rang again, and she walked to the wall phone in the kitchen to pick up.

"Hello?"

"Hi. It's me again."

"Hi." *Why had she called back?*

"Why didn't you tell me that you had a roommate?" Marie's stomach gave a twist. Upstairs, she heard Britt typing.

"Oh, I don't know. It didn't seem important."

"God, I can't imagine you with a roommate. What's the matter, need the dough?"

"No, it wasn't really that." This appeared to be it. Jill was fishing. There was nowhere the conversation could go this time but where it had to go. She should never have called Britt to the phone the first time; what had that accomplished, except probably to get Britt mad at her too?

"Why are you so quiet? Marie, I called back to give you a chance to say *This isn't what it sounds like.*"

*Here goes.* "Yeah. Well, it *is* what it sounds like." Upstairs she heard Britt walk across the floor to the bathroom.

"It is?"

"Yup."

"Are we talking about the same thing?"

"I think so."

"My God." A pause. "How long?"

"Off and on since that party. She's lived here since January."

"I was just over to your place last weekend."

"She was at the law school."

"Just by luck?"

"No. I made sure before you and I arranged it. It wasn't too hard; she's been working at school a lot lately, and her schedule is pretty predictable. I was going to tell you, but the time didn't seem right." The toilet flushed. There was every reason to suspect that Britt hadn't heard the phone ring the second time.

"Well, I guess there's no sense in thinking she might change her mind about going out with my good-looking brother-in-law, is there?" Jill gave a tight laugh.

"I guess not."

"And I guess my son is safe." Marie said nothing. There was a long, silent pause before Jill spoke again: "Are you really, you know . . . a Lesbian?"

"I'm not sure. I guess so."

"I'll see you at school."

"Jill, it will be the same between us."

"I'll see you at school."

"Can we talk about it?"

"I'll see you at school." She hung up and Marie replaced the phone in the cradle, not sure she had ever in her life been hung up on before.

*Well, damn it. God damn it.* Upstairs, Britt was still typing; her Editor-in-Chief, Alex Something, liked for the staff to type their memos to him, which would often take her an hour or so. Marie looked out the window and took a drink of ice cold beer. *Why the fuck didn't I tell her before now?*

She didn't know what to do now. What were the alternatives? She could call Jill back or drive over to her house, but there was little in the second conversation that seemed to invite that. In any event, Jill lived all the way out in Moriarty and it would take an hour to get there. She could ask Britt to stop typing and they could talk. Later, she could cry or come in Britt's arms. Maybe both. That seemed to be the problem, though, not the solution and somehow neither outcome seemed particularly tempting right now. She could hop in her car and drive aimlessly through the south Valley until dawn. She could pick up street corner drug dealers, offering them a ride home and unmarked cash and then beat them unmercifully and sell the story to the *Trib*. Or she could liquidate all of her assets, buy land near Tierra Amarilla and speak present-tense Spanish for the rest of her life. She downed the remainder of her beer, and opened another one.

This was fun. She would set small fires all over the northeast heights, take the tram to the top of the Crest and watch the city burn. She would move to New Brunswick and get a job teaching English to French-speakers. Or *vice versa*. She and the dog would leave for New York City, where she would make a killing speculating in the Armenian rug trade and Ginger would take home the blue ribbon at the Madison Square Garden dog show. She would fly to Tehran, kidnap the Ayatollah and hold him for ransom, dressed in a Rolling Stones tee shirt and running shorts. She would have her entire body tattooed, change her name and join the circus. Angela Sue Boatwright, the illustrated lady. Leslie LaFarbe. Athena Acropolopolis.

After about ten minutes of this game, she wandered upstairs and into the study, where Britt was still typing, with her back to the door, though Marie could see her face reflected in the window. She walked over behind her and rested her hands on Britt's shoulders.

"I think I'll run over to Smith's. Need anything?"

"A shoulder massage?" Marie began squeezing Britt's shoulder muscles. "Mmmm. There. That feels good," Britt moved her shoulders up and down under Marie's hands. "But why Smith's? We just went shopping yesterday. Who just called?"

"Oh, nobody. Telemarketer. Vinyl siding. It's much better than the aluminum kind, you know. I feel like a gimlet, and so I need limes.

"Chicken livers and lime juice?"

"That's *giblet*. Soft *g*. Gimlet, hard *g*. Gin, lime juice and sugar. Yummy."

"Gin on top of beer? Careful, or you're going to feel terrible in the morning. Actually, now that you mention it, cold chicken livers, chopped with onion, and drizzled with lime juice doesn't sound bad."

"Call Julia Child."

"Okay, so to Smith's for limes." She shrugged her shoulders under Marie's hands. "I can't think of anything else we need from the store. I should be done by the time you get back; maybe I'll try one."

Marie kissed Britt on the part, picked up her wallet and keys from the bedroom, and wandered downstairs and out the door, picking up Ginger along the way, and wondering if Britt's famous ability to know when she was lying worked with her back turned, looking at Marie's reflection in the window of the study.

She took her time at the store, first trying to figure out what to say to Jill in the morning, then trying to figure out how to stop trying to figure out what to say to Jill in the morning. Nothing, was her hope; maybe just leaving everything lie for a bit was the best course.

Back at the duplex, Britt had finished her work, and was now downstairs, sitting on the couch, with classical music playing on the FM. She looked tired and about to fall asleep. With her eyes closed she asked, "Is that Mozart?"

"That is Vivaldi. Mozart is right now lying upside-down in his unmarked crypt."

"Why?"

"Because you confused the two. Mozart is famous for having observed that Vivaldi wrote the same song five hundred times. If you fall asleep on the couch, you'll be sorry in the morning."

"I'm not the one who is about to put gin on top of beer." She stood up and stretched. "I was about to take the dog for her walk, but I thought I'd wait for you. Wanna come with us?"

"No, go ahead. I'll make the drinks. You're going to try one?"

"Sure. Right after Ginger pees." Hearing her name, or one of them, anyway, Ginger got herself up, shook, and walked over to them, wagging her tail. "Hey, Virginia. Where's your leash?" Britt spread her hands, turning in a circle in the middle of the living room. "Where *is* it? I don't see it. How can we go for a walk without your leash? Where is it?" Ginger, amazed as always when a human couldn't see something that was in plain sight, walked into the kitchen and sat down next to where her leash hung from its hook, and looked expectantly at Britt, her pink tongue dripping drool onto the kitchen floor. "Oh, there it is! Well, come on then." Britt walked over to the wall, took down the leash and fastened it to Ginger's collar. "Ready? We'll be back. Ten minutes. Fifteen. C'mere, pup."

When Britt and the dog returned, Marie had the gin and lime juice drinks mixed, with sugar on the side to sweeten to taste. Marie had two, to Britt's one, while she explained what she had in mind for next week's civics classes. Being around a law student had changed rather dramatically Marie's take on how to teach that class, for example by emphasizing more the civil, as opposed to the criminal side of the law, which she proposed to do next week, and wanted Britt's advice. They got to bed around midnight.

~

As Britt had predicted, Marie felt terrible in the morning. Still, she managed to drag herself out of bed more or less on time, to breakfast on black coffee, and to drive herself to school without incident. She also managed, with somewhat more difficulty, to avoid seeing Jill, wondering all through the day if the word were out, to her colleagues, or, worse, to the students. But it appeared not, for everyone greeted her normally, though Jill stayed away, and she doubted anyway that Jill would announce what she had learned. And that afternoon, she walked directly from her last-period class to her car in the parking lot, without chit-chat, and drove home and got through dinner that night, without telling Britt that Jill knew.

# 14

## ATHENS

One day, two weeks after she had returned to Athens from the overnight trip to Paros and Thira, Anna bought a pen, a cheap, click-ballpoint pen, red, with a picture of the Acropolis painted on it. She carried it, clipped to the back pocket of her jeans, and buying it was a significant step in her coming to grips with where she was and what she was doing there. From the time when she first came to Athens until she bought the pen, she had never carried anything with her except money, and often no money, either. She would leave the room key at the hotel desk, and her passport was with the hotel clerk, too. She carried no identification, nor did she carry a scrap of paper or book in English, nor even a map, whether she was walking the streets or riding buses, whether she was sipping coffee in the Omonia café with the beasts on the walls in *bas-relief*, or attending movies in Swedish with Greek subtitles.

The day she bought the pen, she had slept late at the hotel and eaten an orange for lunch, sitting in the National Gardens, watching the ducks beg for food. She first thought maybe she would try to go through the entire day without speaking a single word, but then she changed her mind and spoke at length to the ducks about the weather. She felt good and she had stopped looking over her shoulder at last to see if Mike Reid was following her.

After finishing the orange, she had walked aimlessly through the streets west of Syntagma, looking at shoes and scarves and electric appliances in the shop windows. Along Kolokotroni Street at Voulis Street is a kiosk, draped with foreign newspapers and magazines in many languages. She stopped there often on her walks, to buy cigarettes or chocolate, but she always avoided looking at the English-language newspapers, like *USA Today*, as she had no wish to know what was happening at home, or for that matter, anywhere. The day she bought the pen, though, she allowed herself to study the Arabic papers, running her fingers right to left along the beautiful script that could not possibly be language. The numbers, even, were not recognizable, but she could not remember why that was important. She wrinkled her forehead and nodded, pretending that she could read the Arabic and laughing to herself at the people she was fooling.

So, one day, many weeks after she came to Athens, she bought at that kiosk a red pen with the Acropolis painted on it, and she began to carry it with her, as she moved through the streets.

It was another week, though, before she thought of something to write with the pen. She was sitting at lunchtime in a café inside the large indoor market on Aiolou Street. The place bustled with white-jacketed waiters banging the sturdy white plates together and dodging around the working-class patrons who leaned across the tables and talked above the racket. Outside, across the covered alleyway that led into the depths of the market, was a butcher shop, and the hanging, bloody carcasses of goats, chickens and pigs did little for Anna's appetite. The dishes she had ordered, one with ground meat and macaroni, covered in olive oil, and one with a boiled green vegetable they called *horta*, also dowsed in oil, sat hardly touched, though she had managed to drink a glass of wine and eat some of the hard, crusty bread. She shared the table with two old Greek men, men old enough to be her father, who talked loudly, gestured earnestly and ignored her. Though her appetite had disappeared, she sat over the food for an hour or more, watching the customers and the workers in the market.

It came to her without her thinking about it: *I shall see if my brain still works. I shall see if my brain still works.* She pulled the pen from her back pocket, moved the largely untouched dishes to clear a spot on the white paper table cloth, and clicked the point of the pen out deliberately. After a moment she began to write: *Given any Tupolev-class function T, for every $x_0$ in the open interval (0,1) there is a non-negative $y_0$, such that $T(x_0) = $ . . .* She continued to write until she had completed the first equation of her PhD dissertation, beginning simply so that she would have something she knew was true. She clicked the point in, and looked at what she had written. She passed her index finger tip over the letters; the ink smeared a bit on the table cloth and she looked at the trace of blue on her finger, rubbing at it lightly with her thumb.

That statement had been true in Tallahassee, she knew, but was it true here? She puzzled over that question for a moment. It had something important to do with her work, with her life even. How could one be sure that it was true here? Here was not there. Many rules were different here: food was served lukewarm and oily; old women wore black; men danced together. How could one be sure that equation (1) of Anna R. Browning's PhD dissertation was true here?

The matter would take some study. Many things thought to be true were not. So many things were happening here that did not happen at home, it was almost impossible to believe that equation (1) was true here. She wrote equation (2) from her dissertation.

It certainly did not go without saying that these statements were true here. Nor could she think of any particular reason why they should be true here. Nothing was the same here. Anna Browning walked the streets with empty pockets and had sex with men she didn't know here, and that was a difference that made the untruth of equations (1) and (2) of her dissertation seem a minor difference in comparison. She wrote Jablonski's second transformation. Her memory, it seemed, was unimpaired. She wrote, without hesitation and, she knew, with complete accuracy, the last equation she had written on the yellow notebook pages at home on the desk in her study, written in reaction to Jablonski's work before she had left to come here.

She no longer had sex with men she didn't know, she reminded herself.

The old men who shared the table were looking at her. One spoke, gesturing at the equations. It was in Greek, of course, but it was a friendly inquiry by all indications. She could not understand the words, but he appeared to say, "Why do you sit here, my young, blond, foreign friend, and write equations on the table cloth? Is there nothing else for a young woman to do in Athens in the spring?" Anna smiled and shrugged her shoulders. She drew a box around the four lines of writing.

"Equations," she said, in English, rather lamely. "I make them. Well, . . ." The men started to laugh, unable to understand the English. "Well, . . .," Anna began to laugh, too, and decided to go on with her explanation, "actually, ahhh, I made only these three, . . ." She made checkmarks in front of the first, second and fourth. ". . . but someone else made this one. Jablonski is his name." She tapped the third equation with her ballpoint and looked at the two old men, who were talking back to her in Greek. "No, no," she said, using some of the

Greek she had picked up. "Όχι, Όχι. Jablonski. Jablonski." She exaggerated the syllables and one of the men got the idea, pointed to the third equation with a thick, cracked, and not very clean fingernail and said back "Ja-blon-ski."

"Right! Εντάξι!" They all three laughed and clicked together their glasses of white, sour wine. No one else in the crowded restaurant paid them any mind.

The second old man gestured at her untouched food and Anna shook her head, making a face. He nodded and commiserated in Greek, although she doubted that he understood the problem to be lukewarm olive oil. The first man reached over and felt the thinness of her upper arm and shook his head to his friend. More Greek was exchanged, the waiter was called and soon a wide flat bowl of creamy white soup was sitting in front of Anna, on top of the equations. The first old man made eating motions with his hand; the second pushed the bread basket toward her.

The soup had rice in it, and a lemony taste, and it set well on Anna's stomach.

"Ειναι καλώ;" the man asked.

Anna could not understand, but, unknowing, answered correctly anyway: "It's good. Thank you. Ευχάριστώ."

"Πάρακαλώ." The man nodded and smiled. Anna knew that word as *please* but the Greeks must use it for *you're welcome* too, as is true in many languages. She took another spoonful and wiped her mouth on the napkin.

The three of them fell silent now, having exhausted the potential of the conversation they were having. Anna continued to eat the soup, first out of politeness, then to satisfy a genuine bit of hunger that had sprung up. The men seemed satisfied that they had saved the strange blond woman who wrote mathematics on the table cloth, saved her from starvation, and were soon back to their earlier topic, which was entirely beyond Anna's ken.

Anna finished the soup, interrupted the men to say "Ευχάριστώ" again and pushed the bowl over next to her other dishes. A wet, oily ring swooped down through the box she had drawn and cut through the equations. The pen lay beside the writing, and bread crumbs and salt crystals speckled the entire scene. She sat back in her chair, crossed her legs, folded her hands together on her stomach, and looked across the room, past the diners and the waiters, at the cook dishing out food in the kitchen, which was really just an open area at the far end of the dining room. She lowered her eyes to the equations and then raised them back up to the cook, a handsome young man with dark hair and a tight, white tee shirt. Then she unfocused her eyes, as she remembered she used to do, sitting in her office, or in the study at home, when she was thinking, working, once, she recalled, with Rachel on the floor and the rain outside falling straight down.

She shook her head and brought the room back into focus. *Not yet.* She was still Anna Browning, she knew that. And she knew where she was. And why. Partially. At least she was coming to know why she was here. It seemed to have a great deal to do with carrying nothing in her pockets but money and attending Swedish movies with Greek subtitles; with no one in the other world, the home world, knowing where she was, and no one in this one knowing who she was. But she was not yet ready to unfocus her eyes across the room and think as she used to think. She was Anna Browning all right, but she was not yet ready to be the Anna Browning who raised her children, admired her husband, made mathematics, and, however reluctantly, joined the petty battles of academia. Not yet.

She called the waiter, who added up her dishes in his head and spoke a number. She indicated that she couldn't understand and made a writing motion with her right hand into her left palm. He used her pen to write the total on the table cloth, near her equations. She pointed at the soup plate and asked with her eyes and hand whether that was included in the total, he indicated that it was and she paid the bill. She left the small change on the table for the waiter, though his tip was already figured in the tab, picked up the pen, put it in her back pocket and walked around to the side of the table so that she stood next to the old men. She shook both of their hands, slowly, carefully, saying "Ευχάριστώ. Γέια σάς." *Thank you. Goodbye to both of you,* and wound her way between the tables out into the market, where she spent an enjoyable hour walking, inspecting the foods and the wares, until she finally emerged into the late afternoon sun and the smog and the exhaust of the afternoon traffic.

PAROS

Michael Reid opened the fresh paperback, bought in Athens as he passed through, returning from Romania, turned the cover under and creased it with his thumb, and read the first line: *I could think of three good reasons for not going to Moscow, one of which was 26, blond, and upstairs unpacking her suitcase.* He immediately dropped the book into his lap; it slipped off onto the floor of the porch and he looked out over the harbor. It was a cool afternoon with a breeze off the water, and the sun no longer struck the porch, so he sat wrapped in a thin, striped Greek blanket whose texture had been unable to hold the book when he dropped it. Stunning, he thought, a truly stunning first sentence. He let the book rest on the porch floor for a moment as he looked around at the early April afternoon.

That first sentence, he thought, augured well for the rest of this early April afternoon. He had enjoyed the stay on Paros partly because he had been able to read widely—wildly, even—sampling this and that genre, this and that classic. He ordinarily did not read spy novels. At home he had two rather strict rules: he did not read books with red stars or swastikas on the cover, and he did not read science fiction books with maps in the front. But the trip to Paros was designed to give relief from such rules and he had packed and brought an eclectic suitcaseful of paperbacks, mostly now read and passed on to other English-language readers, and supplemented, as now, by fresh stock from the bookstores of Athens, or the tourist shops of Parokia, the main village of the island. He had not been disappointed, and he had had some memorable moments with his books. He had recently finished the *Alexandria Quartet*, which he just now reckoned to be the finest exposition on the subject of love in the entire history of literature, and the first sentence of *Trial Run* suggested that it was the perfect counterpoint to the *Quartet*.

Reading *Jude the Obscure*, he remembered, had been an event remarkable even to the extent of creating the two Anna Browning apparitions in the Café Neon. He shook his head, remembering the staggering similarity he had seen the first time and the very different similarity the second. At the end of the trip to the socialist north, he had had a brandy in the café, but the *Jude*-inspired strangeness was gone. The *Quartet* put another sort of mystery in the air, and the café presented no young blond women, only a very usual crowd of men and one woman who twisted a greasy strand of her hair, and who was decidedly not Anna Browning.

He wondered what Anna had thought of the letter he had sent. He would have to call her when he got back to the States; she was a lousy correspondent and rarely answered his letters or cards. He couldn't remember that she ever had written to him. She was friendly enough when he called, although admittedly the various challenges of presenting mathematical concepts to teenagers did not engage her attention. She had probably thought his letter uninteresting; for all of Anna's brilliance, she lacked a certain imagination that would allow such a coincidence to catch her fancy. Her mathematics also caused her to have a certain lack of awareness of the world around her, an awareness which an event like the one in the Café Neon required in order to be appreciated. For instance, she was the only person in the world who called him *Mike*, a nickname he disliked, but he had given up long ago on trying to correct her and, in a way, he admired her ability so completely to disregard the goings-on around her and to be unaware that everyone else in the room was calling him *Michael*. She was brilliant, that was for sure, much smarter than he, but brilliance, he thought, in the epitome of self-indulgence, was over-glorified, and, in any case, was accompanied by its own special burdens.

He picked the book up off the floor and reopened it to the first page. For some reason, at home at least, he had never particularly enjoyed beginning a book. For some reason it felt better to be finishing a book than beginning it. That had certainly been true of the *Quartet* and he had closed *Clea*, sitting in the second-class dining room of the ΝΆΞΟΣ, with a bit of honeyed pastry, and a cup of very bad ship-board coffee, on the way back to Paros from Athens and the north, with a warm sense of peace. He fancied himself a letter writer of some talent, or at least enthusiasm, but he knew he'd never match the elegance of Clea's last letter to Darley, telling him that she was leaving Alexandria for France. *Write and tell me,* she wrote, wondering about his writing, *or save it for some small café under a chestnut-tree, in smoky autumn weather, by the Seine. I wait, quite serene and happy, a real human being, an artist at last.*

When the book, and the *Quartet* ended a half-page later, he had thought for a moment of returning to *Justine*, with which he had struggled at the start. He had not done so, partly because of the feeling that ending a book was a more enjoyable experience than beginning it. He had never subjected that feeling to careful thought before, but now, here on the porch of the small house on Paros, wrapped against the cool Aegean breeze, it seemed just right to pause and ponder why that was. He looked around at the view of the harbor and of Parokia, down the hill below, and let the problem settle itself in his brain. His landlord's old mother stood in the yard of the next house down the road, hanging out the laundry in the sun and breeze, helped by her granddaughter, Mina. That meant that it wasn't going to rain today; the old lady had an uncanny ability to know for sure when to hang her laundry, and he had never seen her caught by the rain with her linens out. He waved across the barnyard at the old woman and the young girl.

"Κάλη μέρα, Κύριε Μπάρμπαρις." he called to the old lady. *Good morning, Mrs. Barbaris.* "Γία σόυ, Μίνα." *Hi, Mina.*

"Γία σόυ, Μικάλι," Mina called back, using the familiar, with her new, if older, friend, and she ran, all knees and elbows, up the hill to stand at the bottom of the steps where he sat.

"Τι κάνεις, Μίνα;" he asked down to her. *How are you?*

"Καλά!" she said. Then, in careful, accented, school-girl English, "I am well. How are you today, Mikalis?"

"I am well, thank you. How is your grandmother?"

Mina was apparently puzzled by the last word. "Δέν καταλαβένω." She shook her head. *I don't understand.*

He spread his moustache so she could better see his lips move and enunciated carefully. "Grandmother. Η Γιαγιά. Τι κάνει η Γιαγιά σόυ; How is your grandmother?"

"Καταλαβένω," she nodded her head. "My grandmother is very well, thank you."

"Κάι το γουρόυνι σου; Τι κάνει το γουρόυνι σου;" *And how is your pig?* Mina and her father were raising a pig in the small barn that lay next to the house that Michael and Emily were renting. Mina had been teaching Michael the names of the various farm animals—το γουρόυνι, the pig, το κοτόπουλο, the chicken, η κατσίκα, the goat, το γάιδαρος, the donkey—so he had taken to practicing by inquiring after one of the beasts whenever he saw her. She thought this was great fun and always laughed when she answered.

"Πόλυ καλό, ευχάριστώ." *Very well, thank you,* and she tore off toward the barnyard yelling over her shoulder a torrent of Greek that he could not understand. He assumed that she meant for him to follow her and see for himself that the pig was doing very well. He extracted himself from his blanket and walked after her.

It was an hour later, after feeding the animals and struggling with the various Greek names, and laughing with the little Greek girl with the enormous black eyes and the heavy black eyebrows, that he returned to the porch and picked up his spy novel and watched as Mina skipped down the hill to her grandmother's. He had had no time, he realized, to ponder why exactly it was that he enjoyed finishing books more than beginning them. He also preferred the end of a baseball game to the beginning. But, it occurred to him as he sat again in the straight backed chair and tipped it against the wall of the house, he preferred the start of a trip to its finish. In what ways was a book different from a trip? Why the difference? And movies. Let's see. He decided he enjoyed the beginning of a movie. The beginning of a semester. The beginning of a trip. But the end of a book and a ball game. For some reason, it struck him right now that he longed for a root beer float, one of the relatively few things impossible to get on the island of Paros.

This trip was winding down, a fact proved by nothing more, perhaps, than his longing for a root beer float. Or—he shook his head in wonder—by his abandonment of all his travel principles back in Athens and his inconsequential phone call to Marie in Albuquerque. It still surprised him to think that he had done it, given his long distrust of the immediacy of telephones in general and overseas telephones in particular. Yes, surely, this trip was winding down. He and Emily had thought they would stay through Orthodox Easter, but the more the foreigners talked about how moving the Good Friday celebration was, the more they had found themselves thinking that they would be gone by then. The descriptions sounded straight out of some travel guide, and if there was anything they had learned in their travels it was that they usually found little enjoyment in events that made the pages of travel guides. The reasons for travel were to observe the occasions when people were unselfconsciously being themselves, not when they were being, willingly or not, tourist attractions.

So this trip was winding down. Emily, he had discovered via a note on the kitchen table this morning when he got up, had caught an early bus, to catch the early ferry to Antiparos, the small island off the coast of the main island, there to learn what she could from a bouzouki player from the band that they had listened to the night before, an old man whose fingering she had admired, or so she had told him on the walk home last night, with the electric sound of bouzoukis still ringing in his ears. There was no reason to expect her back until dark. Her note said that she might, in fact, stay on Antiparos, if, as she hoped, she was invited to sit in with the band that night at a café she had heard about over there but had never been to. Finding a place to sleep would not be a problem, not in the Greek islands, surely, at least in the off-season, one of the most hospitable places in the world. She would have families standing in line to offer a bed to the American woman who played the bouzouki. In a world without telephones, he wouldn't know until it happened. Michael, on the other hand, had nothing to finish up before they left, nothing but this: to sit on the porch and read his spy novel, to watch the boats enter and leave the harbor, to speak halting Greek with Mina, to have dinner at the tiny restaurant called Το Λεμόνι, to drink too much retsina if he wished, and to go to bed, alone, when he chose. And, now that he thought of it, to plan a drive, after they were home and Emily was in Kansas City with her music, a drive along I-40 to Albuquerque. It has been, what?, two years, which was too long to go without seeing Marie and Richard and Rita and the Dukes and the strange color that was called green in the New Mexico desert. He reached down and picked up *Trial Run* and began again to read. *I could think of three good reasons for not going to Moscow, one of which was 26, blond, and upstairs unpacking her suitcase.*

TALLAHASSEE

Nikki Wallace came across Michael's letter to Anna while she was cleaning Anna's study. Not the letter about the strange sighting at the Café Neon in Athens, but the earlier one, the one about the forgone flight to Amsterdam and Paris, the one that Anna had read in her office, and the one that she had used to mark the place of Jablonski's article in the *American Journal of Probability and Statistics*, the one that Ben had chosen to use to entertain the students at the English department party, the performance that Nikki had missed while lying on George and Mildred's soft double bed, talking on the phone to Britt in Albuquerque and listening to Linda Ronstadt sing the National Anthem. The second letter, the one about the Café Neon, Anna had burned in the kitchen sink, then ground the ashes in the garbage disposer, but the first letter she had left in the *AJP&S* and it was there that Nikki found it while cleaning Anna's study.

She had been told very precisely by Ben that she was to touch nothing on Anna's desk, either when she was cleaning or otherwise. Nothing. Period. Ben had been quite emphatic and unambiguous about it. She was to run the vacuum in Anna's study, and dust the bookshelves and lamp shades and the rungs of the chairs when she was cleaning the house, but she was to touch nothing on Anna's desk. And Nikki had followed his instructions to the letter from the beginning of her job as housekeeper. And she never would have come across the letter, marking the place in the *Journal*, sitting next to a stack of Anna's notes on the problem, except that Nikki had to carry an ash tray around the house with her when she was cleaning, for there was none either in Anna's study nor the children's bedrooms. And, on the day in question, early in April, a week after Anna's second phone call home, she had carefully placed her ashtray on Anna's desk, in a clear spot near the stack of yellow notebook papers sitting next to the *AJP&S*, and had cleaned the study according to instructions. But when she had finished sweeping and had picked up the ashtray, holding the vacuum in one hand, and dust rag in the other, she had been somehow distracted and the ashtray had slipped out of her hand with the dust rag and had fallen back onto the desk, leaving its contents of ashes and eight filtered Kool stubs scattered everywhere.

"Well, shit."

She put the vacuum down on the floor and surveyed the damage, shaking her head at her clumsiness. Now, she had an unpleasant choice: leave the mess where it was, for Ben to clean up, or violate the instructions she had been given about the desk. She thought for a minute or two, looking down at the orderliness of the papers on the desk, and decided that there was really nothing to do other than to carefully remove and dust each paper and book on the near right-hand corner of the desk, and the desk calendar, which showed nothing but white since the time Anna had left. And so she began, picking up the pages of notebook paper on which Anna had been organizing her response to Jablonski's article, including the same equation that she had written on the paper table cloth in the Athens restaurant just days before. Each yellow page Nikki picked up carefully, brushed the ashes onto the floor, which would have to be swept all over again, and she didn't have that much time, as the children would be getting off the bus in half an hour, and she hadn't cleaned their bedrooms yet. Each page she laid carefully aside, upside down, making sure that she could put them back in the same order on the corner of the desk where they had originally been.

On the far upper left-hand corner, as seen from Anna's desk chair—the near right-hand corner from where Nikki stood—sat the *AJP&S*, itself covered with ashes, and two cigarette butts, which threatened, if she didn't pick them off carefully, to leave black marks on the cover. So she picked up the entire journal and moved to brush the offending cigarette scraps into the waste basket, and it was then that Michael's letter to Anna fell out and onto the floor, fluttering the pages out of order, as they had once been out of order on the floor of Anna's office in Love Hall on campus.

"God damn it."

She picked the pages of the letter up off the floor, and noticed happily that the journal easily opened to what was probably the place marked, for that article alone had Anna's marginal notes, and the spine of the journal had been broken there. So the only problem was making sure that these pages were in the right order before folding them together longwise and putting the now-clean journal back where it belonged.

It is a little difficult to explain what exactly caught Nikki's eye about the letter that made her begin to read it. Perhaps it was Michael's odd habit of beginning to write before the actual salutation, in this case, *Madison County, Arkansas. June, nearly July, 1983. Rain, cool rain falls. An owl, hunting, hoots.* Perhaps it was that she had not honed her supposed professional cynicism about amateur poetry to the razor-like edge that Ben possessed, nor anything like it, nor was she inclined to. In fact, she admired the phrase *an owl, hunting, hoots.* It was certainly true that the letter's introduction carried with it none of the personal, historical weight that it did for Anna when she received it, not in terms of who the writer was, nor what was represented by the article whose place the letter marked. *An owl, hunting, hoots.* Somehow the fragment—no, it was a complete sentence, she realized—conjured up in her mind exactly the scene that the writer was describing. She sat down, lit a cigarette, checked the clock on the bookshelf, and began to read.

When she got to the mention of Moriarty, she gasped. Literally. A small enough gasp, to be sure, but still, it took her breath away, and she gave a small, inhaled *ha*, full of smoke from her cigarette. *Moriarty.* She quickly found the last page, on which the writer had signed his name. *Michael.* Had she ever been told the name of Britt's Marie's ex-boyfriend? She thought back. She didn't think so. *Michael.* Maybe, but she wasn't sure. *Michael. Madison County, Arkansas. 1983.* Nearly two years ago. *Madison County, Arkansas. The almanac says that Jupiter is rising just now in the east, above the clouds. It is 11:20 p.m., Central Daylight Time.*

It was easy enough, actually, to find the correct order for the pages of the letter, as Michael numbered his pages. Without reading any farther, Nikki folded the pages and put them back into the *Journal*, at the place marked. She then finished cleaning up Anna's desk, re-swept the floor, checked the desk once more for ashes, which she removed with a wetted fingertip. She then quickly spot-cleaned the children's bedrooms. Then, checking the clock, she saw that she probably had twenty minutes or so before the school bus arrived. Ben himself was not due for another couple of hours. She walked back into Anna's study, picked up the *AJP&S*, and sat down in Anna's desk chair.

It was not her way to read another's mail. She knew she was toying, in a very real sense, with her PhD. Her career. Her future. Ben would both fire her and get her tossed out of graduate school if he caught her in here, reading Anna's personal mail. Furthermore, she thought that he would be entirely justified in doing so. What she was setting about to do was totally inexcusable. Still and all, she opened the *Journal*, checked the clock once again, and read Michael's letter all the way through, and then again.

*Moriarty. Michael. She shouldn't have told you about him.* A very small *thank you.* An utterly, utterly implausible coincidence. She re-folded the pages of the letter, put it back into the *Journal*, placed it back on Anna's desk and left the study, closing the door behind her.

◠

Sam and Janet arrived home, changed out of their school clothes, raided the 'fridge, and ran outside to play.

◠

When Ben himself arrived home around seven, Nikki had dinner ready, the table set, and she sat on the living room couch, reading. "Hello," he said.

Their relations had been strained following the day that Anna had called, Nikki had quit, and then had returned. She had done her work, but had not spoken to him the day she returned, had not eaten dinner with the family, and had left immediately after cleaning up, to meet Connor, waiting in his car in the street. The next day, though, Sam's hurt expression called her back from her early departure, and she had stayed to see the children to bed. By now her banter with Ben had returned pretty much to normal, and they never, directly or indirectly, mentioned Anna's phone call. Nor had Ben told Nikki of Anna's second call.

"That smells good."

"Hungarian goulash. It's ready now, but will be better in another hour, if you can wait. The children have already eaten."

"I'd prefer to wait a bit." He took off his jacket, loosened his tie, and sat in an easy chair across from her. "What are you reading?"

She concealed the cover from him by folding the paperback in two. "Listen to this," she read, "*I think, my dear, you have a mania for exactitude and*

*an impatience with partial knowledge which is . . . well, unfair to knowledge itself.*
*How can it be anything but imperfect?"*

"Who wrote that bullshit?"

"I'm told that, given a substantial passage, you are often able to name the author. So you tell me who wrote it."

"Read it again."

"*I think, my dear, you have a mania for exactitude and an impatience with partial knowledge which is . . . well, unfair to knowledge itself. How can it be anything but imperfect?* This should be easy, as the book is from your own library." She put the book, front cover down, into her lap, her hands folded on top.

"I don't feel like playing this game."

"Why? Because there's no audience of undergraduates to impress. Come on, I'll be impressed, Try me."

"Once more."

"You should have it memorized by now. I have." And she recited the passage without opening the book. "*I think, my dear, you have a mania for exactitude and an impatience with partial knowledge which is . . . well, unfair to knowledge itself. How can it be anything but imperfect?*"

"It sounds like Dewey . . ."

"Wrong.

"Be still. I didn't say it *was* Dewey; only that it sounded like him. I'm thinking."

"Well, think out loud. I want to learn how this is done."

"Dewey's *Quest for Certainty* was written in, oh, nineteen-thirty or so, somewhere around then, and it contained that idea, that all knowledge is imperfect. But the ideas didn't really start to catch on until the late forties. It was a little unpopular to be uncertain of oneself during the war. But to find its way into fiction took even longer, say the fifties or sixties." Ben lit a cigarette, and closed his eyes in thought. "Now, that *my dear*, is a clue. The speaker is either a woman or a fag. So—you say the book is from the library back there?— Durrell was famously influenced by the Dewey crowd . . ." Ben opened his eyes to see if Nikki's expression would give him a clue, but she showed no sign of recognition, "Of course, so was Miller. And van Dusen . . . But I'm thinking Durrell, and I think the only thing I've got back there by him is the *Quartet* . . ."

"That's sort of cheating."

"So, *I think, my dear,* would make it either *Clea* or *Balthazar*. It could be van Dusen, but it doesn't sound like van Dusen. *Mania for exactitude.* A nice phrase, that one. Okay, I'll guess Durrell. Uhhh, *Clea*."

"Ta da. *Clea* it is." She revealed the cover. "Pretty impressive, actually."

"You're too easy. More impressive than recognizing a book by its back cover?"

"What?" She turned the book over and looked at the back cover. "You *are* a cheat; I just didn't know how big a one."

"Thank you, *my dear.*"

"So, it was all an act? Miller? I assumed Henry Miller. But who's this van Dusen."

"You've never heard of Clyde van Dusen?" She shook her head. "Chestnut gelding; son of Man o' War. Won the Derby in twenty-nine. If you're going to go through the routine, you've got to have the patter down."

"You're a fraud, as well as a cheat."

"Listen, honey, if taking advantage of the ignorance of others were fraudulent, half the population would be in jail, including every single car salesman, politician and preacher. Ask your Lesbian law student friend. Assuming, against all odds, that she's interested in something other than the rights of the transgendered."

"Hate to bust your stereotype, Ben, but she seems to be interested in commercial transactions and corporate reorganization."

"Which, now that you mention it, strikes me as pretty damn butch."

"Shut up. She can't win, can she?"

"Nobody can win."

"For whatever it's worth, Robin is very not-butch."

"Whatever. So, why are you reading Durrell?"

"English literary criticism in the mid-twentieth century? My dissertation topic, you'll recall. He fits."

"Well, he was born in India, but so what?"

"I don't know. Robin, my best friend who so fascinates you, asked me about the *Quartet*. Actually, her roommate suggested that she read it . . ."

"That would be the snatch-eating roommate, of course?"

She ignored him. ". . . and Robin wondered what I thought."

"A literary Lesbian lawyer. Fancy that."

She ignored him again. "Well, I hadn't ever tried Durrell, but I found the books here in your library, so I read them this week. Just finished this afternoon, actually, and came across the passage I like, mid-way through *Clea*."

"Second-rate."

"You think so? I like the structure of the series."

"A gimmick."

"Maybe so. But a clever gimmick. So surely the *Quartet* was the subject of some pretty intense English criticism near the end of my time period? I haven't sampled that criticism yet; that's next week's library work. But I'm thinking of using the reaction to the *Quartet* in chapter three. We'll see. Totally aside from all of that, I like this part . . ." She picked up the book again from her lap, and reopened it. "*An impatience with partial knowledge which is . . . well, unfair to knowledge itself.* Unfair to knowledge itself."

"Bullshit."

"No, I don't think so."

"So, go ahead and develop a patience with partial knowledge. Just don't do it around me, and for Christ's sake, don't do it in your dissertation."

But it was not her dissertation that Nikki was thinking about an hour later, when she ladled the veal and spicy paprika sauce into the serving bowl for the table. It was Anna and Marie and this Michael, the implausibility of the coincidence, if it were possibly true. It was *an owl, hunting, hoots,* and *she shouldn't have told you about him,* and it was about a very small *thank you* which she had heard on the telephone, with urban noise in the background, and far off, music playing. She cared not at all for John Dewey, but, as much as Ben might have missed the point, Nikki knew that Clea was speaking directly to her.

～

Later that night, she met Connor at Luna's out on Thomasville Road, for coffee and dessert. He was already there when she arrived, sitting sideways to a small, marble-topped table, with a cup of espresso, and two glasses of sparkling water, hers without ice. He didn't get up as she approached the table, but took her hand when she offered it, kissed it lightly on the knuckles, and continued to hold it as she circled the table and sat down on the other side. They talked lightly until her coffee came, and a few minutes later, two desserts: cheesecake for him and a chocolate mousse for her. They had taken to meeting like this, three or four nights a week after she got done with her chores at the Brownings' to chat and sort over the day.

Half-way through, she pulled *Clea* out from her bag and read for him the two crucial sentences, then went on a bit, skipping over references he wouldn't understand. "*I don't suppose reality ever bears a close resemblance to human truth,*" she read, "*Maybe I should like to be content with the poetic symbolism it presents, the shape of nature as it were.*" She looked up from her reading. "What do you think?"

"I agree," Connor said, still sitting sideways to the table, and licking his fork, while going slow with the cheesecake itself.

"You surprise me, not for the first time. I thought for sure you'd think it was bogus. Well, you might agree as a poet, maybe, but not as a scientist. Surely scientists are more precise than poets."

"No, I think you've got that backwards. Poets are permitted to be perfectionists, but scientists can't afford the luxury. Of course, you're the more serious poet, so you should know about that. It seems to me, though, that poets are always striving to find just exactly the perfect word. *A mania for exactitude* indeed. Every poem is an exercise in such mania."

"Maybe. But scientists don't do the same?"

"Not really. Of course, there's the famous Heisenberg Uncertainty Principle."

"Of course. The famous Heisenberg Uncertainty Principle. Which is?"

"That you can't know both the position and velocity of any individual particle, because to measure either interferes with the other."

"What's that have to do with anything?"

"What was that expression? *The shape of nature . . .*"

". . . *as it were.*"

". . . *as it were.* So Heisenberg showed that the shape of nature was inherently uncertain, and knowledge of it would always be imperfect."

"As Clea says."

"Yes, and more generally, Feynman?" He looked at her, and she shook her head. They were beginning to be able to communicate in fragments. "Nobel prize in Physics. Early sixties. Mid-sixties, maybe. He was a great believer in what he called *the primacy of doubt.* Of course, physicists of his generation immediately followed the Einsteinian revolution, in which everything that everyone had been sure of since Newton got tossed out in about ten years. Well, qualified at least. That would make anyone suspicious that he's ever got anything really figured out." She looked at him over her coffee cup. "Or her," he added.

"Maybe." She smiled at him.

"Take the Apalachicola Bay . . ."

"About which you know a thing or two."

"I do. But think of the bay's complexity. Its chemistry changes daily. Its biology, from microbes to dolphins, is amazingly diverse. Even its physics, with its swirling currents, its tides, its heating and cooling, the way the wind stirs the whole mix. To imagine that one could ever manage to describe the entire system with any kind of precision is folly."

"But you try, don't you."

"Sure, we try. But just as surely we have to be, . . . what was that phrase? . . ."

"*Patient with partial knowledge*."

"Exactly. Now look at a map of the Gulf."

"Don't have one with me."

"Next time you get a chance. Apalachicola Bay is this tiny, minuscule little part of the entire Gulf, which is like a squillion times more complex that the estuary itself."

"That much?" She raised an eyebrow.

"More. Ten squillion. Of course, one would expect an experimental scientist to live with incomplete knowledge, because we do our work in the real, messy world. The remarkable thing is that even the theorists, like Feynman and Heisenberg, found that they had to content themselves with uncertainty. No, I'm with, . . . who did you say the speaker was in that book?"

"Clea."

"Clea's the gal for me. Well, after you."

"High praise; I admire her, too. Listen to this," she leafed through to find a page. "At the end of the book, she writes to her friend Darley that she is *serene and happy, a real human being, an artist at last. I love that*."

"Very nice."

"She also says, though she is quoting someone else at this point, that *the richest love is that which submits to the arbitration of time*."

"Speaking of which, got plans for later tonight?"

"Yeah, sorry, but I've got to scoot tonight. I'm proofreading chapter two of my dissertation, and I've got to get it to Ben by the end of the week, so he can read it over the weekend."

"Scoot, scoot, scoot. I'll take a few minutes more to finish reading the *Times*. See you tomorrow?"

"I think so. Need to know right now?"

"Nope. I'll be here."

Nikki stood up, put *Clea* back into her bag, and walked around the table to kiss him quickly on the lips. "Bye. Need any money?"

"My treat. Good night, honey."

"Good night."

"Hey, speaking of the Bay, I've got to run over there this weekend to pick up some samples. Want to ride with me?"

"Yes, I would. Thanks."

"We could take the Browning kids along, if you want to."

"Nah. Let's just make it a day with the two of us. You can school me some more on the necessity of uncertainty. Wait, I just thought of this: If we go on Saturday, we could continue on over to Pensacola to see the ball game. The Pelicans are playing Birmingham on Saturday night."

"Love to. But it would be a long drive home from Pensacola after the game."

"How long?"

He shrugged. "Two, two-and-a-half hours? It must be two-hundred miles. Maybe we'd have to get a room somewhere." His grin was particularly agreeable.

She kissed him once more, winked and said, "Don't push your luck. I'll either see you here tomorrow night, or I'll call. 'Bye."

"I'll be praying for extra innings."

And she walked out to her car in the parking lot.

But driving home, Nikki came to realize that, notwithstanding Connor's paean to imperfect knowledge, Connor and Clea and Heisenberg and Feyman and Durrell and Dewey aside, *she* needed to know more. After all, what did she know for sure now? That both Anna and Marie received letters from a person, or more likely, persons, named Michael, and that Anna's letter mentioned an obscure New Mexico town called Moriarty, where Marie worked, as did surely hundreds of other people. But maybe the Moriarty in Anna's letter was Moriarty, she didn't know, Colorado or Utah, Oregon or Saskatchewan. Even if it were the same town, she knew nothing in Anna's life that would connect her to a small, rural, high-desert town. Anna's letter-writer was perhaps tied to Marie, but how was Marie tied to Anna? She needed to see if there was a closer connection between Anna's and Marie's letter writers, which meant that she would have to talk to Marie and find out some more about her Michael. Until then, she would continue to consider the coincidence to be utterly implausible.

CORRESPONDENCE

April Fifth
Πάρος

Dear Ριχάρντο –

On the way out of Romania a couple of weeks ago, I found myself involved in a gypsy-run operation to smuggle Tupperware into Yugoslavia, but that's a story that will have to wait until the mood to write strikes. I only wanted you to know that it all came out okay, in case you saw the story in the *Trib* and were worried.

The pace of life has picked up here on Paros a bit, the ferry boats are increasingly crowded, as tourist season approaches, and the ambience that fosters letter-writing is fading fast. We may be moving on soon. South would be my choice, but one does not always get one's choice in such matters. When I re-read the last sentence I realize that such grousing is unseemly from one who has just finished a spasm of unfettered, quite satisfying, Soviet-sphere-of-influence-hopping. *Quick!* An act of contrition. Meeska-Mooska Mumblemumblemumble. As you can see, the ambience that fosters letter-writing is fading fast. Like I said.

Emily is off just now playing the bouzouki at a wedding at a restaurant called Ευκάλυπτος, which means The Eucalyptos Tree, and I am sitting on the dock, not far from the post office, thinking of how sometimes real life looks like bad special effects. The ferry to Athens—a boat called *ΝΑΞΟΣ*—just pulled out of the harbor, and from this low angle, the departing wake looked much like the periscope shot of a Jap battleship in any number of grade B war movies. It is strange, isn't it Richard, how life goes?
As ever,
Μικάλι

After a day trying to sort through the different possibilities—Robin and Marie are both at home; Robin is there but not Marie; Marie but not Robin—Nikki had no good, fool-proof plan for learning more about Marie's connection to Anna's letter-writing friend Michael. She knew that the only way it would work was to find Marie at home by herself, but how to arrange that, without either one knowing that she was trying?

She started by calling the duplex, mid-week, mid-morning, Albuquerque time, getting, as she expected, no one, and leaving a message on the machine: *Robin: Call me.* And when Britt returned the call that evening to the Browning home, Nikki said, "Kiddo. I can't talk now. When's a good time to catch you?"

To which Britt responded perfectly, for Nikki's purposes, "Well, not Tuesday or Friday afternoon or evenings. My life belongs to Randolph on those nights, sometimes quite late. Weekends, late afternoons, would be best."

"Got it. I'll be in touch. Love 'ya. Bye."

So, of course, Nikki called back late Friday afternoon, and Marie answered. "Hello?"

"Hi, Marie. This is Nikki Wallace."

"Oh, hi." Marie was immediately nervous, after the last time the two of them had talked on the phone. "Britt's not here right now. She works with her professor on Tuesday and Friday nights and often doesn't get home until after I'm in bed. But I'll tell her you called."

"Well, actually, I'm glad to get you when she's not around. Is she okay? I haven't heard from her in quite a while."

"She's fine. Just busy. She and her professor have this case coming up in New York in a few weeks, and, God, she's been working like crazy on it. And she's got her class work to keep up with, you know how she is . . ."

"I do."

"And the *Law Review* is winding down at the end of the year, but there's still stuff that she has to do. Training next year's staff, or something."

"But she's okay?"

"Yes. Tired, but okay. She's got honest-to-goodness dark circles under her eyes. But I've gotten her to promise me that we're going to take it easy this weekend. I'll have her call you; it will do her good just to sit on the couch and chat with you. I think you're good for her." Marie paused, not sure what Nikki would say to that overture.

Nikki paused for what she hoped was just the right length of time, before saying, "Thanks." Another pause. "You know, Marie, I felt kind of bad about our last phone conversation, when you called from work. Moriarty, right?"

"Right."

Nikki wrote the word *Moriarty* on the yellow pad she had in front of her, underlined it, then underlined it again. "Right. Anyway, I'm sorry. I was kind of a louse that day. The truth of the matter is that I think you are good for Robin, too."

"Thank you."

"And I don't know you well enough to say the kinds of things I was saying on the phone that day. It's just that Robin leads a difficult life—well, you do too, now—and the assholes of the world can be pretty rough on her for the way she is. I guess you know that there are people out there who just automatically hate her. It really pisses me off."

"It shows."

"I know, and it usually doesn't bother me that it shows. But I didn't have to show it quite so emphatically to you the other day."

"It's okay. It made me know how much you cared for her."

"I do care for her; more than anyone. And I always want her to go slow. Or slow*er*, anyway. Like my father used to say when he was teaching me to play chess: *when in doubt, move a pawn*. Be careful. Move slowly. Do as little as you can get away with, unless you're sure. But Britt has always taken a different path. She's more of a *be bold; take chances* kind of gal. She never could play chess worth a damn, but she was a hell of an equestrian. Fearless."

"That's interesting. I have a friend like that, too."

"Oh? Who?"

"*My married ex-boy friend*, as you put it so indelicately the other day."

*Here goes*, Nikki thought. She hadn't expected the comment about moving-pawns and risk-taking to be the *entre* she needed, but here it was, and now the conversation had to take its dangerous turn.

"Ah. I shouldn't have said what I said about him, either."

"You said it was just a lucky guess."

"Which itself was a snarky thing to say. I'll admit to you now that Robin had mentioned some guy."

"Yes. Michael Reid."

*Michael Reid*, Nikki wrote. "She says you get kind of, I don't know, moody after you hear from him."

"Wow. Did she say that? Do I? Maybe so, but I'll have to watch for that. He's a special friend of mine, I'll admit. Actually, I don't see much of him anymore; it's been a couple of years, I guess. He keeps in touch with these long letters he writes to me from here and there, sometimes his home, but more often when he's travelling. He travels a lot." *Long letters*, Nikki wrote. *Traveler.* "If I get moody, I suppose it's about the travel and the places he visits. I haven't been that many places and his letters make me think about where he is. He's a good describer of places. *Describer.*

"Where's he live?"

"Arkansas. The Ozarks. He teaches at the University of Arkansas."

*Ozarks/Univ. Ark.*

"I'll admit," Marie continued, "that he's a special friend, like I said, though I don't really think of him as my boy friend, or anything like it. But I'll admit, too, that I haven't figured out how to tell him about Britt, but I will by the time he gets back in the country. And I want you to know it's a question of *how* and *when* I'll tell him; not *if*. Actually, of all the people in the world that I know, I expect him to be the most understanding."

"Where is he now?"

"Well," Marie laughed, "one never really knows." It had become remarkably comfortable, she thought, having this conversation with Britt's best friend. "He—they, including the married part—are in Athens for the spring, but he's kind of using that as a central location from which to travel around. Actually, I think they've rented a house down in the Greek islands somewhere.

*Athens/Islands.* Nikki drew a square around the words with her pen, then turned the square into a 3-D box.

"So how do you know him?" she asked innocently.

"Well, we met in a class in grad school, when he was doing his PhD and I was doing my Masters. But we didn't know each other well until we both ended up teaching out in Moriarty. He taught math. Pre-algebra and the like."

*Math/Pre-alg.* She then added an exclamation point. *!*

"He was in grad school part time, on the side at first, then he quit at Moriarty and went full-time, and got his doctorate. Then they left New Mexico and he moved to some other university job, before ending up in Arkansas. His wife's a musician. Right now, I forget exactly where they went. Someplace in the mid-west. We only overlapped as colleagues for a couple of years."

"Did they ever live in Florida?"

"Florida? Why do you ask?"

"Oh, I don't know. You live in Florida for a while and you start thinking that everyone has lived here at some point." Nikki held her breath, closed her eyes and grimaced to herself. She knew it was weak, but it was the only thing she'd been able to think of to test a possible connection to Anna.

Marie seemed not to notice. "No, I don't think so, not Florida. *X Fla.* His first professor job after leaving here was at some university in Kansas. Not one of the big ones. I can't remember. Maybe it will come to me. "

*Kansas.*

"He sounds like an interesting kind of guy."

"Yes, he is that. Washburn. That's where he went after getting his PhD. Washburn. Somewhere in Kansas."

*Washburn.*

"He says that I'm the better teacher, but he's the one who ended up teaching teachers how to teach. He says he's on a mission—to get elementary teachers to stop telling their kids that if they don't behave they were going to do the arithmetic lesson, and if he could do that, he'd be satisfied."

"Did you ever think of going that route?"

"You mean a PhD? Teaching in college? Not really. I like the young students and don't think I'd like to teach adults. There's a certain spark that you see in the eyes of children that I don't think would be there in a college classroom. But Britt says you want to go into university teaching someday."

"Some day. Whenever I get this damn dissertation finished. This Michael does sound like an interesting guy."

"Oh, he lives an odd life, checking out of his responsibilities every now and then and taking off, on his own as often as with his wife. I remember once, back when he was at Moriarty, summer vacation was coming up and he was leaving his address with the secretary. I was standing at her desk with him and he was saying, you know, like *the first week of June, I'll be in San Francisco visiting my sister, and the next two weeks in Yosemite.* Then he said something like, *from then until mid-August, I'll be incommunicado.* I don't remember, somewhere in the Caribbean, maybe. And the secretary was a single mother with two kids and she got this far-away look in her eyes as if to say how wonderful it would be to be totally, absolutely, incommunicado for a while."

"That can make it kind of hard on his friends, I suppose."

"One gets used to it."

"I guess so. Me? I'd rather be able to reach people. And to be reachable, I guess. Incommunicado never appealed to me much."

"Me neither, actually. And that's why you called wondering if Britt is all right? She does, I think, do a pretty good job of keeping in touch with people. She's much better at seeing Bill and Maggie than I am with my parents." It felt nice, Marie thought, to be able to speak so familiarly with Nikki about Britt's parents.

"Yes, but then it's a little difficult *not* to stay in touch with Bill and Maggie, if I remember right."

"That really hasn't been a problem. They've been nice to me. I suppose they are nice to, uh, you know, everybody that Britt sees."

"No, I'll tell you this: they didn't like Lorinda."

"Why not?"

"Too young. Too flighty. Unreliable. Lacking in decorum. I could go on. They're probably beside themselves with relief at your steadiness." Marie accepted the compliment without comment. "Anyway, listen, tell them I said *hey* the next time you see them. I practically grew up at their house, you know. And at the stable, while Robin obsessed over that horse of hers."

"Were you there for the broken arm?"

"No, but I was for the re-mount."

"A week later, right?"

"Right. God, I'll never forget it. I thought Maggie was going to kill someone. I'll say this: Robin has more guts than anyone I know. Which is why I worry about her. But don't tell Robin that I was snooping around after her well-being, okay? I don't want her to feel bad because she hasn't called me recently. I just wanted to be sure about her."

"I won't mention you called. But she's okay, and I'll insist that she sleep in this weekend."

"Okay. Then I'll relax. And I'll be in touch. I enjoyed the talk."

"Really?"

"Really."

"It was good to talk to you, too, Nikki. Thanks."

"You're welcome. And, again, I'm sorry about the last phone call."

"It's okay. Please, call anytime."

"Bye."

"Goodbye."

Nikki picked up her pad of paper. *Moriarty. Michael Reid. Long letters. Traveler. Describer. Ozarks/Univ. Ark. Athens/Islands. Math/Pre-alg! X Fla. Kansas/Washburn.* She thought she had it all, and that now she knew, but oddly enough she was in no particular hurry to fit the final piece of the puzzle into place. So, carrying the pad with her, she wandered through the empty Browning house, picked up some dirty clothes off of the floor of Janet's room, pondered the bookshelves in Ben's library, changed out the towels in the bathroom, before ending up in Anna's study.

And yes, there it was, on the wall across from Anna's desk. A rather chintzy-looking plaque, machined out of what looked like dark walnut, into the rather boring shape of Kansas, with a star marking Topeka, the capital, affixed to which was a brass engraving, attesting to the appreciation that the members of the Washburn University chapter of Kappa Mu Epsilon, the national mathematics honorary fraternity, owed to Professor Anna Browning for her service as their advisor for the years 1976 to '79.

She sat down in the easy chair across from Anna's desk, from where she could see Michael's letter, marking the place of Jablonski's article in the *American Journal of Probability and Statistics*. She was inclined for a moment to read the letter again, but she decided against it. She now knew enough. Enough to know that the Utterly Implausible Coincidence was true, and to know that Anna Browning and Marie Cochran both received letters from the same person. But what was really so implausible about that? A guy writes long letters. Okay, so that was maybe a little nineteenth-century-ish, but it was not utterly implausible. Two women in different parts of the country receive those letters. Unremarkable. No, the only thing implausible was that Nikki Wallace, *ex* of Albuquerque, New Mexico and currently of Tallahassee, Florida, knew both of those women. Sort of. Well, she didn't know either of them, really, but was connected to them in an oddly unsettling way, through the offices of Ben and Robin, two persons who would surely dislike each other instantly upon meeting, and who, actually, probably already disliked each other without ever having met.

That was, in fact, remarkable, and Nikki sat back in the chair, lit a Kool, knowing that she'd have to find an ashtray before the ash got long enough to flick, and felt herself to be sitting at the exact center of the galaxy, with everything spinning in complex patterns over her head. That was the only implausible part, that it would be she who—other than the writer, this Michael Reid—was most likely the only person in the world, the galaxy, who knew both Anna Browning and Marie Cochran. Why she?

Nikki was, beyond everything else, Copernican to her very core, an attribute which she owed to having read *De Revolutionibus Orbium Coelestium* at St. John's years ago. It had made her Copernican, not merely in her belief that the sun was at the center of the solar system, which was difficult not to believe nowadays, but much, much beyond that. *I am not special. Here is not special. Now is not special.* She recalled having written that across the top of her notebook during the junior-year Great Books class discussion of *De Revolutionibus.* Thinking that one, or one's people, or one's religion, or one's nation, was somehow special, she had decided, had led to considerable mischief throughout the history of the world, mischief that she, herself, intended to avoid. Maybe the God of the Entire Universe had made Jerusalem His capital, but she doubted it, and ditto for everywhere else on the planet that claimed that distinction.

But here she was, Nikki Wallace, nobody special, sitting in this chair feeling as if the galaxy were spinning over her head, with her at the exact center. How utterly implausible, if not completely bloody ridiculous, was that? Well, maybe. Maybe not. Does Copernicanism require that *no one ever*, actually be at the center of the galaxy? Surely not. In fact, was it not somehow presumptuous to think that one could never possibly be at the galactic center? Sure, Nikki Wallace was unique in a genetic sense, but until now she had never felt that *unusual,* which she considered the more valuable trait. But the letter, the phone call, the entire situation made her queasy with the unusualness of it all.

But, she would have to leave for later the philosophical implications of the coincidence. What to do now? Nothing, she decided, cupping her hand under her cigarette to catch the ash. She stood up, walked over to the corner of Anna's desk and with one forefinger, the cigarette in her mouth, curling smoke up into her right eye, touched the near corner of Michael's letter. She then dusted her ashy hands into the waste basket, walked out of the study, and, with one last look over her shoulder at the letter, closed the door behind her.

For now, she would tell no one. Who would believe her, at any rate? Nor could she think of how the information, even if true, could possibly be used to help find Anna. Somehow, it seemed entirely too prosaic to think that Anna had left her husband, her children, and her career, to join her lover Michael Reid in Greece; there was little in the letter as Nikki remembered it to suggest that kind of relationship between the two of them. She remembered Anna's very quiet *thank you* at the end of the phone conversation they had had, if you could call it a conversation, and there was the music in the background, the music that Nikki now suspected was bouzouki music, but how would that possibly convince anyone other than her that Anna was now in Athens? Not to mention that to say anything to Ben would be to admit that she had read Anna's private mail, which would lead, she suspected, to the very justified destruction of all she had worked for.

Nor could she think of any reason that Robin should be told of the coincidence. She had managed to find in the letter, very much contrary to what Anna herself, or Ben, had found in it, a warm feeling toward this Michael whom she didn't know, a warmth that, given the present circumstances, she could hardly expect Robin to share. She recalled his description of the Ozark hillside, his fondness for an obscure café on an out-of-the-way plaza in Paris, the draw he felt to both places, the balance he tried to maintain between them. He was, as Marie had said, a good describer. But the attraction she felt went beyond that. What Anna had found tedious, and Ben imbecilic, Nikki had found not far short of profound. She particularly remembered his inclusion in the important things in life of one's ability to turn a double play when the kid pitcher really needed it. She had never experienced that as a player, never, in fact, had she played behind a substantially younger pitcher, but as a minor league baseball fan, she knew exactly what he was talking about. It was not the mechanics of the game, elegant though they can be. Nor was it about winning or losing, advancing to the play-offs or not. It was about the personal side of the game, which she appreciated so much, and about how a young man's entire psyche can sometimes be abetted just by getting out of this inning with minimal damage done. And, if the veteran players behind the kid get done what had to be done, it could make the kid's career. Completely contrary to the reactions that the letter had evoked in Anna herself, and Ben, Nikki found herself liking the guy, and, most surprising of all, the warmth that Nikki felt toward the writer had somehow managed to attach itself to Robin's lover, Marie, whom she had just manipulated into telling her the tale.

Shaking her head at the strangeness of it all, but comfortable in her conclusion that nothing should be said to anyone at this time—not to Ben nor Marie, the principals, nor to Robin, who was tied to Marie, nor even to Connor, who would have been a neutral listener—Nikki walked into the kitchen, carefully tore from the pad the yellow sheet with her notes from the phone call, wadded it up and placed it in the kitchen trash. She then removed the white plastic bag from under the sink, tied a knot to hold it shut, and walked the trash out to her car, parked on the street. She placed the trash in the back seat, to be thrown away next time she bought gasoline. Back inside, she tidied up the kitchen and began to prepare dinner, before deciding that it would be a good night for them all to go out for pizza.

It was only about an hour later, when Marie was busy with her lesson plans for the following week, that she came to notice, in retrospect, the extent to which Michael had dominated so much of her pleasant phone chat with Nikki, who had shown more interest in Michael's past than Britt ever had. Marie could think of no reason why that would have been so except that Britt had asked Nikki to pump her for the information. Britt had never seemed all that curious about Michael, but then, why shouldn't she be? It bothered Marie that Britt would not ask Marie herself, but would use Nikki as the inquisitor. But it bothered her more that Michael might appear out of nowhere before she and Britt had had a frank discussion about him. It was well past time for the two of them to talk about Michael, and what he meant to Marie. This weekend, she thought, if the opportunity presented itself.

Connor picked Nikki up at her apartment before six on Saturday morning.

"Timmy's coming?"

"You bet. In the event of extra innings, I didn't want him to be in the yard all night."

"They'll never let him into the ball park with you. Will they?"

"I'll bet you the price of admission that I can talk his way in."

"Bet."

They stopped at Myra Jean's in Crawfordville for breakfast, and got to the Department of Environmental Protection field office in Apalachicola around eight. Nikki had prepared for a day lounging on the beach, with a stack of books to read, a boom box, and a collection of Linda Ronstadt CDs, which they had sampled on the drive over. It would be too cold to swim in April in the northern Gulf, but the sun was warm and she wore her bikini as underwear. However, at the DEP office, plans quickly changed, as the documentation of the water samples that Connor had driven over to pick up was not to his liking, and he decided that they would all have to be re-done, today, and that he and Nikki would have to do the work. So, instead of a morning on the beach, and an afternoon driving on to Pensacola to see the game, they spent most of the day on the water. Connor would motor the little inboard skiff to a particular location in the estuary, using a satellite positioning device belonging to the DEP, and would take the sample. It was Nikki's job, sitting in her bikini on a deck chair wearing a floppy straw hat and with her feet up on the side of the boat, dropping her spent Kools into a coffee can, Tim curled on the deck beside her, to record neatly the location, time, surface-water temperature, and depth for each of the two-hundred-fifty numbered samples.

When she asked him what the relationship of the surface temperature was to the temperature at the depth of the sample, Connor said, "Good girl. I'll make a scientist of you yet. The answer is *not much*, but to measure the temperature down below is complicated."

"Why not just send a thermometer down with the little bottle?"

"Won't work. You'd have to pull the thermometer up through warmer or colder layers to get it back into the boat. There's a gizmo on the market that will get the job done, by electronically transporting the temp reading up to the boat, but they're pricey. I've got one on the Department wish list, but I don't expect to see it in my lab anytime soon. In the meantime, I must develop, as your friend Clea might say, *a patience with partial knowledge.*"

"*How can it be anything other than imperfect?*" she quoted, and they laughed.

Once, around lunchtime, she had to pee, and didn't know how that was going to be arranged without a trip to shore, but he told her there was a wide-mouthed collection gadget, of the type used to implement the DEP's drug-testing policy, in the small cabin down below, and she found it easily enough, with a little roll of toilet paper next to it.

Back on deck, she asked, "So where do I wash my hands, Mr. Environmental Quality?"

He smiled and said, "Urine is almost sterile, you know," but when she gave him a look, he said, "Over the side is fine," and she did.

They finished the job by late afternoon, packed the samples in ice, *per* EPA specs, in the DEP's coolers for transportation back to Connor's lab in Tallahassee, and then found their way to Papa Joe's for beers and dinner. They took a table out on the deck, overlooking the water, and Connor was a regular, so no one objected to Tim's presence.

"Will he be fired?" Nikki asked, half-way through her first beer.

"Who?"

"The worker who collected the original samples."

"She, actually. And she doesn't work for me, so it's not my call."

"And if it were?"

"I wouldn't fire her. She's new, just out of a bio-tech program at the local community college. I'd just take her aside and let her come to see just how precise the measurements have to be, and how neatly tallied. Say, you could do the job; you've already been trained."

"Yeah, but I don't have an associate's degree from Panama City Tech."

"Don't be such a snob. Actually, I'll bet that she's exceeded her parents' level of education by more than you have exceeded yours. I know she has mine. But actually, I am afraid she will get fired, because her supervisor got embarrassed by what I—*we*—had to do today, and he'll probably want to take it out on her to deflect that embarrassment. What I'm really afraid might happen, and what would be the worst of all, is that the supervisor will give her a little scolding and tell her to make sure the documentation is right next time, wink, wink."

"So you lose another Saturday, and then she *is* fired."

"No, worse. Then she comes to realize that she has to make the documentation *look* precise, even if it isn't. It would be easy enough to fake the precision that we need, and I'd never, never know it." He shook his head. "I'd never know it. Basically, she has me at her mercy, and there's no sense in trying to hide that from her. All you can do is try to get her to buy into the scientific ethics of doing it right, not just making it look like it was done right."

"You know, I found myself thinking of Clea on the boat, even before you quoted her."

"Why the fascination with Clea? Or should I say obsession?"

"Partly because I'm dealing with some imperfect knowledge myself right now."

"How so?"

"An implausible coincidence."

"Go on."

"Let's order, first. I'm hungry." Really what she needed was time to think how much, and how, she was going to tell him about the Utterly Implausible Coincidence. And after the waitress was flagged down, their orders taken, and Tim was walked down the steps to do his business, which included sniffing at every single piling that held up the deck, she decided to deflect the topic. Instead she said, "You know what my dissertation is about, right?"

"Mid-century English critical theory. How could I forget?"

"Right. Say nineteen thirty-five to nineteen sixty-five. So, the first chapter is the introduction. That's done. The second chapter is the theoretical overview, in which I relate the various forms of critical theory coming and going during that time period: modernism, post-modernism, post-colonialism, pre-feminism, the literary version of abstract expressionism, conceptualism, pre-conceptualism, post-conceptualism, anti-conceptualism—those sorts of thing. Long. And boring. But complete, except for a little tweaking to satisfy Ben. Now, the third chapter is an examination of the critical treatment given to one particular literary work, and I've just decided this last week that I'm going to focus on the reception given to Durrell's *Alexandria Quartet*, of which *Clea* is the final volume. So, I brought all four books along, to begin giving them another read before I begin the third chapter."

"Why those books particularly?"

"Partly because of the conversation we had a couple of days ago over coffee, when you surprised me by agreeing with Clea. Actually, you might like to read *The Quartet*. You'd like the structure, at least."

"How so?"

The food came: plates of shrimp, oysters and scallops, nothing fancy, but lots of it, with fries on the side, and two more beers.

"Well, in the first book, called *Justine*, an unnamed narrator tells of his love affair with the title character, in pre-War Alexandria. A very lovely read. Then in the second book, called *Balthazar*, the narrator, still unnamed, and accompanied by a child of complicated origin, retreats to a Greek island, maybe Rhodes, to write *Justine*, the book we have just read. He produces a manuscript of *Justine*, which he sends off for comment to his friend Balthazar, back in Alexandria. The manuscript is returned to him with Balthazar's handwritten notes, now called The Interlineal, wherein Balthazar corrects much of what the narrator said in *Justine*, which we've already read. Like *you thought Justine was in love with you, but she was actually just using her affair with you to camouflage her other affair with the man she was really in love with.* That sort of thing. Okay? With me?"

He nodded while biting into a shrimp, and flipped the tail in an arc over the edge of the table. Timmy, at his feet, caught it on the fly, without comment.

"Now, the third book is called *Mountolive*, and it is told in the third person, and the narrator of the first two books, now identified as one Darley, is a character in the third. It relates the same events, more or less—at least the same time period and same locale—as the first two books, but now focusing on Mountolive, an English diplomat in Egypt, friend of Darley, Balthazar, Justine, and all the rest." She dunked an oyster into hot sauce and slurped it down, followed by a drink of cold beer. "So—see?" She gestured with a French fry, "We've now read essentially the same story from three different spatial perspectives. And the fourth book is *Clea*, with Darley again as the first-person narrator, carrying on the story on the temporal axis, now with the War winding down. Four-dimensional, get it? Very Einsteinian. We learn, for example, that Justine is actually carrying on *both* of her affairs so as to deflect attention away from her husband, Nessim, whom she loves dearly, but who, though a Copt, is involved in some dicey politics relating to the partition of Palestine."

"Using her body for her husband's political ends. How pre-feminist, indeed."

"Exactly. And there were some female critics who noted that. And that Justine is told that she asked for the rape she experienced as a child, and probably enjoyed it."

"Ouch."

"Really."

"How it must pain you to read such crap."

"Well, in nineteen eighty-five, I read words written by Durrell in the late fifties, about something that was supposed to have been said in nineteen forty-five."

"Doesn't it make you angry to read it?"

"Who should I be angry with? Durrell for writing the words, Darley for reporting them, Justine for reacting to them, or Pursewarden for having said them?"

"Lit crit, as you call it, drives me crazy. Still, it must be hard."

"Yes, I'll admit it can be. Justine, and most of the other female characters, are somehow damaged goods. Including Clea, who loses a hand near the end of the fourth book. That's part of what I'm going to write about in the third chapter, how the nascent feminist theorists reacted to the books and to the female characters."

"And you?"

"Me?"

"What do you think about them?"

"That there are too many sentences beginning with the words *Like all women, she . . .*" Nikki paused to eat a scallop, a bit undercooked to Connor's exact specification. "Still I think there is wisdom in the *Quartet,* notwithstanding that Durrell knew less about women than he thought he did. Actually, he could have learned something from you today about Clea's Dewian philosophy of imperfect knowledge."

"Really? What?"

"Well, you, my dear, have a mania for exactitude."

"*Me?*"

"Latitude and longitude to the tenth of a second. Depths to the centimeter. Temperatures to the tenth of a degree, Celsius. Yes, you are very, very exact. I suppose I should have guessed that from what else I knew about you, but seeing you at work today was very impressive, I must say."

"In a manic sort of way."

"Right. But you also made me see what you had only told me about before: the complexity of the Bay. We took two hundred and fifty samples, and it seemed like nothing, when we were out on the water. What? We sampled maybe one-millionth of one per cent of the entire estuary? Plus I came to see the Bay as three-dimensional, when we'd take several samples at different depths at one location, without moving the boat. I never realized what a tremendously complex system it is."

"Eco-bio-chemo-physio-system."

"In four dimensions, because of depth and time. Incredible."

"So?"

"So Clea is wrong. Dead wrong. You, my dear, have *both* a mania for exactitude *and* a patience with partial knowledge. I had read that passage a dozen times, always buying Durrell's notion that the mania and the impatience had to be linked together, and that both had to be rejected to appreciate the true Dewian principle. But you showed me that there is not, necessarily, a linkage. In fact, maybe there can't be."

"The most maniacal are also the most patient?"

"Maybe. But not necessarily that way, either. Ben Browning strikes me as both maniacal and impatient, very anti-Clea-an. He claims Dewey to be full of shit, and is very confident in his own intelligence. But he certainly would have had no patience for the wonderful day that I had today. I learned a lot."

They clinked beer glasses and ordered more seafood, over which they lingered until it was well past the time when it made any sense at all to drive to Pensacola to see the Pelicans game. Instead, as it began to get dark, they got back into Connor's car, the samples on ice in the back seat with Tim, and headed across the Memorial Bridge on US 98, the coast road back to Tallahassee. However, playing with the radio dial, Nikki was able to pick up an AM station from Pensacola carrying the game, and so she sat back to listen, her bare feet up on the dashboard, while Connor drove into the April night, the sky fading to darkness in the west behind them.

The announcer, who was working the game by himself, doing both play-by-play and color commentary, had a nice easy radio-way about him. His baritone was easy to listen to, and—though he was clearly a Pelicans fan, employed by the team—he did not hyperventilate, and was not prone to excessive home-team-ism. And, most importantly for a radio announcer calling a game, he did not jabber away constantly; his silences, sometimes as much as ten seconds long, were not silent at all, with crowd noise in the background—*beer here; come on, Ricky; Charge!*—and these, too, added to the listening experience. It was, Nikki thought, a little like listening to a pleasant Mozart sonata—no, the quality of the underlying product was not up to Mozart; this was, after all, early-season minor league baseball, after all, and Class A at that—it was more like listening to a nice Samuel Barber sonata, played by someone who had not yet made the big time—no recording contracts, no solo gigs with the National Orchestra, no NPR interviews—and maybe never would, a student, maybe, not at Julliard, but at FSU, a nice, competent pianist, playing a nice, quiet composition. They listened, she looking out the passenger-side window at the Gulf slipping by, and he driving quietly.

And, for whatever reason, she found herself not at all surprised when the situation that Michael Reid had described in his letter to Anna began to unfold as the announcer called the game. The Pelicans entered the fifth inning down by two, and the pitcher, a nineteen-year-old kid just out of high school, was in trouble, with runners on first and second and only one out, already having let in two more runs in the fifth. Nikki could almost see the Pelicans' manager, with another guy warm in the bullpen, thinking that it was time to give the hook to the kid. He probably already had his foot on the top step of the dugout, with his hands in his hip pockets, though the announcer didn't say so.

At which point the kid threw a hard slider to the Birmingham DH, who went the other way and sliced the ball down the third baseline, over the bag and headed for the corner, *triple* written all over it. But the third baseman, a guy in his thirties who had rattled around the minors his entire career, his big-league dreams having crumbled to dust in towns like Little Rock, Corpus Christi and Decatur, dove to his right, and snared the ball two inches off the ground, coming to rest with his belt buckle in foul territory. But he got himself to his knees, and with all the strength his sore right shoulder could muster, he threw to the second baseman, who doubled the runner off second. Inning over.

They listened to the announcer's call of the play—detailed and appreciative, but not off-the-charts and his blood pressure well under control—and then to his re-description, before going to the commercial break.

"Nice play," Nikki said.

"The pitcher owes the third baseman a steak dinner," Connor said. In the dark car, Nikki smiled, unfastened her seat belt, slid across the seat, and kissed his ear warmly, ending up with a lick of his earlobe. "What was that for?" he asked.

"For reading my mind. Don't have a wreck; I'm not belted in."

He put his arm across her shoulders and she rested her left hand on his knee, as they rode along the 98, listening to the rest of the game. The Pelicans scratched their way back into it, and were within a run in the eighth, when they lost the signal, and rode the rest of the way in silence.

At the Tallahassee city limits, he asked, "Where to?"

"My place."

They arrived at her apartment around ten, and she invited him in, where they made love until nearly midnight. Feigning sleepiness, she sent him home, but then sat up until almost three, smoking and writing down the thoughts that she had had about *The Quartet* during the day.

# 15

## ALBUQUERQUE

Contrary to Marie's promise to Nikki, Britt was up early, as usual, on Saturday morning, for a quick liquid breakfast, and then off on her bike to a *Law Review* meeting at school. Marie busied herself around the duplex, straightening up the living room and kitchen, defrosting the fridge, brushing the dog, and vacuuming out the front seat of her car, where she had spilled a bag of popcorn about a week earlier and had not yet gotten around to cleaning it up. The postman stopped by as usual at about ten o'clock, and in amongst the mostly junk mail lay a letter from Michael.

*Well, now,* Marie thought to herself, *this may be way to get Michael into a conversation and out of the way.* He had never called back after the message left on the machine, but she assumed that shortly he'd appear at the door, as usual, and she and Britt had to talk about him before that happened. And this letter might be just the means for that conversation to begin. She felt the weight of the letter in her hand, held it up to the light, and then decided that the best way to proceed was for her to read the letter, not alone, but in Britt's company. That might put both Britt's curiosity and Marie's worries about him to rest.

Marie was going to bring the letter out at dinner on Saturday night, she really was, but in the end she got cold feet, and took Saturday night to re-think the idea, at the movies, later for ice cream, and then while waiting for sleep to come in the dark bedroom, with Britt sleeping quietly beside her.

On Sunday morning, Britt did sleep in, while Marie sat at the kitchen table contemplating the still-unopened letter, until shortly before eleven when she heard Britt move around in the bedroom, then wander down the hall to the bathroom and close the door. Marie walked quietly up the stairs to the bedroom, smoothed out the sheets but did not make the bed and lay down, fully dressed. Then, hearing the water begin to run in the shower, she got up, took off her shoes and socks, and changed her jeans into running shorts, and put on a faded red Lobos tee shirt, with the sleeves torn off and which Britt had once said she looked nice in. Marie wondered if the torn sleevelessness was not, in fact, a little butch—a thought, she admitted to herself, she'd never entertained after years of wearing the shirt, until Britt had said she liked her in it—but it might be just right for what she had planned. She sat back down on the bed, leaning against the headboard, and with her legs stretched out in front of her. Then she pulled her knees up under her chin. At first she put the letter, still unopened, on the bedside table, then as an afterthought, put it into the drawer of the table and closed the drawer, and waited for Britt to emerge from the bathroom.

She came in, naked, drying her hair with a towel. "Oh, there you are. Why did you let me sleep so long?"

"Good morning. You needed the sleep."

"I guess I did," Britt said, stepping into her panties, and then her jeans, her breasts bobbing as she pulled up and zipped herself in. "I'm hungry. Have you eaten? I like that shirt on you."

"Nah. I was waiting for you. Why don't you come over here and sit down."

"I have to comb my hair out. Have you seen my comb?"

"It's on top of the dresser. Come on, sit down here."

Britt did so, still without a bra, but holding a tee shirt in her left hand, with the comb. She bent over and kissed Marie on the mouth. "Did you sleep well?"

"Yup." *Okay, here goes.* "Listen, I got a letter from Michael in yesterday's mail, and I'd like to read it to you. What do you think of that?"

"Why?" Britt pulled the tee shirt on, which disappointed Marie, though she didn't say so.

"I know you might have to study . . ."

"Shush." Britt interrupted. "That doesn't matter. Why do you want to read it to me? He wrote to you, not me." She began running the comb through her wet hair.

Marie leaned over to her left and pulled the letter out of the drawer and showed it to Britt. The envelope was hefty and dirty from travel; it had been postmarked from Paros two weeks earlier.

"See. I haven't opened it yet. When it arrived, at first I thought I'd wait until sometime when I was alone. Then, I got the idea of opening it with you and reading it to you, so you would know what it says at the same time that I do. You seem curious about him . . ."

"Not really." Britt's voice was flat, uninflected. Uninterested, maybe.

". . . but then . . .?"

"But then what?"

"Nothing. Never mind. Anyway, I want you to know that they aren't love letters. They're mostly about the places he visits, that's all, and I just wanted you to see that. " she shrugged, "I thought maybe we should do it right now. Right here." She felt like she was blushing a little bit.

Britt said nothing, but continued combing her hair, while looking out the window at the Crest.

"Do you have to go to the library? This can wait."

"No, I'm not going anywhere. Go ahead and read it." Her voice sounded strained to Marie and she wondered if she was making a mistake, but she kept on ahead, though she changed her mind and didn't suggest to Britt that she take her tee shirt back off and lie next to her, as she had thought she might a few minutes ago. Britt was looking back into the room, and she maybe she looked sort of interested in what the letter might say. Her expression was hard for Marie to read.

"We can do this downstairs while you get something to eat, if you want to."

"You're chickening out, aren't you? That's okay; whatever you feel like."

"I just want to sit next to you, so you can see the words and I can feel you next to me." Ginger took this moment, having heard their voices, to walk up the stairs and into the room and around the bed to where they were. Britt put down the comb, pulled the dog's head in her lap and began to scratch her ears. Marie opened the letter the short way and pulled out the pages. She began to read: "*April First*, it says, *Paros*. That's the island that he and Emily have been staying on all spring. It's one of what he calls the Kyclades. *My dear Marie. As I look back on the day, it seems that, except for what Dirck said, the colors are what I remember most. Oh, the sun was pleasant and, with it, the warmth, after several days of cold, grey days in which the sun shone through the clouds as if it were the moon, silly sun, thinking it could be the moon. Yes, the sun was warm on the balcony that day and could be taken full in the face.*

"*And the camaraderie was pleasant as well. There were four of us there on the balcony, before Dirck and Femka came—me, Emily, a friend named Tomas and his friend Sophia. There was rambling unhurried talk of art and motorcycles, Bulgaria and Casablanca, Lessing and Durrell. Talk that explored; thoughts that came up short; talk that flowed effortlessly. The best I can describe it is this: like the way Dylan plays the harp on Visions of Joanna. The talk was a bit like the words there, too. Rambling, a little silly, thoughts for the sake of thinking them. But Mona Lisa musta had the hiway blues/you can tell by the way she smiles. I misplaced Dresden, but no one really cared on the balcony in the sun. Yes, the camaraderie was most pleasant and I will remember it, in addition to the colors and, of course, what Dirck said.*

"This is a little more poetic than he usually writes. I wonder what's gotten into him."

Britt, whose eyes were closed and whose hand still gently stroked the dog's ear, said nothing.

"Anyway: *The timelessness was also memorable—or rather it is remarkable that I don't remember the passage of time. An hour or two, I suppose. But maybe only a few minutes? It is hard to put a measure to the time, except that it was time on the balcony, with the sun and the colors. Surely it wasn't a week, was it? Dirck could not have sat still for a week.*

"*But unmeasurable time is nonetheless time—easy time, relaxed time, time felt passing by with one's fingertips. Time that, looking back on it, seems more a soft breeze than something that ticks away. Time, there on the balcony, that could be taken full in the face like the sun, now that the sun was behaving like the sun, and not the moon.*

"*But there's no getting around it: it was the colors, except for what Dirck said, it was . . .*

" *. . .* Wait a minute," Marie interrupted herself, "Let me try that again: *it was the colors, except for what Dirck said, it was the colors that were the most memorable. Bright, sharp colors. Emily's red sleeves moving up and down, up and down, the blue sky, the white buildings. There was no subtlety of color; no lion-dust brown nor bruise grey, that day on the balcony with the sun and time on the face. Unlike the talk, which was full-contoured and indistinct, the colors were bright and cut sharp lines in space. Red. Blue. White. And orange, of course, orange oranges—they were tangerines, in fact, but the rhythm of the word seems wrong just now. As we talked and felt the sun, Emily sent the oranges, up, around and down, . . .* Oh, I see, she's juggling. Did I tell you that she was a juggler?"

"Just read."

*"Emily sent the oranges, up around and down, up, through and down, around, around, up, over. Down, over. The soft smack on her hands, the red sleeves alternating, blue and white behind, orange oranges sailing around, under, up and over.*

*"As I write, I remember the rhythm of the moment, too. Time did not flow, but brushed the cheek like a breeze. The oranges, though, sailed rhythmically and therefore measured, not time, but the moment: up, around and down, up, through and down. Over, over. The oranges seemed to persuade the rest of life to follow the same rhythm. I felt myself breathe in time with the oranges. The gulls swung around overhead in agreement with the rhythm.*

*"I sat on the balcony and watched the oranges and let the conversation lapse, as it did easily, without being cut off. I watched Emily's effortlessness, her non-concentration, the small smile on her lips, slightly parted, the odd, odd look in her eyes, as she looked at none of the oranges individually and yet watched them all. There is some significant aspect of life caught up in juggling, at least it seemed so, that day on the balcony in the sun. Emily looked at the tops of the arcs, but not at her hands, which caught and tossed, caught and tossed. Her hips swayed just slightly in time with the rhythm; now and again one hand would flash behind her back and an orange would sail over her shoulder, back to front, to fall, just as it should, in time, into her other hand. The oranges rose against the white wall of the building across the street, floated across the blue sky and down to meet her red sleeve. Yes, certainly it was the colors that I remember most, that day on the balcony with the sun.*

*"Dirck, a little Dutch kid, and his older sister, Femka walked along the street below and we called them to come up. He watched for a bit as the oranges spun around and over. Puzzlement. Then, "Why are you doing that?"*

They looked at each other, Marie and Britt, did. Marie paused for a while; Britt said nothing, but waited, still stroking the dog's ear. Marie went back to reading. *My, my, we laughed and Emily quit and laughed too and we—all of us, Dirck too, not sure why we were laughing—we ate the tangerines, spitting the seeds back into the grocery sack and we sat with our backs to the whitewashed wall and let the sun brush our cheeks on a warm Greek spring afternoon. And it was then, it was then that I wished the impossible—that you . . ."*

Marie's voice caught a little at the surprising reference to herself. She went on: *that you could have been there with us and I could have said: Tom,*

*Emily, Sophia. This is my friend Marie. Dirck, Femka, this is Marie. And that you could have closed your eyes to the sun, sensed the gulls spinning over your head and felt some of the peace that was there, a peace that you, more than anyone, deserve.*

"I think I'm going to cry. His letters never made me cry before." Marie took a deep breath; Britt reached over and put her hand on her shoulder.

*"And later we would have held hands and walked to the restaurant of Kyriokos to eat and dance and drink sweet wine."* A long pause. *"Michael."*

She had been placing the pages one at a time on the bed, as she read them, on the side of her away from Britt and now she put the last page down, so that the sheets lay there stacked in reverse order, white note book paper with torn spiral edges and a blue scrawl on both sides. They both sat quietly for a minute.

"I guess it *was* kind of a love letter, wasn't it?" Marie's emotions felt like they had been wrecked. "I'm glad I shared it with you."

Britt still said nothing. Her eyes were closed.

"You haven't said anything. What are you thinking?"

Britt looked up. "Feel like a walk?"

Marie was confused but there seemed to be nothing else to say but, "Sure. Let's walk Ginger over to the park. Let me put something else on."

"What's wrong with what you have on?"

"Nothing, I guess," Marie said, shrugging. *I haven't heard that tone of voice before*, she thought.

The day was cool, but warming, as they walked down Manzano to Marquette, west on Marquette to Jefferson, and up Jefferson to Zia School park, a block short of Lomas. Farther south along Copper, and then on Central, the neighborhoods were turning kind of rough and later tonight the park would be busy with drug dealers, prostitutes and college boys patronizing both. Now, though, in the daylight, the setting was friendly and benign.

The park tables were filling up with picnickers, noonish on a nice Sunday in April, so they sat on the grass and let Ginger run, in violation of the posted notices that no one obeyed. Within minutes the dog had found and returned with a stick, which she placed at Britt's feet and waited for it to be thrown. Britt jumped up and obliged. For a long time Marie sat and watched the two of them play; Britt would throw the stick for a while, then run several steps and fake a throw. Ginger would take off in that direction, waiting for the stick to land in front of her. When she couldn't hear or see it, she would return to Britt who would be hiding the stick behind her back. This time she'd throw it and off Ginger would go, never learning the fake, never tiring of the game.

"Attagirl, Trover. Bring it here."

When she brought the stick back, Britt would have to chase her to get her to drop it. They would wrestle on the ground, Ginger growling with a ferocity that no one would ever believe, Britt squealing and yelling for her to let the god damn stick go. Finally, on what would be the last throw, Britt raced after Ginger, who, confused by this new game, kept looking over her shoulder, nearly tripped over her own legs, but still won the race to the stick easily. When Britt returned to Marie, she collapsed to the ground, out of breath and crying.

"I'm not him."

"I know."

"Do you know what I worry about the most?"

Marie was looking down at Britt, who was lying on her stomach picking at the grass with her fingers. It was easy to know she was still crying, but she didn't seem sad. Marie waited for a minute to see if she would go on by herself. When she didn't, Marie asked, "What?"

"That if something ever happened to you, I wouldn't know right away. They'd tell someone else first. Finally someone would say, *Does her roommate know? You know, what's-her-name.*"

"What are you talking about? What's going to happen to me?"

"I don't know. Anything. A car accident. I'd probably find out after the funeral."

"Nothing's going to happen." Marie, who could not figure out what this was all about, reached out and touched Britt's shoulder, looking around to see if anyone was nearby. Britt shrugged her hand away.

"Someday something will happen. It has to. And I want to know about it and hold your hand by the bed but I won't know. They'll tell your parents and your friend Jill and probably even Michael but they won't tell your so-called *roommate* until somebody thinks of it and it's too late." The emphasis on the word *roommate* was angry.

"Britt, you're driving me crazy! What's going on? What makes you think something is going to happen? Christ, I can't figure you out sometimes."

Britt rolled over and sat up; she was no longer crying. "The letter."

"What does this have to do with the letter?"

"Did you ever stop to think what would happen if *he* had an accident?"

"Who? Michael? No. Why? What do you mean?"

"He loves you, you know. Only partly maybe, and not just you, maybe, and only sometimes maybe, but he loves you. And you love him, too. Maybe not the same way that he loves you or you love me, but you do."

"I don't know. I do know how I feel about you."

"That's the point. What happens if he gets kidnapped by terrorists?"

"That's crazy. This whole conversation is crazy."

"No, really. What happens? How do you find out?"

"I don't know."

"I do. You hear about it on the fucking news. That's how. His wife, or whatever she is, hears, and his friends hear, his parents hear, a bunch of fucking strangers hear. But you are his secret lover and you hear on the fucking NBC Nightly News. Think about it. It's true."

"Maybe it is. Why are you angry?"

"Because that's how I hear about you, God damn it. I'm your fucking secret lover. Your secret *lady* lover. Get it now?"

"But what's this have to do with the letter?"

"You do get it, don't you? That's a bullshit question, Marie. You do get it. The letter isn't important. It was a wonderful letter. I wish you were there with him in Greece. I wish I were too. I wish *his* wish would come true and we could all be friends and lovers. Except, of course, the part where you and he disappear from the restaurant and Emily and I sip our wine and wonder what not to say to each other. But it isn't. It won't be. You'll always get long letters and occasional visits and that's okay because it's part of the deal. But when he gets kidnapped by terrorists, you hear about it on the news. And I'm to you like you are to him. And I'm not sure I want to be."

"I can't believe all this talk about terrorists. Don't you think it's a little dramatic? *I'm* not going to be kidnapped by terrorists, that's for sure."

"It doesn't matter what kind of accident, Marie. I won't be allowed to be the grieving widow, that's all. And I'd like to be. I will need that."

"God, how morbid. Besides, you're the one that's used to this kind of relationship. You knew what it was going to be like."

"It was never like *this* before and don't *you* tell me it was."

"You're angry at me because you love me more than you did the others."

"That's right. And go ahead and suggest that that doesn't make sense. I'll . . ."

"You know, Britt, this is crazy. Nothing is going to happen to me. Come on. Let's go home. It'll be easier to talk there."

But Britt just continued to sit on the grass, her feet pulled up and her arms on her knees. And after a minute, she began to talk. "We got a call from the stable one Saturday afternoon the summer I was sixteen. Transnational was acting a little funny and maybe we should come over and check on him. So my father and I got into the car and drove over to see what was going on.

"By the time we got there, he was seriously colicking, nobody knew why, but it was clear that they had waited too long before calling us or doing anything. His gums were pale and he kept lying down and then standing up again, biting at his flanks, all signs of trouble. So we put him in the trailer and hauled him to the vet's."

Marie moved over next to her, but said nothing.

"He stayed there two nights. I stayed with him, but he never got better. By the end, he was having his stomach pumped every three hours, and when the effluent turned bloody, everyone knew it was time to put him down."

"I'm so sorry, Britt."

"Be quiet; I'm talking. It gets worse. My father told the vet that he knew how to do it, and if the vet would give us the chemicals, we'd take T-man down to a friend of his with a farm near Belen, and we'd do it and bury him there. We called my mother, but she didn't want any part of it, so my father and I loaded T up and took him to the farm. I cried the whole way."

Here she paused for a long time. Marie said nothing.

"My father then proceeded to fuck up the job." Britt shook her head and began to sob. "He didn't have a clue, not a fucking clue. He couldn't find the vein in T-man's neck, and injected into the muscle, instead. So, instead of just quietly going to sleep, Transnational felt the pain of the chemical burning into him, and he fought it—and us—every step of the way. Every God damned step. At the end, he was lying on the ground and I was wishing he would die, wishing he would die, wishing he would die. When he finally did, with his eyes open, staring up at the sky, covered in sweat from the fight, I . . ., I . .."

"You must have been so sad," Marie said.

"I wasn't sad. I was angry, so angry I was sick to my stomach for days."

"Angry? Who could you be angry at?"

"Everyone. My father because he said he knew how to do it, and he didn't. My mother because she couldn't find the time to come with us. The stable manager for not calling us sooner. The vet for trusting my father when he said he could do it. Beth for acting like such a goddam grownup when she heard the news. Everyone. Even T, because I was sure he could have fixed it by himself if he had just calmed down. But especially at myself. For letting it happen. No. More than that: for doing it to him."

"You didn't do it to him."

"You don't know anything."

"Why are you telling me this story now? You never would before."

"Because I want you to know how mad I am at you right now. As mad as then."

"But why?"

"Because, if it had been him, and he had told you a story like that, you would have taken him in your arms, right here in Zia School park, and held him, and petted him, and kissed away his tears. But, there you are . . ." Britt looked up at Marie, her eyes red and swollen, "sitting there so quietly, saying that you're sorry. Why aren't you holding me? Huh?"

The flick of Marie's eyes toward the family at the closest picnic table was involuntary and if she could have she would have commanded them to remain fixed on Britt's face.

"Damn it!" Britt stood up. "Come on, Ginger," she called to the dog, who trotted over and allowed herself to be leashed. "Let's go home. But if you think I'm going to bed with both of you, you're nuts."

"What?"

"You put on your sexy little let's-do-it shirt and say *I think I'd like to read Michael's letter to you here in bed while you happen to be half naked. Wouldn't that be a pleasant way to spend the rest of the morning?*" The mocking in Britt's voice was brutal.

"What? Britt, that's not what I meant . . ."

"Ha!"

"I just wanted it to be an intimate time of trust."

"Bullshit. You just wanted to have both of us between your legs. Do you know just how regularly I feel him in bed with us? Do you know how often I think that you are pretending that my hands are his hands?"

"Oh, Britt. Never."

"The other day, when we were talking about how to pick a father for a child. And I said, *well, we could pick a friend*, your eyes lit up like firecrackers. You immediately thought *Michael*, didn't you?"

"For about ten seconds, before dismissing the idea as crazy."

"Just long enough for you to think that, hey, we could dispense with the insertion gizmo, and you could just fuck him for old time's sake. That was his message on the machine the other day, wasn't it? How many times have you talked to him without telling me?"

"None. Not at all. He never called back."

"Right. Do you know how often it seems like you are thinking that if you were with him you could just be a *girl* again? So you wouldn't be *queer* any longer?"

"Are you blaming me for what you're thinking?"

"Do me the favor of denying that I'm right."

"Look, he's part of my life. He used to be a different part. God, I don't know how a brain works, and maybe I was thinking of having you both in bed at once. But I don't *think* I was thinking that. I don't want that, not on any rational level at least. I don't want to be a *girl* again. But I don't want to pretend that I wasn't his *girl*, his secret *girl*. And I was pleased to be. I would have married him, you know, I would have had his babies, I would have gone to Parents' Night at school, I would have gone on his trips with him, I would have done the whole routine, if he'd asked. You would have been a pale-eyed blond that I saw dancing at the Fargo one night while I was sitting after school holding hands with him. Do you want me to deny all of that? That's what would be bullshit. But that's not the way it has turned out. So I'm here in the park, in love with you and arguing with you and he's in Greece with Emily. And I'm not totally comfortable arguing in the park with you, and maybe I'm not even totally comfortable being in love with you and so I looked around to see if anyone was looking before I would take you into my arms and if I were with him in Greece I'd know exactly what the rules were and even if I didn't, the world would cut me some fucking slack and here in the park with you I don't know what the rules are yet and I'm *so* sorry I read you the goddam letter. Come on, Ginger!" Marie jerked the leash out of Britt's hand and walked quickly away. Over her shoulder she yelled, "And I'm sorry I flunked your lousy dyke test." On the sidewalk on Jefferson Street she waited, not looking to see if Britt was following.

When, after a minute, Britt did not appear behind her, she turned and saw her still standing in the middle of the park, too far away to make out what she was doing. "Fuck," Marie said, "Fuckfuckfuck." She stamped her foot. Ginger looked up at her and let her tail droop, waiting to be punished, for what, she did not understand. Marie turned and walked back to where Britt stood.

"Sorry. I shouldn't have said that."

"Forget it," Britt said.

"Jill knows."

Britt looked down at her. "When?"

"The night she called. You know, the other night. Don't give me any credit for bravery, though, she figured it out on her own. She called back after you went upstairs. I lied to you and said it was someone selling siding, but it was Jill. She asked right out. The Greek term was used. I confirmed it."

Britt laughed a little, apparently in spite of herself. "What now?"

Marie shrugged. "I don't know. I'll see her at school; we'll get it worked out."

"I'm sorry."

"No, you're not."

"No."

"It's hard."

"I know that. You just forget that it's hard for me, too. The hard part for you is deciding. The hard part for me is living with you while you decide."

"You make it sound like it's all my fault."

"Fault is not the relevant concept."

"Shit, I hate that. Don't use your law-talk on me."

"Then don't you treat me like a seventh grader."

"What?"

"You heard me."

"Do I?"

"*Do I?*" Britt spat the words out.

"That's ridiculous. I do not. When?"

"Only every day."

"I do not. That's stupid."

"Well, excuse me, but I'm ten miles behind you. I don't know what you were thinking of, but suggesting that we read that letter in bed was the stupidestassed idea you have ever had. I'm sorry, but I couldn't stand it. I should have said so at the beginning. Then the letter itself made me mad at the predicament I was in."

"Why?"

Britt turned and began walking toward home, Marie and the dog hurrying to keep up. They walked along silently for a while before Britt spoke again. "The letter was so effortless. It seemed so easy for him to be sitting on a balcony in the Greek sunshine with Emily, thinking about you. And where are you? How are you? Does he really care? Does he think about how these letters might affect the lives of the people who receive them?"

"I think he does."

"Spare me."

"I know him pretty well, you know. I think you've got the wrong impression. I suppose I'm the one who has given it to you. What do you want me to do after this? When I get letters, should I hide them from you? Should I tell him to stop writing? Don't ask me to do that, please. You don't want me to do that, do you?" Marie's voice had grown soft.

"There. *That's* your girl-voice. Use it with him, not with me."

"Oh, Christ. Shit. What's going on? What do you want me to do? Who do I have to be to please you?"

"I'm not sure what I want. The next time a letter comes, read it and decide if you want to share it with me. But do not make them, or him, part of our relationship. And keep him the hell out of our bedroom. If you want to get fucked, meet him someplace, and do it, for God's sake, and when you get home, lie to me about where you've been. I'll act as if I don't know. Then life will be perfect and we can pretend we're married."

"You're being very mean, you know. Why?"

"So maybe you'll know what it was like to have that letter read to me. Talk about dyke tricks! Reading me a letter from your boy friend is a trick right out of the straight girls' manual."

"A minute ago, I thought you were going to get over being mad."

"I was, but I decided against it. See that asshole, golden boy, frat rat at the next corner. I hope he propositions us so I can personally kick his balls into testicle jam. And if you want to wonder whether I'd be pretending that it was Michael Reid, go ahead and wonder."

"If you think I'm so straight, maybe I'll pick him up." Marie had reached the point where she had no more energy to figure out what to say, but only to say what came to her mind at the moment.

"That's not funny."

"I suppose not."

But the fellow on the next corner did nothing when they walked by, except smile and say "Hi. Need anything?" for he was selling, not buying, and they walked the rest of the way home silently.

When they got home, Britt, without even going inside, said, "I'll be at the law school. Don't wait up."

"Good. Maybe you can find someone there who is sufficiently committed to the cause."

"I don't give a shit about the quote unquote *cause*, Marie." Britt said, getting on her bike. "But it would be nice to find someone committed to *something*. You and he are a quite a matched pair."

She biked off, and Marie said to her back, "And if you're so curious about Michael Reid, ask me yourself; don't have your friend do it," but it was not clear if Britt even heard the comment.

That night Britt slept on the bed in the study, with the door closed.

～

Britt, who had been awake since before five, lay on the bed in the study, listening to Marie get up and ready for work. There had been a quiet knock at the door, but she did not respond, and waited until she heard the back door close and Marie's car start up and drive away down the alley, heading for Lomas and I-40. Then she waited five minutes more before she got up, used the bathroom and wandered downstairs to make herself a cup of Nescafé. While the water was coming to a boil, she stared out the back window, where Ginger was sniffing around the fenced-in back yard, checking for sign of overnight intruders.

When the kettle whistled, she turned back into the kitchen, poured the water into the cup and sat down. They were out of half-and-half, so she dropped milk into the black liquid, watching each drop leave a splotchy mark before settling into the coffee. She put the milk back into the fridge, then walked to the phone and dialed Nikki's number in Tallahassee. The machine picked up—*I'm not here; deal with it*—and she yelled into the receiver, "Arrrrgh," not exactly a primal scream, but a decent approximation of the universal expression of anguished frustration. She hung up, but then immediately re-dialed. *I'm not here; deal with it.* "Don't call back if you're just going to say you told me so," and she hung up again. She sat down, sipped her coffee and looked at the clock. It was just before eight. She had Corporate Finance at ten-thirty. She took another sip of the coffee, then stood up and carried the cup upstairs, where she showered and dressed.

It took her most of an hour to find Michael's juggling letter. First, twenty minutes upstairs, going through Marie's desk and filing cabinet, then the clothes drawers of her dresser, then the linen closet, then through the pockets of all of Marie's jackets hanging in the closet. Downstairs took fifteen minutes, checking in each of the books on the bookshelf, between the albums, in all the drawers in the kitchen, everywhere. Then another ten minutes re-checking the upstairs.

She finally found it, crumpled up and stuffed down the side of the trash can out by the alley in the back. Britt retrieved it, and brought it back inside, where she smoothed the pages out on the kitchen table, toasted herself an English muffin, and made another cup of coffee. She then sat down and read the letter from beginning to end, dunking her muffin in the coffee, which left crumbs sinking to the bottom of the cup, and a rainbowy sheen of butter fat floating on top.

"God damn it, Michael," she spoke aloud, "you're not playing fair."

She looked at the clock again, put on her shoes, grabbed Ginger's leash from its hook on the wall, then walked back to the phone and dialed Nikki's number one more time. *I'm not here; deal with it.* "Never mind," she said, "I'm on my way to the market to buy her flowers. Stop rolling your eyes." She hung up and went out to collect Ginger, who spun in a circle when she saw the leash, and they walked up Manzano to Lomas, and to the grocery market on the corner. At the store, she tied Ginger to the bike rack and walked inside. She looked at the fresh-cut flowers, but in the end walked up to the check-out with a large bunch of asparagus, a pint of half-and-half, and a six-pack of tonic water.

She knew the checker. "Hey, Oliver."

"Hi, Britt. No classes today?"

"Actually, yes. But it looks like, as my friend Keisha likes to say, I'm about to forgo the opportunity offered by Corporate Finance." She checked her watch. "Yes. I won't make it there in time on my bike, and parking will be iffy at this time of day. Besides, I still have something I have to do."

"Corporate Finance? I thought you were in law school."

"I am. It's about the laws governing how a corporation raises operating funds—public offerings, securities, that kind of thing. And what happens when the company goes bust."

"Sounds wretchedly boring. I did hear, though, on the radio the other day, about some guy who made ten million dollars buying asparagus futures." He weighed and entered the price of her bunch.

She whistled. "That's pricey."

"You wanna put it back?"

"Nah. It's for special. Asparagus futures?"

"Yeah. You invest, say, ten thousand today, for the right to buy asparagus next winter as some fixed price. From Guatemala, or something like that. The guy cleaned up."

"Nice idea, if I had a spare ten grand. And if I were a complete idiot. I say use caution, Oliver."

"Don't worry. It's not for me. I sell asparagus; the boss buys it. I don't care for the stuff."

"Acquired taste. Makes your pee stink, too. Okay. Bye."

"See ya around, Britt."

Back home, she invited the dog into the house, where she had a drink from her bowl, then curled up on her bed in the corner of the kitchen. Britt put the half-and-half in the fridge, the tonic in the pantry, and then set the asparagus in a bowl of ice water on the kitchen table. Upstairs, she found a bit of ribbon, and some nice stationery, and back at the kitchen table, she wrapped the asparagus in the ribbon and sat down to write a note.

*Marie.*

She looked at the page, then wrote *Dear* in front. Then she added an exclamation point.

"What do you think, Trov? You know her better than I do. *Marie* or *Dear Marie*?"

Ginger looked up and flopped her tail on the floor.

"What?"

Flop, flop.

"Be bold, you think?"

Flop.

"I think so, too." She wadded up the piece of note paper and began again.

*Darling,*

*I went to the store to buy you flowers, but came home with this bouquet instead. I hope you like them. Maybe you can make that asparagus thing.*

*I won't be home until late—It's that Law Review hand-over dinner at the Hilton on University, and Alex is sure to make a hash of it. I'll get away as soon as it's polite. Wait up for me, will you?*

*I'm a terrible jerk. And I'm sorry.*

*Be mine.*

*Britt*

*P.S. I don't think you should throw the letter away.*

She propped Michael's juggling letter, back in its original travel-worn envelope, against the bowl holding the asparagus, and placed her note in front of both. She then went upstairs, changed into clothes that she could wear to the *Law Review* dinner, put Ginger back outside, locked the house and drove off to school, where she had to park seven blocks away, making her feet sore from walking in her nice shoes, and late for class.

CORRESPONDENCE

The International Airport, Athens
Awaiting Egyptair 774 to Cairo
April Something

Dear Marie,
I saw my friend Anna again, sitting alone in the cafe on Omonia Square. Except this time she had a different face from before and looked alone, but not lonely. Before, it had been the opposite.
    M.

MORIARTY

Tetherball is a game played with no more intensity anywhere in the world than on the Moriarty Middle School playground at lunch time. It is a game played with the intensity of Olympic volleyball and of Final Four basketball; with a good deal more intensity than minor league baseball. The students line up a dozen at a time to play. The winner stays on, the loser goes to the end of the line—no grousing, no dawdling, the maximum number of games must be played in the allotted twenty-five minutes of recess.

At just about the time that Britt was walking to her carrel after Corporate Finance, having stayed after to apologize to the professor for walking in late, Marie stood at the edge of the tetherball court and watched Thomas Edwards win his fifth game in a row. It was good to see him doing something so well. He was not a great reader, she knew from class, and she had once seen him in study hall multiplying 20 times 3 by drawing three rows of twenty little sticks, then counting them all. At tetherball, though, he was a champ. He was tall for the seventh grade and, while not particularly graceful (nor gracious, she noted, as he won his sixth), he had the knack for giving the ball a flick each time it came around, just beyond the outstretched arms of his opponent. It was not easy, Marie knew; she had tried it. As the rope wound around the pole, the ball spun faster in an orbit tilted to ground level and the flicks had to speed up, and the jumps had to precess around the pole or you'd block your own shot and give your opponent a chance to get back into the game. Thomas was good at it, and another challenger, a chubby little eighth grade girl, tasted defeat.

Marie saw Jill, her co-lunchtime-playground-monitor today, leaning against the building, her jacket zipped against the cool April breeze, which came today out of the high mountain snow fields to the north. She seemed to be enjoying the sun and watching some of the older kids flirt, off toward the fence where a little grey-green grass grew. Marie checked her watch; fifteen minutes before class, and enough time to start up a conversation and try to break through the ice.

Jill had been decidedly icy since the phone calls a week or so earlier. They had barely spoken and Jill had found a seat far from her at the last faculty meeting. Now was the time to begin the reconciliation, if there was to be one.

*What the hell*, she thought, *I've got the one who thinks I'm not gay enough pissed off at me, I'd might as well confront the one who thinks I'm too gay. Lesbian,* she corrected herself.

*Straight as the homestretch.*

*I called back to give you a chance to say This isn't what it sounds like.*

What was she going to say? What *should* she say?

She walked over and stood next to Jill, leaning against the school building.

The bricks were warm on her back, from the sun. Jill moved over a bit to make room, but said nothing.

"Talk to you?", Marie said after a minute.

"Sure," Jill said stiffly, "What would you like to talk about?"

"About that I'm not sure if you're my friend anymore. That you haven't spoken to me since the phone calls. That you acted like you were afraid I was going to put my hand on your knee at the faculty meeting last week."

"Why didn't you tell me?"

"I was going to."

"When? On your fifth anniversary?"

"I don't know. I didn't know what to say." Jill started to walk away. "Jill, it's no big deal. Give me a chance to explain." Jill walked back and leaned against the building. They were looking at each other but their voices were low and their faces plain. The children played nearby without noticing them. They might have been discussing the principal's latest edict. Jill spoke:

"If it weren't a big deal, you'd have told me. If it is a big deal, then yeah, I'm worried you'll put your hand on my knee. You can't change the rules like this, Marie, and expect me not to notice."

"It's not like that. It's actually more like a change of key than a change in the rules. C-sharp to B-natural." She paused. "Well, maybe a bit bigger than that. F-sharp?"

"No details, please."

"I'm in love, Jill. It scares the shit out of me, but I am. And I want you to know. I should have told you before now. Before last week. I'm sorry for that; it was a hell of a way for you to find out. I didn't know what to say. But I'm not sorry for her."

"Look. Let's not talk any more just now, okay?" Jill was now looking away from Marie, out over the playground. In the distance the land sloped up and became forested with the small, crooked piñon and juniper trees of the high desert. The back of the Crest could be seen, a little north of west, the only clouds in the sky collecting on the far side of it, over the city. "You're one of my best friends, Marie. I wonder if you know that. I wonder if you know what I have felt like since the other night. If we talk now, I may say something that will change that and I don't want to. So let's just let it lie for a while, okay? I'm afraid to talk now."

"*Deny cert.*"

"Deny what?"

"*Deny cert.* It's a legal expression. Britt uses it. I'm not sure what it means technically, but she uses it for what you just said, as a response to a question that she doesn't want to answer either way right now. *I deny cert on that one,* she'll say. She tells me that it expresses no opinion at all on the question. Just *ask me again later.* Courts do it sometimes, I think."

"Smart girl, this Britt."

"Unhuh." Marie looked out at the children playing. Thomas was on the defense, the rope about three feet long and the ball spinning against him. His shirt tail was out, his black hair hung limp with sweat and his legs had lost their spring. Defeat was imminent. "She's a little ticked at me right now, actually." Jill turned her head away, but Marie went on ahead. "We had kind of a row on Sunday. I was accused of, let's see, *failure to commit to the relationship* I think is the principal beef. If she were a guy, we'd probably be leaning here, I'd be asking for advice and you'd be giving it. Instead, I'm too embarrassed to ask and you're too disgusted to listen. That's what makes it so hard."

"Rodney! Put Rosa down. Right now. Right now, mister! What," Jill said, turning back to look at Marie, "what are you going to tell Herbert?" Herbert Sandoval was the principal of the Middle School. "What are you going to tell the School Board?"

"I don't know."

"Maybe you should have thought of that before now."

"Well, excuse me for not thinking about how the Moriarty Board of Education was going to react while I was in the process of falling in love."

"What are you going to tell them?" Jill gestured with her forehead toward the children playing in front of them.

"Same as I've always told them about my love life. Nothing."

"If you think this is the same as that, then you're delusional, Marie. Totally off your rocker."

"Well, then, what the fuck am I supposed to do?" She bit off the expletive between her front teeth and lower lip, so that it was little more than an expulsion of air.

"Shhh. Calm down. Don't show them that you're upset." Marie took a couple of deep breaths. Jill continued. "Listen. Let's talk later. Just don't . . .," she shook her head. "Never mind."

"What?"

"Don't make me feel like you're looking down my blouse, okay? This world's full of people trying to look down my blouse."

Now Marie was angry, and had to fight back her tears. "Don't be an asshole, Jill." She was speaking too loudly now and some children nearby snickered to hear their teacher swear. She lowered her voice and looked a Jill. "I don't. I don't want to. That's not how it works."

"I don't care how it works, actually. We'll talk more, sometime later. Give me some time, now." Jill moved away, her hands in her jacket pockets and her eyes on the ground. She kicked a stone with her shoe and the stone skipped across the hard-packed dirt of the playground and pinged against a glass Coke bottle lying in the dust. About thirty feet away, she looked back over her shoulder at Marie, who was inspecting a young boy's skinned knee, through the rip in his jeans. Marie looked up and caught Jill's eye and called, "It'll be okay." Jill grinned, apparently at the ambiguity, and answered, "I suppose it will," not really loudly enough for Marie to hear.

Marie was using her handkerchief to get the gravel out of the wound, rubbing, she knew, harder than she really needed to. The boy's tears and the grip of his hand on her shoulder somehow expressed an anger and frustration she couldn't express directly herself. *It's a lousy trick*, she scolded herself, *taking it out on him*, but she kept working at the wound, ungently, until the boy said, "Miss Cochran, it hurts." And Marie said, "I know it does, Cayetano," so she took the boy's hand and walked him to the nurse's station, across the parking lot at the high school. Did her reaction to Jill's confusion have anything to do with Britt's trip to New York with Randolph? Was the fight in the park really over Michael? Did Cayetano's skinned knee have anything to do with the April breeze? She thought not, but who was ever to know for sure?

∿

Thusly, and as was inevitable, the play-ground, the locker-room, the school-bus rumors began. And, as was equally inevitable, initially these rumors were inaccurate as to a couple of key elements: *Miss Cochran has a new boy friend, and Mrs. Westwood doesn't like him.*

∿

That night, Marie waited up, as she had been asked to do, for Britt to come home after the *Law Review* dinner, and later on, when the phone rang, they let it ring. The machine picked up, but it was Nikki calling, and she left no message.

April 18, Agami, west of Alexandria, Egypt. It is 10:00 a.m. or so. My watch is across the room and just now it seems okay to say *10:00 a.m. or so* when in fact it might be much later than that, though not yet noon. The sun is warm and the breeze off the sea is cool.

Dear Marie,

Years and years ago, you, knowing I had been to and liked the Kyklades, told me to read *The Alexandria Quartet.* You said that the books were the most wonderful that you had ever read, or some such impossible praise. I tried several times to read them as the years went by, but never with any success. *Justine* was too poetic for me then; for reasons that I don't suppose you will ever understand, I liked neither poetry nor scotch whiskey in those days.

It makes me feel good, my friend, to tell you now that I read the *Quartet* this spring and they are, like you said, wonderful. Maybe, when you get this, you'll somehow be pleased to know that after all these years my tastes matured, I had the time and, on the last page, I thought about starting again. Didn't, but thought about it. I did, though, buy a shot of quite expensive scotch at the second-class bar on the ferryboat I was riding back to Paros, walked outside into the damp, salty air, and standing on the starboard rail, sent a toast your way. I hope it arrived in good shape.

It was the *Quartet*, partly, that brought Emily and me here. Xmas to Easter on Paros, with jaunts to the north, was all that it might have been, but as April 1st came and went, as the weather turned spring-like only most reluctantly, as the shops and discos, dormant during the winter, opened and prepared for business, as the ferries became daily more crowded, we decided to call it over. We gave up the house and tolerated with good humor, but just barely, the usual goodbyeing. Darley describes a wonderful goodbye from his island in *Balthazar*, but that was before. As April 1st came and went, we foreigners became more and more tourists to the Greeks, or so it seemed to us. So the goodbyes were mostly from the other foreigners, the exception being the little Greek girl Mina, the daughter of our landlord, who held onto my hand and cried. So, we took the ferry north with mixed feelings, and settled in Athens to decide what to do. I spent the time it takes to drink a coffee, or two, sitting on Syntagma Square wondering, as I often do, how long I'd have to sit there before someone I know walks by. One day I'll do just that, I think, but not this trip, for the weather quickly turned cold again, and after only a day or two, we chose the sun and flew to Cairo.

The train to Alexandria was smooth and comfortable; the delta through the window was touched with poverty, but only touched, in my view. I was surprised how unlike other non-Western, Third-World places Egypt seemed to me. More money, less mystery than I expected. Emily, whose memory is worse or whose sensitivity is better than mine, was more bothered. We disembarked at the main station in Alex and found our way to our hotel on the Corniche east of the harbor.

There is no charm to Alexandria. We tried to find it; the *Quartet* was fresh in my memory. But we looked, we walked, we rode trams, we asked around. There is no charm. The Corniche is a busy highway. Cars and buses roar along, horns steadily honking. A walk along the Cornishe is impossible. Worse, it's unpleasant. After the *Quartet*, it didn't seem possible that a walk along the Cornishe could ever become unpleasant.

I mustn't overstate. Alexandria is not a dreadful city. I will ride the bus in tomorrow, partly to mail this, but partly, I'll admit, to have a little time on my own. There *are* post offices in this town where I write, but it will be nice to wander the uncharming, noisy streets alone for a while. But no, Alex is not a dreadful city; I would return to Alexandria next year. I know a hotel, a restaurant, a tea room, a bakery, an English-language cinema. But from the *Quartet* I expected so much: life, conversation, decadence, verve, sex, love, lust, politics, empire, war, evil, love. (Blinded canaries? I'll pass.) But instead there is a rather ordinary big city with an Egypt Air office, a special tourist rate for currency exchange and automobiles that honk as they approach every intersection.

So we rode the bus to here—Agami—a suburb to the west. We had been told of a hotel and a price, but when we arrived it was not so. But we met some boys who helped, drove us about and finally to a friend of one of their friends who rented us a flat near the beach for ninety Egyptian Pounds per week, much more than the house on Paros, but still not much.

There is no charm to Agami. Side by side by side stand high-rise apartment buildings, mostly unfinished, but some occupied. There are enormous piles of concrete, as far as you can see or walk along the beach in an hour. And the beach itself is strewn with tar balls and plastic bottles, the flotsam and jetsam of the modern Med. It all stands empty now, but the heat of Cairo will soon drive people to the sea and the high-rise apartments.

But to us it seems all right. The flat is spacious, the bed enormous, reminiscent of Smith Field (that being an utterly obscure science fiction reference). Scratchy, lo-fi, feedback-prone loudspeakers call the faithful to prayer five times a day at the mosque the next block over. And the sun is so warm. We let it soak through our skin and burn it, and into our bones and innards. It was cold on Paros and now we lie on the roof and tell each other to roll over. When I go downstairs for a beer, the workers constructing the neighboring high rise throw pebbles down at Emily and speak Arabic to her, which does little for her otherwise cheery attitude.

Nearby, on the road to the village center (but don't let your mind conjure up an image of the center of a small village west of Alexandria on the sea, for it's sure to be the wrong image, unless you are more savvy than I about such things, which I doubt) is a small shop which caters to the exotic needs of foreigners: wine, Nescafé, soy sauce, European cheese. The proprietor claims to speak the language of every customer who has ever walked in the door. Farther down there is a butcher shop, a rug shop, a record shop and a travel agent. A bank, a Kentucky Fried Chicken, a pharmacy. We walk in often, past a several-days-long funeral, to shop for food or beer or just to walk.

This letter, I can see as I reread it, has nowhere to go. And that, I guess captures the feeling of this odd place a little west of Alexandria. We are in fact happy to walk in the sun and be warm, to talk about art or politics or what we've seen. To be warm and to read and write. For soon it will be over and we shall head back. First to Cairo, where we have yet to see the pyramids or the market or the Blue Mosque, none of which I expect to be charming. Then we shall split up for a while, as Emily has compositions she's been working on all spring and has somehow arranged bouzouki gigs in a couple of jazz clubs in K.C., how she managed that from Paros, don't ask me. I, more tolerant of the noise and the dirt and the Arab males, and with nothing really to pull be back home until fall semester, hanker to stay on a bit, to see the Sinai and Israel. It's possible, I'm told, to take a series of public buses from Cairo, across the Canal, across the Sinai, and all the way to the Israeli border, which would be an adventure. Or maybe I'll try Cyprus. There's a ferry from Alex to Limassol, and from there a bus up into the mountains, where a certain monastery is said to house an icon too holy to be looked upon. It would be almost worth the trip just to not see it. But one of those is the next stop, and for now, here is enough. And now. A time to savor being here, not the place of the *Quartet* to be sure, but nevertheless here, in a place I never heard of, with my good friend and a man who speaks all languages.

I hope this reaches you, that you are well and that you don't think I'm crazy.

Yours,

Michael.

P.S. What I *really* hanker for, my friend and love, is to see you, to mess up your hair, and to listen to you tell me what's new in your life. It's not impossible that in a few weeks I'll be back in the States and you'll find me on your doorstep.

## ALBUQUERQUE, TALLAHASSEE AND ATHENS

When it's seven in the evening in Albuquerque, it's nine in Tallahassee, and four the next morning in Athens.

⌁

Britt had said that she would be home around eight, without having eaten, so Marie had shopped at the deli counter for dinner: pastrami and rye bread, some nice mustard, potato salad, and she had made cold asparagus with prosciutto and lemon, *that asparagus thing*, as Britt had put it in her note. And a nice Belgian beer, all laid out on the kitchen table waiting.

Now, Marie was upstairs, in the study, looking at the telephone answering machine. She no longer had the owner's manual, but she thought she could figure out what to do on her own, so she turned the knob to *RECORD*, and spoke into the small little hatched area that she thought must be the microphone. "Hi," she said, "Leave a message for Marie or Britt." She turned the knob to *PLAY* and listened. *Hi. Leave a message for Marie or Britt.*

*Yes*, she thought, *that's better.*

～

"Mom, come here." Christina was kneeling backwards on the couch, looking out the front window onto Harvard Court, the cul-de-sac where they lived, walking distance to the law school, backing up to the golf course. Rita walked over and knelt on the couch next to her. Outside, on the twilit street, Richard could be seen walking back and forth in front of the house, apparently talking to himself. "What's Richard doing?"

"I think he's practicing."

"Practicing what?"

"A speech he has to give in New York City in a few days. He has a case before a court back there, and he has to make a presentation to the judges. He's a little nervous, I think."

"Richard is nervous? But he's a professor."

"Professors get nervous, too, you know. Especially when they have to make speeches away from school."

"I've never seen Richard nervous."

"Well, everyone gets nervous sometimes. Remember when you had to tell your class about that book you read?"

"*Ivanhoe*? He's nervous like that? But I'm just a kid."

"Sure, but it still feels the same to be nervous. Even when you're a grown-up. But he doesn't want to bother us, so he's practicing outside."

"What should we do?"

"Well, do you remember what I did when you were nervous about *Ivanhoe*?"

"You made me hot chocolate, and told me that it was going to be all right."

"And I think that's just what we ought to do now, for Richard."

"Do you think he'd like some? Hot chocolate is just for kids, isn't it?"

"I'm guessing that there's nothing he'd like more than for us to make him some hot chocolate and for you to take a mug out to him, and tell him that it's going to be all right. Want to do it?"

"Okay."

"Come on."

Britt, after the sandwiches, salads and beer, and after cleaning up the kitchen, had disappeared upstairs, and the shower had now been running for longer than usual. Marie had settled down, in sleepwear and silk robe, reading *The Economist* in the living room. She heard the water stop running, and soon thereafter, Britt was at the top of the stairs, singing Ruffles and Flourishes: "Runt-ta-da-da-dah-dah. Runt-ta-da-da-dah-dah. Runt-ta-da-da-dah-dah." Then she walked down the steps, wearing a white towel wrapped around her from just above her breasts to just above her knees. "You ready?"

Marie looked up from her magazine. "Ready for what?"

"Ta-da." Britt put her left hand behind her head, with her elbow out to the side. "Bare as a twelve-year-old."

"Congratulations. How do you like it?"

Britt peered around at her own shaved arm pit. "Actually, the look is okay. It's the *idea* that takes some getting used to."

Marie raised an eyebrow. "Shocking. An idea that takes some getting used to? Fancy that."

"Do I detect a feeble attempt at irony in your response?"

"Me? Ironic? I'm sure I don't know what you mean. Three eighteen-B Manzano Northeast. House of ideas-that-take-some-getting-used-to."

"Okay, okay. You've made your point."

"Of course, you do seem to be bleeding down your left leg."

Britt looked down. "Yeah. I nicked my knee."

"Come here. I'll fix it." Britt walked over to the couch. "Put your foot up here," which she did, causing the towel to fall open. Marie pulled a Kleenex out of the pocket of her robe, wet it with spit, and wiped the line of blood running down Britt's leg, then tore off a corner of the tissue, and stuck it to the nick. "There," she kissed Britt's kneecap. "That'll stop it. Actually, you probably could skip your knees anyway. Knees are difficult. You're blond. And see? You've got nothing much to shave above your knees anyway. I would have stopped here, just below the knee." She drew a line across Britt's leg with her forefinger.

"I'll remember that for next time."

Marie looked up. "Next time?"

"We'll see. You want to watch TV, or read your magazine?"

"You watch. I'll read in bed."

"I'll be up before long."

~

Nikki lay in her dark bedroom, falling in love, in a post-coital sort of way. She was feeling just now quite well taken care of, sexually speaking, thank you very much. Connor lay next to her, quiet as a mouse, sound asleep. *Lord be praised*, she thought, *he doesn't even snore.*

She sat up, swung her feet to the floor, and took a moment for her body to adjust itself to the vertical. She was a little light-headed. She shook her head so that her hair fell loose, let her breasts arrange themselves, and felt that curiously pleasant feeling, as she deposited a dollop of his semen onto the sheets. After a moment, she stood up and padded quietly out of the bedroom and down the hall to the bathroom. Standing with one foot on the toilet lid, she cleaned herself up, gave herself an additional dose of spermicide, then, after the customary wait, took out her diaphragm, cleaned it off and put it away. Wrapping herself in her terry cloth robe, she walked into the dark living room, sat on the couch with the lights off, and lit a cigarette.

They had been having sex for about three weeks now, ever since the night after the night when he had read to her over the telephone, the day that she had answered the phone and it had been Anna, who had said *thank you*, the day that Ben had called her a slut and she had walked out, and she had called Connor and he had read to her. When she had felt herself becoming aroused during his reading of the section of the article on the importance of the fresh-water in-flow to the Bay from the Apalachicola-Chattahoochee River System, his baritone in her ear discussing the threat to both the quality and quantity thereof by the rapid growth of the Atlanta metropolitan area, she had felt herself go loose and damp, and she had known that this relationship was going to be consummated, and quickly, and they had begun to have sex the next night.

It had not gone so well, initially. Nikki liked her sex slow and she liked it neat: no music or talk. No drugs or alcohol. No mood-inducing incense or perfumed body oils. No tools, no toys and only ambient light. And slow. It had taken Connor a while to match her pace. And, even less auspiciously, it had taken him longer than it should have to recognize that, in her humble opinion, it was *his* job to match *her* pace and not the other way around. So, they had stumbled around a bit and, the other night, after the trip to Apalachicola and back, when she had sent him home and not let him spend the night, she had wondered what the future held for them.

But tonight. Tonight he had done well. It was mostly, she thought, that he had slowed his hands down. He had very nice hands, large, with soft palms. But tonight his fingertips had been rough, apparently from some work he had been doing around his house, and the rough edges of his fingertips had caught on the skin of her nipples, and had nicely scratched down her spine. But it had mostly been how slow his hands had been, touching, stroking and massaging, so that she had been in a near-orgasmic frenzy before he had paid attention to anything below her navel. And when he had finally entered her, it had been millimeter by millimeter, and had taken the better part of an hour, or so it had seemed to her at the time. And now he slept, quietly, in her bed, nicely exhausted. She might, she thought, just have to marry this guy.

She sat in the chair in the dark room, and thought over the proposition that she was in love with Connor and might have to get married. She thought, too, of her friend Robin, and she shook her head, laughing quietly to herself at the thought of the three messages from Albuquerque she had found on her machine. *The girl's in love,* she thought, *the girl is in love.* But, then, they had always done things in lock-step, and it seemed appropriate that they would be venturing in this direction, too, at about the same time.

She thought, too, of what Anna and Marie's letter-writer had written about the things that matter in life. How had he put it? *Where one goes. What one does. Who one loves and how well.* Indeed. And she wondered what this Michael Reid would think of Ben and Robin and now Connor, and how well each of them was loved, and was to be loved, by Anna, Marie and Nikki. Speaking for herself, and for her best friend, she though he just might approve.

And at this moment, the Utterly Implausible Coincidence became a secret, almost a conspiracy, between her and Michael, whom she had never met. She felt close to him, and in a special, anti-Copernican, way. It was only she and he who knew both Marie and Anna, though admittedly, she knew them only indirectly, through Robin and Ben. But no one else knew of this triangular—no, quadrilateral—no, polygonal relationship at all, just she and Michael. And the insight he had shown in his letter, insight into both love and baseball and into life in general, had bound her to him in a way that she felt like sharing with no one. No one at all.

"God help all of us," she said aloud, as she got up from the couch, put out her cigarette, and walked back toward her bedroom. Then, on second thought, she returned to the bathroom, re-inserted her diaphragm, because, well, one never knew, and, back in the bedroom, dropped her robe to the floor and slipped in, under the sheets, and next to her new love.

$\sim$

Ben sat alone in his study, with the book he wasn't reading resting in his lap, thinking about the events of two days before, and what he was going to do about them. Rachel had called Nikki *Mommy*, which had, in turn, sent Janet running in tears to her room, while Sam sat quietly in a chair, ostensibly reading.

Nikki, damn her, had known exactly what to do. First, she had dropped to her knees, taken Rachel in her arms and laughed it off. "No, no, honey." She pointed to her own chest. "Nik-ki. Nik-ki." She then had taken Rachel's little hand, made a tiny fist with her index finger sticking out, and tapped her own chest with the finger. "Nik-ki. Nik-ki. Nik-ki," until Rachel had managed something close to *Nikki*. Then she had tousled her hair, said "That's right. Nikki," had stood up and patted her on the butt. Then she had walked to the hallway, silently laying her hand on Sam's head as she passed him by, and knocked on Janet's door. "Take a ride with me."

And the two of them had left the house, without another word spoken, to Ben or anyone, and climbed into Nikki's Saab, parked in the street. Two hours later they had returned, walked hand-in-hand through the front door, both their faces smeared with ice cream, across the living room and down the hall to Janet's room. Passing Ben, Nikki had said, "We won't be hungry for dinner; you're on your own," and nothing else, and then they had closed Janet's door behind them. And for the rest of the night, they had stayed in there together, with talk, music, laughter and maybe crying heard through the door. When it was time for Nikki to leave, she and Janet had hugged at Janet's door, the little girl had gone back inside her room, but had left the door open, and Nikki had said to Ben, on her way out the door, "Pretend like it never happened. Goodnight." And she was gone.

And now, two days later, he sat in his study, listening to Sam and Janet divide up between themselves the chores relating to getting themselves ready for bed, and getting Rachel up and ready for Mrs. Lutz in the morning, and wondered how his well-ordered life had become so completely out of his control.

$\sim$

From her hotel room in Athens, Anna watched the sky begin to lighten. She had been up all night. Working. Working on mathematics, from memory, the first time she had done so since leaving home. Her brain still worked, and now she placed on the desk in front of her a postcard she had bought, with an aerial photograph of Omonia Square. On the back, she wrote one equation, the result of the night's work, an equation that promised, at the very least, to make Jablonski's second transformation a special case of its more general proposition, and perhaps, even, a trivial result. She would have to see.

She addressed the postcard to herself, at the post office box in Tallahassee, the box that contained nothing other than her wallet, an envelope with the key to the box itself, and the junk mail that had accumulated during her stay in Greece. She then let herself out of her room, walked downstairs and through the silent lobby and out the door. She would walk the empty streets of the Plaka, watching the old town wake up, she thought, have herself an early breakfast, and mail the postcard when the post office opened.

# ~ 16

## ALBUQUERQUE AND NEW YORK CITY

I t was early Wednesday morning, on the day Britt was to leave for New York City and Marie lay in bed waiting for the alarm to go off. Britt was still asleep, far on her side of the bed, on her stomach with the blanket pulled up over her shoulders and her feet exposed and draped off the end. Her face was turned away from Marie and toward the open window. Outside, it was that early morning grey light when, back east, early risers wonder if it is overcast or not and can't yet tell. In the desert, the same color is seen, but one never confuses it with soon-to-drizzle overcast. Marie stared across the bed and out the window toward the Crest, invisible in the dark. The alarm would go off in twelve minutes. She reached over and pushed the plunger in. She'd wait a few minutes and wake Britt.

She had not really been awake long and it would not be right to say that she was uneasy about Britt's trip. The best she could say was that she felt peculiar. Out of sorts. She had felt a little peculiar ever since she had been sick at the restaurant two, closer to three, weeks earlier. She had felt ill at ease ever since the phone calls and playground conversation with Jill. She had felt unsure of herself ever since the fight in Zia School park. Sure enough, the fight had cured itself in ways indistinguishable from fights with other lovers in the past, some in parks, some not, with mutual apologies and multiple orgasms, but with little settled, and even this similarity had surprised Marie a little. The surprise unsettled her, too, and she wasn't sure why. She didn't know how to feel, that was the problem, she thought, as she stared out the window. She could just make out the outline of the Crest. She didn't know how to feel. She fell back asleep.

This was her dream: she is in a large room with tables and chairs. A café. Maybe a restaurant. She doesn't know the place. The room is occupied by everyone she has ever known. Her friends stand in small clusters representing different eras of her life. The conversations are cacophonous. She is a character in the dream, as well as an outside observer, usually from above, like a Rod Serling camera angle.

She is calm and still. She is sitting at a small table and her friends drift past. They chat. They smile. Life goes on. She thinks about getting up from the table and introducing to each other her various friends who are strangers, but she doesn't.

Later in the dream she is alone, sitting on a log in dusty cowgirl boots, jeans, a dirty red hooded sweatshirt and a Moriarty Pintos baseball cap. She recognizes the spot, in the Gila, high in the ponderosa pines, off the side of the Forest Service road, with a windmill nearby pumping water for her and the range cattle. She can hear the wind in the pine needles above her head and the buzzing of the flies and the end-of-the-day busyness of the birds and the grate of a flying grasshopper and nothing else. Humanity is silent here. The crackle of her campfire is the only noise human-made.

It is dusk and her campfire burns with bright flame and black smoke of the years-old and desert-dry resinous pine. She sits by the fire alone and wonders what happened to her friends. For a moment, she fears that she has built the fire too large and that she will start a devastating forest fire and get into trouble, but then the fire settles down and she relaxes. The light fades and the flame of the fire flickers out and the moon rises and she sits by the coals until the dream, too, dies away.

⌒

"Marie." Britt was shaking her shoulder. "Don't you have to get up? You're going to be late for school. Marie."

Marie opened her eyes and it was full daylight. "What time is it?"

"Seven forty-five. What happened to the alarm?"

"Oh, I turned it off and went back to sleep." Marie stretched. "Are you going to be late?"

"No, I'm not going to class today. And Randolph and I don't leave for the airport until nine-thirty. I've got time." She flopped on her back. "I slept *good*." She yawned.

"I didn't even hear you come home last night; it must have been late."

Marie rolled over and put her arm across Britt's chest and kissed her on the mouth. "Yuck. You were smoking."

"Only a couple. C'mon, get up. You've gotta get going. You take a shower; I'll fix you coffee. Come on. Be the breadwinner."

Marie stuck her tongue out and staggered to the bathroom, peed, brushed her teeth in the shower and washed her hair, while Britt cleaned herself up in the sink, wiping the mirror clear of the steam. Marie knew, in fact, that there was no hurry, but she wasn't going to tell Britt that. She dressed in a springy yellow skirt and red sweater, dried her hair and went down to breakfast.

"Shouldn't you call and tell them you'll be late?"

"Relax." She put her right hand on the side of Britt's jaw and kissed her again. This time, toothpaste. "There's an assembly first period so no one will notice that I'm late. Are you all packed?"

"Yup. I can't have forgotten anything; I've packed everything I own. I changed my mind three times yesterday on that blouse, so I'm taking both. If you were there tomorrow, you'd tell me which one to wear. I'm going to miss you."

"Me, too." Marie reached across the breakfast table and held both her hands. "Give the Second Circuit the what-for; heroically protect the interests of the moneyed class; remember me to Herald Square. What's secret number one?"

"Be confident."

"And are you confident?"

"Yes."

"Good. Then no need for secret number two." Marie squeezed Britt's hands. "Now, I gotta go. Bring home the blue." She gulped her coffee down, kissed her lover once more, they touched five fingertips, right to left, and she was gone.

Marie drove up Manzano Street, turned right on Lomas and stopped at the gas station at the corner of Lomas and San Pedro. It was going to be a warm, sunny spring day. She filled the tank, then went inside the convenience store, called her principal and said she was ill and wouldn't be in. Back in her car then, she headed east on I-40, into the canyon to Tijeras, and drove up to the top of the Crest.

It was cool so high up in the morning air. The tall pines shaded the west ridge overlooking the city and a light dew lay on the grass. Marie changed into sneakers and walked along the trail, heading south, the city on her right. Below, last evening's showers had left the arroyos wet and they looked like strands of silver heishi strewn from the bottom of the Crest all the way down until they were lost in the irrigated green of the city. She came to a small meadow she knew and sat on a boulder, watching the wild flowers and listening to the breeze in the high pines.

She didn't know how to feel, that was the problem. She wished Michael were here. She had never known how to feel about him either. They had never talked about themselves. They had talked about their relationships with others, about herself or himself, about life and love, but never about them, together or apart. Then why did she wish he were here? Why had she come here, to this place, on the day that Britt was flying to New York City? She and Michael had once come here, had a picnic and talked for hours. Why had she known this morning in the early grey, between wakefulness and the dream, that she would play hooky and come to this place? What was this all about? What had it been about all along?

She didn't know how to feel. How does one feel when one's first woman lover flies off to a challenging career with a man, a man in front of whom Marie had gotten sick, like a child? A man that unsettled her, who seemed, she didn't know, mysterious, in a very subtle way. Mysterious in a way, she suspected, that no one felt but her. A mystery that Britt surely did not see and Marie had only sensed in the hour or so she had spent with him. And how does one feel when one's best friend is afraid you'll make a pass at her? Were there no guidelines? What would Michael say? "It's none of my business who you are in love with. Or sleep with. Or her gender. Sentences that begin with *it's none of my business* are almost always true."

"This *is* your business, Michael." She whispered it, just barely aloud, and she began to sob, quietly, alone in an Alpine meadow, high above a desert city. The last-quarter moon, a week before new, was ahead of the sun, invisible, but made some early morning Eastern sky, somewhere, lovely. "If I just knew where you were; if I knew which way to look."

There was, she came to realize, nowhere to look. There was only the meadow and the dewy wild flowers, the pines and the city below. A memory of an afternoon here with Michael and a memory of a smoky kiss that morning. There was Beirut and Moriarty, Jill and her students and this Richard Randolph and her strange feeling about him. All of these were the galaxy's forces, pulling her, pushing her gently this way and that. She felt like a sea frond, swaying in the tide. Like a woman sitting in a café, watching her friends pass by. This place, though special, was not where she should have come this day; she shook her head and dried her eyes; there were no answers here. There were only wild flowers, and over there long ago she had thought herself a little in love with a man, a man who was no longer here. She sat for a long time with her eyes, now dry, closed and her hands folded in her lap.

Eventually, she walked back along the trail and stood at the look-out, leaning on the rail, watching the city below. She thought for a minute that she might drive on to Moriarty, teach most of her classes and waste the district whatever little money it paid substitute teachers. Maybe Jill would like to go out for a beer after work. No, she was hardly in the mood to do all that that would require. She would just go home. To what? To the way it had been when she lived there alone? To wait for a letter? For a call? The problem was that she didn't yet know how to feel about all this, all this swaying. She needed someone close, and they were all far away, and she was alone.

Off to her left, far below and several miles away, she could see the airport and she watched as a plane took off, banked right, all the way around and headed west, maybe for Phoenix or L.A. It was strange to see the planes from above; it was like she caught them by surprise, rising silently, clumsily, exposed, their backs naked and usually out of view. She looked at her watch, and it occurred to her that Britt would just now be sitting on a plane soon to take off; she watched a few more. Two headed east, to Dallas, maybe, to connect to New York, but she couldn't catch the markings. Marie imagined Britt sitting in the plane and she felt a center-shift. To her the Crest was fixed and the plane moved. She let herself see through Britt's eyes and the airplane was the center and the Crest moved.

That was the place, down there, she knew, that was the place where movement and stability both lived, where Britt and Michael would both be near. She got back in her car and drove down into town and to the airport.

∽

It was true; that's the way it was. Britt, in a left side window seat, watched the Crest as it crawled past. Then they were over the plains. She looked down, trying to spot Moriarty and the school, but she couldn't; it was on the other side of the plane.

∽

Marie and Michael sent each other postcards from airports, writing on the back the words to whatever song was adrift in the cortex. She bought a card with a picture of Dukes Stadium and wrote: *Every light is on but all the rooms/ Are empty except one.* She did not sign her name; he would know from whence it came. It was not meant that he should understand the message; that was part of the idea.

After she mailed the card, she called her tenants and said she had to rush out of town on an emergency and would they look after Ginger until she got back? "Oh, no. Everything is okay, but Britt is gone, too. I should be back on Saturday." Then she bought the *New York Times* and drifted down to the departure lounge, where she read and watched the people come and go.

~

"Well," Richard said to Britt, on the curb in front of the Algonquin Hotel after they had checked in and unpacked, "we have the last of the afternoon and an evening to play. Tomorrow morning we practice one last time, then we argue. What shall it be?"

"My choice?"

"Your choice entirely."

"No, you. I've never been to New York before, and I wouldn't know where to begin. You pick; show me something special."

"Okay, the Empire State Building it is. We can walk." He led her across 44th Street, south on Fifth Avenue, to 34th Street, where they leaned back and looked up, tourists that they were. "Want to see the lobby?"

"Sure."

"It is considered more sophisticated to prefer the Chrysler Building to the Empire State, but . . ."

"But that's why you prefer this one."

"You're beginning to get to know me."

"Reverse snobbism? Like insisting that students not call you Dr. Randolph?"

"Well, I'm not crazy about the *snob* part, but yes. Want to ride up to the top?"

"Nah. That's not something the sophisticated do."

"Okay. Now are you ready for your turn?"

"Come on." She bolted to the right, and ran outside to 34th Street, then down to Fifth Avenue; she was a half block ahead of him and gaining before he turned the corner, dodging pedestrians and yelling over her shoulder at him. At the next corner, she stepped into the street, held up her hand and flagged a taxi, just like she knew exactly how to flag a taxi. *I wouldn't be at all surprised*, he thought, *if she can whistle through her fingers.* By the time he caught up, an empty one was approaching. Richard was out of breath.

"What the hell?"

The taxi stopped, she opened the rear door and said, "Get in." She climbed in after him. "Grand Central Station and step on it," she said. The cab sped away. She sat back in the seat, stretched her legs out and folded her arms over her chest. She looked very pleased.

"Where are we going?"

"That's it."

"That's it?"

"That's it."

"*Grand Central Station and step on it*?"

"I've always wanted to do that." He started to laugh and she did, too. "I've seen it done in the movies."

"That is the craziest thing I have ever heard of. That's it? That's what you want to do in the City?"

"That's it for now. Your turn again."

"Well, how was it?"

"It was great. Everything I imagined it would be. Hoopla!"

"Hoopla?"

"Yeah. It means *hooray*."

"I know what it means. I just didn't know anyone used it but me."

"Really? I never heard it until recently. My roommate uses it. Where's it come from?"

"I'm not sure." Richard thought for a minute. "It's German I guess. I picked it up from the Three Penny Opera. Pirate Jenny says, let's see, . . . *da, da, da*," he tried to find a starting point, "*. . . and when all their heads fall off, I'll say Hoopla!*"

"Pretty cheerful."

"Jenny had a rough life."

"Huh. Well, anyway, we're here."

The trip was short and the driver took the small fare without comment.

Richard tipped him heavily and Britt winked at the cabby and said, "Thanks." He drove off without a word.

"He didn't bat an eye," Richard observed.

"He's probably an actor, practicing dead-pan," she said.

"Dead-pan Pakistani, too?"

"Don't be so provincial."

They walked around and through the terminal, while Richard explained that Grand Central was a *terminal*, not a *station*, because it was the end of the line. "Penn Station is a station."

"Who cares?"

They walked outside and looked at the south facade and he told her about the litigation that had surrounded its preservation. He was hard pressed, though, to match her choice. Alone, he would have gone up to the Bronx and paid his respects to Yankee Stadium, but that was a rough part of town now and he wasn't sure he wanted to take her up there. So, heading nowhere in particular, they walked up Fifth Avenue and into Central Park, at first hardly talking, not forcing a conversation over the racket of the traffic. The park was quieter, but no topic seemed to catch until they walked past the Dakota, where John Lennon had been shot. Then they began telling Beatles stories and enjoyed comparing their two very different experiences, as he had been in high school when *I Want to Hold Your Hand* hit the charts, and she had been in grade school. The talk came more easily as they headed up Central Park West.

Marie's name slid in and out of the conversation, and Britt spoke of her in a way that was both discreet and all the while unambiguous. She called Marie her *roommate*, and never actually said they shared the bedroom of the duplex, but neither did she go out of her way to suggest that they didn't. At one point, emboldened by the spring day, and an hour's comfortable conversation, Richard told her of the image he had of Marie in a seventies-era indie rock and roll band.

"Wrong image," Britt said, "she was an athlete in college. A swimmer. Let me see . . ." She squinted one eye and brought an item up from memory, "she was NCAA Division III champion her junior year in the four-hundred meter individual medley. We call that the *four-hundred I-M*, if you want to know. I really should remember her time. Seems like it was four minutes and something. Is that possible?"

"Beats me. What happened her senior year?"

"She got hurt. Pulled a muscle. Made the finals, but didn't place. Wait. I've got it. Four-twenty-eight-twenty-six."

Richard shrugged. "Sounds impressive, I guess. *Champion* is the key word. How old is she?"

"About like you, I'd guess. When did you graduate from college?"

"Sixty-five."

"And she graduated in sixty-nine. She's a little short of forty."

"And you're around thirty. That's not too bad, not too much of an age difference."

Britt said nothing and they walked on a while.

"How long have you . . ."

Britt interrupted to answer, "We've been together about six months."

"No, I meant *you* singular. How long have you been . . . with women?" His voice faded a little at the end.

"You don't know me well enough yet to ask that." She said it matter-of-factly, without looking at him and still walking.

He was embarrassed, primarily, he supposed, because what she said was true. He hoped the *faux pas* wouldn't ruin the mood. "Sorry." He looked across at her and couldn't read her expression. "I don't know what made me ask."

"It's called *prurient interest*. No First Amendment protection." She looked at him and smiled.

"Can you cite a case for that proposition?"

"You bet. Miller *versus* California. Nineteen seventy-three."

"Impressive. You may pass the bar exam yet. But why couldn't it be *friendly* interest, not *prurient*?"

"Because if you were walking through Central Park with a gay male student, you wouldn't have been interested."

"How do you know that?"

"Shot in the dark. Come on, let's change the subject. Ask me again later. Maybe I'll feel like telling you my life story."

"Okay, sorry. So what do you think the Dodgers' chances are this year?"

"Baseball? Well, what could be less prurient than that?"

"You don't follow the game, do you?"

"Not really. But my best friend does. And she says I should."

"Listen to her. You should."

"Why? Baseball is a metaphor for life, blah, blah, blah?"

Richard laughed. "Okay, some people do get carried away a bit. But, no. I was thinking more along the lines that baseball is the only game compatible with napping."

"As in *boring*?"

"No, no. It's only boring because you don't understand the finer points of the game. And that's true of every sport. There's probably some sport that you find fascinating, but that I would find boring because I don't understand it."

"Dressage."

"The *perfect* example. So, no. What I meant about baseball being compatible with napping is that it's the only game known for which one can plan an afternoon around falling asleep in front of."

"A person can fall asleep in front of anything, if tired enough, no?"

"Sure. But it's only baseball about which one finds himself saying, *I think I'll mow the lawn after lunch, then the game's on at two and I'll be asleep in the recliner by the fifth inning.* It becomes part of the afternoon's schedule. No one would ever *plan* to fall asleep in the third quarter of a football game."

"So, you think I need to nap more? Why?"

"It slows you down."

"And you think I need to slow down?"

"Anyone your age who doesn't need to slow down isn't moving fast enough."

"Does that make sense?"

"I think so."

"I'll have to share the thought with Nikki. By the way, she told me to tell you that she once saw a five-two double play. Whatever that is. She thought it would impress you."

Richard whistled appreciatively. "A third-to-home double play. I've never seen one."

"I think that's what she said. Maybe not. Maybe I got it wrong."

"No, let's see. Score tied in extra innings; bases loaded; infield in. Grounder close to the bag at third. Five steps on the base, then comes home to Two, to prevent the run from scoring. The force is off, so the catcher has to tag the runner trying to score. Probably would have been better if the third baseman hadn't stepped on the base, thrown home for the force, then taken the throw back from the catcher for the force at third. Which would be five-two-five."

Britt shrugged her shoulders. "Beats me. I'll ask Nikki next time I talk to her. Wait. There's a taxi. Let's grab it. I want to see Washington Square."

They spent the rest of the afternoon touristing around, window-shopped in the Village and saw George McGovern walking along Fifth Avenue, looking grey-suited, grey-haired, successful and taller than Richard would have guessed. When they returned to the hotel, they looked like an out-of-town couple, foot-weary and loaded down with souvenirs.

They had an early dinner at an Italian restaurant near the hotel, and then a drink in the lobby of the Algonquin, a confident and optimistic toast, and Richard walked Britt to her room.

"See you in the morning," he said.

"Are you nervous?"

"You'll be great."

"Good night."

Inside, Britt tried to call home, but the machine picked up. *Hi. Leave a message for Marie or Britt.* After the beep, Britt spoke. "Oh, Marie! What a nice surprise! I love the new message. Thank you. Thank you. What a treat. Listen, I'm sorry I missed you. Everything went smoothly, though the plane was a little late leaving Dallas. We spent this afternoon seeing the sights, and had a nice dinner. You wouldn't believe the rooms in this hotel! They're *tiny*. Okay, I'm going to go now before I get cut off by the machine. Maybe you're out walking Ginger. Don't call back, okay? I'd love to talk, but I'm going to take a shower and go to sleep early. I think Randolph is nervous. Can you believe it? Okay, bye. Love you."

～

"That's the last flight, Miss." The Delta gate attendant was closing up for the night. Marie had struck up several conversations with him as the day had unwound. He had been pleasant and a little flirtatious, but she hadn't minded. Twice she had found ways not to tell him her name. She wasn't sure what he would say now. She said:

"I think I'll sit here a while longer; I'm at an interesting place in my book. Do you think anyone will mind?" She had already been there ten hours.

"No, you can't stay here. They're about to close this concourse." *He thinks I'm crazy*, Marie thought. *He'll stop flirting now.* "But if you're still waiting for someone, the main lobby outside the ticketing area stays open all night. Come on; I'll show you."

They walked down the B-concourse into the main departure lounge; a metal grating clattered shut behind them. "Here," he said, "you can watch as the flights come and go on the departure board. Okay? Are you sure you're all right?"

"I'm fine, thank you. Good night."

"Good night," he said and walked across the departure lounge. He glanced over his shoulder as Marie found a seat, and, once out of sight, told the security guard to look after her. She made herself comfortable on a long bench, with her back to a pillar, arranged her skirt around her legs and opened her book. She felt very peaceful.

Later that night, after midnight, Albuquerque time, Marie wandered down to a pay phone, said hello to a janitor emptying the trash cans, and got from information the number for the Algonquin Hotel in Manhattan. She charged the call to the home phone.

"Good morning," the desk clerk answered promptly. "Algonquin Hotel."

"Hi. Could I leave a message for one of your guests?"

"Do you want me to ring the guest's room?"

"Oh, no. It's too late and I don't want to disturb her. Could you just leave a written note for her in the morning?"

"Of course. What is the guest's name?"

"Britt Larsen. L-A-R-S-E-N. I don't know her room number."

"That's all right. And the message?"

"Good luck. Love, Marie."

"*Good luck. Love, Marie.*"

"Yes, that's right."

"And will there be anything else?"

"No, thank you. Good night."

"Good bye."

⌒

Britt and Richard met in the hotel lounge for a light breakfast in the morning, then found an unoccupied conference room, where they went over their arguments one more time, this time with no one playing the judges, just their own presentations, delivered straightforwardly and without interruption.

At the end, Richard said, "Well, if it goes that smoothly, we'll have done well. You want some lunch?"

"You start without me. I'm going to take a walk. There'll be time to get dressed after lunch, right?"

"Right. Okay, see you there. I think I'm going to call my wife, first." They split up, Richard up to his room and Britt out the front door of the hotel.

Britt was a no-show for lunch, which worried Richard a little. He was just finishing up his second cup of coffee, and looking at his watch, when she walked into the lobby.

"Where have you been?"

"Am I late? I thought there was still plenty of time."

"We're okay, but you're going to have to rush to eat and then get dressed."

"I think I'm going to skip food. My stomach is a little iffy, maybe from the pasta last night."

"Where did you go?"

"I've been walking around Grand Central. What an amazing place! There are nooks and crannies that you wouldn't believe. Well, maybe you would. But all kinds of shops and restaurants, trains coming and going, subways, commuters, tourists, pan-handlers, school children. It's incredible. I sat for a long time in the departure lounge, just watching the people coming and going, before I discovered the ceiling. Have you looked at the ceiling?" He nodded. "It's become my current favorite place in the world. Well, I haven't seen all that much, except for the various sites we dug in the Southwest. I'll tell you this: there's nothing like Grand Central in Albuquerque. Did you know it's a *terminal*, not a *station*, because it's the end of the line?"

"I've heard that, yes."

"Penn Station is a *station*. That coffee looks good. I'll have a cup, then go up to dress."

⁓

Early Thursday morning, Marie called Jill from the airport, catching her at home, before she went to school.

"Hi, it's me."

"Hi. Where were you yesterday? I saw that Allison was in your room as a substitute."

"Yeah, I've got a bug of some kind. The doctor says it's going around. He says I might be contagious, and so I'm going to miss today and tomorrow, too. Would you do me a couple of favors?"

"Sure."

"Tell Allison that my lesson plans are in the top drawer of my desk. There's nothing that she shouldn't be able to handle. The Civics class . . ."

"Wait a minute," Jill interrupted. "Let me get a pencil." She was gone for a minute. "Okay. Lesson plans in top drawer. Go on."

"The Civics class is expecting a quiz tomorrow, but I'll just push that over to next week. And Alan Bostwick does *not* have library privileges. *Not*. He'll try to hoodwink Allison, but tell her not to let him."

"Got it. Anything else?" The announcement of the boarding of American 1543 came over the airport PA system. "What's all that noise? Where are you?"

"Oh, I'm filling a prescription at Walgreens and someone is looking for a lost child or something. There, is that better?"

"I can hear you, but why didn't you call from home?"

"I don't know. It hit me while I was here that I should call you before you left. I'd rather have you take care of this for me than anyone in the office. So, that's all I can think of. Tell Herb that I'll be back in on Monday. I can't think of anything else." There was silence on Jill's end of the line for a moment, as if she were thinking about how to say something. "Okay? My prescription is ready, so I'd better go."

"Marie?"

"I'm here."

"Bob and I wondered if maybe you and Britt would like to come over for dinner sometime. Just the four of us. Nothing fancy. After you feel better, of course."

"I feel a little bit better already. Yes, we'd like that. Thank you, Jill. Yes, we'd like that."

"Well, get home and get to bed. I'll see you next week and we can make some plans."

"Okay. Bye." Marie hung up the pay phone, smiled to herself, then found her way to a restroom to wash up.

~

When Richard tapped on Britt's hotel room door a half-hour later, she answered immediately. "Well, I'll be damned," he said, "you did it."

"What do you think?" She turned from the door and walked away from him to the middle of the room, then turned back. "Do I look like a lawyer?"

"One hundred percent."

She did. Her wide shoulders held the suit well. The short heels on her shoes seemed to make her hold her shoulders back and she was his height, or maybe a little more. The collar of her white blouse was buttoned at her neck and would have been a bit too large on a man, but the looseness was attractive on her.

"I don't often dress like this," she said, "if you want to know the truth."

"Some things do go without saying. Are you okay with it? This is not the time for you to be losing your convictions, my dear. We need strength and determination in the courtroom today, not doubt and equivocation."

"Well, so much for that." She pulled her skirt against her knees and looked down at her feet. "Marie had me shave my legs. I feel like a teenager."

"You look nice, and you do *not* look like a teenager. But how about those bracelets? If they jingle when you gesture, it may be distracting."

She took the silver bracelets off, then put one of them back on. "For good luck. Man, I could use a cigarette."

"I can't help you, but they have some in the lobby."

"That's all right; I was made to promise I wouldn't. When do we have to leave? I was just going over my argument again." Her bed was made and her notebook was open on the foot.

He checked his watch. "Forty-five minutes."

"Okay. Go away. I have to use the bathroom. I'll meet you in the lobby in a half an hour. Oh. You look nice too."

Richard rode the elevator to the lobby, bought the *Times* and sat in one of the comfortable chairs near the front, hoping to see someone literary. What had happened up there just now that made this feeling of misgiving?

～

The courtroom of the United States Court of Appeals for the Second Circuit, in the Federal Courthouse in lower Manhattan, was intimidating, even to Richard and he had been in that very room before. There was no audience to speak of, only a few lawyers awaiting later cases and a bored newspaper reporter or two, but the courtroom presented the aura of *the law* as no room in the friendly confines of the law school in New Mexico ever could. The high ceilings, the portraits—there was Learned Hand, for God's sake—the bailiffs, court reporters, functionaries, the marble floors against which their heels clicked, the very dimensions of the room. The lectern was so much farther back, the bench so much higher than at home. Richard was going to comment on the feel of the place, but when he looked at Britt as they arranged their papers on the right hand counsel table, he held his tongue. He saw she felt very small. *Holy shit*, he thought, *she is scared to death*. Richard had known, though she denied it, that she would be nervous and he had tried, with all the practice and role-playing, to prepare her for it. But nervous was not the same as frightened. Who could have guessed that a bright, composed woman like she would ever be frightened? But there she was, looking small. Her suit, honest to God, suddenly looked a size too large for her. When you see a woman like Britt Larsen feeling small, you should know, you should call it off right now. But, no, he couldn't do that. *God help us*, he thought.

The judges came in, everyone in the courtroom stood, then sat down.

While the lawyers on the other side were addressing the court, Richard found himself engaged in a feverish juggling act. He, too, felt the aura of the place and he had to calm his own nerves. At the same time, he had to keep an ear tuned to the arguments of the opponents. As the appellees in the case, the ones whose victory was being appealed, Richard and Britt would speak second, and they would lose that advantage if they didn't keep their wits about them and shape their arguments to attack the other side's weaknesses. He wrote *$14,000,000.00* on the top of his note pad to remind himself what, exactly, was at stake here and tried to concentrate. But on top of this all, he had to keep an eye on Britt and do what he could to help her manage her fear.

Britt was to speak first for their side, which might have been a tactical error, Richard now realized. The plan called for her to begin by re-addressing the facts of the case, to emphasize those that they anticipated the other side would play down, and to get the judges to see the case in a light favorable to the Bank of Commerce. So they conversed very quietly while their opponents spoke to the judges, deciding exactly how she should proceed. During these whispered conversations Richard found Britt distracted and unable to concentrate. When she made notations in the margins of her typed notes, her left hand shook so that he couldn't read what she had written. He didn't know, and had no real confidence, that she could read it either.

As the second speaker neared the end of his time, they fell silent. This was it. He had forgotten the anxiety of this moment. Richard put his left hand on Britt's right, which was cold and clammy, and whispered, "You'll do fine. Just like in Albuquerque. Piece of cake." She squeezed his hand back, but continued to look straight ahead at a point about three feet below the judges' eye level.

He could see that the muscles in her jaw were working and her breathing was shallow.

Their opponent thanked the court for its attention, closed his notes and sat down. The Presiding Judge, sitting in the middle of the panel of three judges, thanked the speaker, looked over his reading glasses at Richard and said, with a flat voice, "Appellees." Britt took a breath, stood up and walked to the lectern, opened her note book and looked up at the judges. She stood with her hands nervously holding the edges of the note book, not with them confidently clasped behind her as he had seen about a million times back in Albuquerque. The Presiding Judge, after a moment, glanced at his colleagues to see that they were ready and then nodded. Britt spoke: "May it please the Court. My name is Britt Larsen and I represent the New Mexico Bank of Commerce. My co-counsel is Richard Randolph." Her voice was tight and unnaturally high; her gesture towards him stiff and perfunctory. She cleared her throat. Richard could see her skirt quiver as her legs shook and her papers rattled in her hands. He kept his face masked with passive confidence for the judges' benefit, but his stomach muscles were tight and he discovered that he was holding his breath. She cleared her throat again and glanced quickly over her shoulder at the water pitcher on their table, then turned and walked back to the table, apparently for a drink. This was acceptable courtroom manners, but just barely, and she had to be getting back to the lectern. He looked up at her standing in front of him, but couldn't catch her eye. She reached for the glass and paused before touching it, her hand shaking. And he watched as she took a breath and visibly willed her hand to stop shaking. It did. By God, it did. *We might just pull this off yet.* She took a sip of water, gave him a small smile and rolled her eyes just a fraction upward, and walked back to the lectern.

"Excuse me, your honors," she said and left it at that, just exactly the right courtroom manners, pulled off naturally, as if she had lost her voice before the United States Circuit Court of Appeals dozens of times before. "May it please the Court. If I may, I would like to review the facts from the perspective of . . ."

"Counselor." The judge on the right spoke.

". . . the appellee."

"*Counselor.*" The judge sitting on the right interrupted her, as was his prerogative, and he spoke without looking up from his notes. *Damn.* Richard closed his eyes. *The bastard. The fucking bastard. The cocksucker. He is going to do it to her. He sees that she is nervous, he knows, if he's got half a brain, that she's a student, but he isn't going to cut her an inch of slack. He isn't going to spend one ounce of his precious judicial temperament helping her relax. He is going to stick it to her, he is going to stick it to her continually for her twenty minutes and he is going to begin right now. Shit.* Richard stared at the judge with a passive face and tried to will that melanomae develop on his bald head. *She's a student, for Christ's sake, you asshole. And you know it. I hope someday your fucking granddaughter is a law student. My law student.*

"Counsellor," the judge on the right repeated a third time, only now looking up, and apparently unaffected by the silent battering administered by Richard. "We don't need to be told the facts again. We know the facts. Let's get right to the heart of the case. The issue is dischargability, is it not? Riley's debt to you is not dischargeable, is it?"

"No, Your Honor." Her voice was tight again as she fumbled, trying to flip through the pages of her notebook. He was asking a question on a point a third of the way into her planned argument and she was trying to find her place in her notes. In the process she was not looking at the judge, not listening to the question and losing control. *Answer it! Do it by instinct!* His mind's voice yelled at her. *You know it. You don't need to look in your notes. You know the answer.* The key was this: she had to begin arguing and stop fumbling around and she had to do it *now.*

The judge was still speaking. "Then doesn't the Greenway case destroy your position, Counselor?"

"Well, sir, I was coming to that in a minute, but I'd be glad to talk about it now." She continued to flip through her notes, not looking at the judges.

"If you don't mind, Ms. Larsen," the judge practically sprayed her with sarcasm, "now would be fine."

"Yes, sir." She had found the spot. "Well, in the Greco case . . ."

"Greenway. *Greenway.* You've heard of the Greenway case?"

"Yes, Your Honor, but . . ." The correct answer was coming; Greco was the case that Britt and Richard were using to counter Greenway. It was *her* case, she had originally found it, and it was her argument. She knew the Greco case better than anyone alive. But the argument had to be done forcefully, confidently and offensively, not defensively. Richard tried to send her the words, words he had heard her say dozens of times in practice: *Your Honor, appellees feel that the Greco case, out of the Bankruptcy Court in California, sheds much more light on the proper analysis than does Greenway . . ."* But Britt was too slow with her response; she was back on her heels in a defensive posture, like an infielder backing away from a short hop. The judge on the left interrupted:

"Doesn't the plain language of section eleven-twenty-nine take care of the problem, Counselor?"

This judge may have been trying to help her, for his voice was kind and the argument based on section 1129 was their strongest argument. It was to have been the first part of her presentation. But now the question was out of order, again. She looked up from her notes at the judge on the left and said, "Well, yes, Your Honor, it does, but, . . .," she turned her attention back to the judge on the right, giving the appearance of being a spectator at a tennis match. ". . . the Greenway case . . ."

The left-hand judge interrupted again. His voice was patronizing: "But why bother with Greenway, when the statute itself solves the problem?"

"Yes, Your Honor, but . . ." She stopped. Silently, but plainly, as if on a puppeteer's thread, her right hand gestured toward the judge on the right, a tiny, frustrated indication that he had gotten her confused and off-balance, a gesture that was truly a breach of courtroom etiquette. One was never to allow one's frustration with the judges' questions to show in the courtroom, and no one, including Britt, spoke for a moment, in quiet recognition that the cherished sanctity of the court had been violated.

"I have an idea, Counselor." The Presiding Judge spoke through the silence, his voice seeming to have to push its way through the heavy atmosphere. "Why don't you begin with the facts and get to your points in order?" He smiled. Britt looked to the right-hand judge, who gave the smallest of nods in agreement, his eyes on his notes and his writing hand in motion. Less than a minute had passed since Britt had returned to the lectern after her drink and she was back where she started; no great loss of time, but she had apparently offended one judge and failed to impress the others and had generally shown herself to be an advocate out of control of her argument, the worst kind of impression, it is thought, that an advocate can give.

"Yes, sir." She paused. Even from the rear, it was obvious that she realized what she had lost in the last minute and that her composure had not returned to her. The silence in the courtroom seemed to last days.

Finally, Britt took a deep breath and began to recite the facts, but barely a minute or two later, she stumbled, got the facts of the case confused and had to correct herself. So many, many practices, and she lost her concentration, apologized and then went on again. Richard wished he were elsewhere.

The questions continued to fly at her from the three judges, who now made it clear that none of them had, as a top priority that day, the relaxation and welcoming of some western woman law student who thought she was the real thing, nor for that matter, her ivory tower mentor. The questions were sharp, the judges continued to interrupt Britt and each other, and were impatient with her if she did not answer the moment she was asked. She looked from one to another, fought to find the right words and would just begin to answer when another question would pommel her.

Before she sat down, Britt had regained some of her composure. She answered the last several questions well and then skipped pretty smoothly to her summation; maybe the judges eased up a little at the end, Richard couldn't tell. She finished, having covered only about two thirds of what they had intended for her to say. She sat down and he guessed that she wanted nothing more than to put her head in her hands and curse herself out, but his hand lightly on her shoulder as he made his way behind her reminded her that she couldn't do that. He approached the lectern, with fourteen million dollars on the line, thinking, oddly enough, that even a ball player, a relief pitcher, say, who lets the game slip away in the ninth, is allowed to put his head in his hands and curse himself out.

Richard's half went smoothly enough and, in fact, though they wouldn't know for a month or more, there was still a good chance that they could win the case, having already won once below. He told her that as they packed up their papers when the judges had left and again as they stood at the top of the steps of the Federal Courthouse and looked out over the small plaza. It had rained while they had been inside arguing and the stone steps were now slippery. The subway entrance lay just across the street and had their mood been different he would have suggested that they brave the underground back to the hotel. Instead, he held her elbow lightly so that she wouldn't take a misstep on the slippery stairs, as they walked down to the curb and tried to flag a taxi. As they waited, the opposing attorneys came down the steps and along the sidewalk, walking back to their nearby office. Richard knew that they would stop and chat, oozing graciousness and interest in the provinces, and they did. They complimented Britt on her performance and commiserated on the harshness of the panel of judges. She smiled and shook hands, but it was clear that she wasn't buying it.

The ride from the courthouse back to the hotel was slow and painful.

They sat in the back of the taxi, caught in cross-town traffic, stalled in mid-block with horns blaring, the rain falling again, New York at its worst. Britt now looked clumsy and uncomfortable in her suit as she stared out the side window, her chin in her right hand, her jacket riding up on the seat cushion and her skirt twisted under her. Richard loosened his tie and put his head against the back of the seat, and stared up through the dirty rear window at the dirty red buildings and dirty grey sky.

"Want to walk the rest of the way? I have an umbrella."

She didn't answer.

The taxi ride took too long, thirty-five minutes, he checked his watch. Time when their minds should have been distracted, but in which they now had nothing to do but to sit in the slow, slow traffic and let the depression sink in. He told her again, for about the fifth time now, that they might still win, as they finally pulled up in front of the Algonquin and climbed out of the taxi.

They had about three hours before they were to go to the theater, so they split up to relax, freshen up and change. He was still in his suit a half an hour later, wishing he were Michael Reid, with nothing more important to worry about than being arrested by the K.G.B., and nothing more taxing to wonder about than whether the woman across the café was an old friend or a total stranger, when Britt knocked at his door. She was now dressed in jeans, sneakers and a dark blue, hooded sweatshirt that said *Del Norte High* in red across the front. She had been crying and, Richard supposed, talking to her girlfriend at home.

"Come in. You can't be thinking about doing Broadway like that."

"I was terrible, wasn't I?"

"Come on in. No, go get dressed. We're going to the theater. We can eat first if you want; you skipped lunch."

"I was terrible, wasn't I?"

"Later."

"Wasn't I?"

"You finished well."

"Translation: *I sucked.*"

"Okay, you win. Come in." He should have known that this was not a time when bullshit would do.

She came in, slammed the door and walked across the room. Richard sat back down.

"Say it."

"Say what?"

"You know."

"Okay. You were terrible, I was mediocre, the judge on the right was a prick and the other side was very, very good. There."

"Why?" She was crying again. She stood behind a wing chair, backed into the far corner of the room and yelled the question at him.

"Let's go to the show, have dinner, have too much to drink, and talk about it when we get back to Albuquerque."

"NOW!" She was choking with rage and tears. "Why? Why couldn't I do it? Why was I so fucking afraid? I *knew* that case. I knew it better than *you*, for Christ's sake. I knew it better than the judges did." Her breathing came in sobs. "But I couldn't say it." She pronounced each word separately. "I. Couldn't. Say. It. I couldn't think up there. Why? God *damn* it! I *knew* that case."

Richard sat silent; there were no answers, not now, not yet. He watched her pace and cry and spit and kick the bathroom door. When she sat at last in the wing chair and put her head in her hands, he picked up the phone and ordered a bottle of Jack Daniel's from room service. Britt put two fingers to her lips, and he ordered cigarettes, too. "What?" he said into the phone. "I don't know. Ahh, Marlboros, I guess." She didn't look up.

When the liquor came, they drank it straight and warm from the bathroom tumblers, without a toast, without a word, and they stayed in their own thoughts. She chain-smoked in what appeared to be a conscious move to make herself feel worse and, while the smell turned his stomach, he felt that this was not the time to complain. By now Richard had figured the problem out, but she wasn't yet ready to hear it, he thought, so he watched and listened as she cried, raged, got drunk and the hour for the show came and went.

It was dark out the window when she got up from her chair, clicked the light on and walked to the mirror on the bedroom wall. She stared at her image and mocked, with chilling accuracy, her bumbling of the facts of the case earlier that day.

"Imbecile."

"Cut it out."

She took a deep breath and pulled her hair back behind her head, holding it there like a pony tail. She wiped her nose and her eyes on the sleeve of the other arm and, holding the cigarette between her thumb and forefinger, took the last, hot and ugly drag, then put the cigarette out. She exhaled the smoke into the air, her head straight back, her eyes closed. She turned and looked him square in the face.

"I want to get laid. I haven't been laid in ten years."

He looked into her eyes and said nothing.

She reached both hands back over her shoulders, grabbed fistfuls of sweatshirt and pulled it off over her head. Underneath, nothing. "I mean it, Richard. Will you fuck me?" Standing there in her sneakers and jeans, the shirt dragging on the floor from her left hand, her eyes angry, hurt and red, her face flushed and blotched, her hair still behind her ears, she was as beautiful as any woman he had ever seen. Her breasts were wonderfully suited to her broad shoulders and her stomach was smooth and flat. A hint of a tan, an early spring burn from the Albuquerque sun left its mark. Smoke from the ashtray curled up through the lamp shade and was jolted by the heat from the bulb; out the window, a jet rose from JFK and banked south of east, bound for Africa.

*I mustn't move,* he thought, *not a muscle. In a minute I'll be able to move.* He could not look away. He said nothing.

"Damn it, Richard, will it always be like this when I argue a case? I can't stand it. Damn it! I quit. I don't need this horseshit. You can take your bankruptcy law, your Uniform Commercial Fucking Code, your god damn *may-it-please-the-court* and you can shove it up the ass of that god damned judge whatever his name was." She turned her back to him, dropped the shirt to the floor and held her hair in her fist again. He couldn't believe it. It was as if she had never said it; he wasn't sure anymore that she had. He sat, and watched, as she walked over to the table and lit another cigarette, her breasts impossibly fluid, her skin impossibly bright in the room's light. She drew hard on the cigarette, then walked over and picked up the sweatshirt from where it lay on the floor. She held it in front of her, her left hand full of her right breast beneath the material of the shirt, and she began to recount the day's argument, walking back and forth across the room, apparently unaware of his excitement. The cigarette, and those before, gave her voice a crude, soft, airy sound, a sound so unlike the tinny, too-high one her nervousness had created earlier, in the courtroom. The smoke came up through her throat and out her mouth when she talked and made her cough.

He sat, quiet and still, and on the edge of ecstasy.

Finally, she lay down on one of the beds, collapsed, really, exhausted, drained, slightly drunk, her right arm now across her eyes, her sweatshirt across her chest. Without looking at him she said, "Damn it, Richard. Say something. I have never known fear like that in my entire life. Where does it come from?"

He cleared his throat and sipped some bourbon. "For Christ's sake, Britt, I am more than a little drunk on very expensive whiskey, you are lying half-naked on my bed in a hotel far from home, calling me *Richard* for the first time ever and looking so God-damned beautiful I've got chest pains, we've just turned one hundred dollars worth of Broadway tickets into scrap paper and we may have screwed up an otherwise perfectly winnable case. This is not a time to expect grand insight."

"I'll take minor insight." She leaned up on one elbow and looked at him; the sweatshirt fell away and onto the bed beside her. Her breasts moved in a way that was inconceivably lovely.

"Sometimes life is so ridiculous it's hardly worth living."

"Oh, shit. Thanks a lot." She fell back on the bed.

"I warned you."

"I have a headache. Do you have anything?" She threw the sweatshirt across the room, in the direction of a chair.

He walked to the bathroom for the aspirin, turned the overhead light out of her eyes and handed her the bottle. She took four in a mouthful of whiskey.

"God *damn* it."

"Here, put your head in my lap." He took off his jacket and sat cross-legged behind her, put a pillow in his lap and her head on the pillow. With the two middle fingers on each hand, he touched her temples and slowly made circles in opposite directions.

"Count with me, quietly. It's a Tai Chi method. Each way, groups of three, then out, like this, through the spot where my fingers touch." He kept his voice low. "Now, out." He made his wrists limp and pulled his hands away from her head. "Quietly. Feel the pool of energy under your butt, under your heels. Feel it come up and out where my fingers touch. You must be relaxed; loosen your joints. Think about lying, afloat on the Caribbean Sea. Imagine a blue, so blue it's five-dimensional." He was remembering a description from one of Michael's letters. "Imagine miles of this blue stuff supporting you. Imagine it supporting your wrists, miles of it deep and miles of it blue, supporting the backs of your knees. Think about what it would feel like to arch your head back, all the way back until your nose was underwater and to breathe this blue stuff into your lungs. Imagine the heavy feel it would have coming in and out of your lungs. Imagine that you could do all of this and stay alive, but thinking about the blue and the breathing of this heavy, heavy blueness, and not about the life around you."

Her face gained a little peace. After several minutes, with her eyes still closed, she said, "I think it works."

"Scary, isn't it? Maybe there *is* a pool of energy under your butt."

For the first time, she laughed, a small, closed-mouth laugh, that didn't reach the walls. "Maybe it was the aspirin."

"Shhhhhh. It doesn't work unless you believe."

～

At about seven o'clock, Albuquerque time, Marie called the Algonquin and had the clerk ring Britt's room. When there was no answer, the clerk came back on the line and asked if she wanted to leave a message, but she declined.

～

Richard continued the Tai Chi and talked, now that it seemed to be his time to talk. Quietly, always quietly, he tried to calm her and make her relax. He talked of Albuquerque and the desert, of the law and its practice, of winning and losing. But mostly he talked about minor league baseball and how a kid can appear to be a wonderful player in Albuquerque or Portland or Salt Lake City. How he can be a *great* Triple A player, a wonderful prospect, a hitter of curve balls, a fielder of bad hops, a sacrifice flier when it counts. But how he can be brought up too quickly, only to flop in the big leagues, go two-for-twenty-one in July and be sent down again. Not that it was his fault, you see, or that his career is over. Only that management had fucked up, been too eager with a resource as rare and fragile as an old, old Indian basket, too greedy, too impatient, in need of a quick fix for second division doldrums in the parent club. Many careers had begun like this and many first-class players had had to suffer through embarrassments like hers of that day.

Her eyes were still closed. Tears ran off the sides of her head and wet the short, fine hairs at her temples where his fingers massaged. He lightly blotted her eyes with his thumbs. She started to say something, but he touched his fingers to her lips. She licked her own salt and relaxed her eyelids and unfurrowed the skin between her eyes.

He continued to talk. Of Rafael Landestoy and Candy Maldenado and Ivan de Jesus. He made her say the names, names that meant nothing to her but she repeated them and he made her concentrate on her throat and tongue and the feel of the sounds against her teeth. *Rafael Landestoy. Candy Maldenado. Ivan de Jesus.* Slowly she calmed down, her chest rose and fell regularly and he didn't know if she was asleep. He continued to move his hand slowly in circles around her temples, then out and in, drawing the pain and the insult and the embarrassment away, and to talk to her.

Somewhere in the hour of quiet talk, Richard leaned forward and reached down with his left hand and unbuttoned her jeans. She was not asleep and she unzipped the fly half-way and wriggled her hips to get comfortable. Her ankles were crossed, her arms at her sides, her eyes still closed and, looking down the length of her body, Richard could see the white line of the top of her panties, just where the zipper closed. He reached down again and very lightly passed his fingers across the smooth skin where her pants lay open. The tips of his fingers just touched the line of white, and he sat back and began again to stroke her temples. She did not move, nor open her eyes. He would remember that tiny stripe of white between her navel and the tight crotch of her jeans forever, and the feel of her skin on his fingertips, because as he sat there, his hands now motionless on her temples and his eyes closed but still seeing her jeans lying open, exposing a tiny bit of white, he knew why they were here. Knew that he had committed an outrage worse even than bringing a player up too soon. Knew that he had put her in the Second Circuit today on the chance that, just about now, after a successful day in court and a cosmopolitan night on the town, they would be in bed, together, here in the Algonquin.

He rebelled at the thought, but in the late night quiet of the room he knew it to be true. He knew it had been true since that first spasm of puzzling excitement he had felt about her the previous summer, as he sat alone, at the ball park. He had been tempted by her looks and her mind. He had been curious about her and her preferences, about his own sexuality, his own power. So he had brought her here, perhaps jeopardizing her career and compromising so much of his life, to see if, in the rush of victory and in the mystery of the Algonquin, she would, . . . what? Choose him.

And he realized that his scheme of manipulation and exploitation might have been his own private burden to bear, except that his hand had reached down and unbuttoned her jeans. Everything else had been counseling, guiding, preparing and later, calming a half-naked and somewhat drunken young woman. The manipulation would have been there, yes, but secret. Unethical, a violation of her trust, but secret, unacted upon.

He had, though, unbuttoned her jeans and with that declared himself to her as something much more than her teacher. That was an act only explicable as a seduction and between the two of them, it could never be otherwise. It could never be that he had not reached down and undone her jeans.

He had no real concern for what others thought, any others, not then. But between the two of them, everything had changed. He felt as though he had just crossed into a different universe. In this one he had manipulated and seduced a very dear person, a friend whose love, he knew, lay elsewhere. He looked down on her face, eyes closed, now calm, and wished he could return to the other universe, in which a half-naked tirade and a Tai Chi exercise alone had established an intimacy between them that now seemed enough. But there was no returning, of course. This one was now the one.

Britt may have sensed these thoughts, though he couldn't believe she knew what he was feeling. She reached up with both of her hands and took his fingers and held them, now looking up into his eyes, the same calm, quiet expression on her face, her lips in the barest of smiles, upside down to him. "You're trembling," she said. She moved his hands down so that his fingertips lay on her collar bones.

His breath would not come to him; for a long moment, his body refused to breathe. For he knew that his high-minded thoughts of minutes ago were bullshit, and if she moved his hands down any farther, on to her breasts, he would do it, he would still do it. *If she speaks to me, if her lips move, if her eyes say it . . .* And he looked down through her pale blue eyes, at the back of her skull and saw a desert as far as he could see.

But she just held his fingers and looked up into his eyes. Not a word, not a sign that he could read. No move to pull him close, nor to push him away. Just her holding his hands, holding an equilibrium, an inertia, a balance of all the forces in the room.

Then she shivered. Richard saw goose-bumps arise on her arms and her nipples perked up.

"Cold?" His voice nearly did not work.

"A little."

"Want your shirt?"

"I'll get it." She swung her feet to the floor and sat up, then put her head down, apparently dizzy. In a moment, she stood up and faced him, her right arm across her breasts.

"Thank you . . ."

He said nothing, but smiled.

". . . and I'm sorry."

He had no idea what she meant.

"We could still eat," he said, moving to sit on the edge of the bed. "It's late, but this is New York."

"I feel like feeling hungry for a while. And I'm not done crying."

"Remember what I said. It's not the end of your career. I just brought you up too soon." Does she know, he wondered, does she sense the lie? Does she know why we're here? Does it matter to her?

Britt gave a little smile, reached her left hand out and touched his right shoulder with her fingers. "I know, but I have a few other things to cry about. Don't worry, I'll be okay." She turned her back and zipped her pants, then fetched the sweatshirt and put it on. He noticed that she had never taken her shoes off. *How close could it have really been?*, he thought. *She still has her shoes on.*

At the door, she turned and said, "I'll see you in the morning."

"Good night, Britt."

"Good night." She was gone. Right there, at the end, instead of saying *Good night*, he had almost said *Stay*. He closed his eyes and heard himself say it. *Stay*. What would she have done? How could he have said it? How could he not have said it? He stretched out on the bed, still dressed in his white shirt, tie and court pants. Across the room, the pack of cigarettes, half gone, sat on a small table under the mirror. The red and white of the package was magnetic; he did not look away as he reached over and took a drink from the bourbon in Britt's glass. Perhaps she would come back for them. It would take him all night to figure out what to say to her in the morning.

～

Marie had to send the postcards to Michael at his Ozark address, though she knew, as much as it was ever possible to know about Michael, that he wasn't there now.

*April 28, 10 p.m.*

*I've spent 34 hours in the Albuquerque airport, awaiting my lover's return. What do you make of that?*

*She calls me "Angel." In the morning. Boy, do we need to talk.*
*Marie.*

~

Back in her room, Britt called Marie. *Hi. Leave a message for Marie or Britt.* "Hi. It's me. Are you there? Pick up." She paused, but when Marie didn't pick up, she went on. "I'm drunk and discouraged. It didn't go well. Where are you? I'll try back in a bit."

She hung up, went into the bathroom, made herself get sick, and then took a cold shower. Her head cleared, and she found that she was dreadfully tired. She tried the duplex once more—"Where *are* you?"—then hung up, collapsed onto the bed and was soon asleep. The bathroom light was still on.

~

Marie walked outside to the post office at the airport, bought a stamp from the machine and listened to the sound of the postcard to Michael falling through the slot and into the bag. Outdoors the air smelled of jet exhaust and sounded of flight, but she walked back inside to the airport bar, ordered a Heineken with ice and watched the late news.

There was a four-car pile-up on I-25 at San Mateo, and a shooting at a Circle K out on Coors to get out of the way first, and some pleasant banter between Dick and Linda, notwithstanding the deaths, and Marie listened with the ten per cent of her attention that the late local news required. A story from the network feed was next: there was tension in the Middle East and the reporter talked grimly, with a white skyline and a bullet-pocked wall behind him. Marie's attention increased when she heard that the report was from Beirut; she grinned and tipped her glass to the screen, high over the bartender's head. "Here's to Beirut," she said aloud.

"Do you want another one?"

"No, thanks, I'm just talking to myself."

Beirut. Michael is over there somewhere, she supposed. His last letter had been from Egypt. No, Greece. She couldn't remember just now. Anyway, that was interesting. "Life imitates travel." She spoke the words aloud. Michael is in Egypt, Britt is in New York, Marie is in Albuquerque thinking of Beirut. She reached for a handful of salted red peanuts from the bowl in front of her and imagined a map of the world lying on the bar. She placed a peanut for her, for Britt and for Michael. Ahhh, the classic triangle. Actually it was pretty much of a straight line the way she envisioned the map; maybe she had Egypt too far to the north. She moved his peanut closer to the edge of the bar. In any case, the classic triangle was much too simple for the situation she found herself in. She placed a small pile of peanuts near Michael's, but above and to the right. Beirut society. She surveyed her map, and then returned her attention to the TV for a minute, where she caught the signoff from Lebanon, and the tease before the commercial break. National news. Reagan was up to something, dressed in a tux, talking to a crowd in tuxes and gowns, she didn't catch about what. Reagan knew how to wear a tux, she'd give him that. She looked again at the pile of peanuts representing Beirut society, picked one out, and looked at it closely over her glasses.

"Lorinda. We meet at last. Nikki says you're flighty. Sanctimonious and flighty. A bad combination, if you want my opinion. You don't belong here, you creep; you're not good enough for us."

*Us.* She paused to contemplate the word. Why was the word *us* so scary? How hard it must be for Britt to wait and wonder if she would ever use the word.

"Where do you belong? Rome? Jerusalem? No. The Dallas Theological Seminary is full of your ilk." Marie placed the peanut south and east of Albuquerque. She added a peanut next to Britt's for Richard Randolph in New York; she nudged them together so they were touching, salt-to-salt, oil-to-oil. No. She separated them to a discreet distance, then farther, placing Richard in Delaware, probably.

Speaking of New York, the sports were now on the news. Or do you say *was* on? She wondered. The Dodgers and the Mets were playing in New York, tied 3-3 in overtime, or whatever they called it in baseball. Michael had always kidded her about her baseball illiteracy, but she knew more than he suspected. Like that the Dukes belonged to the Los Angeles Dodgers and that was why Albuquerque was full of Dodger fans, even though L.A. was far away, and other teams were closer, though she couldn't think of where right now. She added a peanut for Los Angeles and remembered the weekend in Phoenix last summer, missing Michael's plane from LAX. She added Phoenix to the map. She remembered tromping around the Phoenix airport, through the heat and her anger. She added Tallahassee to the map, remembering her conversations with Nikki.

So, what was this all about? She surveyed the bar with its invisible map in front of her. Something was missing; it wasn't yet ready to come together for her. Her mood had changed as the time had passed in the airport and she now found her sobs on the Crest and the fear expressed on the first postcard to Michael to be melodramatic. But there was still an uneasiness around that she couldn't make out. Was there a peanut missing, a place unaccounted for, something or someone, someplace that would make all of this make sense? Maybe it was in Beirut. Maybe it was with Michael, wherever he was, or with his strange friend, or maybe a stranger, who sat and drank brandy in a café that Marie now realized must be the café of her dream. Maybe there was something in that woman's aloneness that completed the picture. Maybe it was just that spending two days in the Albuquerque airport made her think so. She added a peanut for Athens.

Or maybe it was Michael's juggling letter, which she had re-thrown away, in spite of Britt's suggestion that she keep it. Maybe this was much more about juggling than it was about peanuts. She added a peanut for the island where the juggling took place, the name of which escaped her just now. Maybe it was about Jill's peace offering, and the relief that she had felt on hearing the invitation, relief, ignoring for now that she still had to walk with Britt through Jill's front door and stand there in the living room, unambiguously Britt's lover.

"What have we got here?" Marie jumped, but it was just the bartender, looking down at the peanuts and holding a fresh Heineken in his hand.

"Egypt," she said, and picked up the peanut representing Michael and popped it in her mouth. "And Beirut." Another peanut. "This one is rancid; you should toss it out." Using her forefinger, she rolled Lorinda across the bar to him. "Never mind, I'm just fooling around."

"This is for you," the bartender said, flipping the supposedly rancid peanut into the trash and, putting the bottle down next to her glass, "The guy down the bar bought it for you."

"Oh, shit," she said, not looking down the bar. "Tell him, . . ., Christ, I don't know, . . ." Suddenly she felt very tired. "Just tell him I don't want it. Tell him I've got a plane to catch." She scooped up the remaining peanuts on the bar and tossed them into her mouth, downed the last of her beer and walked out onto the concourse, sucking on the ice cubes. She checked her watch and hurried toward the departure gates, wondering if the man in the bar knew, as she did, that the last flight had already left for the night.

～

Late that night, after midnight in Albuquerque, and unable to sleep under the bright lights of the departure lounge, it occurred to Marie for the first time that Britt might well be trying to call her at home, and would be wondering why she didn't answer. The simplest thing to do would be to go home, get whatever messages were there, take a shower, get some sleep in her own bed, and come back tomorrow to meet Britt when she arrived. But she knew that she wouldn't do that; she had become obsessed with the idea of waiting in the airport another night, until Britt arrived. She wasn't crazy, she knew, but she conceded to obsessiveness just now. So she picked up a pay phone again, called the Algonquin, and left a message with the desk clerk, to be delivered in the morning. *Everything is okay. I'm fine. See you tomorrow. Love, Marie.*

⁓

Richard looked up, over his tomato juice, as Britt approached the table to join him at mid-morning breakfast in the Algonquin's lobby. She wore shorts, sneakers and a polo shirt. Her eyes were bloodshot, her hair had lost yesterday's sheen and was pulled back from her face with two barrettes. He had never noticed how her ears stood out just slightly from the sides of her head. Her voice was hoarse from smoke and whiskey and anger, when she sat down and said: "Two days ago at breakfast, I thought I could do anything, but that I didn't have enough time to get it done. This morning I feel the opposite. I'm not sure which I like better. I feel like an adult."

"It's the whiskey."

"Don't be a grouch. I was being profound."

In spite of the ugly sound to her voice, there was some brightness in it, or in her, which gave slight hope that the world was not going to end immediately, a hope he had difficulty sharing. He took a tiny sip of tomato juice and closed his eyes against his stomach's reaction. Cigarette smoke from a nearby table drifted with unerring accuracy across the room and struck him between the eyes.

When the waiter approached the table, Britt looked at Richard.

"I've already ordered. Go ahead."

So Britt looked up at the waiter and said, "Just coffee, please, with cream, and a plain croissant. With a little strawberry jam if you have some."

"Yes, ma'am," the waiter said, and departed.

Richard shook his head. "You just ordered off the menu at the Algonquin. Stunning." She leaned her head to the right, as if to say, *why not?* He closed his eyes and pressed his thumb and fingers into the corners. When he opened them again, she was looking at him.

"Let me try," he said.

"Try what?"

"Profundity. I went to sleep last night thinking of you."

"It was the whiskey. Did you call your wife?"

"Yes. Did you?" He shook his head to clear the cobwebs. "I didn't mean that. I meant did you call your . . ." He spread his hands in frustration.

"Sometimes language just isn't up to the job, is it? No, I didn't. But I got a couple of overnight messages from her. I picked them up at the front desk just now. She probably didn't want to wake me. They came in quite late."

Minutes passed. The waiter brought the food and set it in front of them. Bacon and eggs now revealed themselves to have been a big mistake on Richard's part; he picked the plate up and set it off to the side of the table, on top of a freshly folded *Times*. News and food, equally unappetizing, he thought. He wondered if the paper would contain any reference to yesterday's court case. Surely not, not in the *Times*. But the *Post*? SMALL TOWN LAWYERS EMBARRASSED BY LOCAL FIRM. *"Had spunk," say winners.* He looked up again; she was pouring cream into her coffee very carefully. He watched for a minute and then commented, "You don't stir it?"

"No. You can tell the future in the clouds and swirls of the cream." There was that brightness again.

"Go ahead."

She studied the cup. "Surprise without mystery. Irony. Whimsy. Maybe some change."

"Is that me or you?"

"It's my cup. You stirred yours."

He ordered a fresh cup and followed her directions, pouring the cream down one side and watching the clouds billow up to the top. The pouring had imparted a little rotation to the coffee, so the clouds were swinging lazily clockwise around the center.

"What do you see?"

"That's not how it works. You have to read your own."

"I don't know how."

She looked at him, not into his cup. "Don't stir it. Don't try to smooth it all into one color. Read it as it lies. Let the patterns develop. Admire the complexity; appreciate the asymmetry. Which is right up your alley. Don't inject your own mind into the pattern; if you try to get inside, the pattern will be destroyed. This is not a time for keen rational thought. Look at the clouds and swirls and listen to what your ear hears coming from the moons of Venus."

"Venus hasn't any moons."

"Not that are known. The pattern itself is the message; listen to it; the meaning will come to you."

"I'm not sure I understand," he said. "What if I just let the pattern lie? If I don't read it?"

"It will wait. It will still be there, if you drink without stirring."

He picked up the cup and sipped. His left wrist held the memory of first the resistance and then the release of the button on her jeans. He put the cup down and reached in his pocket.

"You left these in the room last night." He slid the pack of cigarettes over to her. She made a face and raised a cross with her index fingers in front of her eyes.

"Get them away! I quit. I'll never smoke again."

"I think I'll save them. A souvenir." He reached to pick them up.

"Don't be silly, Richard." She snatched them and crushed the pack and the remaining cigarettes in her hand. "Please."

*So much is left unsaid*, he thought to himself. *So many questions have only been asked behind my eyes. There is so much I don't know. I do not know what she thinks. I do not know if she would have stayed. But she seems content that those questions will be mine, for now at least, my version of them, at least. Not hers, not Rita's, not the school's, not her Marie's.* He shook his head and said, "Sometimes I lose track. Things don't always turn out the way I expect them to."

"It's good for one."

He sat back and looked around the Algonquin's lobby. He tried to put his eyes over there, at that other table, and looked back at the two of them sitting here. *What would we appear to be? What would a passerby make of the two of us, sitting here, not talking? What would be made of the still life—the mostly untouched food, fresh flowers, fresh newspaper and a crumpled pack of cigarettes—spread out in front of them?* He studied the image, then looked back to her.

"I almost came to your room last night; the cigarettes would have been my excuse. I thought for a long time about standing at your door, then knocking and what you would be doing and what you would say when you opened it . . ."

"Richard . . ."

He held up his hand. "Let me finish. I want to tell you a story. I have a friend, an old friend, maybe my closest friend in some ways. He's in the midst of a strange circumstance: he keeps seeing someone who reminds him of an old friend of his. Maybe she was his lover; I can't tell. He sees her in bars, across the street, on the bus, you know, again and again. And it can't be her for she doesn't live where he is and the coincidence is just too unlikely. It looks so much like her, but each time she has a different characteristic in common with his friend, so the women he sees don't all even look like each other. Each just looks like his friend.

"So, he tells me about all this, writes me a letter without much detail, really. I'm filling in the blanks he leaves. But here's what I got to thinking of last night after you left: he, my friend, seems to be happier with the mystery of it all than with the solution. He doesn't approach the woman, or women, not even to satisfy himself that she isn't his friend. He just watches and wonders and lets the strangeness be.

"Last night, after you left and I saw the cigarettes on the table, I thought about bringing them to you and I got to thinking of my friend and his wondering if the woman is his friend or what's going on and how she can't be when she seems so like her. And the more I thought of him and her and the more I wanted to come to your room and the more I wondered what you would say at the door, the more comfortable I became with the state of not knowing. And I decided not to come down the hall and knock on your door."

Her eyes had been on him while he talked and she waited a moment for him to go on. When he said nothing more, and she seemed to realize that he was finished for now, she said, "Mystery without surprise."

"What?"

She gestured at the coffee. "*Mystery without surprise.* The mirror image of my fortune. Nice. Tidy. Balanced. I approve."

He stared at her for a moment, trying to read her face. "You're not going to give me a hint, are you?" Her look was inscrutable. "Do *you* know what you would have done if I had knocked?"

She laughed. "Come on, Richard, learn your friend's lesson." Her face showed pleasure at this precise moment and nothing else. He shook his head.

"You are a most wise and remarkable woman, Britt Larsen, and you order off the menu."

"In more ways than one."

He let the thought hang in the air, waiting to see in which of several possible senses she meant it. But she said nothing more, nor did she raise her eyes from her plate. After a moment, he continued. "I count it an honor to have known you."

She looked up at him, smiled, then sipped her coffee and took a small bite of her croissant. "What about the woman?" Her tongue came out to catch a flake of the pastry. She helped it back in with her index finger.

"What about her?"

"What's her lesson? We've learned your friend's. What can be seen through her eyes?"

"I didn't think to wonder."

"That's a nice male perspective." He thought she was teasing him.

"Come on, give me a break. We don't even know who she is. Maybe she's not his old friend at all. We don't even know if *she* is only one person."

"True, her lesson is bound to be more ambiguous to us than is his. That's okay; I could go for a little more ambiguity this morning." It was clear that she was having fun, and that pleased him after her embarrassment of the previous day's work.

"But how can we ever know what she's thinking?" he wondered.

"We can know it in the same way the coffee knows the future. Indefinitely. Quietly. Intuitively."

"Go ahead, then, what do you know about this woman?" He sat back, crossed his arms and watched her.

She was quiet for a minute, looking around the restaurant. Then she lost her smile, lowered her eyes and her voice. "Oh, that she, whoever she is, is not a breakfast-table game."

"Meaning?"

"That I'm not going to read her like a cup of coffee." She looked up at him again. "Maybe a tolerance of ambiguity is her lesson to us. She probably has close friends to whom her message is clearer and to whom your friend's *let-the-mystery-be-unresolved* lesson is ambiguous."

Richard considered the point. The mood was in danger of becoming somber. "So, there she sits, watched by my friend, who enjoys the mystery, and he tells me, and I decide, in a smoky, expensive hotel room, to drink Jack Daniel's and stay put, suspended between the ultimate joy and the ultimate indiscretion." He paused to give her time to show her hand, but still nothing. "Makes me sound like I was afraid of taking the risk."

"Easy does it on the old testosterone level. We know different. And no one else even knows you had the choice."

"Okay, then, . . ." He picked up his cup. ". . . a caffeinated toast to the ambiguous, anonymous female who may be called Ann and maybe not. In either case, may she fare well."

Britt raised her cup and continued the toast, "And thank you, unknown sister, for touching our lives with such a delicate and knowing touch." Their cups met in a *ping* that said much about the china at the Algonquin, and they sipped their coffees.

"Well, Ms. Larsen, I believe we have struck a blow against superficiality."

"I think so. I think we have done that."

"There's one last thing I'd like to do in New York, if you're game."

Her eyes were bright. "Go on."

"There's a way of getting from downtown Manhattan to LaGuardia without using a taxi, and I'd like to try it. I confirmed the route with Professor Johnson, who says it is used only by the most adventuresome of tourists. No New Yorker would think of it."

"What do we have to do?"

"Catch the Eighth Avenue K train uptown, through the tunnel to Roosevelt Drive in Queens and transfer to the Q thirty-three bus. We'll have to carry our suitcases from here over to Eighth Avenue, and then at the transfer point to the bus."

"I'm game. That's only two and a half blocks."

"You think you're pretty smart having mastered Manhattan in a day and a half, don't you?" They laughed. "The blocks are long going across town, remember."

"Let's do it. But I'm going to change into my jeans first."

Richard stood up and picked up the check. "Meet you down here in a half hour."

She remained seated, looking down, twisting a fork in her hand. "One last thing, . . ., about yesterday. In court . . ."

"I still think we win the case."

"Yeah, but . . ."

"Yeah, but nothing. You're going to be a great lawyer."

"How do you know?"

"Trust me. I am an expert in such matters. Do you feel like you have to say you're sorry again? Don't. You don't. Not for anything."

"But . . ."

"Really, you don't. Tell you what: in two weeks we'll re-hash the entire episode and make what we can out of the experience. Both of us. Now, let's get out of here. A half an hour. I'll settle up the bill and be waiting out there in the lobby. I plan to tell the doorman that we're taking the subway to LaGuardia."

A half an hour later, with their bags and in their traveling clothes, they met in the lobby. "Come here," Britt said, "I want to show you something." She walked over to the grand piano which stood near the back, ready for the evening's entertainment. Richard followed. Britt lifted back the cover to expose the keys and struck one.

"What's that?" he asked.

"High B."

"The significance of which is?"

"It's the highest note that the soprano solo has to sing in the *Ode to Joy.*"

"How do you know?"

"I looked it up."

"Hit it again." She did so. "Pretty high."

"Pretty goddam high," she agreed. "I couldn't get there." She struck the key one last time. "Good luck. I hope you get the chance."

They picked up their bags and headed across the lobby and out the door, past the uniformed doorman and the bell captain with his whistle, smiling with the smugness of those heading for the airport without using a taxi. And the taxi-less trip to LaGuardia worked just like Michael had said it would, and they rode quietly home to the Albuquerque Friday afternoon.

## 〜 17

## ALBUQUERQUE

A t the arrival gate, Marie stood waiting, but far back, behind the wives and children, fathers and friends meeting the plane. She was very tired and grimy, though she had sponge-bathed over the sink in the restroom. She had slept little the night before; the unseen man who had tried to buy her a beer in the bar had changed the feel of the airport for her and she had worried all night that he was lurking around, ready to pester her. She had sat up most of the night, reading and dozing in a chair in the brightly lit main baggage area. She had begun drinking coffee at around four o'clock in the morning with the early ground crews, and by noon her stomach was sour and her head ached with caffeine. The last two hours before the plane arrived had moved with a slowness she had never experienced and she had checked the clock almost, it seemed, every minute.

Now she stood watching the passengers file through the de-boarding door into the airport. It would have been easy for Britt to miss her as she wasn't expecting to be met. But she did see her and Marie gave a quiet little wave, and tried to make her hair lie down in the front. Britt walked over, put down the suitcase and hugged her. Richard hung back, giving the two of them time to greet.

"What are you doing here? Why aren't you in school?" Britt said. "It's good to see you. When I couldn't get you last night, I was a little worried, but then I got your messages this morning, . . . You look awful. Are you okay?" Now they stood apart, not touching.

"I know I look terrible. I've been here since you left."

"What?"

"Yes, here. In the airport. Since Wednesday morning."

"Bullshit. That's two days. Two days? More than two days. What about school?"

"I know. I called in sick. I waited over there . . .," she pointed to a bench near the gate. ". . . and slept in the departure lounge. Oh, Britt," she squeezed her eyes shut, moved forward and put her forehead on Britt's shoulder, her hands in her own pockets. "I missed you. I wanted to be close to you. I felt you here. It was like you were on the other side of that door." She kept her head where it was on Britt's shoulder, but pointed with her left hand toward the gate. "I missed you and, I don't know why, but I was afraid . . ."

"Shhhh."

". . . I don't know, afraid that you wouldn't come back."

"Shhhh. Come on. I missed you, too. Shhhh. Don't cry. Relax." Britt pulled Marie's face away, and held her at short arm's length. "Don't think that. Really. Everything's going to be okay. I'm not going to leave you. Don't worry. I'm not. And I don't think you're going to do what Lorinda did. Please don't cry."

"Is that what this is all about?"

"Partly. This trip was about many things."

"And him?"

"He'll be okay. Now, push your hair around and come over and say hi. Richard's staring." She did. "You remember my roommate, Marie?"

"Sure. Hi."

"How were the arguments?"

"Dukes against the Dodgers," he said and Britt smiled. Marie didn't understand. She wasn't really listening very closely. With her finger hooked in Britt's near belt loop and her head on Britt's shoulder, she looked into Richard's eyes and she felt herself being drawn to a place far away, to a place she wished not to go. She shook her head, a short, quick shake. "What?" She felt very tired and confused. People were pushing against her, trying to get around, hurrying down the concourse toward the airport lobby and others were going the other way, toward a departure gate, and these two were talking like they were talking in code. It was very close and for an instant she thought she might faint. *God, no*, she couldn't do that; she had already gotten sick in front of this man, whom Britt, she noticed, was now calling *Richard*. She shook her head again and reached out with her left hand to steady herself. She held onto Richard's forearm.

"What? How were the arguments?" She avoided looking in his eyes.

"Are you okay?" Richard asked. He supported her under her arm and looked at Britt. "Is she okay?"

"She's just tired, I think. Let's go."

Down the escalator into the lobby, Marie felt a surge of energy and she brightened. She ran her fingers through her hair and straightened her shoulders. "Let's not go just yet, all right? Can we stay here in the lobby for a minute? Just a minute. I'm just not quite ready to go yet. Is it all right?" She turned around and faced both of them, under the large black departure board. "Just for a little while. I'm okay. There." She pointed over their shoulders. "There. Let's just stay for a minute and watch all those little numbers and letters flip over. Watch. Here they go." She felt high, a little like she was stoned, and she pointed up as Britt and Richard turned around. "Listen. Chicka-chicka-chicka-chicka-chicka-chick. HaHA!" She laughed and actually clapped her hands, as the board realigned itself. *TW 263 DFW 4:35 4:35 A6,* moved up one row. She moved between them and put her hand in Britt's; their three heads were all bent to look up as *DL 704 ATL 4:45 5:05 A4* moved up.

"You know," she said, "Michael and I once stood here for like an hour and watched those little guys flip over, not saying anything, just watching and listening and going *chicka-chicka-chicka-chicka-chicka-chicka-chicka-chick.* Well, I don't really suppose it was an hour. At the end he got this look on his face and I knew he wanted to be somewhere else, somewhere alone, but he just stood here with me and we watched the flights change. I never loved him any more than I did right then when he wanted to be there and yet he stayed here with me. But you don't know who I'm talking about. A friend."

*AA 586 DFW 4:45 4:45 B1* moved up a row. Britt was looking off to the left, back the way they had come, as if she had forgotten something. Richard looked down at Marie, but she avoided his eyes again; hers were on the departure board.

"No," he said, "but I have a friend like that. His name is Michael, too. I can imagine him doing that. Where did your friend want to go?"

"*Chicka-chicka-chicka-chicka-chicka-chick.*" Marie was copying the noise again, smiling and watching the little letters and numbers flip over. "Here comes the last one."

*SW 1010 LAX 5:00 5:00 C15* moved up and the board was silent. Richard thought that she hadn't heard him, but she looked up at him and said, "I don't think it mattered. I'm ready to go home now. I think I'm going to sleep for a week. How were the arguments? How was New York?" They walked to her car in the parking lot, Britt drove and, on the way home, Marie fell asleep.

## AT CAIRO INTERNATIONAL AIRPORT, HELIOPOLIS, EGYPT

In the Cairo airport, Michael Reid had written his departure lounge postcard to Marie:
*I/ I feel/ feel like/ I am/in a burning building/and I gotta go.*

He was walking to the Post, thinking of the flight to Amsterdam and how the layover might be long enough to give him time to ride the train into town and make a quick visit to the Van Gogh museum, when, walking by the abandoned suitcase, he was surprised by the noise of the bomb. The force of the explosion threw him against the far wall and, unconscious, both of his legs gone below the knees, in the confusion, he bled to death before help could arrive.

## ALBUQUERQUE, ATHENS, TALLAHASSEE AND THE OZARKS

Marie allowed herself to be fussed over by Britt and was put to bed with much ado and, once there she became quite tired again and went to sleep almost immediately. She awoke later, with her glasses off, the evening light fading and Britt sitting on the side of the bed, holding her hand.

"Hi, there." She squeezed Britt's hand. "Here you are, just like you said you wanted to be, in the park."

"How do you feel?"

"I'm okay, just a little tired is all. Tell me about the trip."

"No, you sleep some more."

"Britt, I'm not sick . . ."

"Shhhh." Britt brushed the hair out of Marie's eyes, and laid her palm on her forehead.

". . . and I'm not crazy." She rolled over on her side, still holding Britt's hand, and began to stroke the inside of her forearm, her finger following the thin white scar.

"I like it when you caress me," Britt said.

"Remember when I first noticed the scar?"

"El Norteño. Our first time out in the world together."

Marie leaned over and touched her lips to Britt's forearm. "You called it your reminder. I wanted to kiss it that night, but I was too embarrassed. Then you said something that made me blush."

"It was that blush that won my heart, you know."

Marie lay back. "Really, do tell me about New York. I'll fall asleep if you do."

"Well." Britt shook her head and began to speak in a low voice and very, very slowly. "It didn't go as planned. I didn't do very well." Marie started to say something, but Britt went on. "No, really. I didn't. You're not going to believe this, Marie, but I was so afraid. So afraid I just couldn't think straight. It's strange, looking back on it, I can see myself, standing in front of the court, speechless with fear." She spoke slowly, slowly. "Speechless. I was shaking. Can you believe it? Shaking. I've never felt fear before, not like that, but I was afraid there."

"Everyone gets nervous."

"This was more than that. This was fear. It turned my stomach. Maybe I needed you there to stroke my arm and say *everyone gets nervous.*"

"Nikki says you aren't afraid of anything, and that gets you in trouble sometimes. She says you've been fearless ever since you got this." Marie kissed the scar again.

"The reminder? Was this like that? It's been so long ago I don't remember."

"But you remember the mantra."

"Sarah's jumping mantra?"

"Say it for me."

"*Heels-down-toes-out-squeeze-with-your-calves-shorten-the-rein-grab-his-mane-look-beyond-the-jump-be-ready-for-anything.* I thought I was . . ."

"I like the part about grabbing the horse's mane."

They were talking quietly to each other, but somehow not, stepping on each other's lines, talking over one another.

". . . prepared for anything, with all the practice . . ."

". . . it's like there's something special about a horse letting you hold onto his mane . . ."

". . . I can't believe we could have practiced any more . . ."

". . . it's almost like you and the horse were one being . . ."

". . . Richard says I have a tendency to drown in the details . . ."

"... one being ..."

"... which more practice would have made worse ..."

"... you and the horse. What's the part near the end?"

"*Be ready for anything.*"

"No, before that."

"*Look beyond the jump.*"

"I love the image of you, holding on to T-man's mane, squeezing him with your calves, both of you, as one, looking beyond the jump ..."

"... I think all the practice had me staring at the jump."

"... into the future ..."

"Staring at the jump. You had that figured out, didn't you?"

Marie was suddenly tired again, and the mixed-up conversation, with the two of them talking over each other, had become confusing to her, and she didn't answer.

"I looked down at the jump." Britt smiled. "You're exactly right, my Angel. Exactly. And I'm the one who's supposed to be the accomplished equestrienne. And you figured it out, just like that." She shook her head. "I did. I looked at the jump. When Richard and I walked into that courtroom, it was like, I now see it, it was like I was staring at the jump the week after I broke my arm. *Staring at it.* No wonder the horse balked. T-man would have known that I was sitting on his back, scared to death. He would have known for sure. At one point, I almost got it under control, but then I lost hold and there I was: the horse running headlong toward the jump, me staring at the gate, and the horse knowing for sure that something was wrong up on there. If I could only have seen my mother in the audience, looking worried. If you had been there, or Sarah, you could have reminded me to say the mantra. Maybe, if I had just remembered the scar. Anyway, it was almost tangible this fear. I don't know. I don't know what the next time will be like, but Richard helped, last night, helped me work through that a little." Marie was having difficulty keeping her eyes open. "I don't know. Everything might have been different if you had been there. .... Everything. I said something to Richard that I'm embarrassed about. No, it's worse than that ..."

Marie missed the next bit, but woke when Britt touched her cheek.

"Go to sleep. There's something I need to tell you, but we'll talk in the morning."

"No, I'm okay." The room was dark now and Marie thought that maybe quite a bit of time had passed since the last part of the conversation that she could remember. She could barely see Britt's face. Fatigue kept her eyes from focusing and she closed the left one, trying hard to see, trying to make it so there was only one image of Britt and concentrating on being awake. But when she spoke she wasn't sure at first whether her words were real or dreamed: "How do you feel? Will it be all right?"

"It all makes me feel a very odd feeling." Marie tried to listen closely, but she could hardly make it out. "I don't know how to say it, really. I don't know; kind of warm and smoky here, and rainy and cold over there."

Had she heard right? Marie struggled to stay awake. What a very strange thing to say. "What? What do you mean?"

"I don't know," Britt said, Marie's eyes finally closing. "I don't know. I don't know. . . ."

~

Richard's attention snapped up from his newspaper and he stared past Rita, at the wall. He thought of the stripe of white and remembered the room at the Algonquin, with Britt's head in his lap, his fingers on her collar bones and his mind, he didn't know why, in Egypt.

"Honey, . . .?" Rita began, puzzled by his blank stare over her shoulder. But his stare didn't break and he didn't hear her and she went back to reading the paper.

~

Anna Browning drank Nescafé and nibbled on a pastry at a sidewalk cafe on Syntagma Square in Athens. The *International Herald-Tribune* was on the table in front of her. The *Herald-Tribune*, she had recently discovered, mostly just reprinted articles that had appeared at home in the *New York Times* and the *Washington Post*. Reading the *Times-Post* in Athens in the Eighties was hardly up to the standard of reading the *Herald-Tribune* in Paris in the Sixties, but you take, she guessed, what you are given. What she was given this day was an astoundingly pleasant Greek spring morning with a warm sun, a cloudless sky and an undemanding cup of *nes*, as the Greeks call instant coffee.

She had read the *Herald-Tribune* this morning pretty much from cover to cover, finishing a moment ago with the baseball scores. The world seemed to be getting along. In New York, the Dodgers had taken two from the hometown Mets, one said to be an extra-innings thriller, though she was not enough of a baseball fan to appreciate that. Sam Shepard, whose work she did appreciate, was suing to stop the performance of one of his plays, out in New Mexico, on the grounds, it appeared, that the performance interfered with his privacy. And in Egypt, an airport had been bombed, though no credit had yet been taken for the deed. The world seemed to be getting along pretty much as before. As before. Before. Anna suspected that for the rest of her life, time would be divided into *before* and *after*.

And *during*? What of the *during*? These weeks in Athens had become for her a small and ugly thing that was, in a funny way, also beautiful and erotic in its shriveled, smelly deadness. She thought she would take this *during* and wrap and bind it tight in the ribbon of this Greek morning and store it away, like a fetish, a totem, store it away in a secret place. And once it was put in its secret place, it would be time to go home.

From where she sat she could see an Olympic Airlines office, up the square and to the right, and all it would take was to walk up there with her ticket and make a reservation. This was off-season so there should be no problem finding a seat whenever she chose to leave. She wondered how long she would have to sit here on Syntagma Square before someone she knew walked by. Maybe even Mike Reid. She would be able to handle that now. *Hey, Mike. Long time, no see. Small world. Sit down. Coffee?*

She ordered another cup of *nes*, closed her eyes to the sun and thought about being at home with Ben and the children. Yes, in a moment she'd walk up the street and make reservations home. In a moment. She would be ready in a little while.

～

In the Ozarks, Emily tossed a restless sleep. The owls stayed near the cabin, themselves restless and hungry. And the spirit named Chip, who lived under the spring and who supposedly looked after travelers, sat on the floor near Emily's bed with his back to the wall and his knees drawn up so his heels touched his butt, and he gnawed at a hangnail and tried to explain what had gone wrong. He talked quietly to her about the way things would be, until the moon rose, her dreams quieted and she fell into a deeper sleep.

～

It is difficult to know what Rachel dreamt of that night. Her dreams were still largely inchoate, you see, merely forms and shapes, light and dark, a few colors, drifting through her sleep, her eyes moving under her lids. Not one tiny piece of her self made any effort to interpret what she saw. But perhaps that night she saw the shape of a horseshoe crab, and heard her mother's soft voice, and felt the comforting feel of her thumb in her mouth, where it lay now, and the grainy touch of the damp sand against her palm, and the shape that she had seen, out in Apalachicola Bay, beyond the fog.

～

Marie pulled her robe about her, looked toward the dark and brooding face of the Crest, visible only by the absence of stars behind it, and let the late, late night drift past. An hour ago she had awakened to far-off thunder and had looked around, lying on her back, moving only her eyes. Britt slept quietly next to her, her breathing deep and regular. Nothing moved. She had arisen and had come to stand in the back doorway, while Ginger sniffed along the alleyway fence, and to think by herself.

She didn't remember all of the conversation with Britt earlier, when she was fighting off sleep, but she remembered the fear Britt had described. She remembered her own sad fear, if that was what it had been, up in the meadow on the Crest a couple of days ago. Hers was gone for now, maybe because of the vulnerability shown by Britt, maybe because of some peace she had found at the airport, maybe just from standing with Britt and Richard Randolph under the departure board, thinking of that other time with Michael. In any case, the fear, if that was what it had been, was gone.

What had she been afraid of? She was not bothered by an uncertainty about Britt and Richard Randolph in New York. Britt had been wrong, she thought. This wasn't about fidelity. Whatever was rippling in the universe around her tonight, it wasn't commitment. It wasn't betrayal. She had felt close to Michael in the airport, alone at night, as close as when he lay next to her, but that had not been a betrayal of Britt. Reading his juggling letter to Britt had not been an act of infidelity either, she now knew, not to either of them. Michael represented, had always represented, the uncommitted part of life. The unattached part. Unattached. Marie thought back to that summer in college when she had swum in the AAU meets, had slept in her car and competed unattached. *Marie Cochran. Unattached.* There had always been a part of her life that was unattached. Michael had ratified that part, had made it legitimate and for that they had become so close. The love that was found in the juggling letter from Paros, in all of his letters, really, was not a love that led to faithfulness, but, instead, to non-attachment and to autonomy.

Britt, of course, threatened her unattached part; so did Beirut. Nothing could be very good, she thought, if it was not good enough to be threatening to the unattached, uncommitted part. This threat, she could now see, had resulted in her strange reaction last summer in Phoenix when Michael hadn't appeared on schedule, and she had rushed home to Britt. But, as she had come to know in the airport, that unattached part of her was strong enough and would survive. On the Crest, in the meadow, there may have been a feeling that the uncommitted part was gone and that betrayal was at hand, with Richard Randolph as the agent. But those feelings now were gone, or at least under control. The departure lounge itself, with its movement, its center and its sense of Michael's presence had shown her otherwise. Michael will admire her for having figured that out and she smiled as she imagined telling him.

She called quietly to Ginger, closed and locked the door behind both of them, and walked into the living room, drew open the curtain, and sat on the white couch, looking out the window at Manzano Street, dark and empty.

If it was not a fear of betrayal, then was it the opposite? Had the fear been a fear of commitment? Was she afraid of Britt? Of the Beirut sisterhood? No. Fostering the unattached part of her was not caused by a fear of attachment, it was simply an honoring of unattachment. There are reasons for walking in the mountains other than fear of the water, Michael had once said.

What was left if the fear was gone? Wonder? Suspense? She was uncertain. The fear, now that she thought about it, had been a fear of uncertainty, but tonight, now, uncertainty rested pretty easily on her mind. Earlier, in the airport, she had sensed some twist or tear or doubling over of the fabric of the universe against which she played out her life. When Britt and Richard had walked toward her, it had been as if time had shuddered, and things were changing. What things? Things. She didn't know what lay ahead; didn't know what the next day's light would bring. She wondered how it could be that life would not always be as it was right then. But standing in the airport, under the departure board, the destinations and flights moving up the board, she had known that it would not be. And that, right then, and now, had been all right. The fear was gone. As Britt would say, she was now looking beyond the jump. If she did not exactly welcome these uncertainties, she was determined to watch them pass by this window here as if they were new sights on the way into a strange city.

It was very quiet in the house and, maybe, for a while she slept. Hours passed. Her thoughts traveled widely. Toward morning, the moon rose and, at last, she went upstairs to lie in the arms of Britt.

# ~ 18

## CAIRO

T he young staffer in the American Embassy in Cairo called his young American wife and told her that the trip to Alexandria had to be postponed for a day. Yes, he knew it was terribly hot and yes, most of their friends were heading up for a few days and yes, he knew there was to be a much-anticipated party in Alex tonight at the Swedish consulate, but something had come up. It had been determined that the westerner who had been blown up at the airport was an American and there were details to be arranged and those details had been put onto his desk, yes, this late in the week. Well, certainly, it was all right with him if she went up to Alex earlier with their friends and he would join them as soon as he could get away, probably sometime tomorrow. *No, no,* he could easily take the train; she should take the car. They hung up with perfunctory *love-yous.*

The young embassy staffer looked at Michael Reid's passport, paging idly through the visa stamps. It might be possible to read the entry and exit stamps carefully and reconstruct the poor bastard's itinerary that had put him within a couple of feet of some fanatical Arab's homemade, and just shy of incompetently made, suitcase bomb at just exactly the wrong moment. It was a goddamn miracle that the thing ever went off. Poor bastard. He doubted, though, that anyone would take more than a glance at the passport. The late Mr. Reid was dead, so what did it matter? If he had been lucky enough to have been kidnapped, it would be different. His life would be the country's now, back home. His name would be raised at White House press conferences. Prayers would issue forth from the lips of strangers. Yellow ribbons would festoon the streets of, unmmm, . . . Madison County, Arkansas, wherever the hell that was. Why had he not given his town's name? Who cares? But bombings were not like kidnappings or hijackings; they were over too quickly, and this one looked to the young embassy staffer like one that the press would handle with little ado: *The State Department announced today that in this week's bomb attack in Cairo, one American tourist was killed and two Egyptians were slightly injured. The name of the American is being withheld pending notification of next-of-kin. In other news . . .* The President would express concern, but because this was Egypt and not Greece, the emphasis would be on the evils of international terrorism rather than the host country's sorry attempts at security, the Egyptian regime being deemed too fragile just now to stand such criticism. And that would be it; one American tourist, short, forty and brown-eyed, by the looks of the incident report, would be shipped home in a body bag, embalmed by some crooked Arab who would do a half-assed job and charge the next-of-kin double, the body would arrive slightly ripe, and everyone would forget.

*Christian.* The Egyptian consulate in Athens conformed to the quaint habit of asking visa applicants for their religions. Oh, well. *Mohammad 1, Jesus nil.*

It might have been otherwise. *Let's see, where were you last?* The staffer made a half-hearted effort to find the most recent visa before Egypt and decided on Romania, getting it wrong, of course. He studied the Romanian stamps, issued, he did not know, by a reluctant border guard, speaking poor, suspicious German on the night train from Sophia. *It might have been different*, the staffer thought. *You could have stayed an extra week; you might have left Romania a day earlier and everything would have changed and you would have missed your appointment with the jihad down here. Then you would still be alive, sitting comfortably back home in Arkansas, and you would have died fifty years from now the way we are intended to die, staring at the wall of some rest home, unable to recognize your own grandchildren. And you would have saved yourself the embarrassment of minor martyrdom to the Gods of the Western Industrialized Democracies.*

The young embassy staffer tossed Michael's passport onto his desk, pulled out of his file cabinet the appropriate forms and walked to his office door.

"Asalah, do you know whether the Communications Section is working this weekend because of the bombing?"

"Yes, sir, I believe it is."

"Would you please get Miss Anderson on the phone for me?"

"Yes, sir."

The staffer went back into his office, shut the door and sat back at his desk. *Well, Mr., ahhhh, Reid,* he thought, *perhaps something good will come of your untimely death after all. Will you rest more easily, Mr. Reid, knowing that three otherwise unhappy people will be spending the evening in non-conjugal congress because you chose this weekend to expire?* Four, actually, counting whatever unfortunate fellow his wife would pick up at the Swedish consulate and screw tonight. The young embassy staffer turned to the form for the wire of notification and condolences. *Rest in peace, my friend, rest in peace, and leave everything to me.* He consulted the *In case of emergency* box in the front of Michael's passport and wrote, "Dear Mr. Randolph: It is with great sadness that I must inform you that . . ."

ATHENS

Anna Browning sat in the departure lounge of Athens' west airport, the Olympic airport, the one nearer the sea, and waited for her flight to New York to be called. She didn't have long to wait, for she had cut the timing a little close. At the last minute this morning, she had decided that she needed one more walk around Syntagma, down Stadiou Street to Omonia, one last look through the grime-streaked windows of the café that said ΚΑΦΕΝΕΟΝ over the door. Then she had resisted taking a taxi to the airport and had instead hopped the No. 10 trolley and transferred to the Olympic bus which had dropped her at the airport, still with plenty of time, really. But security was very tight at the airport, apparently due to the bombing in Cairo, so the line into the departure lounge had moved slowly and she had had to submit to a most thorough search by a security matron. Now she sat with less than a half an hour to go before departure time.

The avoidance of a taxi to the airport had been her parting homage to Mike Reid. He hadn't been on her mind all that much lately, not since the obsession of the early part of her stay. But she had awakened this morning thinking of him. She remembered sitting at lunch once in some restaurant in Topeka, years ago, and he had been talking about travel and had told her that he disliked taxis. It is odd how small bits of memory lie in one's brain like that. Since it had been his idea, in a way, that she come to Athens, she determined, this morning, still lying in bed, to leave as he might once have left Athens. It was the kind of sentimentality that would later embarrass her.

She carried no luggage, so the trip by trolley and bus had been easy enough. She had thought about wearing home the clothes she had worn over, but had decided against it. That skirt was too big for her now, and she felt more comfortable in her jeans. So she had left the skirt hanging in the closet at the hotel, along with the few spare clothes she had bought, and set out, first to Omonia and then to the airport, in jeans and shirt, beret and sneakers. She carried only her passport, her ticket, the pen clipped in her back pocket and what was left of her money. She had never in her life felt lighter.

Sitting now in the departure lounge, though, she looked around and with a start realized she was going home. It would not be right to say that she hadn't realized before now that she was going home, but, sitting, looking across the departure lounge at a small tax-free liquor and souvenir shop, she suddenly had a very Tallahasseean thought: the children would probably like a souvenir from Greece. No such thought had passed through her mind in months, and the hominess of it made her know what, exactly, she was doing. For a moment, her heart pounded against her ribs.

The decision to go home had been made and wouldn't stand re-thinking now. She was indeed going home. But she would not let herself deny the fact that part of her longed to walk out of the airport, to stand on the steps leading down to where the Olympic bus back into town waited, to catch a glimpse of the sea sparkling across the parking lot and the road, and to have no one know who she was. Part of her would, right now, turn and walk away from this airplane. But the decision had been made and she was going home, and the Olympic bus and the No. 10 trolley would wait patiently, forever, she supposed, for that part of her.

The flight was called while she was still staring at the row of tee shirts in the shop across the way. She jumped up and ran across the lounge and quickly bought three shirts in various small sizes, with the Parthenon, the Agora and Lykabettos on the front and the word *AΘHNAI* in blue. Ben was harder to shop for, he always was, and time was short. She looked around a bit, as the line to board the plane shortened, and finally settled on a cigarette lighter, with a blue and white Greek flag on it. She imagined that he would have some joke about its chintziness and she almost changed her mind, but the cashier had already rung up the purchase. She paid and waited while the cashier put the purchases in a plastic shopping bag. Plenty of time.

The thought occurred to her that if she missed the plane, she would have a good excuse, because the security had made the line into the airport move so slowly. Then the next thought: for several months, excuses had been unnecessary, absolutely unnecessary. She was returning to a world where excuse must sometimes be made for doing or not, for having done or not having done. She watched the line to the plane shorten, standing at the cashier's station in the gift shop, until it was only ten people long. At the adjacent gate, the attendant announced the departure of a flight to Amsterdam.

Would those at home expect her to have an excuse for her absence? There was none, not really. She had wrapped her fetish successfully and hidden it away and there were no excuses in it or for it. Rachel would expect no excuse; between Anna and Rachel there had always been much without excuse. But with the others, she expected some tight moments, for she intended to make no excuse. At most she had a reason: *I went to Athens to look for a guy I hardly know, and the coffee tasted better than I had expected.* Would that be enough? She would have to see.

The line was gone. The attendant stood at the doorway, with both of her hands full of boarding card stubs. Anna stood for a moment and held her breath, prolonging the tension she felt pulling at her. She felt tightly strung, like a piano, and, yes, it felt good.

She walked across the departure lounge and the agent spotted her and knew she intended to board. Now Anna could not simply miss the plane. Now, if she were to stay, she would have to say "I'm staying." The plastic bag seemed heavier than it should have been and she stopped just short of the podium to check and make sure the cashier hadn't put something in by mistake, but, no, three tee shirts and a cigarette lighter was all. She showed her boarding pass to the attendant, and her passport again, and submitted to one more body search in a curtained enclosure and then walked outside and climbed on the bus for the ride to the airplane.

She took the last walk, from the bus to the plane's loading stairs, very slowly, looking around. Halfway, she pivoted on her right foot, then her left heel, so that she turned a full circle while she walked, still looking. The turning forced the plastic bag out from her side in a circle and that made her spin a little off-center, a little asymmetric. She listened to the sound of her final steps along the tarmac and then climbed the stairs into the airplane, the last passenger to board.

Minutes later, the 747 performed its unlikely trick and lifted itself off the ground and into the air. It immediately banked to the left, to the west, to save the Parthenon the indignity of its vibrations, so that Anna was denied a last view of the city. Instead, she looked down on the water, where an orange ferry boat named ΝΆΞΟΣ, its decks cluttered with tourists, headed south for the islands, leaving behind a straight white wake, like a scratch on the blue Aegean Sea.

# ⁓ EPILOGUE

Those who knew Michael Reid well might say that all the rest of it will happen almost as if Michael himself had scripted it out. Britt Larsen, even, will think this, although she never knew Michael at all, not really. Maybe she had an inkling of it that day in the Albuquerque departure lounge under the flight board. Maybe not. Or maybe she foretold it, in a way, during the fight in Zia School park. Or maybe she should have known that it, or something like it, was to happen from the time, before the first dance at the Café Fargo, when she watched the small, dark-eyed woman drink her beer over ice. Maybe not.

It will turn out like this: The young embassy staffer in Cairo will have been correct, both about how he and his wife would spend the evening of Michael's death, and about the lack of interest the world press would show in the solitary casualty of an amateur bombing, plausible responsibility for which would never be claimed by anyone. Thus, Richard will learn of Michael's death first, in the cable from the embassy in Cairo, and he will grieve for his friend. Rita and the children will do and say the sorts of things that loving family members do and say. Christina will be especially comforting to him, as she will make him a cup of hot chocolate, all on her own, and she will ask him, with her quiet and intense seriousness, whether she might call him *Pops*, even though he wasn't officially her father at all.

Richard will quickly decide to fly to the Ozarks to tell Emily, who will say she already knew, though it will never be clear to Richard how she could have, as the State Department had not yet released Michael's name to the press. And when he walks to his car to catch the flight home, the fledgling owls will watch him go, and he will hear the soft, chromatic notes, as Emily, alone now in the cabin, quietly improvises a Requiem on her ten-string guitar.

Britt will learn of Michael's death almost incidentally, indirectly, from

Harriet, Richard's secretary, actually, and she will react as one who had once read a puzzling postcard, that's all. She will learn of it only somewhat after the event, and with few details, on her way from here to there, busy with this and that: final exams, awards ceremonies, graduation, bar exam studying, job offer, the bankruptcy clerkship. She will never be able to remember exactly when she learned of it, nor exactly what she said, except that it was the kind of thing that one said when one heard that a friend of a friend had died. She will even mention to Marie that a friend of Richard's had died. It will not occur to her that it was more than that, not then. The news will not be as important to her that day, whatever day it will be, as any number of other things that she would soon forget. It would have helped later if she had been able to talk to Marie about just when she heard the news and what she had thought, but she will not be able to.

She will wonder whether Marie had stopped hearing from Michael, as there will have been neither a sign nor a mention of a letter for several months. Marie, of course, will have become reluctant to bring him up very often, or what he was doing or where he was and why wasn't he writing? Marie will worry about him, but she will worry not that he was dead, a fear she might have shared with Britt, but that he no longer cared to write, which she couldn't really share, not after the fight in the park. And she will worry that her last postcard from the airport was the cause of his silence, and this, too, she will not be able to share with Britt.

So, in the end, Britt will figure it out on her own. No, *figure it out* is the wrong phrase, for there will be no *figuring*, and she will do none of the careful calculating that Nikki had done following her own discovery of Michael's letter to Anna. She will be sitting at her desk, upstairs in the room facing west, away from the Crest, studying for the bar exam on a Tuesday morning in June. She will be studying contracts law, if that is important to you, and maybe it is, for that was Richard's subject, and he had taught it to her, back before she even knew Marie. Marie will be at work, teaching summer school, proctoring an exam, keeping an eye on Edgar Jones, who is prone to copy if he can get away with it. It would be appropriate if Richard were to be watching the Dukes play, sitting on the third base side, guessing hit and run, but that isn't where he will be. It will be a weekday morning, you see, which perhaps shows that Michael did not script the whole thing out himself. Richard will be in the backyard, playing four-way catch with the kids, enjoying the summer life of a law professor, and they will be about to surprise Rita at work for lunch. And Britt at that moment will snap off the point on her pencil and she will look up from her notes and out the window to Manzano Street, and she will know that Richard's friend was Marie's lover. Absolutely, she will know. She will be so sure, that it will never occur to her to wonder how she came to know. She will not know what to do, but she will realize that she would have to be the one to tell Marie, and she will not be able to imagine how she will do that. She never knew Michael, remember, nor read any of his letters but the one, so she will not know that his vanishing had always been the basis of the bargain for those who knew and loved Michael. So Britt will close her book, walk downstairs and sit on the white couch with the dog on the floor next to her until Marie walks smiling in through the back door several hours later. And even then Britt will not have figured out any more than to say, "Your Michael is dead."

Nikki Wallace will take her Utterly Implausible Coincidence with her to an early grave. She will have been relieved of her housekeeping duties perfunctorily by Ben upon Anna's return, and will have been paid her wages plus a tip. The tip she will think insulting, not because of its size, but because it was even offered. Ben will never say a word to her, nor to anyone else for that matter, about the circumstances of Anna's departure or her return, and perhaps for that reason, Nikki will not tell him that she had read Michael's letter to Anna. She will eventually hear of Michael's death from Britt, but with him dead, her friend comfortably with Marie, and Anna at home, she will see no reason to tell anyone of the secret that only she and Michael shared, not just yet. So, Nikki will defend her dissertation, which will be published in book form by Yale University Press, will leave Tallahassee, and will begin her rapid rise in academia, as Ben had predicted. In the end, though, and in the face of Ben's angry ridicule, she will choose family, friends and desert air over prestige, and will settle in at the University of New Mexico, where she will be known as Dr. Nikki Wallace Williams, The James and Julie Davis Distinguished Professor of Literary Criticism. And one spring, twelve years after Anna's return, the cigarettes will announce that their toll was now due. Nikki will die a slow and cruel death, with, at the very end, one of her hands held by her husband and the other by the friend she called *Robin*, while Marie plays Crazy 8s with Nikki and Connor's two young children in the family room at the hospice. And if, near the end, Nikki will try to talk about the mysterious interconnectedness of life, in her delirium she will not be able to keep all the names straight, and no one will pay much attention to her.

And finally this: Anna Browning will never know, never learn, never ask about Michael's death, nor will she ever know any of the others in this story.

# ∼ ACKNOWLEDGEMENT

**M**any years ago, an MFA student at the University of Arkansas read an early draft of part of chapter two. She said, "I'd like to have a beer with her." Nothing more. It took ten years or so (while I was otherwise occupied) for it to come to me what she meant, and another three years to write it that way, during which time I managed to forget the MFA student's name. If I ever knew it. I know it's a long shot, but I hope that she sees this, remembers the advice, and gets in touch. For, to the extent that this story is a success, it is her doing.

—R.L.
Hindsville, Arkansas
January 2012

www.ingramcontent.com/pod-product-compliance
Lightning Source LLC
Chambersburg PA
CBHW031025030726
47497CB00004B/1015